THE VIKING POR

WESTERN F

William Kittredge grew up on the MC Ranch in southwestern Oregon, farmed until he was thirty-five, studied in the Writer's Workshop at the University of Iowa, and is currently a professor of English and creative writing at the University of Montana in Missoula, Montana.

Kittredge's writing has been published in magazines including *The Atlantic*, *Harper's*, *Esquire*, and *Outside*. He is the author of two short-story collections, *The Van Gogh Field and Other Stories* (1979) and *We Are Not in This Together* (1984); two collections of essays, *Owning It All* (1987) and *Who Owns the West* (1996); and a memoir, *Hole in the Sky* (1992), which won the PEN West Award for nonfiction book of the year. He co-authored the nine novels in the *Cord* series of Westerns, and co-edited (with Annick Smith) *The Last Best Place: A Montana Anthology* (1988).

The Portable

WESTERN READER

Edited and with an Introduction by

WILLIAM KITTREDGE

PENGUIN BOOKS

PENGUIN BOOKS
Published by the Penguin Group
Penguin Books USA Inc., 375 Hudson Street,
New York, New York 10014, U.S.A.
Penguin Books Ltd, 27 Wrights Lane,
London W8 5TZ, England
Penguin Books Australia Ltd, Ringwood,
Victoria, Australia
Penguin Books Canada Ltd, 10 Alcorn Avenue,
Toronto, Ontario, Canada M4V 3B2
Penguin Books (N.Z.) Ltd, 182–190 Wairau Road,
Auckland 10, New Zealand

Penguin Books Ltd, Registered Offices:
Harmondsworth, Middlesex, England

First published in Penguin Books 1997

1   3   5   7   9   10   8   6   4   2

Copyright © William Kittredge, 1997
Copyright © Penguin Books USA Inc., 1997
All rights reserved

Pages 596–600 constitute an extension of this copyright page.

LIBRARY OF CONGRESS CATALOGING IN PUBLICATION DATA
The portable western reader/edited and with an introduction by
William Kittredge.
    p.   cm.—(The Viking portable library)
ISBN 0 14 02.3026 2 (pbk.)
1. West (U.S.)—Literary collections.   2. American literature—
West (U.S.)   3. Western stories.   I. Kittredge, William.
II. Series.
PS509.W47P67   1997
810.8'03278—dc21   96–47243

Printed in the United States of America
Set in Bembo
Designed by Virginia Norey

Once again, for Annick

ACKNOWLEDGMENTS

THANKS TO ALL the people who helped educate me over all the years. Particular thanks to Gary Holthaus, who got me to read a lot of things I didn't know about.

And thanks to Alex Smith and Andrew Smith, good pals who helped me put together the headnotes.

But most of all I have to thank Dennis Held. Without his good sense and scrupulous attention to detail, this book would not have come to exist. Dennis showed me a lot of poems I would have overlooked. His eye for excellence has a lot to do with the quality of what we have here.

CONTENTS

INTRODUCTION

WEST OF YOUR TOWN:
ANOTHER COUNTRY

ON A JULY AFTERNOON in the vast center of South Dakota, heading west, towing a U-Haul and weary from a going-away party in Iowa City the night before, I came to the Missouri River. Everything changed.

Without expecting it (this was in 1969, and I'd never been across South Dakota before), once the bridge over the river was crossed, I found myself in that big old other country, my homeland, the West. I was back inside my skin again.

Just over the bridge I stopped for gas, and bought a can of beer and walked off from my car. Out a hundred yards from the freeway I stood with my shadow for company, breathing in and trying to acknowledge that maybe I wasn't going to always be so distant from myself as I'd been during my year in the Midwest.

How was it that I could so clearly sense, even to the point of wondering about it at the time, there above the river, near the freeway, that I was back in the West? Maybe it was the humidity. The air was drier and lighter. In Iowa I'd felt I was sort of drowning. Maybe it was the shattering, brilliant quality of the light, in which horizons and each thing at hand seemed distinct, defined, and actual.

The almost endless variety of societies and territories in the American West speak to me in a single voice. Think of the layers of history, both hideous and sweet, which have been acted out on the enormous run of staging grounds between South Dakota and San Francisco Bay. How to name why I know when I am in the West?

———

The motel where I stayed that night—just short of Rapid City—was connected to a construct of tourist attractions based on the mythological past—wagon-train dioramas with real wagons from the so-called frontier days, and so on.

I felt personally invaded. Such make-believe, I thought as I lay down to sleep, was only the playpen of fools of the sort who would live near the freeway. I was dead wrong.

Western lives, for a long time, as understood by outlanders, swirled by inside pretty much pure make-believe. West was always the way Americans were going. Defining the West, what they would find out there, was one of their prime games.

Their defining story in this game was "the Western," a morality play about the invasion and conquest of the wilderness and native savagery which was taken to be the essence of North America. It is a story which details the triumph of European people and their laws (read civility and community) in a conflict with both wild indifferent nature and bad men, some of them native, who are driven by the forces of lust and greed.

The Western was enormously attractive to Eastern audiences right from the beginning, reeking as it did of self-righteous violence, the excitement of romantic places and lives, and the imperialistic triumphs of white people. Around seventeen hundred pulp-paper nickel-dime novels about various sharp-shot escapades of Buffalo Bill came out in the nineteenth century.

It would be comforting to think people who had actually gone to live in the West were not as inclined to understand the world in terms of being saved by heroes, and were capable of seeing the Western as nonsense. But they weren't, not always.

In my ranchland boyhood we used to go to Western movies to see if Hollywood cowboys knew enough to get on their horses from the wrong side (or so we claimed). But we also played endless galloping horseback shoot-out games of cowboys and Indians. We lived inside mythology like any American.

The Western is a story in which we get to have our cake and eat it. Shane does the killing, then rides into the mythical Tetons, carrying all guilt away with him. Our problems have been solved quickly, and we are off the hook, guilt free, ready to go on, no blood on our hands.

The Western is a story as ancient as warfare, about solving problems with violence, the great simple solution, the cutting through, the opening of some unsolvable knot. Westerns, while they are basically about reestablishing community, embody a sexist, racist, imperialist story of conquest and takeover, a deeply pernicious teaching story which is still in our minds and acted out, every day, on our mean streets. Children kill other children, with handguns, settling scores, on playing fields in New Orleans. We have insane bombers getting even in Oklahoma. We try to forget Vietnam.

It would be pretty to think the American version of this ancient showdown shoot-'em-up story of aggression enshrined has vanished. But it hasn't.

The Western mutated and went to the edge of the continent and downtown with Dashiell Hammett and Raymond Chandler and the cops and detectives (think of *Chinatown* as the last Western movie). Lately, the Western has gone to virtual worlds and outer space, where the same old story is being endlessly reenacted by killer androids.

Out West, in the meantime, citizens were mostly inhabiting quite different lives. The settlement and subsequent resettlements of the West have been mostly communal enterprises—think of the wagon trains, which immediately became communities on wheels, and the cowhands on the great drives north from Texas, the Mormons on their handcart journeys to the valley of the Salt Lake in Utah, miners down thousands of feet underground in Butte (and their families, up on the surface, waiting), and cattlemen in Miles City in the 1880s, and sodbusters and their families coming in on Saturday afternoon to shop and talk in little towns like U Bet in central Montana in the years just before World War I, and the little cities growing, Boise and Santa Fe, Fort Collins and Bakersfield. Each was a unique place, but in each, citizens were building houses and businesses, paving their streets, assessing taxes, getting in crops, lumbering, going down into the mines, putting up fences, kissing, dancing, dying alone in a bad rooming house or at home in the arms of their loved ones—all our usual human endeavors.

But it was a long time before writing about the West began to reflect the intricacies of that actual living. There was a lot of bang-up storytelling about adventurous times in the West—journals of traveling upriver on the Missouri, reports from the gold camps—but there was not much sustained attention to the joys and frailties of life as it was ordinarily lived until the decades between the beginning of World War I and the end of World War II. In those years a sequence of writers—

most notably Willa Cather, Mari Sandoz, Walter van Tilburgh Clark, Wallace Stegner, and A. B. Guthrie Jr.—gave us books it is convenient if not elegant to call "antimythological."

They often very deliberately worked against the conventions of the Western in order to celebrate the domestic complexities of communal life in all its variousness. Western writers began to understand that the detailing of so-called ordinary lives was a worthy artistic ambition.

Westerners were beginning the long process of learning to think for themselves, about themselves, learning to understand that while they lived in communities with wildly different ideas of self and destiny, each was capable of identifying and solving its own problems.

It has taken decades, but these days most Westerners take pride in the notion that they inhabit their own societies, that they run them and are no longer inhabitants of an emotional and intellectual colony, and can't be summed up by a story someone else made up about them.

The American West is becoming its own place. In recent years it's fair to say the territory out beyond the short-grass plains has been as much Western, another country, as American.

But it's hard to name social and personal qualities that are specifically Western. How do we identify someone as a Westerner? Maybe it has to do with the way people talk, gestures and ways of going into the world. Maybe it's just that life in the vicinity of great spaces does something to the mind. Maybe people who move into such expanses of territory are already of a certain mind-set. Maybe certain psychic connections holding us together in the West are genetic—maybe there's a combination of genes which dictates a taste for long vistas, living in smallish towns in the vicinity of a natural world which is in some semblance of working order while occasionally honoring a yearning to hit the big road for new country simply in order to witness the sights (or, as the old-timers had it, see the elephant).

If the American West is a place with its own pretty much secure if nebulous sense of itself, it's also an intricate set of local societies and understandings which are as clearly real as those in County Cork or Vermont or New Orleans.

Because it is so enormous and so various in its landforms, from what remains of the tall-grass prairies on the Oklahoma/Kansas border to the red cedar rainforests on highlands in sight of the Pacific, because the original tribal inhabitants (the Hopi, the Sioux, the northern Paiute, for instance) are so different from one another, because the people who moved in have been everything from German/Russians who came from the vicinity of the Volga River to settle in North Dakota in the 1860s to the Laotians who came to western Montana in the 1970s, Western societies are perhaps mostly held together by a common history of existing as outsiders as we learn to be ourselves—what we want to be and sort of are, free and kicking in some vicinity we think of as home.

Wallace Stegner said the West was "the native home of hope." The West has historically been the home of possibility. The vast landforms and skies still seem to imply freedom.

Our societies in the American West—from the Comanche and the Hopi to the mix of cowhands and oil-field geologists in Wyoming to computer experts and multiracial families on the wide streets of Boise and Phoenix—are as various as those anywhere, and often at odds with one another. But they all seem to share some sense that an expansive, generous life is possible in this open place. You can be anything you can manage—that's the message a lot of us get.

But, of course, that message is not necessarily true.

Native people lived a hunting, gardening, seasonal life along the Missouri for centuries. Then Europeans began appearing, a few French traders and, in 1805, an expedition from the United States, organized by Thomas Jefferson and led by Meriwether Lewis and William Clark.

Before long, those native people were increasingly visited by people who can be seen as the cutting edge of the invasion, among them artists. John J. Audubon came upriver by steamboat in 1846, and grieved for what he saw: "thousands multiplied by thousands of Buffaloes are murdered in senseless play."

The Mandan, who sheltered the Lewis and Clark expedition through winter of 1804–1805, were moved upriver to a permanent agency for the Arikara, Hidatsa, and Mandan at Fort Berthold in 1868; today they are culturally extinct.

All this, then, is a prelude to saying that Western writers are learning to tell their own local, particular stories—to have a literature.

By "literature" I mean storytelling that is useful because it helps us to witness ourselves as we are in the world and to think in fresh ways about ourselves as we might become instead of reinforcing our prejudices about who we think we ought to be.

The West is learning to imagine and reimagine itself through ver-

sions of what is and could be in books like *Housekeeping*, Marilynne
Robinson's vision of possibility in the lake district of the Idaho panhandle, and James Galvin's *The Meadow*, a set of interwoven stories about
the ways people have lived out in the silences and light over the highlands south of Laramie, and the poetry of Theodore Roethke and
Richard Hugo and Pattiann Rogers and Philip Levine and Gary Snyder,
and the stories Richard Ford gave us in *Rock Springs*. But this sort of
listing can run on and on, far beyond the boundaries of this book.

After I crossed the Missouri back in 1969, driving on into the twilight
falling over South Dakota, the freeway tracing just north of badlands, I
found that I was sorrowing for myself because I had imagined my way
back inside the Western, seeing myself as a lonely-guy-on-the-road,
Huck-Finn-on-the-Mean-Streets in a story of radical individualism and
dislocation; home but on my way to a bad motel, on the other side of
the gunfighter myth. Think of Shane after the shoot-out, down the trail,
living out a country-and-western song, feeling mostly rootless.

Recalling photographs of the snowy slaughter of native people at
Wounded Knee, just south of badlands, in 1891, I found myself mired
in sad resonances, thinking of Crazy Horse, killed not far away after
being arrested by the military in 1877, just a year after Custer and his
troops suffered their misadventure on the Little Bighorn.

But there are other, more heartening stories of the West, most of
them not so notorious or bloody. I might have felt a connection to a
story like "The Woman and the Horse," compiled by A. L. Kroeber
(the anthropologist who brought Ishi to Berkeley) in the winter of 1901
as he collected Gros Ventre tales at the Fort Belknap Reservation in
northern Montana.

"The Woman and the Horse" ends with the woman speaking:

> "I cannot go back to the tribe now. I have become a horse.
> . . . If you do not loose me, many in the tribe will die." Then
> the young man went to his father and told what the woman
> had said. The old man went outside and cried it out to the
> people. Then they freed her and the horses. They ran amid
> flying dust, the woman far in the lead.

That story is part of what we have left from a treasure-house of
artful and useful metaphoric narratives told by natives on the plains be-

fore the Europeans arrived, stories about embracing that munificence which is as much a part of life as our isolations, stories about making as much of what we have as is possible. The writing in this book, over years, has told me that we cannot help but have connection to one another.

But this collection is not an attempt at defining Western American literature as anything but useful. While most Westerners have have no doubt mostly experienced the history of their region as a single long arc of complexity and ceaseless change, I've divided the selections in this book into four parts as a way of trying to help readers make sense of a discrete series of transitions (or waves of reimagining) in the ways the world has defined the American West in story, and in the ways Westerners have used storytelling to define themselves.

Part One represents the evolution of Native American stories about themselves from early times until now; Part Two represents the ways Westerners have worked to separate themselves from the violence-oriented and mostly nonsensical mythology of the nineteenth-century "Western" in order to examine actual rather than mythological experience; Part Three represents writers telling us their versions of what they took (and take) to be actual Western experience; Part Four represents the work of younger writers who are looking toward our future as part of a global culture.

The collection is a celebration of the West and some of the writing that has helped me understand my territory for what it is and could be. A few important writers are missing for a variety of reasons, mostly financial; but I was eager to include any writing which cast light on our lives in Western America, no matter who wrote it or where they lived. We name ourselves and our futures through narrative. These stories rest on the West in layers, and reach out and out.

The Portable

WESTERN READER

PART ONE

ANCIENT STORIES

NATIVE PEOPLE, WITH THEIR OWN brilliant storytelling traditions, occupied the territories we know as the American West for millennia. They mostly sustained themselves through hunting and gathering, with some gardening on the side (it has been said that Europeans found a Native American garden in America, and called it wilderness). It is testimony to the strength of those cultures and their sustaining stories that Native American cultures were able to survive European diseases, such as smallpox, and genocidal violence during the period of settlement following the Civil War.

Native Americans responded to these overwhelming catastrophes with courage and endurance. They continued to tell their stories, and spent most of a hundred years cherishing their cultures in secret. In the last couple of decades many Native Americans have begun the long and difficult process of recovering their cultures. For a long time Native American writers wrote European stories and poems about their experience. Now, as can be seen in the work of James Welch and Joy Harjo, they are telling their stories and poems in Native American ways, making their own mirrors in which to see their own lives and worth, at large in the world again, in a vividly imaginative and resolutely independent way.

WASHINGTON MATTHEWS

Washington Matthews (1843–1905) was an anthropologist and his-torian of Native American peoples whose translations of Navajo songs and tales, published by the American Museum of Natural History, introduced the "Navajo Night Chant" to Anglo readers in 1902. Matthews's rendering of the chant, one which is traditionally sung in a complex, nine-day healing ceremony, has since become the best-known work of Navajo literature in English translation.

HOUSE MADE OF THE DAWN

In Tse'gihi
In the house made of the dawn,
In the house made of the evening twilight,
In the house made of the dark cloud,
In the house made of the he-rain,
In the house made of the dark mist,
In the house made of the she-rain,
In the house made of pollen,
In the house made of grasshoppers,
Where the dark mist curtains the doorway,
The path to which is on the rainbow,
Where the zigzag lightning stands high on top,
Where the he-rain stands high on top,
Oh, male divinity!
With your moccasins of dark cloud, come to us.
With your leggings of dark cloud, come to us.
With your shirt of dark cloud, come to us.
With your head-dress of dark cloud, come to us.
With your mind enveloped in dark cloud, come to us.
With the dark thunder above you, come to us soaring.
With the shapen cloud at your feet, come to us soaring.
With the far darkness made of the dark cloud over your
    head, come to us soaring.
With the far darkness made of the he-rain over your head,
    come to us soaring.

With the far darkness made of the dark mist over your head,
  come to us soaring.
With the far darkness made of the she-rain over your head,
  come to us soaring.
With the zigzag lightning flung out on high over your head,
  come to us soaring.
With the rainbow hanging high over your head, come to us
  soaring.
With the far darkness made of the dark cloud on the ends of
  your wings, come to us soaring.
With the far darkness made of the he-rain on the ends of
  your wings, come to us soaring.
With the far darkness made of the dark mist on the ends of
  your wings, come to us soaring.
With the far darkness made of the she-rain on the ends of
  your wings, come to us soaring.
With the zigzag lightning flung out on high on the ends of
  your wings, come to us soaring.
With the rainbow hanging high on the ends of your wings,
  come to us soaring.
With the near darkness made of the dark cloud, of the he-
  rain, of the dark mist and of the she-rain, come to us.
With the darkness on the earth, come to us.
With these I wish the foam floating on the flowing water
  over the roots of the great corn.
I have made your sacrifice.
I have prepared a smoke for you.
My feet restore for me.
My limbs restore for me.
My body restore for me.
My mind restore for me.
My voice restore for me.
To-day, take out your spell for me.
To-day, take away your spell for me.
Away from me you have taken it.
Far off from me it is taken.
Far off you have done it.
Happily I recover.
Happily my interior becomes cool.

Happily my eyes regain their power.
Happily my head becomes cool.
Happily my limbs regain their power.
Happily I hear again.
Happily for me (the spell) is taken off.
Happily I walk (or, may I walk).
Impervious to pain, I walk.
Feeling light within, I walk.
With lively feelings, I walk.
Happily (or in beauty) abundant dark clouds I desire.
Happily abundant dark mists I desire.
Happily abundant passing showers I desire.
Happily an abundance of vegetation I desire.
Happily an abundance of pollen I desire.
Happily abundant dew I desire.
Happily may fair white corn, to the ends of the earth, come
    with you.
Happily may fair yellow corn, to the ends of the earth, come
    with you.
Happily may fair blue corn, to the ends of the earth, come
    with you.
Happily may fair corn of all kinds, to the ends of the earth,
    come with you.
Happily may fair plants of all kinds, to the ends of the earth,
    come with you.
Happily may fair goods of all kinds, to the ends of the earth,
    come with you.
Happily may fair jewels of all kinds, to the ends of the earth,
    come with you.
With these before you, happily may they come with you.
With these behind you, happily may they come with you.
With these below you, happily may they come with you.
With these above you, happily may they come with you.
With these all around you, happily may they come with you.
Thus happily you accomplish your tasks.
Happily the old men will regard you.
Happily the old women will regard you.
Happily the young men will regard you.
Happily the young women will regard you.

Happily the boys will regard you.
Happily the girls will regard you.
Happily the children will regard you.
Happily the chiefs will regard you.
Happily, as they scatter in different directions, they will
    regard you.
Happily, as they approach their homes, they will regard you.
Happily may their roads home be on the trail of pollen
    (peace).
Happily may they all get back.
In beauty (happily) I walk.
With beauty before me, I walk.
With beauty behind me, I walk.
With beauty below me, I walk.
With beauty above me, I walk.
With beauty all around me, I walk.
It is finished (again) in beauty,
It is finished in beauty,
It is finished in beauty,
It is finished in beauty.

A. L. KROEBER

*During the first half of 1901, working as a member of the Mrs. Morris
K. Jesup expedition, the anthropologist Alfred L. Kroeber collected
many Gros Ventre myths and tales on the Fort Belknap Indian Reservation in northern Montana. Although some of these stories exist in
modern forms, Kroeber's transcriptions have a precise and vivid language that preserves the flavor of the original tradition. His informant
for this selection was Assiniboine, a middle-aged man. The selection,
from Kroeber's* Gros Ventre Myths and Tales, *is part of the An-
thropological Papers of the American Museum of Natural History (1907).*

THE WOMAN AND THE HORSE

AS TOLD BY ''ASSINIBOINE''

The people sent out two young men to look for buffalo. They killed one and were butchering it. Then one of them said, "I will go to that hill and look around; do you continue to butcher." He went on the hill, and his companion went on with the butchering. The one on the hill looked about him with field-glasses. At Many-Lakes he saw a large herd of wild horses. He continued to look at them. Then he saw a person among them. Then he saw something streaming behind the person. He thought it was a loose breech-cloth. He called his companion, and said to him, "Look!" Then they went nearer. They saw that it was indeed a person. They thought that it was something unnatural (*kaxtawuu*). Therefore they did not try to disturb the person, but went back. They asked the people, "Did you ever miss a person?" An old man said, "Yes. A man once lost his wife as the camp moved. She was not found." Thereupon the young men told what they had seen. The people thought it must be this woman. The whole camp went there. All the people mounted their best horses in order to catch her. When they approached the place, they surrounded the whole country. All of them had mirrors. When they had gone all around, they turned the mirrors and reflected with them, signalling that the circle was complete. Then they drew together. The four that were mounted on the fastest horses started toward the herd. The wild horses ran, but, wherever they went, they saw people. The person in the herd was always in the lead. The people continued to close up on the horses. When they got them into a small space, they began to rope them. Six of the horses and the woman escaped. She was exceedingly swift. The people headed them off, and at last drove them into an enclosure. With much trouble they at last succeeded in fastening one rope on her leg and one on her arm. Then they picketed her at the camp like a horse. *Pubis suæ crines equi caudæ similes facti erant.* At night a young man went out. He lay down on the ground near her, looking at her. Then the woman spoke: "Listen, young man. I will tell you something. You must do what I tell you. It is the truth. Long ago the camp was moving. I was far behind. I saw a large black stallion come. He had a rope on him. I jumped off my horse and caught him, thinking he belonged to some one in camp. When I had hold of the rope, he spoke to me. He said, 'Jump on my back.'

Then I climbed on him. He is the one that took me away. He is my husband. I have seven children by him, seven young horses. There is one, that gray one; there another one, that spotted one; there a black painted one; there a black one." She showed him all her children. "That is my husband," she said of a black horse that was tied near by. "I cannot go back to the tribe now. I have become a horse. Let me go. Let us all go. Tie a bell on a horse of such a color; then you will be lucky in getting horses. If you will let me loose, I will give you forty persons (you will kill forty enemies). If you do not loose me, many of the tribe will die." Then the young man went to his father and told what the woman had said. The old man went outside and cried it out to the people. Then they freed her and the horses. They ran amid flying dust, the woman far in the lead.

CATHARINE McCLELLAN

Dr. Catharine McClellan spent years collecting the stories of native people in western Canada and Alaska, particularly of the Tagish, Tuchone, and Tlingit. Her publications include The Girl Who Married the Bear *(1970),* My Old People Say *(1975), and* Part of Land, Part of Water: A History of the Yukon Indians *(1987). Dr. McClellan writes, "All Indians fear bears, but women seem to have an almost pathological reaction to grizzlies, as much because of their spiritual as their natural aspects."*

THE GIRL WHO MARRIED
THE BEAR

Once there was a girl who picked berries in the summer. She went with her family, and they picked berries and dried them. When she went with her women folk, they would see bear droppings on the trail. Girls have to be careful about bear droppings. They shouldn't walk over it. Men can walk over it, but young girls have to walk around it. But this girl always jumped over it and kicked it. She would disobey her mother. All the time she would see some bear droppings and kick it and step over it. She kept seeing it all around her. She did this from childhood.

When she was quite big they went out picking berries. She picked with her mother and aunts and sisters. She saw some bear droppings. She said all kinds of words to it and kicked it and jumped over it.

When they were all coming home, they carried their baskets of berries. The girl saw some nice berries and stopped to get them. The others went ahead. When she had picked the berries and was starting to get up, her berries all spilled out of her basket. She leaned down and was picking them off the ground.

Soon she saw a young man. He was very good looking. She had never seen him before. He had red paint on his face. He stopped and talked to her. He said, "Those berries you are picking are no good. They are all full of dirt. Let's go up a little ways and fill your baskets up. There are some good berries growing up there. I'll walk home with you. You needn't be afraid."

After they had gotten the basket half full of berries the man said, "There is another bunch of berries up there a little ways. We'll pick them too."

When they had picked them all, he said, "It's time to eat. You must be hungry."

He made a fire. They cooked gopher, quite a lot of it, and they ate some. Then the man said, "It's too late to go home now. We'll go home tomorrow. It's summer, and there's no need to fix a big camp."

So they stayed there. When they went to bed, he said, "Don't lift your head in the morning and look at me, even if you wake up before I do."

So they went to bed. Next morning they woke up. The man said to her, "We might as well go. We'll just eat that cold gopher. We needn't make a fire. Then we'll go pick some berries. Let's get a basket full."

All the time the girl kept talking about her mother and father. All the time she wanted to go home, and she kept talking about it.

He said, "Don't be afraid, I'm going home with you." Then he slapped her right on top of her head, and he put a circle around the girl's head the way the sun goes. He did this so she would forget. Then she forgot. She didn't talk about her home any more.

They left again. He said, "You're all right. I'll go home with you."

Then after this she forgot all about going home. She just went around with him picking berries. Every time they camped, it seemed like a month to her, but it was really only a day. They started in May. They kept traveling and going.

Finally she recognized a place. It looked like a place that she and her family used to dry meat. Then he stopped there at the timberline and slapped her. And he made a circle sunwise, and then another on the ground where she was sitting. He said, "Wait here. I am going hunting gophers. We have no meat. Wait 'till I come back." Then he came back with the gophers. They kept traveling. Late in the evening they made camp and cooked.

Next morning they got up again. At last she knew. They were traveling again, and it was getting late. And she came to her senses and knew it. It was cold. He said, "It's time to make a camp. We must make a home." He started making a home. He was digging a den. She knew he was a bear then.

He got quite a way digging the den, then he said, "Go get some balsam boughs and brush." She went and got some. She broke the branches from as high as she could and brought the bundle.

He said, "That brush is no good. You left a mark, and the people will see it and know we were here. We can't use that. We can't stay here."

So they left. They went up to the head of a valley. She knew her brothers used to go there to hunt and to eat bear. In the spring they took the dogs there, and they hunted bears in April. They would send the dogs into the bear den and then the bear would come out. That's where her brothers used to go. She knew it.

He said, "We'll make camp." He dug a den and sent her out again.

"Get some brush that is just lying on the ground—not from up high. No one will see where you get it, and it will be covered with snow."

She got it from the ground and brought it to him, but she bent the branches up high too. So she let them hang down so her brothers would know. And she rubbed sand all over herself—all over her body and limbs. And then she rubbed the trees all around, so that the dogs would find where she had left her scent. Then she went to the den with her bundle of brush. She brought it.

Just when the man was digging, he looked like a bear. This was the one time. The rest of the time he seemed like a human being. The girl didn't know how else to stay alive, so she stayed with him as long as he was good to her.

"This is better," he said, when she brought back the brush. Then he brushed up and fixed the place. After he fixed the den, they left. The grizzly bear is the last bear to go into his den. They go around in the snow.

They went hunting gophers for winter. She never saw him do it. She always sat around when he was hunting gophers. He dug them up like a grizzly bear, and he didn't want her to see it. He never showed her where he kept the gophers.

Nearly every day they hunted gophers and picked berries. It was quite late in the year. He was just like a human to her.

It was October. It was really late in the fall. He said, "Well, I guess we'll go home now. We have enough food and berries. We'll go down."

So they went home. Really they went into the den. They stayed there and slept. They woke up once a month and got up to eat. They kept doing it and going back to bed. Every month, it seemed like another morning, just like another day. They never really went outside. It just seemed like it.

Soon the girl found that she was carrying a baby. She had two little babies—one was a girl, and one was a boy. She had them in February in the den. This is when bears have their cubs. She had hers then.

The bear used to sing in the night. When she woke up she would hear him. The bear became like a shaman when he started living with the woman. It just came upon him like a shaman.

He sang his song twice. She heard it the first time. The second time the bear made a sound, "Wuf! Wuf!" And she woke up.

"You're my wife, and I am going to leave soon. It looks like your brothers are going to come up here soon, before the snow is gone. I want you to know that I am going to do something bad. I am going to fight back!"

"Don't do it!" she said. "They are my brothers. If you really love me you will love them too. Don't kill them. Let them kill you! If you really love me don't fight! You have treated me good, why did you live with me if you are going to kill them?"

"Well, all right," he said, "I won't fight, but I want you to know what will happen!"

His canines looked like swords to her.

"These are what I fight with," he said. They looked like knives to her. She kept pleading.

"Don't do anything. I'll still have my children if they kill you!" She knew he was a bear then. She really knew.

They went to sleep. She woke again. He was singing again.

"It's true," he said. "They are coming close. If they do kill me, I want them to give you my skull—my head, and my tail. Tell them to give them to you. Wherever they kill me, build a big fire, and burn my head and tail and sing this song while the head is burning. Sing it until they are all burnt up!"

So they ate and went to bed, and another month went by. They didn't sleep the whole month. He kept waking up.

"It's coming close," he said. "I can't sleep well. It's getting to be bare ground. Look out and see if the snow is melted from in front of the den."

She looked, and there was mud and sand. She grabbed some and made it into a ball and rubbed it all over herself. It was full of her scent. She rolled it down the hill. Then the dogs could smell it. She came in and said, "There is bare ground all over in some places."

He asked her why she had made the marks. "Why? Why? Why? They'll find us easy!"

They went to bed again, just for a little while.

Next morning he said, "Well, it's close! It's close! Wake up!"

Just when they were getting up, they heard a noise. "The dogs are barking. Well," he said, "I'll leave. Where are my knives? I want them!"

He took them down. She saw him putting in his teeth. He was a big bear. She pleaded with him.

"Please don't fight. If you wanted me, why did you go this far? Just think of the children. Who will look after my children if you kill them? My brothers will help me. If my brothers hunt you, let them be!"

When he went, he said, "You are not going to see me again!"

He went out and growled. He slapped something back into the den. It was a pet dog, a little bear dog.

When he threw the dog in, she grabbed it and shoved it back in the brush under the nest. She put the dog there to hide it. She sat on it and kept it there so it couldn't get out. She wanted to keep it for a reason.

For a long time there was no noise. She went out of the den. She heard her brothers below. They had already killed the bear. She felt bad, and she sat down. She found an arrow. She picked it up, and then others. Finally she fitted the little dog with a string around his back. She tied the arrows into a bundle. She put them all on the little dog, and he ran to his masters.

The boys were down there dressing the bear. They knew the dog. They noticed the bundle and took it off.

"It's funny," they said. "No one in a bear den would tie this on!" They talked about it. They decided to send the youngest brother up to the den. A younger brother can talk to his sister, but an older brother can't.

The older brothers said to the youngest brother, "We lost our sister a year ago in May. Something could have happened. A bear might have taken her away. You are the youngest brother. Don't be afraid. There is nothing up there but her. You go and see if she is there. Find out!"

He went. She was sitting there crying. The boy came up. She cried when she saw him. She said, "You boys killed your brother-in-law! I went with him last May. You killed him, but tell the others to save me the skull and tail. Leave it there for me. When you get home, tell Mother to sew a dress for me so I can go home. Sew a dress for the girl and pants and a shirt for the boy. And moccasins. And tell her to come and see me."

He left and got down there and told his brothers, "This is my sister up there. She wants the head and tail."

They did this, and they went home. They told their mother. She got busy and sewed. She had a dress and moccasins and clothes for the children. The next day she went up there. They dressed the little kids. Then they went down to where the bear was killed. The boys had left a big fire. She burned the head and tail. Then she sang until all was ashes.

Then they went home, but she didn't go right home. She said, "Get the boys to build a house. I can't come right in to the main camp. It will be quite a while. The boys can build a camp right away."

She stayed there a long while. Towards fall she came and stayed with her mother. All winter. The kids grew.

Next spring her brothers wanted her to act like a bear. They wanted to play with her. They had killed a female bear that had cubs, one male and one female. They wanted their sister to put on the hide and to act like a bear. They fixed little arrows. They pestered her to play with them, and they wanted her two little children to play too. She didn't want it.

She told her mother, "I can't do it! Once I do it, I will turn into a bear. I'm half there already! Hair is already showing on my arms and legs! It is quite long."

If she had stayed there with her bear husband another summer she would have turned into a bear. "If I put on a bearhide, I'll turn into one!" she said.

They kept telling her to play. Then her brothers sneaked up. They threw the hides over her and the little ones. Then she walked off on four legs, and she shook herself just like a bear. It just happened. She was a grizzly bear. She couldn't do a thing. She had to fight against the arrows. She killed them all off, even her mother. But she didn't kill her youngest brother, not him. She couldn't help it. Tears were running down her face.

Then she went on her own. She had her two little cubs with her.

That's why the bear is partly human. That is why you never eat grizzly bear meat. Now people eat black bear meat, but they still don't eat grizzly meat, because grizzlies are half human.

JAROLD RAMSEY

Jarold Ramsey grew up on a ranch in central Oregon, near the Warm Springs Indian Reservation, and attended the universities of Oregon and Washington. His most recent book of poems is Hand-Shadows *(1989); his work on Indian literature includes a popular anthology,* Coyote Was Going There *(1977), and a critical study,* Reading the Fire *(1983). He teaches at the University of Rochester in New York State. This selection, "Coyote and Eagle Go to the Land of the Dead," belongs to the Wasco-Wishram tribe and was recorded in the Curtis text* The North American Indian, *Vol. 8 (1911), and reprinted in* Coyote Was Going There.

COYOTE AND EAGLE GO TO
THE LAND OF THE DEAD

Coyote had a wife and two children, and so had Eagle. Both families lived together. Eagle's wife and children died, and a few days later Coyote experienced the same misfortune. As Coyote wept, Eagle said, "Do not mourn: that will not bring your wife back. Make ready your moccasins, and we will go somewhere." So the two prepared for a long journey, and set out westward.

After four days they were close to the ocean; on the one side of a body of water they saw houses. Coyote called across, "Come with a boat!"—"Never mind; stop calling," said Eagle. He produced an elderberry stalk, made a flute, put the end into the water, and whistled. Soon they saw two persons come out of a house, walk to the water's edge, and enter a canoe. Said Eagle, "Do not look at those people when they land." The boat drew near, but a few yards from the shore it stopped, and Eagle told Coyote to close his eyes. He then took Coyote by the arm and leaped to the boat. The two persons paddled back, and when they stopped a short distance from the other side, Eagle again cautioned Coyote to close his eyes, and then leaped ashore with him.

They went to the village, where there were many houses, but no people were in sight. Everything was still as death. There was a very large underground house, into which they went. In it was an old woman [Frog] sitting with her face to the wall, and lying on the floor on the other side of the room was the moon. They sat down near the wall.

"Coyote," whispered Eagle, "watch that woman and see what she does when the sun goes down!" Just before the sun set they heard a voice outside calling, "Get up! Hurry! The sun is going down, and it will soon be night. Hurry! Hurry!" Coyote and Eagle still sat in a corner of the chamber watching the old woman.

People began to enter, many hundreds of them, men, women, and children. Coyote, as he watched, saw Eagle's wife and two daughters among them, and soon afterward his own family. When the room was filled, Nikshia'mchash, the old woman, cried, "Are all in?" Then she turned about, and from a squatting posture she jumped forward, then again and again, five times in all, until she alighted in a small pit beside the moon. This she raised and swallowed, and at once it was pitch dark. The people wandered about, hither and thither, crowding and jostling, unable to see. About daylight a voice from outside cried,

"Nikshia'mchash, all get through!" The old woman then disgorged the moon, and laid it back in its place on the floor; all the people filed out, and the woman, Eagle, and Coyote were once more alone.

"Now, Coyote," said Eagle, "could you do that?"—"Yes, I can do that," he said. They went out, and Coyote at Eagle's direction made a box of boards, as large as he could carry, and put into it leaves from every kind of tree and blades from every kind of grass. "Well," said Eagle, "if you are sure you remember just how she did this, let us go in and kill her."

So they entered the house and killed her, and buried the body. Her dress they took off and put on Coyote, so that he looked just like her, and he sat down in her place. Eagle then told him to practice what he had seen, by turning around and jumping as the old woman had done. So Coyote turned about and jumped five times, but the last leap was a little short, yet he managed to slide into the hole. He put the moon into his mouth, but, try as he would, a thin edge still showed, and he covered it with his hands. Then he laid the moon back in its place and resumed his seat by the wall, waiting for sunset and the voice of the chief outside.

The day passed, the voice called, and the people entered. Coyote turned about and began to jump. Some [of the people] thought there was something strange about the manner of jumping, but others said it was really the old woman. When he came to the last jump and slipped into the pit, many cried out that this was not the old woman, but Coyote quickly lifted the moon and put it in his mouth, covering the edge with his hands.

When it was completely dark, Eagle placed the box in the doorway. Throughout the long night Coyote retained the moon in his mouth, until he was almost choking, but at last the voice of the chief was heard from the outside, and the dead began to file out. Everyone walked into the box, and Eagle quickly threw the cover over and tied it. The sound was like that of a great swarm of flies.

"Now, my brother, we are through," said Eagle. Coyote removed the dress and laid it down beside the moon, and Eagle threw the moon into the sky, where it remained. The two entered the canoe with the box, and paddled toward the east.

When they landed, Eagle carried the box. Near the end of the third night Coyote heard somebody talking; there seemed to be many voices. He awakened his companion, and said, "There are many people coming."—"Do not worry," said Eagle; "it is all right." The following night Coyote heard the talking again, and, looking about, he discovered that the voices came from the box which Eagle had been carrying. He placed his ear against it, and after a while distinguished the voice of his wife. He smiled, and broke into laughter, but he said nothing to Eagle.

At the end of the fifth night and the beginning of their last day of traveling, Coyote said to his friend, "I will carry the box now; you have carried it a long way."—"No," replied Eagle, "I will take it; I am strong."—"Let me carry it," insisted Coyote; "suppose we come to where people live, and they should see the chief carrying the load. How would that look?" Still Eagle retained his hold on the box, but as they went along Coyote kept begging, and about noon, wearying of the subject, Eagle gave him the box.

So Coyote had the load, and every time he heard the voice of his wife he would laugh. After a while he contrived to fall behind, and when Eagle was out of sight around a hill he began to open the box, in order to release his wife. But no sooner was the cover lifted than it was thrown back violently, and the dead people rushed out into the air with such force that Coyote was thrown to the ground. They quickly disappeared in the west. Eagle saw the cloud of dead people rising in the air, and came hurrying back. He found one man left there, a cripple who had been unable to rise; he threw him into the air, and the dead man floated away swiftly.

"You see what you have done, with your curiosity and haste!" said Eagle. "If we had brought these dead all the way back, people would not die forever, but only for a season, like these plants, whose leaves we have brought. Hereafter trees and grasses will die only in the winter, but in the spring will be green again. So it would have been with the people."—"Let us go back and catch them again," proposed Coyote; but Eagle objected: "They will not go to the same place, and we would not know how to find them; they will be where the moon is, up in the sky."

C. C. UHLENBECK

C. C. Uhlenbeck, a Dutch ethnologist, collected firsthand accounts of traditional Blackfeet life in the summer of 1911. A young Blackfeet interpreter, Joseph Tatsey, helped Uhlenbeck transcribe "How the Ancient Peigans Lived," as told by a Blackfeet man named Blood (Kainaikoan). This account was published in A New Series of Blackfoot Texts *(1912), in both a Blackfeet transcription and an English translation.*

HOW THE ANCIENT
PEIGANS LIVED

AS TOLD BY BLOOD (KAINAIKOAN)

How the ancient Peigans moved about, how they ate, the things they cooked with, the things they had happy times with, how they fought in war, how they played, and how they dressed, the way I heard about them.

Far down on Maria's river [literally: Bear creek], there they stayed till late in the spring. Their horses were really fat, they had done shedding their hair. They [the Peigans] waited for one another. They waited for the bulls, that they had shed their hair. The chiefs talked, they went crying about the camp, they would say: Go about to get lodge-pins. We shall move up [away from the river]. Then they moved up. It was in the Battle-coulee that they camped. In the morning they went round saying: Come on, we shall move. When the buffaloes were far, we overtook them in the Cypress hills; when they were not far, we overtook them in the Small Sweetgrass hills. We would chase the bulls between the Small Sweetgrass hills. The bulls were chased first. And their bodies were oily. They were put straight up [after having been killed]. Their eyes [the bulls' eyes] were dusty. They would rub the knives a little, with them they cut their backs open. They were all skinned from the back down. Then they would throw out their kidneys. And the oil and grease would gather about their navels. They would throw down the yellow back-fat and spread it out. The man would tell his wife: Take and wash the manifold. When she came back, he would say to her: That

leg-bone, the oily leg-bone, just break that. It would be broken for him.
And the manifold and the marrow of the leg would burst by chewing.
He would roll the marrow in the manifold. He would burst it by chew-
ing it.

He had done skinning. Then he began to pack his meat [on a
horse]. Then he came home with the meat. Then the woman [his wife]
brought it [the horse with the meat] home [to her own parents]. He
[her husband] stretched his hand out [that means: gave the meat to his
parents-in-law]. And the man [the husband] just sat [inside of his lodge].
His wife came in with the son-in-law's [that means: her husband's] food.
The broken boss-rib, the short rib, the gut with the blood in it, the
tripe where it is good, with those [four] things he [the son-in-law] was
fed [by his parents-in-law]. He was told by his wife: Give an invitation.
The old men, those were the ones he invited. The women jerked the
skin-meat from the skins which they would make their marks on [the
skins that would be used as parfleches]. They made marks on the parfleches, and the long sacks, the real sacks, and the berry-sack. In that
way we made use of the hide. The chief then again cried about the
camp: When the slices of meat are dry, then we shall move. We shall
move down over on Milk river [literally: Little creek]. Close by [that
river] are the better buffalo. We shall skin [for lodges]. Again he cried
around the camp: We shall move. We shall make a circle [to chase the
buffalo]. We shall camp on Bad-water [a lake]. They camped. The lodges
were all put up. Everything was quiet in the camp [literally: they—the
lodges—were all quiet]. And the chief said: Now begin to catch your
horses. Then they went on a hunt. Then they got to the buffalo. They
began to get on their horses. Then they chased the buffalo. The carcasses
were scattered all over. And they began to skin. They would take the
teats of the cows with sucklings. There was foam on the back-fat from
rubbing. They would go home with the carcasses.

The horses that had meat on them would be taken all over [the
camp]. They were what the married men presented [to their fathers-in-
law]. The cooked ribs, that were all carried about, were the food given
to the sons-in-law. Inviters would go about. When a man was still at
home, [some people on the outside] then would say: A big herd of
buffalo is coming towards the camp. The women would say: Over there
is [a buffalo], that the people try to kill, that we may go to get the
entrails. No one went ahead of them [the women] for the blood, when
they went themselves to the carcasses about. They camped a long time,

where they got food. All their choice pieces of the meat got dry [during the time they were camping]. Then they dried their skinnings [the hides]. The strong women would quickly get the hair off their hides. The chief said: Come on, we shall move to the Manyberries [a local name]. We shall camp there. There is a young man who went far, he found out [that] the berries are ripe. Come on, you women, you may go for berries. And they had many berry-bags [literally: And many were their berry-bags]. In the evening they all came back from picking berries. The pickings of that one [bunch of women] were sarvis-berries, goose-berries, white-berries [red-willow-berries]. That were the pickings of that one bunch of women. Their children would be delighted in eating the berries. The women prepared [an oil out of] the brains and the liver, mixed up [to oil the hides with]. There began to be many [hides] for their future lodges. They had done the oiling of the skins.

When they moved again, the chief said: We shall move. We shall camp at Buffalo-head [a local name]. There are many berries [of all kinds], [especially] cherries. They took them. When they had brought them home, they mashed them with the whole seed in them. They were picked for future use [for winter-time]. Then they moved again. The chief said: The buffalo is near the Seven-persons [a local name], we shall camp there, and there we shall chase elk. And there they camped. They gathered in a circle [to chase the elk]. Then they chased [the elk]. And there was much hot pemmican, tripe, guts. The choice parts were back-fat, flanks, belly-fat. They all had plenty of food. The chiefs would come together to decide, which way to move the camp. They did not move about [far], they only ate food. And there they moved about [just a little]. When the hides were all good, then [the chiefs] said: We shall move to the mountains [the Cypress hills]. We shall cut the lodge-poles. Then they started to move. Then they separated [by bands]. Then they would move this way. They camped over there at Long-lakes [a local name]. Then they moved again. The chief said: We shall move to Where-the-Women-society-left-their-lodgepole [a local name]. And there are some [buffalo], we have still to chase. We moved back [towards the prairie].

The chief said: Come on, we shall move. We shall move to Green lake. And there they camped. Then stray-bulls were chased. They were taken to use their hides for Indian trunks. The women would use their hides to tie their travois with. The hair on the heads [of the buffalo] was taken also. It was made into ropes. The same [hides] were also made into hard ropes. And the women made a string from the sinews [this string was used in tanning]. They began to tan the skins for the lodges. [The chief] would say: We shall move. We shall move to Writing-stone [a local name]. There are many berries, [especially] cherries. They camped there. The women did not go far for picking berries. And the mashed cherries were dry. They put them away. They put them in calf-sacks. They were the berries for future use. In winter they would skim the grease with them, they would mix them with their pemmican, and they would make soup with them. [The chief] would say: We shall move up [alongside Milk river] to Woman's-point [a local name]. We shall camp about along the river. The meat about [the camp] is getting scarce. Then we had moved away [from the river]. Buffalo and antelopes commenced again to be shot. The prairie-antelopes were fat like dog-ribs. They had sweet livers. There was nothing, we would just look at [without killing it]. Wolves, badgers, skunks, prairie-antelopes were those, that we bought tobacco with.

[The chief] said: We shall cut our lodge-poles from Cut-bank river. When we were near to [the place], where we would cut our lodgepoles, the women would have completed their lodges. They would have done sewing them. Then they [the Peigans] moved fast. Then they camped. It is Cut-bank river, where they always cut lodge-poles from. They would watch the lodge-poles. When they were all dry, then they would stretch their lodges with them. And they would look like leaf-lodges. And it was late in the fall, the leaves would all be white. They began to eat guts [and] tripe. They began to make soup with them. One never turned his head away from the soup. They would begin to eat even hard-seed-berries. They were careful [literally: hard] women, [that] never would be hungry. Over there [near the mountains] it was, they camped about. Black-tails, deer, elk, moose, those were [the animals], they hunted for. These [people] were camped about [near the mountains], those were [the animals] they killed. When it snowed [first] in the fall, then they began to hurry, that they moved down [to the lower country]. There [down] on the river, there they would be camped about. There they waited, where the buffalo would come the nearest. To that place they would move. They would carefully look, where they [themselves] would be during the winter. Then they camped in different places all along the river. They would make the corral [for their horses]. In the beginning of the winter they were all happy.

[The chief] would say: The buffalo would not set warm their [un-

born] calves [that means: the buffalo would not have another place than
their own bodies to hide their calves]. Then they [the people] were
happy. When it cleared up, one person would see the buffalo. In the
night he came back, and said: The buffalo are close by, they are many.
In the morning you will hunt. They were all gone on a hunt. Then
they would chase the buffalo. The buffalo's fur was good already. They
[the people] liked the big heifers [four years old], [and] the heifers [two
years old] very much. With those they wintered [that means: they ate
them during the winter]. They would be like as if their hair were
brushed. Oh, happy times there would be in the beginning of the winter,
from the food that they got. They all came back home. [After] two,
three, four, five [days] the buffalo would go away [from the neighbourhood of the Indians]. They [the buffalo] moved back [they would drift
away north]. And here, where they were camped, they would just stay.
They would be in a hurry for their robes [to tan them]. They jerked
the skin-meat from them. Then they scraped them. Then they oiled
them with the brains and the liver. Then they greased them. When they
were soaked with grease, they had already warm water. Then they would
pull the water [from the fire]. They poured the water on them. When
they were soaked with water, they would twist them. [When] the water
was all out of them [by twisting], then they would untie them. Then
they tied them stretched. Then they began to scrape the moisture out
of them. They scraped them with a broken stone. They would brush
their fur with sticks. It [the hide] was a little dry, then they pulled it on
a string. Then they put it down. Then they stretched it by stepping on
it [by holding their feet on the ends]. Then they pulled it again on the
string. There were some buffalo-bones, they were called shoulderbones.
With those they also scraped the hide. Then they [the hides] were completed. Then there was nothing to think about [to worry about]. They
had done making robes for themselves. The woman, and her husband,
and her children, they all had robes for themselves. When they slept,
they would sleep as if they were sleeping with fire [the robes were so
warm!].

[When] the buffalo was far, the girls would cut a big tree over there.
It would fall. She [a girl] would go up to it. Here, where she liked it,
she would knock off the bark of it. She would hit it [the tree] lightly.
Then she would peel from the same place [where she had been hitting].
The same size [as she had peeled] she would tear in two. She would eat
it. It was very sweet. Then the girls and boys—many of them—would

go. Over there on the hill-side they dug for false roots [a kind of eatable roots], rattle-sound-roots, [and] make-bleed-roots. Those they ate also. The children never became sick [because those roots were so healthy]. They would find the other [trees] to eat, they took all those trees. They peeled the bark from them. They ate also roseberries, [and] hard-seed-berries. And then there was earth-medicine [black alcali], it was earth. They licked it. All the mouths would be just white from it. That [the earth-medicine] prevented them from being sick [literally: they would not get sick from]. The women kept bullberries through winter [literally: laid bullberries over night]. They had them also for berries to use them afterwards. When they had real winter, they would provide for wood. The women would go on foot for wood. They would pack the wood on their back. When the wood was far to get, they would put the travois on a horse. They had covered their saddles from one end to the other [with raw-hide]. They carried wood on them [on the travois and the saddles]. They had profit from the travois. They valued it very much. When they had done carrying wood with it, then they began to coil up the ropes, attached to the travois, [for fear] that they might be eaten [by the dogs]. And the old woman had [also] profit from her dog. She would say: Just put it [the dog] short [that means: just put the travois on its neck]. That way she got her wood.

When she had done getting her wood, then she began to put her leg-bones together. She pulled out her stone to hammer the bones on, [and] her stone-hammer. She put her leg-bones down on her half of a hide. She would say: I shall make grease [from the bones]. Then she began to hammer them. She had already put her real pot on the fire. She would make the soup with one of the leg-bones. She had done hammering them. Then she would put the mashed bones in [the pot]. When it had boiled a long time, then she would pull it from the fire. She had already put the cherries [near her]. She took a hornspoon. With that she skimmed. She put her skimmed grease in a big real [wooden] bowl. Then she had done skimming [the grease]. She put the cherries in [the bowl]. There was much [literally: far] of the cherries with skimmed grease. She told the women: You must get hot this soup of the leg-bones. Her daughter was already hammering the sirloin-dried-meat. [When] she had done hammering, she gave it to [her mother]. And she [the mother] mixed it [the dried meat] up with the skimmed grease [and cherries]. Then she made it all into one roll. She gave that to her son-in-law. He invited the old men.

JAMES WELCH

James Welch is a native Montanan, born in Browning in 1940. In 1971, Welch, a member of the Blackfeet and Gros Ventre tribes, published a book of poetry, Riding the Earthboy 40. *Since then he has published four novels:* Winter in the Blood *(1974);* The Death of Jim Loney *(1979);* Fools Crow *(1986), which won the* Los Angeles Times Book Prize; *and* The Indian Lawyer *(1990). Welch received an Emmy for his screenplay for* Last Stand at Little Bighorn, *a documentary produced for PBS; his nonfiction book about the battle,* Killing Custer, *was published in 1994. He lives in the Rattlesnake Canyon above Missoula with his wife, Lois.*

Until the 1970s, most Native American writers in the West (including Welch) tended to write what were essentially European novels about Native American experience. Then, with the sudden popularity of Gabriel García Márquez's One Hundred Years of Solitude, *Latin American so-called magic realist writing gave them a model to use when trying to write from inside animist cultures.* Fools Crow, *in which creatures and humans talk to one another, is one of the first novels to convincingly reproduce the animist nature of Native American lives as they were lived on the plains of the West.*

FROM *FOOLS CROW*

Some time between the moon of flowers and Home Days, with the high hot sun turning the grass from green to pale straw, the Pikuni people began to pack up their camps to begin the four-day journey to Four Persons Butte near the Milk River. Here, the Sacred Vow Woman and her helpers had determined to build a lodge for the Sun Chief, and here they meant to honor him with sacred ceremonies, songs and dances.

Heavy Shield Woman had purchased the Medicine Woman bundle from her predecessor, and her relatives in the camps had procured the sacred bull blackhorn tongues.

On the first day the people assembled near the confluence of the Two Medicine River and Birch Creek. Most of the bands arrived within the compass of the midmorning and midafternoon sun. As each band arrived, members of the All Crazy Dogs, the police society, showed them where to set up. Soon a great circle was formed, as the last of the bands, the Never Laughs, filled the perimeter. The Sacred Vow Woman's lodge was erected in the center and Heavy Shield Woman entered. Then the camp crier rode among the lodges, calling forth all the women who had vowed to come forward to the tongues. He beat his small drum and called for their husbands to accompany them. He stopped before the lodge of Heard-by-both-sides Woman, who had been a Sacred Vow Woman two years earlier, and called her to instruct Heavy Shield Woman in her duties.

When the chosen had been assembled in the lodge, Heard-by-both-sides Woman lifted one of the tongues above her head and asked Sun Chief to affirm that she had been virtuous in all things. All of the women did this. Then the dried tongues were boiled and cut up and placed in parfleches. Heavy Shield Woman began her fast.

The next day she led the procession to the second camp. On her travois she carried the Medicine Woman bundle and the sacred tongues. Four days they camped in four different locations, arriving at last on a flat plain beneath Four Persons Butte. Each day Yellow Kidney and the many-faces man, wise in the ritual of the Sun Dance, purified themselves in the sweat lodge.

The dawn of the fifth day, Low Horn, a celebrated warrior and scout, left his lodge, saddled his buffalo-runner and galloped down off the plain to the valley of the Milk River. As he rode, he examined the big-leaf trees around him. Across the river he spotted one that interested him. It was stout but not too thick. It was true and forked at just the right height. He looked at the tree, the way the sun struck it, and decided it was the chosen one.

When he reached camp—by now everyone was up and the breakfast fires were lit—he rode among the lodges, calling to the men of the Braves society. He ate a chunk of meat while the others saddled their horses. Then he led them back to the spot. Everybody-talks-about-him had been selected to chop it down, and he set upon it with his ax. He had killed many enemies. At midmorning, his bare back shiny with sweat, he gave a final blow and the tree groaned and swayed and toppled into a stand of willows. The men who had been waiting jumped upon the tree and began to slash and hack, cutting off the limbs as though they were the arms and legs of their enemies. Not too long ago, these would have been traditional enemies; now, more than one of the Braves was killing the encroaching Napikwans.

Heavy Shield Woman sat in the Sacred Vow lodge, her face drawn and gray with her fast. Soon it would be over, but the thought of food had become distant and distasteful. She listened to her helpers talk quietly among themselves, but the words were not clear to her ears. She prayed to the Above Ones, to the Below Ones and to the four directions for strength and courage, but each time she began her prayers, her mind drifted and she saw her husband as he had appeared at her lodge door after his long absence. She had greeted him with high feelings, with much crying, hugging and wailing. She was overjoyed to have her man return. But later, as they sat quietly, she had been surprised to feel only pity for him. He was not the strong warrior who had left camp in that moon of the falling leaves. This man was a shadow who looked at her with stone eyes, who no longer showed feelings of love or hate or even warmth. And he had not changed in the ensuing moons. He was no longer a lover, hardly even a father to his children. Was he still a man? Had a bad spirit taken him over? But she, Heavy Shield Woman, had changed too.

Her thoughts were interrupted by the entrance of Heard-by-both-sides Woman and her husband, Ambush Chief. He carried the Medicine Woman bundle and would serve as ceremonial master during the transfer. When all the helpers, clad in gray blankets with red painted stripes, had seated themselves, Ambush Chief began to open the bundle, praying and singing as he did so. The first object he held up was the sacred elkskin dress. He sang of the origin of the garment while the women put the dress on Heavy Shield Woman. Then they draped an elkskin robe over her shoulders. One by one, he removed the sacred objects: the medicine bonnet of weasel skins, feather plumes and a small skin doll stuffed with tobacco seeds and human hair; the sacred digging stick that So-at-sa-ki, Feather Woman, had used to dig turnips when she was married to Morning Star and lived in the sky with him and his parents, Sun Chief and Night Red Light. She and Morning Star had an infant son named Star Boy.

Ambush Chief told of the time So-at-sa-ki, while digging turnips, had dug up the sacred turnip, creating a hole in the sky. She looked down and saw her people, her mother and father, her sister, on the plains and she grew homesick. Night Red Light, upon hearing of her daughter-in-law's act, became angry, for she had warned Feather Woman not to dig up the sacred turnip. Sun Chief, when he returned from his journey, became angry with Morning Star, for he had not kept his wife from doing this, and so he sent Feather Woman back to earth to live with her people. She took Star Boy with her because Sun did not want him in his house. She also took the elkskin dress, the bonnet, the digging stick. She and her son rode down the wolf trail back to her people, and she was happy to be with them. She hugged them and rejoiced, for she was truly glad to be home. But as the sleeps, the moons, went by, she began to miss her husband. Each morning she would watch him rise up. She shunned the company of her mother and father, her sister, even her son, Star Boy. She became obsessed with Morning Star, and soon she began to weep and beg him to take her back. But each morning he would go his own way, and it was not long before Feather Woman died of a broken heart.

As Star Boy began to grow up, a scar appeared on his face. The older he grew, the larger and deeper the scar grew. Soon his friends taunted him and called him Poia, Scar Face, and the girls shunned him. In desperation he went to a many-faces man who gave him directions to Sun Chief's home and whose wife made Scar Face moccasins for his journey. After much traveling, he reached the home of Sun Chief far to the west. Sun had just returned from his long trip across the sky and he was angry with Scar Face for entering his home. Sun Chief decided to kill him, but Night Red Light interceded on behalf of the unlucky young man. Morning Star, not knowing the youth was his son, taught him many things about Sun and Moon, about the many groups of Star People. Once, while on a hunt, seven large birds attacked Morning Star, intending to kill him, but Scar Face got to them first, killing them. When Morning Star told his father of this brave deed, Sun Chief removed the scar and told the youth to return to his people and instruct them to honor him every summer and he would restore their sick to health and cause the growing things and those that fed upon them to grow abundantly. He then gave Poia two raven feathers to wear so that the people would know he came from the Sun. He also gave him the elkskin robe to be worn by a virtuous medicine woman at the time of the ceremony. Star Boy then rode down the wolf trail to earth and instructed the Pikunis in the correct way, and then he returned to Sun's home with a bride. Sun made him a star in the sky. He now rides near to Morning Star and many people mistake him for his father. That is why he is called Mistake Morning Star. And that is how the Sun ceremony came to be.

While Ambush Chief related this story of Scar Face, three helpers were building an altar near the lodge door. They stripped off the sod and dry-painted Sun, Moon and Morning Star. They painted sun dogs on either side of Sun's face to represent his war paint. Then the helpers chanted and shook their rattles to pay homage to Sun and his family. When they finished, Ambush Chief stood and lifted his face.

"Great Sun! We are your people and we live among all your people of the earth. I now pray to you to grant us abundance in summer and health in winter. Many of our people are sick and many are poor. Pity them that they may live long and have enough to eat. We now honor you as Poia taught our long-ago people. Grant that we may perform our ceremony in the right way. Mother Earth, we pray to you to water the plains so that the grass, the berries, the roots may grow. We pray that you will make the four-leggeds abundant on your breast. Morning Star, be merciful to your people as you were to the one called Scar Face. Give us peace and allow us to live in peace. Sun Chief, bless our children and allow them long lives. May we walk straight and treat our fellow creatures in a merciful way. We ask these things with good hearts."

Before they left the lodge, the helpers with brushes obliterated their dry paintings, just as Sun had removed the scar from Poia.

Red Paint stood next to her husband and watched the procession. The ground was already becoming dusty from the people and horses. Earlier the people had been busy setting up their lodges, getting water from the clear, deep creek that came out of Four Persons Butte, gathering firewood. But now they were all here, watching the procession, moving to the beat of a single small drum. Red Paint was shocked at how old and bent her mother looked. She wasn't even certain that the woman was her mother. Her face was hidden by the hanging weasel skins. Two helpers held her up.

The procession circled halfway around the unfinished Medicine Lodge. Then they entered a sun shelter to the west of it. Here, the tongues were distributed to the sick, the poor, the children, to all who desired such communion. The women who had vowed to come forward to the tongues opened the parfleches and distributed pieces to the faithful. Heavy Shield Woman, weak from her lack of food, watched the people chew the tongues and she prayed, moving her lips, without words.

It was nearly dark by the time the men of the warrior societies began the task of erecting the center pole of the Medicine Lodge. With long poles they advanced from the four directions, singing to the steady drumbeat. With rawhide lines attached to their poles, they raised the cottonwood log until it stood in the hole dug to receive it. Heavy Shield Woman watched the proceedings with prayers and apprehension, for if it failed to stand straight, she would be accused of not being a virtuous woman. But it did stand, and the men began hurriedly to attach it to posts and poles around the perimeter of the lodge. Younger men began to pile brush and limbs over the structure. Now Heavy Shield Woman sighed and slumped into the arms of two of her assistants. They carried her back to her lodge, where the hot berry soup awaited her. She could break her fast.

For the next four days the weather dancers danced to the beat of rattles against drum. Warriors enacted their most courageous exploits and hung offerings on the center pole. For each deed they placed a stick on the fire until it blazed high night and day. In other lodges Sacred Pipe men and Beaver Medicine men performed their ceremonies for those who sought their help.

All day and into the night, young men in full regalia paraded their horses around the perimeter of the enormous camp. The All Crazy Dogs had a difficult time policing the grounds. But they had discovered none of the white man's water in the encampment, and for that they were grateful. Sometimes they even had time to enter into the stick games that were being played. Throughout the night, the taunting songs of the various sides increased in volume as the stakes grew higher. During the day there were many horse races. Bands raced against each other, societies had their own horses and riders. The betting was heavy and some men lost their entire herds and possessions, even their weapons. Fights broke out over the close races and the All Crazy Dogs moved in, scattering the participants in all directions. And always there were the drums, the singing and dancing.

White Man's Dog awoke at dawn one day with a terrible dread in his heart. He had eaten and drunk nothing the previous day and he could hear his stomach rumble. He sat up in the robes and his body was wet with sweat. The days and even the nights had been hot, but this sweat had nothing to do with heat. He sat up and listened to the steady *thunk! thunk! thunk!* of a single drum. It was the only sound in camp and it was not a call to celebrate but to let the people know where they were.

White Man's Dog looked down at Red Paint. Her loose dark hair fell down around her shoulder. He touched the soft skin. His hand was rough and dark, and it seemed to him that the hand and the shoulder were made of two different substances. He was awed by the power of their lovemaking, and as he looked at her neck and shoulder he was filled with desire. The quiet camp seemed far away to him as he lay back down and reached for and fondled her breasts. He wanted her to wake up and he wanted this dawn to last. But then the thought of the day's ceremony entered his mind and his desire left him.

He stood at the back of the perimeter of lodges and peed. To the east, the first streak of orange crossed the sky. He smelled the prairie grass and the sagebrush and the sweet mustiness of the horses who watched him. He listened to the clear song of the yellow-breast crouched in the grass to his right. Two long-tails flew through the sky toward Four Persons Butte, their black-and-white bodies bobbing lightly through the morning sky. He looked back toward the camp. Most of the outer lodges were unpainted, or had simply painted designs of ocher earth, black sky and yellow constellations. The sacred tipis of Beaver, Blackhorn, Bear and Otter were on the inside of the perimeter, facing the Medicine Lodge. As he watched the sky lighten, the wisps of smoke grew fainter. White Man's Dog stood in the quiet dawn, his heart beating strong with all the power of the Pikunis. He felt ready for the ordeal ahead of him.

Mik-api sat back on his haunches and looked down at White Man's Dog. They were in a brush shelter just to the side of the big Medicine Lodge. The black paint dots trailing from the corners of the young man's eyes glistened in the dappled sunlight. Mik-api looked satisfied. He and two other old men, Chewing Black Bones and Grass Bull, had painted White Man's Dog's body white with double rows of black dots down each arm and leg. On his head they placed a wreath of sage grass and bound the same grass around his wrists and ankles. As the tear paint dried on his cheeks, the old men prayed that he would acquit himself well so that Sun Chief would smile on him in all his undertakings.

Then they led him into the Medicine Lodge and he lay down on a blanket on the north side of the Medicine Pole. He heard a man on the other side recite war honors, and he felt the hands of Mik-api and Grass Bull on his arms. Chewing Black Bones knelt over him with a real-bear claw longer than a man's finger. The man reciting war honors stopped. White Man's Dog looked into Mik-api's eyes and bit his lower lip. He felt the searing pain in his left breast as Chewing Black Bones pierced it with the bear claw. His breathing made a hissing sound in the quiet lodge. Again he felt the claw pierce his flesh, this time on the right breast. His eyes were squinted tight but the tears leaked from them. And now he felt the sarvisberry sticks being pushed under his skin and he looked down and saw the rich blood pouring down onto his arms. Mik-api and Grass Bull helped him up and held him as Chewing Black Bones attached the rawhide lines that hung from the top of the Medicine Pole to the skewers in his breasts.

"Now go to the Medicine Pole and thank Sun Chief for allowing you to fulfill your vow."

White Man's Dog approached the pole and thanked Sun for helping him on his raid and for protecting him. He asked for forgiveness for desiring his father's young wife and he saw Kills-close-to-the-lake that night running from him and he asked her forgiveness too. He felt his head get light and he almost collapsed with pain. He thanked Sun for his fine new wife and vowed to be good and true to all the people. Finally, he asked Sun to give him strength and courage to endure his torture. Then he backed away from the pole and began to dance. He danced to the west, toward the lodge door. He danced to the drum and rattle. From somewhere behind him he heard the bird-bone whistle of a many-faces man, and he felt the sticky warm blood coursing down from his wounds. Then he heard the drum speed up and he danced harder, pulling harder against the lines attached to his breasts. He danced and twisted and pulled and when he thought he couldn't stand the pain the left skewer broke loose, swinging him around to his knees. He bit his lip until he tasted blood mixed with the salty tears running down into his mouth over the black painted tears. He pushed himself up to his feet again and danced to the east, away from the door. He leaned away from the Medicine Pole and jerked his body back and forth, but the second skewer would not give. His head was fuzzy with red and black images and only the pain kept him there in the lodge. Then he saw the dawn and the long-tails and the patient horses. He heard the yellow-breast singing in his ears and then it turned into a voice, loud and deep, and it recited the victories it had gained over its enemies. Raven flew into the lodge and sat down between Red Paint and Kills-close-to-the-lake. One more step, he cawed, think of Skunk Bear, your power—and he felt the other skewer pull free and he fell backward into the darkness.

Mik-api rose and cut the bloody skewers from their rawhide tethers.

Small strips of flesh hung from them. He carried them to the Medicine Pole and laid them at the base. "Here is the offering of White Man's Dog," he said. "Now he is for certain a man, and Sun Chief will light his way. His friend Mik-api has spoken to you."

White Man's Dog slept that night by himself a good distance from the encampment of the Pikunis. His wounds were raw and swollen and his stomach had become a small knot, for he had still not eaten. In the distance he could hear the thundering rumble of the drums as the dancing picked up. He lay in his robe on the flat ground and watched Seven Persons and the Lost Children in the night sky. To the east, Night Red Light had risen full over the prairie. Once he saw a star feeding, its long white tail a streak across the blackness.

Then he was dreaming of a river he had never seen before. The waters were white and the sky and ground glistened as though covered with frost. As he watched the white water flow over the white stones, his eye caught a dark shape lying in the white brush. Then he was down beside the water and the wolverine looked up at him with a pitiful look.

"It is good to see you again, brother," he said. "I have got myself caught again and there is no one around but you."

"But why is it so white, Skunk Bear?" White Man's Dog had to shield his eyes from the glare.

"That's the way it is now. All the breathing things are gone— except for us. But hurry, brother, for I feel my strength slipping away."

White Man's Dog released the animal for the second time.

Skunk Bear felt of his parts and said, "All there. For a while, brother, I thought I was a shadow." Then he reached into his parfleche and took out a slender white stone. "For you, brother. You carry that with you when you go into battle, and you sing this song:

"Wolverine is my brother, from Wolverine I take my courage,
Wolverine is my brother, from Wolverine I take my strength,
Wolverine walks with me.

"You sing that loudly and boldly and you will never want for power."

White Man's Dog watched the wolverine cross the river and amble up the white bluff on the other side. Near the top, the animal turned and called, "I help you because twice you have rescued me from the Napikwans' steel jaws. But you must do one other thing: When you kill the blackhorns, or any of the four-leggeds, you must leave a chunk of liver for Raven, for it was he who guided you to me. He watches out for all his brothers, and that is why we leave part of our kills for him."

"He will be the first to eat of my kills," called White Man's Dog. "Good luck, my brother!" But Skunk Bear had disappeared over the top of the bluff.

As White Man's Dog turned to leave, he saw in the glittering whiteness a figure approaching the river. He became frightened and hid behind a white tree. As the figure passed, he saw it was a young woman dressed in white furs and carrying two water bladders. He watched her dip the bladders into the river until they were full; then she hung them from a branch and took off her furs. She was slender but her breasts and hips were round. She stepped over the stones to the water's edge, arched her back and dove in. She came up and swung her long hair, and White Man's Dog became rigid with desire for her. He wanted his arms around her smooth brown back and he wanted to lay her down in the white grass. As he approached the riverbank, he began to take off his clothes and he heard a song which seemed to come from him. The young woman turned and looked at him. It was Kills-close-to-the-lake. She made no attempt to cover herself.

White Man's Dog quickly turned away.

"Are you afraid of me?"

"No, I am afraid for myself," he said.

"Why? Do you desire me?"

"I can't say. It is not proper."

"Why not? This is the place of dreams. Here, we may desire each other. But not in that other world, for there you are my husband's son."

White Man's Dog looked at her, and he felt nothing but desire. He tried to feel shame, guilt, but these feelings would not come.

"You may desire me, if you wish. Nothing will happen. You may lie with me, if you like." She moved out of the water and stood before him. She looked into his eyes, and he saw Kills-close-to-the-lake for the first time. He saw the hunger she had kept hidden, he saw her beauty, and he saw her spirit.

So they lay down in the white grass together, their bodies warm and alive. He covered her breasts with his hands and pressed his mouth to her slender neck. He smelled her familiar scent and knew it was her.

She moved beneath him and pulled him down and he closed his eyes. He felt her fingers tracing worlds on his back, and then he slept.

White Man's Dog awoke with his cheek against the damp dawn grass. At first he didn't know where he was. He was all alone and it frightened him. He sat up quickly and felt the sudden pain of his chest. He looked down and saw the strip of trade cloth that had been wound around his torso. Beneath the cloth he saw the leaves and the salve, and he remembered the events of the previous day. He was weak with hunger, and he fell back on his elbows. Sun was not yet up, but he saw Morning Star on the eastern horizon and, above him, Mistake Morning Star. He shook his head as though the whiteness of the stars had blinded him or reminded him of another place.

When he awoke the second time, Red Paint was kneeling beside him, his father and mother standing behind her. Red Paint smiled at him and helped him up and held him tenderly to her. Her hair smelled of sweet grass, and he whispered in her ear, "You are my woman, Red Paint, and I will always be your man." He felt her lips move against his cheek but he couldn't make out the words.

He turned and touched his mother, holding her away from the pain. She looked anxiously into his eyes.

"I am proud of you, my son," said Rides-at-the-door. "Mik-api tells me you did not cry out once."

"Mik-api is kind," said White Man's Dog.

Rides-at-the-door laughed and hugged him vigorously. He let out a howl and then he laughed too. As White Man's Dog gathered up his robe, he saw a small object fall out. It was a white stone almost as big around and long as his little finger. He tucked it into the strip of cloth around his chest and caught up with his wife.

Mountain Chief stood before the gathered people. He was a tall man with a long handsome face creased by the winds of many winters. His shirt and leggings were made of antelope skin with dyed quill trim down the arms and legs. Weasel-skin pendants hung from the neck and shoulders. His bonnet was made of thirty eagle feathers standing upright from a folded rawhide headband, decorated with red flannel and brass disks. He raised his arms and the people fell silent.

"Haiya! Listen, my people, for I speak to you with a good heart. Once again we have constructed the Sun Lodge in the way we were

taught by our long-ago people. Let it stand to remind passersby that the
Pikuni are favored among all peoples. We have smoked the long-pipes
together and are at peace with ourselves. Many have left presents for
Sun Chief, and some among us have fulfilled vows made in times of
trouble. Our children have learned much of the good way. Heavy Shield
Woman and her helpers have shown our young girls the way to virtue.
Our young men have listened to the wisdom of their chiefs. I believe
our father, Sun Chief, is satisfied with us. He will bring us rain at the
proper time so that the grass grows and the berries ripen. He will cause
the blackhorns to be thick and everlasting upon our land. He will heal
our sick and take pity on the poor. . . ."

White Man's Dog heard the sound of horses off to the right, in the
area of Mountain Chief's band's lodges. He stole a glance and saw several
young men sitting on their horses. He recognized Owl Child and Black
Weasel and Bear Chief. The rigidity with which they sat, as they listened
to the head chief, made White Man's Dog tense. They had not been
around during the ceremonies. Some thought they had remained north
of the Medicine Line after Mountain Chief's band fled up there. Others
heard they had gone far south to the country where the Napikwans dug
the yellow dust. But here they were, proud, arrogant, ignoring the people who glanced out of the corners of their eyes, dividing their attention
between these intruders and their chief. Just as he was about to turn
back to Mountain Chief's speech, he glimpsed the black legs and head
of a horse on Owl Child's far side. He watched for a while and soon
the horse, with a shudder, moved forward a couple of steps and he
recognized Fast Horse. Like the other riders, he wore face paint and
earrings and a Napikwan shirt, gartered at the elbows. His hair was
tightly braided with pieces of red flannel. It had been two moons since
White Man's Dog had seen him, and he looked leaner in the face and
harder in the body. He seemed to listen to the speech but his face gave
away nothing.

White Man's Dog stood and slipped behind a near lodge. He circled
the inner lodges until he could see the backs of the riders. Then he
walked forward slowly until he was standing beside the black horse. It
was a good, strong animal but it wasn't the horse Fast Horse had stolen
from the Crow camp. White Man's Dog looked up and at first Fast
Horse would not recognize his presence. Then Fast Horse scratched the
back of his neck, turned and looked down. He looked at White Man's
Dog and a grin slowly spread across his face. It was a triumphant grin

and his eyes remained hard. Then he turned his attention to the remainder of the speech, the grin still in place.

". . . I myself have never liked the Napikwans, and I say to you now I would do anything to rid this land of their presence. But many of our chiefs have spoken against me and I respect their arguments. They say that Napikwan is a way of life now. Some even suggest that we go to his schools and his churches. They say if we learn his language, we can beat him with his own words.

"As you know, the white chiefs soon will move the agency from Many Houses to the Milk River to be nearer to us. I believe this will happen before the falling-leaves moon. Already they have taken much of our land, and now they will want more. They are like the yellow-wings who hop about, eating everything in their path. Soon there will be nothing to feed upon." Mountain Chief paused and looked down at a group of children who sat near his feet. His eyes softened and he almost smiled at these young Pikunis. He lifted his head. "But I will do as my chiefs demand. We will counsel with the whites, and if they do not want too much, we will make a new treaty. My heart is not in this, but I will accede to the wishes of my people."

Owl Child suddenly whirled his horse, and in an instant the other riders followed. White Man's Dog jumped back but the tail of the black horse caught him across the face. He rubbed his cheek and watched the riders gallop out of camp and across a field and out of sight behind a rise. It happened so fast that many people saw only a cloud of dust.

Mountain Chief saw it all, and he waited until the drumming hoofbeats died away. If he had been affected, he gave no sign. He was a chief. "Now we will go our separate ways and rejoin the hunt. Let there be no bickering among you, for our plains are vast and the blackhorns plentiful. You young men keep away from the white man's water. I wish you good traveling and good hunting. Sun Chief has been honored and feels kindly toward his children. I grasp hands with all of you. My words enter your ears from my heart. Farewell."

As White Man's Dog helped pack the lodge furnishings on the travois, he watched the Small Robes leave the encampment. Heavy-charging-in-the-brush rode at the lead, followed by the warriors, who were singing a traveling song. Behind them came the women riding the travois horses. Children and old ones rode the travois, watching the other bands take down their lodges and pack up. The camp dogs, so boisterous dur-

ing the encampment, now trotted patiently beside the packhorses. At
the rear, young boys drove the loose horses, snapping pieces of rawhide
at them and shouting insults.

White Man's Dog was anxious to be gone. He had learned from
his father that they would head for the Sweet Grass Hills. The grass was
always long there, and the buffalo caused the plains to be black as far as
one could see. Also he was happy because the Sweet Grass Hills were
not far from the Medicine Line. He did not like Owl Child's reaction
to Mountain Chief's call for peace with the Napikwans. If trouble came,
the Lone Eaters could run across the line in a day's time. The thought
of running shamed him, but he now had to think of Red Paint as well
as his family.

He walked over to his father's lodge to see if he could help them, but
they were tying on the last of their belongings. His mother told him to get
a kettle of water to douse the fire. He was glad for something to do and
walked swiftly down the path to the small creek. As he neared the dam of
sticks and mud, he saw Heavy Shield Woman bathing her face and arms.
She was his mother-in-law now and according to custom he must not
look at her face again, so he walked through the brush downstream until
he came to a pool close to the bank. He lay on his belly and sucked in
the cool water. He sat back and wiped his mouth. It was pleasant in the
shade of the big-leaf trees, and he was glad to get away from people.
He sighed and closed his eyes but he knew they would be waiting for
him. He dipped the kettle full of water and turned to leave.

Kills-close-to-the-lake stood in the path. White Man's Dog realized
he had not seen much of her during the encampment, but she probably
spent her time with her parents, who were of the Never Laughs band.
They were camped several bands away from the Lone Eaters. As White
Man's Dog looked at her face, he saw something different about her. At
first he thought she looked different because he had not seen her for
several sleeps. Her face was still young but her eyes were deeper, as
though she had become someone else, a woman that White Man's Dog
had never seen before. He started to speak when he noticed that her left
hand was thickly bundled with cloth. He saw only three fingers sticking
out of the bandage.

"You sacrificed a finger," he said quietly.

"It is not uncommon. It is done at the Sun Dance honoring
ceremony."

"You made a vow?"

"I had a dream," she said and walked past him and knelt by the water. He watched her drink from a cupped hand and then splash water on her face and neck. Then she stood and walked a short way upstream. She leaned against a big-leaf tree and shuddered deep down. Her eyes darkened with pain as she lifted the bandaged hand to her breast.

"You should rest—for the journey."

"It was a dream about you," she said. She did not look at him. "It was the moon when the heavy snows come, but it was not cold. It was as warm as it is now. You were down here by this creek and all around it was white. You hid behind this tree but I saw you. You watched me bathe in the waters. I felt your eyes on my body and I got light-headed. I pretended I didn't notice you"—she lowered her eyes to the bandaged hand—"but then I felt something crawling all over my skin as though the water held tiny hot fleas. But when I turned to you, you were gone. In your place stood a short heavy animal with long claws and sharp teeth. He said, 'Come to me, sister, and I will show you magic.' He was the creature that lives by himself in the Backbone. All the others fear him, but I didn't. I came out of the water and let him ravish me. I didn't care; you had gone away. When he had finished, he bit this finger off. Before he left he threw the finger on the ground and it turned into a white stone. 'Let this always remind you of your wickedness, sister. You're lucky I didn't bite your nose off.' I threw myself into the white grass and wept, for he had revealed what I had kept hidden even from myself. And it was so hopeless, this desire! I wept until all my tears, all my desires and hope, were gone and I felt lighter. I could see more clearly and I saw nothing ahead of me and I was content with this vision. I found the white stone and carried it to where you were sleeping after your torture. I placed it in the robe beside you so that you would be reminded of your good fortune."

White Man's Dog watched her run away from him. His mind was tangled with confusion. That white world she described was familiar to him. He had been there and had seen the white river, the white ground. And he had seen a dark creature and, yes, it had been Wolverine. Then he remembered the animal with white fur that had come to drink. It was a slender, lovely animal and he had watched it drink from the white waters. He had been in that world but he hadn't seen Kills-close-to-the-lake.

He felt in his small war bag that hung around his neck and he pulled out the white stone, and as he caressed it, he sang softly:

"Wolverine is my brother, from Wolverine I take my courage,
Wolverine is my brother, from Wolverine I take my strength,
Wolverine walks with me."

White Man's Dog didn't know how or why, but Wolverine had
cleansed both him and Kills-close-to-the-lake. He had also given White
Man's Dog his power, in the white stone and the song.

JAMES MOONEY

James Mooney, the son of Irish immigrants, was born in Indiana in
1861. An ardent Irish nationalist all his life, Mooney was one of the
first ethnologists sympathetic to and respectful of the Indian traditions.
He contributed many irreplaceable reports and studies on the traditional
culture of the Cherokee and Kiowa, on tribal group population in
North America, and—most important—on the Ghost Dance. Some
of Mooney's major monographs are Sacred Formulas of the Cherokee *(1891),* The Ghost-Dance Religion and the Sioux Outbreak of 1890 *(1896), and* Myths of the Cherokee *(1900).*

The Ghost Dance was a millennial cult that, toward the end of
the nineteenth century, swept through many of the American Indian
tribes west of the Mississippi. Working for the Smithsonian's Bureau
of American Ethnology, Mooney described the Ghost Dance as the
response of a tribe to the intolerable stresses laid upon it by oppression,
disease, and poverty.

This excerpt is the testimony of a Shoshone shaman named Cap-
tain Dick, taken down at Fort Bidwell in the northeastern corner of
California (his descendants worked on the ranch where I grew up, only
a couple of dozen miles to the north). It is of course a dream, a yearning
story bound to fail.

FROM *THE GHOST-DANCE RELIGION AND THE SIOUX OUTBREAK OF 1890*

We may now consider details of the doctrine as held by different tribes, beginning with the Paiute, among whom it originated. The best account of the Paiute belief is contained in a report to the War Department by Captain J. M. Lee, who was sent out in the autumn of 1890 to investigate the temper and fighting strength of the Paiute and other Indians in the vicinity of Fort Bidwell in northeastern California. We give the statement obtained by him from Captain Dick, a Paiute, as delivered one day in a conversational way and apparently without reserve, after nearly all the Indians had left the room:

Long time, twenty years ago, Indian medicine-man in Mason's valley at Walker lake talk same way, same as you hear now. In one year, maybe, after he begin talk he die. Three years ago another medicine-man begin same talk. Heap talk all time. Indians hear all about it everywhere. Indians come from long way off to hear him. They come from the east; they make signs. Two years ago me go to Winnemucca and Pyramid lake, me see Indian Sam, a head man, and Johnson Sides. Sam he tell me he just been to see Indian medicine-man to hear him talk. Sam say medicine-man talk this way:

"All Indians must dance, everywhere, keep on dancing. Pretty soon in next spring Big Man [Great Spirit] come. He bring back all game of every kind. The game be thick everywhere. All dead Indians come back and live again. They all be strong just like young men, be young again. Old blind Indian see again and get young and have fine time. When Old Man [God] comes this way, then all the Indians go to mountains, high up away from whites. Whites can't hurt Indians then. Then while Indians way up high, big flood comes like water and all white people die, get drowned. After that water go way and then nobody but Indians everywhere and game all kinds thick. Then medicine-man tell Indians to send word to all Indians to keep up dancing and the good time will come. Indians who don't dance, who don't believe in this word, will grow little, just about a foot high, and stay that way. Some of them will be turned into wood and be burned in fire."

LINDA HOGAN

Linda Hogan, a Chickasaw poet, novelist, playwright, educator, and essayist, was born in 1947 in Denver, Colorado. She is the author of the novel Mean Spirit *(1990) and collections of poetry, including* Eclipse *(1983) and* Book of Medicines *(1993). Her fourth collection of poems,* Seeing Through the Sun *(1985), received an American Book Award from the Before Columbus Foundation. Hogan is the recipient of other awards, including the Guggenheim, the National Endowment for the Arts, and Five Civilized Tribes Playwriting Award. Hogan currently works as a volunteer in wildlife rehabilitation, and has twice served on the NEA poetry panel. She teaches creative writing and Indian Studies at her alma mater, the University of Colorado.*

The early-twentieth-century discovery of oil on northern Oklahoma land led to great wealth for the Osage tribe and a dark story of white efforts to take the wealth away from the Osage. In Mean Spirits, *a retelling of that history, Linda Hogan weaves a Faulknerian thicket of voices which helps us to an intimacy with events and perhaps an ability to re-see our story of who we have been and might be.*

FROM *MEAN SPIRIT*

OKLAHOMA, 1922

That summer a water diviner named Michael Horse forecast a two-week dry spell.

Until then, Horse's predictions were known to be reliable, and since it was a scorching hot summer, a good number of Indians moved their beds outdoors in hopes a chance breeze would pass over and provide relief from the hot nights. They set them up far from the houses that held the sun's heat long after dark. Cots were unfolded in kitchen gardens. White iron beds sat in horse pastures. Four-posters rested in cornfields that were lying fallow.

What a silent bedchamber the world was, just before morning when even the locusts were still. In that darkness, the white beds were ghostly.

They rose up from the black rolling hills and farmlands. Here, a lonely bed sat next to a barbed wire fence, and there, beneath the protection of an oak tree, a man's lantern burned beside his sleeping form. Near the marshland, tents of gauzy mosquito netting sloped down over the bony shoulders and hips of dreamers. A hand hung over the edge of a bed, fingers reaching down toward bluegrass that grew upward in fields. Given half a chance, the vines and leaves would have crept up the beds and overgrown the sleeping bodies of people.

In one yard, a nervy chicken wanted to roost on a bedframe and was shooed away.

"Go on. Scat!" an old woman cried out, raising herself half up in bed to push the clucking hen back down to the ground.

That would be Belle Graycloud. She was a light-skinned Indian woman, the grandmother of her family. She wore a meteorite on a leather thong around her neck. It had been passed on to her by a man named Osage Star-Looking who'd seen it fall from the sky and smolder in a field. It was her prized possession, although she also had a hand-written book by the old healer, Severance.

Belle slept alone in the herb garden. The rest of her family believed, in varying degrees, that they were modern, so they remained inside the oven-hot walls of the house. Belle's grown daughters drowsed off and on throughout the night. The men tossed. The two young people were red-faced and sweating, tangled in their bed linens on sagging mattresses.

Belle frightened away the hen, then turned on her side and settled back into the feather pillow. Her silver hair spread over the pillow. Even resting outside in the iron bed surrounded by night's terrain, she was a commanding woman with the first morning light on her strong-boned face.

A little ways down the road toward Watona, Indian Territory, a forest of burned trees was just becoming visible in morning's red firelight. Not far from there, at the oil fields, the pumps rose and fell, pulling black oil up through layers of rock. Across the way was a greenwood forest. And not even a full mile away from where Belle slept, just a short walk down the dirt road, Grace Blanket and her daughter Nola slept in a bed that was thoughtfully placed in their flower garden. Half covered in white sheets, they were dark-skinned angels dreaming their way through heaven. A dim lantern burned on a small table beside Grace. Its light fell across the shocking red blooms of roses.

Grace Blanket sat up in bed and put out the lamp. It smoked a little, and she smelled the kerosene. She climbed out from between her damp sheets. Standing in her thin nightdress, buried up to her dark ankles in the wild iris leaves that year after year invaded her garden, Grace bent over her sleeping daughter and shook the girl's shoulder. Grace smiled down at Nola, who had a widow's peak identical to her own, and even before the sleeping girl opened her eyes, Grace began to straighten the sheets on her side of the bed. "Make your bed every morning," they used to say, "and you'll never want for a husband." Grace was a woman who took such sayings to heart and she still wanted a husband. She decided to let Nola sleep a few minutes longer.

Lifting the hem of her nightgown, she walked across the yard, and went inside the screen door to the house.

Indoors, Grace pulled a navy blue dress over her head and zipped it. She fastened a strand of pearls around her neck, then brushed her hair in front of the mirror.

It was a strange house for a Hill Indian, as her people had come to be called. And sometimes, even to herself, Grace looked like an apparition from the past walking through the rooms she'd decorated with heavy, carved furniture and glass chandeliers. It seemed odd, too, that the European furniture was so staunch and upright when Grace was known to be lax at times in her own judgments.

She went to the open window and leaned out. "Nola! Come on now." She could see the girl in the growing daylight. She looked like an insect in its cocoon.

Nola turned over.

The Hill Indians were a peaceful group who had gone away from the changing world some sixty years earlier, in the 1860s. Their survival depended on returning to a simpler way of life, so they left behind them everything they could not carry and moved up into the hills and bluffs far above the town of Watona. Grace Blanket had been born of these, and she was the first to go down out of the hills and enter into the quick and wobbly world of mixed-blood Indians, white loggers, cattle ranchers, and most recently, the oil barons. The Hill Indians were known for their runners, a mystical group whose peculiar running discipline and austere habits earned them a special place in both the human world and the world of spirits.

But there were reasons why Grace had left the hills and moved down to Watona. Her mother, Lila Blanket, was a river prophet, which meant that she was a listener to the voice of water, a woman who interpreted the river's story for her people. A river never lied. Unlike humans, it had no need to distort the truth, and she heard the river's voice unfolding like its water across the earth. One day the Blue River told Lila that the white world was going to infringe on the peaceful Hill People. She listened, then she went back to her tribe and told them, "It is probable that we're going to lose everything. Even our cornfields."

The people were quiet and listened.

Lila continued, "Some of our children have to learn about the white world if we're going to ward off our downfall."

The Hill Indians respected the Blue River and Lila's words, but not one of them wanted to give their children up to that limbo between the worlds, that town named Watona, and finally Lila, who had heard the Blue directly, selected her own beautiful daughter, Grace, for the task. She could not say if it was a good thing or bad thing; it was only what had to be done.

Lila was a trader. That was her job at the Hill settlement. She went down to Watona often to trade sweet potatoes for corn, or sometimes corn for sweet potatoes. On her journeys, she was a frequent visitor at the Grayclouds'. Moses Graycloud, the man of the house, was Lila's second cousin. She liked him. He was a good Indian man; a rancher who kept a pasture and barn lot full of cattle and a number of good-looking horses. One day, when she mustered up enough strength, Lila took cornmeal and apples down to the small town, stopped by the Gray-cloud house, and knocked on the door.

As always, Belle was happy to see Lila Blanket. She opened the door for her. "Come in. Welcome." She held Lila's hand and smiled at her. But when she saw Lila's grief, her expression changed to one of concern. "I see you didn't come to trade food," she said. "What is it?"

Lila covered her face with her hands for a moment, then she took a deep breath and looked at Belle Graycloud. "I need to send my daughter to live near town. We've got too far away from the Americans to know how their laws are cutting into our life."

Belle nodded. She knew that a dam was going to be built at the mouth of the Blue River. The water must have told Lila this, about the army engineers and the surveyors with their red flags.

Lila was so overcome with sadness that she could hardly speak, but she asked Belle, "Can Grace stay with you?"

"Yes. I want her here." Belle put her hand on Lila's arm. "You come too, as often as you want. There's always an extra plate at our table."

On the day Lila took Grace to the Grayclouds, she kissed the girl, embraced her, and left immediately, before she could change her mind. She loved her daughter. She cried loudly all the way home, no matter who passed by or heard her. In fact, an old Osage hermit named John Stink heard the woman's wailing and he came down from his campsite, took Lila's hand, and walked much of the way home with her.

Grace Blanket had a ready smile and a good strong way with Belle's wayward chickens, but she paid little attention to the Indian ways. She hardly seemed like the salvation of the Hill Indians. And she was not at all interested in the white laws that affected her own people. After she finished school, Grace took a job at Palmer's store in town, and put aside her money. It wasn't any time at all before Grace bought a small, grassy parcel of land. She rented it out as a pasture for cattlemen, and one day, while Grace was daydreaming a house onto her land—her dream house had large rooms and a cupid fountain—Lila Blanket arrived in Watona, Indian Territory, with Grace's younger sisters. They were twins, ten years old, and the older woman wanted them to live with Grace and go to school. Their American names were Sara and Molene. And they had the same widow's peak that every Blanket woman had. They were wide-eyed girls, looking around at the world of automobiles and blond people. The longer they were there, the more they liked Watona. And the more Lila visited them, the more she hated the shabby little town with its red stone buildings and flat roofs. It was a magnet of evil that attracted and held her good daughters.

But the girls were the last of the Hill Indians ever to move down to Watona. Molene died several summers later, of an illness spread by white men who worked on the railroad. Sara caught the same paralyzing illness and was forced to remain in bed, motionless for over a year while Grace took care of her. By the time Sara was healthy enough to sit up in a wheelchair, both she and Grace wanted to remain in Watona. It was easier to wash clothing in the wringer washers, she reasoned, than to stir hot water tubs at home, and it was a most amazing thing to go for a ride in an automobile, and to turn on electric lights with the flick of a fingertip. And the delicate white women made such beautiful music on their pianos that Grace wanted one desperately and put away some of her earnings in a sugar bowl toward that cause.

There also were more important reasons why they remained; in the early 1900s each Indian had been given their choice of any parcel of land not already claimed by the white Americans. Those pieces of land were called allotments. They consisted of 160 acres a person to farm, sell, or use in any way they desired. The act that offered allotments to the Indians, the Dawes Act, seemed generous at first glance so only a very few people realized how much they were being tricked, since numerous tracts of unclaimed land became open property for white settlers, homesteaders, and ranchers. Grace and Sara, in total ignorance, selected dried-up acreages that no one else wanted. No one guessed that black undercurrents of oil moved beneath that earth's surface.

When Belle Graycloud saw the land Grace selected, and that it was stony and dry, she shook her head in dismay and said to Grace, "It's barren land. What barren, useless land." But Grace wasn't discouraged. With good humor, she named her property "The Barren Land." Later, after oil was found there, she called it "The Baron Land," for the oil moguls.

It was Michael Horse, the small-boned diviner who'd predicted the two-week dry spell, who had been the first person to discover oil on the Indian wasteland, and he found it on Grace's parched allotment.

With his cottonwood dowsing rod, he'd felt a strong underground pull, followed it straight through the dry prairie grass, turned a bit to the left, and said, "Drill here. I feel water." Then he smiled and showed off his three gold teeth. The men put down an auger, bored deep into the earth, and struck oil on Grace Blanket's land.

Michael Horse fingered one of his long gray braids that hung down his chest. "I'll be damned," he said. He was worried. He didn't know how he had gone wrong. He had 363 wells to his credit. There was no water on Grace Blanket's land, just the thick black fluid that had no use at all for growing corn or tomatoes. Not even zucchini squash would grow there. He took off his glasses and he put them in his shirt pocket. He didn't want to see what happened next.

When Grace Blanket's first lease check came in from the oil company, she forgot the cupid fountain and moved into a house with Roman columns. She bought a grand piano, but to her disappointment she was without talent for music. No matter how she pressed down the ivory keys, she couldn't play the songs she'd heard and loved when white women sang them. After several months, she gave up and moved the piano outside to a chicken coop where it sat neglected, out of tune, and swelling up from the humidity. When a neighboring chicken built a nest on the keys, Grace didn't bother to remove the straw and feathers.

After that, she only bought items she could put to good use. She bought crystal champagne glasses that rang like bells when a finger was run over the rim, a tiny typewriter that tapped out the English words she'd learned in school, and a white fur cape that brought out the rich chestnut brown in her dark skin. She wore the cape throughout her pregnancy, even on warmer days, so much that Belle Graycloud poked fun at her. "When that baby comes, it's going to be born with a fan in its tiny hands."

"That's all right," said Grace, flashing a smile. "Just so long as it's electric."

"Say, who is the father, anyway?" Belle asked. But Grace just looked away like she hadn't heard.

After Nola was born, Grace took the child back a few times each year to the world of the Hill society, and while Nola had a stubborn streak, even as an infant, she was peaceful and serene in the midst of her mother's people. As much as the child took to the quieter ways of the Hill Indians, they likewise took to her, and while Grace continued to make her way in life, enjoying the easy pleasures money could buy, not one of those luxuries mattered a whit to Nola. By the time she was five years old, it was apparent to everyone that Nola was ill-suited for town life. She was a gentle child who would wander into the greenwood forest and talk to the animals. She understood their ways. Lila thought that perhaps her granddaughter was going to be the one to return to the people. Nola, not Grace, was the river's godchild.

But what Lila didn't know, even up to the day she died, was that her daughter's oil had forestalled the damming of the Blue River, and that without anyone realizing it, the sacrifice of Grace to the town of Watona had indeed been the salvation of the Hill Indians. The dam would not go in until all the dark wealth was removed from inside the land.

JOHN GRAVES

John Graves was born in Fort Worth, Texas, in 1920. Graves remained there until he attended Rice Institute. After graduation, Graves went to the Marine Corps officers' school at Quantico. When World War II began, he was shipped off to the Pacific, where he served with the Fourth Marine Division until he was wounded at Saipan and invalided home. After the war, he received his M.A. at Columbia University and began writing. He is the author of such distinguished books as Goodbye to a River *(1959),* Hard Scrabble *(1974),* From a Limestone Ledge *(1980), and* Blue and Some Other Dogs *(1981). Graves lives in Glen Rose, Texas.*

"The Last Running," which ran in The Atlantic Monthly *in 1959, is a narrative I've heard spoken of as the "the great father of stories ever written about the 19th Century West." It looks back to the short-lived world of horsemen, Native American and white, warring for possession of the vast interior of the continent, and shows how warfare must be ultimately resolved—by honoring the dreams of onetime enemies, rediscovering humor, and settling down to live in peace.*

THE LAST RUNNING

They called him Pajarito, in literal trader-Spanish interpretation of his surname, or more often Tom Tejano, since he had been there in those early fighting days before the Texans had flooded up onto the plains in such numbers that it became no longer practical to hate them with specificity.

After the first interview, when he had climbed down from the bed where an aching liver held him and had gone out onto the porch to salute them, only to curse in outrage and clump back into the house when he heard what they wanted, the nine of them sat like grackles about the broad gray-painted steps and talked, in Comanche, about Tom Texan the Little Bird and the antique times before wire fences had partitioned the prairies. At least, old Juan the cook said that was what they were talking about.

Mostly it was the old men who talked, three of them, one so de-

crepit that he had had to make the trip from Oklahoma in a lopsided
carryall drawn by a piebald mare, with an odd long bundle sticking out
the back, the rest riding alongside on ponies. Of the other six, two were
middle-aged and four were young.

Their clothes ran a disastrous gamut from buckskin to faded calico
and blue serge, but under dirty Stetsons they wore their hair long and
braided, plains style. Waiting, sucking Durham cigarettes and speaking
Comanche, they sat about the steps and under the cottonwoods in the
yard and ignored those of us who drifted near to watch them, except
the one or two whom they considered to have a right to their attention.
Twice a day for two days they built fires and broiled unsymmetrical
chunks of the fat calf which, from his bed, furiously, Tom Bird had
ordered killed for them. At night—it was early autumn—they rolled up
in blankets about the old carryall and slept on the ground.

"They show any signs of leaving?" Tom Bird asked me when I
went into his room toward evening of the second day.

I said, "No, sir. They told Juan they thought you could spare one
easily enough, since all of them and the land too used to be theirs."

"They didn't used to be nobody's!" he shouted.

"They've eaten half that animal since they got here," I said. "I never
saw anybody that could eat meat like that, and nothing but meat."

"No, nor ever saw anything else worth seeing," he said, his somber
gray eyes brooding. He was one of the real ones, and none of them are
left now. That was in the twenties; he was my great-uncle, and he had
left Mississippi in disgust at sixteen to work his way out on the high
plains to the brawling acquisitive Texas frontier. At the age of eighty-
five he possessed—more or less by accident, since cattle rather than land
had always meant wealth to him—a medium-large ranch in the canyon
country where the Cap Rock falls away to rolling prairies, south of the
Texas Panhandle. He had buried two wives and had had no children
and lived there surrounded by people who worked for him. When I had
showed up there, three years before the Comanches' visit, he had merely
grunted at me on the porch, staring sharply at my frail physique, and
had gone right on arguing with his manager about rock salt in the pastures. But a month later, maybe when he decided I was going to pick
up weight and live, we had abruptly become friends. He was given to
quick gruff judgments and to painful retractions.

He said in his room that afternoon, "God damn it. I'll see them in
hell before they get one, deeper than you can drop an anvil."

"You want me to tell them that?"

"Hell, yes," he said. "No. Listen, have you talked any with that old one? Starlight, they call him."

I said that neither Starlight nor the others had even glanced at any of us.

Tom Bird said, "You tell him you're kin to me. He knows a lot, that one."

"What do you want me to say about the buffalo?"

"Nothing," he said and narrowed his eyes as a jab of pain shot through him from that rebellious organ which was speaking loudly now of long-gone years of drinking at plains mudholes and Kansas saloons. He grunted. "Not a damn thing," he said. "I already told them."

Starlight paid no attention at all when I first spoke to him. I had picked up a poor grade of Spanish from old Juan in three years, but was timid about using it, and to my English he showed a weathered and not even disdainful profile.

I stated my kinship to Tom Bird and said that Tom Bird had told me to speak to him.

Starlight stared at the fourteen pampered bison grazing in their double-fenced pasture near the house, where my great-uncle could watch them from his chair in the evenings. He had bred them from seed stock given him in the nineties by Charles Goodnight, and the only time one of them had ever been killed and eaten was when the governor of the state and a historical society had driven out to give the old man some sort of citation. When the Comanches under Starlight had arrived, they had walked down to the pasture fence and had looked at the buffalo for perhaps two hours, hardly speaking, studying the cows and the one calf and the emasculated males and the two bulls—old Shakespeare, who had killed a horse once and had put innumerable men up mesquite trees and over fences, and his lecherous though rarely productive son, John Milton.

Then they had said, matter-of-factly, that they wanted one of the animals.

Starlight's old-man smell was mixed with something wild, perhaps wood smoke. His braids were a soiled white. One of the young men glanced at me after I had spoken and said something to him in Comanche. Turning then, the old Indian looked at me down his swollen nose. His face was hexagonal and broad, but sunken where teeth were gone. He spoke.

The young man said in English with an exact accent, "He wants to know what's wrong with old Tom Bird, not to talk to friends."

All of them were watching me, the young ones with more affability than the others. I said Tom Bird was sick in the liver and patted my own.

Starlight said in Spanish, "Is he dying?"

I answered in Spanish that I didn't think so but that it was painful.

He snorted much like Tom Bird himself and turned to look again at the buffalo in the pasture. The conversation appeared to have ended, but not knowing how to leave I sat there on the top step beside the old Comanche, the rest of them ranged below us and eyeing me with what I felt to be humor. I took out cigarettes and offered them to the young man, who accepted the package and passed it along, and when it got back to me it was nearly empty. I got the impression that this gave them amusement, too, though no one had smiled. We all sat blowing smoke into the crisp evening air.

Then, it seemed, some ritual biding time had passed. Old Starlight began to talk again. He gazed at the buffalo in the pasture under the fading light and spoke steadily in bad Spanish with occasional phrases of worse English. The young Indian who had translated for me in the beginning lit a small stick fire below the steps. From time to time one of the other old men would obtrude a question or a correction, and they would drop into the angry Comanche gutturals, and the young man, whose name was John Oak Tree, would tell me what they were saying.

The story went on for an hour or so; when Starlight stopped talking they trooped down to the carryall and got their blankets and rolled up in them on the ground. In the morning I let my work in the ranch office wait and sat down again with the Comanches on the steps, and Starlight talked again. The talk was for me, since I was Tom Bird's kinsman. Starlight did not tell the story as I tell it here. Parts I had to fill in later in conversation with Tom Bird, or even from books. But this was the story.

Without knowing his exact age, he knew that he was younger than Tom Bird, about the age of dead Quanah Parker, under whom he had more than once fought. He had come to warrior's age during the big fight the white men had had among themselves over the black men. Born a Peneteka or Honey Eater while the subtribal divisions still had meaning, he remembered the surly exodus from the Brazos reservation to Oklahoma in 1859, the expulsion by law of the Comanches from all of Texas.

But white laws had not meant much for another ten years or so. It was a time of blood and confusion, a good time to be a Comanche and fight the most lost of all causes. The whites at the Oklahoma agencies were Northern and not only tolerated but sometimes egged on and armed the parties striking down across the Red, with the full moon, at the line of settlements established by the abominated and tenacious Texans. In those days, Starlight said, Comanches held Texans to be another breed of white men, and even after they were told that peace had smiled again among whites, they did not consider this to apply to that race which had swarmed over the best of their grass and timber.

In the beginning, the raids had ritual formality and purpose; an individual party would go south either to make war, or to steal horses, or to drive off cattle for trading to the New Mexican *comancheros* at plains rendezvous, or maybe just reminiscently to run deer and buffalo over the old grounds. But the distinctions dimmed. In conservative old age Starlight believed that the Comanches' ultimate destruction was rooted in the loss of the old disciplines. That and smallpox and syphilis and whiskey. And Mackenzie's soldiers. All those things ran in an apocalyptic pack, like wolves in winter.

They had gone horse-raiding down into the Brazos country, a dozen of them, all young and all good riders and fighters. They captured thirty horses here and there in the perfect stealth that pride demanded, without clashes, and were headed back north up the Keechi Valley near Palo Pinto when a Texan with a yellow beard caught them in his corral at dawn and killed two of them with a shotgun. They shot the Texan with arrows; Starlight himself peeled off the yellow scalp. Then, with a casualness bred of long cruelty on both sides, they killed his wife and two children in the log house. She did not scream as white women were said to do, but until a hatchet cleaved her skull kept shouting, "Git out! Git, git, git."

And collecting five more horses there, they continued the trek toward the Territory, driving at night and resting at known secret spots during the days.

The leader was a son of old Iron Shirt, Pohebits Quasho, bullet-dead on the Canadian despite his Spanish coat of mail handed down from the old haughty days. Iron Shirt's son said that it was bad to have

killed the woman and the children, but Starlight, who with others
laughed at him, believed even afterward that it would have been the
same if they had let the woman live.

What was certain was that the Texans followed, a big party with
men among them who could cut trail as cleanly as Indians. They followed quietly, riding hard and resting little, and on the third evening,
when the Comanches were gathering their herd and readying themselves
to leave a broad enclosed creek valley where they had spent the day,
their sentry on a hill yelled and was dead, and the lean horsemen with
the wide hats were pouring down the hillside shouting the long shout
that belonged to them.

When it happened, Starlight was riding near the upper end of the
valley with the leader. The only weapons with them were their knives
and Starlight's lance, with whose butt he had been poking the rumps of
the restive stolen horses as they hazed them toward camp below. As they
watched, the twenty or more Texans overrode the camp, and in the
shooting and confusion the two Comanches heard the end of their five
companions who had been there afoot.

"I knew this," the leader said.

"You knew it," Starlight answered him bitterly. "You should have
been the sentry, Know-much."

Of the other two horse gatherers, who had been working the lower
valley, they could see nothing, but a group of the Texans rode away
from the camp in that direction, yelling and firing. Then others broke
toward Starlight and the leader a half mile above.

"We can run around them to the plain below," the son of Iron
Shirt said. "Up this creek is bad."

Starlight did not know the country up the creek, but he knew what
he felt, and feeling for a Comanche was conviction. He turned his pony
upstream and spurred it.

"Ragh!" he called to the leader in farewell. "You're dirty luck!"
And he was right, for he never saw the son of Iron Shirt again. Or the
other two horse gatherers either.

But the son of Iron Shirt had been right, too, because ten minutes
later Starlight was forcing his pony among big fallen boulders in a root
tangle of small steep canyons, each of which carried a trickle to the
stream below. There was no way even to lead a horse up their walls; he
had the feeling that any one of them would bring him to a blind place.

Behind him shod hoofs rang; he whipped the pony on, but a big

Texan on a bay horse swept fast around a turn in the canyon, jumping the boulders, and with a long lucky shot from a pistol broke Starlight's pony's leg. The Comanche fell with the pony but lit cat-bouncing and turned, and as the Texan came down waited crouched with the lance. The Texan had one of the pistols that shot six times, rare then in that country. Bearing down, he fired three times, missing each shot, and then when it was the moment Starlight feinted forward and watched the Texan lurch aside from the long bright blade, and while he was off balance, Starlight drove it into the Texan's belly until it came out the back. The blade snapped as the big man's weight came onto it, falling.

Starlight sought the pistol for a moment but not finding it ran to the canyon wall and began climbing. He was halfway up the fifty feet of its crumbling face when the other Texan rode around the turn and stopped, and from his unquiet horse, too hastily, fired a rifle shot that blew Starlight's left eye full of powdered sandstone.

He was among swallows' nests. Their molded mud crunched under his hands; the birds flew in long loops, chittering about his head. Climbing, he felt the Texan's absorbed reloading behind and below him as the horse moved closer, and when he knew with certainty that it was time, looked around to see the long caplock rifle rising again.

The bullet smashed through his upper left arm, and he hung only by his right, but with the long wiry strength of trick horsemanship he swung himself up and onto the overhanging turf of the cliff's top. A round rock the size of a buffalo's head lay there. Almost without pausing he tugged it loose from the earth and rolled it back over the cliff. It came close. The Texan grabbed the saddle as his horse reared, and dropped his rifle. They looked at each other. Clutching a blood-greasy, hanging arm, the Comanche stared down at a big nose and a pair of angry gray eyes, and the young Texan stared back.

Wheeling, Starlight set off trotting across the hills. That night before hiding himself he climbed a low tree and quavered for hours like a screech owl, but no one answered. A month later, an infected skeleton, he walked into the Penateka encampment at Fort Sill, the only one of twelve to return.

That had been his first meeting with Tom Bird.

When telling of the fights, Starlight stood up and gestured in proud physical representation of what he and others had done. He did not give it as a story with a point; it was the recountal of his acquaintance with

a man. In the bug-flecked light of a bulb above the house's screen door
the old Indian should have looked absurd—hipshot, ugly, in a greasy
black hat and a greasy dark suit with a gold chain across its vest,
the dirty braids flying as he creaked through the motions of long-
unmeaningful violence.

But I did not feel like smiling. I looked at the younger Indians
expecting perhaps to find amusement among them, or boredom, or cyn-
icism. It was not there. They were listening, most of them probably not
even understanding the Spanish but knowing the stories, to an ancient
man who belonged to a time when their race had been literally terrible.

In the morning Starlight told of the second time. It had been after
the end of the white men's war; he was a war chief with bull horns on
his head. Thirty well-armed warriors rode behind him when he stopped
a trail herd in the Territory for tribute. Although the cowmen were only
eight, their leader, a man with a black mustache, said that four whoa-
haws were too many. He would give maybe two.

"Four," Starlight said. "Texan."

It was an arraignment, and the white man heard it as such. Looking
at the thirty Comanches, he said that he and his people were not Texans
but Kansas men who were returning home with bought cattle.

"Four whoa-haws," Starlight said.

The white man made a sullen sign with his hand and spoke to his
men, who went to cut out the steers. Starlight watched jealously to make
certain they were not culls, and when three of his young men had them
and were driving them away, he rode up face to face with the white
leader, unfooled even though the mustache was new.

"Tejano," he said. "Stink sonabitch." And reached over and twisted
Tom Bird's big nose, hard, enjoying the rage barely held in the gray
eyes. He patted his scarred left biceps and saw that the white man knew
him, too, and reached over to twist the nose again, Tom Bird too prudent to stop him and too proud to duck his head aside.

"Tobacco, Texan," Starlight said.

Close to snarling, Tom Bird took out a plug. After sampling and
examining it and picking a bit of lint from its surface, Starlight tucked
it into his waistband. Then he turned his horse and, followed by his
thirty warriors, rode away.

In those days revenge had still existed.

He had been, too, with Quanah Parker when that half-white chief had made a separate peace with Tom Bird—Tom Tejano the Pajarito now, looming big on the high plains—as with a government, on the old Bird range up along the Canadian. There had been nearly two hundred with Quanah on a hunt in prohibited territory, and they found few buffalo and many cattle. After the peace with Tom Bird they had not eaten any more wing-branded beef, except later when the Oklahoma agency bought Bird steers to distribute among them.

They had clasped hands there in Quanah's presence, knowing each other well, and in the cowman's tolerant grin and the pressure of his hard fingers Starlight had read more clearly the rout of his people than he had read it anywhere else before.

"Yah, Big-nose," he said, returning the grip and the smile. Tom Bird rode alone with them hunting for ten days and led them to a wide valley twenty miles long that the hide hunters had not yet found, and they showed him there how their fathers had run the buffalo in the long good years before the white men. November it had been, with frosted mornings and yellow bright days; their women had followed them to dress the skins and dry the meat. It was the last of the rich hunting years.

After that whenever Tom Bird passed through Oklahoma he would seek out the Indian who had once pulled his nose and would sometimes bring presents.

But Starlight had killed nine white men while the fighting had lasted.

Dressed, Tom Bird came out onto the porch at eleven o'clock, and I knew from the smooth curve of his cheek that the liver had quit hurting. He was affable and shook all their hands again.

"We'll have a big dinner at noon," he told Starlight in the same flowing pidgin Spanish the old Comanche himself used. "Juan's making it especially for my Comanche friends, to send them on their trip full and happy."

Still unfooled, Starlight exhumed the main topic.

"No!" Tom Bird said.

"You have little courtesy," Starlight said. "You had more once."

Tom Bird said, "There were more of you then. Armed."

Starlight's eyes squinted in mirth which his mouth did not let itself reflect. Absently Tom Bird dug out his Days O'Work and bit a chew, then waved the plug apologetically and offered it to the Comanche.

Starlight took it and with three remaining front teeth haggled off a chunk and pretended to put it into his vest pocket.

They both started laughing, phlegmy, hard-earned, old men's laughter, and for the first time—never having seen Tom Bird out-argued before—I knew that it was going to work out.

Tom Bird said, "Son of a coyote, you . . . I've got four fat *castrados,* and you can have your pick. They're good meat, and I'll eat some of it with you."

Starlight waggled his head mulishly. "Those, no," he said. "The big bull."

Tom Bird stared, started to speak, closed his mouth, threw the returned plug of tobacco down on the porch, and clumped back into the house. The Indians all sat down again. One of the other older men reached over and picked up the plug, had a chew, and stuck it into his denim jacket. Immobility settled.

"Liberty," Starlight said out of nowhere, in Spanish. "They speak much of liberty. Not one of you has ever seen liberty, or smelled it. Liberty was grass, and wind, and a horse, and meat to hunt, and no wire."

From beyond the dark screen door Tom Bird said, "The little bull."

Starlight without looking around shook his head. Tom Bird opened the door so hard that it battered back against the house wall, loosening flakes of paint. He stopped above the old Indian and stood there on bowed legs, looking down. "You rusty old bastard!" he shouted in English. "I ain't got but the two, and the big one's the only good one. And he wouldn't eat worth a damn."

Starlight turned his head and eyed him.

"All right," Tom Bird said, slumping. "All right."

"Thank you, Pajarito," Starlight said.

"Jimmy," the old man said to me in a washed-out voice, "go tell the boys to shoot Shakespeare and hang him up down by the washhouse."

"No," John Oak Tree said.

"What the hell you mean, no?" Tom Bird said, turning to him with enraged pleasure. "That's the one he wants. What you think he's been hollering about for two whole days?"

"Not dead," John Oak Tree said. "My grandfather wants him alive."

"Now ain't that sweet?" the old man said. "Ain't that just beautiful?

And I can go around paying for busted fences from here to Oklahoma and maybe to the God damn Arctic Circle, all so a crazy old murdering Comanche can have him a pet bull buffalo."

Starlight spoke in Spanish, having understood most of the English. "Tom Tejano, listen," he said.

"What?"

"Listen," Starlight said. "We're going to kill him, Tom Tejano. We."

"My butt!" said Tom Bird, and sat down.

In the afternoon, after the fried chicken and the rice and mashed beans and the tamales and the blistering chili, after the courteous belching and the smoking on the porch, everyone on the ranch who could leave his work was standing in the yard under the cottonwoods as the nine Comanches brought their horses up from the lot, where they had been eating oats for two days, and tied them outside the picket fence, saddled.

After hitching Starlight's mare to the carryall, without paying any attention to their audience they began to strip down, methodically rolling their shed clothes into bundles with hats on top and putting them into the back of the carryall. Starlight reeled painfully among them, pointing a dried-up forefinger and giving orders. When they had finished, all of them but he wore only trousers and shoes or moccasins with here and there scraps of the old bone and claw and hide and feather paraphernalia. John Oak Tree had slipped off the high-heeled boots he wore and replaced them with tennis sneakers.

A hundred yards away, gargling a bellow from time to time, old Shakespeare stood jammed into a chute where the hands had choused him. Between bellows, his small hating eye peered toward us from beneath a grayed board; there was not much doubt about how *he* felt.

The Indians took the long, blanketed bundle from the carryall and unrolled it.

"For God's sake!" a cowboy said beside me, a man named Abe Reynolds who had worked a good bit with the little buffalo herd. "For God's sake, this is nineteen damn twenty-three?"

I chuckled. Old Tom Bird turned his gray eyes on us and glared, and we shut up. The bundle held short bows, and quivers of arrows, and long, feather-hung, newly reshafted buffalo lances daubed with red and black. Some took bows and others lances, and among the bowmen were the two old men younger than Starlight, who under dry skins still had ridged segmented muscles.

"Those?" I said in protest, forgetting Tom Bird. "Those two couldn't . . ."

"Because they never killed one," he said without looking around. "Because old as they are, they ain't old enough to have hunted the animal that for two whole centuries was the main thing their people ate, and wore, and made tents and ropes and saddles and every other damn thing they had out of. You close your mouth, boy, and watch."

Starlight made John Oak Tree put on a ribboned medal of some kind. Then they sat the restless ponies in a shifting line, motley still but somehow, now, with the feel of that old terribleness coming off of them like a smell, and Starlight walked down the line of them and found them good and turned to raise his hand at Tom Bird.

Tom Bird yelled.

The man at the chute pulled the bars and jumped for the fence, and eight mounted Indians lashed their ponies into a hard run toward the lumpy blackness that had emerged and was standing there swaying his head, bawling-furious.

Starlight screeched. But they were out of his control now and swept in too eagerly, not giving Shakespeare time to decide to run. When the Indian on the fastest pony, one of the middle-aged men, came down on him shooting what looked like a steady jet of arrows from beside the pony's neck, the bull squared at him. The Indian reined aside, but not enough. The big head came up under the pony's belly, and for a moment horse and rider paused reared against the horns and went pinwheeling backward into the middle of the onrushing others.

"Them idiots!" Abe Reynolds said. "Them plumb idiots!"

One swarming pile then, one mass with sharp projecting heads and limbs and weapons, all of them yelling and pounding and hacking and stabbing, and when old Shakespeare shot out from under the pile, shrugging them helter-skelter aside, he made a run for the house. Behind him they came yipping, leaving a gut-ripped dead horse on the ground beside the chute and another running riderless toward the northeast. One of the downed hunters sat on the ground against the chute as though indifferently. The other—one of the two oldsters—was hopping about on his left leg with an arrow through the calf of his right.

But I was scrambling for the high porch with the spectators, those who weren't grabbing for limbs, though Tom Bird stood his ground cursing as Shakespeare smashed through the white picket fence like dry sunflower stalks and whirled to make another stand under the cotton-woods. Some of the Indians jumped the fence and others poured through the hole he had made, all howling until it seemed there could be no breath left in them. For a moment, planted, Shakespeare stood with arrows bristling brightly from his hump and his loins and took someone's lance in his shoulder. Then he gave up that stand, too, and whisked out another eight feet of fence as he leveled into a long run down the dirt road past the corrals.

They rode him close, poking and shooting.

And finally, when it was all far enough down the road to have the perspective of a picture, John Oak Tree swung out leftward and running parallel to the others pulled ahead and abruptly slanted in with the long bubbling shriek, loud and cutting above all the other noise, that you can call rebel yell or cowboy holler or whatever you want, but which deadly exultant men on horseback have likely shrieked since the Assyrians and long, long before. Shakespeare ran desperately free from the sharp-pointed furor behind him, and John Oak Tree took his dun pony in a line converging sharply with the bull's course, and was there, and jammed the lance's blade certainly just behind the ribs and pointing forward, and the bull skidded to his knees, coughed, and rolled onto his side.

"You call that fair?" Abe Reynolds said sourly.

Nobody had. It was not fair. Fair did not seem to have much to do with what it was.

Starlight's carryall was headed for the clump of horsemen down the road, but the rest of us were held to the yard by the erect stability of Tom Bird's back as he stood in one of the gaps in his picket fence. Beside the chute, Starlight picked up the two thrown Indians and the saddle from the dead horse, the old hunter disarrowed and bleeding now, and drove on to where the rest sat on their ponies around Shakespeare's carcass.

Getting down, he spoke to John Oak Tree. The young Indian dismounted and handed his lance to Starlight, who hopped around for a time with one foot in the stirrup and got up onto the dun pony and brought it back toward the house at a run, the lance held high. Against his greasy vest the big gold watch chain bounced, and his coattails flew, but his old legs were locked snugly around the pony's barrel. He ran it straight at Tom Bird where he stood in the fence gap, and pulled it cruelly onto its hocks three yards away, and held out the lance butt first.

"I carried it when I pulled your nose," he said. "The iron, anyhow."

Tom Bird took it.

"We were there, Tom Tejano," Starlight said.

"Yes," my great-uncle said. "Yes, we were there."

The old Comanche turned the pony and ran it back to the little group of his people and gave it to John Oak Tree, who helped him get back into the carryall. Someone had caught the loose pony. For a few moments all of them sat, frozen, looking down at the arrow-quilled black bulk that had been Shakespeare.

Then, leaving it there, they rode off down the road toward Oklahoma, past the fences of barbed steel that would flank them all the way.

A cowhand, surveying the deadly debris along the route of their run, said dryly, "A neat bunch of scutters, be damn if they ain't."

I was standing beside old Tom Bird, and he was crying. He felt my eyes and turned, the bloody lance upright in his hand, paying no heed to the tears running down the sides of his big nose and into his mustache.

"Damn you, boy," he said. "Damn you for not ever getting to know anything worth knowing. Damn me, too. We had a world, once."

LOUISE ERDRICH

*Louise Erdrich was born in 1954 in Little Falls, Minnesota, grew up in North Dakota, is of German-American and Chippewa descent, and is a member of the Turtle Mountain Band of Ojibwa (Chippewa). She is the author of two books of verse—*Jacklight *(1984) and* Baptism of Desire *(1991); four novels—*Love Medicine *(1984),* The Beet Queen *(1986),* Tracks *(1988), and* The Bingo Palace *(1993). With her husband, Michael Dorris, she is the co-author of another novel,* Crown of Columbus *(1991). Her honors include*

the National Book Critics Circle (1984) award and the Los Angeles
Times *prize for fiction.*

"Fleur," first published in Esquire, *is an early chapter from*
Tracks. *In it, technique mirrors the action, the telling hovering near
the intersection between the "realistic" traditions of European storytelling and what we can think of as "magic realist," or fabulistic,
Native American storytelling—just as the events in the story take place
at a time and in a world where traditional animist and rationalist
European ways of understanding values fall into conflict with one
another.*

FLEUR

The first time she drowned in the cold and glassy waters of Lake Turcot,
Fleur Pillager was only a girl. Two men saw the boat tip, saw her struggle
in the waves. They rowed over to the place she went down, and jumped
in. When they dragged her over the gunwales, she was cold to the touch
and stiff, so they slapped her face, shook her by the heels, worked her
arms back and forth, and pounded her back until she coughed up lake
water. She shivered all over like a dog, then took a breath. But it wasn't
long afterward that those two men disappeared. The first wandered off,
and the other, Jean Hat, got himself run over by a cart.

It went to show, my grandma said. It figured to her, all right. By
saving Fleur Pillager, those two men had lost themselves.

The next time she fell in the lake, Fleur Pillager was twenty years
old and no one touched her. She washed onshore, her skin a dull dead
gray, but when George Many Women bent to look closer, he saw her
chest move. Then her eyes spun open, sharp black riprock, and she
looked at him. "You'll take my place," she hissed. Everybody scattered
and left her there, so no one knows how she dragged herself home.
Soon after that we noticed Many Women changed, grew afraid,
wouldn't leave his house, and would not be forced to go near water.
For his caution, he lived until the day that his sons brought him a new
tin bathtub. Then the first time he used the tub he slipped, got knocked
out, and breathed water while his wife stood in the other room frying
breakfast.

Men stayed clear of Fleur Pillager after the second drowning. Even
though she was good-looking, nobody dared to court her because it was

clear that Misshepeshu, the waterman, the monster, wanted her for himself. He's a devil, that one, love-hungry with desire and maddened for the touch of young girls, the strong and daring especially, the ones like Fleur.

Our mothers warn us that we'll think he's handsome, for he appears with green eyes, copper skin, a mouth tender as a child's. But if you fall into his arms, he sprouts horns, fangs, claws, fins. His feet are joined as one and his skin, brass scales, rings to the touch. You're fascinated, cannot move. He casts a shell necklace at your feet, weeps gleaming chips that harden into mica on your breasts. He holds you under. Then he takes the body of a lion or a fat brown worm. He's made of gold. He's made of beach moss. He's a thing of dry foam, a thing of death by drowning, the death a Chippewa cannot survive.

Unless you are Fleur Pillager. We all knew she couldn't swim. After the first time, we thought she'd never go back to Lake Turcot. We thought she'd keep to herself, live quiet, stop killing men off by drowning in the lake. After the first time, we thought she'd keep the good ways. But then, after the second drowning, we knew that we were dealing with something much more serious. She was haywire, out of control. She messed with evil, laughed at the old women's advice, and dressed like a man. She got herself into some half-forgotten medicine, studied ways we shouldn't talk about. Some say she kept the finger of a child in her pocket and a powder of unborn rabbits in a leather thong around her neck. She laid the heart of an owl on her tongue so she could see at night, and went out, hunting, not even in her own body. We know for sure because the next morning, in the snow or dust, we followed the tracks of her bare feet and saw where they changed, where the claws sprang out, the pad broadened and pressed into the dirt. By night we heard her chuffing cough, the bear cough. By day her silence and the wide grin she threw to bring down our guard made us frightened. Some thought that Fleur Pillager should be driven off the reservation, but not a single person who spoke like this had the nerve. And finally, when people were just about to get together and throw her out, she left on her own and didn't come back all summer. That's what this story is about.

During that summer, when she lived a few miles south in Argus, things happened. She almost destroyed that town.

———

When she got down to Argus in the year of 1920, it was just a small grid of six streets on either side of the railroad depot. There were two elevators, one central, the other a few miles west. Two stores competed for the trade of the three hundred citizens, and three churches quarreled with one another for their souls. There was a frame building for Lutherans, a heavy brick one for Episcopalians, and a long narrow shingled Catholic church. This last had a tall slender steeple, twice as high as any building or tree.

No doubt, across the low, flat wheat, watching from the road as she came near Argus on foot, Fleur saw that steeple rise, a shadow thin as a needle. Maybe in that raw space it drew her the way a lone tree draws lightning. Maybe, in the end, the Catholics are to blame. For if she hadn't seen that sign of pride, that slim prayer, that marker, maybe she would have kept walking.

But Fleur Pillager turned, and the first place she went once she came into town was to the back door of the priest's residence attached to the landmark church. She didn't go there for a handout, although she got that, but to ask for work. She got that too, or the town got her. It's hard to tell which came out worse, her or the men or the town, although the upshot of it all was that Fleur lived.

The four men who worked at the butcher's had carved up about a thousand carcasses between them, maybe half of that steers and the other half pigs, sheep, and game animals like deer, elk, and bear. That's not even mentioning the chickens, which were beyond counting. Pete Kozka owned the place, and employed Lily Veddar, Tor Grunewald, and my stepfather, Dutch James, who had brought my mother down from the reservation the year before she disappointed him by dying. Dutch took me out of school to take her place. I kept house half the time and worked the other in the butcher shop, sweeping floors, putting sawdust down, running a hambone across the street to a customer's bean pot or a package of sausage to the corner. I was a good one to have around because until they needed me, I was invisible. I blended into the stained brown walls, a skinny, big-nosed girl with staring eyes. Because I could fade into a corner or squeeze beneath a shelf, I knew everything, what the men said when no one was around, and what they did to Fleur.

Kozka's Meats served farmers for a fifty-mile area, both to slaughter, for it had a stock pen and chute, and to cure the meat by smoking it or spicing it in sausage. The storage locker was a marvel, made of many thicknesses of brick, earth insulation, and Minnesota timber, lined inside with sawdust and vast blocks of ice cut from Lake Turcot, hauled down from home each winter by horse and sledge.

A ramshackle board building, part slaughterhouse, part store, was fixed to the low, thick square of the lockers. That's where Fleur worked. Kozka hired her for her strength. She could lift a haunch or carry a pole of sausages without stumbling, and she soon learned cutting from Pete's wife, a string-thin blonde who chain-smoked and handled the razor-sharp knives with nerveless precision, slicing close to her stained fingers. Fleur and Fritzie Kozka worked afternoons, wrapping their cuts in paper, and Fleur hauled the packages to the lockers. The meat was left outside the heavy oak doors that were only opened at 5:00 each afternoon, before the men ate supper.

Sometimes Dutch, Tor, and Lily ate at the lockers, and when they did I stayed too, cleaned floors, restoked the fires in the front smoke-houses, while the men sat around the squat cast-iron stove spearing slats of herring onto hardtack bread. They played long games of poker or cribbage on a board made from the planed end of a salt crate. They talked and I listened, although there wasn't much to hear since almost nothing ever happened in Argus. Tor was married, Dutch had lost my mother, and Lily read circulars. They mainly discussed about the auctions to come, equipment, or women.

Every so often, Pete Kozka came out front to make a whist, leaving Fritzie to smoke cigarettes and fry raised doughnuts in the back room. He sat and played a few rounds but kept his thoughts to himself. Fritzie did not tolerate him talking behind her back, and the one book he read was the New Testament. If he said something, it concerned weather or a surplus of sheep stomachs, a ham that smoked green or the markets for corn and wheat. He had a good-luck talisman, the opal-white lens of a cow's eye. Playing cards, he rubbed it between his fingers. That soft sound and the slap of cards was about the only conversation.

Fleur finally gave them a subject.

Her cheeks were wide and flat, her hands large, chapped, muscular. Fleur's shoulders were broad as beams, her hips fishlike, slippery, narrow. An old green dress clung to her waist, worn thin where she sat. Her braids were thick like the tails of animals, and swung against her when she moved, deliberately, slowly in her work, held in and half-tamed, but only half. I could tell, but the others never saw. They never looked into her sly brown eyes or noticed her teeth, strong and curved and very white. Her legs were bare, and since she padded around in beadwork moccasins they never saw that her fifth toes were missing. They never knew she'd drowned. They were blinded, they were stupid, they only saw her in the flesh.

And yet it wasn't just that she was a Chippewa, or even that she was a woman, it wasn't that she was good-looking or even that she was alone that made their brains hum. It was how she played cards.

Women didn't usually play with men, so the evening that Fleur drew a chair up to the men's table without being so much as asked, there was a shock of surprise.

"What's this," said Lily. He was fat, with a snake's cold pale eyes and precious skin, smooth and lily-white, which is how he got his name. Lily had a dog, a stumpy mean little bull of a thing with a belly drum-tight from eating pork rinds. The dog liked to play cards just like Lily, and straddled his barrel thighs through games of stud, rum poker, vingt-un. The dog snapped at Fleur's arm that first night, but cringed back, its snarl frozen, when she took her place.

"I thought," she said, her voice soft and stroking, "you might deal me in."

There was a space between the heavy bin of spiced flour and the wall where I just fit. I hunkered down there, kept my eyes open, saw her black hair swing over the chair, her feet solid on the wood floor. I couldn't see up on the table where the cards slapped down, so after they were deep in their game I raised myself up in the shadows, and crouched on a sill of wood.

I watched Fleur's hands stack and ruffle, divide the cards, spill them to each player in a blur, rake them up and shuffle again. Tor, short and scrappy, shut one eye and squinted the other at Fleur. Dutch screwed his lips around a wet cigar.

"Gotta see a man," he mumbled, getting up to go out back to the privy. The others broke, put their cards down, and Fleur sat alone in the lamplight that glowed in a sheen across the push of her breasts. I watched her closely, then she paid me a beam of notice for the first time. She turned, looked straight at me, and grinned the white wolf grin a Pillager turns on its victims, except that she wasn't after me.

"Pauline there," she said, "how much money you got?"

We'd all been paid for the week that day. Eight cents was in my pocket.

"Stake me," she said, holding out her long fingers. I put the coins in her palm and then I melted back to nothing, part of the walls and tables. It was a long time before I understood that the men would not have seen me no matter what I did, how I moved. I wasn't anything like Fleur. My dress hung loose and my back was already curved, an old woman's. Work had roughened me, reading made my eyes sore, caring for my mother before she died had hardened my face. I was not much to look at, so they never saw me.

When the men came back and sat around the table, they had drawn together. They shot each other small glances, stuck their tongues in their cheeks, burst out laughing at odd moments, to rattle Fleur. But she never minded. They played their vingt-un, staying even as Fleur slowly gained. Those pennies I had given her drew nickels and attracted dimes until there was a small pile in front of her.

Then she hooked them with five-card draw, nothing wild. She dealt, discarded, drew, and then she sighed and her cards gave a little shiver. Tor's eye gleamed, and Dutch straightened in his seat.

"I'll pay to see that hand," said Lily Veddar.

Fleur showed, and she had nothing there, nothing at all.

Tor's thin smile cracked open, and he threw his hand in too.

"Well, we know one thing," he said, leaning back in his chair, "the squaw can't bluff."

With that I lowered myself into a mound of swept sawdust and slept. I woke up during the night, but none of them had moved yet, so I couldn't either. Still later, the men must have gone out again, or Fritzie come out to break the game, because I was lifted, soothed, cradled in a woman's arms and rocked so quiet that I kept my eyes shut while Fleur rolled me into a closet of grimy ledgers, oiled paper, balls of string, and thick files that fit beneath me like a mattress.

The game went on after work the next evening. I got my eight cents back five times over, and Fleur kept the rest of the dollar she'd won for a stake. This time they didn't play so late, but they played regular, and then kept going at it night after night. They played poker now, or variations, for one week straight, and each time Fleur won exactly one dollar, no more and no less, too consistent for luck.

By this time, Lily and the other men were so lit with suspense that they got Pete to join the game with them. They concentrated, the fat dog sitting tense in Lily Veddar's lap, Tor suspicious, Dutch stroking his huge square brow, Pete steady. It wasn't that Fleur won that hooked them in so, because she lost hands too. It was rather that she never had a freak hand or even anything above a straight. She only took on her low cards, which didn't sit right. By chance, Fleur should have gotten a full or flush by now. The irritating thing was she beat with pairs and never bluffed, because she couldn't, and still she ended up each night with exactly one dollar. Lily couldn't believe, first of all, that a woman could be smart enough to play cards, but even if she was, that she would then be stupid enough to cheat for a dollar a night. By day I watched him turn the problem over, his hard white face dull, small fingers probing at his knuckles, until he finally thought he had Fleur figured out as a bit-time player, caution her game. Raising the stakes would throw her.

More than anything now, he wanted Fleur to come away with something but a dollar. Two bits less or ten more, the sum didn't matter, just so he broke her streak.

Night after night she played, won her dollar, and left to stay in a place that just Fritzie and I knew about. Fleur bathed in the slaughtering tub, then slept in the unused brick smokehouse behind the lockers, a windowless place tarred on the inside with scorched fats. When I brushed against her skin I noticed that she smelled of the walls, rich and woody, slightly burnt. Since that night she put me in the closet I was no longer afraid of her, but followed her close, stayed with her, became her moving shadow that the men never noticed, the shadow that could have saved her.

August, the month that bears fruit, closed around the shop, and Pete and Fritzie left for Minnesota to escape the heat. Night by night, running, Fleur had won thirty dollars, and only Pete's presence had kept Lily at bay. But Pete was gone now, and one payday, with the heat so bad no one could move but Fleur, the men sat and played and waited while she finished work. The cards sweat, limp in their fingers, the table was slick with grease, and even the walls were warm to the touch. The air was motionless. Fleur was in the next room boiling heads.

Her green dress, drenched, wrapped her like a transparent sheet. A skin of lakeweed. Black snarls of veining clung to her arms. Her braids were loose, half-unraveled, tied behind her neck in a thick loop. She stood in steam, turning skulls through a vat with a wooden paddle. When scraps boiled to the surface, she bent with a round tin sieve and scooped them out. She'd filled two dishpans.

"Ain't that enough now?" called Lily. "We're waiting." The stump of a dog trembled in his lap, alive with rage. It never smelled me or noticed me above Fleur's smoky skin. The air was heavy in my corner, and pressed me down. Fleur sat with them.

"Now what do you say?" Lily asked the dog. It barked. That was the signal for the real game to start.

"Let's up the ante," said Lily, who had been stalking this night all month. He had a roll of money in his pocket. Fleur had five bills in her dress. The men had each saved their full pay.

"Ante a dollar then," said Fleur, and pitched hers in. She lost, but they let her scrape along, cent by cent. And then she won some. She played unevenly, as if chance was all she had. She reeled them in. The game went on. The dog was stiff now, poised on Lily's knees, a ball of vicious muscle with its yellow eyes slit in concentration. It gave advice, seemed to sniff the lay of Fleur's cards, twitched and nudged. Fleur was up, then down, saved by a scratch. Tor dealt seven cards, three down. The pot grew, round by round, until it held all the money. Nobody folded. Then it all rode on one last card and they went silent. Fleur picked hers up and blew a long breath. The heat lowered like a bell. Her card shook, but she stayed in.

Lily smiled and took the dog's head tenderly between his palms.

"Say, Fatso," he said, crooning the words, "you reckon that girl's bluffing?"

The dog whined and Lily laughed. "Me too," he said, "let's show." He swept his bills and coins into the pot and then they turned their cards over.

Lily looked once, looked again, then he squeezed the dog up like a fist of dough and slammed it on the table.

Fleur threw her arms out and drew the money over, grinning that same wolf grin that she'd used on me, the grin that had them. She jammed the bills in her dress, scooped the coins up in waxed white paper that she tied with string.

"Let's go another round," said Lily, his voice choked with burrs. But Fleur opened her mouth and yawned, then walked out back to gather slops for the one big hog that was waiting in the stock pen to be killed.

The men sat still as rocks, their hands spread on the oiled wood table. Dutch had chewed his cigar to damp shreds, Tor's eye was dull. Lily's gaze was the only one to follow Fleur. I didn't move. I felt them gathering, saw my stepfather's veins, the ones in his forehead that stood out in anger. The dog had rolled off the table and curled in a knot below the counter, where none of the men could touch it.

Lily rose and stepped out back to the closet of ledgers where Pete kept his private stock. He brought back a bottle, uncorked and tipped it between his fingers. The lump in his throat moved, then he passed it on. They drank, quickly felt the whiskey's fire, and planned with their eyes things they couldn't say out loud.

When they left, I followed. I hid out back in the clutter of broken boards and chicken crates beside the stock pen, where they waited. Fleur could not be seen at first, and then the moon broke and showed her, slipping cautiously along the rough board chute with a bucket in her hand. Her hair fell, wild and coarse, to her waist, and her dress was a floating patch in the dark. She made a pigcalling sound, rang the tin pail lightly against the wood, froze suspiciously. But too late. In the sound of the ring Lily moved, fat and nimble, stepped right behind Fleur and put out his creamy hands. At his first touch, she whirled and doused him with the bucket of sour slops. He pushed her against the big fence and the package of coins split, went clinking and jumping, winked against the wood. Fleur rolled over once and vanished in the yard.

The moon fell behind a curtain of ragged clouds, and Lily followed into the dark muck. But he tripped, pitched over the huge flank of the pig, who lay mired to the snout, heavily snoring. I sprang out of the weeds and climbed the side of the pen, stuck like glue. I saw the sow rise to her neat, knobby knees, gain her balance, and sway, curious, as Lily stumbled forward. Fleur had backed into the angle of rough wood just beyond, and when Lily tried to jostle past, the sow tipped up on her hind legs and struck, quick and hard as a snake. She plunged her head into Lily's thick side and snatched a mouthful of his shirt. She lunged again, caught him lower, so that he grunted in pained surprise. He seemed to ponder, breathing deep. Then he launched his huge body in a swimmer's dive.

The sow screamed as his body smacked over hers. She rolled, striking out with her knife-sharp hooves, and Lily gathered himself upon her, took her foot-long face by the ears and scraped her snout and cheeks against the trestles of the pen. He hurled the sow's tight skull against an iron post, but instead of knocking her dead, he merely woke her from her dream.

She reared, shrieked, drew him with her so that they posed standing upright. They bowed jerkily to each other, as if to begin. Then his arms

swung and flailed. She sank her black fangs into his shoulder, clasping
him, dancing him forward and backward through the pen. Their steps
picked up pace, went wild. The two dipped as one, boxstepped, tripped
each other. She ran her split foot though his hair. He grabbed her kinked
tail. They went down and came up, the same shape and then the same
color, until the men couldn't tell one from the other in that light and
Fleur was able to launch herself over the gates, swing down, hit gravel.

The men saw, yelled, and chased her at a dead run to the smokehouse. And Lily too, once the sow gave up in disgust and freed him.
That is where I should have gone to Fleur, saved her, thrown myself on
Dutch. But I went stiff with fear and couldn't unlatch myself from the
trestles or move at all. I closed my eyes and put my head in my arms,
tried to hide, so there is nothing to describe but what I couldn't block
out, Fleur's hoarse breath, so loud it filled me, her cry in the old language, and my name repeated over and over among the words.

The heat was still dense the next morning when I came back to work.
Fleur was gone but the men were there, slack-faced, hung over. Lily
was paler and softer than ever, as if his flesh had steamed on his bones.
They smoked, took pulls off a bottle. It wasn't noon yet. I worked
awhile, waiting shop and sharpening steel. But I was sick, I was smothered, I was sweating so hard that my hands slipped on the knives, and
I wiped my fingers clean of the greasy touch of the customers' coins.
Lily opened his mouth and roared once, not in anger. There was no
meaning to the sound. His boxer dog, sprawled limp beside his foot,
never lifted its head. Nor did the other men.

They didn't notice when I stepped outside, hoping for a clear
breath. And then I forgot them because I knew that we were all balanced, ready to tip, to fly, to be crushed as soon as the weather broke.
The sky was so low that I felt the weight of it like a yoke. Clouds hung
down, witch teats, a tornado's green-brown cones, and as I watched one
flicked out and became a delicate probing thumb. Even as I picked up
my heels and ran back inside, the wind blew suddenly, cold, and then
came rain.

Inside, the men had disappeared already and the whole place was
trembling as if a huge hand was pinched at the rafters, shaking it. I ran
straight through, screaming for Dutch or for any of them, and then I
stopped at the heavy doors of the lockers, where they had surely taken
shelter. I stood there a moment. Everything went still. Then I heard a

cry building in the wind, faint at first, a whistle and then a shrill scream
that tore through the walls and gathered around me, spoke plain so I
understood that I should move, put my arms out, and slam down the
great iron bar that fit across the hasp and lock.

Outside, the wind was stronger, like a hand held against me. I
struggled forward. The bushes tossed, the awnings flapped off storefronts,
the rails of porches rattled. The odd cloud became a fat snout that nosed
along the earth and sniffled, jabbed, picked at things, sucked them up,
blew them apart, rooted around as if it was following a certain scent,
then stopped behind me at the butcher shop and bored down like a drill.

I went flying, landed somewhere in a ball. When I opened my eyes
and looked, stranger things were happening.

A herd of cattle flew through the air like giant birds, dropping dung,
their mouths opened in stunned bellows. A candle, still lighted, blew
past, and tables, napkins, garden tools, a whole school of drifting eye-
glasses, jackets on hangers, hams, a checkerboard, a lampshade, and at
last the sow from behind the lockers, on the run, her hooves a blur, set
free, swooping, diving, screaming as everything in Argus fell apart and
got turned upside down, smashed, and thoroughly wrecked.

Days passed before the town went looking for the men. They were
bachelors, after all, except for Tor, whose wife had suffered a blow to
the head that made her forgetful. Everyone was occupied with digging
out, in high relief because even though the Catholic steeple had been
torn off like a peaked cap and sent across five fields, those huddled in
the cellar were unhurt. Walls had fallen, windows were demolished, but
the stores were intact and so were the bankers and shop owners who
had taken refuge in their safes or beneath their cash registers. It was a
fair-minded disaster, no one could be said to have suffered much more
than the next, at least not until Fritzie and Pete came home.

Of all the businesses in Argus, Kozka's Meats had suffered worst.
The boards of the front building had been split to kindling, piled in a
huge pyramid, and the shop equipment was blasted far and wide. Pete
paced off the distance the iron bathtub had been flung—a hundred feet.
The glass candy case went fifty, and landed without so much as a cracked
pane. There were other surprises as well, for the back rooms where
Fritzie and Pete lived were undisturbed. Fritzie said the dust still coated
her china figures, and upon her kitchen table, in the ashtray, perched
the last cigarette she'd put out in haste. She lit it up and finished it,

looking through the window. From there, she could see that the old smokehouse Fleur had slept in was crushed to a reddish sand and the stockpens were completely torn apart, the rails stacked helter-skelter. Fritzie asked for Fleur. People shrugged. Then she asked about the others and, suddenly, the town understood that three men were missing.

There was a rally of help, a gathering of shovels and volunteers. We passed boards from hand to hand, stacked them, uncovered what lay beneath the pile of jagged splinters. The lockers, full of the meat that was Pete and Fritzie's investment, slowly came into sight, still intact. When enough room was made for a man to stand on the roof, there were calls, a general urge to hack through and see what lay below. But Fritzie shouted that she wouldn't allow it because the meat would spoil. And so the work continued, board by board, until at last the heavy oak doors of the freezer were revealed and people pressed to the entry. Everyone wanted to be the first, but since it was my stepfather lost, I was let go in when Pete and Fritzie wedged through into the sudden icy air.

Pete scraped a match on his boot, lit the lamp Fritzie held, and then the three of us stood still in its circle. Light glared off the skinned and hanging carcasses, the crates of wrapped sausages, the bright and cloudy blocks of lake ice, pure as winter. The cold bit into us, pleasant at first, then numbing. We must have stood there a couple of minutes before we saw the men, or more rightly, the humps of fur, the iced and shaggy hides they wore, the bearskins they had taken down and wrapped around themselves. We stepped closer and tilted the lantern beneath the flaps of fur into their faces. The dog was there, perched among them, heavy as a doorstop. The three had hunched around a barrel where the game was still laid out, and a dead lantern and an empty bottle, too. But they had thrown down their last hands and hunkered tight, clutching one another, knuckles raw from beating at the door they had also attacked with hooks. Frost stars gleamed off their eyelashes and the stubble of their beards. Their faces were set in concentration, mouths open as if to speak some careful thought, some agreement they'd come to in each other's arms.

Power travels in the bloodlines, handed out before birth. It comes down through the hands, which in the Pillagers were strong and knotted, big, spidery, and rough, with sensitive fingertips good at dealing cards. It comes through the eyes, too, belligerent, darkest brown, the eyes of those in the bear clan, impolite as they gaze directly at a person.

In my dreams, I look straight back at Fleur, at the men. I am no longer the watcher on the dark sill, the skinny girl.

The blood draws us back, as if it runs through a vein of earth. I've come home and, except for talking to my cousins, live a quiet life. Fleur lives quiet too, down on Lake Turcot with her boat. Some say she's married to the waterman, Misshepeshu, or that she's living in shame with white men or windigos, or that she's killed them all. I'm about the only one here who ever goes to visit her. Last winter, I went to help out in her cabin when she bore the child, whose green eyes and skin the color of an old penny made more talk, as no one could decide if the child was mixed blood or what, fathered in a smokehouse, or by a man with brass scales, or by the lake. The girl is bold, smiling in her sleep, as if she knows what people wonder, as if she hears the old men talk, turning the story over. It comes up different every time and has no ending, no beginning. They get the middle wrong too. They only know that they don't know anything.

JOY HARJO

Joy Harjo, born in 1951 in Tulsa, Oklahoma, is an enrolled member of the Creek Tribe. A graduate of the Writer's Workshop at the University of Iowa, she has published four books of poetry including She Had Some Horses *(1983) and* In Mad Love and War *(1990).* Secrets from the Center of the World, *a collection of prose poems detailing Hopi and Navajo homelands, was published in 1989. Among many honors, she has received the William Carlos Williams Award, the Delmore Schwartz Award, The American Book Award, and the 1990 American Indian Distinguished Achievement Award. She is a professor of creative writing at the University of New Mexico. A children's book,* The Goodluck Cat, *was published recently, as well as an anthology of Native American women's writing,* Reinventing the Enemy's Language.

"Deer Dancer," from In Mad Love and War, *is an evocation of a contemporary tavern world of "broken survivors" infused with dreams of the old native world and "ancestors who never left." It is about a woman in revolution against despair, and the rediscovery of significance and meaning in things even after "the real world collapses."*

DEER DANCER

Nearly everyone had left that bar in the middle of winter except the hardcore. It was the coldest night of the year, every place shut down, but not us. Of course we noticed when she came in. We were Indian ruins. She was the end of beauty. No one knew her, the stranger whose tribe we recognized, her family related to deer, if that's who she was, a people accustomed to hearing songs in pine trees, and making them hearts.

The woman inside the woman who was to dance naked in the bar of misfits blew deer magic. Henry Jack, who could not survive a sober day, thought she was Buffalo Calf Woman come back, passed out, his head by the toilet. All night he dreamed a dream he could not say. The next day he borrowed money, went home, and sent back the money I lent. Now that's a miracle. Some people see vision in a burned tortilla, some in the face of a woman.

This is the bar of broken survivors, the club of shotgun, knife wound, of poison by culture. We who were taught not to stare drank our beer. The players gossiped down their cues. Someone put a quarter in the jukebox to relive despair. Richard's wife dove to kill her. We had to hold her back, empty her pockets of knives and diaper pins, buy her two beers to keep her still, while Richard secretly bought the beauty a drink.

How do I say it? In this language there are no words for how the real world collapses. I could say it in my own and the sacred

mounds would come into focus, but I couldn't take it in this
dingy envelope. So I look at the stars in this strange city, frozen
to the back of the sky, the only promises that ever make sense.

My brother-in-law hung out with white people, went to law
school with a perfect record, quit. Says you can keep your laws,
your words. And practiced law on the street with his hands. He
jimmied to the proverbial dream girl, the face of the moon, while
the players racked a new game. He bragged to us, he told her
magic words and that's when she broke, became human.
But we all heard his bar voice crack:

What's a girl like you doing in a place like this?

That's what I'd like to know, what are we all doing in a place
like this?

You would know she could hear only what she wanted to; don't
we all? Left the drink of betrayal Richard bought her, at the bar.
What was she on? We all wanted some. Put a quarter in the juke.
We all take risks stepping into thin air. Our ceremonies didn't
predict this. Or we expected more.

I had to tell you this, for the baby inside the girl sealed up with a
lick of hope and swimming into praise of nations. This is not a
rooming house, but a dream of winter falls and the deer who
portrayed the relatives of strangers. The way back is deer breath
on icy windows.

The next dance none of us predicted. She borrowed a chair for
the stairway to heaven and stood on a table of names. And
danced in the room of children without shoes.

You picked a fine time to leave me, Lucille.
With four hungry children and a crop in the field.

And then she took off her clothes. She shook loose memory,
waltzed with the empty lover we'd all become.

She was the myth slipped down through dreamtime. The promise of feast we all knew was coming. The deer who crossed through knots of a curse to find us. She was no slouch, and neither were we, watching.

The music ended. And so does the story. I wasn't there. But I imagined her like this, not a stained red dress with tape on her heels but the deer who entered our dream in white dawn, breathed mist into pine trees, her fawn a blessing of meat, the ancestors who never left.

PART TWO

TRANSCENDING
THE WESTERN

THE SPANISH WERE PRESENT in the Southwest for centuries, but Meriwether Lewis and William Clark were the first official citizens of the United States to travel in the American West. They were scouting economic possibilities for President Thomas Jefferson. Over the next century, after the conquest of native peoples, the West was settled and established as an economic and intellectual colony of the East. The story which drove that settlement was one about bringing civilization (law and civility) to a place which already had its own rules. It was a story concocted to justify conquest, and in its most nonsensical manifestation it became the story about heroes and shoot-outs and law-bringing we know as "the Western." The only Western included in this collection, "The Man Who Shot Liberty Valance," by Dorothy Johnson, transcends its origins.

It took the West a long time to outgrow that official mythology. The main way this was done was with the help of writers who knew that "the Western" was mostly cooked up for the entertainment of Eastern audiences, and understood it was their responsibility to present us with a report of what actually transpired while the territory was being settled—writers from Teddy Blue Abbott to Mari Sandoz to Bud Guthrie, Wallace Stegner, Ivan Doig, Larry McMurtry, and Mary Clearman Blew.

WALT WHITMAN

Walt Whitman is the central American poet. As Ezra Pound put it, it was Whitman who "broke the new wood." Leaves of Grass was first published in 1855; the collection underwent numerous "triumphant" revisions and additions by the author throughout his life, resulting in a culminating "deathbed" edition, published in 1891–1892, from which this selection was taken. Born May 31, 1819, in West Hills, New York, Whitman worked as a newspaper editor in Brooklyn, New York City, and New Orleans, and later, as a clerk in the Attorney General's office in Washington, DC. He traveled west on two extensive journeys: in 1848, to New Orleans, returning to Brooklyn by way of the Mississippi, the Great Lakes, and the Hudson; and as far west as Colorado on a reading tour in 1879–1880. He died at his home at 328 Mickle Street in Camden, New Jersey, on March 26, 1892.

"Song of the Redwood-Tree," while not first-rate Whitman, is an expression of his yearning to see a spiritually vital "New Society" evolve into being through connection to what he sees as "sweeter, rarer, healthier . . . fields of Nature" in the West. It assumes a relationship between the natural unexploited place and a good unexploitive society, an idea which echoes down to Whitman from the Romantics, and from Whitman on through so much later writing about the American West by Westerners, from Wallace Stegner and Edward Abbey to Terry Tempest Williams.

SONG OF THE REDWOOD-TREE
FROM *LEAVES OF GRASS*

1

A California song!
A prophecy and indirection—a thought impalpable, to
    breathe, as air;
A chorus of dryads, fading, departing—or hamadryads
    departing;
A murmuring, fateful, giant voice, out of the earth and sky,
Voice of a mighty dying tree in the Redwood forest dense.

Farewell, my brethren,
Farewell, O earth and sky—farewell, ye neighboring waters;
My time has ended, my term has come.

2

Along the northern coast,
Just back from the rock-bound shore, and the caves,
In the saline air from the sea, in the Mendocino country,
With the surge for bass and accompaniment low and hoarse,
With crackling blows of axes, sounding musically, driven by
    strong arms,
Riven deep by the sharp tongues of the axes—there in the
    Redwood forest dense,
I heard the mighty tree its death-chant chanting.

The choppers heard not—the camp shanties echoed not;
The quick-ear'd teamsters, and chain and jack-screw men,
    heard not,
As the wood-spirits came from their haunts of a thousand
    years, to join the refrain;
But in my soul I plainly heard.

Murmuring out of its myriad leaves,
Down from its lofty top, rising two hundred feet high,
Out of its stalwart trunk and limbs—out of its foot-thick
    bark,
That chant of the seasons and time—chant, not of the past
    only, but the future.

3

You untold life of me,
And all you venerable and innocent joys,
Perennial, hardy life of me, with joys, 'mid rain, and many a
    summer sun,
And the white snows, and night, and the wild winds;
O the great patient, rugged joys! my soul's strong joys, unreck'd by
    man;
(For know I bear the soul befitting me—I too have consciousness,
    identity,

And all the rocks and mountains have—and all the earth;)
Joys of the life befitting me and brothers mine,
Our time, our term has come.

Nor yield we mournfully, majestic brothers,
We who have grandly fill'd our time;
With Nature's calm content, and tacit, huge delight,
We welcome what we wrought for through the past,
And leave the field for them.

For them predicted long,
For a superber Race—they too to grandly fill their time,
For them we abdicate—in them ourselves, ye forest kings!
In them these skies and airs—these mountain peaks—Shasta—
    Nevadas,
These huge, precipitous cliffs—this amplitude—these valleys grand
    —Yosemite,
To be in them absorb'd, assimilated.

4

Then to a loftier strain,
Still prouder, more ecstatic, rose the chant,
As if the heirs, the Deities of the West,
Joining, with master-tongue, bore part.

Not wan from Asia's fetishes,
Nor red from Europe's old dynastic slaughter-house,
(Area of murder-plots of thrones, with scent left yet of wars and
    scaffolds every where,)
But come from Nature's long and harmless throes—peacefully
    builded thence,
These virgin lands—Lands of the Western Shore,
To the new Culminating Man—to you, the Empire New,
You, promis'd long, we pledge, we dedicate.
You occult, deep volitions,
You average Spiritual Manhood, purpose of all, pois'd on yourself—
    giving, not taking law,
You Womanhood divine, mistress and source of all, whence life and
    love, and aught that comes from life and love,

You unseen Moral Essence of all the vast materials of America, (age
    upon age, working in Death the same as Life,)
You that, sometimes known, oftener unknown, really shape and
    mould the New World, adjusting it to Time and Space,
You hidden National Will, lying in your abysms, conceal'd, but
    ever alert,
You past and present purposes, tenaciously pursued, may-be
    unconscious of yourselves,
Unswerv'd by all the passing errors, perturbations of the surface;
You vital, universal, deathless germs, beneath all creeds, arts,
    statutes, literatures,
Here build your homes for good—establish here—These areas
    entire, Lands of the Western Shore,
We pledge, we dedicate to you.

For man of you—your characteristic Race,
Here may he hardy, sweet, gigantic grow—here tower, proportionate
    to Nature,
Here climb the vast, pure spaces, unconfined, uncheck'd by wall or
    roof,
Here laugh with storm or sun—here joy—here patiently inure,
Here heed himself, unfold himself (not others' formulas heed)—here
    fill his time,
To duly fall, to aid, unreck'd at last,
To disappear, to serve.

Thus, on the northern coast,
In the echo of teamsters' calls, and the clinking chains, and
    the music of choppers' axes,
The falling trunk and limbs, the crash, the muffled shriek,
    the groan,
Such words combined from the Redwood-tree—as of
    wood-spirits' voices ecstatic, ancient and rustling,
The century-lasting, unseen dryads, singing, withdrawing,
All their recesses of forests and mountains leaving,
From the Cascade range to the Wasatch—or Idaho far, or
    Utah,
To the deities of the Modern henceforth yielding,

The chorus and indications, the vistas of coming humanity—
        the settlements, features all,
In the Mendocino woods I caught.

5

The flashing and golden pageant of California!
The sudden and gorgeous drama—the sunny and ample
        lands;
The long and varied stretch from Puget Sound to Colorado
        south;
Lands bathed in sweeter, rarer, healthier air—valleys and
        mountain cliffs;
The fields of Nature long prepared and fallow—the silent,
        cyclic chemistry;
The slow and steady ages plodding—the unoccupied surface
        ripening—the rich ores forming beneath;
At last the New arriving, assuming, taking possession,
A swarming and busy race settling and organizing every
        where;
Ships coming in from the whole round world, and going out
        to the whole world,
To India and China and Australia, and the thousand island
        paradises of the Pacific;
Populous cities—the latest inventions—the steamers on the
        rivers—the railroads—with many a thrifty farm, with
        machinery,
And wool, and wheat, and the grape—and diggings of
        yellow gold.

6

But more in you than these, Lands of the Western Shore!
(These but the means, the implements, the standing-ground,)
I see in you, certain to come, the promise of thousands of
        years, till now deferr'd,
Promis'd, to be fulfill'd, our common kind, the Race.

The New Society at last, proportionate to Nature,
In Man of you, more than your mountain peaks, or stalwart
        trees imperial,

In Woman more, far more, than all your gold, or vines, or
    even vital air.

Fresh come, to a New World indeed, yet long prepared,
I see the Genius of the Modern, child of the Real and Ideal,
Clearing the ground for broad humanity, the true America,
    heir of the past so grand,
To build a grander future.

e. e. cummings

*"Only so long as we can laugh at ourselves are we nobody else,"
advises Edward Estlin Cummings, one of the true iconoclasts of the
poetic line. Champion of small causes and lower cases, Cummings
began his literary career with* The Enormous Room *(1922), a
semifictional description of his internment in a French concentration
camp during World War I, celebrating the idiosyncratic humor of his
fellow prisoners. The clash between institutional order ("manunkind")
and organic complexity, evident in the title of his first collection of
poetry,* Tulips and Chimneys *(1923), is a major characteristic of his
writing, both in style and content. Other important works include*
ViVa *(1931),* no thanks *(1935), and* XAIPE *(1950). His travels
in Russia are detailed in* Eimi *(1933). His Charles Eliot Norton
lectures, given at Harvard (his alma mater), can be found in* Six
Nonlectures, *published in 1953. Cummings was born October 14,
1894, in Cambridge, Massachusetts, and died in Conway, New
Hampshire, in 1962.*

*   "Buffalo Bill's," one of several "Portraits" in* Tulips and
Chimneys, *is a bullet of a poem that manages to both depict the
Western myth of the gunfighter as hero and shoot its way through the
heart of that myth. Cummings can hardly be thought of as a Western
writer, but the poem encapsulates the constant tension between the
defining pop-story legend of the West and the gritty on-the-ground*

realities of Western lives, a struggle that will continue in the contemporary West so long as Westerners keep trying to live the pop gunslinger legend.

Buffalo Bill's
defunct
　　　who used to
　　　ride a watersmooth-silver
　　　　　　　　　　stallion
and break onetwothreefourfive pigeonsjustlikethat
　　　　　　　　　　　　　　　　　Jesus

he was a handsome man
　　　　　　　　　　and what i want to know is
how do you like your blueeyed boy
Mister Death

D. H. LAWRENCE

D. H. Lawrence was born in Nottinghamshire, England, in 1885. His first novel, The White Peacock, *was published in 1911, the same year he had to give up his career as a schoolteacher due to illness ultimately diagnosed as tuberculosis. After eloping to Germany with Frieda Weekley, the German wife of Lawrence's former tutor, he returned to England in 1914, and wrote his most famous novels,* The Rainbow *and* Women in Love. *The former was suppressed, and he could not find a publisher for the latter. After World War I, Lawrence began his "savage pilgrimage," searching for a more fulfilling way of life, far from the industrial cities of Europe. This took him to Sardinia, Ceylon, Australia, and, finally, an extended sojourn at Taos, New Mexico, where he found a community of artists who shared his joy of life and an entourage of women who admired him.*

He returned to Europe in 1925 and wrote his last novel, Lady
Chatterley's Lover, *in 1928, only to see it banned; he died on
March 4, 1930, at Vence, France.*

In "Fenimore Cooper's Leatherstocking Tales," from Lawrence's
Studies in Classic American Literature, *he confronts the literary
mythologizing of the West, fiercely and humorously indicting Cooper
and other romantic "Western" writers. Lawrence, a pioneer in revi-
sionism, understood that the mythology not only masked the inhumane
nature of Manifest Destiny as it developed, but, in masking it, helped
to perpetuate the barbarism. Lawrence understood that we first had to
expose the possibility of brutality in our nature in order to overcome it.*

FROM "FENIMORE COOPER'S
LEATHERSTOCKING TALES," IN
*STUDIES IN CLASSIC
AMERICAN LITERATURE*

Now the essential history of the people of the United States seems to
me just this: At the Renaissance the old consciousness was becoming a
little tight. Europe sloughed her last skin, and started a new, final phase.

But some Europeans recoiled from the last final phase. They
wouldn't enter the *cul de sac* of post-Renaissance, "liberal" Europe. They
came to America.

They came to America for two reasons:

(1) To slough the old European consciousness completely.

(2) To grow a new skin underneath, a new form. This second is a
hidden process.

The two processes go on, of course, simultaneously. The slow forming of the new skin underneath is the slow sloughing of the old skin.
And sometimes this immortal serpent feels very happy, feeling a new
golden glow of a strangely-patterned skin envelop him: and sometimes
he feels very sick, as if his very entrails were being torn out of him, as
he wrenches once more at his old skin, to get out of it.

Out! Out! he cries, in all kinds of euphemisms.

He's got to have his new skin on him before ever he can get out.

And he's got to get out before his new skin can ever be his own
skin.

So there he is, a torn divided monster.

The true American, who writhes and writhes like a snake that is long in sloughing.

Sometimes snakes can't slough. They can't burst their old skin. Then they go sick and die inside the old skin, and nobody ever sees the new pattern.

It needs a real desperate recklessness to burst your old skin at last. You simply don't care what happens to you, if you rip yourself in two, so long as you do get out.

It also needs a real belief in the new skin. Otherwise you are likely never to make the effort. Then you gradually sicken and go rotten and die in the old skin.

Now Fenimore stayed very safe inside the old skin: a gentleman, almost a European, as proper as proper can be. And, safe inside the old skin, he *imagined* the gorgeous American pattern of a new skin.

He hated democracy. So he evaded it, and had a nice dream of something beyond democracy. But he belonged to democracy all the while.

Evasion!—Yet even that doesn't make the dream worthless.

Democracy in America was never the same as Liberty in Europe. In Europe Liberty was a great life-throb. But in America Democracy was always something anti-life. The greatest democrats, like Abraham Lincoln, had always a sacrificial, self-murdering note in their voices. American Democracy was a form of self-murder, always. Or of murdering somebody else.

Necessarily. It was a *pis aller*. It was the *pis aller* to European Liberty. It was a cruel form of sloughing. Men murdered themselves into this democracy. Democracy is the utter hardening of the old skin, the old form, the old psyche. It hardens till it is tight and fixed and inorganic. Then it *must* burst, like a chrysalis shell. And out must come the soft grub, or the soft damp butterfly of the American-at-last.

America has gone the *pis aller* of her democracy. Now she must slough even that, chiefly that, indeed.

What did Cooper dream beyond democracy? Why, in his immortal friendship of Chingachgook and Natty Bumppo he dreamed the nucleus of a new society. That is, he dreamed a new human relationship. A stark, stripped human relationship of two men, deeper than the deeps of sex. Deeper than property, deeper than fatherhood, deeper than marriage, deeper than love. So deep that it is loveless. The stark, loveless, wordless unison of two men who have come to the bottom of themselves. This is the new nucleus of a new society, the clue to a new world-epoch. It asks for a great and cruel sloughing first of all. Then it finds a great release into a new world, a new moral, a new landscape.

Natty and the Great Serpent are neither equals nor unequals. Each obeys the other when the moment arrives. And each is stark and dumb in the other's presence, starkly himself, without illusion created. Each is just the crude pillar of a man, the crude living column of his own manhood. And each knows the godhead of this crude column of manhood. A new relationship.

The Leatherstocking novels create the myth of this new relation. And they go backwards, from old age to golden youth. That is the true myth of America. She starts old, old, wrinkled and writhing in an old skin. And there is a gradual sloughing of the old skin, towards a new youth. It is the myth of America.

You start with actuality. *Pioneers* is no doubt Cooperstown, when Cooperstown was in the stage of inception: a village of one wild street of log cabins under the forest hills by Lake Champlain: a village of crude, wild frontiersmen, reacting against civilization.

Towards this frontier-village in the winter time, a negro slave drives a sledge through the mountains, over deep snow. In the sledge sits a fair damsel, Miss Temple, with her handsome pioneer father, Judge Temple. They hear a shot in the trees. It is the old hunter and backwoodsman, Natty Bumppo, long and lean and uncouth, with a long rifle and gaps in his teeth.

Judge Temple is "squire" of the village, and he has a ridiculous, commodious "hall" for his residence. It is still the old English form. Miss Temple is a pattern young lady, like Eve Effingham: in fact, she gets a young and very genteel but impoverished Effingham for a husband. The old world holding its own on the edge of the wild. A bit tiresomely too, with rather more prunes and prisms than one can digest. Too romantic.

Against the "hall" and the gentry, the real frontiers-folk, the rebels. The two groups meet at the village inn, and at the frozen church, and at the Christmas sports, and on the ice of the lake, and at the great pigeon shoot. It is a beautiful, resplendent picture of life. Fenimore puts in only the glamor.

Perhaps my taste is childish, but these scenes in *Pioneers* seem to me marvelously beautiful. The raw village street, with woodfires blinking

through the unglazed window-chinks, on a winter's night. The inn, with
the rough woodsman and the drunken Indian John; the church, with
the snowy congregation crowding to the fire. Then the lavish abundance
of Christmas cheer, and turkey-shooting in the snow. Spring coming,
forests all green, maple sugar taken from the trees: and clouds of pigeons
flying from the south, myriads of pigeons shot in heaps; and night-fishing
on the teeming, virgin lake; and deer-hunting.

Pictures! Some of the loveliest, most glamorous pictures in all
literature.

Alas, without the cruel iron of reality. It is all real enough. Except
that one realizes that Fenimore was writing from a safe distance, where
he would idealize and have his wish-fulfilment.

Because, when one comes to America, one finds that there is always
a certain slightly devilish resistance in the American landscape, and a
certain slightly bitter resistance in the white man's heart. Hawthorne
gives this. But Cooper glosses it over.

The American landscape has never been at one with the white man.
Never. And white men have probably never felt so bitter anywhere, as
here in America, where the very landscape, in its very beauty, seems a
bit devilish and grinning, opposed to us.

Cooper, however, glosses over this resistance, which in actuality
can never quite be glossed over. He *wants* the landscape to be at one
with him. So he goes away to Europe and sees it as such. It is a sort of
vision.

And, nevertheless, the oneing will surely take place—some day.

The myth is the story of Natty. The old, lean hunter and backwoodsman lives with his friend, the grey-haired Indian John, an old
Delaware chief, in a hut within reach of the village. The Delaware is
christianized and bears the Christian name of John. He is tribeless and
lost. He humiliates his grey hairs in drunkenness, and dies, thankful to
be dead, in a forest fire, passing back to the fire whence he derived.

And this is Chingachgook, the splendid Great Serpent of the later
novels.

No doubt Cooper, as a boy, knew both Natty and the Indian John.
No doubt they fired his imagination even then. When he is a man,
crystallized in society and sheltering behind the safe pillar of Mrs. Cooper, these two old fellows become a myth to his soul. He traces himself
to a new youth in them.

As for the story: Judge Temple has just been instrumental in passing the wise game laws. But Natty has lived by his gun all his life in the wild woods, and simply childishly cannot understand how he can be poaching on the Judge's land among the pine trees. He shoots a deer in the close season. The Judge is all sympathy, but the law *must* be enforced. Bewildered Natty, an old man of seventy, is put in stocks and in prison. They release him as soon as possible. But the thing was done.

The letter killeth.

Natty's last connection with his own race is broken. John, the Indian, is dead. The old hunter disappears, lonely and severed, into the forest, away, away from his race.

In the new epoch that is coming, there will be no letter of the law.

Chronologically, *The Last of the Mohicans* follows *Pioneers*. But in the myth, *The Prairie* comes next.

Cooper of course knew his own America. He traveled west and saw the prairies, and camped with the Indians of the prairie.

The Prairie, like *Pioneers*, bears a good deal the stamp of actuality. It is a strange, splendid book, full of sense of doom. The figures of the great Kentuckian men, with their wolf-women, loom colossal on the vast prairie, as they camp with their wagons. These are different pioneers from Judge Temple. Lurid, brutal, tinged with the sinisterness of crime; these are the gaunt white men who push west, push on and on against the natural opposition of the continent. On towards a doom. Great wings of vengeful doom seem spread over the west, grim against the intruder. You feel them again in Frank Norris's novel, *The Octopus*. While in the West of Bret Harte there is a very devil in the air, and beneath him are sentimental self-conscious people being wicked and goody by evasion.

In *The Prairie* there is a shadow of violence and dark cruelty flickering in the air. It is the aboriginal demon hovering over the core of the continent. It hovers still, and the dread is still there.

Into such a prairie enters the huge figure of Ishmael, ponderous, pariah-like Ishmael and his huge sons and his were-wolf wife. With their wagons they roll on from the frontiers of Kentucky, like Cyclops into the savage wilderness. Day after day they seem to force their way into oblivion. But their force of penetration ebbs. They are brought to a stop. They recoil in the throes of murder and entrench themselves in isolation on a hillock in the midst of the prairie. There they hold out like demi-gods against the elements and the subtle Indian.

The pioneering brute invasion of the West, crime-tinged!

And into this setting, as a sort of minister of peace, enters the old hunter Natty, and his suave, horse-riding Sioux Indians. But he seems like a shadow.

The hills rise softly west, to the Rockies. There seems a new peace: or is it only suspense, abstraction, waiting? Is it only a sort of beyond?

Natty lives in these hills, in a village of the suave, horse-riding Sioux. They revere him as an old wise father.

In these hills he dies, sitting in his chair and looking far east, to the forest and great sweet waters, whence he came. He dies gently, in physical peace with the land and the Indians. He is an old, old man.

Cooper could see no further than the foothills where Natty died, beyond the prairie.

The other novels bring us back east.

The Last of the Mohicans is divided between real historical narrative and true "romance." For myself, I prefer the romance. It has a myth meaning, whereas the narrative is chiefly record.

For the first time we get actual women: the dark, handsome Cora and her frail sister, the White Lily. The good old division, the dark sensual woman and the clinging, submissive little blonde, who is so "pure."

These sisters are fugitives through the forest, under the protection of a Major Heyward, a young American officer and Englishman. He is just a "white" man, very good and brave and generous, etc., but limited, most definitely *borné*. He would probably love Cora, if he dared, but he finds it safer to adore the clinging White Lily of a younger sister.

This trio is escorted by Natty, now Leatherstocking, a hunter and scout in the prime of life, accompanied by his inseparable friend Chingachgook, and the Delaware's beautiful son—Adonis rather than Apollo—Uncas, The last of the Mohicans.

There is also a "wicked" Indian, Magua, handsome and injured incarnation of evil.

Cora is the scarlet flower of womanhood, fierce, passionate offspring of some mysterious union between the British officer and a Creole woman in the West Indies. Cora loves Uncas, Uncas loves Cora. But Magua also desires Cora, violently desires her. A lurid little circle of sensual fire. So Fenimore kills them all off, Cora, Uncas, and Magua, and leaves the White Lily to carry on the race. She will breed plenty of white children to Major Heyward. These tiresome "lilies that fester," of our day.

Evidently Cooper—or the artist in him—has decided that there can be no blood-mixing of the two races, white and red. He kills 'em off.

Beyond all this heart-beating stand the figures of Natty and Chingachgook: two childless, womanless men, of opposite races. They are the abiding thing. Each of them is alone, and final in his race. And they stand side by side, stark, abstract, beyond emotion, yet eternally together. All the other loves seem frivolous. This is the new great thing, the clue, the inception of a new humanity.

And Natty, what sort of a white man is he? Why, he is a man with a gun. He is a killer, a slayer. Patient and gentle as he is, he is a slayer. Self-effacing, self-forgetting, still he is a killer.

Twice, in the book, he brings an enemy down hurtling in death through the air, downwards. Once it is the beautiful, wicked Magua— shot from a height, and hurtling down ghastly through space, into death.

This is Natty, the white forerunner. A killer. As in *Deerslayer*, he shoots the bird that flies in the high, high sky so that the bird falls out of the invisible into the visible, dead, he symbolizes himself. He will bring the bird of the spirit out of the high air. He is the stoic American killer of the old great life. But he kills, as he says, only to live.

Pathfinder takes us to the Great Lakes, and the glamour and beauty of sailing the great sweet waters. Natty is now called Pathfinder. He is about thirty-five years old, and he falls in love. The damsel is Mabel Dunham, daughter of Sergeant Dunham of the Fort garrison. She is blonde and in all things admirable. No doubt Mrs. Cooper was very much like Mabel.

And Pathfinder doesn't marry her. She won't have him. She wisely prefers a more comfortable Jasper. So Natty goes off to grouch, and to end by thanking his stars. When he had got right clear, and sat by the campfire with Chingachgook, in the forest, didn't he just thank his stars! A lucky escape!

Men of an uncertain age are liable to these infatuations. They aren't always lucky enough to be rejected.

Whatever would poor Mabel have done, had she been Mrs. Bumppo?

Natty had no business marrying. His mission was elsewhere.

The most fascinating Leatherstocking book is the last, *Deerslayer*. Natty is now a fresh youth, called Deerslayer. But the kind of silent prim youth who is never quite young, but reserves himself for different things.

It is a gem of a book. Or a bit of perfect paste. And myself, I like a bit of perfect paste in a perfect setting, so long as I am not fooled by pretense of reality. And the setting of Deerslayer *could* not be more exquisite. Lake Champlain again.

Of course it never rains: it is never cold and muddy and dreary: no one has wet feet or toothache: no one ever feels filthy, when they can't wash for a week. God knows what the women would really have looked like, for they fled through the wilds without soap, comb, or towel. They breakfasted off a chunk of meat, or nothing, lunched the same and supped the same.

Yet at every moment they are elegant, perfect ladies, in correct toilet.

Which isn't quite fair. You need only go camping for a week, and you'll see.

But it is a myth, not a realistic tale. Read it as a lovely myth. Lake Glimmerglass.

Deerslayer, the youth with the long rifle, is found in the woods with a big, handsome, blonde-bearded backwoodsman called Hurry Harry. Deerslayer seems to have been born under a hemlock tree out of a pine-cone: a young man of the woods. He is silent, simple, philosophic, moralistic, and an unerring shot. His simplicity is the simplicity of age rather than of youth. He is race-old. All his reactions and impulses are fixed, static. Almost he is sexless, so race-old. Yet intelligent, hardy, dauntless.

Hurry Harry is a big blusterer, just the opposite of Deerslayer. Deerslayer keeps the center of his own consciousness steady and unperturbed. Hurry Harry is one of those floundering people who bluster from one emotion to another, very self-conscious, without any center to them.

These two young men are making their way to a lovely, smallish lake, Lake Glimmerglass. On this water the Hutter family has established itself. Old Hutter, it is suggested, has a criminal, coarse, buccaneering past, and is a sort of fugitive from justice. But he is a good enough father to his two grown-up girls. The family lives in a log hut "castle," built on piles in the water, and the old man has also constructed an "ark," a sort of houseboat, in which he can take his daughters when he goes on his rounds to trap the beaver.

The two girls are the inevitable dark and light. Judith, dark, fearless, passionate, a little lurid with sin, is the scarlet-and-black blossom. Hetty, the younger, blonde, frail and innocent, is the white lily again. But alas, the lily has begun to fester. She is slightly imbecile.

The two hunters arrive at the lake among the woods just as war has been declared. The Hutters are unaware of the fact. And hostile Indians are on the lake already. So, the story of thrills and perils.

Thomas Hardy's inevitable division of women into dark and fair, sinful and innocent, sensual and pure, is Cooper's division too. It is indicative of the desire in the man. He wants sensuality and sin, and he wants purity and "innocence." If the innocence goes a little rotten, slightly imbecile, bad luck!

Hurry Harry, of course, like a handsome impetuous meatfly, at once wants Judith, the lurid poppy-blossom. Judith rejects him with scorn.

Judith, the sensual woman, at once wants the quiet, reserved, un-mastered Deerslayer. She wants to master him. And Deerslayer is half tempted, but never more than half. He is not going to be mastered. A philosophic old soul, he does not give much for the temptations of sex. Probably he dies virgin.

And he is right of it. Rather than be dragged into a false heat of deliberate sensuality, he will remain alone. His soul is alone, for ever alone. So he will preserve his integrity, and remain alone in the flesh. It is a stoicism which is honest and fearless, and from which Deerslayer never lapses, except when, approaching middle age, he proposes to the buxom Mabel.

He lets his consciousness penetrate in loneliness into the new con-tinent. His contacts are not human. He wrestles with the spirits of the forest and the American wild, as a hermit wrestles with God and Satan. His one meeting is with Chingachgook, and this meeting is silent, re-served, across an unpassable distance.

Hetty, the White Lily, being imbecile, although full of vaporous religion and the dear, good God, "who governs all things by his prov-idence," is hopelessly infatuated with Hurry Harry. Being innocence gone imbecile, like Dostoevsky's Idiot, she longs to give herself to the handsome meat-fly. Of course he doesn't want her.

And so nothing happens: in that direction. Deerslayer goes off to meet Chingachgook, and help him woo an Indian maid. Vicarious.

It is the miserable story of the collapse of the white psyche. The white man's mind and soul are divided between these two things: in-nocence and lust, the Spirit and Sensuality. Sensuality always carries a stigma, and is therefore more deeply desired, or lusted after. But spiri-tuality alone gives the sense of uplift, exaltation, and "winged life," with the inevitable reaction into sin and spite. So the white man is divided against himself. He plays off one side of himself against the other side, till it is really a tale told by an idiot, and nauseating.

Against this, one is forced to admire the stark, enduring figure of Deerslayer. He is neither spiritual nor sensual. He is a moralizer, but he always tries to moralize from actual experience, not from theory. He says: "Hurt nothing unless you're forced to." Yet he gets his deepest thrill of gratification, perhaps, when he puts a bullet through the heart of a beautiful buck, as it stoops to drink at the lake. Or when he brings the invisible bird fluttering down in death, out of the high blue. "Hurt nothing unless you're forced to." And yet he lives by death, by killing the wild things of the air and earth.

It's not good enough.

But you have there the myth of the essential white America. All the other stuff, the love, the democracy, the floundering into lust, is a sort of by-play. The essential American soul is hard, isolate, stoic, and a killer. It has never yet melted.

Of course, the soul often breaks down into disintegration, and you have lurid sin and Judith, imbecile innocence lusting, in Hetty, and bluster, bragging, and self-conscious strength, in Harry. But there are the disintegration products.

What true myth concerns itself with is not the disintegration product. True myth concerns itself centrally with the onward adventure of the integral soul. And this, for America, is Deerslayer. A man who turns his back on white society. A man who keeps his moral integrity hard and intact. An isolate, almost selfless, stoic, enduring man, who lives by death, by killing, but who is pure white.

This is the very intrinsic-most American. He is at the core of all the other flux and fluff. And when *this* man breaks from his static isolation, and makes a new move, then look out, something will be happening.

MERIWETHER LEWIS AND
WILLIAM CLARK

Meriwether Lewis (1774–1809) and William Clark (1770–1838) were commissioned by President Thomas Jefferson to explore the vast territory of the Louisiana Purchase, from the Mississippi River to the Pacific Ocean. Lewis was both Jefferson's secretary and a scientist, while Clark was a mapmaker and navigator, and was skilled in negotiating with the Indians.

Their discoveries, recorded in the Original Journals of the Lewis and Clark Expedition, 1804–1806, *one of the world's great stories of exploration, cannot be overvalued in terms of their importance to the opening of the American West to settlement by white pioneers —and to the ways Americans have defined and understood themselves in the West for two hundred years. The West, they told us, is a difficult place, but it is a place where possibility lives, which can be used—where people can reinvent their lives in a kind of freeman paradise—and people came, and still come, intent on the using.*

FROM THE *JOURNALS*

THURSDAY, MAY 23D, 1805

Last night the frost was severe, and this morning the ice appeared along the edges of the river, and the water froze on our oars. At the distance of a mile we passed the entrance of a creek on the north, which we named Teapot creek; it is fifteen yards wide, and although it has running water at a small distance from its mouth, yet it discharges none into the Missouri, resembling, we believe, most of the creeks in this hilly country, the waters of which are absorbed by the thirsty soil near the river. They indeed afford but little water in any part, and even that is so strongly tainted with salts that it is unfit for use, though all the wild animals are very fond of it. On experiment it was found to be moderately purgative, but painful to the intestines in its operation. This creek seems to come from a range of low hills, which run from east to west for seventy miles, and have their eastern extremity thirty miles to the north of Teapot creek. Just above its entrance is a large assemblage of the burrowing squirrels on the north side of the river. At nine miles we reached the upper point of an island in a bend on the south, and opposite the centre of the island, a small dry creek on the north. Half a mile further a small creek falls in on the same side; and six and a half miles beyond this another on the south. At four and a half we passed a small island in a deep bend to the north, and on the same side in a deep northeastern bend of the river another small island. None of these creeks however possessed any water, and at the entrances of the islands, the two first are covered with tall cottonwood timber, and the last with willows only. The river has become more rapid, the country much the same as yesterday, except that there is rather more rocks on the face of the hills, and some small spruce pine appears among the pitch. The wild roses are very abundant and now in bloom; they differ from those of the United States only in having the leaves and the bush itself of a somewhat smaller size. We find the mosquitoes troublesome, notwithstanding the coolness of the morning. The buffalo is scarce to-day, but the elk, deer, and antelope, are very numerous. The geese begin to lose the feathers of the wings, and are unable to fly. We saw five bears, one of which we wounded, but in swimming from us across the river, he became entangled in some driftwood and sank. We formed our camp on the north opposite to a hill and a point of wood in a bend to the south, having made twenty-seven miles.

FRIDAY, MAY 24TH

The water in the kettles froze one eighth of an inch during the night; the ice appears along the margin of the river, and the cottonwood trees which have lost nearly all their leaves by the frost, are putting forth other buds. We proceeded with the line principally till about nine o'clock, when a fine breeze sprung up from the S. E. and enabled us to sail very well, notwithstanding the rapidity of the current. At one mile and a half is a large creek thirty yards wide, and containing some water which it empties on the north side, over a gravelly bed, intermixed with some stone. A man who was sent up to explore the country returned in the evening, after having gone ten miles directly towards the ridge of mountains to the north, which is the source of this as well as of Teapot creek.

The air of these highlands is so pure, that objects appear much nearer than they really are, so that although our man went ten miles without thinking himself by any means half way to the mountains, they do not from the river appear more than fifteen miles distant; this stream we called Northmountain creek. Two and a half miles higher is a creek on the south which is fifteen yards wide, but without any water, and to which we gave the name of Littledog creek, from a village of burrowing squirrels opposite to its entrance, that being the name given by the French watermen to those animals. Three miles from this a small creek enters on the north, five beyond which is an island a quarter of a mile in length, and two miles further a small river: this falls in on the south, is forty yards wide, and discharges a handsome stream of water; its bed rocky with gravel and sand, and the banks high: we called it South-mountain creek, as from its direction it seemed to rise in a range of mountains about fifty or sixty miles to the S. W. of its entrance.

The low grounds are narrow and without timber; the country high and broken; a large portion of black rock, and brown sandy rock appears in the face of the hills, the tops of which are covered with scattered pine, spruce and dwarf cedar; the soil is generally poor, sandy near the tops of the hills, and nowhere producing much grass, the low grounds being covered with little else than the hyssop, or southern wood, and the pulpy-leafed thorn. Game is more scarce, particularly beaver, of which we have seen but few for several days, and the abundance or scarcity of which seems to depend on the greater or less quantity of timber. At twenty-four and a half miles we reached a point of woodland on the south, where we observed that the trees had no leaves, and encamped for the night.

The high country through which we have passed for some days, and where we now are, we suppose to be a continuation of what the French traders called the Côte Noire or Black hills. The country thus denominated consists of high broken irregular hills and short chains of mountains, sometimes one hundred and twenty miles in width, sometimes narrower, but always much higher than the country on either side. They commence about the head of the Kanzas, where they diverge; the first ridge going westward, along the northern shore of the Arkansaw; the second approaches the Rock mountains obliquely in a course a little to the W. of N. W. and after passing the Platte above its forks, and intersecting the Yellowstone near the Bigbend, crosses the Missouri at this place, and probably swell the country as far as the Saskashawan, though as they are represented much smaller here than to the south, they may not reach that river.

SATURDAY, MAY 25TH

Two canoes which were left behind yesterday to bring on the game, did not join us till eight o'clock this morning, when we set out with the towline, the use of which the banks permitted. The wind was, however, ahead, the current strong, particularly round the points against which it happened to set, and the gullies from the hills having brought down quantities of stone, these projected into the river, forming barriers for forty or fifty feet round, which it was very difficult to pass. At the distance of two and three quarter miles we passed a small island in a deep bend on the south, and on the same side a creek twenty yards wide, but with no running water. About a mile further is an island between two and three miles in length, separated from the northern shore by a narrow channel, in which is a sand island at the distance of half a mile from its lower extremity. To this large island we gave the name of Teapot island; two miles above which is an island a mile long, and situated on the south. At three and a half miles is another small island, and one mile beyond it a second three quarters of a mile in length, on the north side. In the middle of the river two miles above this is an island with no timber, and of the same extent as this last.

The country on each side is high, broken, and rocky; the rock being either a soft brown sandstone, covered with a thin stratum of limestone, or else a hard black rugged granite, both usually in horizontal stratas, and the sandrock overlaying the other. Salts and quartz as well as some coal and pumicestone still appear: the bars of the river are composed principally of gravel; the river low grounds are narrow, and afford scarcely any timber; nor is there much pine on the hills. The buffalo have now become scarce: we saw a polecat this evening, which was the first for several days: in the course of the day we also saw several herds of the big-horned animals among the steep cliffs on the north, and killed several of them. At the distance of eighteen miles we encamped on the south, and the next morning, *Sunday, 26th,* proceeded on at an early hour by means of the towline, using our oars merely in passing the river, to take advantage of the best banks. There are now scarcely any low grounds on the river, the hills being high and in many places pressing on both sides to the verge of the water. The black rock has given place to a very soft sandstone, which seems to be washed away fast by the river, and being thrown into the river renders its navigation more difficult than it was yesterday: above this sandstone, and towards the summits of the hills, a hard freestone of a yellowish brown colour shows itself in several stratas of unequal thickness, frequently overlaid or incrusted by a thin stratum of limestone, which seems to be formed of concreted shells. At eight and a quarter miles we came to the mouth of a creek on the north, thirty yards wide, with some running water and a rocky bed: we called it Windsor creek, after one of the party. Four and three-quarter miles beyond this we came to another creek in a bend to the north, which is twenty yards wide, with a handsome little stream of water: there is however no timber on either side of the river except a few pines on the hills. Here we saw for the first time since we left the Mandans several soft shelled turtles, though this may be owing rather to the season of the year than to any scarcity of the animal.

It was here that after ascending the highest summits of the hills on the north side of the river, that captain Lewis first caught a distant view of the Rock [Rocky] mountains, the object of all our hopes, and the reward of all our ambition. On both sides of the river and at no great distance from it, the mountains followed its course: above these, at the distance of fifty miles from us, an irregular range of mountains spread themselves from west to northwest from his position. To the north of these a few elevated points, the most remarkable of which bore north 65° west, appeared above the horizon, and as the sun shone on the snows of their summits he obtained a clear and satisfactory view of those mountains which close on the Missouri the passage to the Pacific.

Four and a half miles beyond this creek we came to the upper point of a small sand island. At the distance of five miles between high bluffs, we passed a very difficult rapid, reaching quite across the river, where the water is deep, the channel narrow, and gravel obstructing it on each side: we had great difficulty in ascending it, although we used both the rope and the pole, and doubled the crews. This is the most considerable rapid on the Missouri, and in fact the only place where there is a sudden descent. As we were labouring over them, a female elk with its fawn swam down through the waves, which ran very high, and obtained for the place the name of the Elk Rapids. Just above them is a small low

ground of cottonwood trees, where at twenty-two and a quarter miles
we fixed our encampment, and were joined by captain Lewis, who had
been on the hills during the afternoon.

The country has now become desert and barren: the appearances
of coal, burnt earth, pumicestone, salts, and quartz, continue as yesterday:
but there is no timber except the thinly scattered pine and spruce on
the summits of the hills, or along the sides. The only animals we have
observed are the elk, the bighorn, and the hare, common in this country.
In the plain where we lie are two Indian cabins [wickiups] made of
sticks, and during the last few days we have passed several others in the
points of timber on the river.

MONDAY, MAY 27TH

The wind was so high that we did not start till ten o'clock, and even
then were obliged to use the line during the greater part of the day. The
river has become very rapid with a very perceptible descent: its general
width is about two hundred yards: the shoals too are more frequent, and
the rocky points at the mouth of the gullies more troublesome to pass:
great quantities of this stone lie in the river and on its banks, and seem
to have fallen down as the rain washed away the clay and sand in which
they were imbedded. The water is bordered by high rugged bluffs, composed of irregular but horizontal stratas of yellow and brown or black
clay, brown and yellowish white sand, soft yellowish white sandstone:
hard dark brown freestone; and also large round kidney formed irregular
separate masses of a hard black ironstone, imbedded in the clay and sand;
some coal or carbonated wood also makes its appearance in the cliffs, as
do also its usual attendants the pumicestone and burnt earth. The salts
and quartz are less abundant, and generally speaking the country is if
possible more rugged and barren than that we passed yesterday; the only
growth of the hills being a few pine, spruce, and dwarf cedar, inter-
spersed with an occasional contrast once in the course of some miles, of
several acres of level ground, which supply a scanty subsistence for a few
little cottonwood trees.

Soon after setting out we passed a small untimbered island on the
south: at about seven miles we reached a considerable bend which the
river makes towards the southeast, and in the evening, after making
twelve and a half miles, encamped on the south near two dead cotton-

wood trees, the only timber for fuel which we could discover in the neighbourhood.

TUESDAY, MAY 28TH

The weather was dark and cloudy; the air smoky, and there fell a few drops of rain. At ten o'clock we had again a slight sprinkling of rain, attended with distant thunder, which is the first we have heard since leaving the Mandans. We employed the line generally, with the addition of the pole at the ripples and rocky points, which we find more numerous and troublesome than those we passed yesterday. The water is very rapid round these points, and we are sometimes obliged to steer the canoes through the points of sharp rocks rising a few inches above the surface of the water, and so near to each other that if our ropes give way the force of the current drives the sides of the canoe against them, and must inevitably upset them or dash them to pieces. These cords are very slender, being almost all made of elkskin, and much worn and rotted by exposure to the weather: several times they gave way, but fortunately always in places where there was room for the canoe to turn without striking the rock; yet with all our precautions it was with infinite risk and labour that we passed these points. An Indian pole for building floated down the river, and was worn at one end as if dragged along the ground in travelling; several other articles were also brought down by the current, which indicate that the Indians are probably at no great distance above us, and judging from a football which resembles those used by the Minnetarees near the Mandans, we conjecture that they must be a band of the Minnetarees of fort de Prairie.

The appearance of the river and the surrounding country continued as usual, till towards evening, at about fifteen miles, we reached a large creek on the north thirty-five yards wide, discharging some water, and named after one of our men Thompson's creek. Here the country assumed a totally different aspect; the hills retired on both sides from the river which now spreads to more than three times its former size, and is filled with a number of small handsome islands covered with cottonwood. The low grounds on the river are again wide, fertile, and enriched with trees; those on the north are particularly wide, the hills being comparatively low and opening into three large vallies, which extend themselves for a considerable distance towards the north: these appearances of vegetation are delightful after the dreary hills over which we have passed, and we have now to congratulate ourselves at having escaped from the last ridges of the Black mountains. On leaving Thompson's creek we passed two small islands, and at twenty-three miles distance encamped among some timber on the north, opposite to a small creek, which we named Bull creek. The bighorn is in great quantities, and must bring forth their young at a very early season, as they are now half grown. One of the party saw a large bear also, but being at a distance from the river, and having no timber to conceal him, he would not venture to fire.

WEDNESDAY, MAY 29TH

Last night we were alarmed by a new sort of enemy. A buffalo swam over from the opposite side and to the spot where lay one of our canoes, over which he clambered to the shore; then taking fright he ran full speed up the bank towards our fires, and passed within eighteen inches of the heads of some of the men, before the sentinel could make him change his course: still more alarmed he ran down between four fires and within a few inches of the heads of a second row of the men, and would have broken into our lodge if the barking of the dog had not stopped him. He suddenly turned to the right and was out of sight in a moment, leaving us all in confusion, every one seizing his rifle and inquiring the cause of the alarm. On learning what had happened, we had to rejoice at suffering no more injury than the damage to some guns which were in the canoe which the buffalo crossed.

In the morning early we left our camp, and proceeded as usual by the cord. We passed an island and two sandbars, and at the distance of two and a half miles we came to a handsome river which discharges itself on the south, and which we ascended to the distance of a mile and a half: we called it Judith's river: it rises in the Rock mountains in about the same place with the Muscleshell and near the Yellowstone river. Its entrance is one hundred yards wide from one bank to the other, the water occupying about seventy-five yards, and in greater quantity than that of the Muscleshell river, and though more rapid equally navigable, there being no stones or rocks in the bed, which is composed entirely of gravel and mud with some sand: the water too is clearer than any which we have yet seen; and the low grounds, as far as we could discern, wider and more woody than those of the Missouri: along its banks we observed some box-alder intermixed with the cottonwood and the willow; the undergrowth consisting of rosebushes, honeysuckles, and a little red willow. There was a great abundance of the argalea or big-horned animals in the high country through which it passes, and a great number of the beaver in its waters.

Just above the entrance of it we saw the fires of one hundred and twenty-six lodges, which appeared to have been deserted about twelve or fifteen days, and on the other side of the Missouri a large encampment, apparently made by the same nation. On examining some moccasins which we found there, our Indian woman said that they do not belong to her own nation the Snake Indians, but she thought that they indicated a tribe on this side of the Rocky mountains, and to the north of the Missouri; indeed it is probable that these are the Minnetarees of fort de Prairie.

At the distance of six and a half miles the hills again approached the brink of the river, and the stones and rocks washed down from them form a very bad rapid, with rocks and ripples more numerous and difficult than those we passed on the *27th* and *28th:* here the same scene was renewed, and we had again to struggle and labour to preserve our small craft from being lost. Near this spot are a few trees of the ash, the first we have seen for a great distance, and from which we named the place Ash Rapids. On these hills there is but little timber, but the salts, coal, and other mineral appearances continue.

On the north we passed a precipice about one hundred and twenty feet high, under which lay scattered the fragments of at least one hundred carcases of buffaloes, although the water which had washed away the lower part of the hill must have carried off many of the dead. These buffaloes had been chased down the precipice in a way very common on the Missouri, and by which vast herds are destroyed in a moment. The mode of hunting is to select one of the most active and fleet young men, who is disguised by a buffalo skin round his body; the skin of the head with the ears and horns fastened on his own head in such a way as to deceive the buffalo: thus dressed, he fixes himself at a convenient distance between a herd of buffalo and any of the river precipices, which sometimes extend for some miles. His companions in the meantime get in the rear and side of the herd, and at a given signal show themselves, and advance towards the buffalo: they instantly take the alarm, and finding the hunters beside them, they run towards the disguised Indian or decoy, who leads them on at full speed towards the river, when suddenly securing himself in some crevice of the cliff which he had previously fixed on, the herd is left on the brink of the precipice: it is then in vain for the foremost to retreat or even to stop; they are pressed on by the hindmost rank, who, seeing no danger but from the hunters, goad on those before them till the whole are precipitated and the shore is strewed with their dead bodies. Sometimes in this perilous seduction the Indian is himself either trodden underfoot by the rapid movements of the buffalo, or missing his footing in the cliff is urged down the precipice by the falling herd. The Indians then select as much meat as they wish, and the rest is abandoned to the wolves, and creates a most dreadful stench. The wolves who had been feasting on these carcases were very fat, and so gentle that one of them was killed with a spontoon.

Above this place we came to for dinner at the distance of seventeen miles, opposite to a bold running river of twenty yards wide, and falling in on the south. From the objects we had just passed we called this stream Slaughter river. Its low grounds are narrow, and contain scarcely any timber. Soon after landing it began to blow and rain, and as there was no prospect of getting wood for fuel farther on, we fixed our camp on the north, three quarters of a mile above Slaughter river. After the labours of the day we gave to each man a dram, and such was the effect of long abstinence from spirituous liquors, that from the small quantity of half a gill of rum, several of the men were considerably affected by it, and all very much exhilarated. Our game to-day consisted of an elk and two beaver.

THURSDAY, MAY 30TH

The rain which commenced last evening continued with little intermission till eleven this morning, when the high wind which accompanied it having abated, we set out. More rain has now fallen than we have had since the 1st of September last, and many circumstances indicate our approach to a climate differing considerably from that of the country through which we have been passing: the air of the open country is astonishingly dry and pure. Observing that the case of our sextant, though perfectly seasoned, shrank and the joints opened, we tried several experiments, by which it appeared that a tablespoonful of water exposed in a saucer to the air would evaporate in thirty-six hours, when the mercury did not stand higher than the temperate point at the greatest heat of the day. The river, notwithstanding the rain, is much clearer than it was a few days past; but we advance with great labour and difficulty; the rapid current, the ripples and rocky points rendering the navigation more embarrassing than even that of yesterday, in addition to which the banks are now so slippery after the rain, that the men who draw the canoes can scarcely walk, and the earth and stone constantly falling down the high bluffs make it dangerous to pass under them; still however we are obliged to make use of the cord, as the wind is strong ahead, the current too rapid for oars, and too deep for the pole. In this way we passed at the distance of five and a half miles a small rivulet in a bend on the north, two miles further an island on the same side, half a mile beyond which came to a grove of trees at the entrance of a run in a bend to the south, and encamped for the night on the northern shore. The eight miles which we made to-day cost us much trouble. The air was cold and rendered more disagreeable by the rain, which fell in several slight showers in the course of the day; our cords too broke several times, but fortunately without injury to the boats.

On ascending the hills near the river, one of the party found that there was snow mixed with the rain on the heights: a little back of these the country becomes perfectly level on both sides of the river. There is now no timber on the hills, and only a few scattering cottonwood, ash, box-alder, and willows, along the water. In the course of the day we passed several encampments of Indians, the most recent of which seemed to have been evacuated about five weeks since, and from the several apparent dates we supposed that they were made by a band of about one hundred lodges who were travelling slowly up the river. Although no part of the Missouri from the Minnetarees to this place exhibit signs of permanent settlements, yet none seem exempt from the transient visits of hunting parties. We know that the Minnetarees of the Missouri extend their excursions on the south side of the river, as high as the Yellowstone; and the Assiniboins visit the northern side, most probably as high as Porcupine river. All the lodges between that place and the Rocky mountains we supposed to belong to the Minnetarees of fort de Prairie, who live on the south fork of the Saskashawan.

FRIDAY, MAY 31ST

We proceeded in two periogues, leaving the canoes to bring on the meat of two buffaloes killed last evening. Soon after we set off it began to rain, and though it ceased at noon, the weather continued cloudy during the rest of the day. The obstructions of yesterday still remain and fatigue the men excessively: the banks are so slippery in some places and the mud so adhesive that they are unable to wear their moccasins; one fourth of the time they are obliged to be up to their armpits in the cold water, and sometimes walk for several yards over the sharp fragments of rocks which have fallen from the hills: all this added to the burden of dragging the heavy canoes is very painful, yet the men bear it with great patience and good humour. Once the rope of one of the periogues, the only one we had made of hemp, broke short, and the periogue swung and just touched a point of rock which almost overset her.

At nine miles we came to a high wall of black rock rising from the water's edge on the south, above the cliffs of the river: this continued about a quarter of a mile, and was succeeded by a high open plain, till three miles further a second wall two hundred feet high rose on the same side. Three miles further a wall of the same kind about two hundred feet high and twelve in thickness, appeared to the north. These hills and river cliffs exhibit a most extraordinary and romantic appearance: they rise in most places nearly perpendicular from the water, to the height of between two and three hundred feet, and are formed of very white sandstone, so soft as to yield readily to the impression of water, in the upper part of which lie imbedded two or three thin horizontal strata of white freestone insensible to the rain, and on the top is a dark rich loam, which forms a gradually ascending plain, from a mile to a mile and a half in extent, when the hills again rise abruptly to the height of about three hundred feet more. In trickling down the cliffs, the water has worn the soft sandstone into a thousand grotesque figures, among which with a little fancy may be discerned elegant ranges of freestone buildings, with columns variously sculptured, and supporting long and elegant galleries, while the parapets are adorned with statuary: on a nearer approach they represent every form of elegant ruins; columns, some with pedestals and capitals entire, others mutilated and prostrate, and some rising pyramidally over each other till they terminate in a sharp point. These are varied by niches, alcoves, and the customary appearances of desolated magnificence: the illusion is increased by the number of martins, who have built their globular nests in the niches and hover over these columns; as in our country they are accustomed to frequent large stone structures.

As we advance there seems no end to the visionary enchantment which surrounds us. In the midst of this fantastic scenery are vast ranges of walls, which seem the productions of art, so regular is the workmanship: they rise perpendicularly from the river, sometimes to the height of one hundred feet, varying in thickness from one to twelve feet, being equally broad at the top as below. The stones of which they are formed are black, thick, and durable, and composed of a large portion of earth, intermixed and cemented with a small quantity of sand, and a considerable proportion of talc or quartz. These stones are almost invariably regular parallelipeds of unequal sizes in the wall, but equally deep, and laid regularly in ranges over each other like bricks, each breaking and covering the interstice of the two on which it rests; but though the perpendicular interstice be destroyed, the horizontal one extends entirely through the whole work: the stones too are proportioned to the thickness of the wall in which they are employed, being largest in the thickest walls. The thinner walls are composed of a single depth of the paralleliped, while the thicker ones consist of two or more depths: these walls pass the river at several places, rising from the water's edge much above the sandstone bluffs which they seem to penetrate; thence they cross in a straight line on either side of the river, the plains over which they tower to the height of from ten to seventy feet, until they lose themselves in the second range of hills: sometimes they run parallel in several ranges near to each other, sometimes intersect each other at right angles, and have the appearance of walls of ancient houses or gardens.

The face of some of these river hills, is composed of very excellent freestone of a light yellowish brown colour, and among the cliffs we found a species of pine which we had not yet seen, and differing from the Virginia pitch-pine in having a shorter leaf, and a longer and more pointed cone. The coal appears only in small quantities, as do the burnt earth and pumice-stone: the mineral salts have abated. Among the animals are a great number of the bighorn, a few buffalo and elk, and some mule-deer, but none of the common deer nor any antelopes. We saw but could not procure a beautiful fox, of a colour varied with orange, yellow, white, and black, rather smaller than the common fox of this country, and about the same size as the red fox of the United States.

The river to-day has been from about one hundred and fifty to two

hundred and fifty yards wide, with but little timber. At the distance of
two miles and a half from the last stone wall, is a stream on the north
side, twenty-eight yards in width, and with some running water. We
encamped just above its mouth, having made eighteen miles.

SATURDAY, JUNE 1ST, 1805

The weather was cloudy with a few drops of rain. As we proceeded by
the aid of our cord we found the river cliffs and bluffs not so high as
yesterday, and the country more level. The timber too is in greater
abundance on the river, though there is no wood on the high ground;
coal however appears in the bluffs. The river is from two hundred to
two hundred and fifty feet wide, the current more gentle, the water
becoming still clearer and fewer rocky points and shoals than we met
yesterday, though those which we did encounter were equally difficult
to pass. Game is by no means in such plenty as below; all that we
obtained were one bighorn, and a mule-deer, though we saw in the
plains a quantity of buffalo, particularly near a small lake about eight
miles from the river to the south. Notwithstanding the wind was ahead
all day, we dragged the canoes along the distance of twenty-three miles.
At fourteen and a quarter miles, we came to a small island opposite a
bend of the river to the north: two and a half miles to the upper point
of a small island on the north; five miles to another island on the south
side and opposite to a bluff. In the next two miles we passed an island
on the south, a second beyond it on the north, and reached near a high
bluff on the north a third on which we encamped.

In the plains near the river are the chokecherry, yellow and red
currant-bushes, as well as the wild rose and prickly pear, both of which
are now in bloom. From the tops of the river hills, which are lower
than usual, we enjoyed a delightful view of the rich fertile plains on both
sides, in many places extending from the river cliffs to a great distance
back. In these plains we meet occasionally large banks of pure sand,
which were driven apparently by the southwest winds, and there de-
posited. The plains are more fertile some distance from the river than
near its banks, where the surface of the earth is very generally strewed
with small pebbles, which appear to be smoothed and worn by the
agitation of the waters with which they were no doubt once covered.
A mountain or part of the North mountain approaches the river within

eight or ten miles, bearing north from our encampment of last evening; and this morning a range of high mountains bearing S. W. from us and apparently running to the westward, are seen at a great distance covered with snow. In the evening we had a little more rain.

SUNDAY, JUNE 2D

The wind blew violently last night, and a slight shower of rain fell, but this morning was fair. We set out at an early hour, and although the wind was ahead by means of the cord went on much better than for the last two days, as the banks were well calculated for towing. The current of the river is strong but regular, its timber increases in quantity, the low grounds become more level and extensive, and the bluffs on the rivers are lower than usual. In the course of the day we had a small shower of rain, which lasted a few minutes only.

As the game is very abundant we think it necessary to begin a collection of hides for the purpose of making a leathern boat, which we intend constructing shortly. The hunters who were out the greater part of the day brought in six elk, two buffalo, two mule-deer and a bear. This last animal had nearly cost us the lives of two of our hunters who were together when he attacked them; one of them narrowly escaped being caught, and the other after running a considerable distance, concealed himself in some thick bushes, and while the bear was in quick pursuit of his hiding place, his companion came up and fortunately shot the animal through the head.

At six and a half miles we reached an island on the northern side; one mile and a quarter thence is a timbered low ground on the south: and in the next two and three quarter miles we passed three small islands, and came to a dark bluff on the south: within the following mile are two small islands on the same side. At three and a quarter miles we reached the lower part of a much larger island near a northern point, and as we coasted along its side, within two miles passed a smaller island, and half a mile above reached the head of another. All these islands are small, and most of them contain some timber. Three quarters of a mile beyond the last, and at the distance of eighteen miles from our encampment, we came to for the night in a handsome low cottonwood plain on the south, where we remained for the purpose of making some ce-

lestial observations during the night, and of examining in the morning
a large river which comes in opposite to us.

MONDAY, JUNE 3D

Accordingly at an early hour, we crossed and fixed our camp in the
point, formed by the junction of the river with the Missouri. It now
became an interesting question which of these two streams is what the
Minnetarees call Ahmateahza or the Missouri, which they described as
approaching very near to the Columbia. On our right decision much of
the fate of the expedition depends; since if after ascending to the Rocky
mountains or beyond them, we should find that the river we were following did not come near the Columbia, and be obliged to return, we
should not only lose the travelling season, two months of which had
already elapsed, but probably dishearten the men so much as to induce
them either to abandon the enterprise, or yield us a cold obedience
instead of the warm and zealous support which they had hitherto afforded us. We determined, therefore, to examine well before we decided
on our future course; and for this purpose despatched two canoes with
three men up each of the streams with orders to ascertain the width,
depth, and rapidity of the current, so as to judge of their comparative
bodies of water. At the same time parties were sent out by land to
penetrate the country, and discover from the rising grounds, if possible,
the distant bearings of the two rivers; and all were directed to return
towards evening.

While they were gone we ascended together the high grounds in
the fork of these two rivers, whence we had a very extensive prospect
of the surrounding country: on every side it was spread into one vast
plain covered with verdure, in which innumerable herds of buffalo were
roaming, attended by their enemies the wolves: some flocks of elk also
were seen, and the solitary antelopes were scattered with their young
over the face of the plain. To the south was a range of lofty mountains,
which we supposed to be a continuation of the South mountain, stretching themselves from southeast to northwest, and terminating abruptly
about southwest from us. These were partially covered with snow; but
at a great distance behind them was a more lofty ridge completely covered with snow, which seemed to follow the same direction as the first,
reaching from west to the north of northwest, where their snowy tops

were blended with the horizon. The direction of the rivers could not however be long distinguished, as they were soon lost in the extent of the plain. On our return we continued our examination; the width of the north branch is two hundred yards, that of the south is three hundred and seventy-two. The north, although narrower and with a gentler current, is deeper than the south: its waters too are of the same whitish brown colour, thickness, and turbidness: they run in the same boiling and rolling manner which has uniformly characterized the Missouri; and its bed is composed of some gravel, but principally mud. The south fork is deeper, but its waters are perfectly transparent: its current is rapid, but the surface smooth and unruffled; and its bed too is composed of round and flat smooth stones like those of rivers issuing from a mountainous country.

The air and character of the north fork so much resemble those of the Missouri that almost all the party believe that to be the true course to be pursued. We however, although we have given no decided opinion, are inclined to think otherwise, because, although this branch does give the colour and character to the Missouri, yet these very circumstances induce an opinion that it rises in and runs through an open plain country, since if it came from the mountains it would be clearer, unless, which from the position of the country is improbable, it passed through a vast extent of low ground after leaving them: we thought it probable that it did not even penetrate the Rocky mountains, but drew its sources from the open country towards the lower and middle parts of the Saskashawan, in a direction north of this place. What embarrasses us most is, that the Indians who appeared to be well acquainted with the geography of the country, have not mentioned this northern river; for "the river which scolds at all others," as it is termed, must be according to their account one of the rivers which we have passed; and if this north fork be the Missouri, why have they not designated the south branch which they must also have passed, in order to reach the great falls which they mention on the Missouri?

In the evening our parties returned, after ascending the rivers in canoes for some distance, then continuing on foot, just leaving themselves time to return by night. The north fork was less rapid, and therefore afforded the easiest navigation: the shallowest water of the north was five feet deep, that of the south six feet. At two and a half miles up the north fork is a small river coming in on the left or western side, sixty feet wide, with a bold current three feet in depth. The party by land had gone up the south fork in a straight line, somewhat north of west for seven miles, where they discovered that this little river came within one hundred yards of the south fork, and on returning down it found it a handsome stream, with as much timber as either of the larger rivers, consisting of the narrow and wide-leafed cottonwood, some birch and box-alder, and undergrowth of willows, rosebushes, and currants: they also saw on this river a great number of elk and some beaver.

All these accounts were however very far from deciding the important question of our future route, and we therefore determined each of us to ascend one of the rivers during a day and a half's march, or farther if necessary, for our satisfaction. Our hunters killed two buffalo, six elk, and four deer to-day. Along the plains near the junction are to be found the prickly pear in great quantities; the chokecherry is also very abundant in the river low grounds, as well as the ravines along the river bluffs; the yellow and red currants are not yet ripe; the gooseberry is beginning to ripen, and the wild rose which now covers all the low grounds near the rivers is in full bloom. The fatigues of the last few days have occasioned some falling off in the appearance of the men, who not having been able to wear moccasins, had their feet much bruised and mangled in passing over the stones and rough ground. They are however perfectly cheerful, and have an undiminished ardour for the expedition.

TUESDAY, JUNE 4TH

At the same hour this morning captain Lewis and captain Clark set out to explore the two rivers; captain Lewis with six men crossed the north fork near the camp, below a small island from which he took a course N. 30° W. for four and a half miles to a commanding eminence. Here he observed that the North mountain, changing its direction parallel to the Missouri, turned towards the north and terminated abruptly at the distance of about thirty miles, the point of termination bearing N. 48° E. The South mountain too diverges to the south, and terminates abruptly, its extremity bearing S. 8° W. distant about twenty miles: to the right of, and retreating from this extremity, is a separate mountain at the distance of thirty-five miles in a direction S. 38° W. which from its resemblance to the roof of a barn, we called the Barn mountain. The north fork, which is now on the left, makes a considerable bend to the northwest, and on its western border a range of hills about ten miles

long, and bearing from this spot N. 60° W. runs parallel with it: north
of this range of hills is an elevated point of the river bluff on its south
side, bearing N. 72° W. about twelve miles from us; towards this he
directed his course across a high, level, dry open plain; which in fact
embraces the whole country to the foot of the mountains. The soil is
dark, rich, and fertile, yet the grass by no means so luxuriant as might
have been expected, for it is short and scarcely more than sufficient to
cover the ground. There are vast quantities of prickly pears, and myriads
of grasshoppers, which afford food for a species of curlew which is in
great numbers in the plain.

He then proceeded up the river to the point of observation they
had fixed on; from which he went two miles N. 15° W. to a bluff point
on the north side of the river: thence his course was N. 30° W. for two
miles to the entrance of a large creek on the south. The part of the river
along which he passed is from forty to sixty yards wide, the current
strong, the water deep and turbid, the banks falling in, the salts, coal and
mineral appearances are as usual, and in every respect, except as to size,
this river resembles the Missouri. The low grounds are narrow but well
supplied with wood: the bluffs are principally of dark brown yellow, and
some white clay with freestone in some places. From this point the river
bore N. 20° E. to a bluff on the south, at the distance of twelve miles:
towards this he directed his course, ascending the hills which are about
two hundred feet high, and passing through plains for three miles, till
he found the dry ravines so steep and numerous that he resolved to
return to the river and follow its banks. He reached it about four miles
from the beginning of his course, and encamped on the north in a bend
among some bushes which sheltered the party from the wind: the air
was very cold, the northwest wind high, and the rain wet them to the
skin. Besides the game just mentioned, he observed buffalo, elk, wolves,
foxes, and we got a blaireau and a weasel, and wounded a large brown
bear, whom it was too late to pursue. Along the river are immense
quantities of roses which are now in full bloom, and which make the
low grounds a perfect garden.

WEDNESDAY, JUNE 5TH

The rain fell during the greater part of the last night, and in the morning
the weather was cloudy and cold, with a high northwest wind: at sunrise

he proceeded up the river eight miles to the bluff on the left side, towards which he had been directing his course yesterday. Here he found
the bed of a creek twenty-five yards wide at the entrance, with some
timber, but no water, notwithstanding the rain: it is, indeed, astonishing
to observe the vast quantities of water absorbed by the soil of the plains,
which being opened in large crevices presents a fine rich loam: at the
mouth of this stream (which he called Lark creek) the bluffs are very
steep and approach the river so that he ascended them, and crossing the
plains reached the river, which from the last point bore N. 50° W.: four
miles from this place it extended north two miles. Here he discovered
a lofty mountain standing alone at the distance of more than eighty miles
in the direction of N. 30° W. and which from its conical figure he called
Tower mountain.

He then proceeded on these two hills and afterwards in different
courses six miles, when he again changed for a western course across a
deep bend along the south side: in making this passage over the plains
he found them like those of yesterday, level and beautiful, with great
quantities of buffalo, and some wolves, foxes, and antelopes, and intersected near the river by deep ravines. Here at the distance of from one
to nine miles from the river, he met the largest village of barking squirrels
which we had yet seen: for he passed a skirt of their territory for seven
miles. He also saw near the hills a flock of the mountain cock or a large
species of heath hen with a long pointed tail, which the Indians below
had informed us were common among the Rock mountains. Having
finished his course of ten miles west across a bend, he continued two
miles N. 80° W. and from that point discovered some lofty mountains
to the northwest of Tower mountain and bearing N. 65° W. at eighty
or one hundred miles distance: here he encamped on the north side in
a handsome low ground, on which were several old stick lodges: there
had been but little timber on the river in the forepart of the day, but
now there is a greater quantity than usual. The river itself is about eighty
yards wide, from six to ten feet deep, and has a strong steady current.
The party had killed five elk, and a mule-deer; and by way of experiment
roasted the burrowing squirrels, which they found to be well flavoured
and tender.

THURSDAY, JUNE 6TH

Captain Lewis was now convinced that this river pursued a direction too far north for our route to the Pacific, and therefore resolved to return; but waited till noon to take a meridian altitude. The clouds, however, which had gathered during the latter part of the night continued and prevented the observation: part of the men were sent forward to a commanding eminence, six miles S. 70° W.; from which they saw at the distance of about fifteen miles S. 80° W. a point of the south bluff of the river, which thence bore northwardly. In their absence two rafts had been prepared, and when they returned about noon, the party embarked: but they soon found that the rafts were so small and slender that the baggage was wet, and therefore it was necessary to abandon them, and go by land. They therefore crossed the plains, and at the distance of twelve miles came to the river, through a cold storm from the northeast, accompanied by showers of rain. The abruptness of the cliffs compelled them, after going a few miles, to leave the river and meet the storm in the plains. Here they directed their course too far northward, in consequence of which they did not meet the river till late at night, after having travelled twenty-three miles since noon, and halted at a little below the entrance of Lark creek.

They had the good fortune to kill two buffalo which supplied them with supper: but spent a very uncomfortable night without any shelter from the rain, which continued till morning, *Friday, 7th,* when at an early hour they continued down the river. The route was extremely unpleasant, as the wind was high from the N. E. accompanied with rain, which made the ground so slippery that they were unable to walk over the bluffs which they had passed on ascending the river. The land is the most thirsty we have ever seen; notwithstanding all the rain which has fallen, the earth is not wet for more than two inches deep, and resembles thawed ground; but if it requires more water to saturate it than the common soils, on the other hand it yields its moisture with equal difficulty.

In passing along the side of one of these bluffs at a narrow pass thirty yards in length, captain Lewis slipped, and but for a fortunate recovery, by means of his spontoon, would have been precipitated into the river over a precipice of about ninety feet. He had just reached a spot where by the assistance of his spontoon he could stand with tolerable safety, when he heard a voice behind him cry out, "Good God, captain, what shall I do?" He turned instantly and found it was Windsor, who had lost his foothold about the middle of the narrow pass, and had slipped down to the very verge of the precipice, where he lay on his belly, with his right arm and leg over the precipice, while with the other leg and arm he was with difficulty holding on to keep himself from being dashed to pieces below. His dreadful situation was instantly perceived by captain Lewis, who stifling his alarm, calmly told him that he was in no danger; that he should take his knife out of his belt with the right hand, and dig a hole in the side of the bluff to receive his right foot. With great presence of mind he did this, and then raised himself on his knees; captain Lewis then told him to take off his moccasins and come forward on his hands and knees, holding the knife in one hand and his rifle in the other. He immediately crawled in this way till he came to a secure spot. The men who had not attempted this passage were ordered to return and wade the river at the foot of the bluff, where they found the water breast high.

This adventure taught them the danger of crossing the slippery heights of the river; but as the plains were intersected by deep ravines almost as difficult to pass, they continued down the river, sometimes in the mud of the low grounds, sometimes up to their arms in the water, and when it became too deep to wade, they cut footholds with their knives in the sides of the banks. In this way they travelled through the rain, mud, and water, and having made only eighteen miles during the whole day, encamped in an old Indian lodge of sticks, which afforded them a dry shelter. Here they cooked part of six deer they had killed in the course of their walk, and having eaten the only morsel they had tasted during the whole day slept comfortably on some willow boughs.

A. B. GUTHRIE JR.

A. B. "Bud" Guthrie Jr. (1901–1991) was born in Indiana and raised in Choteau, Montana, where his father was high school principal; he graduated from the University of Montana in 1923, then moved to Kentucky, where he worked as a journalist and teacher. After twenty years and a stint as a Nieman Fellow at Harvard, he returned to Choteau, where he finished writing The Big Sky *(1947). In 1950, his novel* The Way West *was awarded the Pulitzer prize. In 1953, he wrote the screenplay for the film* Shane. *Guthrie published eight other novels, one juvenile fable, a volume of short fiction,* The Big It and Other Stories *(1960), and a memorable autobiography of his early years,* The Blue Hen's Chick *(1965). Guthrie was a long-standing advocate of wilderness protection. He died at his home near Choteau.*

The following chapter, taken midstream from The Big Sky, *depicts a mountain man's misery as he decries the change his own efforts have wrought upon the land. "She's gone, goddam it! Gone!" he tells his young nephew, an aspiring trapper. "This was man's country onc't. Every water full of beaver and a galore of buffler any ways a man looked, and no crampin' and crowdin'. Christ sake." It's a chanson de geste of the West, a familiar lament in the literature of this territory.*

FROM *THE BIG SKY*

The long western sun lay flat on the river and plain. Down the hills to the northeast a string of pack animals filed, looking black against the summer tan of the bluffs.

"Could be that's Zeb," Summers said, squinting. "McKenzie said likely he'd get in afore dark." He and Jim Deakins and Boone stood behind the fort. The *Mandan* was moored two miles up river, where Jourdonnais was watching cargo and crew. Summers had suggested that the three of them come back to the fort to talk to Calloway. "That hoss knows a heap," he had said to Jourdonnais, "besides bein' kin to Caudill. I figger I better see him."

A little piece from where they stood a dozen lodges of the Assiniboines, set in a half-circle, pointed at the sky. Once in a while smoke came from one of them, rising from the smoke hole at the top in a thin wisp, as if a man with a pipe was blowing through it. The voices of the Indians, of the men talking and the squaws laughing and squabbling and a baby squalling came clear in the evening air. Dogs nosed around the lodges and sometimes faced around in the direction of the three white men and barked as if they had suddenly remembered to do something forgotten.

"Let's set," said Summers, letting himself down to the ground.

The pack string snaked down from the hills and headed toward them across the plain. A mounted man was at the head of it, and another one at its tail.

Summers smoked and watched and said presently, "I do believe it's your Uncle Zeb, Caudill."

It was Uncle Zeb, all right, looking older, and gray as a coon. A man couldn't go wrong on that long nose and the eyes that peered out from under brows as bushy as a bird's nest.

Boone wanted to get up and shout hello and go out and give his hand, but something held him in.

Summers got to his feet easy, so's not to affright the mules that were packed high and wide with meat. "H'ar ye, Zeb?"

Uncle Zeb stared out of his tangle of brow like a man sighting a rifle. "How," he answered, his voice stiff and cracked as a man's is after a long silence. Then, "This child'll be a Digger if it ain't Dick Summers."

Summers motioned. "This here's someone you seen afore."

Uncle Zeb fixed his gaze on Boone. He spit a brown stream over the shoulder of his horse. "So?"

Summers waited, and Uncle Zeb looked at Boone again and said, "Ain't my pup, I'm thinkin'."

"Close," answered Summers. "Don't you know your own nephy, old hoss?"

Boone asked, "How you, Uncle Zeb?"

"For Christ sake!"

"I reckon you don't know me, I've changed that much."

Uncle Zeb spit again and put his mind to remembering. "One of Serenee's young'ns, ain't ye?"

"Boone Caudill."

"For Christ sake!"

Uncle Zeb didn't smile. He sat on his horse, his shoulders slumped and his mouth over at one side, making his face look crooked. A calf was bawling inside the fort as if he had lost his ma. "Stay thar," Uncle Zeb said at last. "I'll get shet of these here mules. Ho, Deschamps." The string got into slow motion, the heads of the mules jerking as the slack went out of the tie ropes. The rider at the tail was an Indian, or a half-breed anyway. For a bridle he had a long hair rope tied about the lower jaw of his horse. The stirrups of his saddle were made of skin and shaped like shoes. He stared as he went by, lounging on his horse, with his rifle carried crosswise before him.

Jim and Summers glanced at Boone. He picked up a blade of grass and tied a knot in it. "It's a spell since he seed me."

The Assiniboine squaws were playing a game, laughing and squealing as they played. Three bucks passed by, making toward the fort. They stopped on the way to ask for some tobacco. A little sand rat that Summers called a gopher came out of a hole and sat up, straight as a peg. He whistled a thin pipe of a whistle that struck the ears like the point of an awl. Boone tossed a pebble at him, and he dived into his hole and then nosed back up, just his head showing, and the black unwinking eye. The sun had got behind a bank of clouds and painted them blood red. It was like an Indian had spit into a hand of vermilion and rubbed the western sky with it. Boone got out the pipe he had traded for down river.

In a little while Uncle Zeb came back, walking stiff and uneven from the saddle. His leggings were black and worn, with no more than a half-dozen pieces of fringe left. He wore an old Indian shirt smeared with blood, which had a colored circle on the chest made of porcupine quills. Instead of a hat he had a red handkerchief tied around his head. He took a bottle out of his shirt and sat down and got the cork out, not saying anything. Summers brought out another bottle. Uncle Zeb passed the first one round, watching it go from hand to hand as if he could hardly wait. The first thing he said was, "Can't buy a drink on'y at night, goddam McKenzie!"

It was getting cold, with the sun low and hid, too cold even for the gnats that like to ate a man alive. A little breeze ran along the ground, making Boone draw into himself. Off a piece he could see some whitened bones, and beyond them some more, and beyond them still more where buffalo had been butchered. Three Indian dogs that looked like wolves except for one that was blotched black and white were smelling around them. The dogs were just bones themselves, with spines that humped up and ran crooked so that the feet didn't set square underneath them. The calf inside the fort was still bawling.

As if it didn't make much difference Uncle Zeb asked, "How's Serenee makin' out?"

"All right, last I seen her."

Uncle Zeb grunted and lifted the bottle and took a powerful drink.

He slumped back, in a mood, as if waiting for the whisky to put life into him. He said, "Christ sake!" and took another drink.

Summers said, "This here's Jim Deakins, crew of the *Mandan*."

"Pleased to meetcha," Jim said.

Uncle Zeb got out tobacco and stuffed it in his cheek and let it soak. "Why're you here?"

"I fit with Pap."

"Measly son of a bitch. By God! If'n you're any part like him——?" He spit and sucked in his lower lip afterward to get the drop off.

"He's some now," Summers said. "He's true beaver. Catched the clap and fit Indians and killed a white b'ar a'ready."

Uncle Zeb looked at Summers. "Never could figger why my sister teamed up with that skunk, less'n she had to." He turned. "How old be ye?"

"Comin' eighteen."

Uncle Zeb thought for a while, then said, "You got no cause to be set up, account of your pap."

"Be goddammed to you! You take after Pap your own self."

"Sic 'im, Boone!" It was Jim, looking across at him with a gleam in his blue eye.

Uncle Zeb only grunted. He started the bottle around again, taking a swig of it first himself and ending the round with another. "This nigger's got a turrible dry."

Summers was smiling at the ground as if he was pleased. "Caudill and Deakins, here, aim to be mountain men."

"Huh! They better be borned ag'in."

"How so?"

"Ten year too late anyhow." Uncle Zeb's jaw worked on the tobacco. "She's gone, goddam it! Gone!"

"What's gone?" asked Summers.

Boone could see the whisky in Uncle Zeb's face. It was a face that had known a sight of whisky, likely, red as it was and swollen-looking.

"The whole shitaree. Gone, by God, and naught to care savin' some of us who seen 'er new." He took the knife from his belt and started jabbing at the ground with it, as if it eased his feelings. He was silent for a while.

"This was man's country onc't. Every water full of beaver and a galore of buffler any ways a man looked, and no crampin' and crowdin'. Christ sake!"

To the east, where the hill and sky met, Boone saw a surge of movement and guessed that it was buffalo until it streamed down the slope, making for them, and came to be a horse herd.

Summers' gray eye slipped from Boone to Uncle Zeb. "She ain't sp'iled, Zeb," he said quietly. "Depends on who's lookin'."

"Not sp'iled! Forts all up and down the river, and folk everywhere a man might think to lay a trap. And greenhorns comin' up, a heap of 'em—greenhorns on every boat, hornin' in and sp'ilin' the fun. Christ sake! Why'n't they stay to home? Why'n't they leave it to us as found it? By God, she's ours by rights." His mouth lifted for the bottle. "God, she was purty onc't. Purty and new, and not a man track, savin' Injuns', on the whole scoop of her."

The horses were coming in fast, running and kicking like colts with the coolness that had come on the land. The gopher was out of his hole again, moving in little flirts and looking up and piping. It was beginning to get dark. The fire in the west was about out; low in the east one star burned. Boone wished someone would quiet that calf.

Summers said, " 'Pears you swallered a prickly pear, hoss."

"Huh!" Uncle Zeb reached in and fingered the cud from his mouth and put a fresh one in.

"Beaver's a fair price, a mighty fair price. It is, now."

"Price don't figger without a man's got the beaver," Uncle Zeb said while his mouth moved to set the chew right.

The horses trotted by, kicking up a dust, shying and snorting as they passed the seated men. Behind them came four riders, dressed in the white blanket coats that the workmen at the fort wore.

"I mind the time beaver was everywhere," Uncle Zeb said. His voice had turned milder and had a faraway tone in it, as if the whisky had started to work deep and easy in him. Or was it that he was just old and couldn't hold to a feeling? "I do now. Everywhere. It was poor doin's, them days, not to trap a good pack every hunt. And now?" He fell silent as if there was nothing fitting a man could lay tongue to.

"Look," he said, straightening a little, "another five year and there'll be naught but coarse fur, and it goin' fast. You, Boone, and you, Deakins, stay here and you'll be out on the prairie, hide huntin', chasin' buffler and skinnin' 'em, and seein' the end come to that, too."

"Not five year," said Summers. "More like fifty."

"Ahh! The beaver's nigh gone now. Buffler's next. Won't be even a goddam poor bull fifty years ahead. You'll see plows comin' across the plains, and people settin' out to farm." He leaned forward, bringing his hands up. "They laugh at this nigger, but it's truth all the same. Can't be t'otherwise. The Company alone's sendin' twenty-five thousand beaver skins out in a year, and forty thousand or more hides. Besides, a heap of buffler's killed by hunters and never skinned, and a heap of skins is used by the Injuns, and a passel of 'em drownds every spring. Ahh!"

"There's beaver aplenty yit," replied Summers. "A man's got to go after them. He don't catch 'em inside a fort, or while makin' meat."

"Amen and go to hell, Dick! On'y, whisky's hard to come by off on a hunt. Gimme a pull on your bottle. I got a turrible dry."

Boone heard his own voice, sounding tight and toneless. "She still looks new to me, new and purty." In the growing darkness he could feel Uncle Zeb's eyes on him, looking at him from under their thickets—tired old eyes that whisky had run red rivers in.

"We're pushin' on," said Summers, "beyant the Milk, to Blackfoot country."

"This child heerd tell."

"Well, now?"

"This nigger don't know, Dick. It's risky—powerful risky, like you know. Like as not you'll go under."

"We got a heap of whisky, and powder and ball and guns, and beads and vermilion and such."

"You seen Blackfeet drunk, Dick?"

"A few."

"They're mean. Oh, by God, they're mean! An' tricky and onreliable. But you know that as good as me. Got a interpreter?"

"Just this hoss. I know it a little, and sign talk, of course. We ain't got beaver for a passel of interpreters."

"You dodged Blackfeet enough to learn a little, I'm thinkin'."

"Plenty plews there."

"They don't do a dead nigger no good. Pass the bottle."

"How are you and McKenzie?"

"The bourgeway bastard, with his fancy getup and his tablecloth and his nose in the air like a man stinks! Y'know the clerks can't set to his table without a coat on? And the chinchin' company, squeezin' hell out of a man and chargin' him Christ knows what for belly rot! McKenzie pays this child, and this child kills his meat, but that's as fur as she goes. I'm just tradin' meat for whisky."

"Zeb," Summers said, "this here's secret as the grave. Wouldn't do for it to get out. It wouldn't now."

"My mouth don't run to them cayutes, drunk or sober."

"We got a little squaw, daughter of a Blackfoot chief, she says, that was stole by the Crows and made a getaway. A boat picked her up, nigh dead, and took her on to St. Louis last fall. We're takin' her back."

"Umm. Injuns don't set much store by squaws."

"Blackfeet like their young'ns more'n most."

"A squaw?"

"I know, but still?"

"Might be." Uncle Zeb was silent for what seemed a long time. "This nigger heerd something from the Rocks about that Crow party. Heavy Otter—ain't that the chief?"

"That's the name she gave. We're countin' on her a heap, Zeb."

"Umm."

"We make talk purty slick, what with her l'arnin' a little white man's talk and me knowin' some Blackfoot. Me and her together, we don't need no interpreter."

"This nigger don't like it."

"Your stick wouldn't float that way? We'll cut you in, and handsome. Better'n bein' a fort hunter."

In the darkness Boone could see Uncle Zeb's head shake. "It ain't a go, Dick. It ain't now."

"I recollect when it would be."

It seemed to Boone that all of time was in Uncle Zeb's voice. "Not now, hoss. Not any more. This child ain't scared, like you know, but it ain't worth it. It's tolerable here, and whisky's plenty even if it costs a heap."

"What you hear about the Blackfeet?"

"The Rocks say they're away from the river, gone north and east to buffler. Me, now, I'd say go to Maria's River, or along there, and fort up, quicker'n scat."

"Too fur. Take a month, even with Jourdonnais blisterin' the crew. Buffler an' Blackfeet would be back afore we could set ourselves."

"Uh-huh. There's mostly some Injuns around Maria's River all the time. Anyways, get your fort up fast."

"That's how this child figgered. A little fort, quick, ready for 'em when they come back to the river."

"It's risky doin's, anyways you lay your sights."

"You figger the Company's like to take a hand in this game?"

"McKenzie's got plans for the Blackfeet. He's makin' medicine. He is, now. Come fall or winter, he'll p'int that way, or try to. But he'll let ye be, likely, thinkin' the Blackfeet and the British'll handle things. He's slick. He ain't wantin' a finger p'inted at him, now you're so fur up."

"He said he might send a boat up, to buck us."

"No sech. He ain't got the hands right now. If this nigger smells a stink afore you pass the Milk, he'll get word to you one way or t'other."

"Heap obliged, hoss."

Uncle Zeb got up unsteadily, his knees cracking as he straightened them out. "If it gits to talk, ask for Big Leg of the Piegans, and give a present, sayin' it's from me. We're brothers, he said onc't."

"That's some, now. Obliged again."

Uncle Zeb walked away, swaying some and not saying goodbye. The three others made off in the direction of the *Mandan,* waking the Indian dogs, which started barking all at once. They could hear loud voices and laughs and sometimes a whoop from inside the fort. "Liquorin' up," said Summers. The calf had stopped bawling.

Boone's head swam with the whisky. It was the first he had let himself drink much of in a long time. "I reckon old age just come on Uncle Zeb," he said. After a silence he added, "It's fair country yit." Summers was keeping them in the open, away from the river.

"It's fair, sure enough," Deakins agreed.

Summers said, "Watch out for them pesky prickly pear. They go right through a moccasin."

TEDDY BLUE ABBOTT

E. C. "Teddy Blue" Abbott rode the cattle-drive trails from Texas to Montana during the 1870s and 1880s. His memoirs, We Pointed Them North: Recollections of a Cowpuncher, *written in collaboration with Helena Huntington Smith, were published in 1939.*

Abbott, as the following illustrates, was an authentic cowboy. His encounters with idiot ranchers, reasonable Cheyenne, and an aging Calamity Jane are described with wit, insight, and kindness. His steady accounts of real Western life give us an unglamorous, nonfictive, and nonrevisionist description of things "nobody will ever see . . . again."

FROM *WE POINTED THEM NORTH: RECOLLECTIONS OF A COWPUNCHER*

[1883]

In spite of the good pay I didn't like that outfit; you couldn't like it, the way it was run. Half the orders Fuller gave us was all wrong, and that's the hardest kind of a job, to do something when you know it is wrong. A man like that had no business trying to run a cow outfit. He didn't know nothing and he couldn't get along with cowpunchers. He was one of these pious New Englanders, that would say his prayers at night and then give you ten dollars to steal a calf the next day.

And I can tell you more than that about what his religion was like. When we were putting up the herd at Fort Kearney, we bought a lot of horses and cattle in Missouri and took them to Fort Kearney by train, and I went down there to help bring them up. We had a couple of trainloads, and the first train was mostly horses. By order of Mr. Fuller all the cars was bedded with straw instead of sand—because it was cheaper, I suppose. And going uphill against the wind the sparks from the engine set the front car on fire. We didn't discover it for quite awhile, back there in the caboose, and when we did see it we couldn't get the engineer to stop. I was running along over the top of the train toward the engine, shooting at the bell with my six-shooter, and he caught on that something was wrong finally and we got them out as fast as we could. But it was too late. Those horses—oh, God, I never want to see anything like that again. Some of them was still alive. Their eyes burned out, and all their hair was gone, and blood was coming out of their nostrils with every breath. We was going to shoot them, but that old man wouldn't let us. He said if we did he might not be able to collect his damages from the railroad company. So we went off and left them there. The man in charge of the second train shot them when he came along.

Although Mr. Fuller didn't know one end of a cow from the other, that didn't stop him from trying to revolutionize the cowboys. He told us down on the Platte that those was his intentions, and when we got up to the Yellowstone he went to work to carry them out. He issued orders forbidding us to bring the *Police Gazette* to the ranch. And when we went to town we were not to take a drink, and he went along to see that the order was obeyed. We couldn't do nothing but give in to him, more or less. We were strangers up north, and winter was coming on. We were getting big wages. We had to take a tumble.

Along toward the end of that fall the outfit was all in Miles City. One day the old man was sitting in the hotel lobby, where he could keep his eye on the bar and see that none of his boys was in there, when in walked Calamity Jane. The first time I ever saw her was five years before this, in the Black Hills in '78, when I went up there from the Platte River with that beef herd. I didn't meet her then, but I got a good look at her, when she was at the height of her fame and looks. I remember she was dressed in purple velvet, with diamonds on her and everything. As I recall it, she was some sort of a madam at that time, running a great big gambling hall in Deadwood.

In Miles City in the fall of '83, I had met her and bought her a few drinks. We knew a lot of the same people. So when she came into the hotel lobby where old man Fuller was, I went over and told her about him, and I said: "I'll give you two dollars and a half if you'll go and sit on his lap and kiss him."

And she was game. She walked up to him with everybody watching her, and sat down on his lap, and throwed both her arms around him so his arms were pinned to his sides and he couldn't help himself—she was strong as a bear. And then she began kissing him and saying: "Why don't you ever come to see me any more, honey? You know I love you." And so forth.

I told him: "Go ahead. Have a good time. It's customary here. I won't write home and tell your folks about it."

The old man spluttered and spit and wiped his mouth on his handkerchief. And he left the hotel and that was the last we saw of him that night.

Later that winter I met Calamity Jane again at Belly-Ups stage station, which was the first station out of Miles City on the Miles-Deadwood stage line. They named it that in honor of the buffalo hunters, who all went belly-ups in the winter of '83 because the buffalo was all gone. Anyway, I met her there, and I borrowed fifty cents from her to buy a meal. I wasn't broke, because I had plenty of money at the ranch, but I had blowed all I had with me, so it come to the same thing.

I thanked her for the fifty cents and said: "Some day I'll pay you." And she said: "I don't give a damn if you never pay me." She meant it, because she was always the kind that would share her last cent.

And I never saw her again until twenty-four years later. It was in 1907, and she was standing on a street corner in Gilt Edge; which was more of a town then than it is now, since they took half the buildings away. I walked up to her and said: "Don't you know me?" and gave her the fifty cents. She recognized me then and said: "I told you, Blue, that I didn't give a damn if you never paid me," and we went and drank it up. She had been famous a long time then, traveling with Buffalo Bill's show and so on, and she was getting old. A few years before I met her in Gilt Edge some friends of hers had taken up a collection and sent her East to make a lady of her, and now she was back. I joked her about her trip and asked her: "How'd you like it when they sent you East to get reformed and civilized?"

Her eyes filled with tears. She said: "Blue, why don't the sons of bitches leave me alone and let me go to hell my own route? All I ask is to be allowed to live out the rest of my life with you boys who speak my language. And I hope they lay me beside Bill Hickok when I die."

[1884]

It was just about the time of the big chinook that came in March of '84, and a few snowdrifts still showed up, when a Cheyenne named Black Wolf and his immediate family of seven lodges came over from Tongue River to the Rosebud on a visit to the other Indians. They camped at the mouth of Lame Deer Creek, near where two partners named Zook and Alderson had a ranch. One day the chief, Black Wolf, went up to this ranch by himself, and the boys gave him dinner. There was just two of them there at the time, a fellow named Sawney Tolliver, from Kentucky originally, and another one whose name I don't remember.

After Black Wolf had filled up, like an Indian would, he walked out and sat down in the sun on some poles, and he went to sleep. He had an old black stovepipe hat on, and this Tolliver stood at the door of the ranch house and said to the other fellow: "I'll bet you a dollar I can shoot a hole through his hat without hitting his head."

The fellow took him up, and Tolliver throwed down on the Indian, and he just creased him along his scalp. You could lay your finger in the mark. It knocked him out and they thought they had killed him. So they got on their horses and rode to the next ranch to get help, because they expected to have hell with the Indians, and they expected right. When they got back to the ranch with their reinforcements, Black Wolf was gone. But they knew the Indians would be coming just the same, and pretty soon they come and commenced shooting. When the other cowboys saw how many Indians there was, they just stampeded off, because they had no stomach for the business anyhow. It was a damn fool trick that caused the trouble. Tolliver left, too, quit the country. If he'd been caught, he'd have gone to jail, you bet, and he knew it. The soldiers would have seen to that.

The Indians went to work and burnt the house down, and shot the dog, and then they quit right there. Hank Thompson told me that in talking about it afterwards they put their two forefingers together, which is the sign meaning "We are even." Some people claim that they stole some provisions out of the house, coffee and so on, and that the stuff was found in their tepees after they surrendered. I don't know, I didn't go in the tepees. My sympathies was with the Indians.

The cowboys who ran away got word to the soldiers and to the sheriff in Miles City that the Cheyennes had broke out. The first we knew of it over at the F U F was when my friend Billy Smith, the stock inspector, who was in charge of the sheriff's posse, turned up at the ranch calling for help to arrest the Indians and protect a couple of white families that were in danger at the mouth of Lame Deer. By this time it was two days after the shooting, because it was one long day's ride of ninety or a hundred miles to Miles City, and another one to the F U F. We ate dinner and got on our horses, and along about 2:00 A.M., we got to one of these white families at the mouth of Lame Deer, where the posse was supposed to rendezvous. We found them all up and scared to death—though the Indians hadn't done a damn thing yet, only burn down the house where their man had been shot. It was lucky he didn't die, or there would have been hell.

Next day the posse divided, and fourteen of us, keeping this side of the Rosebud, rode away around and tied our horses in some brush, left two men with them, and after dark crawled up to where we were in between the Rosebud and the Indian camp. It makes me shiver yet when I think of the chance we took. There was no shelter whatever. We were right up against a high cut bank, with the river running fast and churning ice below us, so there was no way out in that direction. The tepees were about seventy-five yards in front of us and a bright moon was shining. Some of the others said the Indians were asleep. My God, I could look into the tepee right opposite me and see the moon-light shining off the barrel of his gun—because they always polish off that black stuff—and I imagined I could see the hole at the end of the barrel, and it followed me everywhere.

At daylight Hank Thompson and the deputy from Miles City rode into the Indian camp, and believe me that was a brave thing to do. But the Indians liked Hank and trusted him completely. He called to Black Wolf in Cheyenne who they were, and Black Wolf invited them into his tepee and called all the other warriors into council. That's when they told Hank they were even. They hadn't done nothing wrong in their estimation.

The old fellow, Black Wolf, was very tall and dignified, and he had a great big piece of buffalo manure tied on his head over the wound. Hank told them they were surrounded and asked them to surrender, and they all talked and argued. One Indian, Howling Wolf, was determined to fight, not surrender, and he kept tongue-lashing the others; he was all hate, and the white men knew he was dangerous and they was watching him.

Out on the bank we could hear the talking going on, but we couldn't hear what they said or which way it was going until all of a sudden Hank Thompson's voice rang out clear, in English, speaking to Louis King. He said: "If anything starts, get that Indian that's doing the talking."

And Louis said: "I'll get him right between the eyes."

We expected any second to hear the shooting start, after that, and if it had started, God help us. I figure they would have got at least six of us outside, beside the two in the tepee. And we laid there cramped and shivering in the early morning cold—we had been there three hours already—and we waited. And we waited some more. During the World War I read about men going over the top, and I know what it is like.

It's the waiting that gets you. You feel your whole self go down in your boots, and you feel the gun in your hand—and then you wait another half hour.

And all the time Hank Thompson was talking, talking in Cheyenne, explaining things to the Indians and promising that they would get a square deal if they surrendered. And after awhile Black Wolf, who was the subchief at the head of this little bunch, agreed. And the Indians all walked out, thirteen of them, and gave up their guns. They built a big fire then, and we came in and surrounded them and searched them for knives. All but one young brave named Pine had given them up, and he put up a big fight for his knife, which he had in his breech clout, and they couldn't get it away from him. But Black Wolf made him give it up. They're obedient in all things to the chief.

We had an awful narrow squeak in that camp, even after the surrender. When we came in and surrounded them, we didn't bother the women, naturally. It was breakfast time and they were busy around the camp, going back and forth to the river for water. And four or five would go down to the river, and three or four would come back. And three would go down, and two would come back. . . . And they kept that up until there was only one old woman left in that camp. There was a trail that led around through some brush, on the top of the cut bank, and they was crawling along that trail on their hands and knees, going to get word to the whole tribe, which was camped only six miles away.[1]

One of our posse happened to see the head and shoulders of one squaw, as she crawled along where the trail went out of the brush a little way, and that woke him up. He took one look around the camp and yelled: "Where the hell's all them women?" After that they rounded them up and brought them back. There was two or three hundred Indians in that bunch six miles away, and if those women had gotten through to them, it would have been the end of us.

After we had disarmed the Indians, we marched them down to Gaffney's house, that was one of the white families I mentioned at the mouth of Lame Deer. And there I was sworn in as a special deputy, on account of Billy Smith knowing me before. Billy Smith was in charge

---

1. Why were all the women trying to make their getaway, when one alone could have taken word to the tribe? I asked Mr. Abbott this, and he pointed out that in numerous instances atrocities had been committed by white soldiers on Indian women and children. All the Indians knew of these occurrences, and they were afraid for their lives.

of the posse. We got our breakfast down there, and Mrs. Gaffney done the cooking for all of us and the Indians, too. After breakfast we loaded the Indians in a wagon and started off for Miles City, where they were to be tried.

There was a lot of things happened in that Indian camp after I left that I only know about through hearsay. Frank Abbott, who came over with the rest of us from the F U F, says there was a young squaw, Pine's squaw, that had only been married two weeks, and she tried to follow her husband, and he says he has always been sorry for the way they had to treat her to make her go back. But he was disgusted to beat everything with the whole affair, and we was all disgusted when we found out what it was all about, and what danger we had been in for a damn fool trick. Frank says this squaw tried to go to Miles City, while the Indians were in prison before the trial, and was drowned crossing Tongue River. But I couldn't say as to that, because I never heard anything more about it.

We got down to Carpenter and Robinson's ranch just before dark, and there we heard that the Tollivers hadn't made enough trouble yet, because Sawney Tolliver's brother, Brownie, had said he was going to follow us with a bunch of men and going to shoot the Indians in the wagon. Unarmed Indians. Sawney was in Wyoming by this time. Billy Smith left word at the ranch that if anybody followed us and tried to meddle with the Indians, we would shoot them down like dogs. Those Indians had surrendered without firing a shot.

And that wasn't the only reason that we felt as we did. There was only six of us in the posse that took them to Miles City, and if those thirteen Indians had all give a yell and jumped for it out of the wagon, in the night, we'd never have hit a one of them. But they'd given their word. Or Black Wolf had, and what he said went for the rest of them. They always looked to the chief.

In the meanwhile there was still this main bunch of two or three hundred Indians only six miles up from the mouth of Lame Deer, and they'd have jumped the whole United States Army if their chief had given the word. But he didn't give the word. And there again we owed everything to the honor of an Indian.

For on our way to Carpenter and Robinson's that afternoon we saw this one tepee, out from the side of the road. It was the tepee of Little Wolf, the war chief of all the Cheyennes, who was camped out there by himself. And Hank Thompson rode over to him and begged and pleaded with him to give his word that he would stay where he was for another twenty-four hours instead of going in to join his tribe. This would give us a chance to get to Miles City. For Little Wolf was the Cheyennes' great chief, who had led them up here in '78, and they would not move without him.

He finally promised to stay where he was, and he kept his promise, and that saved all our lives. He was a wise leader as well as a great fighter, Little Wolf was, and I believe he was wise enough not to want any more trouble with the white man. He had had a plenty of it, and I believe he knew that the white man was bound to win in the end.

We traveled all that night, the six of us and the Indians. I kept going to sleep in the saddle, because it was the second night for me, and I remember Billy Smith jerking my horse's head up when he went to grazing on me. About daybreak we got to Rosebud station on the Northern Pacific, and we waited there for the train to take us to Miles City. And there I claimed this young Indian, Pine, that wouldn't give up his knife, for my Indian, my friend, and I looked after him as best I could. He was one of the best-looking Indians I ever saw, six feet, one or two inches tall and as straight as a string. And he was brave—he fought for his knife—and I was sure stuck on him.

We all ate there, while we was waiting for the train, and I handed Pine the grub and water first, but he always handed them up to the chief—everything for the chief. And after they had eaten they all wrapped up in their blankets and laid down on their stomachs and went to sleep. And so did I—right beside Pine.

By and by the train came, and we all got on it and went to Miles City. The whole town was out to see us come in with the Indians. At the station we loaded them all in a bus, to take them to the jail at the fort, and I was on top of the bus, so everybody thought I was the cowboy that done the shooting. There was a very popular demi-mondaine by the name of Willie Johnson, who was running Kit Hardiman's honky-tonk, as I have mentioned before, and I remember she came to the door of the house and hollered: "Stay with it, Blue! Don't you weaken!"

When we turned the Indians over to the authorities at Fort Keogh, Major Logan, the commanding officer, was as sore as a boil. He said, here was the Indians, but where was the fellow that started the trouble? And when they told him he was out of the country by that time, Major Logan said the posse was a hell of an outfit and gave us the devil, until, as Billy Smith said afterwards, if he'd had one more word out of him, he'd have hit him over the head with his six-shooter.

I'll tell you something about soldiers. At the first news of the outbreak they started a company of them from Fort Keogh, with a cannon. And when we got up to Miles City with the Indians, these soldiers had gone just forty miles, which was less than half the distance to the scene of the trouble, in the same time it took the sheriff's posse to go clear down to the mouth of Lame Deer and get the Indians and get back. But that's the way they always was in the army—had to go by West Point regulations; had to build their campfire in a certain position from the tent regardless of the way the wind was blowing. They was no earthly good on the frontier.

Well, the thirteen Indians was shut up under guard, and the next morning the whole Cheyenne tribe rode into Miles City. The people were scared to death. They didn't know what was going to happen. But the Indian prisoners had been guaranteed a fair trial, and Hank Thompson was among the Cheyennes all the time, talking to them like a Dutch uncle. So nothing happened. They finally fixed it all up. Four of the Indians pled guilty to burning the ranch house and got a year apiece in the pen, and they turned the rest loose. One of them died up there of grief.

While they were all in jail, I went to see Pine every day, and took him presents of tailor-made cigarettes and candy and stuff. And I told him I'd get him out of it, and luckily he did get out of it, and he was my friend for life. The last day he took a silver ring off his finger and gave it to me. The ring had a little shield, and on the shield it said "C Co 7 Cav." That was Tom Custer's company, and Pine took it off the finger of one of Tom Custer's soldiers at the fight, and he was in that fight when he was not yet fourteen years old.[2] The ring was too small for me, and I wore it around my neck for years, but in the end somebody got away with it.

That business at the mouth of Lame Deer opened my eyes to a lot of things about the Indians. I had it in for them before that, but it was due to ignorance. I had seen a lot of them, but I never associated with them

2. Pine is still living on the Tongue River Reservation and he and Mr. Abbott renewed their acquaintance in the summer of 1938.

the way I did after I got up to Montana. From that time I was on their side, because I saw that when trouble started, more often than not it was the white man's fault.

Not three months after the so-called outbreak I have been telling about, there was another mix-up with the Cheyennes, and it started in the very same outfit—Zook and Alderson. After the Indians burned their ranch on Lame Deer, they moved the outfit, and instead of staying away from these Indians they moved right up into the thick of them, on Hanging Woman, which is another creek in the Tongue River country. It almost seemed like they were looking for trouble; yet that couldn't have been true, because Alderson and his partner were both nice fellows and I believe they were away, both times, when the trouble occurred.

It was during the spring roundup, and they were all out with the roundup except a cowboy named Packsaddle Jack and a couple of others, who were breaking horses at the ranch. Packsaddle Jack was bringing in his horses, early one morning, and there was a Cheyenne named Iron Shirt who had a little garden near there—corn and pumpkins and stuff. And Packsaddle drove his horses right over the Indian's garden, and when the Indian come out and objected Packsaddle shot him in the arm.

Well, there was a lot of riding around and excitement, the same story all over again. Except that some of the cowpunchers had got their bellyful by this time. And when a couple of fellows from Zook and Alderson's rode over to the roundup and asked for men to help defend the ranch, Jesse Garland, the roundup captain, told them to go to hell. He said: "You got us into one jackpot this spring, and I won't allow a man to leave this roundup."

It all blew over. The Cheyennes knew they were beaten, and they were trying to keep the peace. Packsaddle Jack was tried in Miles City that fall and acquitted. And the rest of us weren't going against those fighting Indians on account of any more damned foolishness like that.

But it led to more and still more trouble. Several white men were found dead. Then another white man got killed by two young Indians in a fuss over a cow, which he said they had butchered, and I don't doubt they had. The chief sent word for them to come in, as the tribe would get into trouble for it, and he was going to punish them. They sent word back that they would come, but in their own way.

And they went up on top of a hill, and they sang their death songs, and painted themselves, and braided their horses' manes. And then they rode down from the hill, just the two of them, and charged two companies of soldiers that were sent out to arrest them. Which shows you the desperate courage of those Cheyennes.

I forgot to tell you about one thing that happened that morning on the Rosebud. While we were lying out there in the grass, half froze and waiting for all hell to break loose out of that tepee, I saw an old Indian go up a hill and pray to the sun. It was just coming up, and the top of the hill was red with it, and we were down there shivering in the shadow. And he was away off on the hill, and he held up his arms, and oh, God, but did he talk to the Great Spirit about the wrongs the white man had done to his people. I never have heard such a voice. It must have carried a couple of miles.

I have noticed that what you see when you are cold and scared is what you remember, and that is a sight I will never forget. I am glad that I saw it. Because nobody will ever see it again.

O. E. RÖLVAAG

Ole Edvart Rölvaag was born in 1876 on a small island fishing settlement off the coast of Norway. Raised as an uneducated fisherman, Rölvaag became an avid reader during his teenage years and, at age twenty, chose immigrating to America over fishing in Norway. After three years of farming on his uncle's land in South Dakota, Rölvaag began his education at Augustana College, a grammar school in Canton, South Dakota. Two years later he enrolled at Saint Olaf College and, in 1905, graduated with honors at the age of twenty-eight. Soon afterward he became a professor at his alma mater and occupied the chair of Norwegian literature. He is the author of several books, all written in his native Norwegian. Giants in the Earth, an epic about Norwegian immigration to America, was published in Norway in two volumes in 1924 and 1925 and was a huge success. It was translated into English in 1927 and was a best-seller in America. Rölvaag died in 1931.

The homesteading immigrants, Scandinavian and otherwise, who

*attempted to inhabit the West faced the brutal transition of moving
from an intimate communal setting to the vast American plains. Rölvaag's themes revolve around the problems of setting up a new community and the consequences of the resulting isolation. In this chapter
from* Giants in the Earth, *the harsh landscape, "giantlike and full
of cunning," creates a solitude capable of generating madness.*

FROM *GIANTS IN THE EARTH*

During the first day, both she and the boys found so much to do that
they hardly took time to eat. They unloaded both the wagons, set up
the stove, and carried out the table. Then Beret arranged their bedroom
in the larger wagon. With all the things taken out it was quite roomy
in there; it made a tidy bedroom when everything had been put in order.
The boys thought this work great fun, and she herself found some relief
in it for her troubled mind. But something vague and intangible hovering in the air would not allow her to be wholly at ease; she had to
stop often and look about, or stand erect and listen. . . . Was that a
sound she heard? . . . All the while, the thought that had struck her
yesterday when she had first got down from the wagon, stood vividly
before her mind: here there was nothing even to hide behind! . . . When
the room was finished, and a blanket had been hung up to serve as a
door, she seemed a little less conscious of this feeling. But back in the
recesses of her mind it still was there. . . .

After they had milked the cow, eaten their evening porridge, and
talked awhile to the oxen, she took the boys and And-Ongen and
strolled away from camp. With a common impulse, they went toward
the hill; when they had reached the summit, Beret sat down and let her
gaze wander aimlessly around. . . . In a certain sense, she had to admit
to herself, it was lovely up here. The broad expanse stretching away
endlessly in every direction, seemed almost like the ocean—especially
now, when darkness was falling. It reminded her strongly of the sea, and
yet it was very different. . . . This formless prairie had no heart that beat,
no waves that sang, no soul that could be touched . . . or cared. . . .

The infinitude surrounding her on every hand might not have been
so oppressive, might even have brought her a measure of peace, if it had
not been for the deep silence, which lay heavier here than in a church.
Indeed, what was there to break it? She had passed beyond the outposts

of civilization; the nearest dwelling places of men were far away. Here no warbling of birds rose on the air, no buzzing of insects sounded; even the wind had died away; the waving blades of grass that trembled to the faintest breath now stood erect and quiet, as if listening, in the great hush of the evening. . . . All along the way, coming out, she had noticed this strange thing: the stillness had grown deeper, the silence more depressing, the farther west they journeyed; it must have been over two weeks now since she had heard a bird sing! Had they traveled into some nameless, abandoned region? Could no living thing exist out here, in the empty, desolate, endless wastes of green and blue? . . . How *could* existence go on? she thought, desperately. If life is to thrive and endure, it must at least have something to hide behind! . . .

IX

By noon the next day they had finished the wheat field. Today Tönseten was of a different mind—there really was no great hurry; the weather kept cool, and the grain didn't look any riper today than yesterday, either at his own place or at Hans Olsa's; if this spell of cool weather should last, the wheat would profit by yet another week; but then they might prepare to harvest a crop unique in the history of wheat growing.

Tönseten felt highly well pleased with himself and the rest of the world; he had now proved his prowess before his neighbors; the field was almost finished here, and it wouldn't do any harm to rest and visit awhile. . . . "Don't fret, boys, I won't need to hurry at all! Those four acres of oats will only be play for the afternoon!"

And Per Hansa felt very much the same way. He and the other men were sitting in the shade on the north side of the house, with their backs up against the wall, enjoying the cool breeze that had sprung up from the west. . . . What was the use of hurrying? . . . Per Hansa had told the Solum boys that he wouldn't need them that afternoon, as he and Hans Olsa could easily bind the oats; but it was so pleasant to rest here and spin yarns that the boys didn't feel like stirring until the others went to the field.

As they got up at last and returned to their work, the northwest breeze struck them full in the face with its cool, fresh fragrance; Tönseten sniffed it approvingly, declaring that if this weather kept on, he and Hans Olsa would be sure to steal a march on Per Hansa in the end; never had the Lord sent finer weather for wheat to ripen in! He chuckled and talked away, his rotund body bobbing up and down with an irresistible merriment. . . . "Well, boys, in my opinion the Land of Canaan didn't have much on this country—no, I'm damned if it had! Do you suppose the children of Israel ever smelt a westerly breeze like this? Why, folks, it's blowing honey!" . . . His festive mood was still possessing him as he began to hitch up the horses; in the midst of it he had to turn around and ask them shyly, "Now, wasn't it remarkable that I should discover just *this* place for you?"

Hans Olsa burst into a laugh. "Yes, it surely was wonderful, Syvert!"

But Tönseten felt that this praise wasn't enough—he wanted to carry the joke a little farther. Turning to his other neighbor, he asked with the same roguish air, "What did you say, Per Hansa?"

Per Hansa remained strangely silent; he was standing a little distance away, shading his eyes with his right hand and looking into the west; an intent, troubled expression had come over his face.

. . . "What in the devil? . . ." he muttered to himself. Off in the western sky he had caught sight of something he couldn't understand—something that sent a nameless chill through his blood. . . . Could that be a storm coming on?

He hurried over to the wheat shock where Hans Olsa was sitting, pointed westward, and asked in a low voice, "Tell me, can you see anything over there?"

Hans Olsa was on his feet in an instant. . . . "Well, look at that! . . . It must be going to storm!"

Tönseten had finished hitching the horses to the reaper, and had just mounted the seat when he saw Per Hansa run over, pointing to the west. Now both his neighbors were shouting at him:

"What's that, Syvert?"

Tönseten turned in his seat, to face a sight such as he had never seen or heard before. From out of the west layers of clouds came rolling—thin layers that rose and sank on the breeze; they had none of the look or manner of ordinary clouds; they came in waves, like the surges of the sea, and cast a glittering sheen before them as they came; they seemed to be made of some solid murky substance that threw out small sparks along its face.

The three men stood spellbound, watching the oncoming terror; their voices died in their throats; their minds were blank. The horses snorted as they, too, caught sight of it, and became very restless.

The ominous waves of cloud seemed to advance with terrific speed, breaking now and then like a huge surf, and with the deep, dull roaring sound as of a heavy undertow rolling into caverns in a mountain side. . . . But they were neither breakers nor foam, these waves. . . . It seemed more as if the unseen hand of a giant were shaking an immense tablecloth of iridescent colors! . . .

"For God's sake, what——!" . . . Tönseten didn't finish; unconsciously he had been hauling so hard on the lines that the horses began backing the machine.

Just then Ole and Store-Hans came running wildly up, shouting breathlessly, "A snowstorm is coming! . . . *See!*"

. . . The next moment the first wave of the weird cloud engulfed them, spewing over them its hideous, unearthly contents. The horses became uncontrollable. "Come here and give me some help!" cried Tönseten through the eerie hail, but the others, standing like statues, heard nothing and paid no heed; the impact of the solid surge had forced them to turn their backs to the wind. Tönseten could not hold the horses; they bolted across the field, cutting a wide semi-circle through the oats; not until he had the stern of his craft well into the wind could he stop them long enough to scramble down and unhitch them from the reaper.

At that moment two women came running up—Kjersti first, with her skirt thrown over her head, Sörine a little way behind, beating the air with frantic motions. The Solum boys, too, had now joined the terror-stricken little crowd. Down by the creek the grazing cows had hoisted their tails straight in the air and run for the nearest shelter; and no sooner had the horses been turned loose, than they followed suit; man and beast alike were overcome by a nameless fear.

And now from out the sky gushed down with cruel force a living, pulsating stream, striking the backs of the helpless folk like pebbles thrown by an unseen hand; but that which fell out of the heavens was not pebbles, nor raindrops, nor hail, for then it would have lain inanimate where it fell; this substance had no sooner fallen than it popped up again, crackling, and snapping—rose up and disappeared in the twinkling of an eye; it flared and flittered around them like light gone mad; it chirped and buzzed through the air; it snapped and hopped along the ground; the whole place was a weltering turmoil of raging little demons; if one looked for a moment into the wind, one saw nothing but glittering, lightninglike flashes—flashes that came and went, in the heart of a cloud made up of innumerable dark-brown clicking bodies! All the while the roaring sound continued.

"Father!" shrieked Store-Hans through the storm. "They're little birds—they have regular wings! Look here!" . . . The boy had caught one in his hand; spreading the wings and holding it out by their tips, he showed it to his father. The body of the unearthly creature had a dark-brown color; it was about an inch in length, or perhaps a trifle longer; it was plump around the middle and tapered at both ends; on either side of its head sparkled a tiny black eye that seemed to look out with a supernatural intelligence; underneath it were long, slender legs with rusty bands around them; the wings were transparent and of a pale, light color.

"For God's sake, child, throw it away!" moaned Kjersti.

The boy dropped it in fright. No sooner had he let it go than there sounded a snap, a twinkling flash was seen, and the creature had merged itself with the countless legions of flickering devils which now filled all space. They whizzed by in the air; they literally covered the ground; they lit on the heads of grain, on the stubble, on everything in sight— popping and glittering, millions on millions of them. . . . The people watched it, stricken with fear and awe. Here was *Another One* speaking! . . .

Kjersti was crying bitterly; Sörine's kind face was deathly pale as she glanced at the men, trying to bolster up her courage; but the big frame of her husband was bent in fright and dismay. He spoke slowly and solemnly: "This must be one of the plagues mentioned in the Bible!"

"Yes! and the devil take it!" muttered Per Hansa, darkly. . . . "But it can't last forever."

To Tönseten the words of Per Hansa, in an hour like this, sounded like the sheerest blasphemy; they would surely call down upon them a still darker wrath! He turned to reprove his neighbor: "Now the Lord is taking back what he has given," he said, impressively. "I might have guessed that I would never be permitted to harvest such wheat. That was asking too much!"

"Stop your silly gabble!" snarled Per Hansa. "Do you really suppose *He* needs to take the bread out of your mouth?"

There was a certain consolation in Per Hansa's outburst of angry rationalism; Kjersti ceased weeping, though it was her own husband that had been put to shame. "I believe Per Hansa is right," she said, the sobs still choking her. "The Lord can't have any use for our wheat. He doesn't need bread, anyway. He certainly wouldn't take it from us in this way!"

But her open unbelief only confirmed her husband in his position; clearing his throat, he began to take Kjersti to task: "Don't you remember your catechism, and your Bible history? Isn't it plainly stated that this is one of the seven plagues that fell upon Egypt? Look out for your tongue, woman, lest He send us the other six, too! . . . It states as plain as day that it was because the people *hardened themselves!*" . . .

Tönseten would probably have gone on indefinitely expounding the Scriptures to his wife if Henry Solum hadn't interrupted just then with a practical idea. Turning to his brother, he said, "Go fetch the horses, so we can finish this field; by tomorrow there won't be anything left!"

Per Hansa looked at Henry and nodded approvingly; the simple practicability of the suggestion had touched the chord of action again; he jumped to his feet and walked across to the field, where the work of devastation was already in full progress. As he saw the fine, ripe grain being ruthlessly destroyed before his eyes, he felt but one impulse—to stop the inroads of these demons in any possible way. He began to jump up and down and wave his hat, stamping and yelling like one possessed. But the hosts of horrid creatures frolicking about him never so much as noticed his presence; the brown bodies whizzed by on every hand, alighting wherever they pleased, chirping wherever they went; as many as half a dozen of them would perch on a single head of grain, while the stem would be covered with them all the way to the ground; even his own body seemed to be a desirable halting place; they lit on his arms; his back, his neck—they even dared to light on his bared head and on the very hat he waved.

His utter impotence in the face of this tragedy threw him into an uncontrollable fury; he lost all restraint over himself. "You, Ola!" he shouted, hoarsely. "Run home after Old Maria, and bring the caps!"

The boy was soon back with the old musket. His father, hardly able to wait, ran to meet him and snatched the weapon out of his hands. Hurriedly putting on a cap, he settled himself in a firm foothold—for he still had sense enough to remember how hard the rifle kicked when it had been lying loaded a long time.

As Hans Olsa caught wind of what he intended to do he tried to stop it. "Don't do that, Per Hansa! If the Lord has sent this affliction on us, then . . ."

Per Hansa glowered at him with a look of angry determination; then, facing squarely the hurricane of flying bodies, he fired straight into the thickest of the welter! . . . The awful detonation of the old, rusty muzzle-loader had a singular effect; at first, as the shattering sound died away, nothing appeared to have happened—the glittering demons flickered by as unconcernedly as before; but presently a new movement seemed to originate within the body of the main cloud; it began to heave and roll with a lifting motion; in a few minutes the cloud had left the ground and was sailing over their heads, with only an intermittent hail of bodies pelting down on them out of its lower fringe; the roaring becoming more muffled.

"Do you suppose you've actually driven them off?" cried Henry, breathlessly, marvelling as he watched.

"Yes, from *here!*" said Hans Olsa in the same solemn tone, as he pointed down the hill. "But see *our* fields . . . !"

Per Hansa was still in the grip of the strange spell that had taken possession of him; he apparently did not hear what the others were saying; without looking again he hurried off to help Sam with the horses. "Let's get the reaper started!" he cried. "No sense in sitting here like a row of dummies!"

His example roused them once more, and without further words they followed his lead; just before sundown that night they finished the oat field at Per Hansa's. All the while fresh clouds of marauders were passing over. As soon as he could get away each man hurried to his own place; they were all terribly anxious to see how much damage had been done at home. . . . Couldn't they start cutting tomorrow, even if the grain wasn't quite ripe? they thought as they hurried on. Wouldn't it be possible to save *something* out of the wreck? What in God's name could they do if the whole crop were destroyed? . . . Anxiety tugged at their heartstrings. Yes, what could they do? . . .

Ole and Store-Hans went home with Hans Olsa to bring back word as to whether it would be possible to start harvesting his field in the morning. Per Hansa walked home alone; the spell had lifted now, and the reaction had left him in a troubled, irresolute frame of mind. The things that had happened that afternoon seemed harsh and inexplicable. . . . To be sure, *he* had saved his whole crop—but how and why? He had saved it—partly because of his own foolish, headstrong acts, and partly because his land chanced to lie so much higher than that of his neighbors, that it had been the first to dry out in the spring. . . . Well,

great luck for him! But at this moment gladness and happiness were the
last things that he could feel. . . . There were his neighbors—poor devils!
Hadn't they worked just as faithfully, hadn't they struggled just as hard
—and with a great deal more common sense than he had shown? Why
should they have to suffer this terrible calamity while he went scot-free?
. . . And there was something else that worried him desperately.
Throughout the afternoon, while he had been working, vague misgivings of how it was going at home had visited him, an uneasy sense of
oppression and impending disaster; he had found himself constantly
watching his own house, and had every moment expected to see Beret
come around the corner. But not a soul had he caught sight of in all
this time, moving about down there, though the hard labor and the
fiends of the air had left him scant chance to think about it till now.

As he approached the house his misgivings grew more pronounced,
till suddenly they leaped into an overmastering fear which he tried to
assuage by telling himself that she had kept indoors because she had not
dared to leave the children, and that in doing so she had acted wisely.
. . . The house lay in deep twilight as he drew near; there was no sign
of life to be seen or heard, except the malign beings that still snapped
and flared through the air; the sod hut, surrounded as it was by flowing
shapes, looked like a quay thrust out into a turbulent current; in the
deepening twilight, the pale, shimmering sails of the flying creatures had
taken on a still more unearthly sheen; they came, flickered by, and were
gone in an instant, only to give place to myriads more.

. . . Can she have gone over to one of the neighbors'? he wondered
as he came up to the door. No, she hasn't—the door can't be closed
from the outside. . . . Per Hansa gasped for breath as he knocked on
the door of his own house. . . . He rapped harder . . . called, with his
voice tearing from his throat:

"Open the door, Beret!"

He found himself listening intently, his ears strained to catch the
least sound; at length he thought he heard a movement inside, and a
great wave of relief swept over him.

. . . "Thank God!" . . . He waited for the door to be opened—
but nothing happened; nothing more could be heard. . . . What can she
be doing? Didn't she hear me? What in Heaven's name has she put in
front of the door? . . .

Per Hansa had begun to shove against the panel.

"Open the door, I tell you! . . . Beret—where are you?" . . .

Once more he listened; once more he caught a faint sound; but the blood pounding in his ears deafened him now. Pulling himself together, he shoved against the door with all his strength—shoved until red streaks were flashing before his eyes. The door began to give—the opening widened; at last he had pushed it wide enough to slip through.

. . . *"Beret!"* . . . The anguish of his cry cut through the air. . . . "Beret!" . . .

Now he stood in the middle of the room. It was absolutely dark before his eyes; he looked wildly around, but could see nothing.

. . . "Beret, where are you?"

No answer came—there was no one to be seen. But wasn't that a sound? "Beret!" he called again, sharply. He heard it now distinctly. Was it coming from one of the beds, or over there by the door? . . . It was a faint, whimpering sound. He rushed to the beds and threw off the bedclothes—no one in this one, no one in that one—it must be over by the door! . . . He staggered back—the big chest was standing in front of the door. Who could have dragged it there? . . . Per Hansa flung the cover open with frantic haste. The sight that met his eyes made his blood run cold. Down in the depths of the great chest lay Beret, huddled up and holding the baby in her arms; And-Ongen was crouching at her feet—the whimpering sound had come from her.

It seemed for a moment as if he would go mad; the room swam and receded in dizzy circles. . . . But things had to be done. First he lifted And-Ongen out and carried her to the bed—then the baby. At last he took Beret up in his arms, slammed down the lid of the chest, and set her on it.

. . . "Beret, Beret!" . . . he kept whispering.

All his strength seemed to leave him as he looked into her tear-swollen face; yet it wasn't her tears that drained his heart dry—the face was that of a stranger, behind which her own face seemed to be hidden.

He gazed at her helplessly, imploringly; she returned the gaze in a fixed stare, and whispered hoarsely:

"Hasn't the devil got you yet? He has been all around here today. . . . Put the chest back in front of the door right away! He doesn't dare to take the chest, you see. . . . We must hide in it—all of us!"

"Oh, Beret!" begged Per Hansa, his very soul in the cry. Speechless and all undone, he sank down before her, threw his arms around her waist, and buried his head in her lap—as if he were a child needing comfort.

The action touched her; she began to pat his head, running her fingers through his hair and stroking his cheek. . . . "That's right!" she crooned. . . . "Weep now, weep much and long because of your sin! . . . So I have done every night—not that it helps much. . . . Out here nobody pays attention to our tears . . . it's too open and wild . . . but it does no harm to try."

"Oh, Beret, my own girl!"

"Yes, yes, I know," she said, as if to hush him. She grew more loving, caressed him tenderly, bent over to lift him up to her. . . . "Don't be afraid, dear boy of mine! . . . For . . . well . . . it's always worst just before it's over!"

Per Hansa gazed deep into her eyes; a sound of agony came from his throat; he sank down suddenly in a heap and knew nothing more. . . .

Outside, the fiendish shapes flickered and danced in the dying glow of the day. The breeze had died down; the air seemed unaccountably lighter.

. . . That night the Great Prairie stretched herself voluptuously; giantlike and full of cunning, she laughed softly into the reddish moon. "Now we will see what human might may avail against us! . . . Now we'll see!" . . .

ELINORE RUPERT STEWART

Elinore Rupert Stewart, a widowed "washlady," in 1909 traveled from Denver, Colorado, to Burnt Fork, Wyoming, with her ten-year-old daughter in order to become a housekeeper for a Scotch-American Wyoming rancher. A true woman homesteader, Stewart married the rancher and braved the fierce weather of the high Wyoming plains, of which she wrote, "They have just three seasons here, winter and July and August." Stewart wrote twenty-six letters to a friend back in Colorado describing her rough times and indomitable will with precise language and stoic humor. The letters were published as a collection in

1914, Letters of a Woman Homesteader, *and were the inspiration
for the critically acclaimed motion picture* Heartland.

*This optimistic excerpt tells of the joys of staking a claim. "I am
very enthusiastic about women homesteading," Stewart writes, envi-
sioning the hard work of improving land as a better alternative to
slaving away in the city. Any woman who wants to follow suit, she
recommends, "will have independence, plenty to eat all the time, and
a home of her own in the end."*

FROM *LETTERS OF A WOMAN HOMESTEADER*

When I read of the hard times among the Denver poor, I feel like urging
them every one to get out and file on land. I am very enthusiastic about
women homesteading. It really requires less strength and labor to raise
plenty to satisfy a large family than it does to go out to wash, with the
added satisfaction of knowing that their job will not be lost to them if
they care to keep it. Even if improving the place does go slowly, it is
that much done to stay done. Whatever is raised is the homesteader's
own, and there is no house-rent to pay. This year Jerrine cut and
dropped enough potatoes to raise a ton of fine potatoes. She wanted to
try, so we let her, and you will remember that she is but six years old.
We had a man to break the ground and cover the potatoes for her and
the man irrigated them once. That was all that was done until digging
time, when they were ploughed out and Jerrine picked them up. Any
woman strong enough to go out by the day could have done every bit
of the work and put in two or three times that much, and it would have
been so much more pleasant than to work so hard in the city and then
be on starvation rations in the winter.

To me, homesteading is the solution of all poverty's problems, but
I realize that temperament has much to do with success in any under-
taking, and persons afraid of coyotes and work and loneliness had better
let ranching alone. At the same time, any woman who can stand her
own company, can see the beauty of the sunset, loves growing things,
and is willing to put in as much time at careful labor as she does over
the washtub, will certainly succeed; will have independence, plenty to
eat all the time, and a home of her own in the end.

Experimenting need cost the homesteader no more than the work, because by applying to the Department of Agriculture at Washington he can get enough of any seed and as many kinds as he wants to make a thorough trial, and it does n't even cost postage. Also one can always get bulletins from there and from the Experiment Station of one's own State concerning any problem or as many problems as may come up. I would not, for anything, allow Mr. Stewart to do anything toward improving my place, for I want the fun and the experience myself. And I want to be able to speak from experience when I tell others what they can do. Theories are very beautiful, but facts are what must be had, and what I intend to give some time.

Here I am boring you to death with things that cannot interest you! You'd think I wanted you to homestead, would n't you? But I am only thinking of the troops of tired, worried women, sometimes even cold and hungry, scared to death of losing their places to work, who could have plenty to eat, who could have good fires by gathering the wood, and comfortable homes of their own, if they but had the courage and determination to get them.

I must stop right now before you get so tired you will not answer. With much love to you from Jerrine and myself, I am

Yours affectionately,

ELINORE RUPERT STEWART.

WALLACE STEGNER

Wallace Stegner was a true citizen of the entire West. Born in 1909, he grew up in North Dakota, Washington, Saskatchewan, Montana, and Utah. Stegner received a Ph.D. from the University of Iowa in 1935, and taught at Wisconsin and Harvard before moving on to Stanford University, where he directed the creative writing program until he retired in 1969. Author of nearly forty books, Stegner won the Pulitzer prize in 1972 for Angle of Repose *(1971), and won the National Book Award for fiction in 1977 for* The Spectator Bird *(1976). Among his best-known books are* The Big Rock

Candy Mountain *(1943) and* Wolf Willow *(1963). Stegner was known for his pioneering work in conservation. The West lost one of its most articulate and passionate statesmen when he died in 1993.*

This selection, "Carrion Spring," from Wolf Willow, *shows Stegner, one of the principal antimythological writers of the West, working* against *the legacy of the West as an exalted place. The metaphor of thaw, of uncovering the awful-yet-genuine crap and rot that lies beneath the shining virgin snow, is used to illuminate the frustration and despair which overwhelmed so many settlers and immigrants. Stegner revered the West, for all its difficulties along with its glories, as a* real *place and not a make-believe paradise.*

CARRION SPRING
FROM *WOLF WILLOW*

The moment she came to the door she could smell it, not really rotten and not coming from any particular direction, but sweetish, faintly sickening, sourceless, filling the whole air the way a river's water can taste of weeds—the carrion smell of a whole country breathing out in the first warmth across hundreds of square miles.

Three days of chinook had uncovered everything that had been under snow since November. The yard lay discolored and ugly, gray ashpile, rusted cans, spilled lignite, bones. The clinkers that had given them winter footing to privy and stable lay in raised gray wavers across the mud; the strung lariats they had used for lifelines in blizzardy weather had dried out and sagged to the ground. Muck was knee deep down in the corrals by the sod-roofed stable; the whitewashed logs were yellowed at the corners from dogs lifting their legs against them. Sunken drifts around the hay yard were a reminder of how many times the boys had had to shovel out there to keep the calves from walking into the stacks across the top of them. Across the wan and disheveled yard the willows were bare, and beyond them the floodplain hill was brown. The sky was roiled with gray cloud.

Matted, filthy, lifeless, littered, the place of her winter imprisonment was exposed, ugly enough to put gooseflesh up her backbone, and with the carrion smell over all of it. It was like a bad and disgusting wound, infected wire cut or proud flesh or the gangrene of frostbite, with the bandage off. With her packed trunk and her telescope bag and two loaded grain sacks behind her, she stood in the door waiting for Ray to come with the buckboard, and she was sick to be gone.

Yet when he did come, with the boys all slopping through the mud behind him, and they threw her trunk and telescope and bags into the buckboard and tied the tarp down and there was nothing left to do but go, she faced them with a sudden, desolating desire to cry. She laughed, and caught her lower lip under her teeth and bit down hard on it, and went around to shake one hoof-like hand after the other, staring into each face in turn and seeing in each something that made it all the harder to say something easy: Goodbye. Red-bearded, black-bearded, gray-bristled, clean-shaven (for her?), two of them with puckered sunken scars on the cheekbones, all of them seedy, matted-haired, weathered and cracked as old lumber left out for years, they looked sheepish, or sober, or cheerful, and said things like, "Well, Molly, have you a nice trip, now," or "See you in Malta maybe." They had been her family. She had looked after them, fed them, patched their clothes, unraveled old socks to knit them new ones, cut their hair, lanced their boils, tended their wounds. Now it was like the gathered-in family parting at the graveside after someone's funeral.

She had begun quite openly to cry. She pulled her cheeks down, opened her mouth, dabbed at her eyes with her knuckles, laughed. "Now you all take care," she said. "And come see us, you hear? Jesse? Rusty? Slip? Buck, when you come I'll fix you a better patch on your pants than that one. Goodbye, Panguingue, you were the best man I had on the coal scuttle. Don't you forget me. Little Horn, I'm *sorry* we ran out of pie fixings. When you come to Malta I'll make you a peach pie a yard across."

She could not have helped speaking their names, as if to name them were to insure their permanence. But she knew that though she might see them, or most of them, when Ray brought the drive in to Malta in July, these were friends who would soon be lost for good. They had already got the word: sweep the range and sell everything—steers, bulls, calves, cows—for whatever it would bring. Put a For Sale sign on the ranch, or simply abandon it. The country had rubbed its lesson in. Like half the outfits between the Milk and the CPR, the T-Down was quitting. As for her, she was quitting first.

She saw Ray slumping, glooming down from the buckboard seat with the reins wrapped around one gloved hand. Dude and Dinger were hipshot in the harness. As Rusty and Little Horn gave Molly a hand up to climb the wheel, Dude raised his tail and dropped an oaty bundle of dung on the singletree, but she did not even bother to make a face or say something provoked and joking. She was watching Ray, looking right into his gray eyes and his somber dark face and seeing all at once what the winter of disaster had done to him. His cheek, like Ed's and Rusty's, was puckered with frost scars; frost had nibbled at the lobes of his ears; she could see the strain of bone-cracking labor, the bitterness of failure, in the lines from his nose to the corners of his mouth. Making room for her, he did not smile. With her back momentarily to the others, speaking only for him, she said through her tight teeth, "Let's git!"

Promptly—he was always prompt and ready—he plucked whip from whipsocket. The tip snapped on Dinger's haunch, the lurch of the buggy threw her so that she could cling and not have to turn to reveal her face. "Goodbye!" she cried, more into the collar of her mackinaw than to them, throwing the words over her shoulder like a flower or a coin, and tossed her left hand in the air and shook it. The single burst of their voices chopped off into silence. She heard only the grate of the tires in gravel; beside her the wheel poured yellow drip. She concentrated on it, fighting her lips that wanted to blubber.

"This could be bad for a minute," Ray said. She looked up. Obediently she clamped thumb and finger over her nose. To their right, filling half of Frying Pan Flat, was the boneyard, two acres of carcasses scattered where the boys had dragged them after skinning them out when they found them dead in the brush. It did not seem that off there they could smell, for the chinook was blowing out in light airs from the west. But when she let go her nose she smelled it rich and rotten, as if it rolled upwind the way water runs upstream in an eddy.

Beside her Ray was silent. The horses were trotting now in the soft sand of the patrol trail. On both sides the willows were gnawed down to stubs, broken and mouthed and gummed off by starving cattle. There was floodwater in the low spots, and the sound of running water under the drifts of every side coulee.

Once Ray said, "Harry Willis says a railroad survey's coming right up the Whitemud valley this summer. S'pose that'll mean homesteaders in here, maybe a town."

"I s'pose."

"Make it a little easier when you run out of prunes, if there was a store at Whitemud."

"Well," she said, "we won't be here to run out," and then immediately, as she caught a whiff that gagged her, "Pee-you! Hurry up!"

Ray did not touch up the team. "What for?" he said. "To get to the next one quicker?"

She appraised the surliness of his voice, and judged that some of it was general disgust and some of it was aimed at her. But what did he want? Every time she made a suggestion of some outfit around Malta or Chinook where he might get a job he humped his back and looked impenetrable. What *did* he want? To come back here and take another licking? When there wasn't even a cattle outfit left, except maybe the little ones like the Z-X and the Lazy-S? And where one winter could kill you, as it had just killed the T-Down? She felt like yelling at him, "Look at your face. Look at your hands—you can't open them even halfway, for calluses. For what? Maybe three thousand cattle left out of ten thousand, and them skin and bone. Why wouldn't I be glad to get out? Who *cares* if there's a store at Whitemud? You're just like an old bulldog with his teeth clinched in somebody's behind, and it'll take a pry-bar to make you unclinch!" She said nothing; she forced herself to breathe evenly the tainted air.

Floodwater forced them out of the bottoms and up onto the second floodplain. Below them Molly saw the river astonishingly wide, pushing across willow bars and pressing deep into the cutbank bends. She could hear it, when the wheels went quietly—a hushed roar like wind. Cattle were balloonily afloat in the brush where they had died. She saw a brindle longhorn waltz around the deep water of a bend with his legs in the air, and farther on a whiteface that stranded momentarily among flooded rosebushes, and rotated free, and stranded again.

Their bench was cut by a side coulee, and they tipped and rocked down, the rumps of the horses back against the dashboard, Ray's hand on the brake, the shoes screeching mud from the tires. There was brush in the bottom, and stained drifts still unmelted. Their wheels sank in slush, she hung to the seat rail, they righted, the lines cracked across the muscling rumps as the team dug in and lifted them out of the cold, snowbank breath of the draw. Then abruptly, in a hollow on the right, dead eyeballs stared at her from between spraddled legs, horns and tails and legs were tangled in a starved mass of bone and hide not yet, in that cold bottom, puffing with the gases of decay. They must have been three deep—piled on one another, she supposed, while drifting before some one of the winter's blizzards.

A little later, accosted by a stench so overpowering that she breathed it in deeply as if to sample the worst, she looked to the left and saw a longhorn, its belly blown up ready to pop, hanging by neck and horns from a tight clump of alder and black birch where the snow had left him. She saw the wind make catspaws in the heavy winter hair.

"Jesus," Ray said, "when you find 'em in *trees!*"

His boots, worn and whitened by many wettings, were braced against the dash. From the corner of her eye Molly could see his glove, its wrist-lace open. His wrist looked as wide as a doubletree, the sleeve of his Levi jacket was tight with forearm. The very sight of his strength made her hate the tone of defeat and outrage in his voice. Yet she appraised the tone cunningly, for she did not want him somehow butting his bullheaded way back into it. There were better things they could do than break their backs and hearts in a hopeless country a hundred miles from anywhere.

With narrowed eyes, caught in an instant vision, she saw the lilac bushes by the front porch of her father's house, heard the screen door bang behind her brother Charley (screen doors!), saw people passing, women in dresses, maybe all going to a picnic or a ballgame down in the park by the river. She passed the front of McCabe's General Store and through the window saw the counters and shelves: dried apples, dried peaches, prunes, tapioca, Karo syrup, everything they had done without for six weeks; and new white-stitched overalls, yellow horsehide gloves, varnished axe handles, barrels of flour and bags of sugar, shiny boots and workshoes, counters full of calico and flowered voile and crepe de chine and curtain net, whole stacks of flypaper stuck sheet to sheet, jars of peppermints and striped candy and horehound. . . . She giggled.

"What?" Ray's neck and shoulders were so stiff with muscle that he all but creaked when he turned his head.

"I was just thinking. Remember the night I used our last sugar to make that batch of divinity, and dragged all the boys in after bedtime to eat it?"

"Kind of saved the day," Ray said. "Took the edge off ever'body."

"Kind of left us starving for sugar, too. I can still see them picking up those little bitty dabs of fluff with their fingers like tongs, and stuffing them in among their whiskers and making faces, *yum yum,* and wondering what on earth had got into me."

"Nothing got into you. You was just fed up. We all was."

"Remember when Slip picked up that pincushion I was tatting a cover for, and I got sort of hysterical and asked him if he knew what it was? Remember what he said? 'It a doll piller, ain't it, Molly?' I thought I'd die."

She shook her head angrily. Ray was looking sideward at her in alarm. She turned her face away and stared down across the water that spread nearly a half-mile wide in the bottoms. Dirty foam and brush circled in the eddies. She saw a slab cave from an almost drowned cutbank and sink bubbling. From where they drove, between the water and the outer slope that rolled up to the high prairie, the Cypress Hills made a snow-patched, tree-darkened dome across the west. The wind came off them mild as milk. Poisoned! she told herself, and dragged it deep into her lungs.

She was aware again of Ray's gray eye. "Hard on you," he said. For some reason he made her mad, as if he were accusing her of bellyaching. She felt how all the time they bumped and rolled along the shoulder of the river valley they had this antagonism between them like a snarl of barbed wire. You couldn't reach out anywhere without running into it. Did he blame her for going home, or what? What did he expect her to do, come along with a whole bunch of men on that roundup, spend six or eight weeks in pants out among the carcasses? And then what?

A high, sharp whicker came downwind. The team chuckled and surged into their collars. Looking ahead, she saw a horse—picketed or hobbled—and a man who leaned on something—rifle?—watching them. "Young Schulz," Ray said, and then here came the dogs, four big bony hounds. The team began to dance. Ray held them in tight and whistled the buggywhip in the air when the hounds got too close.

Young Schulz, Molly saw as they got closer, was leaning on a shovel, not a rifle. He had dug a trench two or three feet deep and ten or twelve long. He dragged a bare forearm across his forehead under a muskrat cap: a sullen-faced boy with eyes like dirty ice. She supposed he had been living all alone since his father had disappeared. Somehow he made her want to turn her lips inside out. A wild man, worse than an Indian. She had not liked his father and she did not like him.

The hounds below her were sniffing at the wheels and testing the air up in her direction, wagging slow tails. "What've you got, wolves?" Ray asked.

"Coyotes."

"Old ones down there?"

"One, anyway. Chased her in."

"Find any escape holes?"

"One. Plugged it."

"You get 'em the hard way," Ray said. "How've you been doing on wolves?"

The boy said a hard four-letter word, slanted his eyes sideward at Molly in something less than apology—acknowledgment, maybe. "The dogs ain't worth a damn without Puma to kill for 'em. Since he got killed they just catch up with a wolf and run alongside him. I dug out a couple dens."

With his thumb and finger he worked at a pimple under his jaw. The soft wind blew over them, the taint of carrion only a suspicion, perhaps imaginary. The roily sky had begun to break up in patches of blue. Beside her Molly felt the solid bump of Ray's shoulder as he twisted to cast a weather eye upward. "Going to be a real spring day," he said. To young Schulz he said, "How far in that burrow go, d'you s'pose?"

"Wouldn't ordinarily go more'n twenty feet or so."

"Need any help diggin'?"

The Schulz boy spat. "Never turn it down."

"Ray . . ." Molly said. But she stopped when she saw his face.

"Been a long time since I helped dig out a coyote," he said. He watched her as if waiting for a reaction. "Been a long time since I did anything for *fun*."

"Oh, go ahead!" she said. "Long as we don't miss that train."

"I guess we can make Maple Creek by noon tomorrow. And you ain't in such a hurry you have to be there sooner, are you?"

She had never heard so much edge in his voice. He looked at her as if he hated her. She turned so as to keep the Schulz boy from seeing her face, and for just a second she and Ray were all alone up there, eye to eye. She laid a hand on his knee. "I don't know what it is," she said. "Honestly I don't. But you better work it off."

Young Schulz went back to his digging while Ray unhitched and looped the tugs and tied the horses to the wheels. Then Ray took the shovel and began to fill the air with clods. He moved more dirt than the Fresno scrapers she had seen grading the railroad back home; he worked as if exercising his muscles after a long layoff, as if spring had fired him up and set him to running. The soil was sandy and came out in clean brown shovelfuls. The hounds lay back out of range and watched. Ray did not look toward Molly, or say anything to Schulz. He just moved dirt as if dirt was his worst enemy. After a few minutes Molly pulled the buffalo robe out of the buckboard and spread it on the drying prairie. By that time it was getting close to noon. The sun was full out; she felt it warm on her face and hands.

The coyote hole ran along about three feet underground. From where she sat she could look right up the trench, and see the black opening at the bottom when the shovel broke into it. She could imagine the coyotes crammed back at the end of their burrow, hearing the noises and seeing the growing light as their death dug toward them, and no way out, nothing to do but wait.

Young Schulz took the shovel and Ray stood out of the trench, blowing. The violent work seemed to have made him more cheerful. He said to Schulz, when the boy stopped and reached a gloved hand up the hole, "She comes out of there in a hurry she'll run right up your sleeve."

Schulz grunted and resumed his digging. The untroubled sun went over, hanging almost overhead, and an untroubled wind stirred the old grass. Over where the last terrace of the floodplain rolled up to the prairie the first gopher of the season sat up and looked them over. A dog moved, and he disappeared with a flirt of his tail. Ray was rolling up his sleeves, whistling loosely between his teeth. His forearms were white, his hands blackened and cracked as the charred ends of sticks. His eyes touched her—speculatively, she thought. She smiled, making a forgiving, kissing motion of her mouth, but all he did in reply was work his eyebrows, and she could not tell what he was thinking.

Young Schulz was poking up the hole with the shovel handle. Crouching in the trench in his muskrat cap, he looked like some digging animal; she half expected him to put his nose into the hole and sniff and then start throwing dirt out between his hind legs.

Then in a single convulsion of movement Schulz rolled sideward. A naked-gummed thing of teeth and gray fur shot into sight, scrambled at the edge, and disappeared in a pinwheel of dogs. Molly leaped to the heads of the horses, rearing and wall-eyed and yanking the light buckboard sideways, and with a hand in each bridle steadied them down. Schulz, she saw, was circling the dogs with the shotgun, but the dogs had already done it for him. The roaring and snapping tailed off. Schulz kicked the dogs away and with one quick flash and circle and rip tore the scalp and ears off the coyote. It lay there wet, mauled, bloody, with its pink skull bare—a little dog brutally murdered. One of the hounds came up, sniffed with its neck stretched out, sank its teeth in the coyote's shoulder, dragged it a foot or two.

"Ray . . ." Molly said.

He did not hear her; he was blocking the burrow with the shovel blade while Schulz went over to his horse. The boy came back with a red willow stick seven or eight feet long, forked like a small slingshot at the end. Ray pulled away the shovel and Schulz twisted in the hole with the forked end of the stick. A hard grunt came out of him, and he backed up, pulling the stick from the hole. At the last moment he yanked hard, and a squirm of gray broke free and rolled and was pounced on by the hounds.

This time Ray kicked them aside. He picked up the pup by the tail, and it hung down and kicked its hind legs a little. Schulz was down again, probing the burrow, twisting, probing again, twisting hard.

Again he backed up, working the entangled pup out carefully until it was in the open, and then landing it over his head like a sucker from the river. The pup landed within three feet of the buckboard wheel, and floundered, stunned. In an instant Molly dropped down and smothered it in clothes, hands, arms. There was snarling in her very ear, she was bumped hard, she heard Ray yelling, and then he had her on her feet. From his face, she thought he was going to hit her. Against her middle, held by the scruff and grappled with the other arm, the pup snapped and slavered with needle teeth. She felt the sting of bites on her hands and wrists. The dogs ringed her, ready to jump, kept off by Ray's kicking boot.

"God a'mighty," Ray said, "you want to get yourself killed?"

"I didn't want the dogs to get him."

"No. What are you going to do with him? We'll just have to knock him in the head."

"I'm going to keep him."

"In Malta?"

"Why not?"

He let go his clutch on her arm. "He'll be a cute pup for a month and then he'll be a chicken thief and then somebody'll shoot him."

"At least he'll have a little bit of a life. Get *away,* you dirty, murdering . . . !" She cradled the thudding little body along one arm under her mackinaw, keeping her hold in the scruff with her right hand, and turned herself away from the crowding hounds. "I'm going to tame him," she said. "I don't care what you say."

"Scalp's worth three dollars," Schulz said from the edge of the ditch.

Ray kicked the dogs back. His eyes, ordinarily so cool and gray, looked hot. The digging and the excitement did not seem to have taken the edge off whatever was eating him. He said, "Look, maybe you have to go back home to your folks, but you don't have to take a menagerie along. What are you going to do with him on the train?"

But now it was out. He did blame her. "You think I'm running out on you," she said.

"I just said you can't take a menagerie back to town."

"You said *maybe* I had to go home. Where else would I go? You're going to be on roundup till July. The ranch is going to be sold. Where on earth *would* I go but home?"

"You don't have to stay. You don't have to make me go back to ridin' for some outfit for twenty a month and found."

His dark, battered, scarred face told her to be quiet. Dipping far down in the tight pocket of his Levi's he brought up his snap purse and took from it three silver dollars. Young Schulz, who had been probing the den to see if anything else was there, climbed out of the ditch and took the money in his dirty chapped hand. He gave Molly one cool look with his dirty-ice eyes, scalped the dead pup, picked up shotgun and twisting-stick and shovel, tied them behind the saddle, mounted, whistled at the dogs, and with barely a nod rode off toward the northeastern flank of the Hills. The hounds fanned out ahead of him, running loose and easy. In the silence their departure left behind, a clod broke and rolled into the ditch. A gopher piped somewhere. The wind moved quiet as breathing in the grass.

Molly drew a breath that caught a little—a sigh for their quarreling, for whatever bothered him so deeply that he gloomed and grumped and asked something impossible of her—but when she spoke she spoke around it. "No thanks for your digging."

"He don't know much about living with people."

"He's like everything else in this country, wild and dirty and thankless."

In a minute she would really start feeling sorry for herself. But why not? Did it ever occur to him that since November, when they came across the prairie on their honeymoon in this same buckboard, she had seen exactly one woman, for one day and a night? Did he have any idea how she had felt, a bride of three weeks, when he went out with the boys on late fall roundup and was gone two weeks, through three different blizzards, while she stayed home and didn't know whether he was dead or alive?

"If you mean me," Ray said, "I may be wild and I'm probably dirty, but I ain't thankless, honey." Shamed, she opened her mouth to reply, but he was already turning away to rummage up a strap and a piece of whang leather to make a collar and leash for her pup.

"Are you hungry?" she said to his shoulders.

"Any time."

"I put up some sandwiches."

"O.K."

"Oh, Ray," she said, "let's not crab at each other! Sure I'm glad we're getting out. Is that so awful? I hate to see you killing yourself bucking this *hopeless* country. But does that mean we have to fight? I thought maybe we could have a picnic like we had coming in, back on that slough where the ducks kept coming in and landing on the ice and skidding end over end. I don't know, it don't hardly seem we've laughed since."

"Well," he said, "it ain't been much of a laughing winter, for a fact." He had cut down a cheekstrap and tied a rawhide thong to it. Carefully she brought out the pup and he buckled the collar around its neck, but when she set it on the ground it backed up to the end of the thong, cringing and showing its naked gums, so that she picked it up again and let it dig along her arm, hunting darkness under her mackinaw.

"Shall we eat here?" Ray said. "Kind of a lot of chewed-up coyote around."

"Let's go up on the bench."

"Want to tie the pup in the buckboard?"

"I'll take him. I want to get him used to me."

"O.K.," he said. "You go on. I'll tie a nosebag on these nags and bring the robe and the lunchbox."

She walked slowly, not to scare the pup, until she was up the little bench and onto the prairie. From up there she could see not only the Cypress Hills across the west, but the valley of the Whitemud breaking out of them, and a big slough, spread by floodwater, and watercourses going both ways out of it, marked by thin willows. Just where the

Whitemud emerged from the hills were three white dots—the Mountie post, probably, or the Lazy-S, or both. The sun was surprisingly warm, until she counted up and found that it was May 8. It ought to be warm.

Ray brought the buffalo robe and spread it, and she sat down. One-handed because she had the thong of the leash wrapped around her palm, she doled out sandwiches and hard-boiled eggs. Ray popped a whole egg in his mouth and chewing, pointed. "There goes the South Fork of the Swift Current, out of the slough. The one this side, that little scraggle of willows you can see, empties into the Whitemud. That slough sits right on the divide and runs both ways. You don't see that very often."

She appraised his tone. He was feeling better. For that matter, so was she. It had turned out a beautiful day, with big fair-weather clouds coasting over. She saw the flooded river bottoms below them, on the left, darken to winter and then sweep bright back to spring again while she could have counted no more than ten. As she moved, the coyote pup clawed and scrambled against her side, and she said, wrinkling her nose in her freckleface smile, "If he started eating me, I wonder if I could keep from yelling? Did you ever read that story about the boy that hid the fox under his clothes and the fox started eating a hole in him and the boy never batted an eye, just let himself be chewed?"

"No, I never heard that one," Ray said. "Don't seem very likely, does it?" He lay back and turned his face, shut-eyed, into the sun. Now and then his hand rose to feed bites of sandwich into his mouth.

"The pup's quieter," Molly said. "I bet he'll tame. I wonder if he'd eat a piece of sandwich?"

"Leave him be for a while, I would."

"I guess."

His hand reached over blindly and she put another sandwich into its pincer claws. Chewing, he came up on an elbow; his eyes opened, he stared a long time down into the flooded bottoms and then across toward the slough and the hills. "Soon as the sun comes out, she don't look like the same country, does she?"

Molly said nothing. She watched his nostrils fan in and out as he sniffed. "No smell up here, do you think?" he said. But she heard the direction he was groping in, the regret that could lead, if they did not watch out, to some renewed and futile hope, and she said tartly, "I can smell it, all right."

He sighed. He lay back and closed his eyes. After about three minutes he said, "Boy, what a day, though. I won't get through on the patrol trail goin' back. The ice'll be breakin' up before tonight, at this rate. Did you hear it crackin' and poppin' a minute ago?"

"I didn't hear it."

"Listen."

They were still. She heard the soft wind move in the prairie wool, and beyond it, filling the background, the hushed and hollow noise of the floodwater, sigh of drowned willows, suck of whirlpools, splash and guggle as cutbanks caved, and the steady push and swash and ripple of moving water. Into the soft rush of sound came a muffled report like a tree cracking, or a shot a long way off. "Is that it?" she said. "Is that the ice letting loose?"

"Stick around till tomorrow and you'll see that whole channel full of ice."

Another shadow from one of the big flat-bottomed clouds chilled across them and passed. Ray said into the air, "Harry Willis said this railroad survey will go right through to Medicine Hat. Open up this whole country."

Now she sat very still, stroking the soft bulge of the pup through the cloth.

"Probably mean a town at Whitemud."

"You told me."

"With a store that close we couldn't get quite so snowed in as we did this winter."

Molly said nothing, because she dared not. They were a couple that, like the slough spread out northwest of them, flowed two ways, he to this wild range, she back to town and friends and family. And yet in the thaw of one bright day, their last together up here north of the Line, she teetered. She feared the softening that could start her draining toward his side.

"Molly," Ray said, and made her look at him. She saw him as the country and the winter had left him, weathered and scarred. His eyes were gray and steady, marksman's eyes.

She made a wordless sound that sounded in her own ears almost a groan. "You want awful bad to stay," she said.

His tong fingers plucked a strand of grass, he bit it between his teeth, his head went slowly up and down.

"But how?" she said. "Do you want to strike the Z-X for a job, or the Lazy-S, or somebody? Do you want to open a store in Whitemud for when the railroad comes through, or what?"

"Haven't you figured that out yet?" he said. "Kept waitin' for you to see it. I want to buy the T-Down."

"You *what?*"

"I want us to buy the T-Down and make her go."

She felt that she went all to pieces. She laughed. She threw her hands around so that the pup scrambled and clawed at her side. "Ray Henry," she said, "you're crazy as a bedbug. Even if it made any sense, which it doesn't, where'd we get the money?"

"Borrow it."

"Go in debt to stay up *here?*"

"Molly," he said, and she heard the slow gather of determination in his voice, "when else could we pick up cattle for twenty dollars a head with sucking calves thrown in? When else could we get a whole ranch layout for a few hundred bucks? That Goodnight herd we were running was the best herd in Canada, maybe anywhere. This spring roundup we could take our pick of what's left, including bulls, and put our brand on 'em and turn 'em into summer range and drive everything else to Malta. We wouldn't want more than three-four hundred head. We can swing that much, and we can cut enough hay to bring that many through even a winter like this last one."

She watched him; her eyes groped and slipped. He said, "We're never goin' to have another chance like this as long as we live. This country's goin' to change; there'll be homesteaders in here soon as the railroad comes. Towns, stores, what you've been missin'. Women folks. And we can sit out here on the Whitemud with good hay land and good range and just make this God darned country holler uncle."

"How long?" she said. "How long have you been thinking this way?"

"Since we got John's letter."

"You never said anything."

"I kept waitin' for you to get the idea yourself. But you were hell bent to get out."

She escaped his eyes, looked down, shifted carefully to accommodate the wild thing snuggled in darkness at her waist, and as she moved, her foot scuffed up the scalloped felt edge of the buffalo robe. By her toe was a half-crushed crocus, palely lavender, a thing so tender and unbelievable in the waste of brown grass under the great pour of sky that she cried out, "Why, good land, look at that!"—taking advantage of it both as discovery and as diversion.

"Crocus?" Ray said, bending. "Don't take long, once the snow goes."

It lay in her palm, a thing lucky as a four-leaf clover, and as if it had had some effect in clearing her sight, Molly looked down the south-facing slope and saw it tinged with faintest green. She put the crocus to her nose, but smelled only a mild freshness, an odor no more showy than that of grass. But maybe enough to cover the scent of carrion.

Her eyes came up and found Ray's watching her steadily. "You think we could do it," she said.

"I know we could."

"It's a funny time to start talking that way, when I'm on my way out."

"You don't have to stay out."

Sniffing the crocus, she put her right hand under the mackinaw until her fingers touched fur. The pup stiffened but did not turn or snap. She moved her fingers softly along his back, willing him tame. For some reason she felt as if she might burst out crying.

"Haven't you got any ambition to be the first white woman in five hundred miles?" Ray said.

Past and below him, three or four miles off, she saw the great slough darken under a driving cloud shadow and then brighten to a blue that danced with little wind-whipped waves. She wondered what happened to the ice in a slough like that, whether it went on down the little flooded creeks to add to the jams in the Whitemud and Swift Current, or whether it just rose to the surface and gradually melted there. She didn't suppose it would be spectacular like the break-up in the river.

"Mumma and Dad would think we'd lost our minds," she said. "How much would we have to borrow?"

"Maybe six or eight thousand."

"Oh, Lord!" She contemplated the sum, a burden of debt heavy enough to pin them down for life. She remembered the winter, six months of unremitting slavery and imprisonment. She lifted the crocus and laid it against Ray's dark scarred cheek.

"You should never wear lavender," she said, and giggled at the very idea, and let her eyes come up to his and stared at him, sick and scared. "All right," she said. "If it's what you want."

MARI SANDOZ

Mari Sandoz (1896–1966) received the 1955 National Achievement Award of The Westerners for having more books (four) than any other author, living or dead, on the One Hundred Best Books about the West list. Her central achievement, The Trans-Missouri Series, was conceived during Sandoz's teenage years. The series began with the classical Old Jules *(1935), and continued with* Crazy Horse: The Strange Man of the Oglalas *(1942),* Cheyenne Autumn *(1953),* The Buffalo Hunters: The Story of the Hide Men *(1954), and* The Cattlemen: From the Rio Grande Across the Far Marias *(1958). Sandoz is the author of several other books of fiction and nonfiction, including* Son of the Gamblin' Man *(1960),* Love Song to the Plains *(1961),* These Were the Sioux *(1961), and a collection of short writings,* Hostiles and Friendlies *(1959).*

Sandoz drew upon her pioneer upbringing in her Trans-Missouri Series, as well as in her other work, and in this excerpt from her masterpiece, Old Jules. *Her books were some of the first written by a Westerner to turn away from mythic concerns and confront the grim hardships and bleak biographies of settlers who went out to conquer the West but were so often brutalized by the life, and lived their days mostly trying to survive it.*

FROM *OLD JULES*

Once more that dream of every frontier, a boom, struck the Panhandle. Twenty years after the influx of settlers into the hard-land fringe north and west of the sandhills, another, and this time a swifter, more spectacular, wave surged over the free-land region and broke about Alliance, the land-office town.

The Kinkaid Act, allowing every *bona fide* settler six hundred forty acres of free land for a filing fee of fourteen dollars, went into effect June 28, 1904. Weeks earlier big shipments of cases, kegs, and barrels had arrived. Several new saloons were built in strategic spots in the little prairie town. Soft-spoken men, with knife-edged, peg-topped trousers and beautifully kept hands, appeared out of nowhere. A little weather-beaten church was suddenly overshadowed by the house next door, gay in a yellow coat of paint, a mechanical piano, a crystal chandelier, and painted glass lamps about which lolled women in lace blouses and wasp-ish waists, chaperoned by Silver Nell, in wine-colored velvet and a dog collar of imitation pearls, winter or summer.

Two weeks before the opening, covered wagons, horsebackers, men afoot, toiled into Alliance, got information at the land office, and van-ished eastward over the level prairie. Many turned back at the first soft yellow chophills, pockmarked by blowouts and warted with soapweeds. Others kept on, through this protective border, into the broad valley region, with high hills reaching towards the whitish sky. Many came in hired livery rigs and generally went away again, for the drivers knew how to keep in the bewildering border of waste land all day. So stories spread through the East of a new Great American Desert, the sandhills of western Nebraska. The cattlemen should be paid to live in it.

Before the opening Jules spent weeks in the hills, only to find that every good flat was either covered or cut up by filings upon which no one lived. But after a lot of preliminary contesting he had over two dozen men ready to file. In Alliance they found board shacks thrown together and lined with rows of occupied beds and extra landseekers sleeping on the floor. Tents and covered wagons fringed the town. Pas-ture and hay were sky high. Jules stayed with Broome, his land attorney. His settlers shifted for themselves as they could.

In the evening Jules, his rifle across his arm, limped about among the newcomers and felt young again. It was like Valentine in the eighties, but different too—many more people and not so young, not nearly so young. Many of these were old—defeated old men. And about the hotels and the rude boarding houses were women with graying hair and fuzzy cheeks, women who spoke meticulous English and were horrified at the locator. They would never trust themselves alone with such a man. They wondered at his acquaintance with the wives of prominent people: bankers, newspapermen, attorneys, land officials. "The standards here—well, really!" a high-bosomed old soldier's widow remarked through her lace handkerchief as Jules limped through the packed lobby of a hotel, his rifle still across his arm.

The day of the opening long queues of homeseekers waited for hours, only to find that even the sad choice of land that was free had been filed earlier in the day. There was talk of cattleman agents who made up baskets full of filing papers beforehand and ran them through the first thing. One woman was said to have filed on forty sections, under forty names, at five dollars a shot. The land was covered by filings that would never turn into farms. Yes, the Kinkaid Act was a cattleman law, as it was intended to be.

Nevertheless Jules was busy. His buckskin team, colts of Old Daisy, threaded in and out between the hills. In six months all unoccupied filings would be subject to contest. For twenty-five dollars Jules showed the land, ascertained the numbers, took the settler to Alliance to the land office, helped him make his filings, and later, when he was ready to fence, surveyed the homestead completely. If the homeseeker found nothing to please him, there was no charge. Otherwise Jules pocketed a twenty-five-dollar fee.

"That way you run around, skinning your team all over the sandhills, and for nothing half the time," Mary protested.

Jules's neighbors argued with him, too. What prevented a settler from getting the numbers of the land and then going to Alliance alone to file, giving the locator nothing for his work?

"That would be crooked," Jules pointed out.

"Funny how he reads his own honesty and his own cussedness into everything and everybody!" Nell Sears, married twice and now back and living with her brother Charley, commented to Mary.

And every few days some land agent or attorney from, say, Chicago suggested that Jules charge fifty or a hundred dollars and give him a fourth or half of the fee for steering the prospects to him. Jules stuck his cob pipe between his bearded lips and threw the letters into the wood box.

"I am not in this business for the money. I'm trying to build up the country."

After the grandmother died, Jules announced that he was getting a convict on parole from Governor Mickey.

"What kind?" Mary looked up dubiously from the children's plates.

"A Bohemian, forty years old."

"I mean—what 's he locked up for?"

Jules had planned to avoid the question, but faced with it now he filled his mouth with potatoes and spoke through them. "Sent up for thirteen years. Trumped-up charge of criminal intercourse with a little girl three years old."

Mary wiped the baby's chin. "I do not like it."

Two weeks later a livery man from Rushville brought the convict

Jim, a former packing-house worker speaking broken English. He was pale as tallow, could n't draw a bucket of water, and had never touched a live horse or cow. He walked gingerly through the six inches of snow in his slip-on rubbers, shivering behind Jules, who took him to the edge of the hill and showed him the snow-bound orchard.

As soon as the two men were out of the house the Sunday crowd buzzed. "Old Jules is crazy, bringing a man like that into his home," Mary overheard Charley Sears say. She was putting up another bed in the lean-to for Marie and the baby, who slept with her because he disturbed Jules. Jim would have the attic to himself.

"Cold as the devil up there—freeze the poor Bohunk stiff," Jules objected.

"He has two good feather beds and I don't remember you ever complaining about the cold for the children up there."

"Oho."

At supper time Jim was still overhead, unpacking probably. They could hear him walk four steps this way and then four back, although the attic was made up of two rooms, each sixteen feet long. Four steps, always four.

The boys were sent up to call him. He came down the outside stairs into the house and stood, his hands behind the thin back, his head down.

"Pull up—what you waiting for?" Jules demanded impatiently.

The man looked about him without turning his head; only his brown eyes glinting in the light showed that there was movement at all.

"Here," Mary indicated the foot of the table.

Slowly the man came to the backless chair. Jules was already eating, seeing nothing, but the children eyed Jim over their spoons. When Mary had dished out for them all with little Fritz on her arm, she noticed in surprise that the man still stood.

"Sit down."

The heavy lines in Jim's face crumpled and broke as his reddish moustache spread into a reticent little smile, showing well-kept teeth.

"You mean it I should sit?"

"Of course."

"Thank you, lady." He slipped sidewise into the chair, without moving it, without a sound. He did n't seem to notice the quarrels of the children, or Jules's growls because his wife had overlooked his pointing finger.

"Don't go back upstairs until you want to go to bed," Mary advised.

So Jim sat back in a corner, far from the lamp and the stove, his head between his hands. But she knew that his eyes followed her about.

The spring after Jim came to the river Jules put him to farming. The former meat-cutter had a lot to learn, but he worked, grew tanned, strong. He learned to laugh again, too, and sometimes he sang prison favorites, "Nearer, My God, to Thee," "Darling Nelly Gray," and "Till We Meet Again," during the evenings. Jules taught him to handle a repeating shotgun, to track the wily jack rabbit that made so cunning an end to his trail, to judge the speed of flying ducks. He made even a quail hunter of Jim.

The first Fourth of July Jim was on the river he took Jule, James, and Marie fishing in Spring Creek, in the school section. All the neighbors went to Palmer's grove, down the river, passing Jules's house with bunting-trimmed wagons and buggies, waving flags and shooting firecrackers. And the children, would they not go? Jim asked. Ah, but that was bad, and so he made a fishing holiday. They caught a dishpan full of sunfish and had a fine time.

"Are n't you worried—those children with such a man?" Mrs. Surber asked.

"Ach, no." Mary washed her hands preparatory to working her bread into buns and loaves. "He 's a nice man with a family in Chicago and a little girl about Marie's age. It was the strike made him go to Omaha, away from them. Too bad—and he likes his schnapps much now his wife got a divorce."

The golden ash clung to its leaves until they were brown and wrinkled, the cottonwoods still yellow-green at the time when Mary and the children usually raked up big piles of dry leaves for the bottom bed ticks. She liked cottonwood leaves better than straw or husks; they lumped less and shook up easier and, with a loose quilt of wild duck feathers over the top, lay well. But at last the ticks were all stuffed high, the root crops carefully put away in the cellar, and the ledge lined with cauliflower, cabbage, and endive. And still the smoke of fall hung blue along the bluffs.

Then, at three one morning, Jules awakened them all with a loud hullabaloo to see the northern lights. From east to west stretched a wall of reddish light, long tongues of cold rose reaching towards the zenith, rising and falling as though fanned by an Indian robe.

Winter was upon them.

All fall the farmers waited on freight cars to ship their big crops. Now it was as Jones and Sturgeon and Jules recalled, the land they saw in '84. Everyone was optimistic and borrowing money on future good times, including Jules. The Koller and Peters settlement gave him a lease at twenty-five dollars a year as long as he wanted it on the quarter across the road; the adjoining quarter he bought for two hundred fifty dollars. In return he dismissed three contests, a protest against a proof, and his mineral claims against land in the ambitious neighbors' range.

"Your papa is a thief—he stole land from our papa," one of the Peters girls said to Marie on the bridge one day. But Jules's children were accustomed to such things. She giggled, turned, and ran up the road homeward, kicking sand back with her bare feet as she went, the nearest thing to nose-thumbing her mother permitted.

Christmas time Paul from the Platte and William, both just back from California, where they went to look around a little, came to the river for a visit. They brought their wives and Ferdinand. Emile, they apologized, had a cold. Mary understood. But the others came for Sunday dinner and stayed until late in the night. Fanny, Paul's wife, with one boy and a fine house, put on airs, bragged about her indigestion, and took soda and charcoal tablets. Her sister Lena, with no children, and still living in the old sod house full of fleas, was her own impulsive self, quick to anger and equally quick to laugh in unrestraint.

They drank a couple of bottles of wine they brought back with them, compared it sadly to that of the Old Country, and talked about the fruit possibilities of western Nebraska. Paul was starting an orchard. William had dammed Box Butte Creek, stocked the pond with government fish, and grew a fine garden.

And as the evening came on and the red firelight played over them they talked of the old days and the Old Country. Mary was the only one of them who did not speak French. But William, and particularly Paul, in contrast with the unchallenged leader Jules, gave her a phrase here and there in German and in English. They made her feel that her dinner was good and that her family was a nice one. She needed that, for she had heard that Paul's wife compared her to a rabbit in prolificacy. Jules only laughed. "Fanny would n't be sick all the time if she raised a big family."

"They seem healthy enough, our children, but they don't grow,"

Mary said when they spoke of the young ones. "And handsome they never will be."

"Every child is beautiful to his mother," Fanny said sweetly as she pushed her chair back to avoid the ashes from Jules's pipe.

William grinned a little, sucked in his breath, and looked into Mary's eyes.

"They will do well. They have a sensible mother," he said.

The new year promised to be an interesting one for Jules. The *Standard* reprinted a section of his discussion of tree culture before the State Horticultural Society. Gray wolves were dragging down strong fat steers and horses and eating them alive as they did the big bull in the cottonwood grove in Wyoming, where Jules shot seven. That was after one of his wives,—which one?—Emelia, left him. He heard she went from bad to worse, the way with women who won't work for a living. And here he had already this crop of little cotton-tops growing up about him from another.

The wolves were so bad that the Spade, Springlake, and Modisett ranches offered a hundred dollars for each gray killed in their region. Jules wanted to start as soon as he heard about the bounty, but the thermometer was down to twenty below zero.

"You can't go until it gets warmer," Mary pointed out. "You forget you 're not used to sleeping out like you were ten years ago, and not so young."

Yes, not so young. Then he rose to contradict her. "I feel as young as I ever did."

"You feel—but you are not."

The next two weeks of cold wave were severe. Range riders nursed protruding, purpled ears and frozen feet. The schools were closed. And as in the early days close confinement brought out quarrels, aroused dormant conflicts. Four wives left their husbands when the sun came again. One could n't wait. She ran out into the storm and was lost for a day. Two men advertised: "I will not be responsible for any debts contracted by anyone except myself."

Jules spent the cold weather about the stove with his guns, his stamps, and his correspondence. He tried to get a pardon for Jim, who was a good honest fellow even though he could never learn to trap muskrats as well as little Jule. While he was writing to Lincoln, he complained about the new game laws. "Pay to hunt on my land, where I feed the game? Can't kill the grouse and the rabbits that eat the buds and bark off my trees! To hell with such laws. I found the country open and free and I don't recognize any restrictions imposed by a bunch of cheap politicians grafting on the taxpayer."

To emphasize his contempt Jules ordered a new lot of high-powered shells and another forty-foot fish net. But his interest soon changed. A letter from Washington informed him that hundreds of fraudulent filings were subject to cancellation whenever a *bona fide* settler applied for a filing. In a couple of months still another block would be opened. That meant another boom. Jules took his compass to town to have the needle remagnetized, put new red rags on his surveying pins, looped the chain neatly, and waited for the snow to go.

Twenty-two years brought many changes to the land of promise into which Jules drove so confidently in '84. By 1906 the Indians along the Niobrara, the big game,—elk, deer, even antelope,—were gone. The winters were still cold, but now there were railroads, good houses, fuel, warm clothing, better roads. The summers were still dry, and although Jules had moved out of the gumbo, as the southsiders called the Flats, the farmers on the table from Alliance to Gordon were doing what Jules said must be done: learning how to handle their soil, practising diversified farming, finding drouth-resisting crops. When corn failed, wheat often succeeded, and despite bugs and early freezes there were usually potatoes and Indians from Pine Ridge to pick them up behind the digger, in return for hard money every evening. The irrigation project was gone and with it its exponents. Where others lost everything, Jules Tissot sold his land and cattle for twenty thousand dollars.

"Did n't have a damned cent when I located him in '84, and all he ever did for me was drop me in a well," Jules told Ferdinand when he heard of the sale.

"He may come to see you before he leaves for the Old Country," Nana suggested, anxious to please. Paul, tired of having the younger brother drunk around the saloons, had sent him to Jules, who had even less patience with him. But Ferdinand stayed most of the winter, going to Pine Creek to his claim for his relapses. "No, a drunken man I won't have around the place," Mary said. Jules agreed. "A man ought to know when he has enough."

Other things were changing too. Most of the towns were alternately wet and dry, with the saloon element a strong factor in every election. But with or without saloons the towns, except Alliance, were the drab, quiet trading centres of a stock-farming region. Even the small stations in the sandhills went to sleep the instant the cowboys vanished over the hill. The blatant bad man was gone and the thieves and murderers pretended respectability, often most convincingly. Better roads cut down the necessity of halfway stations, and age did for the roadhouse girls what community censure failed to do.

Jules himself was changed, but much of it was only external—the crippled foot, gray hair, graying beard, a forward plumpness at the middle, and a fleshiness about the wings of his nose. Mary cooked food as he liked it, and in large quantities. When Mrs. Surber first saw him heap mashed potatoes in the centre of his plate, cover the plate with slabs of fried ham and two big dippers of unthickened gravy,—three thick slabs of bread stacked beside his plate,—she held up her hands in actual horror. When he repeated the portion in the same meal she was silenced.

"A man must eat if he is going to do a good day's work," he argued.

"Then you think you work?"

"I work my head. I 'm not a *Grobian* with a strong back and a weak mind."

"No, you leave the strong back to your wife. Nu-un, you will pay for such eating. It cannot go otherwise."

But at forty-seven Jules seemed annoyingly healthy even without the daily bath essential to a Surber. He was a little heavier, with pouches under his eyes, still the pessimist about anything anyone else was to do, satisfied the country was going to the dogs. He talked socialism to Ferdinand until late at night, but without the accustomed glass of wine, for Nana must not be encouraged. Evidently this Jules still hoped to build the community he planned, somewhere—Canada perhaps, or Mexico.

When Marie, learning to read a little, found Jules's name in the *Appeal to Reason*,[1] she took it in pride to her mother. Mary glanced at the item, an acknowledgment of a contribution of twenty-five dollars to the defense fund of the embattled Warren. So—throw money away-

1. The *Appeal to Reason*, 1895–1922, a Socialist sheet, was moved to Girard, Kansas, in 1897, by Publisher Wayland, who set the vogue for muckraking. Under the pyrotechnics of Fred Warren, managing editor after 1901, the circulation ran into the millions. In 1905 he serialized Upton Sinclair's *The Jungle*.

—while she skimped and slaved, the children not in school because they had no shoes. She saw nothing in the ideal of a free press while she and the children were in need.

Jules could not very well strike her with the baby in her arms; besides, he was no longer certain that she would n't fight back. So he whipped Marie until he was breathless and left for a hunt on Pine Creek.

But age and Mary's resolution to make her man as comfortable as possible, with her determination to send as good as she got, were mellowing Jules. They got along well enough now—very well, the neighbors said, considering how William and Lena quarreled. When he sent the life-insurance agent flying to his buggy it was not entirely from a sense of persecution. Partly it was the imp and the devil in him that made him torment Mary by saying, "I don't intend to hire the Old Woman to kill me."

Although Mary sometimes said Jules told all he knew, he did n't talk about the man with the Winchester he had seen at Valentine and at the foot of the Big Horns until Marie was seven. They had been hunting, Marie following behind with her hands full of young grouse. As usual, Jules stopped on Freese Hill to rest his foot. With the sun glinting tardy rays along the blue barrel of the new repeating shotgun he held between his knees, he talked; looking away down upon the place where Freese once lived, now in young trees in neat rows, and over the dark block of Henriette's house to the shadowed bluffs beyond, he talked.

"He saved my life—when everybody else endangers it."

Marie liked the story, but dared not say so. Instead she stroked the head of a grouse, closed the soft blue eyelids. Here on this dark spot of gravel the Indians once built signal fires to be seen for miles along the twisting blue band of river and on the table from Box Butte to Hay Springs. Once Pete had shown her how to make wreaths of bluebells and yellow sweet peas here, but that was long ago too, before Victoria's trouble.

"Marie!" The mother's call came faintly up to them.

"Mama is calling—I better go," Marie stammered, grasping the scattered grouse by the necks.

"Heah?—Oho, yes, go. I be home after I rest."

Not until the sun was gone and the blued steel of his new gun was dark and cold to the touch did Jules limp down the hill and home.

———

A good wheat crop brought several new threshing crews into the community, and two of them crossed the river and pushed into the south region. Jules threshed two hundred bushels of wheat, assuring a bread supply—dark, because it was macaroni, but rich and nutlike. Pat Burke, living a mile east, raised a little too, the break in his bad luck. First the lightning had struck his haystack, then killed his team, and finally, during a morning storm, it struck his little house, ripping out all four corners, breaking the stove, tossing the lids about, and knocking Pat unconscious.

"He had it coming. He bin working against me ever since he lived there."

"Ach, you are crazy."

"Hold your mouth."

But Mary was in good spirits. "Now, you can tell me to hold my mouth, but that don't change things. You still talk like a crazy man. Pat Burke has too much trouble getting enough to drink to think about you."

It was true that as soon as the Koller and Peters troubles were over Jules and Pat quarreled over the fence, took up each other's stock for damage, lawed. Pat put up "no hunting" signs and, although there was no game on his bare little place, Jules immediately hunted there, with only the satisfaction of defying the little boards that said in black paint, NO HUNTING ALOUD. Next thing Jules would be arrested for shooting at Pat.

"But what can I do?" Mary asked.

Late one night in August someone pounded on the bedroom window, calling, "Hey, Jules, hey!"

Mary nudged her snoring husband, grabbed her dress, and, slipping it over her short gown, lit the lamp. Framed in the window was the befuddled, red face of Pat Burke.

"What you want?" Jules demanded, reaching for his rifle.

"Oh, nothing—just a match. Gotta match?"

Mary brought a full box from the kitchen. Pat tried to take one and spilled them all. But finally he got his pipe going and with elaborate thanks he stumbled away into the darkness.

"The drunken fool—wake me up at three o'clock!" Jules roared, and hung up his rifle. But before Mary got the light out Pat was back.

"Shay—" he asked thickly, "could I sleep here? It 's raining. M-my feet are wet."

"What 's the matter? Where 's your team?"

"Ghosts got them—ghosts under the b-bridge."

Jules got up, pulled on his pants, and with Mary carrying the lantern they went down through the soft starlight. One horse and most of the buggy were on the bridge, but two wheels hung over the four-foot railing and in the water below lay the other horse, tangled in harness and broken doubletrees.

They got the team out and Pat slept on the couch in the kitchen. In the morning while Mary was getting breakfast he sat up, rubbed his eyes, opened them cautiously, looking between his blunt fingers. She was still there.

"Where did you come from?"

"Maybe I do live here," Mary answered indulgently.

Pat buried his face in the pillow, moved his head until one eye could see, got up, walked all about the woman in blue calico. "An' it looks like you was intending to stay!"

After a breakfast of fried young grouse, biscuits, and hot chocolate, he was sober enough to go home.

"Why do you fight with the poor drunk?" Mary inquired of Jules. Surely his "no hunting" signs seemed unimportant enough to-day.

After threshing Pat took a load of wheat to town. On the way home he gave an acquaintance a drink from a gallon jug of whiskey. The next man on the road found him on his knees, his throat across the front endgate of the double bed, his face black, his tongue out, dead. He had fallen off the high seat and was too drunk to get up.

The *Standard* was caustic. "We want such blood money to run our schools, so keep the saloon door open. It may catch another victim." It had already, at Rushville. Carl Fisher left town with a team and wagon, did not reach home. A neighbor searching the breaks of Rush Creek found the wagon upset at the foot of the bank, both horses dead, and Fisher crushed under the box. He left a wife and six children.

The Crawford *Bulletin*, taking the stand that anything happening in the Panhandle reflected on the entire section, carried a fiery editorial. "The county of Sheridan, in the state of Nebraska, lost two citizens last week through intoxication beyond human standard, and nothing is done, yet the marshal at Rushville chokes off free speech by the handcuff and bludgeon route, as he did when A. L. Schiermeyer, member of the state socialistic lecture bureau, attempted to say a few words to his fellow men."

Jules, usually an energetic exponent of free speech and leaning towards socialism, lost sight of these issues entirely when the saloons were attacked. "Just because a few fools don't know when they have enough they would prevent a decent man from having a glass of beer now and then."

"You think a man like Fisher, with a family on the county now, ought to be allowed to drink himself under the ground?" a neighbor asked.

Mary, down on her knees scrubbing up where Jules had greased his guns, looked up.

"Maybe some families would be better off if their men drank themselves into the grave."

But as usual Jules only heard what he wanted to hear, and that afternoon they all went buffalo-berrying. Jules ahead, with his shotgun for game, Mary carrying the pails, an old sheet, and the axe, the boys trailing along behind with the dishpan and broomsticks. Marie had to stay home with the baby.

Where the silvery buffalo-berry bushes were solid clumps of yellow or orange, the tiny, shot-like berries in round clusters all along the thorny stems, Mary held the bushes back while Jules chopped them off, to be threshed with broomsticks over the sheet.

Dishpans full of berries were taken to the river for preliminary washing, the worm-lightened fruit floated away, until all the pails were full. Then there was a day of jelly making in the big copper boiler and the wine press, until six- and eight-gallon stone jars were filled with the wine-red liquor to cool and set into firmest jelly for winter.

With the fall, animosity against the cattlemen flared higher. A man was murdered at the Spade ranch. Just a bum's quarrel, it was said at first. Then it was recalled that Dave Tate, who was still accused of murdering Musfeldt, had worked there, that Bartlett Richards was under indictment for land frauds, and that a relative of his was setting up a sheep ranch on the Spade range along the Niobrara, in a settled community, with thirty-five hundred sheep and two Mexican herders. Sheep would eat the grass roots out of the ground, cut up the sod, leave nothing but blowouts and wool-tufted fences, destroy the value of the surrounding land. There were more settler meetings. Richards, hearing of them, offered a reward for the murder of the man at the Spade and made overtures of compromise to the neighbors about the sheep ranch. Trying to make a good impression on the government now, the settlers said.

Jules's children were sent to bed or whipped to silence when he did n't want to be bothered. But when he talked of the sky, plants, and rocks, strange people and places over the world, of the coal age and the lumbering animals that lived then, they drew slyly near. Even the older ones, remembering his earlier violence, somehow lost their fear for the moment.

Jules taught them useful things: to pick the thick green worms from his trees and to trap the wily gopher. When a particularly clever one would n't be caught, Jules ordered the boys to bring the spade and help dig along the gopher's tunnel, leaving only a very thin crust over it, and a point of light at the end.

"Now fetch me my twelve-bore," he ordered. With the gun aimed upon the tunnel, Jules waited, and the boys behind him. Ten minutes, twelve, of absolute silence. Then suddenly the top of the tunnel boiled with fresh earth. The twelve-gauge roared and the boys ran through the black powder smoke to the hole splattered across the gopher's runway. Jule dug with his fingers, brought up a shattered mass that was gopher.

"Ach, your papa is so nervous he can't wait a minute on anybody, but he can sit still for hours hunting," Mary complained.

Often Jules took the two eldest, seven and eight, small, twin-like, to trail noiselessly behind him when he went on a hunt. Carefully they stepped through the rose-brush thickets, stooping to pull sand burrs and cactus from their feet. At his motion of command they ran ahead to scare up quail, dropping at the first whir of wings and watching where the birds fell. When the gun was silent they ran to retrieve the game, catching all the cripples, crushing the backs of the brittle skulls between their teeth as they had seen Jules do.

"Why, I never saw anything like it! Those children are better than any dog!" an Eastern hunter exclaimed.

"I learn my kids to obey instantly or I lick hell out of them," Jules chuckled. The man turned to look back at the two, slipping through the clearing, avoiding the dry rose-brush stems scattered about, each with two handfuls of quail held by the feet. Jule was whispering about the man's high-laced boots.

"He don't have to get stickers, I bet."

Marie nodded, caught the stranger's eyes upon her, and fell back behind her brother. The man did n't have a beard like Papa, but he was fat, and she was almost as much afraid of fat men as of beards. For once she let her brother lead.

The Surbers built a house and barn. Sundays they came to the Running Water, Mrs. Surber and the girls in the carriage with side lights, one of their young Swiss helpers driving, several riding alongside. Sometimes Felix and Gus, sons of Jules's Uncle Paul living beyond the Koller and Peters homes, came down in goat-hair chaps with their horse-breaking friends. They ran the bunch of ponies up from the school section. When the plank gate of the high board corral finally clanked behind Old Red, the Surber girls and their friends climbed upon the fence and watched.

The wild horses pushed into a far corner about the wily-eyed old sorrel, noses aquiver, manes blowing. At the flick of a clod they ran about the corral, crowding the wall. The arm of the roper shot out, his heels tore up the dirt until he got a turn of the rope about the snubbing post. Perhaps the horse leaped into the air as the noose shut off his wind. Perhaps he just sat back stubbornly, wavering on his feet until he went down. Perhaps another rope jerked a foot away and Felix was on his neck, his strong hand on the blood-flecked nostrils.

Finally the saddle was on the fighting horse, hunched up into a balloon, or with legs spraddled out, dun belly swaying to the ground. When Gus was securely anchored in the saddle the horse was given his head and the sky opened over them. With what skill the seventeen-year-old giant could muster he rode his horse, fanned him, scratched him, showing white teeth in his brown face for the approval of his audience. Perhaps a sunfisher left him in the dust, or a low-withered gray threw saddle and bridle clean, setting Gus ignominiously afoot.

Another horse, another rider.

Sometimes there were twisted ankles, hips, or a broken collar bone. Perhaps a cunning five-year-old, sensing the flying oval of rope was for him, bolted the high gate, crashing it down as he jumped, Old Red and the rest running at his heels, away over the hills, splashing the Niobrara high over them as they plunged through, stopping only when they reached the security of the school section north of Henriette's.

In the meantime Mrs. Surber and Mary walked through the garden pulling young carrots, picking a mess of peas or beans for the visitors to take home. Jules read or talked to Henri Surber or other visitors. He never went near the corral while horses were being handled. "I can't stand to see anybody get crippled," he said.

This spring Victoria and her pretty baby were leaving. Not so long ago even the Johansen girls, school-teachers, with an organ and a rose garden, stopped their side-lighted carriage for the little Polish girl on their way to dances and literaries. Now nobody came near her except Mrs. Van Dorn.

People began to talk again. Ed had been fooled. He had n't known how it was with Victoria, but the older sister had, and telling the frightened girl to keep her mouth shut, Maggie threatened Ed with the penitentiary. So he had been in the bushes with both. And here it was almost a year and his wife still flat as a board. But it was n't so fine for her. Mrs. Fluckiger told around that she saw the new bride with a black eye when it got out about Victoria. Her parasol with the ruffles and her fine, feathered hats were gone. Maybe Ed burned them that day he found out. Anyway, he rode down to see Victoria. Together they walked along the river over an hour, talking. Finally Ed kissed her, right out in the open, and then he rode away. Once when he was drunk he talked about it in Jules's kitchen. "I make that damn woman pitch hay till she have to burn her pants."

Pete never came over to take the boys fishing any more. His dog got poison somewhere and almost died. She dropped her pups and was n't much good for over a month afterward. Jules heard that they thought it was the strychnine of an old coyote bait he put out.

"If that damn dog got any of my poison he must have been on my place, and I have no use for stray dogs!"

One Sunday afternoon Marie sneaked away from the baby-tending to sit with her feet dangling over the river, looking down upon its dark green spring flow until the bridge began to fly upstream, carrying her far away. Suddenly Pete stood behind her. He did n't say anything, just stood there, looking at her, a long, tow-headed Polander. Finally he whistled to his dog and started his cows for home. Marie went slowly up the road, her game spoiled. The next day Steve Staskiewicz moved away to a sandy place in the Schwartz range, and young Ignatz from Posen settled his family in the grove across the Running Water. Jules saw that the young Pole was a fool for the accordion and for whiskey, but also that he needed work, and so he sent him to Modisett's hay camp and got him a job raking hay. Sometimes Ignatz and Pete, who drove the stacker team, rode down to the river on Sundays. Once or twice Victoria came too, pretty in her red waist and her tan divided skirt.

But the move into a new community did n't help the Polish girl.

Before two years were gone she shocked the community again, this time by dying. She was taken by violent cramps, and before her father could make the sign of the cross over her she was dead. Everyone remembered now what a lovely, motherless little girl she had been. Gardens were stripped of flowers, and the funeral procession to the church was the longest ever seen in the neighborhood.

Then it got out that the week before young Ignatz went to town to have his wife arrested for trying to poison him. He said she put green stuff in his coffee, the stuff he had for bugs on cabbages. But perhaps because she was the one to get sick the officials would n't do anything.

Several days after Victoria's funeral a stranger stopped at Jules's door and asked to see his record of strychnine sales. The large book showed that he sold an eighth of an ounce to Victoria Staskiewicz two weeks before, for gopher poisoning, price one dollar. Mary remembered that when the girl bought the poison on her way home from church with her baby and her father, Ignatz was with them, riding along beside the buggy. He admitted now that he knew about the poison. She told him "I got it" in English when she came back to the buggy. Yes, he had given her the dollar. He was working at Modisett's the day she died.

There was considerable trouble about it in the Catholic congregation. A suicide buried in consecrated ground!

"Ach, poor girl," Mary said sorrowfully.

Jules scraped the inside of his cob pipe with his pocket knife.

"When she was here for cherries last time she asked me if strychnine works on people like on dogs." He stopped, sucked the stem, and spit the nicotine into the fire.

"What did you say?"

"I told her all I know was wait on nature."

"Poor, poor girl," Mary murmured to herself. Then, louder: "But it 's good with her now."

"Heah?" Jules asked.

"Nothing."

"Oho," Jules dismissed it as woman's grumbling. Already his mind was on other things. Deep down in the hills, farther than the little blue lake he saw from Deer Hill, was a large block of good land: deep, broad valleys, sheltered by high ridges of hills from the northwest wind. Here, away from corrupt politicians and pettifogging lawyers, a man could live. Good neighbors, good talk, and his family growing up strong to carry on his work.

DOROTHY M. JOHNSON

Dorothy M. Johnson was one of a very few white honorary members
of the Blackfeet tribe. She became well known for her sensitive and
accurate depictions of Indian and Western life in historical stories col-
lected in Indian Country *(1953),* The Hanging Tree *(1957), and*
her novel Buffalo Woman *(1977). Born December 19, 1905, in*
McGregor, Iowa, she moved to Montana with her family when she
was a child. She graduated from Montana State University in 1928,
moved to New York City, and became a magazine editor. She re-
turned to Montana in 1950. In 1952, she began a fifteen-year tenure
as a professor of journalism at the University of Montana. When "The
Hanging Tree" was produced as a motion picture by Warner Brothers
in 1959, she began a third career, adapting screenplays from her short
stories, including scripts for the classic Westerns The Man Who Shot
Liberty Valance *and* A Man Called Horse. *Johnson also wrote six*
children's novels and several nonfiction books, including the authori-
tative biography of the Sioux chieftain Sitting Bull, Warrior for a
Lost Nation *(1969). When Jimmy Stewart resignedly remarked,*
"Print the legend," at the end of The Man Who Shot Liberty
Valance *(directed by John Ford in 1962), he was speaking for John-*
son, in a powerful ironic way, against the kind of solve-your-problems-
with-violence myth-making typical of "Westerns." Dorothy Johnson
died of Parkinson's disease on November 11, 1984, in Missoula,
Montana.

THE MAN WHO SHOT
LIBERTY VALANCE

Bert Barricune died in 1910. Not more than a dozen persons showed
up for his funeral. Among them was an earnest young reporter who
hoped for a human-interest story; there were legends that the old man
had been something of a gunfighter in the early days. A few aging men
tiptoed in, singly or in pairs, scowling and edgy, clutching their battered
hats—men who had been Bert's companions at drinking or penny ante
while the world passed them by. One woman came, wearing a heavy
veil that concealed her face. White and yellow streaks showed in her

black-dyed hair. The reporter made a mental note: Old friend from the old District. But no story there—can't mention that.

One by one they filed past the casket, looking into the still face of old Bert Barricune, who had been nobody. His stubbly hair was white, and his lined face was as empty in death as his life had been. But death had added dignity.

One great spray of flowers spread behind the casket. The card read, "Senator and Mrs. Ransome Foster." There were no other flowers except, almost unnoticed, a few pale, leafless, pink and yellow blossoms scattered on the carpeted step. The reporter, squinting, finally identified them: son of a gun! Blossoms of the prickly pear. Cactus flowers. Seems suitable for the old man—flowers that grow on prairie wasteland. Well, they're free if you want to pick 'em, and Barricune's friends don't look prosperous. But how come the Senator sends a bouquet?

There was a delay, and the funeral director fidgeted a little, waiting. The reporter sat up straighter when he saw the last two mourners enter.

Senator Foster—sure, there's the crippled arm—and that must be his wife. Congress is still in session; he came all the way from Washington. Why would he bother, for an old wreck like Bert Barricune?

After the funeral was decently over, the reporter asked him. The Senator almost told the truth, but he caught himself in time. He said, "Bert Barricune was my friend for more than thirty years."

He could not give the true answer: He was my enemy; he was my conscience; he made me whatever I am.

Ransome Foster had been in the Territory for seven months when he ran into Liberty Valance. He had been afoot on the prairie for two days when he met Bert Barricune. Up to that time, Ranse Foster had been nobody in particular—a dude from the East, quietly inquisitive, moving from one shack town to another; just another tenderfoot with his own reasons for being there and no aim in life at all.

When Barricune found him on the prairie, Foster was indeed a tenderfoot. In his boots there was a warm, damp squidging where his feet had blistered, and the blisters had broken to bleed. He was bruised, sunburned, and filthy. He had been crawling, but when he saw Barricune riding toward him, he sat up. He had no horse, no saddle and, by that time, no pride.

Barricune looked down at him, not saying anything. Finally Ranse Foster asked, "Water?"

Barricune shook his head. "I don't carry none, but we can go where it is."

He stepped down from the saddle, a casual Samaritan, and with one heave pulled Foster upright.

"Git you in the saddle, can you stay there?" he inquired.

"If I can't," Foster answered through swollen lips, "shoot me."

Bert said amiably, "All right," and pulled the horse around. By twisting its ear, he held the animal quiet long enough to help the anguished stranger to the saddle. Then, on foot—and like any cowboy Bert Barricune hated walking—he led the horse five miles to the river. He let Foster lie where he fell in the cottonwood grove and brought him a hat full of water.

After that, Foster made three attempts to stand up. After the third failure, Barricune asked, grinning, "Want me to shoot you after all?"

"No," Foster answered. "There's something I want to do first."

Barricune looked at the bruises and commented, "Well, I should think so." He got on his horse and rode away. After an hour he returned with bedding and grub and asked, "Ain't you dead yet?"

The bruised and battered man opened his uninjured eye and said, "Not yet, but soon." Bert was amused. He brought a bucket of water and set up camp—a bedroll on a tarp, an armload of wood for a fire. He crouched on his heels while the tenderfoot, with cautious movements that told of pain, got his clothes off and splashed water on his body. No gunshot wounds, Barricune observed, but marks of kicks, and a couple that must have been made with a quirt.

After a while he asked, not inquisitively, but as one who has a right to know how matters stood, "Anybody looking for you?"

Foster rubbed dust from his clothes, being too full of pain to shake them.

"No," he said. "But I'm looking for somebody."

"I ain't going to help you look," Bert informed him. "Town's over that way, two miles, when you get ready to come. Cache the stuff when you leave. I'll pick it up."

Three days later they met in the town marshal's office. They glanced at each other but did not speak. This time it was Bert Barricune who was bruised, though not much. The marshal was just letting him out of the one-cell jail when Foster limped into the office. Nobody said anything until Barricune, blinking and walking not quite steadily, had left.

Foster saw him stop in front of the next building to speak to a girl. They walked away together, and it looked as if the young man were being scolded.

The marshal cleared his throat. "You wanted something, Mister?"

Foster answered, "Three men set me afoot on the prairie. Is that an offense against the law around here?"

The marshal eased himself and his stomach into a chair and frowned judiciously. "It ain't customary," he admitted. "Who was they?"

"The boss was a big man with black hair, dark eyes, and two gold teeth in front. The other two—"

"I know. Liberty Valance and a couple of his boys. Just what's your complaint, now?" Foster began to understand that no help was going to come from the marshal.

"They rob you?" the marshal asked.

"They didn't search me."

"Take your gun?"

"I didn't have one."

"Steal your horse?"

"Gave him a crack with a quirt, and he left."

"Saddle on him?"

"No. I left it out there."

The marshal shook his head. "Can't see you got any legal complaint," he said with relief. "Where was this?"

"On a road in the woods, by a creek. Two days' walk from here."

The marshal got to his feet. "You don't even know what jurisdiction it was in. They knocked you around; well, that could happen. Man gets in a fight—could happen to anybody."

Foster said dryly, "Thanks a lot."

The marshal stopped him as he reached the door. "There's a reward for Liberty Valance."

"I still haven't got a gun," Foster said. "Does he come here often?"

"Nope. Nothing he'd want in Twotrees. Hard man to find." The marshal looked Foster up and down. "He won't come after you here." It was as if he had added, *Sonny!* "Beat you up once, he won't come again for that."

And I, Foster realized, am not man enough to go after him.

"Fact is," the marshal added, "I can't think of any bait that would bring him in. Pretty quiet here. Yes sir." He put his thumbs in his galluses and looked out the window, taking credit for the quietness.

Bait, Foster thought. He went out thinking about it. For the first time in a couple of years he had an ambition—not a laudable one, but something to aim at. He was going to be the bait for Liberty Valance and, as far as he could be, the trap as well.

At the Elite Cafe he stood meekly in the doorway, hat in hand, like a man who expects and deserves to be refused anything he might ask for. Clearing his throat, he asked, "Could I work for a meal?"

The girl who was filling sugar bowls looked up and pitied him. "Why, I should think so. Mr. Anderson!" She was the girl who had walked away with Barricune, scolding him.

The proprietor came from the kitchen, and Ranse Foster repeated his question, cringing, but with a suggestion of a sneer.

"Go around back and split some wood," Anderson answered, turning back to the kitchen.

"He could just as well eat first," the waitress suggested. "I'll dish up some stew to begin with."

Ranse ate fast, as if he expected the plate to be snatched away. He knew the girl glanced at him several times, and he hated her for it. He had not counted on anyone's pitying him in his new role of sneering humility, but he knew he might as well get used to it.

When she brought his pie, she said, "If you was looking for a job . . ."

He forced himself to look at her suspiciously. "Yes?"

"You could try the Prairie Belle. I heard they needed a swamper."

Bert Barricune, riding out to the river camp for his bedroll, hardly knew the man he met there. Ranse Foster was haughty, condescending, and cringing all at once. He spoke with a faint sneer, and stood as if he expected to be kicked.

"I assumed you'd be back for your belongings," he said. "I realized that you would change your mind."

Barricune, strapping up his bedroll, looked blank. "Never changed it," he disagreed. "Doing just what I planned. I never give you my bedroll."

"Of course not, of course not," the new Ranse Foster agreed with sneering humility. "It's yours. You have every right to reclaim it."

Barricune looked at him narrowly and hoisted the bedroll to sling it up behind his saddle. "I should have left you for the buzzards," he remarked.

Foster agreed, with a smile that should have got him a fist in the teeth. "Thank you, my friend," he said with no gratitude. "Thank you for all your kindness, which I have done nothing to deserve and shall do nothing to repay."

Barricune rode off, scowling, with the memory of his good deed irritating him like lice. The new Foster followed, far behind, on foot.

Sometimes in later life Ranse Foster thought of the several men he had been through the years. He did not admire any of them very much. He was by no means ashamed of the man he finally became, except that he owed too much to other people. One man he had been when he was young, a serious student, gullible and quick-tempered. Another man had been reckless and without an aim; he went West, with two thousand dollars of his own, after a quarrel with the executor of his father's estate. That man did not last long. Liberty Valance had whipped him with a quirt and kicked him into unconsciousness, for no reason except that Liberty, meeting him and knowing him for a tenderfoot, was able to do so. That man died on the prairie. After that, there was the man who set out to be the bait that would bring Liberty Valance into Twotrees.

Ranse Foster had never hated anyone before he met Liberty Valance, but Liberty was not the last man he learned to hate. He hated the man he himself had been while he waited to meet Liberty again.

The swamper's job at the Prairie Belle was not disgraceful until Ranse Foster made it so. When he swept floors, he was so obviously contemptuous of the work and of himself for doing it that other men saw him as contemptible. He watched the customers with a curled lip as if they were beneath him. But when a poker player threw a white chip on the floor, the swamper looked at him with half-veiled hatred— and picked up the chip. They talked about him at the Prairie Belle, because he could not be ignored.

At the end of the first month, he bought a Colt .45 from a drunken cowboy who needed money worse than he needed two guns. After that, Ranse went without part of his sleep in order to walk out, seven mornings a week, to where his first camp had been and practice target shooting. And the second time he overslept from exhaustion, Joe Mosten of the Prairie Belle fired him.

"Here's your pay," Joe growled, and dropped the money on the floor.

A week passed before he got another job. He ate his meals frugally in the Elite Cafe and let himself be seen stealing scraps off plates that other diners had left. Lillian, the older of the two waitresses, yelled her disgust, but Hallie, who was young, pitied him.

"Come to the back door when it's dark," she murmured, "and I'll give you a bite. There's plenty to spare."

The second evening he went to the back door, Bert Barricune was there ahead of him. He said gently, "Hallie is my girl."

"No offense intended," Foster answered. "The young lady offered me food, and I have come to get it."

"A dog eats where it can," young Barricune drawled.

Ranse's muscles tensed and rage mounted in his throat, but he caught himself in time and shrugged. Bert said something then that scared him: "If you wanted to get talked about, it's working fine. They're talking clean over in Dunbar."

"What they do or say in Dunbar," Foster answered, "is nothing to me."

"It's where Liberty Valance hangs out," the other man said casually. "In case you care."

Ranse almost confided then, but instead said stiffly, "I do not quite appreciate your strange interest in my affairs."

Barricune pushed back his hat and scratched his head. "I don't understand it myself. But leave my girl alone."

"As charming as Miss Hallie may be," Ranse told him, "I am interested only in keeping my stomach filled."

"Then why don't you work for a living? The clerk at Dowitts' quit this afternoon."

Jake Dowitt hired him as a clerk because nobody else wanted the job.

"Read and write, do you?" Dowitt asked. "Work with figures?"

Foster drew himself up. "Sir, whatever may be said against me, I believe I may lay claim to being a scholar. That much I claim, if nothing more. I have read law."

"Maybe the job ain't good enough for you," Dowitt suggested.

Foster became humble again. "Any job is good enough for me. I will also sweep the floor."

"You will also keep up the fire in the stove," Dowitt told him. "Seven in the morning till nine at night. Got a place to live?"

"I sleep in the livery stable in return for keeping it shoveled out."

Dowitt had intended to house his clerk in a small room over the store, but he changed his mind. "Got a shed out back you can bunk in," he offered. "You'll have to clean it out first. Used to keep chickens there."

"There is one thing," Foster said. "I want two half-days off a week."

Dowitt looked over the top of his spectacles. "Now what would you do with time off? Never mind. You can have it—for less pay. I give you a discount on what you buy in the store."

The only purchase Foster made consisted of four boxes of cartridges a week.

In the store, he weighed salt pork as if it were low stuff but himself still lower, humbly measured lengths of dress goods for the women customers. He added vanity to his other unpleasantnesses and let customers discover him combing his hair admiringly before a small mirror. He let himself be seen reading a small black book, which aroused curiosity.

It was while he worked at the store that he started Twotrees' first school. Hallie was responsible for that. Handing him a plate heaped higher than other customers got at the café, she said gently, "You're a learned man, they say, Mr. Foster."

With Hallie he could no longer sneer or pretend humility, for Hallie was herself humble, as well as gentle and kind. He protected himself from her by not speaking unless he had to.

He answered, "I have had advantages, Miss Hallie, before fate brought me here."

"That book you read," she asked wistfully, "what's it about?"

"It was written by a man named Plato," Ranse told her stiffly. "It was written in Greek."

She brought him a cup of coffee, hesitated for a moment, and then asked, "You can read and write American, too, can't you?"

"English, Miss Hallie," he corrected. "English is our mother tongue. I am quite familiar with English."

She put her red hands on the café counter. "Mr. Foster," she whispered, "will you teach me to read?"

He was too startled to think of an answer she could not defeat.

"Bert wouldn't like it," he said. "You're a grown woman besides. It wouldn't look right for you to be learning to read now."

She shook her head. "I can't learn any younger." She sighed. "I always wanted to know how to read and write." She walked away toward the kitchen, and Ranse Foster was struck with an emotion he knew he could not afford. He was swept with pity. He called her back.

"Miss Hallie. Not you alone—people would talk about you. But if you brought Bert—"

"Bert can already read some. He don't care about it. But there's some kids in town." Her face was so lighted that Ranse looked away.

He still tried to escape. "Won't you be ashamed, learning with children?"

"Why, I'll be proud to learn any way at all," she said.

He had three little girls, two restless little boys, and Hallie in Twotrees' first school sessions—one hour each afternoon, in Dowitt's storeroom. Dowitt did not dock his pay for the time spent, but he puzzled a great deal. So did the children's parents. The children themselves were puzzled at some of the things he read aloud, but they were patient. After all, lessons lasted only an hour.

"When you are older, you will understand this," he promised, not looking at Hallie, and then he read Shakespeare's sonnet that begins:

> *No longer mourn for me when I am dead*
> *Than you shall hear the surly sullen bell*

and ends:

> *Do not so much as my poor name rehearse,*
> *But let your love even with my life decay,*
> *Lest the wise world should look into your moan*
> *And mock you with me after I am gone.*

Hallie understood the warning, he knew. He read another sonnet, too:

> *When in disgrace with Fortune and men's eyes,*
> *I all alone beweep my outcast state,*

and carefully did not look up at her as he finished it:

> *For thy sweet love rememb'red such wealth brings*
> *That then I scorn to change my state with kings.*

Her earnestness in learning was distasteful to him—the anxious way she grasped a pencil and formed letters, the little gasp with which she always began to read aloud. Twice he made her cry, but she never missed a lesson.

He wished he had a teacher for his own learning, but he could not trust anyone, and so he did his lessons alone. Bert Barricune caught him at it on one of those free afternoons when Foster, on a horse from the livery stable, had ridden miles out of town to a secluded spot.

Ranse Foster had an empty gun in his hand when Barricune stepped out from behind a sandstone column and remarked, "I've seen better."

Foster whirled, and Barricune added, "I could have been somebody else—and your gun's empty."

"When I see somebody else, it won't be," Foster promised.

"If you'd asked me," Barricune mused, "I could've helped you. But you didn't want no helping. A man shouldn't be ashamed to ask somebody that knows better than him." His gun was suddenly in his hand, and five shots cracked their echoes around the skull-white sandstone pillars. Half an inch above each of five cards that Ranse had tacked to a dead tree, at the level of a man's waist, a splintered hole appeared in the wood. "Didn't want to spoil your targets," Barricune explained.

"I'm not ashamed to ask you," Foster told him angrily, "since you know so much. I shoot straight but slow. I'm asking you now."

Barricune, reloading his gun, shook his head. "It's kind of late for that. I come out to tell you that Liberty Valance is in town. He's interested in the dude that anybody can kick around—this here tenderfoot that boasts how he can read Greek."

"Well," said Foster softly. "Well, so the time has come."

"Don't figure you're riding into town with me," Bert warned. "You're coming in all by yourself."

Ranse rode into town with his gun belt buckled on. Always before, he had carried it wrapped in a slicker. In town, he allowed himself the luxury of one last vanity. He went to the barbershop, neither sneering nor cringing, and said sharply, "Cut my hair. Short."

The barber was nervous, but he worked understandably fast.

"Thought you was partial to that long wavy hair of yourn," he remarked.

"I don't know why you thought so," Foster said coldly.

Out in the street again, he realized that he did not know how to go about the job. He did not know where Liberty Valance was, and he was determined not to be caught like a rat. He intended to look for Liberty.

Joe Mosten's right-hand man was lounging at the door of the Prairie Belle. He moved over to bar the way.

"Not in there, Foster," he said gently. It was the first time in months that Ranse Foster had heard another man address him respectfully. His presence was recognized—as a menace to the fixtures of the Prairie Belle.

When I die, sometime today, he thought, they won't say I was a coward. They may say I was a damn fool, but I won't care by that time.

"Where is he?" Ranse asked.

"I couldn't tell you that," the man said apologetically. "I'm young and healthy, and where he is is none of my business. Joe'd be obliged if you stay out of the bar, that's all."

Ranse looked across toward Dowitt's store. The padlock was on the door. He glanced north, toward the marshal's office.

"That's closed, too," the saloon man told him courteously. "Marshal was called out of town an hour ago."

Ranse threw back his head and laughed. The sound echoed back from the false-fronted buildings across the street. There was nobody walking in the street; there were not even any horses tied to the hitching racks.

"Send Liberty word," he ordered in the tone of one who has a right to command. "Tell him the tenderfoot wants to see him again."

The saloon man cleared his throat. "Guess it won't be necessary. That's him coming down at the end of the street, wouldn't you say?"

Ranse looked, knowing the saloon man was watching him curiously.

"I'd say it is," he agreed. "Yes, I'd say that was Liberty Valance."

"I'll be going inside now," the other man remarked apologetically. "Well, take care of yourself." He was gone without a sound.

This is the classic situation, Ranse realized. Two enemies walking to meet each other along the dusty, waiting street of a western town. What reasons other men have had, I will never know. There are so many things I have never learned! And now there is no time left.

He was an actor who knew the end of the scene but had forgotten the lines and never knew the cue for them. One of us ought to say something, he realized. I should have planned this all out in advance. But all I ever saw was the end of it.

Liberty Valance, burly and broad-shouldered, walked stiff-legged, with his elbows bent.

When he is close enough for me to see whether he is smiling, Ranse Foster thought, somebody's got to speak.

He looked into his own mind and realized, This man is afraid, this Ransome Foster. But nobody else knows it. He walks and is afraid, but he is no coward. Let them remember that. Let Hallie remember that.

Liberty Valance gave the cue. "Looking for me?" he called between his teeth. He was grinning.

Ranse was almost grateful to him; it was as if Liberty had said, The time is now!

"I owe you something," Ranse answered. "I want to pay my debt."

Liberty's hand flashed with his own. The gun in Foster's hand exploded, and so did the whole world.

Two shots to my one, he thought—his last thought for a while.

He looked up at a strange, unsteady ceiling and a face that wavered like a reflection in water. The bed beneath him swung even after he closed his eyes. Far away someone said, "Shove some more cloth in the wound. It slows the bleeding."

He knew with certain agony where the wound was—in his right shoulder. When they touched it, he heard himself cry out.

The face that wavered above him was a new one, Bert Barricune's.

"He's dead," Barricune said.

Foster answered from far away, "I am not."

Barricune said, "I didn't mean you."

Ranse turned his head away from the pain, and the face that had shivered above him before was Hallie's, white and big-eyed. She put a hesitant hand on his, and he was annoyed to see that hers was trembling.

"Are you shaking," he asked, "because there's blood on my hands?"

"No," she answered. "It's because they might have been getting cold."

He was aware then that other people were in the room; they stirred and moved aside as the doctor entered.

"Maybe you're gonna keep that arm," the doctor told him at last. "But it's never gonna be much use to you."

The trial was held three weeks after the shooting, in the hotel room where Ranse lay in bed. The charge was disturbing the peace; he pleaded guilty and was fined ten dollars.

When the others had gone, he told Bert Barricune, "There was a reward, I heard. That would pay the doctor and the hotel."

"You ain't going to collect it," Bert informed him. "It'd make you too big for your britches." Barricune sat looking at him for a moment and then remarked, "You didn't kill Liberty."

Foster frowned. "They buried him."

"Liberty fired once. You fired once and missed. I fired once, and I don't generally miss. I ain't going to collect the reward, neither. Hallie don't hold with violence."

Foster said thoughtfully, "That was all I had to be proud of."

"You faced him," Barricune said. "You went to meet him. If you got to be proud of something, you can remember that. It's a fact you ain't got much else."

Ranse looked at him with narrowed eyes. "Bert, are you a friend of mine?"

Bert smiled without humor. "You know I ain't. I picked you up off the prairie, but I'd do that for the lowest scum that crawls. I wisht I hadn't."

"Then why—"

Bert looked at the toe of his boot. "Hallie likes you. I'm a friend of Hallie's. That's all I ever will be, long as you're around."

Ranse said, "Then I shot Liberty Valance." That was the nearest he ever dared come to saying "Thank you." And that was when Bert Barricune started being his conscience, his Nemesis, his lifelong enemy and the man who made him great.

"Would she be happy living back East?" Foster asked. "There's money waiting for me there if I go back."

Bert answered, "What do you think?" He stood up and stretched. "You got quite a problem, ain't you? You could solve it easy by just going back alone. There ain't much a man can do here with a crippled arm."

He went out and shut the door behind him.

There is always a way out, Foster thought, if a man wants to take it. Bert had been his way out when he met Liberty on the street of Twotrees. To go home was the way out of this.

I learned to live without pride, he told himself. I could learn to forget about Hallie.

When she came, between the dinner dishes and setting the tables for supper at the café, he told her.

She did not cry. Sitting in the chair beside his bed, she winced and jerked one hand in protest when he said, "As soon as I can travel, I'll be going back where I came from."

She did not argue. She said only, "I wish you good luck, Ransome. Bert and me, we'll look after you long as you stay. And remember you after you're gone."

"How will you remember me?" he demanded harshly.

As his student she had been humble, but as a woman she had her pride. "Don't ask that," she said, and got up from the chair.

"Hallie, Hallie," he pleaded, "how can I stay? How can I earn a living?"

She said indignantly, as if someone else had insulted him, "Ranse Foster, I just guess you could do anything you wanted to."

"Hallie," he said gently, "sit down."

He never really wanted to be outstanding. He had two aims in life: to make Hallie happy and to keep Bert Barricune out of trouble. He defended Bert on charges ranging from drunkenness to stealing cattle, and Bert served time twice.

Ranse Foster did not want to run for judge, but Bert remarked, "I think Hallie would kind of like it if you was His Honor." Hallie was pleased but not surprised when he was elected. Ranse was surprised but not pleased.

He was not eager to run for the legislature—that was after the territory became a state—but there was Bert Barricune in the background, never urging, never advising, but watching with half-closed, bloodshot eyes. Bert Barricune, who never amounted to anything, but never intruded, was a living, silent reminder of three debts: a hat full of water under the cottonwoods, gunfire in a dusty street, and Hallie, quietly sewing beside a lamp in the parlor. And the Fosters had four sons.

All the things the opposition said about Ranse Foster when he ran for the state legislature were true, except one. He had been a lowly swamper in a frontier saloon; he had been a dead beat, accepting handouts at the alley entrance of a café; he had been despicable and despised. But the accusation that lost him the election was false. He had not killed Liberty Valance. He never served in the state legislature.

When there was talk of his running for governor, he refused. Handy Strong, who knew politics, tried to persuade him.

"That shooting, we'll get around that. 'The Honorable Ransome Foster walked down a street in broad daylight to meet an enemy of society. He shot him down in a fair fight, of necessity, the way you'd shoot a mad dog—but Liberty Valance could shoot back, and he did. Ranse Foster carries the mark of that encounter today in a crippled right arm. He is still paying the price for protecting law-abiding citizens. And he was the first teacher west of Rosy Buttes. He served without pay.' You've come a long way, Ranse, and you're going further."

"A long way," Foster agreed, "for a man who never wanted to go anywhere. I don't want to be governor."

When Handy had gone, Bert Barricune sagged in, unwashed, unshaven. He sat down stiffly. At the age of fifty, he was an old man, an unwanted relic of the frontier that was gone, a legacy to more civilized times that had no place for him. He filled his pipe deliberately. After a while he remarked, "The other side is gonna say you ain't fitten to be governor. Because your wife ain't fancy enough. They're gonna say Hallie didn't even learn to read till she was growed up."

Ranse was on his feet, white with fury. "Then I'm going to win this election if it kills me."

"I don't reckon it'll kill you," Bert drawled. "Liberty Valance couldn't."

"I could have got rid of the weight of that affair long ago," Ranse reminded him, "by telling the truth."

"You could yet," Bert answered. "Why don't you?"

Ranse said bitterly, "Because I owe you too much. . . . I don't think Hallie wants to be the governor's lady. She's shy."

"Hallie don't never want nothing for herself. She wants things for you. The way I feel, I wouldn't mourn at your funeral. But what Hallie wants, I'm gonna try to see she gets."

"So am I," Ranse promised grimly.

"Then I don't mind telling you," Bert admitted, "that it was me reminded the opposition to dig up that matter of how she couldn't read."

As the Senator and his wife rode home after old Bert Barricune's barren funeral, Hallie sighed. "Bert never had much of anything. I guess he never wanted much."

He wanted you to be happy, Ranse Foster thought, and he did the best he knew how.

"I wonder where those prickly-pear blossoms came from," he mused.

Hallie glanced up at him, smiling. "From me," she said.

JACK LONDON

Jack London, the illegitimate son of an astrologer, was born in California in 1876. Raised in extreme poverty, London supported himself with dangerous jobs; by the age of eighteen he had worked as a seaman, a jutemill worker, a fish patrolman, and a coal shoveler. After crossing the country with an organized group of unemployed people, London was jailed for vagrancy for thirty days, and decided to educate himself to improve his own condition and that of others. After a futile winter of gold prospecting in the Klondike, London began to write professionally. A prolific writer whose credo was a thousand words a day, six days a week, London became the highest-paid writer of his time. His novels ranged in tone and style from rugged adventures of man in and against nature like The Call of the Wild *(1903),* The Sea Wolf *(1904), and* White Fang *(1906) to more political and polemic books like* The People of the Abyss *(1903),* The Iron Heel *(1908), and* Martin Eden *(1909), a patently autobiographical story. London died broke and brokenhearted in 1916, a few months after his painstakingly built Wolf House (the ruins of which now form a California State Monument) burned down. He died of a "gastrointestinal type of uraemia," although his death was widely supposed to have been a suicide.*

"A Raid on the Oyster Pirates" exemplifies London's style of affectionately writing about the desires and humanity of the rough-and-tumble people who inhabited the West.

A RAID ON THE
OYSTER PIRATES

Of the fish patrolmen under whom we served at various times, Charley Le Grant and I were agreed, I think, that Neil Partington was the best. He was neither dishonest nor cowardly; and while he demanded strict obedience when we were under his orders, at the same time our relations were those of easy comradeship, and he permitted us a freedom to which we were ordinarily unaccustomed, as the present story will show.

Neil's family lived in Oakland, which is on the Lower Bay, not more than six miles across the water from San Francisco. One day, while scouting among the Chinese shrimp-catchers of Point Pedro, he received word that his wife was very ill; and within the hour the Reindeer was bowling along for Oakland, with a stiff northwest breeze astern. We ran up the Oakland Estuary and came to anchor, and in the days that followed, while Neil was ashore, we tightened up the Reindeer's rigging, overhauled the ballast, scraped down, and put the sloop into thorough shape.

This done, time hung heavy on our hands. Neil's wife was dangerously ill, and the outlook was a week's lie-over, awaiting the crisis. Charley and I roamed the docks, wondering what we should do, and so came upon the oyster fleet lying at the Oakland City Wharf. In the main they were trim, natty boats, made for speed and bad weather, and we sat down on the stringer-piece of the dock to study them.

"A good catch, I guess," Charley said, pointing to the heaps of oysters, assorted in three sizes, which lay upon their decks.

Peddlers were backing their wagons to the edge of the wharf, and from the bargaining and chaffering that went on, I managed to learn the selling price of the oysters.

"That boat must have at least two hundred dollars' worth aboard," I calculated. "I wonder how long it took to get the load?"

"Three or four days," Charley answered. "Not bad wages for two men—twenty-five dollars a day apiece."

The boat we were discussing, the Ghost, lay directly beneath us. Two men composed its crew. One was a squat, broad-shouldered fellow with remarkably long and gorilla-like arms, while the other was tall and well proportioned, with clear blue eyes and a mat of straight black hair. So unusual and striking was this combination of hair and eyes that Charley and I remained somewhat longer than we intended.

And it was well that we did. A stout, elderly man, with the dress and carriage of a successful merchant, came up and stood beside us, looking down upon the deck of the Ghost. He appeared angry, and the longer he looked the angrier he grew.

"Those are my oysters," he said at last. "I know they are my oysters. You raided my beds last night and robbed me of them."

The tall man and the short man on the Ghost looked up.

"Hello, Taft," the short man said, with insolent familiarity. (Among the bayfarers he had gained the nickname of "The Centipede" on account of his long arms.) "Hello, Taft," he repeated, with the same touch of insolence. "Wot'r you growlin' about now?"

"Those are my oysters—that's what I said. You've stolen them from my beds."

"Yer mighty wise, ain't ye?" was the Centipede's sneering reply. "S'pose you can tell your oysters wherever you see 'em?"

"Now, in my experience," broke in the tall man, "oysters is oysters wherever you find 'em, an' they're pretty much alike all the Bay over, and the world over, too, for that matter. We're not wantin' to quarrel with you, Mr. Taft, but we jes' wish you wouldn't insinuate that them oysters is yours an' that we're thieves an' robbers till you can prove the goods."

"I know they're mine; I'd stake my life on it!" Mr. Taft snorted.

"Prove it," challenged the tall man, who we afterward learned was known as "The Porpoise" because of his wonderful swimming abilities.

Mr. Taft shrugged his shoulders helplessly. Of course he could not prove the oysters to be his, no matter how certain he might be.

"I'd give a thousand dollars to have you men behind the bars!" he cried. "I'll give fifty dollars a head for your arrest and conviction, all of you!"

A roar of laughter went up from the different boats, for the rest of the pirates had been listening to the discussion.

"There's more money in oysters," the Porpoise remarked dryly.

Mr. Taft turned impatiently on his heel and walked away. From out of the corner of his eye, Charley noted the way he went. Several minutes later, when he had disappeared around a corner, Charley rose lazily to his feet. I followed him, and we sauntered off in the opposite direction to that taken by Mr. Taft.

"Come on! Lively!" Charley whispered, when we passed from the view of the oyster fleet.

Our course was changed at once, and we dodged around corners and raced up and down side-streets till Mr. Taft's generous form loomed up ahead of us.

"I'm going to interview him about that reward," Charley explained, as we rapidly overhauled the oyster-bed owner. "Neil will be delayed here for a week, and you and I might as well be doing something in the meantime. What do you say?"

"Of course, of course," Mr. Taft said, when Charley had introduced himself and explained his errand. "Those thieves are robbing me of thousands of dollars every year, and I shall be glad to break them up at any price—yes, sir, at any price. As I said, I'll give fifty dollars a head, and call it cheap at that. They've robbed my beds, torn down my signs, terrorized my watchmen, and last year killed one of them. Couldn't prove it. All done in the blackness of night. All I had was a dead watch-man and no evidence. The detectives could do nothing. Nobody has been able to do anything with those men. We have never succeeded in arresting one of them. So I say, Mr.—What did you say your name was?"

"Le Grant," Charley answered.

"So I say, Mr. Le Grant, I am deeply obliged to you for the assistance you offer. And I shall be glad, most glad, sir, to cooperate with you in every way. My watchmen and boats are at your disposal. Come and see me at the San Francisco offices any time, or telephone at my expense. And don't be afraid of spending money. I'll foot your expenses, whatever they are, so long as they are within reason. The situation is growing desperate, and something must be done to determine whether I or that band of ruffians own those oyster beds."

"Now we'll see Neil," Charley said, when he had seen Mr. Taft upon his train to San Francisco.

Not only did Neil Partington interpose no obstacle to our adventure, but he proved to be of the greatest assistance. Charley and I knew nothing of the oyster industry, while his head was an encyclopedia of facts concerning it. Also, within an hour or so, he was able to bring to us a Greek boy of seventeen or eighteen who knew thoroughly well the ins and outs of oyster piracy.

At this point I may as well explain that we of the fish patrol were free lances in a way. While Neil Partington, who was a patrolman proper, received a regular salary, Charley and I, being merely deputies, received only what we earned—that is to say, a certain percentage of

the fines imposed on convicted violators of the fish laws. Also, any rewards that chanced our way were ours. We offered to share with Partington whatever we should get from Mr. Taft, but the patrolman would
not hear of it. He was only too happy, he said, to do a good turn for
us, who had done so many for him.

We held a long council of war, and mapped out the following line
of action. Our faces were unfamiliar on the Lower Bay, but as the Reindeer was well known as a fish-patrol sloop, the Greek boy, whose name
was Nicholas, and I were to sail some innocent-looking craft down to
Asparagus Island and join the oyster pirates' fleet. Here, according to
Nicholas's description of the beds and the manner of raiding, it was
possible for us to catch the pirates in the act of stealing oysters, and at
the same time to get them in our power. Charley was to be on the
shore, with Mr. Taft's watchmen and a posse of constables, to help us
at the right time.

"I know just the boat," Neil said, at the conclusion of the discussion, "a crazy old sloop that's lying over at Tiburon. You and Nicholas
can go over by the ferry, charter it for a song, and sail direct for the
beds."

"Good luck be with you, boys," he said at parting, two days later.
"Remember, they are dangerous men, so be careful."

Nicholas and I succeeded in chartering the sloop very cheaply; and
between laughs, while getting up sail, we agreed that she was even cra-
zier and older than she had been described. She was a big, flat-bottomed,
square-sterned craft, sloop-rigged, with a sprung mast, slack rigging,
dilapidated sails, and rotten running-gear, clumsy to handle and uncertain
in bringing about, and she smelled vilely of coal tar, with which strange
stuff she had been smeared from stem to stern and from cabin-roof to
centreboard. And to cap it all, Coal Tar Maggie was printed in great
white letters the whole length of either side.

It was an uneventful though laughable run from Tiburon to Asparagus Island, where we arrived in the afternoon of the following day.
The oyster pirates, a fleet of a dozen sloops, were lying at anchor on
what was known as the "Deserted Beds." The Coal Tar Maggie came
sloshing into their midst with a light breeze astern, and they crowded
on deck to see us. Nicholas and I had caught the spirit of the crazy craft,
and we handled her in most lubberly fashion.

"Wot is it?" someone called.

"Name it 'n' ye kin have it!" called another.

"I swan naow, ef it ain't the old Ark itself!" mimicked the Centipede from the deck of the Ghost.

"Hey! Ahoy there, clipper ship!" another wag shouted. "Wot's yer port?"

We took no notice of the joking, but acted, after the manner of greenhorns, as though the Coal Tar Maggie required our undivided attention. I rounded her well to windward of the Ghost, and Nicholas ran for'ard to drop the anchor. To all appearances it was a bungle, the way the chain tangled and kept the anchor from reaching the bottom. And to all appearances Nicholas and I were terribly excited as we strove to clear it. At any rate, we quite deceived the pirates, who took huge delight in our predicament.

But the chain remained tangled, and amid all kinds of mocking advice we drifted down upon and fouled the Ghost, whose bowsprit poked square through our mainsail and ripped a hole in it as big as a barn door. The Centipede and the Porpoise doubled up on the cabin in paroxysms of laughter, and left us to get clear as best we could. This, with much unseamanlike performance, we succeeded in doing, and likewise in clearing the anchor-chain, of which we let out about three hundred feet. With only ten feet of water under us, this would permit the Coal Tar Maggie to swing in a circle six hundred feet in diameter, in which circle she would be able to foul at least half the fleet.

The oyster pirates lay snugly together at short hawsers, the weather being fine, and they protested loudly at our ignorance in putting out such an unwarranted length of anchor-chain. And not only did they protest, for they made us heave it in again, all but thirty feet.

Having sufficiently impressed them with our general lubberliness, Nicholas and I went below to congratulate ourselves and to cook supper. Hardly had we finished the meal and washed the dishes, when a skiff ground against the Coal Tar Maggie's side, and heavy feet trampled on deck. Then the Centipede's brutal face appeared in the companionway, and he descended into the cabin, followed by the Porpoise. Before they could seat themselves on a bunk, another skiff came alongside, and another, and another, till the whole fleet was represented by the gathering in the cabin.

"Where'd you swipe the old tub?" asked a squat and hairy man, with cruel eyes and Mexican features.

"Didn't swipe it," Nicholas answered, meeting them on their own ground and encouraging the idea that we had stolen the Coal Tar Maggie. "And if we did, what of it?"

"Well, I don't admire your taste, that's all," sneered he of the Mexican features. "I'd rot on the beach first before I'd take a tub that couldn't get out of its own way."

"How were we to know till we tried her?" Nicholas asked, so innocently as to cause a laugh. "And how do you get the oysters?" he hurried on. "We want a load of them; that's what we came for, a load of oysters."

"What d'ye want 'em for?" demanded the Porpoise.

"Oh, to give away to our friends, of course," Nicholas retorted. "That's what you do with yours, I suppose."

This started another laugh, and as our visitors grew more genial we could see that they had not the slightest suspicion of our identity or purpose.

"Didn't I see you on the dock in Oakland the other day?" the Centipede asked suddenly of me.

"Yep," I answered boldly, taking the bull by the horns. "I was watching you fellows and figuring out whether we'd go oystering or not. It's a pretty good business, I calculate, and so we're going in for it. That is," I hastened to add, "if you fellows don't mind."

"I'll tell you one thing, which ain't two things," he replied, "and that is you'll have to hump yerself an' get a better boat. We won't stand to be disgraced by any such box as this. Understand?"

"Sure," I said. "Soon as we sell some oysters we'll outfit in style."

"And if you show yerself square an' the right sort," he went on, "why, you kin run with us. But if you don't" (here his voice became stern and menacing), "why, it'll be the sickest day of yer life. Understand?"

"Sure," I said.

After that and more warning and advice of similar nature, the conversation became general, and we learned that the beds were to be raided that very night. As they got into their boats, after an hour's stay, we were invited to join them in the raid with the assurance of "the more the merrier."

"Did you notice that short, Mexican-looking chap?" Nicholas asked, when they had departed to their various sloops. "He's Barchi, of the Sporting Life Gang, and the fellow that came with him is Skilling. They're both out now on five thousand dollars' bail."

I had heard of the Sporting Life Gang before, a crowd of hoodlums and criminals that terrorized the lower quarters of Oakland, and two-thirds of which were usually to be found in state's prison for crimes that ranged from perjury and ballot-box stuffing to murder.

"They are not regular oyster pirates," Nicholas continued. "They've just come down for the lark and to make a few dollars. But we'll have to watch out for them."

We sat in the cockpit and discussed the details of our plan till eleven o'clock had passed, when we heard the rattle of an oar in a boat from the direction of the Ghost. We hauled up our own skiff, tossed in a few sacks, and rowed over. There we found all the skiffs assembling, it being the intention to raid the beds in a body.

To my surprise, I found barely a foot of water where we had dropped anchor in ten feet. It was the big June run-out of the full moon, and as the ebb had yet an hour and a half to run, I knew that our anchorage would be dry ground before slack water.

Mr. Taft's beds were three miles away, and for a long time we rowed silently in the wake of the other boats, once in a while grounding and our oar blades constantly striking bottom. At last we came upon soft mud covered with not more than two inches of water—not enough to float the boats. But the pirates at once were over the side, and by pushing and pulling on the flat-bottomed skiffs, we moved steadily along.

The full moon was partly obscured by high-flying clouds, but the pirates went their way with the familiarity born of long practice. After half a mile of the mud, we came upon a deep channel, up which we rowed, with dead oyster shoals looming high and dry on either side. At last we reached the picking grounds. Two men, on one of the shoals, hailed us and warned us off. But the Centipede, the Porpoise, Barchi, and Skilling took the lead, and followed by the rest of us, at least thirty men in half as many boats, rowed right up to the watchmen.

"You'd better slide outa this here," Barchi said threateningly, "or we'll fill you so full of holes you wouldn't float in molasses."

The watchmen wisely retreated before so overwhelming a force, and rowed their boat along the channel toward where the shore should be. Besides, it was in the plan for them to retreat.

We hauled the noses of the boats up on the shore side of a big shoal, and all hands, with sacks, spread out and began picking. Every now and again the clouds thinned before the face of the moon, and we could see the big oysters quite distinctly. In almost no time sacks were filled and carried back to the boats, where fresh ones were obtained. Nicholas and I returned often and anxiously to the boats with our little loads, but always found some one of the pirates coming or going.

"Never mind," he said; "no hurry. As they pick farther and farther away, it will take too long to carry to the boats. Then they'll stand the full sacks on end and pick them up when the tide comes in and the skiffs will float to them."

Fully half an hour went by, and the tide had begun to flood, when this came to pass. Leaving the pirates at their work, we stole back to the boats. One by one, and noiselessly, we shoved them off and made them fast in an awkward flotilla. Just as we were shoving off the last skiff, our own, one of the men came upon us. It was Barchi. His quick eye took in the situation at a glance, and he sprang for us; but we went clear with a mighty shove, and he was left floundering in the water over his head. As soon as he got back to the shoal he raised his voice and gave the alarm.

We rowed with all our strength, but it was slow going with so many boats in tow. A pistol cracked from the shoal, a second, and a third; then a regular fusillade began. The bullets spat and spat all about us; but thick clouds had covered the moon, and in the dim darkness it was no more than random firing. It was only by chance that we could be hit.

"Wish we had a little steam launch," I panted.

"I'd just as soon the moon stayed hidden," Nicholas panted back.

It was slow work, but every stroke carried us farther away from the shoal and nearer the shore, till at last the shooting died down, and when the moon did come out we were too far away to be in danger. Not long afterward we answered a shoreward hail, and two Whitehall boats, each pulled by three pairs of oars, darted up to us. Charley's welcome face bent over to us, and he gripped us by the hands while he cried, "Oh, you joys! You joys! Both of you!"

When the flotilla had been landed, Nicholas and I and a watchman rowed out in one of the Whitehalls, with Charley in the sternsheets. Two other Whitehalls followed us, and as the moon now shone brightly, we easily made out the oyster pirates on their lonely shoal. As we drew closer, they fired a rattling volley from their revolvers, and we promptly retreated beyond range.

"Lot of time," Charley said. "The flood is setting in fast, and by the time it's up to their necks there won't be any fight left in them."

So we lay on our oars and waited for the tide to do its work. This was the predicament of the pirates: because of the big run-out, the tide was now rushing back like a mill-race, and it was impossible for the strongest swimmer in the world to make against it the three miles to the sloops. Between the pirates and the shore were we, precluding escape in that direction. On the other hand, the water was rising rapidly over the shoals, and it was only a question of a few hours when it would be over their heads.

It was beautifully calm, and in the brilliant white moonlight we watched them through our night glasses and told Charley of the voyage of the Coal Tar Maggie. One o'clock came, and two o'clock, and the pirates were clustering on the highest shoal, waist-deep in water.

"Now this illustrates the value of imagination," Charley was saying. "Taft has been trying for years to get them, but he went at it with bull strength and failed. Now we used our heads . . ."

Just then I heard a scarcely audible gurgle of water, and holding up my hand for silence, I turned and pointed to a ripple slowly widening out in a growing circle. It was not more than fifty feet from us. We kept perfectly quiet and waited. After a minute the water broke six feet away, and a black head and white shoulder showed in the moonlight. With a snort of surprise and of suddenly expelled breath, the head and shoulder went down.

We pulled ahead several strokes and drifted with the current. Four pairs of eyes searched the surface of the water, but never another ripple showed, and never another glimpse did we catch of the black head and white shoulder.

"It's the Porpoise," Nicholas said. "It would take broad daylight for us to catch him."

At a quarter to three the pirates gave their first sign of weakening. We heard cries for help, in the unmistakable voice of the Centipede, and this time, on rowing closer, we were not fired upon. The Centipede was in a truly perilous plight. Only the heads and shoulders of his fellow-marauders showed above the water as they braced themselves against the current, while his feet were off the bottom and they were supporting him.

"Now, lads," Charley said briskly, "we have got you, and you can't get away. If you cut up rough, we'll have to leave you alone and the water will finish you. But if you're good, we'll take you aboard, one man at a time, and you'll all be saved. What do you say?"

"Ay," they chorused hoarsely between their chattering teeth.

"Then one man at a time, and the short men first."

The Centipede was the first to be pulled aboard, and he came willingly, though he objected when the constable put the handcuffs on him. Barchi was next hauled in, quite meek and resigned from his soaking. When we had ten in our boat we drew back, and the second Whitehall was loaded. The third Whitehall received nine prisoners only—a catch of twenty-nine in all.

"You didn't get the Porpoise," the Centipede said exultantly, as though his escape materially diminished our success.

Charley laughed. "But we saw him just the same, a-snorting for shore like a puffing pig."

It was a mild and shivering band of pirates that we marched up the beach to the oyster house. In answer to Charley's knock, the door was flung open, and a pleasant wave of warm air rushed out upon us.

"You can dry your clothes here, lads, and get some hot coffee," Charley announced, as they filed in.

And there, sitting ruefully by the fire, with a steaming mug in his hand, was the Porpoise. With one accord Nicholas and I looked at Charley. He laughed gleefully.

"That comes of imagination," he said. "When you see a thing, you've got to see it all around, or what's the good of seeing it at all? I saw the beach, so I left a couple of constables behind to keep an eye on it. That's all."

JOHN STEINBECK

John Steinbeck was born in Salinas, California, in 1902 and died in 1968. He was awarded the Nobel prize for literature in 1962. Not a great scholar, Steinbeck attended Stanford intermittently in the 1920s but never finished. Tortilla Flat *(1935) first gained him popular success, and it was followed by three powerful novels that focused on the woes of the working man and forever connected Steinbeck with the*

struggles of America's proletariat—In Dubious Battle *(1936)*; Of
Mice and Men *(1937), which became a successful stage play and
has been made into several films; and* The Grapes of Wrath *(1939),
which sparked political action and became an immensely popular film.
In 1952, he published what he considered to be his masterwork,* East
of Eden.

The Harvest Gypsies *was originally published as a series of
newspaper columns in the San Francisco* News, *written while Steinbeck was doing research for* The Grapes of Wrath. *They were re-
published in 1938 in pamphlet form by the Simon J. Lubin Society,
under the original title,* Their Blood Is Strong. *In contrast to the
Jack London selection, this excerpt, "The Squatters' Camps," is pure
reportage, without the slightest hint of romance.*

THE SQUATTERS' CAMPS
FROM *THE HARVEST GYPSIES*

The squatters' camps are located all over California. Let us see what a
typical one is like. It is located on the banks of a river, near an irrigation
ditch or on a side road where a spring of water is available. From a
distance it looks like a city dump, and well it may, for the city dumps
are the sources for the material of which it is built. You can see a litter
of dirty rags and scrap iron, of houses built of weeds, of flattened cans
or of paper. It is only on close approach that it can be seen that these
are homes.

Here is a house built by a family who have tried to maintain a
neatness. The house is about 10 feet by 10 feet, and it is built completely
of corrugated paper. The roof is peaked, the walls are tacked to a
wooden frame. The dirt floor is swept clean, and along the irrigation
ditch or in the muddy river the wife of the family scrubs clothes without
soap and tries to rinse out the mud in muddy water. The spirit of this
family is not quite broken, for the children, three of them, still have
clothes, and the family possesses three old quilts and a soggy, lumpy
mattress. But the money so needed for food cannot be used for soap nor
for clothes.

With the first rain the carefully built house will slop down into a
brown, pulpy mush; in a few months the clothes will fray off the chil-

dren's bodies while the lack of nourishing food will subject the whole family to pneumonia when the first cold comes.

Five years ago this family had fifty acres of land and a thousand dollars in the bank. The wife belonged to a sewing circle and the man was a member of the grange. They raised chickens, pigs, pigeons and vegetables and fruit for their own use; and their land produced the tall corn of the middle west. Now they have nothing.

If the husband hits every harvest without delay and works the maximum time, he may make four hundred dollars this year. But if anything happens, if his old car breaks down, if he is late and misses a harvest or two, he will have to feed his whole family on as little as one hundred and fifty.

But there is still pride in this family. Wherever they stop they try to put the children in school. It may be that the children will be in a school for as much as a month before they are moved to another locality.

Here, in the faces of the husband and his wife, you begin to see an expression you will notice on every face; not worry, but absolute terror of the starvation that crowds in against the borders of the camp. This man has tried to make a toilet by digging a hole in the ground near his paper house and surrounding it with an old piece of burlap. But he will only do things like that this year. He is a newcomer and his spirit and decency and his sense of his own dignity have not been quite wiped out. Next year he will be like his next door neighbor.

This is a family of six; a man, his wife and four children. They live in a tent the color of the ground. Rot has set in on the canvas so that the flaps and the sides hang in tatters and are held together with bits of rusty baling wire. There is one bed in the family and that is a big tick lying on the ground inside the tent.

They have one quilt and a piece of canvas for bedding. The sleeping arrangement is clever. Mother and father lie down together and two children lie between them. Then, heading the other way, the other two children lie, the littler ones. If the mother and father sleep with their legs spread wide, there is room for the legs of the children.

There is more filth here. The tent is full of flies clinging to the apple box that is the dinner table, buzzing about the foul clothes of the children, particularly the baby, who has not been bathed nor cleaned for several days. This family has been on the road longer than the builder of the paper house. There is no toilet here, but there is a clump of willows nearby where human feces lie exposed to the flies—the same flies that are in the tent.

Two weeks ago there was another child, a four year old boy. For a few weeks they had noticed that he was kind of lackadaisical, that his eyes had been feverish. They had given him the best place in the bed, between father and mother. But one night he went into convulsions and died, and the next morning the coroner's wagon took him away. It was one step down.

They know pretty well that it was a diet of fresh fruit, beans and little else that caused his death. He had no milk for months. With this death there came a change of mind in his family. The father and mother now feel that paralyzed dullness with which the mind protects itself against too much sorrow and too much pain.

And this father will not be able to make a maximum of four hundred dollars a year any more because he is no longer alert; he isn't quick at piecework, and he is not able to fight clear of the dullness that has settled on him. His spirit is losing caste rapidly.

The dullness shows in the faces of this family, and in addition there is a sullenness that makes them taciturn. Sometimes they still start the older children off to school, but the ragged little things will not go; they hide in ditches or wander off by themselves until it is time to go back to the tent, because they are scorned in the school.

The better-dressed children shout and jeer, the teachers are quite often impatient with these additions to their duties, and the parents of the "nice" children do not want to have disease carriers in the schools.

The father of this family once had a little grocery store and his family lived in back of it so that even the children could wait on the counter. When the drought set in there was no trade for the store any more.

This is the middle class of the squatters' camp. In a few months this family will slip down to the lower class. Dignity is all gone, and spirit has turned to sullen anger before it dies.

The next door neighbor family of man, wife and three children of from three to nine years of age, have built a house by driving willow branches into the ground and wattling weeds, tin, old paper and strips of carpet against them. A few branches are placed over the top to keep out the noonday sun. It would not turn water at all. There is no bed. Somewhere the family has found a big piece of old carpet. It is on the ground. To go to bed the members of the family lie on the ground and fold the carpet up over them.

The three year old child has a gunny sack tied about his middle for clothing. He has the swollen belly caused by malnutrition.

He sits on the ground in the sun in front of the house, and the little black fruit flies buzz in circles and land on his closed eyes and crawl up his nose until he weakly brushes them away.

They try to get at the mucous in the eye-corners. This child seems to have the reactions of a baby much younger. The first year he had a little milk, but he has had none since.

He will die in a very short time. The older children may survive. Four nights ago the mother had a baby in the tent, on the dirty carpet. It was born dead, which was just as well because she could not have fed it at the breast; her own diet will not produce milk.

After it was born and she had seen that it was dead, the mother rolled over and lay still for two days. She is up today, tottering around. The last baby, born less than a year ago, lived a week. This woman's eyes have the glazed, far-away look of a sleep walker's eyes. She does not wash clothes any more. The drive that makes for cleanliness has been drained out of her and she hasn't the energy. The husband was a share-cropper once, but he couldn't make it go. Now he has lost even the desire to talk. He will not look directly at you for that requires will, and will needs strength. He is a bad field worker for the same reason. It takes him a long time to make up his mind, so he is always late in moving and late in arriving in the fields. His top wage, when he can find work now, which isn't often, is a dollar a day.

The children do not even go to the willow clump any more. They squat where they are and kick a little dirt. The father is vaguely aware that there is a culture of hookworm in the mud along the river bank. He knows the children will get it on their bare feet. But he hasn't the will nor the energy to resist. Too many things have happened to him. This is the lower class of the camp.

This is what the man in the tent will be in six months; what the man in the paper house with its peaked roof will be in a year, after his house has washed down and his children have sickened or died, after the loss of dignity and spirit have cut him down to a kind of subhumanity.

Helpful strangers are not well-received in this camp. The local sheriff makes a raid now and then for a wanted man, and if there is labor trouble the vigilantes may burn the poor houses. Social workers, survey workers have taken case histories. They are filed and open for inspection. These families have been questioned over and over about their origins, number of children living and dead. The information is taken down and filed. That is that. It has been done so often and so little has come of it.

And there is another way for them to get attention. Let an epidemic break out, say typhoid or scarlet fever, and the country doctor will come to the camp and hurry the infected cases to the pest house. But malnutrition is not infectious, nor is dysentery, which is almost the rule among the children.

The county hospital has no room for measles, mumps, whooping cough; and yet these are often deadly to hunger-weakened children. And although we hear much about the free clinics for the poor, these people do not know how to get the aid and they do not get it. Also, since most of their dealings with authority are painful to them, they prefer not to take the chance.

This is the squatters' camp. Some are a little better, some much worse. I have described three typical families. In some of the camps there are as many as three hundred families like these. Some are so far from water that it must be bought at five cents a bucket.

And if these men steal, if there is developing among them a suspicion and hatred of well-dressed, satisfied people, the reason is not to be sought in their origin nor in any tendency to weakness in their character.

ROBINSON JEFFERS

Robinson Jeffers, whose hand-built home, Hawk Tower, in Carmel, California, is preserved as a Historical Landmark, was born in Pittsburgh on January 10, 1887. Son of a prominent classics professor, he was sent off to boarding schools in Geneva, Lausanne, Zurich, and

Leipzig, mastering French, Italian, German, and Greek. He returned stateside in 1903, and after his family moved to California, he entered Occidental College, graduating at the ripe age of eighteen. As Richard Ellman put it, Jeffers "lived intensely but with few outward incidents," finding inspiration in the rocky crags, hawks and seabirds, and the relative isolation of his Pacific coast sanctuary, where he settled in 1913. A prolific writer who published over twenty volumes of lyric poetry and drama, he earned his greatest fame in 1946, when he translated Euripides' Medea into his own idiom (Judith Anderson played the leading role on Broadway).

His best-known works include the long poems Roan Stallion *(1925) and* The Double Axe *(1948), which raised a stir with its unpopular rage against World War II. Two volumes of selected poems, the first in 1938, and the second a posthumous edition published in 1965, contain most of the important shorter poems. In his lifetime Jeffers was censured for celebrating the blood-stained glories of wildness. Critical reevaluation since Jeffers's death in 1962 has acknowledged that he was an antiwar poet of considerable moral and political vision.*

EAGLE VALOR, CHICKEN MIND

Unhappy country, what wings you have! Even here,
Nothing important to protect, and ocean-far from the nearest
    enemy, what a cloud
Of bombers amazes the coast mountain, what a hornet-
    swarm of fighters,
And day and night the guns practicing.

Unhappy, eagle wings and beak, chicken brain.
Weep (it is frequent in human affairs), weep for the terrible
    magnificence of the means,
The ridiculous incompetence of the reasons, the bloody and
    shabby
Pathos of the result.

ERNEST HEMINGWAY

Ernest Hemingway was the best-known writer of his generation, and, perhaps, of twentieth-century American literature. Born in 1899 in Oak Park, Illinois, Hemingway twice ran away from home before becoming a cub reporter for the Kansas City Star *in 1917. A year later he volunteered as an ambulance driver and was badly wounded on the Italian front. Returning to America, he began writing for the* Toronto Star Weekly, *was married in 1921, and moved to Europe as a roving correspondent. In France, he came into contact with Gertrude Stein, Ezra Pound, and James Joyce. His book* Three Stories and Ten Poems *was given a limited publication in Paris in 1923. From then on, he took to a life of writing, bull-fighting, big-game hunting, and deep-sea fishing. He was in Spain during its civil war, and immortalized the bravery of the rebel Communists in* For Whom the Bell Tolls *(1940). Toward the end of his life he lived mostly in Cuba and in Ketchum, Idaho, where he committed suicide in 1961. From early on, Hemingway established himself as a master of a peculiarly American writing style and became a legend during his lifetime. His best-known books include* The Sun Also Rises *(1926),* A Farewell to Arms *(1929), and* The Old Man and the Sea *(1952), which won the Pulitzer prize in 1953. In 1954, he was awarded a Nobel prize for literature.*

The following essay, "The Clark's Fork Valley, Wyoming," taken from a 1939 issue of Vogue, *clearly shows Hemingway's style and the reasons he chose to weather the closing seasons of his life in the West. He shows how significant places connect us to memory; he talks about loving the love of good country.*

THE CLARK'S FORK VALLEY, WYOMING

At the end of summer, the big trout would be out in the centre of the stream; they were leaving the pools along the upper part of the river and dropping down to spend the winter in the deep water of the canyon. It was wonderful fly-fishing then in the first weeks of September. The native trout were sleek, shining, and heavy, and nearly all of them leaped when they took the fly. If you fished two flies, you would often have two big trout on and the need to handle them very delicately in that heavy current.

The nights were cold, and, if you woke in the night, you would hear the coyotes. But you did not want to get out on the stream too early in the day because the nights were so cold they chilled the water, and the sun had to be on the river until almost noon before the trout would start to feed.

You could ride in the morning, or sit in front of the cabin, lazy in the sun, and look across the valley where the hay was cut so the meadows were cropped brown and smooth to the line of quaking aspens along the river, now turning yellow in the fall. And on the hills rising beyond, the sage was silvery grey.

Up the river were the two peaks of Pilot and Index, where we would hunt mountain-sheep later in the month, and you sat in the sun and marvelled at the formal, clean-lined shape mountains can have at a distance, so that you remember them in the shapes they show from far away, and not as the broken rock-slides you crossed, the jagged edges you pulled up by, and the narrow shelves you sweated along, afraid to look down, to round that peak that looked so smooth and geometrical. You climbed around it to come out on a clear space to look down to where an old ram and three young rams were feeding in the juniper bushes in a high, grassy pocket cupped against the broken rock of the peak.

The old ram was purple-grey, his rump was white, and when he raised his head you saw the great heavy curl of his horns. It was the white of his rump that had betrayed him to you in the green of the junipers when you had lain in the lee of a rock, out of the wind, three miles away, looking carefully at every yard of the high country through a pair of good Zeiss glasses.

Now as you sat in front of the cabin, you remembered that downhill shot and the young rams standing, their heads turned, staring at him, waiting for him to get up. They could not see you on that high ledge, nor wind you, and the shot made no more impression on them than a boulder falling.

You remembered the year we had built a cabin at the head of Timber Creek, and the big grizzly that tore it open every time we were away. The snow came late that year, and this bear would not hibernate, but spent his autumn tearing open cabins and ruining a trap-line. But he was so smart you never saw him in the day. Then you remembered coming on the three grizzlies in the high country at the head of Crandall Creek. You heard a crash of timber and thought it was a cow elk bolting, and then there they were, in the broken shadow, running with an easy, lurching smoothness, the afternoon sun making their coats a soft, bristling silver.

You remembered elk bugling in the fall, the bull so close you could see his chest muscles swell as he lifted his head, and still not see his head in the thick timber; but hear that deep, high mounting whistle and the answer from across another valley. You thought of all the heads you had turned down and refused to shoot, and you were pleased about every one of them.

You remembered the children learning to ride; how they did with different horses; and how they loved the country. You remembered how this country had looked when you first came into it, and the year you had to stay four months after you had brought the first car ever to come in for the swamp roads to freeze solid enough to get the car out. You could remember all the hunting and all the fishing and the riding in the summer sun and the dust of the pack-train, the silent riding in the hills in the sharp cold of fall going up after the cattle on the high range, finding them wild as deer and as quiet, only bawling noisily when they were all herded together being forced along down into the lower country.

Then there was the winter; the trees bare now, the snow blowing so you could not see, the saddle wet, then frozen as you came downhill, breaking a trail through the snow, trying to keep your legs moving, and the sharp, warming taste of whiskey when you hit the ranch and changed your clothes in front of the big open fireplace. It's a good country.

THEODORE ROETHKE

*Theodore Roethke was born May 25, 1908, in Saginaw, Michigan,
and grew up in the garden world of his parents' family greenhouse
business. He attended the University of Michigan and took graduate
courses at Harvard. He taught at several colleges and universities, and
was particularly generous in devoting time and energy to his students
—even coaching tennis at one point. His organic, elegiac verse shows
the influence of Eliot and Yeats, and his poetry had a profound influence on his students, including James Wright and the Western poets
Richard Hugo and David Wagoner. His first volume of poetry,* Open
House *(1941), brought considerable attention, and his potential was
fulfilled when Roethke won the Pulitzer prize for* The Waking *in
1953. His first volume of collected poems,* Words for the Wind,
won a National Book Award, as did The Far Field, *published posthumously in 1964. He died in Seattle on August 1, 1963, after a
strenuous swim in cold water.*

*The poems here, "All Morning" and "The Far Field," both
from* The Far Field, *are dreams of a paradise where the calling of life
drowns out technology, where living things, if not permanent, remain
saving, central in our imaginations as we invent and reinvent the stories
which we use to define our lives and societies.*

ALL MORNING

Here in our aging district the wood pigeon lives with us,
His deep-throated cooing part of the early morning,
Far away, close-at-hand, his call floating over the on-coming
    traffic,
The lugubriously beautiful plaint uttered at regular intervals,
A protest from the past, a reminder.

They sit, three or four, high in the fir-trees back of the
    house,
Flapping away heavily when a car blasts too close,
And one drops down to the garden, the high rhododendron,

Only to fly over to his favorite perch, the cross-bar of a
    telephone pole;
Grave, hieratic, a piece of Assyrian sculpture,
A thing carved of stone or wood, with the dull iridescence
    of long-polished wood,
Looking at you without turning his small head,
With a round vireo's eye, quiet and contained,
Part of the landscape.

And the Steller jay, raucous, sooty headed, lives with us,
Conducting his long wars with the neighborhood cats,
All during mating season,
Making a racket to wake the dead,
To distract attention from the short-tailed ridiculous young
    ones
Hiding deep in the blackberry bushes—
What a scuttling and rapping along the drainpipes,
A fury of jays, diving and squawking,
When our spayed female cat yawns and stretches out in the
    sunshine—
And the wrens scold, and the chickadees frisk and frolic,
Pitching lightly over the high hedgerows, dee-deeing,
And the ducks near Lake Washington waddle down the
    highway after a rain,
Stopping traffic, indignant as addled old ladies,
Pecking at crusts and peanuts, their green necks glittering;
And the hummingbird dips in and around the quince tree,
Veering close to my head,
Then whirring off sideways to the top of the hawthorn,
Its almost-invisible wings, buzzing, hitting the loose leaves
    intermittently—
A delirium of birds!
Peripheral dippers come to rest on the short grass,
Their heads jod-jodding like pigeons;
The gulls, the gulls far from their waves
Rising, wheeling away with harsh cries,
Coming down on a patch of lawn:

It is neither spring nor summer: it is Always,
With towhees, finches, chickadees, California quail, wood
    doves,
With wrens, sparrows, juncos, cedar waxwings, flickers,
With Baltimore orioles, Michigan bobolinks,
And those birds forever dead,
The passenger pigeon, the great auk, the Carolina paraquet,
All birds remembered, O never forgotten!
All in my yard, of a perpetual Sunday,
All morning! All morning!

THE FAR FIELD

1

I dream of journeys repeatedly:
Of flying like a bat deep into a narrowing tunnel,
Of driving alone, without luggage, out a long peninsula,
The road lined with snow-laden second growth,
A fine dry snow ticking the windshield,
Alternate snow and sleet, no on-coming traffic,
And no lights behind, in the blurred side-mirror,
The road changing from glazed tarface to a rubble of stone,
Ending at last in a hopeless sand-rut,
Where the car stalls,
Churning in a snowdrift
Until the headlights darken.

2

At the field's end, in the corner missed by the mower,
Where the turf drops off into a grass-hidden culvert,
Haunt of the cat-bird, nesting-place of the field-mouse,
Not too far away from the ever-changing flower-dump,
Among the tin cans, tires, rusted pipes, broken machinery,—
One learned of the eternal;
And in the shrunken face of a dead rat, eaten by rain and
    ground-beetles
(I found it lying among the rubble of an old coal bin)

And the tom-cat, caught near the pheasant-run,
Its entrails strewn over the half-grown flowers,
Blasted to death by the night watchman.

I suffered for birds, for young rabbits caught in the mower,
My grief was not excessive.
For to come upon warblers in early May
Was to forget time and death:
How they filled the oriole's elm, a twittering restless cloud,
    all one morning,
And I watched and watched till my eyes blurred from the
    bird shapes,—
Cape May, Blackburnian, Cerulean,—
Moving, elusive as fish, fearless,
Hanging, bunched like young fruit, bending the end
    branches,
Still for a moment,
Then pitching away in half-flight,
Lighter than finches,
While the wrens bickered and sang in the half-green
    hedgerows,
And the flicker drummed from his dead tree in the chicken-
    yard.

—Or to lie naked in sand,
In the silted shallows of a slow river,
Fingering a shell,
Thinking:
Once I was something like this, mindless,
Or perhaps with another mind, less peculiar;
Or to sink down to the hips in a mossy quagmire;
Or, with skinny knees, to sit astride a wet log,
Believing:
I'll return again,
As a snake or a raucous bird,
Or, with luck, as a lion.

I learned not to fear infinity,
The far field, the windy cliffs of forever,

The dying of time in the white light of tomorrow,
The wheel turning away from itself,
The sprawl of the wave,
The on-coming water.

3

The river turns on itself,
The tree retreats into its own shadow.
I feel a weightless change, a moving forward
As of water quickening before a narrowing channel
When banks converge, and the wide river whitens;
Or when two rivers combine, the blue glacial torrent
And the yellowish-green from the mountainy upland,—
At first a swift rippling between rocks,
Then a long running over flat stones
Before descending to the alluvial plain,
To the clay banks, and the wild grapes hanging from the
    elmtrees.
The slightly trembling water
Dropping a fine yellow silt where the sun stays;
And the crabs bask near the edge,
The weedy edge, alive with small snakes and bloodsuckers,—
I have come to a still, but not a deep center,
A point outside the glittering current;
My eyes stare at the bottom of a river,
At the irregular stones, iridescent sandgrains,
My mind moves in more than one place,
In a country half-land, half-water.

I am renewed by death, thought of my death,
The dry scent of a dying garden in September,
The wind fanning the ash of a low fire.
What I love is near at hand,
Always, in earth and air.

4

The lost self changes,
Turning toward the sea,
A sea-shape turning around,—

An old man with his feet before the fire,
In robes of green, in garments of adieu.

A man faced with his own immensity
Wakes all the waves, all their loose wandering fire.
The murmur of the absolute, the why
Of being born fails on his naked ears.
His spirit moves like monumental wind
That gentles on a sunny blue plateau.
He is the end of things, the final man.

All finite things reveal infinitude:
The mountain with its singular bright shade
Like the blue shine on freshly frozen snow,
The after-light upon ice-burdened pines;
Odor of basswood on a mountain-slope,
A scent beloved of bees;
Silence of water above a sunken tree:
The pure serene of memory in one man,—
A ripple widening from a single stone
Winding around the waters of the world.

NORMAN MACLEAN

Norman Maclean was born in Iowa in 1902 and grew up in Missoula, Montana, under the strict tutelage of his father, a Presbyterian minister. From age fourteen through his college years at Dartmouth, Maclean worked summers for the Forest Service in the Bitterroot Mountains. With a doctorate from the University of Chicago, Maclean joined the English department there, where he remained until he retired in 1973 as William Rainey Harper Professor of English. While living at his family's log cabin on Seeley Lake, Montana, Maclean spent most of his summers fly-fishing the Blackfoot River. In 1976, he published

A River Runs Through It and Other Stories, *which was nomi-nated for a Pulitzer prize and was subsequently made into an Academy Award–winning motion picture. His second book,* Young Men and Fire *(1992), about the disastrous Mann Gulch forest fire of 1949, was published posthumously. Maclean died in 1990.*

"In our family, there was no clear line between religion and fly-fishing." So begins A River Runs Through It; *in the selection here, taken from the conclusion to the novel, Maclean earns that sen-tence. We are given a vision of utopia where the sun gleams on the water, where we catch all we need, where all fish are beautiful. From this memory of grace we can connect to our sorrows and intuit an understanding of the words beneath the water.*

FROM *A RIVER RUNS THROUGH IT*

Not only was I on the wrong side of the river to fish with drowned stone flies, but Paul was a good enough roll caster to have already fished most of my side from his own. But I caught two more. They also started as little circles that looked like little fish feeding on the surface but were broken arches of big rainbows under water. After I caught these two, I quit. They made ten, and the last three were the finest fish I ever caught. They weren't the biggest or most spectacular fish I ever caught, but they were three fish I caught because my brother waded across the river to give me the fly that would catch them and because they were the last fish I ever caught fishing with him.

After cleaning my fish, I set these three apart with a layer of grass and wild mint.

Then I lifted the heavy basket, shook myself into the shoulder strap until it didn't cut any more, and thought, "I'm through for the day. I'll go down and sit on the bank by my father and talk." Then I added, "If he doesn't feel like talking, I'll just sit."

I could see the sun ahead. The coming burst of light made it look from the shadows that I and a river inside the earth were about to appear on earth. Although I could as yet see only the sunlight and not anything in it, I knew my father was sitting somewhere on the bank. I knew partly because he and I shared many of the same impulses, even to quitting at about the same time. I was sure without as yet being able to see into what was in front of me that he was sitting somewhere in the sunshine reading the New Testament in Greek. I knew this both from instinct and experience.

Old age had brought him moments of complete peace. Even when we went duck hunting and the roar of the early morning shooting was over, he would sit in the blind wrapped in an old army blanket with his Greek New Testament in one hand and his shotgun in the other. When a stray duck happened by, he would drop the book and raise the gun, and, after the shooting was over, he would raise the book again, occasionally interrupting his reading to thank his dog for retrieving the duck.

The voices of the subterranean river in the shadows were different from the voices of the sunlit river ahead. In the shadows against the cliff the river was deep and engaged in profundities, circling back on itself now and then to say things over to be sure it had understood itself. But the river ahead came out into the sunny world like a chatterbox, doing its best to be friendly. It bowed to one shore and then to the other so nothing would feel neglected.

By now I could see inside the sunshine and had located my father. He was sitting high on the bank. He wore no hat. Inside the sunlight, his faded red hair was once again ablaze and again in glory. He was reading, although evidently only by sentences because he often looked away from the book. He did not close the book until some time after he saw me.

I scrambled up the bank and asked him, "How many did you get?" He said, "I got all I want." I said, "But how many did you get?" He said, "I got four or five." I asked, "Are they any good?" He said, "They are beautiful."

He was about the only man I ever knew who used the word "beautiful" as a natural form of speech, and I guess I picked up the habit from hanging around him when I was little.

"How many did you catch?" he asked. "I also caught all I want," I told him. He omitted asking me just how many that was, but he did ask me, "Are they any good?" "They are beautiful," I told him, and sat down beside him.

"What have you been reading?" I asked. "A book," he said. It was on the ground on the other side of him. So I would not have to bother to look over his knees to see it, he said, "A good book."

Then he told me, "In the part I was reading it says the Word was in the beginning, and that's right. I used to think water was first, but if you listen carefully you will hear that the words are underneath the water."

"That's because you are a preacher first and then a fisherman," I told him. "If you ask Paul, he will tell you that the words are formed out of water."

"No," my father said, "you are not listening carefully. The water runs over the words. Paul will tell you the same thing. Where is Paul anyway?"

I told him he had gone back to fish the first hole over again. "But he promised to be here soon," I assured him. "He'll be here when he catches his limit," he said. "He'll be here soon," I reassured him, partly because I could already see him in the subterranean shadows.

My father went back to reading and I tried to check what we had said by listening. Paul was fishing fast, picking up one here and there and wasting no time in walking them to shore. When he got directly across from us, he held up a finger on each hand and my father said, "He needs two more for his limit."

I looked to see where the book was left open and knew just enough Greek to recognize λόγος as the Word. I guessed from it and the argument that I was looking at the first verse of John. While I was looking, Father said, "He has one on."

It was hard to believe, because he was fishing in front of us on the other side of the hole that Father had just fished. Father slowly rose, found a good-sized rock and held it behind his back. Paul landed the fish, and waded out again for number twenty and his limit. Just as he was making the first cast, Father threw the rock. He was old enough so that he threw awkwardly and afterward had to rub his shoulder, but the rock landed in the river about where Paul's fly landed and at about the same time, so you can see where my brother learned to throw rocks into his partner's fishing water when he couldn't bear to see his partner catch any more fish.

Paul was startled for only a moment. Then he spotted Father on the bank rubbing his shoulder, and Paul laughed, shook his fist at him, backed to shore and went downstream until he was out of rock range. From there he waded into the water and began to cast again, but now he was far enough away so we couldn't see his line or loops. He was a man with a wand in a river, and whatever happened we had to guess from what the man and the wand and the river did.

As he waded out, his big right arm swung back and forth. Each circle of his arm inflated his chest. Each circle was faster and higher and longer until his arm became defiant and his chest breasted the sky. On shore we were sure, although we could see no line, that the air above him was singing with loops of line that never touched the water but got bigger and bigger each time they passed and sang. And we knew what was in his mind from the lengthening defiance of his arm. He was not going to let his fly touch any water close to shore where the small and middle-sized fish were. We knew from his arm and chest that all parts of him were saying, "No small one for the last one." Everything was going into one big cast for one last big fish.

From our angle high on the bank, my father and I could see where in the distance the wand was going to let the fly first touch water. In the middle of the river was a rock iceberg, just its tip exposed above water and underneath it a rock house. It met all the residential requirements for big fish—powerful water carrying food to the front and back doors, and rest and shade behind them.

My father said, "There has to be a big one out there."

I said, "A little one couldn't live out there."

My father said, "The big one wouldn't let it."

My father could tell by the width of Paul's chest that he was going to let the next loop sail. It couldn't get any wider. "I wanted to fish out there," he said, "but I couldn't cast that far."

Paul's body pivoted as if he were going to drive a golf ball three hundred yards, and his arm went high into the great arc and the tip of his wand bent like a spring, and then everything sprang and sang.

Suddenly, there was an end of action. The man was immobile. There was no bend, no power in the wand. It pointed at ten o'clock and ten o'clock pointed at the rock. For a moment the man looked like a teacher with a pointer illustrating something about a rock to a rock. Only water moved. Somewhere above the top of the rock house a fly was swept in water so powerful only a big fish could be there to see it.

Then the universe stepped on its third rail. The wand jumped convulsively as it made contact with the magic current of the world. The wand tried to jump out of the man's right hand. His left hand seemed to be frantically waving good-bye to a fish, but actually was trying to throw enough line into the rod to reduce the voltage and ease the shock of what had struck.

Everything seemed electrically charged but electrically unconnected. Electrical sparks appeared here and there on the river. A fish jumped so far downstream that it seemed outside the man's electrical field, but, when the fish had jumped, the man had leaned back on the rod and it was then that the fish had toppled back into the water not guided in its reentry by itself. The connections between the convulsions and the sparks became clearer by repetition. When the man leaned back on the wand and the fish reentered the water not altogether under its own power, the wand recharged with convulsions, the man's hand waved frantically at another departure, and much farther below a fish jumped again. Because of the connections, it became the same fish.

The fish made three such long runs before another act in the performance began. Although the act involved a big man and a big fish, it looked more like children playing. The man's left hand sneakily began recapturing line, and then, as if caught in the act, threw it all back into the rod as the fish got wise and made still another run.

"He'll get him," I assured my father.

"Beyond doubt," my father said. The line going out became shorter than what the left hand took in.

When Paul peered into the water behind him, we knew he was going to start working the fish to shore and didn't want to back into a hole or rock. We could tell he had worked the fish into shallow water because he held the rod higher and higher to keep the fish from bumping into anything on the bottom. Just when we thought the performance was over, the wand convulsed and the man thrashed through the water after some unseen power departing for the deep.

"The son of a bitch still has fight in him," I thought I said to myself, but unmistakably I said it out loud, and was embarrassed for having said it out loud in front of my father. He said nothing.

Two or three more times Paul worked him close to shore, only to have him swirl and return to the deep, but even at that distance my father and I could feel the ebbing of the underwater power. The rod went high in the air, and the man moved backwards swiftly but evenly, motions which when translated into events meant the fish had tried to rest for a moment on top of the water and the man had quickly raised the rod high and skidded him to shore before the fish thought of getting under water again. He skidded him across the rocks clear back to a sandbar before the shocked fish gasped and discovered he could not live in oxygen. In belated despair, he rose in the sand and consumed the rest of momentary life dancing the Dance of Death on his tail.

The man put the wand down, got on his hands and knees in the sand, and, like an animal, circled another animal and waited. Then the shoulder shot straight out, and my brother stood up, faced us, and, with uplifted arm proclaimed himself the victor. Something giant dangled from his fist. Had Romans been watching they would have thought that what was dangling had a helmet on it.

"That's his limit," I said to my father.

"He is beautiful," my father said, although my brother had just finished catching his limit in the hole my father had already fished.

This was the last fish we were ever to see Paul catch. My father and I talked about this moment several times later, and whatever our other feelings, we always felt it fitting that, when we saw him catch his last fish, we never saw the fish but only the artistry of the fisherman.

While my father was watching my brother, he reached over to pat me, but he missed, so he had to turn his eyes and look for my knee and try again. He must have thought that I felt neglected and that he should tell me he was proud of me also but for other reasons.

It was a little too deep and fast where Paul was trying to wade the river, and he knew it. He was crouched over the water and his arms were spread wide for balance. If you were a wader of big rivers you could have felt with him even at a distance the power of the water making his legs weak and wavy and ready to swim out from under him. He looked downstream to estimate how far it was to an easier place to wade.

My father said, "He won't take the trouble to walk downstream. He'll swim it." At the same time Paul thought the same thing, and put his cigarettes and matches in his hat.

My father and I sat on the bank and laughed at each other. It never occurred to either of us to hurry to the shore in case he needed help with a rod in his right hand and a basket loaded with fish on his left shoulder. In our family it was no great thing for a fisherman to swim a river with matches in his hair. We laughed at each other because we knew he was getting damn good and wet, and we lived in him, and were swept over the rocks with him and held his rod high in one of our hands.

As he moved to shore he caught himself on his feet and then was washed off them, and, when he stood again, more of him showed and he staggered to shore. He never stopped to shake himself. He came charging up the bank showering molecules of water and images of himself to show what was sticking out of his basket, and he dripped all over us, like a young duck dog that in its joy forgets to shake itself before getting close.

"Let's put them all out on the grass and take a picture of them," he said. So we emptied our baskets and arranged them by size and took turns photographing each other admiring them and ourselves. The photographs turned out to be like most amateur snapshots of fishing catches—the fish were white from overexposure and didn't look as big as they actually were and the fishermen looked self-conscious as if some guide had to catch the fish for them.

However, one closeup picture of him at the end of this day remains in my mind, as if fixed by some chemical bath. Usually, just after he finished fishing he had little to say unless he saw he could have fished better. Otherwise, he merely smiled. Now flies danced around his hatband. Large drops of water ran from under his hat on to his face and then into his lips when he smiled.

At the end of this day, then, I remember him both as a distant abstraction in artistry and as a closeup in water and laughter.

My father always felt shy when compelled to praise one of his family, and his family always felt shy when he praised them. My father said, "You are a fine fisherman."

My brother said, "I'm pretty good with a rod, but I need three more years before I can think like a fish."

Remembering that he had caught his limit by switching to George's No. 2 Yellow Hackle with a feather wing, I said without knowing how much I said, "You already know how to think like a dead stone fly."

We sat on the bank and the river went by. As always, it was making sounds to itself, and now it made sounds to us. It would be hard to find three men sitting side by side who knew better what a river was saying.

On the Big Blackfoot River above the mouth of Belmont Creek the banks are fringed by large Ponderosa pines. In the slanting sun of late afternoon the shadows of great branches reached from across the river, and the trees took the river in their arms. The shadows continued up the bank, until they included us.

A river, though, has so many things to say that it is hard to know what it says to each of us. As we were packing our tackle and fish in the car, Paul repeated, "Just give me three more years." At the time, I was surprised at the repetition, but later I realized that the river somewhere, sometime, must have told me, too, that he would receive no such gift. For, when the police sergeant early next May wakened me before daybreak, I rose and asked no questions. Together we drove across the Continental Divide and down the length of the Big Blackfoot River over forest floors yellow and sometimes white with glacier lilies to tell my father and mother that my brother had been beaten to death by the butt of a revolver and his body dumped in an alley.

My mother turned and went to her bedroom where, in a house full of men and rods and rifles, she had faced most of her great problems alone. She was never to ask me a question about the man she loved most and understood least. Perhaps she knew enough to know that for her it was enough to have loved him. He was probably the only man in the world who had held her in his arms and leaned back and laughed.

When I finished talking to my father, he asked, "Is there anything else you can tell me?"

Finally, I said, "Nearly all the bones in his hand were broken."

He almost reached the door and then turned back for reassurance. "Are you sure that the bones in his hand were broken?" he asked. I repeated, "Nearly all the bones in his hand were broken." "In which hand?" he asked. "In his right hand," I answered.

After my brother's death, my father never walked very well again. He had to struggle to lift his feet, and, when he did get them up, they came down slightly out of control. From time to time Paul's right hand had to be reaffirmed; then my father would shuffle away again. He could not shuffle in a straight line from trying to lift his feet. Like many Scottish ministers before him, he had to derive what comfort he could from the faith that his son had died fighting.

For some time, though, he struggled for more to hold on to. "Are you sure you have told me everything you know about his death?" he asked. I said, "Everything." "It's not much, is it?" "No," I replied, "but you can love completely without complete understanding." "That I have known and preached," my father said.

Once my father came back with another question. "Do you think I could have helped him?" he asked. Even if I might have thought longer, I would have made the same answer. "Do you think I could have helped him?" I answered. We stood waiting in deference to each other. How can a question be answered that asks a lifetime of questions?

After a long time he came with something he must have wanted to ask from the first. "Do you think it was just a stick-up and foolishly he tried to fight his way out? You know what I mean—that it wasn't connected with anything in his past."

"The police don't know," I said.

"But do you?" he asked, and I felt the implication.

"I've said I've told you all I know. If you push me far enough, all I really know is that he was a fine fisherman."

"You know more than that," my father said. "He was beautiful."

"Yes," I said, "he was beautiful. He should have been—you taught him."

My father looked at me for a long time—he just looked at me. So this was the last he and I ever said to each other about Paul's death.

Indirectly, though, he was present in many of our conversations. Once, for instance, my father asked me a series of questions that suddenly made me wonder whether I understood even my father whom I felt closer to than any man I have ever known. "You like to tell true stories, don't you?" he asked, and I answered, "Yes, I like to tell stories that are true."

Then he asked, "After you have finished your true stories sometime, why don't you make up a story and the people to go with it?

"Only then will you understand what happened and why.

"It is those we live with and love and should know who elude us."

Now nearly all those I loved and did not understand when I was young are dead, but I still reach out to them.

Of course, now I am too old to be much of a fisherman, and now of course I usually fish the big waters alone, although some friends think I shouldn't. Like many fly fishermen in western Montana where the summer days are almost Arctic in length, I often do not start fishing until the cool of the evening. Then in the Arctic half-light of the canyon, all existence fades to a being with my soul and memories and the sounds of the Big Blackfoot River and a four-count rhythm and the hope that a fish will rise.

Eventually, all things merge into one, and a river runs through it. The river was cut by the world's great flood and runs over rocks from the basement of time. On some of the rocks are timeless raindrops. Under the rocks are the words, and some of the words are theirs.

I am haunted by waters.

WRIGHT MORRIS

Wright Morris was born in Central City, Nebraska, in 1910. The first ten years of his life "were spent in the whistle-stops along the Platte Valley to the West." His novel The Field of Vision *(1956) won the National Book Award in 1956, and* Plains Song *(1980) won the 1981 American Book Award for fiction. Morris is the author of nearly twenty other novels, including another of my favorites,* The Works of Love, *several collections of short fiction, three memoirs, numerous books of criticism, and a number of photo-text volumes. He resides in Mill Valley, California.*

Morris, one of the most underrecognized major writers from the West, opens Ceremony in Lone Tree *with "Come to the window." And then, as in many of his other novels, he takes us out to a place where the slow rhythms of isolated life on the short-grass plains intersect with the contemporary, which in contrast is bound to seem helter-skelter, inhuman.*

FROM *CEREMONY IN LONE TREE*

Come to the window. The one at the rear of the Lone Tree Hotel. The view is to the west. There is no obstruction but the sky. Although there is no one outside to look in, the yellow blind is drawn low at the window, and between it and the pane a fly is trapped. He has stopped buzzing. Only the crawling shadow can be seen. Before the whistle of the train is heard the loose pane rattles like a simmering pot, then stops, as if pressed by a hand, as the train goes past. The blind sucks inward and the dangling cord drags in the dust on the sill.

At a child's level in the pane there is a flaw that is round, like an eye in the glass. An eye to that eye, a scud seems to blow on a sea of grass. Waves of plain seem to roll up, then break like a surf. Is it a flaw in the eye, or in the window, that transforms a dry place into a wet one? Above it towers a sky, like the sky at sea, a wind blows like the wind at sea, and like the sea it has no shade: there is no place to hide. One thing it is that the sea is not: it is dry, not wet.

Drawn up to the window is a horsehair sofa covered with a quilt.

On the floor at its side, garlanded with flowers, is a nightpot full of cigar butts and ashes. Around it, scattered like seed, are the stubs of half-burned kitchen matches, the charcoal tips honed to a point for picking the teeth. They also serve to aid the digestion and sweeten the breath. The man who smokes the cigars and chews on the matches spends most of the day on the sofa; he is not there now, but the sagging springs hold his shape. He has passed his life, if it can be said he has lived one, in the rooms of the Lone Tree Hotel. His coat hangs in the lobby, his shoes are under the stove, and a runner of ashes marks his trail up and down the halls. His hat, however, never leaves his head. It is the hat, with its wicker sides, the drayman's license at the front, that comes to mind when his children think of him. He has never run a dray, but never mind. The badge is what they see, through the hole where his sleeve has smudged the window, on those rare occasions when they visit him. If the hat is not there, they look for him in the lobby, dozing in one of the hardwood rockers or in one of the beds drawn to a window facing the west. There is little to see, but plenty of room to look.

Scanlon's eyes, a cloudy phlegm color, let in more light than they give out. What he sees are the scenic props of his own mind. His eye to the window, the flaw in the pane, such light as there is illuminates Scanlon, his face like that of a gobbler in the drayman's hat. What he sees is his own business, but the stranger might find the view familiar. A man accustomed to the ruins of war might even feel at home. In the blowouts on the rise are flint arrowheads, and pieces of farm machinery, half buried in sand, resemble nothing so much as artillery equipment, abandoned when the dust began to blow. The tidal shift of the sand reveals one ruin in order to conceal another. It is all there to be seen, but little evidence that Tom Scanlon sees it. Not through the clouded eye he puts to the glass. The emptiness of the plain generates illusions that require little moisture, and grow better, like tall stories, where the mind is dry. The tall corn may flower or burn in the wind, but the plain is a metaphysical landscape and the bumper crop is the one Scanlon sees through the flaw in the glass.

Nothing irked him more than to hear from his children that the place was empty, the town deserted, and that there was nothing to see. He saw plenty. No matter where he looked. Down the tracks to the east, like a headless bird, the bloody neck still raw and dripping, a tub-shaped water tank sits high on stilts. Scanlon once saw a coon crawl out the chute and drink from the spout. Bunches of long-stemmed grass, in this short-grass country, grow where the water drips between the rails, and Scanlon will tell you he has seen a buffalo crop it up. A big bull, of course, high in the shoulders, his short tail like the knot in a whip, walking on the ties like a woman with her skirts tucked up. Another time a wolf, half crazed by the drought, licked the moisture from the rails like ice and chewed on the grass like a dog out of sorts. On occasion stray geese circle the tank like a water hole. All common sights, according to Scanlon, where other men squinted and saw nothing but the waves of heat, as if the cinders of the railbed were still on fire.

It seldom rains in Lone Tree, but he has often seen it raining somewhere else. A blue veil of it will hang like the half-drawn curtain at Scanlon's window. Pillars of cloud loom on the horizon, at night there is much lightning and claps of thunder, and from one window or another rain may be seen falling somewhere. Wind from that direction will smell wet, and Scanlon will complain, if there is someone to listen, about the rheumatic pains in his knees. He suffered greater pains, however, back when he had neighbors who complained, of all things, about the lack of rain.

In the heat of the day, when there is no shadow, the plain seems to be drawn up into the sky, and through the hole in the window it is hard to be sure if the town is still there. It takes on, like a sunning lizard, the colors of the plain. The lines drawn around the weathered buildings smoke and blur. At this time of day Scanlon takes his nap, and by the time he awakes the town is back in its place. The lone tree, a dead cottonwood, can be seen by the shadow it leans to the east, a zigzag line with a fishhook curve at the end. According to Scanlon, Indians once asked permission to bury their dead in the crotch of the tree, and while the body was there the tree had been full of crows. A small boy at the time, Scanlon had shot at them with his father's squirrel gun, using soft lead pellets that he dug out of the trunk of the tree and used over again.

From the highway a half mile to the north, the town sits on the plain as if delivered on a flatcar—as though it were a movie set thrown up during the night. Dry as it is, something about it resembles an ark from which the waters have receded. In the winter it appears to be locked in a sea of ice. In the summer, like the plain around it, the town seems to float on a watery surface, stray cattle stand knee-deep in a blur of reflections, and waves of light and heat flow across the highway like schools of fish. Everywhere the tongue is dry, but the mind is wet. According to his daughters, who should know, the dirt caked around

Tom Scanlon's teeth settled there in the thirties when the dust began to blow. More of it can be seen, fine as talcum, on the linoleum floor in the lobby, where the mice raised in the basement move to their winter quarters in the cobs behind the stove.

To the east, relatively speaking, there is much to see, a lone tree, a water tank, sheets of rain and heat lightning: to the west a strip of torn screen blurs the view. The effect is that of now-you-see-it, now-you-don't. As a rule, there is nothing to see, and if there is, one doubts it. The pane is smeared where Scanlon's nose has rubbed the glass. The fact that there is little to see seems to be what he likes about it. He can see what he pleases. It need not please anybody else. Trains come from both directions, but from the east they come without warning, the whistle blown away by the wind. From the west, thin and wild or strumming like a wire fastened to the building, the sound wakes Scanlon from his sleep before the building rocks. It gives him time, that is, to prepare himself. The upgrade freights rock the building and leave nothing but the noise in his head, but the downgrade trains leave a vacuum he sometimes raises the window to look at. A hole? He often thought he might see one there. A cloud of dust would veil the caboose, on the stove one of the pots or the lids would rattle, and if the lamp was lit, the flame would blow as if in a draft.

One day as the dust settled he saw a team of mares, the traces dragging, cantering down the bank where the train had just passed. On the wires above the tracks, dangling like a scarecrow, he saw the body of Emil Bickel, in whose vest pocket the key-wound watch had stopped. At 7:34, proving the train that hit him had been right on time.

To the west the towns are thin and sparse, like the grass, and in a place called Indian Bow the white faces of cattle peer out of the soddies on the slope across the dry bed of the river. They belong to one of Scanlon's grandchildren who married well. On the rise behind the soddies are sunken graves, one of the headstones bearing the name of Will Brady, a railroad man who occasionally stopped off at Lone Tree. Until he married and went east, Scanlon thought him a sensible man.

Down the grade to the east the towns are greener and thicker, like the grass. The town of Polk, the home of Walter McKee, who married Scanlon's eldest daughter, Lois, has elm-shaded streets and a sign on the highway telling you to slow down. There is also a park with a Civil

War cannon, the name of Walter McKee carved on the breech and that of his friend, Gordon Boyd, on one of the cannon balls. In the house where Walter McKee was born grass still grows between the slats on the porch, and the neighbor's chickens still lay their eggs under the stoop. At the corner of the porch a tar barrel catches and stores the rain from the roof. At the turn of the century, when McKee was a boy, he buried the white hairs from a mare's tail in the rain barrel, confident they would turn up next as garter snakes. In the middle of the century that isn't done, and a TV aerial, like a giant Martian insect, crouches on the roof as if about to fly off with the house. That is a change, but on its side in the yard is a man's bicycle with the seat missing. The small boy who rides it straddles it through the bars: he never sits down. He mounts it slantwise, like a bareback rider, grease from the chain rubbing off on one leg and soiling the cuff of the pants leg rolled to the knee. Gordon Boyd still bears the scar where the teeth of the sprocket dug into his calf. Bolder than McKee, he liked to ride on the gravel around the patch of grass in the railroad station, leaning forward to hold a strip of berry-box wood against the twirling spokes.

The short cut in the yard, worn there by McKee, still points across the street to a wide vacant lot and to the tree where McKee, taunted by Boyd, climbed to where the sway and the height made him dizzy. He fell on a milk-can lid, breaking his arm. Mrs. Boyd, a white-haired woman, had put his arm to soak in a cold tub of water while Gordon went for the doctor on McKee's new bike. Over that summer Boyd had grown so fast he could pump it from the seat.

The Boyd house, having no basement, had a storm cave at the back of the yard where McKee smoked corn silk and Boyd smoked Fourth of July punk. The white frame house still has no basement, and the upstairs bedroom, looking out on the porch, is still heated by a pipe that comes up from the stove below. When McKee spent the night with Boyd, Mrs. Boyd would rap a spoon on the pipe to make them quiet, or turn down the damper so the room would get cold. The old coke burner, with the isinglass windows through which Boyd and McKee liked to watch the coke settle, now sits in the woodshed, crowned with the horn of the Victrola. The stove board, however, the floral design worn away where Boyd liked to dress on winter mornings, is now in the corner where the floor boards have sagged, under the new TV. Since the house has no porch high enough to crawl under, Boyd kept his sled and Irish Mail under the porch of a neighbor. Along with Hershey bar tinfoil, several pop bottles, a knife with a woman's leg for a handle, and a tin for condoms, thought to be balloons and blown up till they popped on the Fourth of July, the sled is still there. The boys don't use the ones with wooden runners any more. The chain swing no longer creaks on the porch or spends the winter, cocoonlike, drawn to the ceiling, but the paint still peels where it grazed the clapboards and thumped on the railing warm summer nights. Long after it was gone Mrs. Boyd was kept awake by its creak.

The people change—according to a survey conducted by a new supermarket—but the life in Polk remains much the same. The new trailer park on the east edge of town boasts the latest and best in portable living, but the small fry still fish, like McKee, for crawdads with hunks of liver, and bring them home to mothers who hastily dump them back in the creek. The men live in Polk, where there is plenty of room, and commute to those places where the schools are overcrowded, the rents inflated, but where there is work. At the western edge of town an air-conditioned motel with a stainless-steel diner blinks at night like an airport, just across the street from where McKee chipped his front teeth on the drinking fountain. Once or twice a year on his way to Lone Tree, McKee stops off in Polk for what he calls a real shave, in the shop where he got his haircuts as a boy. The price for a shave and a haircut has changed, but the mirror on the wall is the same. In it, somewhere, is the face McKee had as a boy. Stretched out horizontal, his eyes on the tin ceiling, his lips frothy with the scented lather, he sometimes fancies he hears the mocking voice of Boyd:

> *Walter McKee,*
> *Button your fly.*
> *Pee in the road*
> *And you'll get a sty.*

Although he comes from the south, McKee goes out of his way to enter town from the west, passing the water stack with the word P O L K like a shadow under the new paint. Just beyond the water stack is the grain elevator, the roof flashing like a mirror in the sun, the name T. P. CRETE in black on the fresh coat of aluminum. The same letters were stamped like a legend on McKee's mind. The great man himself was seldom seen in the streets of Polk, or in the rooms of his mansion, but his name, in paint or gold leaf, stared at McKee from walls and windows and the high board fence that went along the lumberyard. T. P. Crete's wife, like a bird in a cage, sometimes went by in her electric car, making no more noise than the strum of the wires on the telephone poles. It was this creature who deprived McKee of his friend Boyd. She sent him, when he proved to be smart, to those high-toned schools in the East that indirectly led to the ruin he made of his life. Destiny manifested itself through the Cretes, and the sight of the name affected McKee like a choir marching in or the sound of his mother humming hymns.

Beyond the grain elevator is the railroad station, the iron wheels of the baggage truck sunk in the gravel, an OUT OF ORDER sign pasted on the face of the penny scales in the lobby. On the east side of the station is a patch of grass. Around it is a fence of heavy wrought iron, the top rail studded to discourage loafers, pigeons and small fry like McKee and Boyd. Polk is full of wide lawns and freshly cropped grass healthy enough for a boy to walk on, but for McKee the greenest grass in the world is the patch inside the wrought-iron fence. He never enters town without a glance at it. If it looks greener than other grass it might be due to the cinder-blackened earth, and the relative sparseness and tenderness of the shoots. But the secret lies in McKee, not in the grass. No man raised on the plains, in the short-grass country, takes a patch of grass for granted, and it is not for nothing they protect it with a fence or iron bars. When McKee thinks of spring, or of his boyhood, or of what the world would be like if men came to their senses, in his mind's eye he sees the patch of green in the cage at Polk. Tall grass now grows between the Burlington tracks that lead south of town to the bottomless sand pit where Boyd, before the eyes of McKee, attempted to walk on water for the first time. But not the last. Nothing seemed to teach him anything.

Southeast of Polk is Lincoln, capital of the state, the present home of McKee and his wife Lois, as well as of Lois's sister Maxine and her family. Tom Scanlon's youngest girl, Edna, married Clyde Ewing, an Oklahoma horse breeder, who found oil on his farm in the Panhandle. The view from their modern air-conditioned house is so much like that around Lone Tree, Edna Ewing felt sure her father would feel right at home in it. Tom Scanlon, however, didn't like the place. For one thing, there were no windows, only those gleaming walls of glass. He had walked from room to room as he did outside, with his head drawn in. Although the floor and walls radiated heat, Scanlon felt cold, since it lacked a stove with an oven door or a rail where he could put his feet. Only in the back door was there something like a window, an opening about the size of a porthole framing the view, with a flaw in the glass to which he could put his eye. Through it he saw, three hundred miles to the north, the forked branches of the lone tree like bleached cattle horns on the railroad embankment that half concealed the town, the false fronts of the buildings like battered remnants of a board fence. Even the hotel, with its MAIL POUCH sign peeling like a circus poster, might be taken for a signboard along an abandoned road. That is how it is, but not how it looks to Scanlon. He stands as if at the screen, gazing down the tracks to where the long-stemmed grass spurts from the cinders like leaks in a garden hose. The mindless wind in his face seems damp with the prospect of rain.

Three stories high, made of the rough-faced brick brought out from Omaha on a flatcar, the Lone Tree Hotel sits where the coaches on the westbound caboose once came to a stop. Eastbound, there were few who troubled to stop. In the westbound caboose were the men who helped Lone Tree to believe in itself. The hotel faces the south, the empty pits that were dug for homes never erected and the shadowy trails, like Inca roads, indicating what were meant to be streets. The door at the front, set in slantwise on the corner, with a floral design in the frosted glass, opens on the prospect of the town. Slabs of imported Italian marble face what was once the bank, the windows boarded like a looted tomb, the vault at the rear once having served as a jail. A sign:

$5. FINE FOR TALKING

TO

PRISONERS

once hung over one of the barred windows, but a brakeman who was something of a card made off with it.

The lobby of the hotel, level with the hitching bar, affords a view of the barbershop interior, the mirror on the wall and whoever might be sitting in the one chair. Only the lower half of the window is curtained, screening off the man who is being shaved but offering him a view of the street and the plain when he sits erect, just his hair being cut. Tucked into the frame of the mirror are the post cards sent back by citizens who left or went traveling to those who were crazy enough to stay on in Lone Tree. The incumbent barber usually doubled as the postmaster. In the glass razor case, laid out on a towel still peppered with his day-old beard, is the razor that shaved William Jennings Bryan. In Lone Tree, at the turn of the century, he pleaded the lost cause of silver, then descended from the platform of the caboose for a shampoo and a shave. On that day a balloon, brought out on a flatcar, reached the altitude of two hundred forty-five feet with Edna Scanlon, who was something of a tomboy, visible in the basket that hung beneath. The century turned that memorable summer, and most of the men in Lone Tree turned with it; like the engines on the roundhouse platform they wheeled from west to east. But neither Scanlon, anchored in the lobby, nor the town of Lone Tree turned with it. The century went its own way after that, and Scanlon went his.

From a rocker in the lobby Scanlon can see the gap between the barbershop and the building on the west, the yellow blind shadowed with the remaining letters of the word MIL NE Y. On the floor above the millinery is the office of Dr. Twomey, where a cigar-store Indian with human teeth guards the door. He stands grimacing, tomahawk upraised, with what are left of the molars known to drop out when the building is shaken by a downgrade freight. When Twomey set up his practice, the barber chair served very nicely as an operating table, a place for lancing boils, removing adenoids or pulling teeth. A flight of wooden steps without a railing mounted to his office on the second floor, but they collapsed within a week or so after he died. He was a huge man, weighing some three hundred pounds, and it took four men to lower his body to the casket on the wagon in the street. The stairs survived the strain, then collapsed under their own weight.

A hand-cranked gas pump, the crank in a sling, sits several yards in front of the livery stable, as if to disassociate itself from the horses once stabled inside. At the back of the stable, inhabited by bats, is the covered wagon Scanlon was born in, the bottom sloped up at both ends like a river boat. Strips of faded canvas, awning remnants, partially cover the ribs. Until the hotel was built in the eighties, the Scanlon family lived in the rear of the millinery, and the covered wagon, like a gypsy encampment, sat under the lone tree. Before the railroad went through, the pony express stopped in the shade of the tree for water. Scanlon remembers the sweat on the horses, and once being lifted to the pommel of the saddle, but most of the things he remembers took place long before he was born.

In the weeds behind the stable are a rubber-tired fire-hose cart without the hose, two short lengths of ladder and the iron frame for the fire bell. When the water-pressure system proved too expensive, the order for the hose and the fire bell was canceled. On the east side of the stable, the wheels sunk in the sand, a water sprinkler is garlanded with morning glories and painted with the legend VISIT THE LYRIC TO-NITE. The Lyric, a wooden frame building, has a front of galvanized tin weathered to the leaden color of the drainpipes on the hotel. It stands like a souvenir book end at the east end of the town, holding up the row of false-front stores between it and the bank. Most of the year these shops face the sun, the light glaring on the curtained windows, like a row of blindfolded Confederate soldiers lined up to be shot. A board-walk, like a fence blown on its side, is half concealed by the tidal drift of the sand—nothing could be drier, but the look of the place is wet. The wash of the sand is rippled as if by the movement of water, and stretches of the walk have the look of a battered pier. The town itself seems to face what is left of a vanished lake. Even the lone tree, stripped of its foliage, rises from the deck of the plain like a mast, and from the highway or the bluffs along the river, the crows'-nest at the top might be that on a ship. The bowl of the sky seems higher, the plain wider, because of it.

A street light still swings at the crossing corner but in the summer it casts no shadow, glowing like a bolthole in a stove until after nine o'clock. The plain is dark, but the bowl of the sky is full of light. On his horsehair sofa, drawn up to the window, Scanlon can see the hands on his watch until ten o'clock. The light is there after the sun has set and will be there in the morning before it rises, as if a property of the sky itself. The moon, rather than the sun, might be the source of it. In the summer the bats wing in and out of the stable as if it were dark, their radar clicking, wheel on the sky, then wing into the stable again. At this time of the evening coins come out to be found. The rails gleam like ice in the cinders, and the drayman's badge on Scanlon's hat, bright as a buckle, can be seen through the hole he has rubbed in the glass.

If a grass fire has been smoldering during the day you will see it flicker on the plain at night, and smoke from these fires, like Scanlon himself, has seldom left the rooms of the Lone Tree Hotel. It is there in the curtains like the smell of his cigars. His daughter Lois, the moment she arrives, goes up and down the halls opening the windows, and leaves a bottle of Air Wick in the room where she plans to spend the night.

For better or worse—as she often tells McKee—she was born and raised
in it.

The last time Lois spent a night in Lone Tree was after her father had
been found wrapped up like a mummy, his cold feet in a colder oven,
and paraded big as life on the front page of the Omaha *Bee*. The caption
of the story read:

MAN WHO KNEW BUFFALO BILL

SPENDS LONELY XMAS

although both his daughter and McKee were out there in time to spend
part of Christmas with him. The story brought him many letters and
made him famous, and put an end to his Lone Tree hibernation. To
keep him entertained, as well as out of mischief, his daughter and her
husband took him along the following winter on their trip to Mexico.
There he saw a bullfight and met McKee's old friend, Gordon Boyd.

In Claremore, Oklahoma, on their way back, they stopped to see
Edna and Clyde Ewing. Clyde claimed to be one fifth Cherokee Indian
and an old friend of Will Rogers, whoever that might be. Although they
had this new modern home, the Ewings spent most of their time going
up and down the country in a house trailer just a few feet shorter than
a flatcar. It had two bedrooms, a shower and a bath, with a rumpus
room said to be soundproof. In the rumpus room, since they had no
children, they kept an English bulldog named Shiloh, whose daddy had
been sold for thirty thousand dollars. Scanlon never cared for dogs, and
being too old to ride any of the Ewings' prize horses he was put in a
buggy, between Ewing and McKee, and allowed to hold the reins while
a white mare cantered. It made him hmmmphh. The Ewings were having a family reunion, but Scanlon saw no Cherokees present.

While they were there, they got on the Ewings' TV the report of a
tragedy in Lincoln: a high-school boy with a hot-rod had run down and
killed two of his classmates. An accident? No, he had run them down
as they stood in the street, taunting him. On the TV screen they showed
the boy's car, the muffler sticking up beside the windshield like a funnel,
the fenders dented where he had smashed into the boys. Then they
showed the killer, a boy with glasses, looking like a spaceman in his
crash helmet. His name was Lee Roy Momeyer—pronounced *Lee* Roy
by his family—the son of a Calloway machine-shop mechanic, and re-

lated to Scanlon by marriage. At the time he ran down and killed his classmates, he was working in a grease pit at the gasoline station where Walter McKee had used his influence to get him the job. Eighteen years of age, serious-minded, studious-looking in his thick-lensed glasses, Lee Roy was well intentioned to the point that it hurt—but a little slow. Talking to him, McKee fell into the habit of repeating himself.

"Mr. McKee," Lee Roy would say, "what can I do you for?" and McKee never quite got accustomed to it. And there he was, famous, with his picture on TV. In the morning they had a telegram from Lois's sister, Maxine Momeyer, asking if McKee would go his bail, which he did. Two days later, as they drove into Lincoln, coming in the back way so nobody would see them, there was no mention of Lee Roy Momeyer on the radio. A man and his wife had just been found murdered, but it couldn't have been Lee Roy. They had *him,* as the reporter said, in custody. Before that week was out there had been eight more, shot down like ducks by the mad-dog killer, and then he was captured out in the sand hills not far from Lone Tree. His name was Charlie Munger, and he was well known to Lee Roy Momeyer, who often greased his car. Between them they had killed twelve people in ten days.

Why did they do it?

When they asked Lee Roy Momeyer he replied that he just got tired of being pushed around. Who was pushing *who?* Never mind, that was what he said. The other one, Charlie Munger, said that he wanted to be somebody. Didn't everybody? Almost anybody, that is, but who he happened to be? McKee's little grandson thought he was Davy Crockett, and wore a coonskin hat with a squirrel's tail dangling, and Tom Scanlon, the great-grandfather, seemed to think he was Buffalo Bill. But when McKee read that statement in the paper there was just one person he thought of. His old boyhood chum, Gordon Boyd. Anybody could run over people or shoot them, but so far as McKee knew there was only one other man in history who had tried to walk on water—and He had got away with it.

McKee filed his clippings on these matters in a book entitled *The Walk on the Water,* written by Boyd after he had tried it himself. When it came to wanting to be somebody, and wanting, that is, to be it the hard way, there was no one in the same class as Boyd.

JOHN HAINES

John Haines was born in Norfolk, Virginia, in 1924, and home-steaded in Alaska for more than twenty years. He has taught creative writing at many universities, including the University of Montana, Ohio University, George Washington University, and the University of Cincinnati. His collected poems, The Owl in the Mask of the Dreamer, *were published in 1993. He has also published a collection of reviews, essays, interviews, and autobiography,* Living off the Country *(1981), and a memoir,* The Stars, the Snow, the Fire *(1989). A two-time Guggenheim fellow and a recent winner of the Western State Arts Federation Lifetime Achievement Award, Haines is currently a freelance writer, traveler, and teacher, and still spends part of each year in Alaska.*

Both "If the Owl Calls Again" (from The Owl in the Mask of the Dreamer*) and the excerpt from "Three Days" (from* The Stars, the Snow, the Fire*) provide us with a sense of the deep calm in the "wildest" landscape of the West—Alaska, where nature is both law and order, and isolation is the rule. Haines tells us not to challenge the environment, but to "take wing and glide to meet" it.*

IF THE OWL CALLS AGAIN

at dusk
from the island in the river,
and it's not too cold,

I'll wait for the moon
to rise,
then take wing and glide
to meet him.

We will not speak,
but hooded against the frost
soar above
the alder flats, searching
with tawny eyes.

And then we'll sit
in the shadowy spruce
and pick the bones
of careless mice,

while the long moon drifts
toward Asia
and the river mutters
in its icy bed.

And when the morning climbs
the limbs
we'll part without a sound,

fulfilled, floating
homeward as
the cold world awakens.

(1960)

FROM "THREE DAYS"
IN *THE STARS, THE SNOW,*
THE FIRE

The cabin is hidden in a dense stand of spruce on a bench overlooking a small, brushy creek. The creek has no name on the maps, but I have called it Cabin Creek for the sake of this camp. The ground is perhaps 1700 feet in elevation, and from the cabin I can look up and see the clear slope of Banner Dome another thousand feet above.

With its shed roof sloping north, the cabin sits low and compact in the snow, a pair of moose antlers nailed above a window in the high south wall. There are four dog houses to the rear of it, each of them roofed with a pile of snow-covered hay. A meat rack stands to one side, built high between two stout spruces, and a ladder made of dry poles leans against a tree next to it. A hindquarter of moose hangs from the rack; it is frozen rock hard and well wrapped with canvas to keep it from birds. Just the same, I see that camp-robbers have pecked at it and torn a hole in the canvas. Nothing else can reach it there, seven feet above the ground.

Nothing has changed since I was last here, and there has been no new snow. Squirrel and marten tracks are all around the cabin, and some of them look fresh; I must set a trap somewhere in the yard.

I leave the dead lynx in the snow beside the cabin; I will skin it later. I lean my walking stick by the door and ease the pack from my shoulders—I am a little stiff from the long walk, and it feels good to straighten my back. A thermometer beside the door reads thirty below.

I open the door, go inside, and set my pack down by the bunk. The cabin is cold, as cold as the outdoors, but there is birch bark and kindling by the stove, and I soon have a fire going. The small sheet-iron stove gets hot in a hurry; I watch the pipe to see that it does not burn.

As the cabin warms up I take off my parka, shake the frost from it, and hang it from a hook near the ceiling. The last time I was here I left a pot of moose stew on the floor beside the stove. Now I lift the pot and set it on the edge of the stove to thaw.

I will need water. Much of the time here I scoop up buckets of clean snow to melt on the stove. There is not much water in a bucketful of dry snow, even when the snow is packed firm, and many buckets are needed to make a gallon or two of water. But this year the snow is shallow, and it is dirty from the wind, with dust and twigs and cones from the trees around the cabin.

And so while the light stays I take a bucket and an ice-chisel, and go down to a small pond below the cabin. Under the snow the ice is clear, and in a short time I chop enough of it to fill the bucket. There is water under the ice, but I know from past use of it that the ice itself is cleaner and has a fresher taste.

Before going back up to the cabin I stand for a moment and take in the cold landscape around me. The sun has long gone, light on the hills is deepening, the gold and rose gone to a deeper blue. The cold, still forest, the slim, black spruce, the willows and few gnarled birches are slowly absorbed in the darkness. I stand here in complete silence and solitude, as alone on the ice of this small pond as I would be on the icecap of Greenland. Only far above in the blue depth of the night I hear a little wind on the dome.

I stir myself and begin walking back up the hill to the cabin with my bucket of ice. Before it is dark completely I will want to get in more wood. There are still a few dry, standing poles on the slope behind the cabin, and they are easy to cut. There will be time for that.

Past three o'clock, and it is dark once more. I am done with my chores. Inside the cabin I light a kerosene lamp by the window, and hang my cap and mittens to dry above the stove. The ice has half-melted in the bucket, and the stew is hot and steaming. I have eaten little this day, and I am hungry. I put on the kettle for tea, set out a plate, and cut some bread. The stew is thick and rich; I eat it with the bread and cold, sweetened cranberries from a jar beneath the table.

Fed and feeling at ease, I sit here by the window, drinking tea, relaxing in the warmth of the cabin. The one lamp sends a soft glow over the yellow, peeled logs. When we built this cabin I set the windows low in the walls so that we could look out easily while sitting. That is the way of most old cabins in the woods, where windows must be small and we often sit for hours in the winter, watching the snow. Now I look out the double panes of glass; there is nothing to see out there but the warm light from the window falling to the snow. Beyond that light there is darkness.

I get up from my chair, to put another stick of wood in the stove and more water in the kettle. I am tired from the long walk, and sleepy with the warmth and food. I take off my moccasins and lie down on the bunk with a book, one of a half dozen I keep here. It is Virgil's *Aeneid*, in English. I open the book to the beginning of the poem and read the first few lines. Almost immediately I fall asleep. When I wake up, it is nearly six o'clock; the fire has burned down and the cabin is chilly.

I feel lazy and contented here with nothing urgent to do, but I get up anyway and feed more wood to the stove. On my feet again, moving around, I find that I am still hungry—all day out in the cold, one uses a lot of fuel. So I heat up what remains of the stew and finish it off. Tomorrow I will cut more meat from the quarter hanging outside, and make another pot. What I do not eat, I will leave here to freeze for another day.

Having eaten and rested, I feel a surge of energy. I go outside to bring in the lynx, intending to skin it; I don't want to carry that heavy carcass home. The lynx is already stiff, beginning to freeze. I carry it in and lay it on the floor near the stove to thaw, while I make myself another cup of tea. When I can move its legs easily, I pull one of the big hind feet into my lap and begin to cut with my pocket knife below the heel where the footpad begins. The skin is stiff and cold under thick fur as it comes slowly free from the sinew.

But soon in the warmth of the room I begin to see fleas, red fleas, crawling out of the fur. One of them, suddenly strong, jumps onto me, and then to the bunk. That is enough. I put down my knife and take the lynx back outdoors. I will leave it here to freeze, and when I come again the fleas will be dead. I am in no hurry about it, and I do not want fleas in my clothing and in my bunk. Already I begin to itch.

Outside, I leave the lynx in the snow once more, and for a brief time I stand in front of the cabin, to watch and listen. The cold air feels good on my bare skin. The stars are brilliant—Polaris and the Dipper overhead. Through a space in the trees to the south I can see part of the familiar winter figure of Orion, his belt and sword; in the north I see a single bright star I think is Vega. I hear an occasional wind-sigh from the dome, and now and then moving air pulls at the spruces around me.

What does a person do in a place like this, so far away and alone? For one thing, he watches the weather—the stars, the snow and the fire. These are the books he reads most of all. And everything that he does, from bringing in firewood and buckets of snow, to carrying the waste water back outdoors, requires that he stand in the open, away from his walls, out of his man-written books and his dreaming head for a while. As I stand here, refreshed by the stillness and closeness of the night, I think it is a good way to live.

But now the snow is cold through my stocking feet, and I go back indoors. I wash the dishes and clean the small table, putting things away for the night. I hang up my trousers and wool shirts, and hang my socks on a line near the ceiling. There is still some hot water in the kettle; I pour it into a basin, cool it with a cup of cold water from the bucket, and wash my face and hands. Having dried myself and brushed my teeth, I am ready for bed.

Lying on the bunk once more, with the lamp by my left shoulder, I pick up my book and try to read again. A page, and then another. My mind fills with images: a fire in the night, Aeneas, and the flight from Troy. I drowse, then wake again. I remember Fred Campbell lying on his cot in the Lake cabin that good fall many years ago, the Bible held overhead in his hand as he tried to read. And soon he was sleeping, the book fallen to his chest. The same page night after night. I was amused at him then, but older now I see the same thing happens to me. It is the plain life, the air, the cold, the hard work; and having eaten, the body rests and the mind turns to sleep.

I wake once more and put away my book. I get up from the bunk and bank the fire, laying some half-green sticks of birch on the coals, and close down the draft. Ice has melted in the bucket, there is plenty of water for the morning.

I blow out the lamp and settle down in the sleeping bag, pulling it around my shoulders. I look into the dark cabin, and to the starlight on the snow outside. At any time here, away from the river and the sound of traffic on the road, I may hear other sounds—a moose in the creek bottom, breaking brush, a coyote on a ridge a mile away, or an owl in the spruce branches above the cabin. Often it is the wind I hear, a whispering, rushy sound in the boughs. Only sometimes when the wind blows strongly from the south I hear a diesel on the road toward Fairbanks, changing gears in the canyon. And once, far away on a warm south wind, the sound of dogs barking at Richardson.

IVAN DOIG

Ivan Doig, born in 1939, is a native of White Sulphur Springs, Montana, and was raised in a family of Scottish ranchers and sheepherders. Doig received his M.S. in journalism from Northwestern University in 1962, and worked as a reporter in the Midwest before moving to Seattle, where he earned a Ph.D. in American history from the University of Washington in 1969. This House of Sky *(1978), Doig's memoir of growing up in Montana, was nominated for a National Book Award. His other books include* Winter Brothers *(1980);* The Sea Runners *(1982);* Dancing at the Rascal Fair *(1987);* Ride with Me, Mariah Montana *(1990), a memoir focused on his mother's short life;* Heart Earth *(1993); and a novel about the building of Fort Peck Dam in eastern Montana in the 1930s,* Bucking the Sun *(1996).*

Focusing on social detail, the textures of life in the northern West as against the mythological and more often than not nonsensical bronco-busting gunfighter stories he calls "Wisterns," Doig believes "we've had too damn much of the cowboy West." In that he's right; the West was and is partways a cowboy culture, but it also was and is many other cultures—Mormon and Navajo and Chicano and Hutterite and Scottish and Basque and Baptist and wheat-farming. Doig reminds us that we are a complex set of local societies, and that our strengths arise from our diversity.

FROM *THIS HOUSE OF SKY*

By the time I was born in 1939, Dad had settled into managing, on shares, a cattle ranch owned by Jap Stewart's brother, beneath the east slope of Grass Mountain. The years there made steady money, but my mother's asthma was clenching worse and worse. The final winter of World War Two, the three of us went to Arizona to try the climate for her there. Dad started work in an aircraft factory, and almost before he was in the door was made a foreman. It may have been that my parents would have chosen Arizona for good, once the war was over and they could have had some time to talk themselves into a new direction of life. But they had arranged to run a thousand head of sheep on shares the next summer, and to give themselves one more season of the mountains. And so we came back to Montana and rode the high trail into the Bridger Range, one to her last hard breaths ever and the other two of us to the bruised time after her death.

This journey of life, then, my father had come by the autumn of 1945, when he and I began to blink awake to find ourselves with the stunted ranch he had managed to rent, and with my situation as the boy he now had to raise alone. It seems to me now that the ranch, even though it was our entire livelihood, counted little in this time. A few thousand acres hugging onto the Smith River just as it began kinking through sage foothills into the southern edge of the valley, the place had more to offer me than it did a man trying to coax a profit from it. Its shale gulches and slab-rocked slopes pulled me off into more pretend games alone than ever, more *kchews* of rock bullets flung zinging off boulders, more dream-times as I wandered and poked and hid among the stone silences. For Dad, the reaches of rock can only have been one more obstacle which cattle and sheep had to be grazed around, and my wandering games the unneeded reminder that he had a peculiar small person on his hands.

It may have been that he thought back to what his own boyhood had been like after his father died, how quickly he had grown up from the push of having to help the family struggle through. It may have been only habit, out of his years of drawing the fullest from those reluctant crews. Or maybe simple desperation. From whatever quarter it came, Dad took his decision about me. My boyhood would be the miniature of how he himself lived.

That policy of his corded us together at once, twined us in the hours of riding to look over the livestock, the mending of barbed-wire fences, all the prodding tasks of the ranch. But more than that. Dad's notion that I was fit for anything he himself might do carried me, in this time when I was a six-seven-eight-year-old, on a journey which stands in my memory as dappled and bold as the stories I heard of his own youth. For after our early months on the ranch, Dad had mended himself enough to enter the life of the valley again in full—and in the valley's terms, and his, this meant nights in White Sulphur Springs and its nine saloons.

Although he could tip down a glass of beer willingly enough, Dad was not what the valley called *a genuine drinking man*. With him, alcohol stood a distant second to the company he found along the barstools. The pattern is gone now, even from White Sulphur Springs, but in its time it was as ordered and enlivening as a regimental trooping of the colors. I come to it yet, even as Dad with me at his waist did, a night or two in mid-week and Saturday nights without miss, as a traveler into a street lit with festival.

The Stockman Bar started us for the night. Just walking through its door stepped you up onto a different deck of life. Earlier the lanky old building had been the town's movie house, and it stretched so far back from the sidewalk that its rear corners began to sidle up the hill behind the main street of town. The builder could have scooped out at the back so the floor would have come out level with the street at the front. Instead, he saved on shovels by carpentering from back to front much the way things were, and when the floorboards came out at the street about the height of a man's waist, a little ramp was angled up through them from the doorway.

It made a fine effect, the customers all at a purposeful tilt as they came climbing toward the long dark-brown span of bar. Then, sitting up on one of the Stockman's three-foot stools, you could glance out and down through the street window at passersby going along below your kneecaps. In early evening, it was a chance to look out at humanity as unseen as if you were hidden away on a shed roof, and Dad and I would settle in to watch the town's night begin to take shape.

The Stockman had other likable lines besides its lofty floor. From end to end, the wall behind the bar was almost all mirror and whiskey bottles, held in regiments by a great dark-wooded breakfront. Glass and liquor and liquor and glass reflected each other until my eyes couldn't take in the bounce of patterns. The label print and emblems would have added up to a book, and the ranks of bottles with their mirror images shouldering behind them seemed to crowd out toward us as we sat at the bar. But in gaps along the bottom shelf, saved for the clean glasses which rested mouth down on white towels, were propped the curiosities I would pick out to look at long and often—the tiny cellophane packs of white salted nuts or smoked meat strips. Every so often, someone might buy a packet and share it along the bar. Every time, the white nuts tasted as chalky as they looked, and the smoked meat let loose a seasoning which made us work each piece around in our mouths as if our tongues were gradually catching fire. These samples would disgust us all for a while, but before long I would forget just what the tastes had been, and start all over again the staring at the packets and the wondering what the snow-colored nuts or the blades of meat must be like.

Untasty as it was, the cellophane food offered the harmless choice I could focus on back of the bar. What I would look at with a peeper's stealth a hundred times an evening was the nakedness of the calendar lady.

You could depend on her year after year: some passing salesman from a brewery would provide the saloon with a long calendar to put up next to the cash register, and on the calendar just above the brewery's name would be a figure big as a sitting cat—the naked lady with breasts coming out like footballs. The style then was to photograph the kneeling calendar lady under a bluish-purple light. The play of this cold tint onto her breasts shaded the nipples down to dark pointed circles like the ends of ripe plums, and tended to make a brunette—as calendar ladies generally seemed to be, across the years—look as if she were only waiting

for the shadows to deepen one notch more before lunging points-first
right at you.

The single thing I knew about women was that I wasn't supposed
to be seeing them in this condition. I felt I had to resort to great casual
sweeps of looking: start my eyes at a high innocent corner of the whiskey
shelves, work like an inventory-taker along the bottle labels until the
neighborhood of the cash register, loiter around the cellophane snacks
while trying to sense out of the corners of my eyes whether anyone was
watching my peeping. Then straight and fast as I could, the peek right
onto the glorious purplish-blue breasts. Hard-earned gazes, every one,
but I was willing to work at it.

The Stockman had even another night-in, night-out attraction.
Against the wall opposite the bar, a smeary rainbow of colors glowed
out of the jukebox. Each shade slid in behind the fluted glass front as
you watched, maybe a dim red followed by a tired green, a mild orange
forever chased by a bruiselike purple, which was likely to remind a
person of the calendar lady again.

This slow spin of colors seemed to be the chief job of the jukebox,
because it rarely put out music. A song from it meant either there were
strangers in the saloon, or one of Dad's friends had pressed a dime into
my hand and steered me off to play a tune while he said something I
shouldn't hear. Months on end somewhere in that span of time, I spent
each bonus dime on *Good Night, Irene.* The record would slide out of
hiding and flip into place, I would press my nose against the jukebox
glass to see the needle jab down, and then I would feel the sound strum
out: *Sometimes I live in the countreeee, sometimes I live in townnnn. . . .* A
lot of times, men would turn sideways along the bar to listen as the sad
chorus went on. *Sometimes I take a great notionnnn, to jump into the river
and drownnnn . . .*

With its movie house length—long enough, in fact, to make the
trip back to the toilet a hazard for a drinker too full of beer—the Stockman at dusk would be as open and uncrowded as a sleepy depot. And
like a depot, it had someone veteran and capable in charge when the
clientele did start showing up. Always, Pete McCabe would be waiting,
watching. His soft gray shirt and the long oval of his face and bald brow
seemed fixed behind the spigot handles which thumbed up at the center
of the long bar. A dozen barrels of beer a week purled out of the spigots
under his steady pull, and never a glass of it came along the bar without
a good word from Pete McCabe.

There are listening bartenders, who are the storied ones, and there are talky bartenders, trying to jaw away the everlasting sameness of their hours. Pete was neither, and better—a bartender who knew how to visit with his customers.

When the two of us straddled onto stools across the slick bar wood from him, Pete would push a schooner of beer in front of Dad, listen close as a minister to whatever he had on his mind, and in turn begin quietly telling Dad who had come into town that day and what price they were getting for their lambs or wool or calves and how far along they were with the haying, and on into bigger currencies: *Hear they had a little flabble down the street last night. Couple of fellows squared off and pushed each other around a little. I just don't care too much for that fightin', Charlie. I don't let it get goin' in here, just have to slap 'em a little before they start in on it . . . Hear a lot about turnin' this into a big gamblin' state. I don't want to see that. It's just a sharpshooter's game, that gamblin'; you'll see the cross-roaders comin' in here like they were flies after a bunch of dead guts. . . . Government trapper was through, said they got an early snow down in that Sixteen country. About six inches of wet, heavy as bread dough. . . .*

Pete's rich ration of talk wasn't done for the business of it. In White Sulphur Springs there was steady thirsty commerce no matter how a bartender behaved. Pete simply had made it a hobby to size up people, and to work out a routine of friendship with those deserving. He had a tribute for the few best men he knew. Glancing off into the glass hodge-podge behind the bar, Pete would say slowly: *He's a nice fellow.* Slow nod, and slower again: *A real nice fellow.* When that was said, you knew the fellow must be a prince of the world. And plainly enough, Pete deemed this wry-smiling father at my side a real nice fellow.

Only now do I understand how starved my father was for that listening and gossip from Pete McCabe. Nowhere else, never in the silences of the life we led most of the time on the ranch, could he hear the valley news which touched our own situation, and in a tone of voice which counted him special. Nowhere else, either, did Dad's past as a ranchman glow alive as it did in the Stockman. Just then in its history, White Sulphur was seeing the last of a generation of aging sheepherders and cowboys and other ranch hands. Several of them, I remember, had nicknames of a style which would pass when they did: Diamond Tony, who had a baffling Middle European name and an odd, chomping accent to go with it; Mulligan John, called so for the meal which had become a habit with him in the aloneness of sheep camps; George Washington

Hopkins, the little Missourian who insisted he was from Texas, and insisted too on being called simply Hoppy; a dressy little foreigner who had been dubbed Bowtie Frenchy; other immigrant herders who rated only Swede, Bohunk, Dutchy; towering Long John and silent Deaf John. Maybe half a hundred of these men, gray and gimpy and familyless, making their rounds downtown, coming out for a few hours to escape living with themselves. Any time after dusk, you began to find them in the saloons in pairs or threes, sitting hunched toward one another, nodding their heads wise as parsons as they reheard one another's stories, remembering them before they were spoken. *Just waitin' for the marble farm,* Pete McCabe said of them with sorrow, for he enjoyed the old gaffers and would set them up a free beer now and again, *you know they'd like to have one and don't have the money for it and I never lost anything doing it for 'em.* Dad had worked with most of these men, on the Dogie or elsewhere, and their company seemed to warm him from the cold agony he had been through.

Other valuable friends could be met in the Stockman. The two I remember above the rest were as alike and different as salt and sugar. Lloyd Robinson was the unsweetened one. Some time before, he had pulled out of his saloon partnership with Pete McCabe, but he still strolled in at least once a day like a landlord who couldn't get out of the habit of counting the lightbulbs. Lloyd was a nondrinker, or at least a seldom drinker. He came by the saloon just to give his tongue some exercise. His wolfish style of teasing kept me wary, but also taught me how to put in sharp licks of my own. Usually a mock uproar broke out between us. When Lloyd glared down the slope of his belly at me and rumbled that if he had been unlucky enough to have Scotch blood in him he'd have cut his throat to let it out, it was my cue to chirp back that he might as well get at it because a Missourian like him was nothing but a Scotchman with his brains kicked out anyhow. He would glower harder and I would try to squint back through giggles, until our truce came with Lloyd's grump that he might as well buy me a soda pop as argue with a redheaded Scotchman.

Nels Nelson had a spread of belly to challenge Lloyd's, but the disposition of a kitten. Nellie drove the grader, the huge bladed machine which scraped down the ruts or cleared the snow from the county's hundreds of miles of dirt roads. He handled machinery with the touch my father had for livestock, and it may have been this turn of skill they recognized in each other that made them friends.

This big open man Nellie had almost all that a small town could offer: a job he liked and did as if born to it, a pretty home of shellacked logs looking across the end of the valley to the Castle Mountains, a wife as handsome and spirited as the palomino horses which she pastured behind their house. He also had an almighty thirst.

It was said in admiration that Nellie was a happy drinker. Each fresh head on a glass of beer delighted him more, until it seemed the next spigot's worth would send him delirious. He would parrot dialects, spiel jokes, greet any newcomer as if the fellow were his long-lost twin, spread every generosity he could think of into the knot of friends around him—and of course was destroying himself. One particular episode of Nellie's that we all laughed about when it happened was actually the worst kind of omen. One midnight, he had wobbled home, lost his footing on the kitchen linoleum, and passed out where he crashed. As he went down, one forearm flopped into the slop bucket beside the sink. He came to in the daylight to find that forearm still dangling into the curdled gray swill of greasy dishwater, potato peelings, and table scraps. A man who could wake up to that in the morning and be back downtown the very evening again drinking—and worse, telling the story on himself—was a man doomed.

Side by side with a friend splintering apart this way, I suppose my father was in a mood to simply accept that life is fatal to us all, one way or another. If he ever tried to warn off Nellie from the fierce drinking, I never heard the words. The flow of booze into his best friend or the behavior of anybody else in the Stockman, Dad took without a blink of judgment. I cannot know whether he ever thought it out entirely, but I believe that in him was the notion that anyone who began his night along the bar with us must have been tussling life in his own right, just as we were. Pete McCabe's Stockman offered a few hours of neutral ground, and the wrong words, even wise ones, might snap that truce.

Three more saloons elbowed into each other on the same block with the Stockman. Next door stood the Melody Lane, with a neon cheeriness about it which probably was supposed to go with the name. Only about a third the size of the Stockman and with plump booths where couples might be sitting and cooing, the Melody Lane seemed always to be showing off its manners more than we liked. It was the kind of enterprise better suited to mixed drinks than beer, and Dad and I seldom invested much time there. But next on the block came a favorite of ours, the Maverick, hard drinking and rollicking. Under its low

ceiling the air hazed into a murky blue, probably as much from accu-
mulating cusswords as cigarette smoke. Opening the door from the street
was like finding yourself in a sudden roaring fog. But if you had lungs
and ears for it, the Maverick was the inevitable place to find one old
friend or another bellied up sometime during the night, and it made a
good sociable stop for Dad after the warmup beer at the Stockman.

For a time, the Maverick even offered gambling. Other saloons
might slyly slip in a poker table or two, but the Maverick set up an
entire side room. If you could wedge your way in, your money might
change hands several different ways. In my memory is all of one evening
spent perched on a corner of the roulette table, boosted kindly by someone who noticed me teetering on tiptoe as I tried to see across to the
white marble whirling around the wheel. Roulette impressed me. I liked
the practiced flip of the wheel man's thumb as he sent the marble whirring around its rim of circle, the hypnotic slow fan of the wheel moving
the opposite direction, the surprise drop and glassy clatter as the marble
fell onto the wheel and skittered for a slot. I probably liked to watch
the stacks of silver dollars being pushed bravely onto the hunch numbers,
too. It was noticeable even to me that roulette players suffered out loud,
and hard, while the poker players farther back in the side room spoke
only to raise, call, and ask whether everybody had put in their ante.

You can see that the Maverick could take up all of a person's night,
if you would let it. But there were six more saloons in town, and Dad
liked to keep on the move. Across a rutted alley from the Maverick
stood a big square-fronted saloon which had earned a hard name even
in this damnless town—the Grand Central. Generally, only spreeing
sheepherders and the most derelict of drunks drank at the Grand Central,
and you could catch a case of brooding glumness just by being around
them. The upstairs floors served as the town's flophouse. *It's a stiffs' outfit,*
Pete McCabe said down his nose. The bleary way of life there was
beyond the understanding of anybody who hadn't sprawled into it, and
the ragtag men of the Grand Central were known to the rest of us only
by the stories which reeked out of the place like the stink of vomited
wine. It was told, and thoroughly believed, that one time the undertaker
had been called about a body lying head down across the stairs leading
up to the flop rooms. He was baffled to find the corpse wedged hard in
the stairwell, stiff as a side of frozen meat and apparently dead for at least
the past twenty-four hours. He was exactly right. Thinking the sprawled
victim was only drunk and sleeping it off upside down, the other in-

habitants had been lurching carefully across him on the stairs for the past day and night.

Even without tales of this sort, the Grand Central made me uneasy. Almost anything else we might meet up with while I was downtown at Dad's elbow had its excitement for me. But not the hopeless sag of those sour-smelling men. We deigned into the Grand Central only when Dad had to find someone to herd sheep or do the lowest ranch chores for a few days, and that was often enough for me.

The saloons went quicker after the Grand Central, as if we were hurrying on from its sights and smells. The place on the next block, the Mint, was the first new saloon in town in years and stood out like a salesman in a white suit. It took up half of a long stucco building, side by side with the dry goods store under a single square front as if they were the facing pages of an argument in an open book. The Mint was inky inside—which must have been thought to be modern—with the light for the entire saloon washing pale and thin from a few tubes of fluorescence behind the bar. The owner was a three-chinned man in a white shirt, which always looked milky-bluish as he bulled around carrying glasses in the squinty light. This was the one saloon in town besides the uppity Melody Lane where drinkers used the booths almost as much as the bar stools. Some Saturday nights the Mint would have two or three people plinking music at the back of the room, and couples would crowd into the booths to sit with their sides snuggled into one another from knee to shoulder.

The Mint made a start toward the politer behavior across on the south side of Main Street, which counted only four saloons to the north side's five. Politest of any in town was the saloon tucked away at the rear of the big brick hotel. Always near-empty, it seemed to have given up to the pack of busy competition down the street and simply forgotten to tell the bartender to stay home. Dad and I dropped in only when he wanted to telephone long distance to a livestock buyer in Bozeman or Great Falls. The hotel lobby had the only phone booth in town, and it did a business steadier than the house saloon ever seemed to have done.

A block or so from there stood a mix of saloon and short-order cafe, as if the owner was absentminded about just what the enterprise was supposed to be. The town long since had supposed that the size of his stomach meant he really preferred the cafe side, and so had nick-named him Ham and Eggs. Ham and Eggs' shacky little building stood almost squarely across from the Grand Central, and seemed to have caught a pall from over there. Night in, night out, there never would be anyone on the bar side of this place except Ham and Eggs himself and a few blank-eyed old sheepherders as unmoving as doorstops, and the short-order side made your stomach somersault just to glance in through the fly-specked window at it. Dad and I generally steered clear, as did anybody who had standards about saloons.

Close by, but a mile further up in likeableness, stood the Pioneer. Oldfangled but not coming-apart-at-the-heels like the Grand Central, earnest enough but not as hard drinking as the Maverick, the Pioneer felt and looked most like a cowtown saloon. Its enormous dark-wood bar and breakfront had been carved and sheened like the woodwork for a cathedral, and at the back, poker tables caught the eye like pretty wheels of green velvet. A small, sad-faced bartender stood on duty at the row of beer taps. *Hullo, Charlie; hullo, Red,* he would murmur as we stepped in, silently pull a glass of beer for Dad, and say no more until a quiet *Take it easy, Charlie; take it easy, Red,* as we went out the door.

Perhaps because of the stony bartender who had nothing else in the world on his mind except what somebody happened to recite into it, the Pioneer served as the town's hiring saloon. Ranch hands looking for a job would leave word with the bartender. Knowing this, ranchers would stride in to ask about a haying hand or somebody who knew how to irrigate. The ranch hand might have his bedroll right there along the back saloon wall, and minutes later be in the rancher's pickup on his way to the new job.

The Pioneer did its businesslike chore for the valley, and the last saloon of all, the Rainbow, did a darker one. The Rainbow gathered in the hardest drinkers of the valley and let them encourage one another.

The middling-sized saloon seemed innocent enough at first glimpse. Next door was one of the town's two cafes, also named the Rainbow, and in back, a large hall where dances were held every month or so. A sizeable portion of the county's social life took place inside the two Rainbows and the hall behind them. But soon enough, you noticed that the drinkers who came to the Rainbow night after night did not take their beer slowly and with plenty of talk, as most of the Stockman's regulars did. The Rainbow crowd—several of the town's professional men, some big ranchers, some of the showy younger cowboys—tossed down whiskey shots and quickly bought one another a next round.

The Rainbow was the one place of this night route which made me uneasy for Dad. Whenever I got sleepy in one of the other saloons,

I would go out to our pickup, clutch the gearshift up away from the edge of the seat, and curl myself down, the steering wheel over me like a hollowed moon, beneath Dad's winter mackinaw. If even that didn't keep me warm or something woke me, I would blink myself up again and hunt down Dad to start asking when we were going home. Most times his answer was, *We'll go in just a minute, son* and three or four of these automatic replies later, we would be on the road. But the rule didn't seem to hold at the Rainbow. Whatever he told me there about how soon we would be leaving, the drink buying would go on, and time stretched longer and longer into the night.

Yet not even the Rainbow became the peril to us that it could have. Dad never enlisted as one of its night-after-night drinkers; he must have seen the risk clear. Every fourth or fifth trip to town, he might end up there and we would be in for a later stay, but otherwise the routine which carried us through the other saloons and their attractions was enough for him.

For me, this span of episode at my father's side carried rewards such as few other times of my life. I cannot put a calendar on this time— more than a year, less than two—but during it, I learned an emotion for the ranchmen of the valley which has lasted far beyond their, and my, leaving of it. Judging it now, I believe what I felt most was gratitude—an awareness that I was being counted special by being allowed into this blazing grownup world, with its diamonds of mirror and incense of talk. I knew, without knowing how I knew, that there was much to live up to in this.

Past those first hard-edged months after my mother's death, then, and on into my father's wise instinct of treating me as though I already was grown and raised, my sixth-seventh-eighth years of boyhood became lit with the lives we found in the Stockman and the Maverick and the others. The widower and his son had begun to steady. But one more time, something turned my father's life, our life. A woman stepped inside the outline where my mother had been.

LARRY MCMURTRY

Larry McMurtry was born in Wichita Falls, Texas, in 1936, into a family of ranchers and cowboys. The author of eighteen novels, McMurtry won the Pulitzer prize in 1986 for his frontier epic Lonesome Dove *(1985), a book that was adapted into a successful television miniseries, as was its sequel,* The Streets of Laredo *(1993). McMurtry is one of America's most popular Western writers, and his books have been made into a long string of successful films, beginning with his first novel,* Horseman, Pass By *(1961), which was made into the award-winning* Hud; *continuing with* The Last Picture Show *(1963);* Terms of Endearment *(1975), the film version of which won the Academy Award for Best Picture in 1984; and* Texasville *(1987). In addition, he has written two books of essays—*In a Narrow Grave *(1968), and* Film Flam *(1987), about his adventures in the film business. McMurtry also owns Booked Up Inc., an enterprise specializing in antiquarian books.*

In "Take My Saddle from the Wall: A Valediction," the concluding essay to In a Narrow Grave, *McMurtry examines ways the myth of the cowboy defined the reality in which his ranch family lived. In his Western fictions, contemporary and historical, and in this essay, recognizing that horseback cowhands and ruling-class ranchers are very different creatures, McMurtry explores the culture and archetypes of the cowboy in a manner which manages to both censure and partways humanely condone the horseman's aesthetic.*

TAKE MY SADDLE FROM THE WALL: A VALEDICTION

Stranger: "Mr. Goodnight, you have been a man of vision."
Charles Goodnight: "Yes, a hell of a vision."
      —J. Frank Dobie, Cow People

Oh, when I die take my saddle from the wall,
Put it on my pony, lead him from the stall,

Tie my bones to his back, turn our faces to the West,
And we'll ride the prairie that we love the best. . . .
— *"Goodbye, Old Paint"*

For braiding I have no gift. During the time when I was nominally a cowboy I would sometimes try to braid a halter, a rope, or a bridle rein, usually with sad results. I could seldom make the strands I worked with lay easily or neatly together; and so it may be, I fear, with the braid of this book.

The reader who has attended thus far will have noticed a certain inconsistency in my treatment of Texas past and present—a contradiction of attractions, one might call it. I am critical of the past, yet apparently attracted to it; and though I am even more critical of the present I am also quite clearly attracted to *it*. Such contradictions are always a bit awkward to work with, but in this case there is even an added difficulty: the strands of subject which I have attempted to braid are not of equal width, and I have only managed to twist them into a very rough plait. That I have not been able to do a smoother job is probably due to the fact that I am a novelist, and thus quite unaccustomed to the strain of prolonged thought. My first concern has commonly been with textures, not structures; with motions, rather than methods. What in this book appear to be inconsistencies of attitude are the manifestations of my ambivalence in regard to Texas—and a very deep ambivalence it is, as deep as the bone. Such ambivalence is not helpful in a discursive book, but it can be the very blood of a novel.

I realize that in closing with the McMurtrys I may only succeed in twisting a final, awkward knot into this uneven braid, for they bespeak the region—indeed, are eloquent of it—and I am quite as often split in my feelings about them as I am in my feelings about Texas. They pertain, of course, both to the Old Texas and the New, but I choose them here particularly because of another pertinence. All of them gave such religious allegiance as they had to give to that god I mentioned in my introduction: the god whose principal myth was the myth of the Cowboy, the ground of whose divinity was the Range. They were many things, the McMurtrys, but to themselves they were cowboys first and last, and the rituals of that faith they strictly kept.

Now the god has departed, thousands of old cowboys in his train. Among them went most of the McMurtrys, and in a few more years the tail-end of the train will pass from sight. All of them lived to see the ideals of the faith degenerate, the rituals fall from use, the principal myth become corrupt. In my youth, when they were old men, I often heard them yearn aloud for the days when the rituals had all their power, when they themselves had enacted the pure, the original myth, and I know that they found it bitter to leave the land to which they were always faithful to the strange and godless heirs that they had bred. I write of them here not to pay them homage, for the kind of homage I could pay they would neither want nor understand; but as a gesture of recognition, a wave such as riders sometimes give one another as they start down opposite sides of a hill. The kind of recognition I would hope to achieve is a kind that kinsmen are so frequently only able to make in a time of parting.

I have never considered genealogy much of an aid to recognition, and thus have never pursued my lineage any distance at all. I remember my McMurtry grandparents only dimly, and in very slight detail, and only a few of the many stories I have heard about them strike me as generative. My grandfather, William Jefferson McMurtry, was the first man I ever saw who wore a mustache—a heavy grey one—and when I think of him I think first of that mustache. He died when I was four and only three stories about him have stuck in my mind.

The first was that he was a drunkard in his middle age, and that my grandmother, burdened with many children and unburdened by any conveniences, had found his drunkenness tiresome and threatened to leave him if he didn't stop drinking. The threat was undoubtedly made in earnest, and he took it so immediately to heart that he stopped drinking then and there, with a jug half-full of whiskey hanging in the saddleroom of the barn. The jug of whiskey hung untouched for nineteen years, until the nail rusted out and it fell.

I remember, too, that it was said he could stand on the back porch of the ranch-house and give a dinner call that his boys could hear plainly in the lower field, two miles away. As a boy, riding across the lower field, I would sometimes look back at the speck of the ranch-house and imagine that I heard the old man's dinner call carrying across the flats.

My grandmother's name was Louisa Francis. By the time I was old enough to turn outward, she had turned inward and was deaf, chairbound, and dying. She lived until I was nine, but I cannot recall that we ever communicated. She was a small woman, wizened by hardship, and I thought her very stern. One day when I was in my teens I went down the crude stone steps to the spring that had been for years the family's only source of water, and it occurred to me that carrying water up those steps year after year would make a lady stern. The children all spoke of William Jefferson as if they had liked him and got on with him well enough, but they spoke of Louisa Francis as one speaks of the Power. I have since thought that an element in her sternness might have been a grim, old-lady recognition that the ideal of the family was in the end a bitter joke; for she had struggled and kept one together, and now, after all, they had grown and gone and left her, and in that hard country what was there to do but rock to death?

William Jefferson, however, sustained himself well to the end, mostly I judge, on inquisitiveness. Since eleven of the twelve children were gone, my father bore the brunt of this inquisitiveness, and one can imagine that it became oppressive at times. When my father returned to the ranch late at night from a trip or a dance the old man would invariably hear his car cross the rattly cattleguard and would hasten out in the darkness to get the news, as it were. Generally the two would meet halfway between the barn and the backyard gate, William Jefferson fresh with queries and midnight speculations on the weather or this or that, my father—mindful that the morning chores were just over the hill—anxious to get to bed. By the time grandfather died the habit had grown so strong that three years passed before my father could walk at night from the barn to the backyard gate without encountering the ghost of William Jefferson somewhere near the chickenhouse.

Pioneers didn't hasten to West Texas like they hastened to the southern and eastern parts of the state. At first glance, the region seemed neither safe nor desirable; indeed, it wasn't safe, and it took the developing cattle industry to render it desirable. My grandparents arrived in 1877 and prudently paused for ten years in Denton County, some sixty miles west of Dallas and not quite on the lip of the plains. The fearsome Comanche had been but recently subdued—in fact, it was still too early to tell whether they *were* subdued. The last battle of Adobe Walls was fought in the Panhandle in 1874, and Quanah Parker surrendered himself and his warriors in 1875. The very next year, sensing a power vacuum, Charles Goodnight drove his herds into the Palo Duro; Satanta, the last great war chief of the Kiowa killed himself in prison in 1878. Remnants of the two nations trickled into the reservation for the next few years; there were occasional minor hostilities on the South Plains as late as

1879. The Northern Cheyenne broke out in 1878—who could be sure the Comanches wouldn't follow their example? To those brought up on tales of Comanche terror the psychological barrier did not immediately fall. The Comanche never committed themselves readily to the reservation concept, and for a time there remained the chance that one might awaken in the night in that lonely country to find oneself and one's family being butchered by a few pitiless, reactionary warriors bent on a minor hostility.

At any rate, in the eighties William Jefferson and Louisa Francis and their first six children moved a hundred miles farther west, to Archer County, where, for three dollars an acre, they purchased a half-section of land. They settled near a good seeping spring, one of the favorite watering places on a military road that then ran from Fort Belknap to Buffalo Springs. The forts that the road connected soon fell from use, but cattle drivers continued to use the trail and the spring for many years. The young McMurtry boys had only to step out their door to see their hero figures riding past.

Indeed, from the pictures I have seen of the original house, they could have ignored the door altogether and squeezed through one of the walls. Life in such a house, in such a country, must surely have presented formidable difficulties and the boys (there were eventually nine, as against three girls) quite sensibly left home as soon as they had mastered their directions.

The median age for leave-taking seems to have been seventeen, and the fact that the surrounding country was rapidly filling up with farmers merely served as an added incentive to departure. The cowboy and the farmer are genuinely inimical types: they have seldom mixed easily. To the McMurtrys, the plow and the cotton-patch symbolized not only tasks they loathed but an orientation toward the earth and, by extension, a quality of soul which most of them not-so-covertly despised. A "one-gallus farmer" ranked very low in their esteem, and there were even McMurtrys who would champion the company of Negroes and Mexicans over the company of farmers—particularly if the farmers happened to be German. The land just to the north of the McMurtry holdings was settled by an industrious colony of German dairymen, and the Dutchmen (as they were called) were thought to be a ridiculous and unsightly thorn in the fair flesh of the range.

In later years two or three of the McMurtry brothers increased their fortunes through farming, but this was a fact one seldom heard bruited about. Indeed, I heard no discussion of the matter until fairly recently, when one of the farms sold for an even million dollars, a figure capable of removing the blight from almost any scutcheon.

The cowboy's contempt of the farmer was not unmixed with pity. The farmer walked in the dust all his life, a hard and ignominious fate. Cowboys could perform terrible labors and endure bone-grinding hardships and yet consider themselves the chosen of the earth; and the grace that redeemed it all in their own estimation was the fact that they had gone a-horseback. They were riders, first and last. I have known cowboys broken in body and twisted in spirit, bruised by debt, failure, loneliness, disease and most of the other afflictions of man, but I have seldom known one who did not consider himself phenom-enally blessed to have been a cowboy, or one who could not cancel half the miseries of existence by dwelling on the horses he had ridden, the comrades he had ridden them with, and the manly times he had had. If the cowboy is a tragic figure, he is certainly one who will not accept the tragic view. Instead, he helps his delineators wring pathos out of tragedy by ameliorating his own loss into the heroic myth of the horseman.

To be a cowboy meant, first of all, to be a horseman. Mr. Dobie was quite right when he pointed out that the seat of the cowboy's man-hood is the saddle. I imagine, too, that he understood the consequences of that fact for most cowboys and their women, but if so he was too kindly a man to spell out the consequences in his books. I would not wish to make the point crudely, but I do find it possible to doubt that I have ever known a cowboy who liked women as well as he liked horses, and I know that I have never known a cowboy who was as comfortable in the company of women as he was in the company of his fellow cowboys.

I pointed out in Chapter 4 that I did not believe this was the result of repressed homosexuality, but of a commitment to a heroic concept of life that simply takes little account of women. Certainly the myth of the cowboy is a very efficacious myth, one based first of all upon a deep response to nature. Riding out at sunup with a group of cowboys, I have often felt the power of that myth myself. The horses pick their way delicately through the dewy country, the brightness of sunrise has not yet fallen from the air, the sky is blue and all-covering, and the cowboys are full of jokes and morning ribaldries. It is a fine action, compelling in itself and suggestive beyond itself of other centuries and other horsemen who have ridden the earth.

Unfortunately, the social structure of which that action is a part began to collapse almost a hundred years ago, and the day of the cowboy is now well into its evening. Commitment to the myth today carries with it a terrible emotional price—very often the cowboy becomes a victim of his own ritual. His women, too, are victims, though for the most part acquiescent victims. They usually buy the myth of cowboying and the ideal of manhood it involves, even though both exclude them. A few even buy it to the point of attempting to assimilate the all-valuable masculine qualities to themselves, producing that awful phenomenon, the cowgirl.

If, as I suggested earlier, the cowboy is a tragic figure, one element of the tragedy is that he is committed to an orientation that includes but does not recognize the female, which produces, in day-to-day life, an extraordinary range of frustrations. Curiously, the form the cowboy's recognition does take is literary: he handles women through a romantic convention. The view is often proffered by worshippers of the cowboy that he is a realist of the first order, but that view is an extravagant and imperceptive fiction. Cowboys are romantics, extreme romantics, and ninety-nine out of a hundred of them are sentimental to the core. They are oriented toward the past and face the present only under duress, and then with extreme reluctance.

People who think cowboys are realists generally think so because the cowboy's speech is salty and apparently straight-forward, replete with the wisdom of natural men. What that generally means is that cowboy talk sounds shrewd and perceptive, and so it does. In fact, however, both the effect and the intention of much cowboy talk is literary: cowboys are aphorists. Whenever possible, they turn their observations into aphorisms. Some are brilliant aphorists, scarcely inferior to Wilde or La Rochefoucauld; one is proud to steal from them. I plucked a nice one several years ago, to wit: "A woman's love is like the morning dew: it's just as apt to fall on a horseturd as it is on a rose." In such a remark the phrasing is worth more than the perception, and I think the same might be said for the realism of most cowboys. It is a realism in tone only: its insights are either wildly romantic, mock-cynical, or solemnly sentimental. The average cowboy is an excellent judge of horseflesh, only a fair judge of men, and a terrible judge of women, particularly "good women." Teddy Blue stated it succinctly forty years ago:

I'd been traveling and moving around all the time and I can't say I ever went out of my way to seek the company of respectable ladies. We (cowboys) didn't consider we were fit to associate with them on account of the company we kept. We didn't know how to talk to them anyhow. That was what I meant by saying that the cowpunchers was afraid of a decent woman. We were so damned scared that we'd do or say something wrong . . .[1]

That was written of the nineteenth century cowboy, but it would hold good for most of their descendants, right down to now. Most of them marry, and love their wives sincerely, but since their sociology idealizes woman and their mythology excludes her the impasse which results is often little short of tragic. Now, as then, the cowboy escapes to the horse, the range, the work, and the company of comrades, most of whom are in the same unacknowledged fix.

Once more I might repeat what cannot be stressed too often: that the master symbol for handling the cowboy is the symbol of the horseman.[2] The gunman had his place in the mythology of the West, but the cowboy did not realize himself with a gun. Neither did he realize himself with a penis, nor with a bankroll. Movies fault the myth when they dramatize gunfighting, rather than horsemanship, as the dominant skill. The cowboy realized himself on a horse, and a man might be broke, impotent, and a poor shot and still hold up his head if he could ride.

Holding up the head had its importance too, for with horsemanship went pride, and with that, stoicism. The cowboy, like Mithridates, survived by preparing for ill and not for good—after all, it sometimes only took a prairie-dog hole to bring a man down. Where emotion was concerned, the cowboy's ethic was Roman: emotion, but always emotion within measure. An uncle of mine put it as nicely as one could want. This one was no McMurtry, but an uncle-by-marriage named Jeff Dobbs. He had

1. *We Pointed Them North.*
2. *Singing Cowboy*, ed. Margaret Larkin, Oak Publications, New York, 1963, p. 60. See in this regard the well-known song "My Love Is a Rider," a song said to have been composed by Belle Starr: *He made me some presents among them a ring. The return that I made him was a far better thing. 'Twas a young maiden's heart I would have you all know, He won it by riding his bucking bronco. Now listen young maidens where e'er you reside, Don't list to the cowboy who swings the rawhide. He'll court you and pet you and leave you and go Up the trail in the spring on his bucking bronco.*

been a cowboy and a Texas Ranger, and when he had had enough of the great world he retired to the backwoods of Oklahoma to farm peanuts and meditate on the Gospels. He was a self-styled Primitive Baptist, which meant that he had a theology all his own, and he had honed his scriptural knife to a fine edge in some forty years of nightly arguments with his wife, my Aunt Minta. Neither of them ever yielded a point, and when my aunt was killed I don't think they even agreed on the book of Zechariah.

One morning not unlike any other, Aunt Minta went out in her car, was hit by a truck, and killed instantly. At this time I was in graduate school in Houston, doctoral longings in me, and I wrote Uncle Jeff to offer condolence. His reply is *echt*-cowboy:

Will answer your welcome letter.

Was glad to heare from you again, well it has rained a-plenty here the last week, the grass is good and everything is lovely . . .

Would like for you to visit me, we could talk the things over that we are interested in. What does PhD stand for? to me its post-hole digger, guess that would be about what it would stand for with all the other old Texas cowpokes . . .

I never could understand why a man wanted to spend all his life going to school, ide get to thinking about the Rancho Grandy, and get rambling on my mind, freedom to quote O. M. Roberts:

to what avail the plow or sail or land.

or life if freedom fail . . .

going to school was always like being in jail to me, life is too short, sweet and uncertain to spend it in jail.

Well, Larry, am still having trouble with my sore eye, have had it five months now, it looks like pinkeye to me, might have took it from the pink-eyed cow.

Yes it was an awful tragidy to have Mint crushed in the smashup, my car was a total loss too.

Things like that will just hoppen though. It is lonesome dreary out here in the backwoods by myself.

Don't ever join the army, if you do you will have to stay in for four years, that would be a long time to stay in the danged army, this conscription is not according to the constitution of the U.S. its involuntary servitude which is slavery . . .

Well I have just had a couple of Jehovah's witnesses visit me but I soon got them told, I think they are as crazy as a betsie bug and I don't like to be bothered with them, with this sore eye I am in a bad humour most of the time anyway, yours truly

Jeff Dobbs

I doubt that Seneca himself could have balanced the car and the wife that simply, and this about one week after she was gone.

But mention of horses and horsemanship brings me back to the Mc-Murtrys, all of whom were devoted to the horse. Indeed, so complete was their devotion that some of them were scarcely competent to move except on horseback. They walk reluctantly and with difficulty, and clearly do not care to be dependent upon their own legs for locomotion. That a person might walk for pleasure is a notion so foreign to them that they can only acquaint it with lunacy or a bad upbringing.

Much as their walking leaves to be desired, it is infinitely to be preferred to their driving. A few of them developed a driver's psychology and a driver's skills, but most of them remained unrepentent horsemen to the end; and an unrepentent horseman at the wheel of a Cadillac is not the sort of person with whom one cares to share a road. That their names are not writ large in the annals of the Highway Patrol is only due to the fact that they lived amid the lightly-habited wastes of West Texas and were thus allowed a wider margin of error than most mortals get.

As horsemen their talents varied, but only one or two were without flair. When it came to riding broncs, Jim, the second eldest, was apparently supreme. If he ever saw a horse he was afraid of no one ever knew about it, and in early Archer County his only rival as a bronc-rider was a legendary cowpuncher named Nigger Bones Hook. If the latter's skills were as remarkable as his name he must indeed have been a rider to contend with, but there are those who considered Uncle Jim his equal. Unfortunately, Uncle Jim over-matched himself early in his life and as a consequence was reduced to riding wheel chairs for some forty years. When he was fifteen, William Jefferson let him ride a strong, wild bronc that had been running loose for some years; Uncle Jim stayed on him, but he was not experienced enough to ride him safely and before the ride was over his head was popping uncontrollably. When the horse exhausted himself neither it nor Uncle Jim were able to bring their heads back to a normal position. William Jefferson took both hands and set his son's head straight, but Uncle Jim's neck was broken and he left the field that day with a pinched nerve which would eventually result in a crippling arthritis. Despite the kickback from that one early ride he went on to acquire a large ranch, a wife and family, a couple of banks and a commensurate fortune. The horse that crippled him never raised its head again and died within two days.

When Jim reached the Panhandle in 1900 he was far from done as a rider; indeed, his most celebrated feat was recorded shortly thereafter. He hired on with the ROs, a ranch owned by an extraordinary and very eccentric Englishman named Alfred Rowe, who was later to go down on the Titanic. Uncle Jim's wages were fifteen dollars a month. One day Rowe bought seventeen horses from the army, all incorrigibles that had been condemned as too wild to be ridden. Rowe offered Uncle Jim a dollar a head to ride them, and he rode them all that same afternoon, after which, convinced that he had made his fortune, he soon went into business for himself.

Roy McMurtry was apparently the only one of the nine boys to rival Jim's skill with a bucking horse, but few of the others were loath to try their hand (or their seat) with a bronc. It is quite clear that riding was the physical skill most crucially connected with the entrance into manhood. In the spring of 1910 Johnny McMurtry, then still in his teens, borrowed a horse and made his way to the Panhandle, looking for a job as a cowboy. He immediately found one with his brothers Charley and Jim, who were then partners in an operation which at times involved as many as 4,000 cattle. One would have thought that with that many cattle to hassle, a young and extraordinarily willing brother would have been an entirely welcome addition to the staff; but McMurtrys, like most cattlemen, take willingness for granted and judge solely on performance. On almost his first drive Johnny came near to achieving permanent disgrace through a lapse in horsemanship. Some eight hundred nervous yearlings were involved; the older brothers were in the process of calming them after several rather hectic stampedes, one of which had flattened a six wire fence. The cattle were almost quiet when the lapse occurred; the account I quote is from an unpublished memoir left me by Uncle Johnny:

> I rode up the bank of Sadler Creek on an old silly horse, he
> got to pitching and pitched under a cottonwood tree and
> dragged me off, then into the herd he went and stampeded
> them again, Jim didn't see it so thought the horse had pitched

me off, he caught him and brought him back to me, he was
as mad as a gray lobo wolf with hydrophobia, he told me that
if I couldn't ride that horse I had better go back to Archer
County and catch rabbits for a living, that was about the only
horse I had that I could really ride pitching and I was proud
of it and was down right insulted for Jim to think I couldn't
ride him . . .

The distinction between being drug off and being pitched off might
seem obscure to many, but not to a young man whose ego-needs were
closely bound up with horsemanship.

At any rate, all the McMurtrys could ride well enough to get themselves
out of Archer County at an early age. Invariably, the direction they rode
was northwest, toward the open and still comparatively empty plains of
the Panhandle. Specifically they rode to the town of Clarendon, near
the Palo Duro canyon, a town which in those days serviced and supplied
most of the great Panhandle ranchers, among them the JAs and the ROs.
For better or worse, Clarendon was their Paris. Charlie arrived in '96,
Bob in '99, Jim in 1900, Ed in 1902, Roy in 1910, Lawrence, Grace
and May at dates now unremembered, Jo and Jeff in 1916, and Margaret
in 1919. Even the old folks went to Clarendon for a time (1919–1925),
but doubtless found it impossible to live peacefully with so many of their
children about, and soon retreated to the balmier latitudes of Archer
County, my father with them.

That that bare and windy little town on the plains should have been
so much to my family I find a bit sad, but not inexplicable. Youth is
youth and a heyday a heyday, wherever one spends it, and it would
appear that at the turn of the century Clarendon was to cowboys what
Paris was soon to be for writers. It was the center of the action. If one
merely wanted to cowboy, there were the great ranches; and if one was
more ambitious the plains was the one place where land in quantity
could still be had cheap.

In time the McMurtrys got—and no doubt earned—their share of
that land. Most of them started as twenty dollar a month cowboys and
quit when they were far enough ahead to buy some land of their own.
Seven of the boys and two of the girls lived out their lives within a
hundred miles of Clarendon, and in time the nine boys between them

owned almost a hundred and fifty thousand acres of Texas land and grazed on it many many thousand head of cattle.

I do not intend here to attempt to describe the McMurtrys one by one. In truth, I didn't know them all that well, not as individuals, and individual character sketches would be neither very interesting nor very authoritative. Most of them were old men when I was very young, and I almost never saw them singly or for any length of time. When I saw them I saw them as a family, grouped with their wives and multitudinous progeny at the family reunions which were held more or less annually from the late forties until the middle sixties. Most of the reunions were held in Clarendon, or, to be more accurate, were held at the Clarendon Country Club, which fact alone is indicative enough of the direction the family had moved.

The Country Club sits some fifteen miles to the northwest of Clarendon, on a ridge not far from the Salt Fork of the Red. Fifteen miles is a short trot in that country and the wives of the local elite would think nothing of driving that far for some minor social function, though as I remember the clubhouse about the only social functions to which it could be adapted were dancing and drinking. Once long ago some cousins and I discovered a couple of rusty slot-machines in a broom closet, indicating that that particular form of gambling had, in those regions at least, passed out of vogue. There was a swimming pool (the one essential of all country clubs), a grove of trees for shade, a windmill for water, and a pond, I suppose, for decor. Of the sights and sounds which one associates with big-city country clubs in Texas—the polished foliage, the liveried staff, the well-parked rows of Mercedes and Lincolns, the tinkle of ice and the ploop of badly-hit tennis balls—there was nothing.

.   Thus, when I saw the McMurtrys, I saw them on the ground that had always held them, the great ring of the plains, with the deep sky and the brown ridges and the restless grass being shaken by the wind as it passed on its long journey from the Rockies south. Teddy Blue mayhap and Old Man Goodnight surely had left their horsetracks on that ridge; there one might have witnessed the coming and going of the god. One by one the old men arrived, in heavy cars with predominantly heavy wives, followed now and then by cautious off-spring in Chevrolets. The day was given over to feasting and anecdotage, in almost equal division. The barbecuing was entrusted to a Negro and a County Agent and generally consisted of about a hundred chickens (for the women and youngsters) and a side of beef (for the men, who, being cattlemen, scorned all other meat if beef were available). Vegetables were irrelevant, but there was usually a washpot full of beans, and of course, twenty or thirty cakes brought by the twenty or thirty wives. Later, should the season be opportune, a pickup full of watermelons might arrive, easily sufficient to bloat such children as were not already bloated on soda pop. Gourmandry was encouraged, indeed, almost demanded, and I recall one occasion when the son of someone's hired hand put all the young McMurtrys to shame by consuming twenty-six Dr. Peppers in the course of a single day.

In the forenoon the family normally split itself into three groups, the division following the traditional dividing line of Western gatherings: men, women, and children, or each to his own kind. After lunch every-one was too stuffed to move and mingled freely if somewhat heavily. My hundred or so cousins and I found generally that we could do with-out one another with no ill effects, and in the afternoons I picked my way gingerly among the bulging uncles and aunts, eavesdropping on such conversations as interested me. With most of my uncles I had no rapport at all. To their practiced eye it must have been evident from the first that I was not going to turn out to be a cattleman. For one thing, I wasn't particularly mean, and in the West the mischief quotient is still a popular standard for measuring the appearance of approvable masculine qualities in a youngster. Any boy worth his salt was expected to be a nuisance, if not to the adults at least to the weaker members of his own age group. I was a weaker member myself; indeed, though I don't re-member it, I believe at some early and very primitive reunion I was cast into a hog wallow or pelted with ordure or something; though the atrocity may be apocryphal it would not have been out of keeping with the spirit of such occasions. Mean kids meant strength in time of need, and how could the elders be sure that a bookish and suspiciously obser-vant youngster like myself might not in time disgrace the line? I knew from an early age that I could never meet their standard, and since in those days theirs was the only standard I knew existed I was the more defensive around them. Indeed, scared. One was mild and two were gentle: the rest, with one exception, were neither harder nor softer than saddle leather. The one exception, was, in my estimation, harder than your average saddle. Tolerance was a quality I think no McMurtry ever understood, much less appreciated, and though one or two of them came to understand mercy it was never the family's long suit.

Strength was quite obviously the family's long suit: strength of body, strength of will, and, over it all, strength of character. One of my difficulties with them was that their strength of character was totally and inflexibly committed to a system of values that I found not wholly admirable. The talk beneath the reunion tent was the talk of men whose wills had begun to resent their weakening bodies. They had all, like Hector, been tamers of horses once—adventure and physical hardship had been the very ground of their manhood. The talk was often of the hardships of their youth, hardships that time with its strange craft had turned into golden memories. As I listened and grew older I became, each year, more sharply aware of the irony of the setting: that those men, who in their youth had ridden these same plains and faced their winds and dangers, should in their age buy so puny a symbol as the Clarendon Country Club, the exultantly unbourgeois and undomestic ideal of the Cowboy expiring in the shade of that most bourgeois and most domestic institution. To give them credit, though, I doubt that any of them were happy about it.

Of all the hardship stories I heard, the one which remains most resonant in my mind is the story of the molasses barrel. It was, for all witnesses, a traumatic event. Late one fall, not long after the turn of the century, William Jefferson had gone to the small town of Archer City to purchase the winter's provisions. Archer City was eighteen miles from the ranch, a tedious trip by wagon. He returned late in the afternoon, and among the supplies he brought back was an eighty-pound barrel of good sorghum molasses, in those days the nearest thing to sugar that could be procured. Such sweetening as the family would have for the whole winter was in the barrel, and all gathered around to watch it being unloaded. Two of the boys rolled the barrel to the back of the wagon and two more reached to lift it down, but in the exchange of responsibilities someone failed to secure a hold and the barrel fell to the ground and burst. Eighty pounds of sweetness quivered, spread out, and began to seep unrecoverably into the earth. Grace, the oldest girl, unable to accept the loss, held her breath and made three desperate circles of the house before anyone could recover himself sufficiently to catch her and pound her on the back. Indeed, the story was usually told as a story on Grace, for most of them had suppressed the calamity so effectively that they could not remember how anyone else had responded. They could speak with less emotion of death and dismemberment than of that moment when they stood and watched the winter's sweetness soak into the chickenyard.[3]

Uncle Johnny, the seventh boy, was born in 1891. He was my favorite uncle and in many ways the family's darling, and I should like to write of him in some detail. Of them all, he fought the suburb most successfully, and hewed closest to the nineteenth century ideal of the cowboy. He was the last to be domesticated, if indeed he ever was domesticated, and at one point he almost abandoned the struggle to be a rancher in order to remain a free cowboy. Indeed, according to the memoir he left me, the desire to be a cowboy was his first conscious desire:

> Dad had built two log barns and we boys would climb on
> top of those barns and watch the herds go by, never since then
> have I wanted to be anything except a cowboy . . .

By the time he was twelve he could chop cotton well enough to consider himself financially independent, and after only a month or two of labor was able to buy a secondhand saddle. By that time he had completed such text-books as the little school-house on Idiot Ridge possessed, and he was not again impeded by education until 1909, when Louisa Francis persuaded him to enroll in a business college in McKinney. The school was teeming with chiggers, but Uncle Johnny applied himself grimly and in only four months acquired a diploma stating that he was a Bachelor of Accounts. He was the only McMurtry to achieve such eminence, and was also, ironically, the only McMurtry ever to go formally broke.

As soon as his course was finished he had to begin to think about paying for it. He went home, borrowed a horse, and headed for the Panhandle, equipped with his original secondhand saddle and seven dollars in cash. He meant to hire on with the JAs, but stopped by first to visit Charley and Jim at their ranch on the Salt Fork of the Red. They

---

3. It now appears that the uncle who first told me this sad story had added a few flowers of his own. What "really happened," it seems, is that the barrel of molasses had a wooden spigot, and was unloaded safely and laid across two supportbeams so that when the spigot was opened the molasses would drain into the molasses pitcher. Unfortunately, a sow came along one day, walked under the barrel, and rooted the spigot out. The molasses drained from the barrel and ran down a footpath all the way to the lots. The catastrophe was thus discovered and the children lined up beside the path to weep. As with many family stories, I think I prefer the fiction to the truth.

were shrewd men and doubtless knew a good thing when they saw it riding up. They hired him immediately at twenty dollars a month and keep, which meant, apparently, that he was allowed to eat whatever small vermin he could catch. Not that Uncle Johnny cared: at this time his eagerness for the cowboy life was little short of mystical. He was willing to forego eating, if necessary, and fortunately had never much liked to sleep either. Fortunately, since to his brothers 3 A.M. was traditionally the end of the night.

He worked for Charley and Jim three years, much of that time in a bachelor camp on the baldies, as the high plains were then called. His possessions consisted of a saddle, shirt, pants, and chaps, two quilts, a six-shooter, and a horse called Sugar-in-the-Gourd. In coolish weather his brothers generously provided him with a teepee, a small stove, and a bucket of sourdough. He spent his wages on cattle—there being nothing else in his vicinity to spend them on—and when his brothers phased him out in 1913 he had paid off the business college and was fifteen hundred dollars to the good.

The yen to work for a really big ranch was still strong in him, so he drifted southwest to the Matadors and hired on with them two days before the wagons pulled out for the spring roundup in 1913. The Matador, like the ROs, was English-owned; they then ran 50,000 head of cattle on slightly over a half-million acres of land. By August Uncle Johnny had helped in the rounding up and shipping of some 19,000 steers, and by early December had assisted in the branding of 11,000 calves.

From the minute he saw the Matador wagons he seemed to realize that he had found his blood's country, and he often said that if he could choose three years to live over they would be the years he had spent with the Matadors. Much of the memoir is devoted to those years, and to the men he worked with: Weary Willie Drace, his wagon-boss, Rang Thornton, Pelada Vivian, and the Pitchfork Kid, names which mean nothing now. In speaking of their departed comrades, men once renowned but soon to be forgotten, old cowboys invariably draw upon the same few images, all of them images taken from their work. Thus, here is Teddy Blue, speaking of the men who had gone with him in the seventies up the long trail to the Yellowstone:

Only a few of us are left now, and they are scattered from Texas to Canada. The rest have left the wagon and gone ahead

across the big divide, looking for a new range. I hope they
find good water and plenty of grass. But wherever they are is
where I want to go.[4]

And here, a generation later, is Uncle Johnny, speaking of his buddy the
Pitchfork Kid:

His equal will never be seen on earth again and if he is
camping the wagon and catching beeves in the great perhaps
and I am fortunate enough to get there I won't be foolish
enough to try and run ahead of him and catch the beef, I know
it can't be done . . .

By October of 1915 he had increased his savings to $2500 and he de-
cided to take the leap from cowboying to ranching, clearly one of the
harder decisions he ever made:

I left the wagon at the Turtle Hole, I have never before or
since hated to do anything as bad as I hated to leave that wagon
and to this day when I go down through there I am filled with
nostalgia, just looking at the old red hill in Croton, the breaks
on the Tongue River and the Roaring Springs, if I had known
that leaving was going to be that hard I would have stayed and
worn myself out right there . . .

Where he went was a ranch in the sandy country south of Muleshoe,
near the New Mexico line, and he stayed there the rest of his life. He
struggled for more than ten years to keep the first ranch he bought, lost
it and went stone broke in 1930, struggled back, and died owning several
thousand acres, several hundred cows, and a Cadillac.

I saw Uncle Johnny's ranch for the first time when I was in my early
teens and went there for a reunion. Three times in all he managed to
capture the reunion for Muleshoe, and for the children of the family
those were high occasions, quite different in quality from anything Clarendon offered. To begin with, Uncle Johnny lived far out in the
country—and such country. I thought the first time I saw it that only

4. *We Pointed Them North.*

a man who considered himself forsaken of God would live in such country, and nothing I have found out since has caused me to alter that view.
The more I saw of it the more I knew that he had been well-punished
for casting over the Edenic simplicity of the Matador wagons.

Then too, the house in which he lived, or, at least, in which he
might have lived, was a bit out of the ordinary. It was a towering three-
story edifice, reminiscent of the house in *Giant*. Every grain of paint had
long since been abraded away by the blowing sand. The house had been
built by an extremely eccentric New York architect, who must also have
considered himself forsaken of God. Indeed, in the long run he probably
was, for solitude and his wife's chirpings eventually drove him mad and
he came in one morning from chopping wood, called her into the basement, and killed her on the spot with the flat of his axe, or so legend
had it. No one had ever bothered to remove the basement carpet, and
the spot, or splotch, remained. Nothing could have had a more Dos-
toevskian impact on such simple Texas kids as we were than that large
irregular stain on the basement rug. A good part of every Muleshoe
reunion was given over to staring at it, while we mentally or in whispers
tried to reconstruct the crime.

When we grew tired of staring at the spot we usually turned our
attentions to the player piano. The architect had apparently been as nos-
talgic for Gotham as Uncle Johnny was for the Matador wagons, since
the piano was equipped with duplicate rolls of "The Sidewalks of New
York" and a number of other ditties that must have evoked really choking memories amid those wastes. There were also a few spiritual items
such as "The Old Rugged Cross," meant, no doubt, for his wife's Bible
group. Over the years Uncle Johnny had developed a keen distaste for
the piano, or perhaps for the selection of rolls, and he was always dashing
in and attempting to lock it, an endeavour in which he was somehow
never successful.

He himself appeared not to care for the house, and slept in the little
bunk-house. The only sign that he ever inhabited the big house was
that the bed in the master bedroom had eleven quilts on it, compensation, no doubt, for having wintered on the baldies with one blanket,
one soogan and a wagon sheet. He generally had in his employ a decrepit
cook of sorts (male) and one or two desperately inept cowboys, usually
Mexican. These slept in the bunkhouse too, or did if they were allowed
the leisure to sleep. All the McMurtrys were near-fanatic workers, but
Uncle Johnny was by all accounts the most relentless in this regard. His

brothers often said, with a certain admiration, that Johnny never had learned how much a horse or a human being could stand. Such humans as worked for him stood as much as he could stand, or else left; and he had to an extraordinary degree that kind of wiry endurance which is fairly common in the cow country. His health broke when he was thirty-three and he was partially crippled the rest of his life, but it hardly seems to have slowed him down. He could not be kept in bed more than five hours a night, and even with one leg virtually useless sometimes branded as many as eight hundred cattle in one day; once, indeed, he vaccinated 730 off the end of a calf-draggers rope in one afternoon.

In the last ten years of his life he sustained an almost incredible sequence of injuries, one following on another so rapidly that he could scarcely get from one hospital to the next without something nearly fatal happening to him. His arthritis was complicated by the fact that his right leg had been broken numerous times. Horses were always falling with him and on him, or throwing him into trees, or kicking him across corrals. The McMurtrys seemed to consider that these minor injuries were no more than he deserved, for being too tight to buy good horses instead of young half-broken broncs. He appreciated good horses, of course, but when he had something to do would get on any horse that stood to hand. One leg was broken almost a dozen times in such manner and near the end he was so stiff that he had his cowboys wire him on his horses with baling wire, a lunatic thing to do considering the roughness of the country and the temperament of most of the horses he rode.

In the late fifties he got cancer of the throat and had his entire larynx removed. For awhile he spoke with an electric voice-box, a device which rendered his dry, wry wit even dryer and wryer. He soon grew dissatisfied with that, however, and learned to speak with a esophigal voice; it left him clear but barely audible and greatly reduced his effectiveness as a raconteur. No sooner was he home from the hospital after his throat operation than he got out to shut a gate and let his own pickup run over him, crushing one hip and leg horribly. He managed to dig himself out and crawl back to his ranch, and was immediately flown back to the same hospital.

In time he recovered and went home to Muleshoe and got married, this in his sixty-fifth year. The day after his wedding, so I am told, he and Aunt Ida, his bride, spent some eleven hours horseback, sorting out a herd of cattle he had bought in Louisiana. Two years later, while on their way to Lubbock, a car ran into them on the highway and broke them both up like eggshells. Aunt Ida got a broken back and knee, Uncle Johnny two broken knees and a bad rebreakage of his crippled leg. In time they both recovered but Uncle Johnny was scarcely home before he allowed a whole feedhouse full of hundred-pound sacks of cattlefeed to fall on top of him, breaking his leg yet again.

In the days of the Muleshoe reunions, most of these disasters were still in the future and he was very much his vigorous self. He owned a Cadillac at this time, but did almost all of his driving in an army surplus jeep of ancient vintage, so ancient, in fact, that it lacked both roof and seats. The small matter of the seat Uncle Johnny took care of by turning a syrup-bucket upside down in the floorboards and balancing a piece of two-by-four across it. This worked well enough for day-to-day driving, but once when he set out to haul a trailerful of pigs to Lubbock the arrangement proved imperfect. The pigs turned over the trailer, the wrench threw Uncle Johnny off the syrup bucket, and jeep, trailer, uncle and swine ended up in a heap in the bar-ditch. He was not much hurt in the accident but was very out of temper before he managed, afoot and with only one usable leg, to get the seven wild pigs rounded up again.

Few of the McMurtrys were devoid of temper and he was not one of those who lacked it, yet I think no child ever sensed his temper. Children found him extraordinarily winning, the perfect uncle and instant confidant. He brought a quality to uncleship that only certain childless men can bring—adult, and yet not domestic. I had always supposed him a truly gentle man and was very shocked, one night, to hear him say that the way to handle Mexicans was to kick loose a few of their ribs ever now and then. I had only to reflect on that awhile to realize that I had never known a cowboy who was also a truly gentle man. The cowboy's working life is spent in one sort of violent activity or other; an ability to absorb violence and hardship is part of the proving of any cowboy, and it is only to be expected that the violence will extend itself occasionally from animals to humans, and particularly to those humans that class would have one regard as animals.

One of the more dramatic manifestations of Uncle Johnny's temper occurred just prior to the last of the Muleshoe reunions. For nostalgia's sake he grazed a few animals of even greater vintage than his jeep, among them a large male elk and an aging buffalo bull. The two animals were never on very good terms, and indeed the old buffalo was regarded as a great nuisance by everyone attached to the ranch. A few days before the reunion someone, Uncle Johnny most likely, made the mistake of leaving the elk and the buffalo alone in the same pen for an hour. The two soon joined in battle, and the battle raged freely for quite some time, neither combatant able to gain a clear advantage. When Uncle Johnny happened on the scene, half of his corrals had been flattened and much of the rest knocked hopelessly awry. Enraged, he at once found in favor of the elk and shot the buffalo dead on the spot. An hour later, when he was somewhat cooler, the Scotch took precedence over the Irish in him and he decided that it might be a novelty (as it would certainly be an economy) to barbecue the buffalo and serve him to the clan. He thus set free the fatted calf that had been meant for that fate and had the buffalo towed to the barbecue pit. It was barbecued, I believe, for forty-eight hours and on the day of the reunion its flesh proved precisely consistent with the McMurtry character: neither harder nor softer than saddle leather. How long one should have had to chew it to break down its resistance I did not find out.

There is yet one more story about Uncle Johnny, and it is the story which slides the panel, as Mr. Durrell might put it. We have seen him so far as the dashing young cowboy and the lovable family eccentric, and I should probably have always thought of him in those terms if the last story had not come to me. It came as I left for college and was offered as a safeguard and an admonition.

While still young, Uncle Johnny had the misfortune to catch what in those days was called a social disease. Where he got it one can easily imagine: some grim clapboard house on the plains, with the wind moaning, Model A's parked in the grassless yard, and the girls no prettier than Belle Starr. His condition became quite serious, and had my father not gone with him to a hospital and attended him during a prolonged critical period he might well have died.

Instead, he recovered, and in gratitude gave my father a present. Times were hard and Uncle Johnny poor but the present was a pair of spurs with my father's brand mounted on them in gold—extraordinary spurs for this plain country.

Since then, my father has worn no other spurs, and for a very long time Uncle Johnny took on himself the cloth of penance—the sort of penance appropriate to the faith he held. For all McMurtrys and perhaps all cowboys are essentially pantheists: to them the Almighty is the name of drought, the Good Lord the name of rain and grass. Nature is the only deity they really recognize and nature's order the only order they hold truly sacred.

The most mysterious and most respected part of nature's order was the good woman. Even the most innocent cowboy was scarcely good enough for a good woman, and the cowboy who was manifestly not innocent might never be good enough, however much he might crave one. Instead, he might choose just such a setting as Uncle Johnny chose: a country forsaken of God and women, the rough bunkhouse, the raw horses and the unused mansion, the sandstorms and the blue northers— accoutrements enough for any penance.

At sixty-five he married a woman he had known for a very long time. When he began to court her he discovered, to quote the memoir, that "she was a much better woman than I was entitled to." Even after they married it was some time before he considered himself quite worthy to occupy the same house with her. Perhaps when he did he let the penance go. Despite the series of injuries, his optimism grew, he bought new land, began to talk of a long-postponed world cruise, and wrote on the last page of his memoir:

> I have had my share of fun and am still having it, we have a lot of plans for the future and expect to carry them out . . .

Ruin had not taught him well at all. A short while after the feed fell on him he learned that he had cancer of the colon. From that time on he was in great pain. His will to live never weakened, indeed, seemed to increase, but this time the cancer was inexorable and he died within three years, his world cruise untaken.

In July of 1965, eight months before he died, Uncle Johnny attended his last reunion. It was held at the Clarendon Country Club, on a fine summer day, and as reunions went it was a quiet, sparsely attended affair. There was a light turnout of cousins and no more than a dozen or two small children scattered about. The food was catered this time, and just as well, too; the Homeric magnificence of some of the earlier feasts would have been largely wasted on the tired and dyspeptic McMurtrys who managed to drag themselves to the plains that day. Charlie and Jim were dead, several of the others were sick, and most of the survivors had long since ruined their digestions.

The talk was what the talk had always been, only the tones had more audible cracks and the rhythms were shorter. Once I saw Uncle Bob, who was just recovering from a broken hip, trying to talk to Uncle Johnny, who was still recovering from his final broken leg. It was a fine paradigm of the existential condition, for the two brothers were standing on a windy curve of the ridge, moving their mouths quite uselessly. Uncle Johnny had almost no voice and Uncle Bob even less hearing, and indeed, had they been able to communicate they would probably only have got in a fight and injured themselves further, for they were not always in accord and it was rumoured that only a few months earlier they had encountered one another on the streets of Amarillo and almost come to blows.

Uncle Johnny, all day, was in very great pain, and only the talk and the sight of the children seemed to lift him above it. Finally it was three o'clock and the white sun began to dip just slightly in its arch. It was time for he and Aunt Ida to start the two hundred mile drive back to Muleshoe. Uncle Johnny reached for his white Stetson and put it on and all of his brothers and sisters rose to help him down the gentle slope to the Cadillac. Most of the women were weeping, and in the confusion of the moment Aunt Ida had forgotten her purse and went back to the tables to get it, while Uncle Johnny, helped by the lame and attended by the halt, worked his way around the open door of the car and stood there a few minutes, kissing his sisters goodbye. Though he was seventy-five and dying there was yet something boyish about him as he stood taking leave of the family. He stood in the frame that had always contained him, the great circular frame of the plains, with the wind blowing the grey hair at his temples and the whole of the Llano Estacado at his back. When he smiled at the children who were near the pain left his face for a second and he gave them the look that had always been his greatest appeal—the look of a man who saw life to the last as a youth sees it, and who sees in any youth all that he himself had been.

The family stood awkwardly around the car, looking now at Uncle Johnny, now at the shadow-flecked plains, and they were as close in that moment to a tragic recognition as they would ever be: for to them he had always been the darling, young Adonis, and most of them would never see him alive again. There were no words—they were not a wordy people. Aunt Ida returned with her purse and Uncle Johnny's last young grin blended with his grimace as he began the painful task of fitting himself into the car. In a few minutes the Cadillac had disappeared behind the first brown ridge, and the family was left with its silence and the failing day.

There, I think, this book should end: with that place and that group, witnesses both to the coming and going of the god. Though one could make many more observations about the place, about the people, about the myth, I would rather stop there, on the sort of silence where fiction starts. Texas soaks up commentary like the plains soak up a rain, but the images from which fiction draws its vibrancy are often very few and often silent, like those I have touched on in this chapter. The whiskey jug hanging in the barn for nineteen years; the children, rent with disappointment around the puddle of molasses; the whorehouse and the goldmounted spurs. And Uncle Jeff, alone in the backwoods with his bad eye and his memories of the Rancho Grandy; and Uncle Johnny, riding up the Canadian in 1911 on a horse called Sugar-in-the-Gourd, and, only four years later, riding away bereft from the Roaring Springs, the dream of innocence and fullness never to be redeemed.

Those images, as it happens, all come from Old Texas, but it would not be hard to find in today's experience, or tomorrow's, moments that are just as eloquent, just as suggestive of gallantry or strength or disappointment. Indeed, had I more taste for lawsuits I would list a few for balance. Texas is rich in unredeemed dreams, and now that the dust of its herds is settling the writers will be out on their pencils, looking for them in the suburbs and along the mythical Pecos. And except to paper riders, the Pecos is a lonely and a bitter stream.

I have that from men who rode it and who knew that country round—such as it was, such as it can never be again.

MARY CLEARMAN BLEW

Mary Clearman Blew was born in Lewiston, Montana, in 1939. She grew up on the site of her great-grandfather's homestead in Fergus County, Montana. She holds B.A. and M.A. degrees from the Uni-

*versity of Montana, and received her Ph.D. from the University of
Missouri at Columbia. Currently she lives in Moscow, Idaho, with
her youngest daughter, Rachel, and teaches creative writing at the University of Idaho. All But the Waltz (1991) won the 1992 Pacific
Northwest Booksellers Association Award. Her most recent book, Bal-
samroot: A Memoir, was published in 1994. She is also the author
of two collections of short stories—Lambing Out (1977) and Runaway (1989)—and was one of the co-editors of The Last Best
Place: A Montana Anthology (1988), and is co-editor, with Kim
Barnes, of Circle of Women (1994), an anthology of contemporary
Western women writers.*

*This selection, from the autobiographical All But the Waltz,
tells us of a woman on the Eastern front of the Rockies who, after
escaping the poor-farmer life she was born to, is now faced with di-
vorcing her wildcatting free-flying husband, again escaping the con-
straints of the conventional map of womanhood in the West. A native
of the Montana highline, Mary Clearman Blew writes about working
her way toward freedom.*

FROM *ALL BUT THE WALTZ*

During the long summer of 1982 I could forget for weeks at a time
what was wrong with my husband. Those mornings dawned, one after
another, in the transparent blue that foretold hundred-degree heat by
noon, and he slept while I woke slowly in the pattern of light cast
through the birch leaves outside our window, and he slept while I show-
ered and pulled on a cotton dress and sandals for the office. I was expecting a baby in September, and my every exertion, heaving myself out
of a chair, carrying the breakfast plates to the sink, letting myself out the
back door and down the steps to my car in the already sweltering morning, cost me a deeper investment in my cocoon of self-absorption.

I had never supposed I would be pregnant again, not after twenty
years. As my body swelled and my pace slowed in a sensation of suspended time, I remembered the pregnant teenager I had been as I might
have remembered another woman, a passing acquaintance turned up
again after more than twenty years. I drove to work already panting for
breath in what passed for morning cool, along the residential streets of

Havre where sprinklers plied the lawns for their allotted hours in the drought, and at five o'clock, arching my back against the ache, I drove home through the haze of dust that had filtered in from the fields. My feet and hands had swollen from the heat until I could not wear my shoes or wedding ring. I felt as though I would always be pregnant.

Except for occasional shortness of breath, Bob was still himself. Earlier in the spring he had driven out to the farm every day at first light for the brief frenetic weeks of spring seeding, but now, in the midsummer space between seeding and harvest, he had little to do but worry about the drought. He got up at noon, had breakfast downtown, drank coffee, and talked about rain with the other farmers.

By the beginning of the 1980s, Havre no longer rocked all night long as it had in the glory days of oil and gas exploration on the highline. The big poker games downtown had closed when the mudmen and the landmen and the drillers and toolpushers and roughnecks went broke or moved to Wyoming in search of new oil developments or, like Bob, went into soberer lines of work. But there were little poker games around town, at the Oxford Bar or PJ's Lounge, for a man looking for a distraction from the weather. At two or three in the morning I would hear the familiar sound of his Wagoneer in the driveway and rouse as Bob slipped into bed beside me, his arm raised to encompass mine as I turned, heavy-bellied, into the curve of his back. He had not yet, not perceptibly, begun to lose muscle tone.

In January he had had the flu, and it seemed to hang on. Sometimes, heading down the three back steps toward his Wagoneer, he had to stop and double over, gasping to get his breath in great racking heaves that left him exhausted. There seemed to be no reason for his lack of breath; he had no other symptoms.

"You ought to see a doctor," I said.

"Oh hell, I'm all right."

As the winter wore on he admitted that the boys down at the coffee shop were urging him to get in and see the doc. Hell, maybe it was mono.

I made an appointment with the doctor for him, but he didn't show up for it.

I had plenty else to think about. Bob and I had been married four years, had been together seven years, and my pregnancy seemed too good to be true. I was undergoing amniocentesis and furnishing a nursery and dreaming about this baby as I had not had the time or inclination when, in my teens, my other children had been born.

Besides, it didn't seem possible that Bob could be sick. He was too crazy, too lucky, too full of the zest of living.

The son of a Kansas cattleman, Bob had left the ranch early for the glamour of the oil patch. Starting out as a roughneck, he went on to sell tools and oil field supplies, then to operate a fleet of water trucks, then to his own drilling rigs. He rode the roller coaster of oil and gas exploration and production, addicted like a gambler to the upward swoops and the adrenaline rushes, landing on his feet when he hit bottom, starting over on another of his nine lives. He came to Havre in the early 1970s, broke, to make a new start drilling gas wells into the shallow Judith River and Eagle formations. He went broke again and lost his rigs, but then he hit a lucky streak, scalping oil field pipe. When I met him, he was rolling in money.

"Hell, I'm the luckiest son of a bitch I know," he told me.

He bought himself an airplane and a new Wagoneer, and he bought electric guitars for his sons in Kansas. When he began spending money on my children, buying them new cowboy boots and saddles, I was transfixed; I'd never seen money flow like . . . well, like water. Born in a drought myself, brought up in the hard-luck tradition of the depression, I could no more have spent money the way Bob did than I could have let water run, wasted, out of a tap. And yet, God, I liked to watch him spend it.

Bob had a jester's license to pull off every audacious stunt I might have longed to try but been afraid to all my life. Under his tutelage I learned to pilot a plane. I let him initiate me into the mile-high club in sweet daylight at ten thousand feet, with the plane on automatic pilot through pillows of cumulus; I flew with him to Calgary, to Houston; and I drank with him in petroleum clubs in the blue haze of the Marlboros he chain-smoked. Through him I met the ragtag and bobtail, newly rich and newly busted exotics of the oil patch, and I listened to their boasting, fatalistic stories of success and disaster. After living twenty years of my life in diligence on college campuses, Bob's exuberance, his grasshopper's delight in the sunlit present, flowed through me like an elixir. I loved his soft Kansas voice, just touched with the flat twang of the Oklahoma border, and I loved his blond hair and diamond-blue eyes and his grin, and I loved his loving me.

After he had spent most of his money, he bought farmland north of Havre and gambled all over again on the weather. I married him in 1978. I wasn't worried; I had a good enough job to pay the bills.

The trees that used to arch over the streets in the heart of Great Falls have been cut down. Ancient cottonwoods with their upper branches lopped against the rot still cast shade over the rambling old residences in the central district, but the Great Falls Clinic abuts the pavement and seems to levitate in the sun. In June of 1982 I used to sit in one of its windowless waiting rooms, stabbing away at a piece of needlepoint and listening to the air-conditioning until I could listen no longer and would heave myself out of the chair and limp through the doors and into the scorching heat.

Across from the clinic was a sandwich shop called the Graham Cracker. I would limp across the street and sit at a tiny Formica table where I sipped bitter coffee and listened to the vibrations of another air conditioner and watched the heat shimmer off the cement on the other side of the plate glass until that, too, became intolerable. As I limped back across the street to the clinic my feet felt like hot sponges. I imagined a tiny squirt of fluid out of my sandals with every step I took.

A week earlier I had gone to a state humanities committee meeting at Big Sky Resort, south of Bozeman, Montana, and Bob had thrown his golf clubs in the back of my car and gone along. It was a chance for us to have a few days away together, and I looked forward to it. Surely, once he got away from the dust of the highline and his fields of shriveled crops, Bob would be himself again.

But as we turned off the interstate and left the plains, climbing along a highway that follows the Gallatin River where it plunges and dashes from its source, twisting through crags and pines and extravagant outcroppings, Bob grew moody. When we reached the resort and checked into our room, he dropped on the bed and closed his eyes.

"You go ahead," he finally muttered. "I don't want anything to eat."

"Where's Bob?" friends asked when I went down to dinner alone, and I answered, "He isn't feeling well."

I felt more annoyed than alarmed. He had no symptoms that I could see but his inexplicable fatigue. I knew he had fought secret bouts with depression for years, but what was he depressed about?

His crops? But every farmer was a gambler, every farmer faced the perils of drought, blight, rain at the wrong time. When had Bob ever backed away from a gamble?

The baby?

No, I couldn't believe that. But there had always been about Bob a hidden sadness, a deep private well into which the jester sometimes retreated while the face went on smiling.

By lunch the next day he pulled himself together and came downstairs to sit on the terrace under the firs with everyone else, but he had little to say, and when one of my friends made an offhand remark, Bob snarled a retort that briefly stopped all conversation. That evening he would not leave the room at all.

"You need to eat something," I argued. "You missed dinner last night, and again tonight—no wonder you're exhausted."

"I don't want a thing," he said. He lay on the bed with his eyes closed, breathing in short gasps.

"What's wrong?"

"Nothing. I just feel like hell. I'm tired."

"Could you eat if I carried you some soup on a tray?"

"Just let me alone!"

I went downstairs alone. I was angry and frightened. What I had hoped would be a tiny vacation with my husband had turned ugly, and I didn't know why.

The next morning was Saturday. The committee concluded its business and adjourned. Everyone was hurrying back and forth with luggage to check out of the resort by eleven. I went upstairs and let myself into the room with my key. The windows were darkened, and Bob slept, naked, on the bed. His clothing and shaving gear were scattered where he had dropped them.

"Just—lemme rest," he muttered.

I sat down on the bed. "We have to check out."

He opened his eyes, closed them and sighed.

"Do you want me to try to find a doctor?" I asked. We were thirty miles from Bozeman and the nearest medical facilities.

He raised his head off the pillow, let it drop. "Hell no, just—lemme rest a minute."

I sat on the bed a moment longer, trying to decide what to do. I couldn't lift him. He still had, at that time, the frame and weight of the college halfback he once had been, and all 185 pounds of him was inert on the bed. The unreality of it all was defeating me. Call an ambulance?

All the way from Bozeman? Surely not. After all, I had seen Bob sink into spells of lassitude before, go into strange fugues of enervation when he seemed incapable of getting out of bed—was this one any different? *Well, yes, it was.* But how?

At last I gathered up the folds of my dress, got up from the bed, and moved slowly around the room, picking up his clothing and packing his shaving kit. Then I made two trips to carry two suitcases down to the lobby, putting my feet carefully down in front of me on stairs I could not see. I brought the car around and parked it in the no-parking zone, as close to the main doors of the resort as I could get it.

"Can you get dressed?" I asked him, back in the darkened room once more.

He roused and nodded. He swung his legs off the bed and then doubled over, his head between his knees.

"Shall I try to find a doctor?" I asked again.

The word *doctor* irritated him into effort. "Don't need a goddamned doctor," he growled, and he sat up and eased his arm into the shirtsleeve I held. Shirt, pants, loafers, and then he stood up, white-faced. Leaning on me, he managed the corridor and the stairs. Once in the lobby, in the sight of other people, he made the effort to straighten and walk by himself out to the car.

I drove down the twisting highway along the Gallatin River while Bob lay back in the passenger seat with his eyes closed. *I'll drive to the emergency room in Bozeman,* I thought. But when I reached the Bozeman exit, I glanced at his face and saw that his color had come back and his breathing was slow and relaxed.

"Hell, keep driving," he said without opening his eyes, and I kept driving.

With the mountains behind us, we drove down through the Gallatin Valley and into the plains. Another thirty miles and we had descended eight thousand feet and come to the little river town of Townsend, halfway between Bozeman and Helena. As I watched the blue outline of the mountains recede in the rearview mirror I thought about Big Sky Resort and the thin cool air at eleven thousand feet above sea level. Bob opened his eyes and sat up in the seat.

"I'm hungry," he said.

I pulled over at a café on Townsend's main street and came around to help him out of the car. His legs were shaky, but he made it into the café and wolfed down a couple of hamburgers.

"Nothing's wrong with me. I just felt like I was worn out," he said.

When we reached Helena, he asked me to pull over and let him drive the rest of the way home.

"You've got to see a doctor."

"Hell, nothing's wrong! I been tired."

"You've got to see a doctor!"

"I'll see how I feel after harvest."

"You aren't going to make it through harvest at this rate! Here's the specialist's number. Will you call him, or shall I?"

"Jesus Christ!" he exploded, finally. "If that's what it takes to shut you up—"

Our doctor in Havre had sounded shaken. "The X rays show a film over the lungs," he said. "I don't know what it is."

The pulmonary specialist in Great Falls did a series of blood oxygen tests and recommended a lung biopsy.

"Hell no, I ain't letting him go down my throat and snip out a piece of my lungs!"

"But we have to find out what's wrong—"

"Nothing's wrong!"

I raged, begged, pleaded with him until he fled the house for the peace and quiet of the all-night coffee shop. Nothing was the matter with him, just a little fatigue, and he could not understand why I was getting so worked up about nothing. The night I threw myself on the kitchen floor and accused him of deliberately intending to leave me a widow with an unborn child, he was shaken by the state I was in. To quiet me, and not because he believed he was sick, he agreed to the biopsy.

After all those hours of waiting in the Great Falls Clinic came the verdict. Refusing to make eye contact, forcing out his words as though each one came with a price tag, the young specialist explained to us that the film that had shown up on the X rays was pulmonary fibrosis, the incurable, progressive spread of fibrous connective tissues that gradually would choke the capacity of the lungs to take in oxygen and supply it to the body. Bob's blood oxygen level was already about 45 percent, compared with a normal level of 98 percent.

While the growth of the fibroids could not be halted or reversed, the specialist said, it could sometimes be slowed. He recommended a massive therapy of steroids and warned us that mood swings could be among the side effects. Bob should be careful and exact in taking his doses.

"And quit smoking," he told him.

Smoking didn't cause pulmonary fibrosis, although it would exacerbate it. A likely cause was contact with asbestos.

Bob shook his head. Didn't believe he'd ever handled the stuff, he said.

"We may never know where it started," said the specialist, and I wondered why it mattered. He wrote out prescriptions for prednisone and scheduled another appointment in a month's time.

The world must be full of battered souls who stayed on the track because the idea of being run over by a train was more preposterous than the evidence of their own eyes.

For me, the sun rises and another day begins to burn without hope of rain. I pull on a fresh cotton tent dress over my enormous self and cram my feet into sandals and drive to the office for another day of the trivia that pester a college campus in the summer. I cannot believe in September and the end of this pregnancy any more than I can believe in the finality of breath. Bob seems himself these days. More than himself. The steroids have infused him with energy.

"Yeah, I'm runnin' on Prestone," he tells his friends at first.

But he does not like the idea of his body being altered in ways he cannot control by these opaque white pills. When he begins to tinker with his dosage, he drives me nearly crazy with apprehension. Feeling better one day, he takes half his pills. Worse the next, he takes double.

"But the doctor warned us about exact dosages!" I scream.

"Hell, that doc doesn't know a goddamned thing about the way I feel."

"What about the cigarettes?"

"I'll quit after harvest."

In my own way I am as certain as Bob that I can control the invisible menace growing in his lungs. Take the medication, follow the doctor's instructions to the letter, and the menace will be slowed, perhaps for years, and meanwhile we can live as we always have, going our separate ways by day and holding each other by night, delighting in each other's pulse and breath, looking forward to the baby.

Bob's denial, on the other hand, is less complex.

"I don't know why, but the prednisone has stopped working," says the specialist on our next visit to the Great Falls Clinic. "I'm going to start you on interferon. It's a drug used in transplant cases to break down the body's natural immune system, and it must be monitored with extreme care."

I listen, panicky, to his instructions. Was Bob's tinkering with his prednisone dosage the reason for its failure to slow the growth of his fibrosis? What will he do with this potential dynamite? What can I do about it?

On the way home, I find out.

"Hell," he says flatly. "I ain't gonna touch that shit. I'm going to wait until after harvest, and then"—he takes his eyes off the road, looks squarely at me—"then I'm going find out what the hell it is I'm allergic to."

Rachel was born at the end of September, and Bob drove us home from the hospital through the last blaze of autumnal color. I carried her into the nursery I had furnished and laid her, sleeping, in her crib. Bob dropped down in a chair beside the crib without taking off his coat or gloves. He watched as she slept: the transparent eyelids of the newborn, the little fists thrown back on either side of her head, the rise and fall of her tiny chest. When I looked in an hour later, neither Rachel nor Bob had moved.

But he had begun to lose weight. Down to 175, then 165 pounds. He bruised easily. Once, while he was holding Rachel, her little fist flailed out and nicked his face with a fingernail, and blood seeped down his cheek for an hour.

He refused to see the specialist again, or any other doctor, but I gleaned information about the progress of his disease where I could find it. "It's the fibrosis that causes the weight loss," explained Rachel's pediatrician when I took her in for her six weeks' checkup. "His body can't maintain itself."

But what caused the mood swings? Was it last summer's dosage of prednisone, still wreaking its roller-coaster damage on his reactions? Was he depressed over an illness he insisted he'd been misdiagnosed with? Or had the dark impulse run within Bob from the beginning, hidden until the combination of drugs and debilitation broke down his defenses? Which was the real Bob?

How much financial havoc can a man cause when he sets a farming operation into motion and then watches as through a haze of detachment while fields go uncultivated, obligations unmet, notes unrenewed? How many additional difficulties can he bring down around his shoulders as well as his family's when he fails to file his corporation reports? His FICA and W-4 forms? What if he fails to file his income taxes? Answer: more difficulties than I ever dreamed possible.

I lay awake at two, three, four o'clock in the morning while birch twigs brushed against the bedroom window and cast a maze of shadows as complex and random as the maze my life had become. Hundreds of thousands of dollars whirred through my brain on a squirrel-wheel frequency, organizing themselves into columns and disintegrating to form new totals at rising interest rates. What was I to do? What to do, what to do? Every hope for a way out of the maze was as treacherous as false dawn. The bank would foreclose on the farm in lieu of the $450,000 note? Very well, but the bank would report the transaction to the IRS as a forgiven debt. What, I wondered, did the IRS do with people like me who owed income tax on $450,000? Did they have jails with squirrel wheels in them?

By this time I lay awake alone, usually, in the bed in the shadows of birch twigs. In the mornings I rose and dressed, drove Rachel to her sitter, and hammered away at the solutions that had eluded me in the small hours. By confronting every debt and filing every delinquent report, I could still cling to my illusions. *Face it! Fight it! If we can once deal with the finances, we can still live comfortably on my salary, and surely the disease can be slowed, maybe for years—if you don't believe in the diagnosis, we'll find another specialist. We'll go to Seattle or San Francisco and find another course of treatment, and surely, surely we can buy time, we can have years together. You'll see Rachel grow up—*

But Bob was away from home most of the time now, driven by my frantic tirades and his own denial of the disease that was slowly strangling him. Fired with the idea of getting back into the oil business, of another chance of striking it lucky, he went back to his native Kansas for weeks and then months at a stretch, coming home only to try to raise money for the leases he was buying.

———

"I found another oil well!"

He looks up from the logbook he has unfolded on the dining room table. Another thirty or forty logbooks are stacked around him or strewn on the floor. Cigarette smoke hangs blue over his head.

"See here? Where the line wavers? I don't see how they could have overlooked it. When they perforated, they missed the zone entirely. I can go in there, unplug it and reperforate, maybe run acid, get the well on stream for fifty, sixty barrels a day, initially—"

Sometimes he finds two or three oil wells in an evening.

"—cost?"

His eyes go opaque for an instant, as though my question has traveled on some dim transmission from outer space.

"What? The cost to rework one well? Hell, I don't know, honey, it'd be just one part of my program—twelve wells, say, at fifteen or twenty thousand—Hell, the cost of one well don't make no nevermind. I'll be talking to my old buddy the banker when I go back to Kansas next week. Now, can you see this? This jiggle on the graph? That's another oil-producing zone they missed when they finished this well—"

"Honey, I realize you don't know a goddamn thing about the oil business, but I don't understand why you can't *see* it! Hell, it's right there on the log! And fifty, sixty barrels a day, even at thirteen dollars a barrel—"

He's down to 150 pounds now. His skin has shrunken over his cheekbones, and his nails are cyanosed. Still, he's drawing on some invisible source of energy; his eyes are huge, his voice urgent as he stabs out one cigarette, lights another, and uses it to gesture at his logbook. All he needs to get on his feet again is a few thousand dollars I have in a savings account. Listening to his fevered chatter, I feel drawn into his dream, his certainty that out there somewhere, in the next fold of the graph, the next thousand feet of well pipe, is the ultimate fountainhead of wealth and health. I could drift with him, believe in him . . . *It was the drought, it was the farm crisis that bankrupted us, it wasn't his fault—and he knows the oil business, knows what he's talking about, it's just a matter of giving him his chance—*

But no.

He flies into a rage at my refusal. "You make me want to puke! *Puke! Puke! Puke! Puke! Puke!*"

A week of verbal bludgeoning is more than enough. I hand over the money, and he sets off for Kansas, serene in his knowledge that the next throw of the dice is his.

A month later he calls home, jabbering, ecstatic. His old buddy the banker believes in him.

"It's growing on trees down here! The money's growing on trees!"

We don't hear from him after that. Another spring deepens into another hot summer, and the lawns and evergreens in Havre suffer the stress from curtailed watering. After work I pick Rachel up from her sitter's and play with her in the swing I have hung in the backyard willow. Rachel has seen so little rain in her life that when a brief deceptive shower fits its way overhead and a few raindrops lash the willow leaves, she asks, "What's that, Mom?"

Swing, swing, every day a bead on a string. Take Rachel to the sitter's and go to work in the mornings, pick her up and come home at night, swing her in the swing and bathe her and feed her and put her to bed. A whiskey and a book and Emmylou Harris for me. Swing, swing, the phone doesn't ring.

"Why don't you divorce him?" one of the attorneys had asked last summer.

This summer I file for divorce.

"Honey, *why?*"

In the hum of the long-distance line between Montana and Kansas, I try to think why.

"I'm coming home," he says after the silence. "I don't really have the time, I got a well just coming into production, but I can see you ain't left me no other choice."

Rachel and I drive to Great Falls to meet him at the airport. I recognize the man who appears on the ramp by his fair hair. He walks a step or two, gasps for breath. A ghost's eyes glow at us.

"Sure missed my two honeys," says the ghost. "Sure hated being away."

One of the disembarking flight attendants touches my arm. "Something's really wrong with this man," she says. "He's having terrible trouble breathing."

I nod.

She hesitates, glancing over our small sick circle. "Well—just so somebody knows," she says finally, and hurries off with her flight bag rolling behind her on its little wheels.

Rachel cuddles up to him. "My honey," he says, teary-eyed.

When we reach the car, he gets in the driver's seat and lights a cigarette. "We'll get rid of this pig," he says, "and buy you a new Lincoln as soon as the well comes on stream. They got new dealers' models in Kansas for under twenty thou. Helluva deal. There's a house down there I want you to see. It's an estate, actually."

"Let me drive."

"Hell, I feel fine! Long as I stay on my medication, I'm fine."

"Medication?"

"My Primatene Mist."

"The banker here in Havre don't want to make me a loan. He says he heard you've filed for divorce. But I told him you're dropping the action. You are dropping the action, aren't you?"

Hell, we got no problems, honey!

If only I could suspend my disbelief, accept the invitation to waltz with this rattling skeleton. But I hear him shouting into the phone at someone in Kansas: *It's still pumping water? Guess we'll have to go down further and shoot the second zone! What? Hell, I don't know! I'm planning to come back down to Kansas by the end of the week! At least by Monday! Hell yes, you'll get paid!*

"I'm having to sue my old buddy the banker for that sixty thousand he still owes me," he explains. "Sonovabitch got cold feet. Hell, can't blame him, in a sense. He don't know a goddamn thing about the oil patch."

No, I won't descend any further with him into his shadow world. I'll murder him instead with disbelief. From the light's edge I will watch as he walks under dead trees where dreams hang like leaves, as he fades into transparency and gibbers at me from the dim reaches: *It sure makes me feel good to know how much confidence my wife's got in me, Mary!*

"You've got to get him out of the house," says the attorney.

You try to divorce me, and you'll never see that little girl again, Mary! Hell no, I'm not talking about custody! I'm just telling you, Mary! You'll never see her again!

"But how can I take him seriously?" I plead.

"We have to take his threats seriously," says the attorney.

The second or third time the police have to come and drag him out of the house, the attorney applies to the judge for a restraining order. So he hides behind a hedge in a borrowed car until a new neighbor comes running across the street: "Quick! A man's trying to coax your little girl into his car with him!"

"We can't put him in jail," says the police lieutenant. "My God, the man's on oxygen."

I don't know why you can't see it, Mary! Hell, that lawyer's just running up his fees. I know I can't tell you a goddamn thing. You think you know it all. But eventually you're going to find out—

I have my phone number changed, and changed again, and still there comes at midnight or one A.M. the single ring. I pick it up to dial tone or to the hesitant whisper: *Honey? Hell, I'll forgive you. I just don't understand how you could throw me out.*

He has hired himself an attorney by now, and the paperwork blizzards back and forth. He demands a division of property, a maintenance allowance, and custody of Rachel. But when it comes to settlement, he backs off; when a hearing date is set, he calls the judge and gets an extension. What he really wants is not to be divorced.

"We could leave it like this," says the attorney finally, wearily. "You have a restraining order and temporary child custody, pending settlement. And you're leaving Montana in a month or two."

So it will never end.

"You don't think he'd try to follow you?" the attorney asks.

"I think he's too sick to follow far."

He lives in a room in the Havre Hotel. Bed, dresser, air-conditioning unit in the window. He can sit in the lobby downstairs and watch TV or watch the traffic on First Street. He can walk around the corner to PJ's Lounge and play a little poker, but he has to carry his portable oxygen supply everywhere he goes. He's a walking skeleton. He has nothing to do, nothing to look forward to— How could she have done it to him?

No, it will never end. Not with the ringing of a telephone, three Octobers later in the golden Palouse. Not when I agree with his sister that yes, we should lay him beside his parents; yes, I will want to bring Rachel. And it will not end with the late-night flight into Wichita, and not with the familiar faces of my kind brother-in-law and his wife waiting to drive us through the murky country roads to the small-town parlor where he waits. Rachel goes wild in the car, kicking, struggling; but when we get to Little River, she calms down and walks up the porch steps and through the door with its oval of Victorian glass.

"Why are his eyes shut?"

It is the first time I have seen him in the flesh since that day three years ago, just before I left Montana for good, when he cornered me in public and ranted, raged, finally slapped my face with all the feeble fury he could muster at my refusal to his waltz. For a moment I fight off the irrational feeling that, sensing my presence, he will sit up in his coffin, chattering, his ghost's eyes glowing: *Why, Mary? Why?*

"How old are you?" the Methodist minister asks Rachel.

"Seven," she whispers.

The Little River cemetery holds the only high ground for miles, and the grass is as stiff and sere as it would be in Montana in October. The wind snarls at the grass and roars in the canopy they have pitched over the open grave, and I remember another cemetery ridge a long time ago, and another dry-eyed woman named Mary.

At the end they fold the flag and hand it to me, the technical widow; and I turn as prearranged and hand it to one of his sons. No, it never ends. Perhaps my grandmother could have told me that. Her shade follows, as does his, through the windswept grass as Rachel and I walk hand in hand down the gravel track from the knoll.

PART THREE

OUR OWN STORIES

IN HINDSIGHT IT IS POSSIBLE to see the turning of a generation in writing about the American West sometime around 1965. The writers who had helped release us from the grip of the genre "Western" as our official story had done their work, and writers with little interest in the "Western" one way or the other were free to investigate the particularities of their own experience.

"All that fascinates us," Jean Baudrillard wrote in *America*, "is the spectacle of the brain and its workings."

Or, as Harold Bloom writes, learning "how to talk to ourselves and how to endure ourselves . . . the proper use of one's own solitude . . . one's confrontation with one's own mortality."

Writers like William Stafford and Ken Kesey and Richard Hugo and Ray Carver and Tom McGuane, though they mostly write out of their Western experiences, haven't been so much interested in illustrating for us local "truths" about our regional society and history as in involving us, through the use of language both as articulate and particular as possible, in the circumstances of what it is like to invent yourself yet again, to be human.

W. H. AUDEN

In 1939, W. H. Auden, already one of Britain's most renowned poets at a youthful thirty-two, crossed the Atlantic for America, where he took up permanent residence. Auden became an American citizen in 1946 and spent most of his later years in New York City's Greenwich Village, moving back to Oxford only in 1972, a year before he died. A lifelong traveler who wrote extensively about his voyages, Auden spent time in Spain, Iceland, China, Germany, Austria, and near the Mediterranean. He published over twenty-five editions of his poetry, and he remains one of the major Modern poets.

In this excerpt from his prose book The Dyer's Hand, *Auden looks down on the West as an outsider, seeing what he takes to be a vast place "where human activity seems a tiny thing in comparison to the magnitude of the earth, and the equality of men not some dogma of politics or jurisprudence but a self-evident fact." It's a notion which is simply not particularly true of the West. Auden confronts the other side of that coin when he speaks of "social fluidity" and "an attitude towards personal relationships in which impermanence is taken for granted." It's another defining notion about the West, which is occasionally but not entirely true, the sort of sweeping generalization which the particularities of experience in the actual West, and writing by those who have spent some time on the ground, disprove as often as not. What emerges from behind Auden's words, however, is a profound respect for often difficult individual lives in the West as anywhere—the West as metaphor for human existence everywhere.*

"THE WEST FROM THE AIR,"
FROM *THE DYER'S HAND*

It is an unforgettable experience for anyone born on the other side of the Atlantic to take a plane journey by night across the United States. Looking down he will see the lights of some town like a last outpost in a darkness stretching for hours ahead, and realize that, even if there is no longer an actual frontier, this is still a continent only partially settled and developed, where human activity seems a tiny thing in comparison to the magnitude of the earth, and the equality of men not some dogma

of politics or jurisprudence but a self-evident fact. He will behold a wild
nature, compared with which the landscapes of Salvator Rosa are as cosy
as Arcadia and which cannot possibly be thought of in human or personal
terms. If Henry Adams could write:

> When Adams was a boy in Boston, the best chemist in the
> place had probably never heard of Venus except by way of
> scandal, or of the Virgin except as idolatry. . . . The force of
> the Virgin was still felt at Lourdes, and seemed to be as potent
> as X-rays; but in America neither Venus nor Virgin ever had
> value as force—at most as sentiment. No American had ever
> been truly afraid of either

the reason for this was not simply that the *Mayflower* carried iconophobic
dissenters but also that the nature which Americans, even in New England, had every reason to fear could not possibly be imagined as a
mother. A white whale whom man can neither understand nor be understood by, whom only a madman like Gabriel can worship, the only
relationship with whom is a combat to the death by which a man's
courage and skill are tested and judged, or the great buck who answers
the poet's prayer for "someone else additional to him" in "The Most
of It" are more apt symbols. Thoreau, who certainly tried his best to
become intimate with nature, had to confess

> I walk in nature still alone
>   And know no one,
> Discern no lineament nor feature
>   Of any creature.
> Though all the firmament
>   Is o'er me bent,
> Yet still I miss the grace
> Of an intelligent and kindred face.
> I still must seek the friend
> Who does with nature blend,
> Who is the person in her mask,
> He is the man I ask. . . .

Many poets in the Old World have become disgusted with human
civilization but what the earth would be like if the race became extinct

they cannot imagine; an American like Robinson Jeffers can quite easily, for he has seen with his own eyes country as yet untouched by history.

In a land which is fully settled, most men must accept their local environment or try to change it by political means; only the exceptionally gifted or adventurous can leave to seek his fortune elsewhere. In America, on the other hand, to move on and make a fresh start somewhere else is still the normal reaction to dissatisfaction or failure. Such social fluidity has important psychological effects. Since movement involves breaking social and personal ties, the habit creates an attitude towards personal relationships in which impermanence is taken for granted.

GALWAY KINNELL

Galway Kinnell has taught poetry for forty-five years at twenty-five colleges and universities, has published over twenty-five volumes of poetry, and has received nearly every major literary award, including Ford, Fulbright, Guggenheim, Lowell, MacArthur, Merrill, Rockefeller, American Academy of Poets, and Pulitzer prizes. Born in Providence, Rhode Island, in 1927, Galway studied at Princeton and the University of Rochester, served in the U.S. Navy during World War II, and began teaching English at Alfred University in 1949. Essential collections of his poetry include Flower Herding on Mount Monadnock *(1964),* Body Rags *(1968),* The Book of Nightmares *(1971),* Mortal Acts, Mortal Words, *(1980), and* The Past *(1985). He has translated French poetry widely, especially the work of François Villon, and has published several books of essays and interviews. He lives in Vermont and New York, where he is associated with the creative writing program at New York University.*

In "The Bear," from Body Rags, *Kinnell fuses the fate of the predator with that of the prey. As in Native American creation myths, the hunter merges with the hunted; the hunger continues, and another round of astonishment, by which I mean life, begins.*

THE BEAR

1

In late winter
I sometimes glimpse bits of steam
coming up from
some fault in the old snow
and bend close and see it is lung-colored
and put down my nose
and know
the chilly, enduring odor of bear.

2

I take a wolf's rib and whittle
it sharp at both ends
and coil it up
and freeze it in blubber and place it out
on the fairway of the bears.

And when it has vanished
I move out on the bear tracks,
roaming in circles
until I come to the first, tentative, dark
splash on the earth.

And I set out
running, following the splashes
of blood wandering over the world.
At the cut, gashed resting places
I stop and rest,
at the crawl-marks
where he lay out on his belly
to overpass some stretch of bauchy ice
I lie out
dragging myself forward with bear-knives in my fists.

3

On the third day I begin to starve,
at nightfall I bend down as I knew I would

at a turd sopped in blood,
and hesitate, and pick it up,
and thrust it in my mouth, and gnash it down,
and rise
and go on running.

4

On the seventh day,
living by now on bear blood alone,
I can see his upturned carcass far out ahead, a scraggled,
steamy hulk,
the heavy fur riffling in the wind.

I come up to him
and stare at the narrow-spaced, petty eyes,
the dismayed
face laid back on the shoulder, the nostrils
flared, catching
perhaps the first taint of me as he
died.

I hack
a ravine in his thigh, and eat and drink,
and tear him down his whole length
and open him and climb in
and close him up after me, against the wind,
and sleep.

5

And dream
of lumbering flatfooted
over the tundra,
stabbed twice from within,
splattering a trail behind me,
splattering it out no matter which way I lurch,
no matter which parabola of bear-transcendence,
which dance of solitude I attempt,

which gravity-clutched leap,
which trudge, which groan.

6

Until one day I totter and fall—
fall on this
stomach that has tried so hard to keep up,
to digest the blood as it leaked in,
to break up
and digest the bone itself: and now the breeze
blows over me, blows off
the hideous belches of ill-digested bear blood
and rotted stomach
and the ordinary, wretched odor of bear,

blows across
my sore, lolled tongue a song
or screech, until I think I must rise up
and dance. And I lie still.

7

I awaken I think. Marshlights
reappear, geese
come trailing again up the flyway.
In her ravine under old snow the dam-bear
lies, licking
lumps of smeared fur
and drizzly eyes into shapes
with her tongue. And one
hairy-soled trudge stuck out before me,
the next groaned out,
the next,
the next,
the rest of my days I spend
wandering: wondering
what, anyway,
was that sticky infusion, that rank flavor of blood, that
    poetry, by which I lived?

WILLIAM STAFFORD

*William Stafford was born in Hutchinson, Kansas, in 1914, and
received his B.A. and M.A. degrees from the University of Kansas,
and his Ph.D. from the University of Iowa. He served in civilian
public service camps as a conscientious objector during World War II.
Author of more than twenty books of poetry and prose, Stafford won
the National Book Award in 1963 for his second book of poems,*
Traveling Through the Dark. *For many years he lived in Lake
Oswego, Oregon, and, for over thirty-five years, taught English at
Lewis and Clark College, traveling tirelessly all the while, across the
United States, and in Europe, Egypt, Iran, and India. Modestly
appraising his own work, Stafford commented, "It is much like talk,
with some enhancement." His most recent book,* The Darkness
Around Us Is Deep: Selected Poems, *was published in 1993.
Stafford died of heart failure in August of that year. Stafford was a
widely present, avuncular figure among writers in the West, a constant
force for decency; his calm, judicious advocacy of fairness and human
commonalities is already deeply missed.*

TRAVELING THROUGH
THE DARK

Traveling through the dark I found a deer
dead on the edge of the Wilson River road.
It is usually best to roll them into the canyon:
that road is narrow; to swerve might make more dead.

By glow of the tail-light I stumbled back of the car
and stood by the heap, a doe, a recent killing;
she had stiffened already, almost cold.
I dragged her off; she was large in the belly.

My fingers touching her side brought me the reason—
her side was warm; her fawn lay there waiting,

alive, still, never to be born.
Beside that mountain road I hesitated.

The car aimed ahead its lowered parking lights;
under the hood purred the steady engine.
I stood in the glare of the warm exhaust turning red;
around our group I could hear the wilderness listen.

I thought hard for us all—my only swerving—,
then pushed her over the edge into the river.

HELP FROM HISTORY

Please help me know it happened, that life I thought we
     had—

Our friends holding out their hands to us—
Our enemies mistaken, infected by unaccountable
     prejudice—
Our country benevolent, a model for all governments, good-
     willed—
Those mad rulers at times elsewhere, inhuman and yet mob-
     worshipped, leaders of monstrous doctrine, unspeakable
     beyond belief, yet strangely attractive to the uninstructed.

And please let me believe these incredible legends that have
     dignified our lives—

The wife or husband helplessly loving us, the children full of
     awe and affection, the dog insanely faithful—
Our growing up hard—hard times, being industrious and
     reliable—
The places we lived arched full of serene golden light—

Now, menaced by judgments, overheard revisions, let me
     retain what ignorance it takes to preserve what we need—
     a past that redeems any future.

PASO POR AQUÍ

Comanches tell how the buffalo
wore down their own pass through these hills,
herds pouring over for years, not finding
a way but making it by going there.
Comanche myself, I bow my head
in the graveyard at Buffalo Gap and begin
to know the world as a land invented
by breath, its hills and plains guided
and anchored in place by thought, by feet.

Tombstones lean all around—marble, and pitiful
limestone agonies, recording in worn-out words
the travailed, the loved bodies that rest here.
No one comes quietly enough to surprise them;
the earth brims with whatever they gave. It spills
long horizons ahead of us, and we part its grass
from above, staring hard enough to begin
to see a world, long like Texas,
deep as history goes after it happens,
and ahead of us, pawed by our impatience.

We came over the plains. Where are we going?

LATE, PASSING PRAIRIE FARM

All night like a star a single bulb
shines from the eave of the barn.
Light extends itself more and more
feebly into farther angles and overhead
into the trees. Where light ends
the world ends.

Someone left the light burning, but
the farm is alone. There is so much
silence that the house leans toward
the road. The last echo from dust

falling through floor joists happened
years ago.

Owls made a few dark lines across
that glow, but now the light has
erased all but itself—is now a pearl for
birds that move in the dark. They polish
this jewel by air from their wings. This glow
is their still dream.

The sill of the house is worn by
steps of travelers, gone—boards tell
their passage, their ending, copied
into the race. When you pass here, traveler,
you too can't keep from making sounds,
like theirs, that will last.

DAVID WAGONER

*David Wagoner was born in Massillon, Ohio, in 1926; he moved
to Whiting, Indiana, as a young child, and remained in the Great
Lakes region throughout his college years. In 1954, Wagoner, a student of Theodore Roethke at Pennsylvania State University, was invited by Roethke to join him as a professor at the University of
Washington. Wagoner became one of the leading literary forces of the
Pacific Northwest, both in terms of his influence as a teacher and editor
(he taught for over thirty years, and has been the editor of* Poetry
Northwest *since 1966), and through the power of his writing. Wagoner has published many books of poetry, and he received the National
Book Award in 1978 for* Traveling Light: Collected Poems,
1956–1976. *A later volume,* Through the Forest, *takes his work
through the late 1980s. A fiction writer with almost a dozen novels
to his credit, including* The Escape Artist *(which was filmed by Fran-*

cis Ford Coppola in 1980) and Where Is My Wandering Boy
Tonight?, *Wagoner also edited and arranged selections from the notebooks of Theodore Roethke (*Straw for the Fire, *1972).*

"*A Guide to Dungeness Spit,*" *from* Traveling Light: Collected Poems, 1956–1976, *is a poem of journey, of the discovery
of what we are on this Pacific coast where life is tidal, and where "We
are called lovers."*

A GUIDE TO DUNGENESS SPIT

Out of wild roses down from the switching road between
   pools
We step to an arm of land washed from the sea.
On the windward shore
The combers come from the strait, from narrows and shoals
Far below sight. To leeward, floating on trees
In a blue cove, the cormorants
Stretch to a point above us, their wings held out like skysails.
Where shall we walk? First, put your prints to the sea,
Fill them, and pause there:
Seven miles to the lighthouse, curved yellow-and-grey miles
Tossed among kelp, abandoned with bleaching rooftrees,
Past reaches and currents;
And we must go afoot at a time when the tide is heeling.
Those whistling overhead are Canada geese;
Some on the waves are loons,
And more on the sand are pipers. There, Bonaparte's gulls
Settle a single perch. Those are sponges.
Those are the ends of bones.
If we cross to the inner shore, the grebes and goldeneyes
Rear themselves and plunge through the still surface,
Fishing below the dunes
And rising alarmed, higher than waves. Those are
   cockleshells.
And these are the dead. I said we would come to these.
Stoop to the stones.
Overturn one: the grey-and-white, inch-long crabs come
   pulsing

And clambering from their hollows, tiptoeing sideways.
They lift their pincers
To defend the dark. Let us step this way. Follow me closely
Past snowy plovers bustling among sand-fleas.
The air grows dense.
You must decide now whether we shall walk for miles and
     miles
And whether all birds are the young of other creatures
Or their own young ones,
Or simply their old selves because they die. One falls,
And the others touch him webfoot or with claws,
Treading him for the ocean.
This is called sanctuary. Those are feathers and scales.
We both go into mist, and it hooks behind us.
Those are foghorns.
Wait, and the bird on the high root is a snowy owl
Facing the sea. Its flashing yellow eyes
Turn past us and return;
And turning from the calm shore to the breakers, utterly still,
They lead us by the bay and through the shallows,
Buoy us into the wind.
Those are tears. Those are called houses, and those are
     people.
Here is a stairway past the whites of our eyes.
All our distance
Has ended in the light. We climb to the light in spirals,
And look, between us we have come all the way,
And it never ends
In the ocean, the spit and image of our guided travels.
Those are called ships. We are called lovers.
There lie the mountains.

KEN KESEY

Ken Kesey was born in La Junta, Colorado, in 1935, grew up around Springfield, Oregon, graduated from the University of Oregon in 1957, and went to Stanford for graduate work. One Flew Over the Cuckoo's Nest *(1962) was enormously successful and was later made into a multi–Academy Award–winning film. His second novel,* Some-times a Great Notion *(1964), was also a popular success and made into a film. Along with his renegade and hugely publicized life— which became the subject of Tom Wolfe's* The Electric Kool-aid Acid Test *in 1968—these two novels gave Kesey a cult status in the late 1960s. The author of several other books, including* Kesey's Garage Sale *(1973),* Demon Box *(1986), and* Sailor Song *(1992), Kesey has also written two children's books,* Little Tricker the Squirrel Meets Big Double the Bear *(1988) and* The Sea Lion *(1991). Kesey still lives in Oregon and, with Ken Babbs, recently co-wrote a historical rodeo novel,* Last Go Round *(1994).*

In this pivotal chapter from One Flew Over the Cuckoo's Nest, *Kesey depicts the root of the narrator's loss. As in so much Western writing, "progress" in the West leaves in its wake the detritus of diminishment. The sense of possibility discovered by Lewis and Clark shrinks as we go on remaking the things that define our world in order to use and inhabit them.*

FROM *ONE FLEW OVER THE CUCKOO'S NEST*

After that, McMurphy had things his way for a good long while. The nurse was biding her time till another idea came to her that would put her on top again. She knew she'd lost one big round and was losing another, but she wasn't in any hurry. For one thing, she wasn't about to recommend release; the fight could go on as long as she wanted, till he made a mistake or till he just gave out, or until she could come up with some new tactic that would put her back on top in everybody's eyes.

A good lot happened before she came up with that new tactic. After

McMurphy was drawn out of what you might call a short retirement and had announced he was back in the hassle by breaking out her personal window, he made things on the ward pretty interesting. He took part in every meeting, every discussion—drawling, winking, joking his best to wheedle a skinny laugh out of some Acute who'd been scared to grin since he was twelve. He got together enough guys for a basketball team and some way talked the doctor into letting him bring a ball back from the gym to get the team used to handling it. The nurse objected, said the next thing they'd be playing soccer in the day room and polo games up and down the hall, but the doctor held firm for once and said let them go. "A number of the players, Miss Ratched, have shown marked progress since that basketball team was organized; I think it has proven its therapeutic value."

She looked at him a while in amazement. So he was doing a little muscle-flexing too. She marked the tone of his voice for later, for when her time came again, and just nodded and went to sit in her Nurses' Station and fiddle with the controls on her equipment. The janitors had put a cardboard in the frame over her desk till they could get another window pane cut to fit, and she sat there behind it every day like it wasn't even there, just like she could still see right into the day room. Behind that square of cardboard she was like a picture turned to the wall.

She waited, without comment, while McMurphy continued to run around the halls in the mornings in his white-whale shorts, or pitched pennies in the dorms, or ran up and down the hall blowing a nickel-plated ref's whistle, teaching Acutes the fast break from ward door to the Seclusion Room at the other end, the ball pounding in the corridor like cannon shots and McMurphy roaring like a sergeant, "Drive, you puny mothers, *drive!*"

When either one spoke to the other it was always in the most polite fashion. He would ask her nice as you please if he could use her fountain pen to write a request for an Unaccompanied Leave from the hospital, wrote it out in front of her on her desk, and handed her the request and the pen back at the same time with such a nice "Thank you," and she would look at it and say just as polite that she would "take it up with the staff"—which took maybe three minutes—and come back to tell him she certainly was sorry but a pass was not considered therapeutic at this time. He would thank her again and walk out of the Nurses'

Station and blow that whistle loud enough to break windows for miles, and holler, "Practice, you mothers, get that ball and let's get a little sweat rollin'."

He'd been on the ward a month, long enough to sign the bulletin board in the hall to request a hearing in group meeting about an Accompanied Pass. He went to the bulletin board with her pen and put down under TO BE ACCOMPANIED BY: "A twitch I know from Portland named Candy Starr."—and ruined the pen point on the period. The pass request was brought up in group meeting a few days later, the same day, in fact, that workmen put a new glass window in front of the Big Nurse's desk, and after his request had been turned down on the grounds that this Miss Starr didn't seem like the most wholesome person for a patient to go pass with, he shrugged and said that's how she bounces I guess, and got up and walked to the Nurses' Station, to the window that still had the sticker from the glass company down in the corner, and ran his fist through it again—explained to the nurse while blood poured from his fingers that he thought the cardboard had been left out and the frame was open. "When did they sneak that danged glass in there? Why that thing is a *menace!*"

The nurse taped his hand in the station while Scanlon and Harding dug the cardboard out of the garbage and taped it back in the frame, using adhesive from the same roll the nurse was bandaging McMurphy's wrist and fingers with. McMurphy sat on a stool, grimacing something awful while he got his cuts tended, winking at Scanlon and Harding over the nurse's head. The expression on her face was calm and blank as enamel, but the strain was beginning to show in other ways. By the way she jerked the adhesive tight as she could, showing her remote patience wasn't what it used to be.

We got to go to the gym and watch our basketball team—Harding, Billy Bibbit, Scanlon, Fredrickson, Martini, and McMurphy whenever his hand would stop bleeding long enough for him to get in the game —play a team of aides. Our two big black boys played for the aides. They were the best players on the court, running up and down the floor together like a pair of shadows in red trunks, scoring basket after basket with mechanical accuracy. Our team was too short and too slow, and Martini kept throwing passes to men that nobody but him could see, and the aides beat us by twenty points. But something happened that let most of us come away feeling there'd been a kind of victory, anyhow: in one scramble for the ball our big black boy named Washington got cracked with somebody's elbow, and his team had to hold him back as he stood straining to where McMurphy was sitting on the ball—not paying the least bit of heed to the thrashing black boy with red pouring out of his big nose and down his chest like paint splashed on a blackboard and hollering to the guys holding him, "He beggin' for it! The sonabitch jus' *beggin'* for it!"

McMurphy composed more notes for the nurse to find in the latrine with her mirror. He wrote long outlandish tales about himself in the log book and signed them Anon. Sometimes he slept till eight o'clock. She would reprimand him, without heat at all, and he would stand and listen till she was finished and then destroy her whole effect by asking something like did she wear a B cup, he wondered, or a C cup, or any ol' cup at all?

The other Acutes were beginning to follow his lead. Harding began flirting with all the student nurses, and Billy Bibbit completely quit writing what he used to call his "observations" in the log book, and when the window in front of her desk got replaced again, with a big X across it in whitewash to make sure McMurphy didn't have any excuse for not knowing it was there, Scanlon did it in by accidentally bouncing our basketball through it before the whitewashed X was even dry. The ball punctured, and Martini picked it off the floor like a dead bird and carried it to the nurse in the station, where she was staring at the new splash of broken glass all over her desk, and asked couldn't she please fix it with tape or something? Make it well again? Without a word she jerked it out of his hand and stuffed it in the garbage.

So, with basketball season obviously over, McMurphy decided fishing was the thing. He requested another pass after telling the doctor he had some friends at the Siuslaw Bay at Florence who would like to take eight or nine of the patients out deep-sea fishing if it was okay with the staff, and he wrote on the request list out in the hall that this time he would be accompanied by "two sweet old aunts from a little place outside of Oregon City." In the meeting his pass was granted for the next weekend. When the nurse finished officially noting his pass in her roll book, she reached into her wicker bag beside her feet and drew out a clipping that she had taken from the paper that morning, and read out loud that although fishing off the coast of Oregon was having a peak year, the salmon were running quite late in the season and the sea was rough and dangerous. And she would suggest the men give that some thought.

"Good idea," McMurphy said. He closed his eyes and sucked a deep breath through his teeth. "Yes sir! The salt smell o' the poundin' sea, the crack o' the bow against the waves—braving the elements, where men are men and boats are boats. Miss Ratched, you've talked me into it. I'll call and rent that boat this very night. Shall I sign you on?"

Instead of answering she walked to the bulletin board and pinned up the clipping.

The next day he started signing up the guys that wanted to go and that had ten bucks to chip in on boat rent, and the nurse started steadily bringing in clippings from the newspapers that told about wrecked boats and sudden storms on the coast. McMurphy pooh-poohed her and her clippings, saying that his two aunts had spent most of their lives bouncing around the waves in one port or another with this sailor or that, and they both guaranteed the trip was safe as pie, safe as pudding, not a thing to worry about. But the nurse still knew her patients. The clippings scared them more than McMurphy'd figured. He'd figured there would be a rush to sign up, but he'd had to talk and wheedle to get the guys he did. The day before the trip he still needed a couple more before he could pay for the boat.

I didn't have the money, but I kept getting this notion that I wanted to sign the list. And the more he talked about fishing for Chinook salmon the more I wanted to go. I knew it was a fool thing to want; if I signed up it'd be the same as coming right out and telling everybody I wasn't deaf. If I'd been hearing all this talk about boats and fishing it'd show I'd been hearing everything else that'd been said in confidence around me for the past ten years. And if the Big Nurse found out about that, that I'd heard all the scheming and treachery that had gone on when she didn't think anybody was listening, she'd hunt me down with an electric saw, fix me where she *knew* I was deaf and dumb. Bad as I wanted to go, it still made me smile a little to think about it: I had to keep on acting deaf if I wanted to hear at all.

I lay in bed the night before the fishing trip and thought it over, about my being deaf, about the years of not letting on I heard what was said, and I wondered if I could ever act any other way again. But I remembered one thing: it wasn't me that started acting deaf; it was people that first started acting like I was too dumb to hear or see or say anything at all.

It hadn't been just since I came in the hospital, either; people first took to acting like I couldn't hear or talk a long time before that. In the Army anybody with more stripes acted that way toward me. That was the way they figured you were supposed to act around someone looked like I did. And even as far back as grade school I can remember people saying that they didn't think I was listening, so they quit listening to the things I was saying. Lying there in bed, I tried to think back when I first noticed it. I think it was once when we were still living in the village on the Columbia. It was summer. . . .

. . . and I'm about ten years old and I'm out in front of the shack sprinkling salt on salmon for the racks behind the house, when I see a car turn off the highway and come lumbering across the ruts through the sage, towing a load of red dust behind it as solid as a string of boxcars.

I watch the car pull up the hill and stop down a piece from our yard, and the dust keeps coming, crashing into the rear of it and busting in every direction and finally settling on the sage and soapweed round about and making it look like chunks of red, smoking wreckage. The car sits there while the dust settles, shimmering in the sun. I know it isn't tourists with cameras because they never drive this close to the village. If they want to buy fish they buy them back at the highway; they don't come to the village because they probably think we still scalp people and burn them around a post. They don't know some of our people are lawyers in Portland, probably wouldn't believe it if I told them. In fact, one of my uncles became a real lawyer and Papa says he did it purely to prove he could, when he'd rather poke salmon in the fall than anything. Papa says if you don't watch it people will force you one way or the other, into doing what they think you should do, or into just being mule-stubborn and doing the opposite out of spite.

The doors of the car open all at once and three people get out, two out of the front and one out of the back. They come climbing up the slope toward our village and I see the first two are men in blue suits, and the behind one, the one that got out of the back, is an old white-haired woman in an outfit so stiff and heavy it must be armor plate. They're puffing and sweating by the time they break out of the sage into our bald yard.

The first man stops and looks the village over. He's short and round and wearing a white Stetson hat. He shakes his head at the rickety clutter of fishracks and secondhand cars and chicken coops and motorcycles and dogs.

"Have you ever in all your born days seen the like? Have you now? I swear to heaven, have you *ever?*"

He pulls off the hat and pats his red rubber ball of a head with a handkerchief, careful, like he's afraid of getting one or the other mussed up—the handkerchief or the dab of damp stringy hair.

"Can you imagine people wanting to live this way? Tell me, John, can you?" He talks loud on account of not being used to the roar of the falls.

John's next to him, got a thick gray mustache lifted tight up under his nose to stop out the smell of the salmon I'm working on. He's sweated down his neck and cheeks, and he's sweated clean out through the back of his blue suit. He's making notes in a book, and he keeps turning in a circle, looking at our shack, our little garden, at Mama's red and green and yellow Saturday-night dresses drying out back on a stretch of bedcord—keeps turning till he makes a full circle and comes back to me, looks at me like he just sees me for the first time, and me not but two yards away from him. He bends toward me and squints and lifts his mustache up to his nose again like it's me stinking instead of the fish.

"Where do you suppose his parents are?" John asks. "Inside the house? Or out on the falls? We might as well talk this over with the man while we're out here."

"I, for one, am not going inside that hovel," the fat guy says.

"That hovel," John says through his mustache, "is where the Chief lives, Brickenridge, the man we are here to deal with, the noble leader of these people."

"Deal with? Not me, not my job. They pay me to appraise, not fraternize."

This gets a laugh out of John.

"Yes, that's true. But someone should inform them of the government's plans."

"If they don't already know, they'll know soon enough."

"It would be very simple to go in and talk with him."

"Inside in that squalor? Why, I'll just bet you anything that place is acrawl with black widows. They say these 'dobe shacks always house a regular civilization in the walls between the sods. And *hot,* lord-a-mercy, I hope to tell you. I'll wager it's a regular oven in there. Look, look how overdone little Hiawatha is here. Ho. Burnt to a fair turn, he is."

He laughs and dabs at his head and when the woman looks at him he stops laughing. He clears his throat and spits into the dust and then walks over and sits down in the swing Papa built for me in the juniper tree, and sits there swinging back and forth a little bit and fanning himself with his Stetson.

What he said makes me madder the more I think about it. He and John go ahead talking about our house and village and property and what they are worth, and I get the notion they're talking about these things around me because they don't know I speak English. They are probably from the East someplace, where people don't know anything about Indians but what they see in the movies. I think how ashamed they're going to be when they find out I know what they are saying.

I let them say another thing or two about the heat and the house; then I stand up and tell the fat man, in my very best schoolbook language, that our sod house is likely to be cooler than any one of the houses in town, *lots* cooler! "I know for a *fact* that it's cooler'n that school I go to and even cooler'n that movie house in The Dalles that advertises on that sign drawn with icicle letters that it's 'cool inside'!"

And I'm just about to go and tell them, how, if they'll come on in, I'll go get Papa from the scaffolds on the falls, when I see that they don't look like they'd heard me talk at all. They aren't even looking at me. The fat man is swinging back and forth, looking off down the ridge of lava to where the men are standing their places on the scaffolding in the falls, just plaid-shirted shapes in the mist from this distance. Every so often you can see somebody shoot out an arm and take a step forward like a swordfighter, and then hold up his fifteen-foot forked spear for somebody on the scaffold above him to pull off the flopping salmon. The fat guy watches the men standing in their places in the fifty-foot veil of water, and bats his eyes and grunts every time one of them makes a lunge for a salmon.

The other two, John and the woman, are just standing. Not a one of the three acts like they heard a thing I said; in fact they're all looking off from me like they'd as soon I wasn't there at all.

And everything stops and hangs this way for a minute.

I get the funniest feeling that the sun is turned up brighter than before on the three of them. Everything else looks like it usually does —the chickens fussing around in the grass on top of the 'dobe houses, the grasshoppers batting from bush to bush, the flies being stirred into black clouds around the fish racks by the little kids with sage flails, just like every other summer day. Except the sun, on these three strangers, is all of a sudden way the hell brighter than usual and I can see the . . . *seams* where they're put together. And, almost, see the apparatus inside them take the words I just said and try to fit the words in here and there, this place and that, and when they find the words don't have any place ready-made where they'll fit, the machinery disposes of the words like they weren't even spoken.

The three are stock still while this goes on. Even the swing's stopped, nailed out at a slant by the sun, with the fat man petrified in it like a rubber doll. Then Papa's guinea hen wakes up in the juniper branches and sees we got strangers on the premises and goes to barking at them like a dog, and the spell breaks.

The fat man hollers and jumps out of the swing and sidles away through the dust, holding his hat up in front of the sun so's he can see what's up there in the juniper tree making such a racket. When he sees it's nothing but a speckled chicken he spits on the ground and puts his hat on.

"I, myself, sincerely *feel*," he says, "that whatever offer we make on this . . . metropolis will be quite sufficient."

"Could be. I still think we should make some effort to speak with the Chief—"

The old woman interrupts him by taking one ringing step forward. "No." This is the first thing she's said. "No," she says again in a way that reminds me of the Big Nurse. She lifts her eyebrows and looks the place over. Her eyes spring up like the numbers in a cash register; she's looking at Mama's dresses hung so careful on the line, and she's nodding her head.

"No. We don't talk with the Chief today. Not yet. I think . . . that I agree with Brickenridge for once. Only for a different reason. You recall the record we have shows the wife is not Indian but white? White. A woman from town. Her name is Bromden. He took her name, not she his. Oh, yes, I think if we just leave now and go back into town, and, of course, spread the word with the townspeople about the government's plans so they understand the advantages of having a hydro-electric dam and a lake instead of a cluster of shacks beside a falls, *then* type up an offer—and mail it to the wife, you see, by mistake? I feel our job will be a great deal easier."

She looks off to the men on the ancient, rickety, zigzagging scaffolding that has been growing and branching out among the rocks of the falls for hundreds of years.

"Whereas if we meet now with the husband and make some abrupt offer, we may run up against an un*told* amount of Navaho stubbornness and love of—I suppose we must call it home."

I start to tell them he's *not* Navaho, but think what's the use if they don't listen? They don't care what tribe he is.

The woman smiles and nods at both the men, a smile and a nod to each, and her eyes ring them up, and she begins to move stiffly back to their car, talking in a light, young voice.

"As my sociology professor used to emphasize, 'There is generally one person in every situation you must never underestimate the power *of*.' "

And they get back in the car and drive away, with me standing there wondering if they ever even *saw* me.

I was kind of amazed that I'd remembered that. It was the first time in what seemed to me centuries that I'd been able to remember much about my childhood. It fascinated me to discover I could still do it. I lay in bed awake, remembering other happenings, and just about that time, while I was half in a kind of dream, I heard a sound under my bed like a mouse with a walnut. I leaned over the edge of the bed and saw the shine of metal biting off pieces of gum I knew by heart. The black boy named Geever had found where I'd been hiding my chewing gum; was scraping the pieces off into a sack with a long, lean pair of scissors open like jaws.

I jerked back up under the covers before he saw me looking. My heart was banging in my ears, scared he'd seen me. I wanted to tell him to get away, to mind his own business and leave my chewing gum alone, but I couldn't even let on I heard. I lay still to see if he'd caught me bending over to peek under the bed at him, but he didn't give any sign—all I heard was the zzzth-zzzth of his scissors and pieces falling into the sack, reminded me of hailstones the way they used to rattle on our tar-paper roof. He clacked his tongue and giggled to himself.

"Um-ummm. Lord gawd amighty. Hee. I wonder how many times this muthuh chewed some o' this stuff? Just as *hard*."

McMurphy heard the black boy muttering to himself and woke and rolled up to one elbow to look at what he was up to at this hour down on his knees under my bed. He watched the black boy a minute, rubbing his eyes to be sure of what he was seeing, just like you see little kids rub their eyes; then he sat up completely.

"I will be a sonofabitch if he ain't in here at eleven-thirty at night, fartin' around in the dark with a pair of scissors and a paper sack." The black boy jumped and swung his flashlight up in McMurphy's eyes. "Now tell me, Sam: what the devil are you collectin' that needs the cover of night?"

"Go back to sleep, McMurphy. It don't concern nobody else."

McMurphy let his lips spread in a slow grin, but he didn't look away from the light. The black boy got uneasy after about half a minute of shining that light on McMurphy sitting there, on that glossy new-healed scar and those teeth and that tattooed panther on his shoulder, and took the light away. He bent back to his work, grunting and puffing like it was a mighty effort prying off dried gum.

"One of the duties of a night aide," he explained between grunts, trying to sound friendly, "is to keep the bedside area cleaned up."

"In the dead of night?"

"McMurphy, we got a thing posted called a *Job* Description, say cleanliness is a *twenty-fo'-hour job!*"

"You might of done your twenty-four hours' worth before we got in bed, don't you think, instead of sittin' out there watching TV till ten-thirty. Does Old Lady Ratched know you boys watch TV most of your shift? What do you reckon she'd do if she found out about that?"

The black boy got up and sat on the edge of my bed. He tapped the flashlight against his teeth, grinning and giggling. The light lit his face up like a black jack o'lantern.

"Well, let me tell you about this gum," he said and leaned close to McMurphy like an old chum. "You see, for years I been wondering where Chief Bromden got his chewin' gum—never havin' any money for the canteen, never havin' anybody give him a stick that I saw, never askin' the Red Cross lady—so I *watched,* and I *waited.* And look here." He got back on his knees and lifted the edge of my bedspread and shined the light under. "How 'bout that? I bet they's pieces of gum under here been used a *thousand* times!"

This tickled McMurphy. He went to giggling at what he saw. The black boy held up the sack and rattled it, and they laughed some more about it. The black boy told McMurphy good night and rolled the top of the sack like it was his lunch and went off somewhere to hide it for later.

"Chief?" McMurphy whispered. "I want you to tell me something." And he started to sing a little song, a hillbilly song, popular a long time ago: " 'Oh, does the Spearmint lose its flavor on the bedpost overnight?' "

At first I started getting real mad. I thought he was making fun of me like other people had.

" 'When you chew it in the morning,' " he sang in a whisper, " 'will it be too hard to bite?' "

But the more I thought about it the funnier it seemed to me. I tried to stop it but I could feel I was about to laugh—not at McMurphy's singing, but at my own self.

" 'This question's got me goin', won't somebody set me right; does the Spearmint lose its flavor on the bedpost o-ver niiiiiite?' "

He held out that last note and twiddled it down me like a feather. I couldn't help but start to chuckle, and this made me scared I'd get to laughing and not be able to stop. But just then McMurphy jumped off his bed and went to rustling through his nightstand, and I hushed. I clenched my teeth, wondering what to do now. It'd been a long time since I'd let anyone hear me do any more than grunt or bellow. I heard him shut the bedstand, and it echoed like a boiler door. I heard him say, "Here," and something lit on my bed. Little. Just the size of a lizard or a snake . . .

"Juicy Fruit is the best I can do for you at the moment, Chief. Package I won off Scanlon pitchin' pennies." And he got back in bed.

And before I realized what I was doing, I told him Thank you.

He didn't say anything right off. He was up on his elbow, watching me the way he'd watched the black boy, waiting for me to say something else. I picked up the package of gum from the bedspread and held it in my hand and told him Thank you.

It didn't sound like much because my throat was rusty and my tongue creaked. He told me I sounded a little out of practice and laughed at that. I tried to laugh with him, but it was a squawking sound, like a pullet trying to crow. It sounded more like crying than laughing.

He told me not to hurry, that he had till six-thirty in the morning to listen if I wanted to practice. He said a man been still long as me probably had a considerable lot to talk about, and he lay back on his pillow and waited. I thought for a minute for something to say to him, but the only thing that came to my mind was the kind of thing one man can't say to another because it sounds wrong in words. When he saw I couldn't say anything he crossed his hands behind his head and started talking himself.

"Ya know, Chief, I was just rememberin' a time down in the Willamette Valley—I was pickin' beans outside of Eugene and considering myself damn lucky to get the job. It was in the early thirties so there wasn't many kids able to get jobs. I got the job by proving to the bean boss I could pick just as fast and clean as any of the adults. Anyway, I was the only kid in the rows. Nobody else around me but grown-ups. And after I tried a time or two to talk to them I saw they weren't for listening to me—scrawny little patchquilt redhead anyhow. So I hushed. I was so peeved at them not listening to me I kept hushed the livelong four weeks I picked that field, workin' right along side of them, listening to them prattle on about this uncle or that cousin. Or if somebody didn't show up for work, gossip about him. Four weeks and not a peep out of me. Till I think by God they forgot I *could* talk, the mossbacked old bastards. I bided my time. Then, on the last day, I opened up and went to telling them what a petty bunch of farts they were. I told each one just how his buddy had drug him over the coals when he was absent. Hooee, did they listen then! They finally got to arguing with each other and created such a shitstorm I lost my quarter-cent-a-pound bonus I had comin' for not missin' a day because I already had a bad reputation around town and the bean boss claimed the disturbance was likely my fault even if he couldn't prove it. I cussed him out too. My shootin' off my mouth that time probably cost me twenty dollars or so. Well worth it, too."

He chuckled a while to himself, remembering, then turned his head on his pillow and looked at me.

"What I was wonderin', Chief, are you biding your time towards the day you decide to lay into them?"

"No," I told him. "I couldn't."

"Couldn't tell them off? It's easier than you think."

"You're . . . lot bigger, tougher'n I am," I mumbled.

"How's that? I didn't get you, Chief."

I worked some spit down in my throat. "You are bigger and tougher than I am. You can do it."

"Me? Are you kidding? Criminy, look at you: you stand a head taller'n any man on the ward. There ain't a man here you couldn't turn every way but loose, and that's a fact!"

"No. I'm way too little. I used to be big, but not no more. You're twice the size of me."

"Hoo boy, you *are* crazy, aren't you? The first thing I saw when I came in this place was you sitting over in that chair, big as a damn mountain. I tell you, I lived all over Klamath and Texas and Oklahoma and all over around Gallup, and I swear you're the biggest Indian I ever saw."

"I'm from the Columbia Gorge," I said, and he waited for me to go on. "My Papa was a full Chief and his name was Tee Ah Millatoona. That means The-Pine-That-Stands-Tallest-on-the-Mountain, and we didn't live on a mountain. He was real big when I was a kid. My mother got twice his size."

"You must of had a real moose of an old lady. How big was she?"

"Oh—big, big."

"I mean how many feet and inches?"

"Feet and inches? A guy at the carnival looked her over and says five feet nine and weight a hundred and thirty pounds, but that was because he'd just *saw* her. She got bigger all the time."

"Yeah? How much bigger?"

"Bigger than Papa and me together."

"Just one day took to growin', huh? Well, that's a new one on me: I never heard of an Indian woman doing something like that."

"She wasn't Indian. She was a town woman from The Dalles."

"And her name was what? Bromden? Yeah, I see, wait a minute." He thinks for a while and says, "And when a town woman marries an Indian that's marryin' somebody beneath her, ain't it? Yeah, I think I see."

"No. It wasn't just her that made him little. Everybody worked on him because he was big, and wouldn't give in, and did like he pleased. Everybody worked on him just the way they're working on you."

"They who, Chief?" he asked in a soft voice, suddenly serious.

"The Combine. It worked on him for years. He was big enough to fight it for a while. It wanted us to live in inspected houses. It wanted to take the falls. It was even in the tribe, and they worked on him. In the town they beat him up in the alleys and cut his hair short once. Oh, the Combine's big—big. He fought it a long time till my mother made him too little to fight any more and he gave up."

McMurphy didn't say anything for a long time after that. Then he raised up on his elbow and looked at me again, and asked why they beat him up in the alleys, and I told him that they wanted to make him see what he had in store for him only worse if he didn't sign the papers giving everything to the government."

"What did they want him to give to the government?"

"Everything. The tribe, the village, the falls . . ."

"Now I remember; you're talking about the falls where the Indians used to spear salmon—long time ago. Yeah. But the way I remember it the tribe got paid some huge amount."

"That's what they said to him. He said, What can you pay for the way a man lives? He said, What can you pay for what a man is? They didn't understand. Not even the tribe. They stood out in front of our door all holding those checks and they wanted him to tell them what to do now. They kept asking him to invest for them, or tell them where to go, or to buy a farm. But he was too little anymore. And he was too drunk, too. The Combine had whipped him. It beats everybody. It'll beat you too. They can't have somebody as big as Papa running around unless he's one of them. You can see that."

"Yeah, I reckon I can."

"That's why you shouldn't of broke that window. They see you're big, now. Now they got to bust you."

"Like bustin' a mustang, huh?"

"No. No, listen. They don't bust you that way; they work on you ways you can't fight! They put things in! They *install* things. They start as quick as they see you're gonna be big and go to working and installing their filthy machinery when you're little, and keep on and on and on till you're *fixed!*"

"Take 'er easy, buddy; shhhh."

"And if you *fight* they lock you someplace and make you stop—"

"Easy, easy, Chief. Just cool it for a while. They heard you."

He lay down and kept still. My bed was hot, I noticed. I could hear the squeak of rubber soles as the black boy came in with a flashlight to see what the noise was. We lay still till he left.

"He finally just drank," I whispered. I didn't seem to be able to stop talking, not till I finished telling what I thought was all of it. "And the last I see him he's blind in the cedars from drinking and every time I see him put the bottle to his mouth he don't suck out of it, it sucks out of him until he's shrunk so wrinkled and yellow even the dogs don't know him, and we had to cart him out of the cedars, in a pickup, to a place in Portland, to die. I'm not saying they kill. They didn't kill him. They did something else."

I was feeling awfully sleepy. I didn't want to talk any more. I tried to think back on what I'd been saying, and it didn't seem like what I'd wanted to say.

"I been talking crazy, ain't I?"

"Yeah, Chief"—he rolled over in his bed—"you been talkin' crazy."

"It wasn't what I wanted to say. I can't say it all. It don't make sense."

"I didn't say it didn't make sense, Chief, I just said it was talkin' crazy."

He didn't say anything after that for so long I thought he'd gone to sleep. I wished I'd told him good night. I looked over at him, and he was turned away from me. His arm wasn't under the covers, and I could just make out the aces and eights tattooed there. It's big, I thought, big as my arms used to be when I played football. I wanted to reach over and touch the place where he was tattooed, to see if he was still alive. He's layin' awful quiet, I told myself, I ought to touch him to see if he's still alive. . . .

That's a lie. I know he's still alive. That ain't the reason I want to touch him.

I want to touch him because he's a man.

That's a lie too. There's other men around. I could touch them.

I want to touch him because I'm one of these queers!

But that's a lie too. That's one fear hiding behind another. If I was one of these queers I'd want to do other things with him. I just want to touch him because he's who he is.

But as I was about to reach over to that arm he said, "Say, Chief," and rolled in bed with a lurch of covers, facing me, "Say, Chief, why don't you come on this fishin' trip with us tomorrow?"

I didn't answer.

"Come on, what do ya say? I look for it to be one hell of an occasion. You know these two aunts of mine comin' to pick us up? Why, those ain't aunts, man, no; both those girls are workin' shimmy dancers and hustlers I know from Portland. What do you say to that?"

I finally told him I was one of the Indigents.

"You're *what?*"

"I'm broke."

"Oh," he said. "Yeah, I hadn't thought of that."

He was quiet for a time again, rubbing that scar on his nose with his finger. The finger stopped. He raised up on his elbow and looked at me.

"Chief," he said slowly, looking me over, "when you were full-sized, when you used to be, let's say, six seven or eight and weighed two eighty or so—were you strong enough to, say, lift something the size of that control panel in the tub room?"

I thought about that panel. It probably didn't weigh a lot more'n oil drums I'd lifted in the Army. I told him I probably could of at one time.

"If you got that big again, could you still lift it?"

I told him I thought so.

"To hell with what you think; I want to know can you *promise* to lift it if I get you big as you used to be? You promise me that, and you not only get my special body-buildin' course for nothing but you get yourself a ten-buck fishin' trip, *free!*" He licked his lips and lay back. "Get me good odds too, I bet."

He lay there chuckling over some thought of his own. When I asked him how he was going to get me big again he shushed me with a finger to his lips.

"Man, we can't let a secret like this out. I didn't say I'd tell you *how,* did I? Hoo boy, blowin' a man back up to full size is a secret you can't share with everybody, be dangerous in the hands of an enemy. You won't even know it's happening most of the time yourself. But I give you my solemn word, you follow my training program, and here's what'll happen."

He swung his legs out of bed and sat on the edge with his hands on his knees. The dim light coming in over his shoulder from the Nurses' Station caught the shine of his teeth and the one eye glinting down his nose at me. The rollicking auctioneer's voice spun softly through the dorm.

"*There* you'll be. It's the Big Chief Bromden, cuttin' down the boulevard—men, women, and kids rockin' back on their heels to peer up at him: 'Well well well, what giant's this *here,* takin' ten feet at a step and duckin' for telephone wires?' Comes stompin' through town, stops just long enough for virgins, the rest of you twitches might's well not even line up 'less you got tits like muskmelons, nice strong white legs long enough to lock around his mighty back, and a little cup of poozle warm and juicy and sweet as butter an' honey. . . ."

In the dark there he went on, spinning his tale about how it would be, with all the men scared and all the beautiful young girls panting after me. Then he said he was going out right this very minute and sign my name up as one of his fishing crew. He stood up, got the towel from his bedstand and wrapped it around his hips and put on his cap, and stood over my bed.

"Oh man, I tell you, I tell you, you'll have women trippin' you and beatin' you to the floor."

And all of a sudden his hand shot out and with a swing of his arm untied my sheet, cleared my bed of covers, and left me lying there naked.

"Look there, Chief. Haw. What'd I tell ya? You growed a half a foot already."

Laughing, he walked down the row of beds to the hall.

THOMAS MCGRATH

Thomas McGrath, born in 1916, was a leftist, a radical, a sometime Communist, and a cofounder of the Ramshackle Socialist Victory Party; he worked as a farmer, welder, labor organizer, writer of pulp fiction, soldier, logger, woodworker, writer of documentary films, and long-time teacher. First and foremost, McGrath was a poet of the Western vernacular and landscape. His political activism (and antagonism toward HUAC in the 1950s) having forced him away from Los Angeles, McGrath found sanctuary in North Dakota, where he lived and taught for years, and began the major poem Letter to an Imaginary Friend. *McGrath also wrote a novel with the prescient title* This Coffin Has No Handles *(1988). McGrath's selected poetry was published in 1988. He died in 1990.*

Just months before he died, McGrath was writing some of the finest poetry of his life. These epigrammatic poems were collected in a posthumous volume called Death Songs *(1992), from which the se-*

*lections here were taken. McGrath sugarcoats nothing, not the selling
out of the true West to myth-makers and tourists who are blind to
sacred places, not the inevitable autumning of our lives. McGrath calls
his shots as he sees them. His candor is invaluable. "So the nation
became / What the legend made of it: / Half exaggeration / Half
pure bullshit."*

LEGENDS, HEROES, MYTH-FIGURES AND OTHER AMERICAN LIARS

Start with Davy Crockett—
A legend for hire—
His nose as long
As a telephone wire.

And he fought a b'ar
With his pants on f'ar
And won at the Alamo—
Or someone's a l'ar.

Or take Solomon Snap,
The peddin' man—
Sold a sheep in wolf's clothing
And a bird-out-of-hand—
(And the bush it wasn't in)

And a false false tooth
Made of a mumbly peg
And a squirrel to nest in
Your basic wooden leg;

Or wooden nutmegs
Or the wild north wind:
By the thirty inch yard
Or in powder kegs—

Last seen heading out
To the Western Lands
With a trainload of postholes
For the farmers in Kansas.

Old stormalong began it—
Windjammer from the sea—
Who made windies and lies
Part of our history

Or maybe Barney Beal
Who could knock down a bull
Until the bull got so deep
He went over the hill.

Or Sam Patch the mill-
Hand—made clothes without seams:
Stripped away our fig leaves
And clothed us in jeans

Or in moon-milky habiliments—
A patch on our pride—
Or in spangled chaparejos
In which to ride

Westward, always westerly,
Toward all desires,
Toward mountain and ocean
And the great Western liars:

Mike Fink, Joe Stink—
Who gave the lie luster—
Helped by Windy Bill
And G.A. Custer.

So the nation became

What legend made of it:

Half exaggeration

Half pure bullshit.

THE PLEASURES OF
THE GREAT SALT LAKE

The great salt moon, that plunges at
The sky, and mirror-like reclaims
A Utah of astonishment
And sunlight, snares no second glance
From jaded tourists roaring down
Nevada's tired and faded hills.

The road slants ruler straight; and salt
The world hangs from the tourist eye
Across the salt-crust mesas swim,
Like dinosaurs the shallow sea,
Miraged, or leap and come to rest
Their bases planted on the clouds.

Yet all this fine and ponderous play
Where the Rockies skip like young rams
Does not amuse the voyaging soul.
In mad and dedicated calm,
He eyes the inscape's decorous hills
Or guidebooks' foolproof scenery.

Tired from their weighty levitation
Mountain and mesa settle down
To race at ninety miles an hour
Past the tourist's crawling car,
All their hop-scotch reality
Boring the dull sight-seer's eye.

LONGING

In these days,
When the winds wear no wedding rings,
Everything seems to be going away:
My sweet son filling his sails at a distant college,
My springtime friends on trail to the ultimate West,
And, even in central summer,
I feel the days shortening,
The stealthy lengthening of the night.

And so, in the imperial extension of the dark,
Against which, all my life, I opposed my body,
I long to pass from this anguish of passings
Into the calm of an indifferent joy . . .

To enter October's frail canoe and drift down
Down with the bright leaves among the raucous wildfowl
On the narrowing autumn rivers where, in these longer
    nights,
Secretly, in the shallows or on reedy shorelines,
Ice is already forming.

KEITH WILSON

Keith Wilson was born in Clovis, New Mexico, in 1927, and has spent most of his life in the southwest Rocky Mountains. He is professor emeritus at New Mexico State University in Las Cruces. In more than twenty volumes of poetry published in the last forty years, consistent themes of violence and history can be traced throughout his work—both in the long and violent history of human inhabitation in his native Southwest, and in his personal experience with violence as a naval officer during the Korean War. Although he began his adult

life as a career navy officer, Wilson fell under the influence of the
"projective verse" methods of Charles Olson, and began using verse
to connect the violent past to the future, promoting hope through com-
passion and forgiveness. Wilson's collections include Sketches *for a*
New Mexico Hill Town *(1966),* Homestead *(1969),* Mid-
watch *(1972),* The Shaman Deer *(1978), and* Lion's Gate: Selected Poems, 1963–1986 *(1987). "The Poem Politic 10: A Note*
for Future Historians" was published in Graves Registry *(1992).*

THE POEM POLITIC 10:
A NOTE FOR FUTURE
HISTORIANS

When writing of us, state
as your first premise
THEY VALUED WAR MORE THAN ANYTHING
You will never understand us
otherwise, say that we

cherished war

   over peace and comfort
   over feeding the poor
   over our own health
   over love, even the act of it
   over religion, all of them, except
   perhaps certain forms of Buddhism

that we never failed to pass bills of war through our legislatures,
using the pressures of imminent invasion or disaster (potential)
abroad as absolution for not spending moneys on projects which
might make us happy or even save us from clear and evident
crises at home

Write of us that we spent millions educating the best of our
youth and then slaughtered them capturing some hill or swamp of
no value and bragged for several months about how well they
died following orders that were admittedly stupid, ill-conceived

Explain how the military virtues, best practiced by robots, are
most valued by us. You will never come to understand us unless
you realize, from the first, that we love killing and kill our own
youth, our own great men FIRST. Enemies can be forgiven,
their broken bodies mourned over, but our own are rarely spoken
of except in political speeches when we "honor" the dead and
encourage the living young to follow their example and be glori-
ously dead also

NOTE: Almost all religious training, in all our countries, dedi-
cates itself to preparing the people for war. Catholic chaplains
rage against "peaceniks," forgetting Christ's title in the Church is
Prince of Peace; Baptists shout of the ungodly and the necessity
of ritual holy wars while preaching of the Ten Commandments
each Sunday; Mohammedans, Shintoists look forward to days of
bloody retribution while Jews march across the sands of Palestine
deserts, Rabbis urging them on. . . .

THEY VALUED WAR MORE THAN ANYTHING

Will expose our children, our homes to murder and devastation
on the chance that we can murder or devastate FIRST and thus
gain honor. No scientist is respected whose inventions help mankind, for its own sake, but only when those discoveries also help
to destroy, or to heal soldiers, that they may destroy other men
and living things

                                                            Be aware that
Destiny has caught us up, our choices made subtly over the ages
have spun a web about us: It is unlikely we will escape, having
geared everything in our societies toward war and combat. It is
probably too late for us to survive in anything like our present
form.

THEY VALUED WAR MORE THAN ANYTHING

If you build us monuments let them all say that, as warning, as a
poison label on a bottle, that you may not ever repeat our follies,
feel our griefs.

EDWARD ABBEY

*Edward Abbey, born in Home, Pennsylvania, in 1927, found many
other homes throughout the West and in the minds and imaginations
of his readers. After twice flunking journalism in high school, Abbey
hitchhiked across the country, fought in Italy, studied philosophy in
Scotland, worked as a welfare caseworker, and spent sixteen summers
as a fire lookout and a park ranger, living close to the land. The author
of two dozen works of fiction and nonfiction, Abbey was a considerable
influence on the literary and environmental scene in the West for more
than twenty years, and his legacy as one of the forefathers of the "eco-
guerrillas" continues since his death. His second novel,* The Brave
Cowboy *(1958), was made into the award-winning film* Lonely
Are the Brave. *His novel* The Monkey Wrench Gang *(1975)
has become a favorite among the environmentally conscious and politically active.*

*Abbey's masterpiece, however, the rock on which his reputation
stands, is* Desert Solitaire *(1969), an evocation of his growing iden-
tification with life connected to the landforms and plants and creatures
of the Southwest, and his awakening to a political determination to
preserve some of the country in what we think of as its naturally evolved
condition. Abbey died in 1989 and lies buried in the desert somewhere
outside Tucson, Arizona.*

FROM *DESERT SOLITAIRE*

Most of my wandering in the desert I've done alone. Not so much from
choice as from necessity—I generally prefer to go into places where no
one else wants to go. I find that in contemplating the natural world my
pleasure is greater if there are not too many others contemplating it with
me, at the same time. However, there are special hazards in traveling
alone. Your chances of dying, in case of sickness or accident, are much
improved, simply because there is no one around to go for help.

Exploring a side canyon off Havasu Canyon one day, I was unable
to resist the temptation to climb up out of it onto what corresponds in
that region to the Tonto Bench. Late in the afternoon I realized that I
would not have enough time to get back to my camp before dark, unless

I could find a much shorter route than the one by which I had come. I looked for a shortcut.

Nearby was another little side canyon which appeared to lead down into Havasu Canyon. It was a steep, shadowy, extremely narrow defile with the usual meandering course and overhanging walls; from where I stood, near its head, I could not tell if the route was feasible all the way down to the floor of the main canyon. I had no rope with me—only my walking stick. But I was hungry and thirsty, as always. I started down.

For a while everything went well. The floor of the little canyon began as a bed of dry sand, scattered with rocks. Farther down a few boulders were wedged between the walls; I climbed over and under them. Then the canyon took on the slickrock character—smooth, sheer, slippery sandstone carved by erosion into a series of scoops and potholes which got bigger as I descended. In some of these basins there was a little water left over from the last flood, warm and fetid water under an oily-looking scum, condensed by prolonged evaporation to a sort of broth, rich in dead and dying organisms. My canteen was empty and I was very thirsty but I felt that I could wait.

I came to a lip on the canyon floor which overhung by twelve feet the largest so far of these stagnant pools. On each side rose the canyon walls, roughly perpendicular. There was no way to continue except by dropping into the pool. I hesitated. Beyond this point there could hardly be any returning, yet the main canyon was still not visible below. Obviously the only sensible thing to do was to turn back. I edged over the lip of stone and dropped feet first into the water.

Deeper than I expected. The warm, thick fluid came up and closed over my head as my feet touched the muck at the bottom. I had to swim to the farther side. And here I found myself on the verge of another drop-off, with one more huge bowl of green soup below.

This drop-off was about the same height as the one before, but not overhanging. It resembled a children's playground slide, concave and S-curved, only steeper, wider, with a vertical pitch in the middle. It did not lead directly into the water but ended in a series of steplike ledges above the pool. Beyond the pool lay another edge, another drop-off into an unknown depth. Again I paused, and for a much longer time. But I no longer had the option of turning around and going back. I eased myself into the chute and let go of everything—except my faithful stick.

I hit rock bottom hard, but without any physical injury. I swam the stinking pond dog-paddle style, pushing the heavy scum away from my face, and crawled out on the far side to see what my fate was going to be.

Fatal. Death by starvation, slow and tedious. For I was looking straight down an overhanging cliff to a rubble pile of broken rocks eighty feet below.

After the first wave of utter panic had passed I began to try to think. First of all I was not going to die immediately, unless another flash flood came down the gorge; there was the pond of stagnant water on hand to save me from thirst and a man can live, they say, for thirty days or more without food. My sun-bleached bones, dramatically sprawled at the bottom of the chasm, would provide the diversion of the picturesque for future wanderers—if any man ever came this way again.

My second thought was to scream for help, although I knew very well there could be no other human being within miles. I even tried it but the sound of that anxious shout, cut short in the dead air within the canyon walls, was so inhuman, so detached as it seemed from myself, that it terrified me and I didn't attempt it again.

I thought of tearing my clothes into strips and plaiting a rope. But what was I wearing?—boots, socks, a pair of old and ragged blue jeans, a flimsy T-shirt, an ancient and rotten sombrero of straw. Not a chance of weaving such a wardrobe into a rope eighty feet long, or even twenty feet long.

How about a signal fire? There was nothing to burn but my clothes; not a tree, not a shrub, not even a weed grew in this stony cul-de-sac. Even if I burned my clothing the chances of the smoke being seen by some Hualapai Indian high on the south rim were very small; and if he did see the smoke, what then? He'd shrug his shoulders, sigh, and take another pull from his Tokay bottle. Furthermore, without clothes, the sun would soon bake me to death.

There was only one thing I could do. I had a tiny notebook in my hip pocket and a stub of pencil. When these dried out I could at least record my final thoughts. I would have plenty of time to write not only my epitaph but my own elegy.

But not yet.

There were a few loose stones scattered about the edge of the pool. Taking the biggest first, I swam with it back to the foot of the slickrock chute and placed it there. One by one I brought the others and made a shaky little pile about two feet high leaning against the chute. Hopeless, of course, but there was nothing else to do. I stood on the top of the pile and stretched upward, straining my arms to their utmost limit and groped with fingers and fingernails for a hold on something firm. There was nothing. I crept back down. I began to cry. It was easy. All alone, I didn't have to be brave.

Through the tears I noticed my old walking stick lying nearby. I took it and stood it on the most solid stone in the pile, behind the two topmost stones. I took off my boots, tied them together and hung them around my neck, on my back. I got up on the little pile again and lifted one leg and set my big toe on the top of the stick. This could never work. Slowly and painfully, leaning as much of my weight as I could against the sandstone slide, I applied more and more pressure to the stick, pushing my body upward until I was again stretched out full length above it. Again I felt about for a fingerhold. There was none. The chute was smooth as polished marble.

No, not quite that smooth. This was sandstone, soft and porous, not marble, and between it and my wet body and wet clothing a certain friction was created. In addition, the stick had enabled me to reach a higher section of the S-curved chute, where the angle was more favorable. I discovered that I could move upward, inch by inch, through adhesion and with the help of the leveling tendency of the curve. I gave an extra little push with my big toe—the stones collapsed below, the stick clattered down—and crawled rather like a snail or slug, oozing slime, up over the rounded summit of the slide.

The next obstacle, the overhanging spout twelve feet above a deep plunge pool, looked impossible. It *was* impossible, but with the blind faith of despair I slogged into the water and swam underneath the drop-off and floundered around for a while, scrabbling at the slippery rock until my nerves and tiring muscles convinced my numbed brain that *this was not the way*. I swam back to solid ground and lay down to rest and die in comfort.

Far above I could see the sky, an irregular strip of blue between the dark, hard-edged canyon walls that seemed to lean toward each other as they towered above me. Across that narrow opening a small white cloud was passing, so lovely and precious and delicate and forever inaccessible that it broke the heart and made me weep like a woman, like a child. In all my life I had never seen anything so beautiful.

The walls that rose on either side of the drop-off were literally perpendicular. Eroded by weathering, however, and not by the corrosion of rushing floodwater, they had a rough surface, chipped, broken, cracked. Where the walls joined the face of the overhang they formed almost a square corner, with a number of minute crevices and inch-wide shelves on either side. It might, after all, be possible. What did I have to lose?

When I had regained some measure of nerve and steadiness I got up off my back and tried the wall beside the pond, clinging to the rock with bare toes and fingertips and inching my way crabwise toward the corner. The watersoaked, heavy boots dangling from my neck, swinging back and forth with my every movement, threw me off balance and I fell into the pool. I swam out to the bank, unslung the boots and threw them up over the drop-off, out of sight. They'd be there if I ever needed them again. Once more I attached myself to the wall, tenderly, sensitively, like a limpet, and very slowly, very cautiously, worked my way into the corner. Here I was able to climb upward, a few centimeters at a time, by bracing myself against the opposite sides and finding sufficient niches for fingers and toes. As I neared the top and the overhang became noticeable I prepared for a slip, planning to push myself away from the rock so as to fall into the center of the pool where the water was deepest. But it wasn't necessary. Somehow, with a skill and tenacity I could never have found in myself under ordinary circumstances, I managed to creep straight up that gloomy cliff and over the brink of the drop-off and into the flower of safety. My boots were floating under the surface of the little puddle above. As I poured the stinking water out of them and pulled them on and laced them up I discovered myself bawling again for the third time in three hours, the hot delicious tears of victory. And up above the clouds replied—thunder.

I emerged from that treacherous little canyon at sundown, with an enormous fire in the western sky and lightning overhead. Through sweet twilight and the sudden dazzling flare of lightning I hiked back along the Tonto Bench, bellowing the *Ode to Joy*. Long before I reached the place where I could descend safely to the main canyon and my camp, however, darkness set in, the clouds opened their bays and the rain poured down. I took shelter under a ledge in a shallow cave about three feet high—hardly room to sit up in. Others had been here before: the dusty floor of the little hole was littered with the droppings of birds, rats, jackrabbits and coyotes. There were also a few long gray pieces of scat with a curious twist at one tip—cougar? I didn't care. I had some matches with me, sealed in paraffin (the prudent explorer); I scraped

together the handiest twigs and animal droppings and built a little fire
and waited for the rain to stop.

It didn't stop. The rain came down for hours in alternate waves of
storm and drizzle and I very soon had burnt up all the fuel within reach.
No matter. I stretched out in the coyote den, pillowed my head on my
arm and suffered through the long long night, wet, cold, aching, hungry,
wretched, dreaming claustrophobic nightmares. It was one of the hap-
piest nights of my life.

GARY SNYDER

*Gary Snyder was born in San Francisco in 1930, and grew up on
the Washington and Oregon coast, receiving a B.A. in anthropology
from Reed College in 1951. After stints as a logger and Forest Service
trailbreaker (he served as the inspiration for Japhy Ryder, the protag-
onist of Jack Kerouac's* The Dharma Bums*), Snyder returned to
California to study Oriental languages in 1953 (he also helped foment
the Beat movement), and wrote the poems later published in* Riprap
(1959) and Myths and Texts *(1960). For fifteen years, Snyder lived
mostly in China and Japan, studying Buddhism with Zen masters.
His first prose book,* Earth House Hold *(1969), written in the
Japanese form of a poetic travel journal, details his experiences in the
Orient. Snyder returned to the United States in 1968 and became a
leading spokesperson for the ecology movement. In 1975, he won the
Pulitzer prize for his collection* Turtle Island. *A prolific translator of
ancient and modern Japanese poetry, he lives in California and teaches
at the University of California at Davis. Recent publications include
a collection of nature essays,* The Practice of the Wild *(1990), and*
No Nature: New and Selected Poems *(1992).*

*Snyder writes about the workaday zen of living in the West, a
place full of both destruction and calamity (blades and saws) and sweet
epiphanies. His poems are often concerned with "the pain of the work
of wrecking the world," which is driven by the idea that people have*

to survive by reaping that which they did not sow—the indispensable complexity of what has evolved, which we call nature. We see his themes working in the poems here, from Riprap and Cold Mountain Poems *(1965) and* Axe Handles *(1983).*

ABOVE PATE VALLEY

We finished clearing the last
Section of trail by noon,
High on the ridge-side
Two thousand feet above the creek
Reached the pass, went on
Beyond the white pine groves,
Granite shoulders, to a small
Green meadow watered by the snow,
Edged with Aspen—sun
Straight high and blazing
But the air was cool.
Ate a cold fried trout in the
Trembling shadows. I spied
A glitter, and found a flake
Black volcanic glass—obsidian—
By a flower. Hands and knees
Pushing the Bear grass, thousands
Of arrowhead leavings over a
Hundred yards. Not one good
Head, just razor flakes
On a hill snowed all but summer,
A land of fat summer deer,
They came to camp. On their
Own trails. I followed my own
Trail here. Picked up the cold-drill,
Pick, singlejack, and sack
Of dynamite.
Ten thousand years.

PAINTING THE NORTH
SAN JUAN SCHOOL

White paint splotches on blue head bandanas
Dusty transistor with wired-on antenna
    plays sixties rock and roll;
Little kids came with us are on teeter-totters
    tilting under shade of oak
This building good for ten years more.
The shingled bell-cupola trembles
    at every log truck rolling by—

The radio speaks:
    today it will be one hundred degrees in the valley.
—Franquette walnuts grafted on the
    local native rootstock do o.k.
    nursery stock of cherry all has fungus;
Lucky if a bare-root planting lives,

This paint thins with water.
This year the busses will run only
    on paved roads,
Somehow the children will be taught:
How to record their mother tongue
    with written signs,

Names to call the landscape of the continent
                they live on
Assigned it by the ruling people of the last
    three hundred years,
The games of numbers,
What went before, as told by those who
    think they know it,

A drunken man with chestnut mustache
Stumbles off the road to ask if he can help.

Children drinking chocolate milk

Ladders resting on the shaky porch.

GETTING IN THE WOOD

The sour smell,
      blue stain,
            water squirts out round the wedge,

Lifting quarters of rounds
      covered with ants,
      "a living glove of ants upon my hand"
the poll of the sledge a bit peened over
so the wedge springs off and tumbles
      ringing like high-pitched bells
            into the complex duff of twigs
            poison oak, bark, sawdust,
            shards of logs,

And the sweat drips down.
      Smell of crushed ants.
The lean and heave on the peavey
that breaks free the last of a bucked
      three-foot round,
            it lies flat on smashed oaklings—

Wedge and sledge, peavey and maul,
      little axe, canteen, piggyback can
      of saw-mix gas and oil for the chain,
knapsack of files and goggles and rags,

All to gather the dead and the down.
      The young men throw splits on the piles
      bodies hardening, learning the pace
and the smell of tools from this delve
      in the winter
            death-topple of elderly oak.
Four cords.

DILLINGHAM, ALASKA,
THE WILLOW TREE BAR

Drills chatter full of mud and compressed air
all across the globe,
        low-ceilinged bars, we hear the same new songs

All the new songs.
In the working bars of the world.
After you done drive Cat. After the truck
        went home.
        Caribou slip,
        front legs folded first
        under the warm oil pipeline
        set four feet off the ground—

On the wood floor, glass in hand,
        laugh and cuss with
        somebody else's wife.
        Texans, Hawaiians, Eskimos,
        Filipinos, Workers, always
        on the edge of a brawl—
        In the bars of the world.
        Hearing those same new songs
                in Abadan,
        Naples, Galveston, Darwin, Fairbanks,
        White or brown,
Drinking it down,

the pain
of the work
of wrecking the world.

RICHARD HUGO

*Richard Hugo was born in Seattle in 1923, and grew up near the
Duwamish River, in White Center, an industrial suburb. In World
War II, Hugo was stationed in Italy, and earned a Distinguished
Flying Cross for his leadership in bombardier missions. He studied
under Theodore Roethke at the University of Washington, receiving
an M.A. in 1952. A Run of Jacks, the first of eight critically
acclaimed collections of poetry, was published in 1961, while Hugo
worked as a technical writer at Boeing and played fast-pitch softball in
the city league. In 1964, Hugo moved to Missoula, Montana, where
he began his tenure at the University of Montana, teaching and directing the creative writing program until his death, in 1982. Hugo's
influential book on writing,* The Triggering Town, *originally published in 1979, is a standard creative writing text. He wrote one
mystery novel,* Death and the Good Life; *a collection of autobiographical essays,* The Real West Marginal Way, *was published
posthumously in 1986. Hugo died in October 1982, in the middle
of the World Series, at Virginia Mason Hospital in Seattle, not far
from where he was born.*

These poems from his collected works, Making Certain It Goes
On, *are testament to Hugo's continued insistence on our need for
humility when confronting conflicting human needs, the enormous and
often bewildering complexities of desire.*

DEGREES OF GRAY IN
PHILIPSBURG

You might come here Sunday on a whim.
Say your life broke down. The last good kiss
you had was years ago. You walk these streets
laid out by the insane, past hotels
that didn't last, bars that did, the tortured try
of local drivers to accelerate their lives.
Only churches are kept up. The jail

turned 70 this year. The only prisoner
is always in, not knowing what he's done.

The principal supporting business now
is rage. Hatred of the various grays
the mountain sends, hatred of the mill,
The Silver Bill repeal, the best liked girls
who leave each year for Butte. One good
restaurant and bars can't wipe the boredom out.
The 1907 boom, eight going silver mines,
a dance floor built on springs—
all memory resolves itself in gaze,
in panoramic green you know the cattle eat
or two stacks high above the town,
two dead kilns, the huge mill in collapse
for fifty years that won't fall finally down.

Isn't this your life? That ancient kiss
still burning out your eyes? Isn't this defeat
so accurate, the church bell simply seems
a pure announcement: ring and no one comes?
Don't empty houses ring? Are magnesium
and scorn sufficient to support a town,
not just Philipsburg, but towns
of towering blondes, good jazz and booze
the world will never let you have
until the town you came from dies inside?

Say no to yourself. The old man, twenty
when the jail was built, still laughs
although his lips collapse. Someday soon,
he says, I'll go to sleep and not wake up.
You tell him no. You're talking to yourself.
The car that brought you here still runs.
The money you buy lunch with,
no matter where it's mined, is silver
and the girl who serves your food
is slender and her red hair lights the wall.

THE FREAKS AT
SPURGIN ROAD FIELD

The dim boy claps because the others clap.
The polite word, handicapped, is muttered in the stands.
Isn't it wrong, the way the mind moves back.

One whole day I sit, contrite, dirt, L.A.
Union Station, '46, sweating through last night.
The dim boy claps because the others clap.

Score, 5 to 3. Pitcher fading badly in the heat.
Isn't it wrong to be or not be spastic?
Isn't it wrong, the way the mind moves back.

I'm laughing at a neighbor girl beaten to scream
by a savage father and I'm ashamed to look.
The dim boy claps because the others clap.

The score is always close, the rally always short.
I've left more wreckage than a quake.
Isn't it wrong, the way the mind moves back.

The afflicted never cheer in unison.
Isn't it wrong, the way the mind moves back
to stammering pastures where the picnic should have
    worked.
The dim boy claps because the others clap.

SILVER STAR

for Bill Kittredge

This is the final resting place of engines,
farm equipment and that rare, never more
than occasional man. Population:
17. Altitude: unknown. For no
good reason you can guess, the woman

in the local store is kind. Old steam trains
have been rusting here so long, you feel
the urge to oil them, to lay new track, to start
the west again. The Jefferson
drifts by in no great hurry on its way
to wed the Madison, to be a tributary
of the ultimately dirty brown Missouri.
This town supports your need to run alone.

What if you'd lived here young, gone full of fear
to that stark brick school, the cruel teacher
supported by your guardian? Think well
of the day you ran away to Whitehall.
Think evil of the cop who found you starving
and returned you, siren open, to the house
you cannot find today. You question
everyone you see. The answer comes back wrong.
There was no house. They never heard your name.

When you leave here, leave in a flashy car
and wave goodbye. You are a stranger
every day. Let the engines and the farm
equipment die, and know that rivers
end and never end, lose and never lose
their famous names. What if your first girl
ended certain she was animal, barking
at the aides and licking floors? You know
you have no answers. The empty school
burns red in heavy snow.

DRIVING MONTANA

The day is a woman who loves you. Open.
Deer drink close to the road and magpies
spray from your car. Miles from any town
your radio comes in strong, unlikely
Mozart from Belgrade, rock and roll
from Butte. Whatever the next number,

you want to hear it. Never has your Buick
found this forward a gear. Even
the tuna salad in Reedpoint is good.

Towns arrive ahead of imagined schedule.
Absorakee at one. Or arrive so late—
Silesia at nine—you recreate the day.
Where did you stop along the road
and have fun? Was there a runaway horse?
Did you park at that house, the one
alone in a void of grain, white with green
trim and red fence, where you know you lived
once? You remembered the ringing creek,
the soft brown forms of far off bison.
You must have stayed hours, then drove on.
In the motel you know you'd never seen it before.

Tomorrow will open again, the sky wide
as the mouth of a wild girl, friable
clouds you lose yourself to. You are lost
in miles of land without people, without
one fear of being found, in the dash
of rabbits, soar of antelope, swirl
merge and clatter of streams.

FORT BENTON

for Jan

This was the last name west on charts.
West of here the world turned that indefinite white
of blank paper and settlers faded one at a time alone.
What had been promised in Saint Louis proved
little more than battering weather and resolve.
Hungry for women and mail, this town
turned out to watch the Mandan dock.

Church was a desperate gesture, prayer
something muttered bitter. One we called friend
the long Missouri here followed his babble
into the breaks and no one looked for his bones.
We still don't look for friends who turn into air.
Given the right seed and seasonal luck
a love of land becomes a need for each other.

The river slides into the breaks. Nothing comes back,
man, Mandan, the latest word on sin.
Trains killed boats and died in their turn.
Where we look deep the river smirks.
Let's recognize "hello there" and "nice day"
spare us those improvements that give way
beneath us like the bank someday for sure.

The best towns, no matter how solvent, seem
to barely hang on. This is the town to leave
for the void and come back to needing a home.
It may be the aged river or the brick hotel
on the bank, heavy as water, or the ritual
that shouldn't be hard to start: the whole town out
shouting "come back" at the breaks one day a year.

DUWAMISH

Midwestern in the heat, this river's
curves are slow and sick. Water knocks
at mills and concrete plants, and crud
compounds the gray. On the out-tide,
water, half salt water from the sea,
rambles by a barrel of molded nails,
gray lumber piles, moss on ovens
in the brickyard no one owns.
Boys are snapping tom cod spines
and jeering at the Greek who bribes
the river with his sailing coins.

Because the name is Indian, Indians
ignore the river as it cruises
past the tavern. Gulls are diving crazy
where boys nail porgies to the pile.
No Indian would interrupt his beer
to tell the story of the snipe
who dove to steal the nailed girl
late one autumn, with the final salmon in.

This river colors day. On bright days
here, the sun is always setting or obscured
by one cloud. Or the shade extended
to the far bank just before you came.
And what should flare, the Chinese red
of a searun's-fin, the futile roses,
unkept cherry trees in spring, is muted.
For the river, there is late November
only, and the color of a slow winter.

On the short days, looking for a word,
knowing the smoke from the small homes
turns me colder than wind from
the cold river, knowing this poverty
is not a lack of money but of friends,
I come here to be cold. Not silver cold
like ice, for ice has glitter. Gray
cold like the river. Cold like 4 P.M.
on Sunday. Cold like a decaying porgy.

But cold is a word. There is no word along
this river I can understand or say.
Not Greek threats to a fishless moon
nor Slavic chants. All words are Indian.
Love is Indian for water, and madness
means, to Redmen, I am going home.

SALT WATER STORY

He loved his cabin: there
nothing had happened. Then his friends were dead.
The new neighbors had different ways.
Days came heavy with regret.
He studied sea charts and charted
sea lanes out. He calculated times
to ride the tide rip, times to go ashore and rest.
He memorized the names of bays: those
with plenty of driftwood for fire,
those with oysters. He found a forest
he could draw back into
when the Coast Guard came looking, news
of him missing by now broadcast state-wide.
He made no move. He turned out lights
and lit candles and watched his face
in the window glow red.

He dreamed a raft
and dreamed this sea lane out, past
long dormant cannons and the pale hermit
who begged to go with him. A blue heron
trailed him. A second heron trailed the first,
a third the second and so on. Those who looked for him
checked the skies for a long blue line
of laboring wings.
The birds broke formation, and the world
of search and rescue lost track of his wake.
His face glowed red on the glass.
If found, he'd declare himself pro-cloud
and pro-wind and anti-flat hot days.

Then he dreamed wrong
what we owe Egypt, what we owe
sea lanes out of the slaves to ourselves
we become one morning, nothing
for us in dawn, and nothing for us in tide.
What we owe Egypt fades

into what we owe Greece and then Rome.
What we owe Rome keeps repeating
like what we owe time—namely our lives
and whatever laughter we find to pass on.
He knew grief repeats on its own.

One night late, the face in the window
glowed back at him pale. He believed that face
some bum peeking in
and waved "hi." The old face told him,
to navigate a lasting way out
he must learn how coins gleam
one way through water, how bones of dead fish
gleam another, and he must learn both gleams
and dive deep. He learned both gleams
and learned to dive fast and come up slow
as sky every day.

And we might think someday we'll find him
dead over his charts, the water ways out
a failed dream. Nothing like that.
His cabin stands empty and he
sails the straits. We often see him
from shore or the deck of a ferry.
We can't tell him by craft. Some days
he passes by on a yacht, some days a tug.
He's young and, captain or deckhand,
he is the one who waves.

PHILIP LEVINE

*Philip Levine is a poet who "tries to write poetry for people for whom
there is no poetry." He was born in 1928 in Detroit, and was formally
educated there at public schools and at Wayne University. After a*

succession of self-alleged "stupid jobs," he left the city for good, living in various parts of the country, including Iowa City, where he received an M.F.A. in poetry, before settling in Fresno, California, in 1958. He taught at the University of California at Fresno for more than thirty years, with time off for residencies at schools in Massachusetts, New Jersey, New York, Ohio, and Australia, and has won multiple National Endowment for the Arts and Guggenheim fellowships. His books of poetry include Not This Pig *(1968),* They Feed the Lion *(1972),* The Names of the Lost *(1976),* Sweet Will *(1985), and* A Walk with Thomas Jefferson *(1988).* What Work Is *(1991) won the National Book Award.* The Bread of Time: Notes Toward an Autobiography *was published in 1994, as was* Collected Poems, *which won the Pulitzer prize for poetry.*

Levine is a poet who has lived a long time in the West, yet who writes for every territory. In "Sierra Kid," from On the Edge *(1963), he gives us a condensed history of the West from the point of view of a pulp hero turned anchorite. What we learn of history we learn too late. "Soloing" shows us another West, a contemporary version, where humans have defaced nature yet can still attain grace by remembering the music of their beginnings.*

SIERRA KID

"I've been where it hurts." the Kid

He becomes Sierra Kid

I passed Slimgullion, Morgan Mine,
Camp Seco, and the rotting Lode.
    Dark walls of sugar pine—,
    And where I left the road

    I left myself behind;
    Talked to no one, thought
Of nothing. When my luck ran out
Lived on berries, nuts, bleached grass.
    Driven by the wind
    Through great Sonora Pass,

I found an Indian's teeth;
    Turned and climbed again
Without direction, compass, path,
Without a way of coming down,
    Until I stopped somewhere
    And gave the place a name.

    I called the forests mine;
        Whatever I could hear
I took to be a voice: a man
Was something I would never hear.

He faces his second winter in the Sierra

A hard brown bug, maybe a beetle,
Packing a ball of sparrow shit—
    What shall I call it?
Shit beetle? Why's it pushing here
At this great height in the thin air
    With its ridiculous waddle
Up the hard side of Hard Luck Hill?
And the furred thing that frightened me—
    Bobcat, coyote, wild dog—
Flat eyes in winter bush, stiff tail,
Holding his ground, a rotted log.
    Grass snakes that wouldn't die,

And night hawks hanging on the rim
Of what was mine. I know them now;
    They have absorbed a mind
Which must endure the freezing snow
They endure and, freezing, find
    A clear sustaining stream.

He learns to lose

    She was afraid
    Of everything,

The little Digger girl.
  Pah Utes had killed
  Her older brother
Who may have been her lover
  The way she cried
  Over his ring—

  The heavy brass
  On the heavy hand.
She carried it for weeks
  Clenched in her fist
  As if it might
Keep out the loneliness
  Or the plain fact
  That he was gone.

  When the first snows
  Began to fall
She stopped her crying, picked
  Berries, sweet grass,
  Mended her clothes
And sewed a patchwork shawl.
  We slept together
  But did not speak.

  It may have been
  The Pah Utes took
Her off, perhaps her kin.
  I came back
  To find her gone
With half the winter left
  To face alone—
  The slow gray dark

  Moving along
  The dark tipped grass
Between the numbed pines.
  Night after night

For four long months
My face to her dark face
   We two had lain
   Till the first light.

Civilization comes to Sierra Kid

They levelled Tater Hill
   And I was sick.
First sun, and the chain saws
   Coming on; blue haze,
      Dull blue exhaust
Rising, dust rising, and the smell.

   Moving from their thatched huts
      The crazed wood rats
By the thousand; grouse, spotted quail
   Abandoning the hills
      For the sparse trail
On which, exposed, I also packed.

   Six weeks. I went back down
      Through my own woods
Afraid of what I knew they'd done.
   There, there, an A&P,
      And not a tree
For miles, and mammoth hills of goods.

   Fat men in uniforms,
      Young men in aprons
With one face shouting, "He is mad!"
   I answered: "I am Lincoln,
      Aaron Burr,
The aging son of Appleseed.

   "I am American
      And I am cold."
But not a one would hear me out.
   Oh God, what have I seen

That was not sold!
They shot an old man in the gut.

Mad, dying, Sierra Kid enters the capital

What have I changed?
I unwound burdocks from my hair
    And scalded stains
    Of the black grape
And hid beneath long underwear
    The yellowed tape.

Who will they find
In the dark woods of the dark mind
    Now I have gone
    Into the world?
Across the blazing civic lawn
    A shadow's hurled

And I must follow.
Something slides beneath my vest
    Like melted tallow,
    Thick but thin,
Burning where it comes to rest
    On what was skin.

Who will they find?
A man with no eyes in his head?
    Or just a mind
    Calm and alone?
Or just a mouth, silent, dead,
    The lips half gone?

Will they presume
That someone once was half alive
    And that the air
    Was massive where
The sickening pyracanthas thrive
    Staining his tomb?

         I came to touch
The great heart of a dying state.
         Here is the wound!
         It makes no sound.
All that we learn we learn too late,
         And it's not much.

SOLOING

My mother tells me she dreamed
of John Coltrane, a young Trane
playing his music with such joy
and contained energy and rage
she could not hold back her tears.
And sitting awake now, her hands
crossed in her lap, the tears start
in her blind eyes. The TV set
behind her is gray, expressionless.
It is late, the neighbors quiet,
even the city—Los Angeles—quiet.
I have driven for hours down 99,
over the Grapevine into heaven
to be here. I place my left hand
on her shoulder, and she smiles.
What a world, a mother and son
finding solace in California
just where we were told it would
be, among the palm trees and all-
night super markets pushing orange
back-lighted oranges at 2 A.M.
"He was alone," she says, and does
not say, just as I am, "soloing."
What a world, a great man half
her age comes to my mother
in sleep to give her the gift
of song, which—shaking the tears
away—she passes on to me, for now
I can hear the music of the world

in the silence and that word:
soloing. What a world—when I
arrived the great bowl of mountains
was hidden in a cloud of exhaust,
the sea spread out like a carpet
of oil, the roses I had brought
from Fresno browned on the seat
beside me, and I could have
turned back and lost the music.

RICHARD SHELTON

Richard Shelton has lived on the Sonoran Desert, outside Tucson, for more than thirty-five years. Born in Boise, Idaho, in 1933, Shelton spent time in Arkansas and Texas before moving to Tucson in 1960, when he began teaching English at the University of Arizona. Fifteen volumes of poetry, starting with Journal of Return *(1969), have earned him National Endowment for the Arts grants, Western States Book Awards, and the International Poetry Forum United States Award. His prose meditation on life in southern Arizona,* Driving to Bisbee, *won the Western States Book Award in 1992. In these selections, from* The Other Side of the Story *(1987), we see our fragility and transience playing out against the actuality and metaphor of red rocks in the timelessness of the Sonoran Desert.*

THE HOLE

I have dug a hole. It is not an extremely large hole, about four feet across and perhaps three feet deep; but it is a wonderful hole, a magnificent hole. I was planning to encase it in concrete and fill it with water to make a pool, a trap for goldfish. But once I had seen the hole, once I became aware of the *holeness* of it, I could not bear to destroy it. It exists and has a function: to be a hole. It has as much right to exist as a mountain or a tree. And I have gotten over the notion that I created it. It was there from the beginning, waiting to be uncovered. I merely found it.

Everything conspires to destroy a hole. Leaves blow into it. Sand and water creep in to fill it. And people have an overpowering urge to throw things into it: stones, trash, cigarette butts, anything. When they have nothing to throw into it, they often fall into it. They seem unable to leave it alone, as if it were something evil, something threatening. But a hole is the least aggressive of things. It asks only to exist and to be what it is.

So I am building a wall around the hole to help protect it. Tourists will go to see anything; and when they come to see my hole, I will put up a sign which says: NO PART OF THIS HOLE MAY BE REMOVED UPON PENALTY OF LAW. There is no law to protect holes; but it will be a small deception which harms no one, and holes need all the help they can get.

A hole is only distantly related to a cave, although it might appear that a cave is just a hole lying down. Actually, in the hierarchy of negative space, holes have much more status than caves. Holes are more courageous, exposing themselves to constant danger, while caves hide under their roofs and protective banks. And people do not seem to have the urge to destroy caves. We simply explore them and deface them. But when we encounter a hole, we want to fill it.

And while each hole is a quite distinct hole, all have two things in common. They love shadows and sound. They hold shadows as long as they can, caressing them. And they do the same thing with sounds, especially the sound of a voice. When I speak into the hole, it cherishes and amplifies my voice, reluctant to let it go. The hole seems quite grateful when it has the opportunity to roll words around, enhancing them in subtle ways. And it takes no real effort for me to throw it a few words now and then. I rather enjoy talking to it. I have come to admire the way it takes pride in being what it is—not the absence of anything, but the presence of something—a hole.

But where is the surface of a hole? I once believed that the surface of a hole is level with the surface of the ground around it. From observation I have come to realize that this is not true. The earth has a surface, and the sea has a surface, but a hole has no surface. A hole has only sides and a bottom from which it extends infinitely upward, like a shaft of light; and as the earth revolves, it moves with great care and precision between the stars.

THE STONES

I love to go out on summer nights and watch the stones grow. I think they grow better here in the desert, where it is warm and dry, than almost anywhere. Or perhaps it is only that the young ones are more active here.

Young stones tend to move about more than their elders consider good for them. Most young stones have a secret desire which their parents had before them but have forgotten ages ago. And because this desire involves water, it is never mentioned. The older stones disapprove of water and say, "Water is a gadfly who never stays in one place long enough to learn anything." But the young stones try to work themselves into a position, slowly and without their elders noticing it, in which a sizable stream of water during a summer storm might catch them broadside and unknowing, so to speak, and push them along over a slope or down an arroyo. In spite of the danger this involves, they want to travel and see something of the world and settle in a new place, far from home, where they can raise their own dynasties away from the domination of their parents.

And although family ties are very strong among stones, many of the more daring young ones have succeeded; and they carry scars to prove to their children that they once went on a journey, helter-skelter and high water, and traveled perhaps fifteen feet, an incredible distance. As they grow older, they cease to brag about such clandestine adventures.

It is true that old stones get to be very conservative. They consider all movement either dangerous or downright sinful. They remain comfortably where they are and often get fat. Fatness, as a matter of fact, is a mark of distinction.

And on summer nights, after the young stones are asleep, the elders turn to a serious and frightening subject—the moon, which is always spoken of in whispers. "See how it glows and whips across the sky, always changing its shape," one says. And another says, "Feel how it pulls at us, urging us to follow." And a third whispers, "It is a stone gone mad."

MAXINE HONG KINGSTON

Maxine Hong Kingston was born in 1940 in Stockton, California,
and was educated at the University of California, Berkeley. A second-
generation Chinese American, Kingston drew much of the background
for her first book, The Woman Warrior: Memoirs of a Girlhood
Among Ghosts *(1976), from history and myth related to her by*
members of her family and other Chinese-American "story-talkers" in
her childhood community. This recollection went on to win the 1978
Anisfield-Wolf Race Relations Award, as well as the nonfiction award
from the National Book Critics Circle. Kingston's other books are
China Men *(1980), which won an American Book Award for non-*
fiction, and Tripmaster Monkey: His Fake Book *(1988).*

China Men *tells of the hardships of immigrants in the twentieth-*
century Far West, of urban homesteading, as bleak, cruel, and desolate
as in any rural landscape. Kingston's America is neither mythic nor
environmental; she finds refuge in the paradise her parents were able
to nurture—an orchard, a duck pond, a garden, alive and blooming.

AMERICAN FATHER
FROM *CHINA MEN*

In 1903 my father was born in San Francisco, where my grandmother
had come disguised as a man. Or, Chinese women once magical, she
gave birth at a distance, she in China, my grandfather and father in San
Francisco. She was good at sending. Or the men of those days had the
power to have babies. If my grandparents did no such wonders, my
father nevertheless turned up in San Francisco an American citizen.

He was also married at a distance. My mother and a few farm
women went out into the chicken yard, and said words over a rooster,
a fierce rooster, red of comb and feathers; then she went back inside,
married, a wife. She laughs telling this wedding story; he doesn't say one
way or the other.

When I asked MaMa why she speaks different from BaBa, she says
their parents lived across the river from one another. Maybe his village
was America, the river an ocean, his accent American.

My father's magic was also different from my mother's. He pulled the two ends of a chalk stub or a cigarette butt, and between his fingers a new stick of chalk or a fresh cigarette grew long and white. Coins appeared around his knuckles, and number cards turned into face cards. He did not have a patter but was a silent magician. I would learn these tricks when I became a grown-up and never need for cigarettes, money, face cards, or chalk.

He also had the power of going places where nobody else went, and making places belong to him. I could smell his presence. He owned special places the way he owned special things like his copper ashtray from the 1939 World's Fair and his Parker 51. When I explored his closet and desk, I thought, This is a father place; a father belongs here.

One of his places was the dirt cellar. That was under the house where owls bounced against the screens. Rats as big as cats sunned in the garden, fat dust balls among the greens. The rats ran up on the table where the rice or the grapes or the beans were drying and ate with their hands, then took extra in their teeth and leapt off the table like a circus, one rat after another. My mother swung her broom at them, the straw swooping through the air in yellow arcs. That was the house where the bunny lived in a hole in the kitchen. My mother had carried it home from the fields in her apron. Whenever it was hopping noiselessly on the linoleum, and I was there to see it, I felt the honor and blessing of it.

When I asked why the cellar door was kept locked, MaMa said there was a "well" down there. "I don't want you children to fall in the well," she said. Bottomless.

I ran around a corner one day and found the cellar door open. BaBa's white-shirted back moved in the dark. I had been following him, spying on him. I went into the cellar and hid behind some boxes. He lifted the lid that covered the bottomless well. Before he could stop me, I burst out of hiding and saw it—a hole full of shining, bulging, black water, alive, alive, like an eye, deep and alive. BaBa shouted, "Get away." "Let me look. Let me look," I said. "Be careful," he said as I stood on the brink of a well, the end and edge of the ground, the opening to the inside of the world. "What's it called?" I asked to hear him say it. "A well." I wanted to hear him say it again, to tell me again, "Well." My mother had poured rust water from old nails into my ears to improve them.

"What's a well?"

"Water comes out of it," BaBa said. "People draw water out of wells."

"Do they drink it? Where does the water come from?"

"It comes from the earth. I don't think we should drink it without boiling it for at least twenty minutes. Germs."

Poison water.

The well was like a wobble of black jello. I saw silver stars in it. It sparked. It was the black sparkling eye of the planet. The well must lead to the other side of the world. If I fall in, I will come out in China. After a long, long fall, I would appear feet first out of the ground, out of another well, and the Chinese would laugh to see me do that. The way to arrive in China less obtrusively was to dive in head first. The trick would be not to get scared during the long time in the middle of the world. The journey would be worse than the mines.

My father pulled the wooden cover, which was the round lid of a barrel, back over the well. I stepped on the boards, stood in the middle of them, and thought about the bottomless black well beneath my feet, my very feet. What if the cover skidded aside? My father finished with what he was doing; we walked out of the cellar, and he locked the door behind us.

Another father place was the attic of our next house. Once I had seen his foot break through the ceiling. He was in the attic, and suddenly his foot broke through the plaster overhead.

I watched for the day when he left a ladder under the open trap door. I climbed the ladder through the kitchen ceiling. The attic air was hot, too thick, smelling like pigeons, their hot feathers. Rafters and floor beams extended in parallels to a faraway wall, where slats of light slanted from shutters. I did not know we owned such an extravagance of empty space. I raised myself up on my forearms like a prairie dog, then balanced sure-footed on the beams, careful not to step between them and fall through. I climbed down before he returned.

The best of the father places I did not have to win by cunning; he showed me it himself. I had been young enough to hold his hand, which felt splintery with calluses "caused by physical labor," according to MaMa. As we walked, he pointed out sights; he named the plants, told time on the clocks, explained a neon sign in the shape of an owl, which shut one eye in daylight. "It will wink at night," he said. He read signs, and I learned the recurring words: *Company, Association, Hui, Tong.* He greeted the old men with a finger to the hat. At the candy-and-tobacco store, BaBa bought Lucky Strikes and beef jerky, and the old men gave me plum wafers. The tobacconist gave me a cigar box and a candy box. The secret place was not on the busiest Chinatown street but the street across from the park. A pedestrian would look into the barrels and cans in front of the store next door, then walk on to the herbalist's with the school supplies and saucers of herbs in the window, examine the dead flies and larvae, and overlook the secret place completely. (The herbs inside the hundred drawers did not have flies.) BaBa stepped between the grocery store and the herb shop into the kind of sheltered doorway where skid-row men pee and sleep and leave liquor bottles. The place seemed out of business; no one would rent it because it was not eye-catching. It might have been a family association office. On the window were dull gold Chinese words and the number the same as our house number. And delightful, delightful, a big old orange cat sat dozing in the window; it had pushed the shut venetian blinds aside, and its fur was flat against the glass. An iron grillwork with many hinges protected the glass. I tapped on it to see whether the cat was asleep or dead; it blinked.

BaBa found the keys on his chain and unlocked the grating, then the door. Inside was an immense room like a bank or a post office. Suddenly no city street, no noise, no people, no sun. Here was horizontal and vertical order, counters and tables in cool gray twilight. It was safe in here. The cat ran across the cement floor. The place smelled like cat piss or eucalyptus berries. Brass and porcelain spittoons squatted in corners. Another cat, a gray one, walked into the open, and I tried following it, but it ran off. I walked under the tables, which had thick legs.

BaBa filled a bucket with sawdust and water. He and I scattered handfuls of the mixture on the floors, and the place smelled like a carnival. With our pushbrooms leaving wet streaks, we swept the sawdust together, which turned gray as it picked up the dirt. BaBa threw his cigarette butts in it. The cat shit got picked up too. He scooped everything into the dustpan he had made out of an oil can.

We put away our brooms, and I followed him to the wall where sheaves of paper hung by their corners, diamond shaped. "Pigeon lottery," he called them. "Pigeon lottery tickets." Yes, in the wind of the paddle fan the soft thick sheaves ruffled like feathers and wings. He gave me some used sheets. Gamblers had circled green and blue words in pink ink. They had bet on those words. You had to be a poet to win, finding lucky ways words go together. My father showed me the winning words from last night's games: "white jade that grows in water," "red jade that grows in earth," or—not so many words in Chinese— "white waterjade," "redearthjade," "firedragon," "waterdragon." He gave me pen and ink, and I linked words of my own: "rivercloud," "riverfire," the many combinations with *horse, cloud,* and *bird.* The lines and loops connecting the words, which were in squares, a word to a square, made designs too. So this was where my father worked and what he did for a living, keeping track of the gamblers' schemes of words.

We were getting the gambling house ready. Tonight the gamblers would come here from the towns and the fields; they would sail from San Francisco all the way up the river through the Delta to Stockton, which had more gambling than any city on the coast. It would be a party tonight. The gamblers would eat free food and drink free whiskey, and if times were bad, only tea. They'd laugh and exclaim over the poems they made, which were plain and very beautiful: "Shiny water, bright moon." They'd cheer when they won. BaBa let me crank the drum that spun words. It had a little door on top to reach in for the winning words and looked like the cradle that the Forty-niner ancestors had used to sift for gold, and like the drum for the lottery at the Stockton Chinese Community Fourth of July Picnic.

He also let me play with the hole puncher, which was a heavy instrument with a wrought-iron handle that took some strength to raise. I played gambler punching words to win—"cloudswallow," "riverswallow," "river forking," "swallow forking." I also punched perfect round holes in the corners so that I could hang the papers like diamonds and like pigeons. I collected round and crescent confetti in my cigar box.

While I worked on the floor under the tables, BaBa sat behind a counter on his tall stool. With black elastic armbands around his shirtsleeves and an eyeshade on his forehead, he clicked the abacus fast and steadily, stopping to write the numbers down in ledgers. He melted red wax in candle flame and made seals. He checked the pigeon papers, and set out fresh stacks of them. Then we twirled the dials of the safe, wound the grandfather clock, which had a long brass pendulum, meowed at the cats, and locked up. We bought crackly pork on the way home.

According to MaMa, the gambling house belonged to the most powerful Chinese American in Stockton. He paid my father to manage it and to pretend to be the owner. BaBa took the blame for the real owner. When the cop on the beat walked in, BaBa gave him a plate of food, a carton of cigarettes, and a bottle of whiskey. Once a month, the police raided with a paddy wagon, and it was also part of my father's job to be arrested. He never got a record, however, because he thought up a new name for himself every time. Sometimes it came to him while the city sped past the barred windows; sometimes just when the white demon at the desk asked him for it, a name came to him, a new name befitting the situation. They never found out his real names or that he had an American name at all. "I got away with aliases," he said, "because the white demons can't tell one Chinese name from another or one face from another." He had the power of naming. He had a hundred dollars ready in an envelope with which he bribed the demon in charge. It may have been a fine, not a bribe, but BaBa saw him pocket the hundred dollars. After that, the police let him walk out the door. He either walked home or back to the empty gambling house to straighten out the books.

Two of the first white people we children met were customers at the gambling house, one small and skinny man, one fat and jolly. They lived in a little house on the edge of the slough across the street from our house. Their arms were covered with orange and yellow hair. The round one's name was Johnson, but what everyone called him was Water Shining, and his partner was White Cloud. They had once won big on those words. Also *Johnson* resembles *Water Shining*, which also has *o, s,* and *n* sounds. Like two old China Men, they lived together lonely with no families. They sat in front of stores; they sat on their porch. They fenced a part of the slough for their vegetable patch, which had a wooden sign declaring the names of the vegetables and who they belonged to. They also had a wooden sign over their front door: TRAN-QUILITY, a wish or blessing or the name of their house. They gave us nickels and quarters; they made dimes come out of noses, ears, and elbows and waved coins in and out between their knuckles. They were white men, but they lived like China Men.

When we came home from school and a wino or hobo was trying the doors and windows, Water Shining came out of his little house. "There's a wino breaking into our house," we told him. It did occur to me that he might be offended at our calling his fellow white man a wino. "It's not just a poor man taking a drink from the hose or picking some fruit and going," I explained.

"What? What? Where? Let's take a look-see," he said, and walked with us to our house, saving our house without a fight.

The old men disappeared one by one before I noticed their going. White Cloud told the gamblers that Water Shining was killed in a farming accident, run over by a tractor. His body had been churned and plowed. White Cloud lived alone until the railroad tracks were leveled, the slough drained, the blackbirds flown, and his house torn down.

My father found a name for me too at the gambling house. "He named you," said MaMa, "after a blonde gambler who always won. He gave you her lucky American name." My blonde namesake must have talked with a cigarette out of the side of her mouth and left red lip prints. She wore a low-cut red or green gambling dress, or she dressed cowgirl in white boots with baton-twirler tassels and spurs; a Stetson hung at her back. When she threw down her aces, the leather fringe danced along her arm. And there was applause and buying of presents when she won. "Your father likes blondes," MaMa said. "Look how beautiful," they both exclaimed when a blonde walked by.

But my mother keeps saying those were dismal years. "He worked twelve hours a day, no holidays," she said. "Even on New Year's, no day off. He couldn't come home until two in the morning. He stood on his feet gambling twelve hours straight."

"I saw a tall stool," I said.

"He only got to sit when there were no customers," she said. "He got paid almost nothing. He was a slave; I was a slave." She is angry recalling those days.

After my father's partners stole his New York laundry, the owner of the gambling house, a fellow ex-villager, paid my parents' fares to Stockton, where the brick buildings reminded them of New York. The way my mother repaid him—only the money is repayable—was to be a servant to his, the owner's, family. She ironed for twelve people and bathed ten children. Bitterly, she kept their house. When my father came home from work at two in the morning, she told him how badly the owner's family had treated her, but he told her to stop exaggerating. "He's a generous man," he said.

The owner also had a black servant, whose name was Harry. The rumor was that Harry was a half-man/half-woman, a half-and-half. Two servants could not keep that house clean, where children drew on the wallpaper and dug holes in the plaster. I listened to Harry sing "Sioux City Sue." "Lay down my rag with a hoo hoo hoo," he sang. He squeezed his rag out in the bucket and led the children singing the chorus. Though my father was also as foolishly happy over his job, my mother was not deceived.

When my mother was pregnant, the owner's wife bought her a dozen baby chicks, not a gift; my mother would owe her the money. MaMa would be allowed to raise the chicks in the owner's yard if she also tended his chickens. When the baby was born, she would have chicken to give for birth announcements. Upon his coming home from work one night, the owner's wife lied to him, "The aunt forgot to feed her chickens. Will you do it?" Grumbling about my lazy mother, the owner went out in the rain and slipped in the mud, which was mixed with chicken shit. He hurt his legs and lay there yelling that my mother had almost killed him. "And she makes our whole yard stink with chicken shit," he accused. When the baby was born, the owner's wife picked out the scrawny old roosters and said they were my mother's twelve.

Ironing for the children, who changed clothes several times a day, MaMa had been standing for hours while pregnant when the veins in her legs rippled and burst. After that she had to wear support stockings and to wrap her legs in bandages.

The owner gave BaBa a hundred-and-twenty-dollar bonus when the baby was born. His wife found out and scolded him for "giving charity."

"You deserve that money," MaMa said to BaBa. "He takes all your time. You're never home. The babies could die, and you wouldn't know it."

When their free time coincided, my parents sat with us on apple and orange crates at the tiny table, our knees touching under it. We ate rice and salted fish, which is what peasants in China eat. Everything was nice except what MaMa was saying, "We've turned into slaves. We're the slaves of these villagers who were nothing when they were in China. I've turned into the servant of a woman who can't read. Maybe we should go back to China. I'm tired of being Wah Q," that is, a Sojourner from Wah.

My father said, "No." Angry. He did not like her female intrigues about the chickens and the ironing and the half-man/half-woman.

They saved his pay and the bonuses, and decided to buy a house, the very house they were renting. This was the two-story house around the corner from the owner's house, convenient for my mother to walk to her servant job and my father to the gambling house. We could rent out the bottom floor and make a profit. BaBa had five thousand dollars. Would the owner, who spoke English, negotiate the cash sale? Days and weeks passed, and when he asked the owner what was happening, the owner said, "I decided to buy it myself. I'll let you rent from me. It'll save you money, especially since you're saving to go back to China. You're going back to China anyway." But BaBa had indeed decided to buy a house on the Gold Mountain. And this was before Pearl Harbor and before the Chinese Revolution.

He found another house farther away, not as new or big. He again asked the owner to buy it for him. You would think we could trust him, our fellow villager with the same surname, almost a relative, but the owner bought up this house too—the one with the well in the cellar—and became our landlord again.

My parents secretly looked for another house. They told everyone, "We're saving our money to go back to China when the war is over." But what they really did was to buy the house across from the railroad tracks. It was exactly like the owner's house, the same size, the same floor plan and gingerbread. BaBa paid six thousand dollars cash for it, not a check but dollar bills, and he signed the papers himself. It was the biggest but most run-down of the houses; it had been a boarding house for old China Men. Rose bushes with thorns grew around it, wooden lace hung broken from the porch eaves, the top step was missing like a moat. The rooms echoed. This was the house with the attic and basement. The owner's wife accused her husband of giving us the money, but she was lying. We made our escape from them. "You don't have to be afraid of the owner any more," MaMa keeps telling us.

Sometimes we waited up until BaBa came home from work. In addition to a table and crates, we had for furniture an ironing board and an army cot, which MaMa unfolded next to the gas stove in the wintertime. While she ironed our clothes, she sang and talked story, and I sat on the cot holding one or two of the babies. When BaBa came home, he and MaMa got into the cot and pretended they were refugees under a blanket tent. He brought out his hardbound brown book with the gray and white photographs of white men standing before a flag, sitting in rows of chairs, shaking hands in the street, hand-signaling from car windows. A teacher with a suit stood at a blackboard and pointed out things with a stick. There were no children or women or animals in this book. "Before you came to New York," he told my mother, "I went to school to study English. The classroom looked like this, and every student came from another country." He read words to my mother and told her what they meant. He also wrote them on the blackboard, it and the daruma, the doll which always rights itself when knocked down, the only toys we owned at that time. The little *h*'s looked like chairs, the *e*'s like lidded eyes, but those words were not *chair* and *eye*. " 'Do you speak English?' " He read and translated. " 'Yes, I am learning to speak English better.' 'I speak English a little.' " " 'How are you?' 'I am fine, and you?' " My mother forgot what she learned from one reading to the next. The words had no crags, windows, or hooks to grasp. No pictures. The same *a, b, c*'s for everything. She couldn't make out ducks, cats, and mice in American cartoons either.

During World War II, a gang of police demons charged into the gambling house with drawn guns. They handcuffed the gamblers and assigned them to paddy wagons and patrol cars, which lined the street. The wagons were so full, people had to stand with their hands up on the ceiling to keep their balance. My father was not jailed or deported, but neither he nor the owner worked in gambling again. They went straight. Stockton became a clean town. From the outside the gambling house looks the same closed down as when it flourished.

My father brought his abacus, the hole punch, and extra tickets home, but those were the last presents for a while. A dismal time began for him.

He became a disheartened man. He was always home. He sat in his chair and stared, or he sat on the floor and stared. He stopped showing the boys the few kung fu moves he knew. He suddenly turned angry and quiet. For a few days he walked up and down on the sidewalk in front of businesses and did not bring himself to enter. He walked right past them in his beautiful clothes and acted very busy, as if having an important other place to go for a job interview. "You're nothing but a gambler," MaMa scolded. "You're spoiled and won't go looking for a job." "The only thing you're trained for is writing poems," she said. "I know you," she said. (I hated her sentences that started with "I know you.") "You poet. You scholar. You gambler. What use is any of that?" "It's a wife's job to scold her husband into working," she explained to us.

My father sat. "You're so scared," MaMa accused. "You're shy. You're lazy." "Do something. You never do anything." "You let your so-called friends steal your laundry. You let your brothers and the Communists take your land. You have no head for business." She nagged him and pampered him. MaMa and we kids scraped his back with a porcelain spoon. We did not know whether it was the spoon or the porcelain or the massage that was supposed to be efficacious. "Quit being so shy," she advised. "Take a walk through Chinatown and see if any of the uncles has heard of a job. Just ask. You don't even need to apply. Go find out the gossip." "He's shy," she explained him to us, but she was not one to understand shyness, being entirely bold herself. "Why are you so shy? People invite you and go out of their way for you, and you act like a snob or a king. It's only human to reciprocate." "You act like a piece of liver. Who do you think you are? A piece of liver?" She did not understand how some of us run down and stop. Some of us use up all our life force getting out of bed in the morning, and it's a wonder we can get to a chair and sit in it. "You piece of liver. You poet. You scholar. What's the use of a poet and a scholar on the Gold Mountain? You're so skinny. You're not supposed to be so skinny in this country. You have to be tough. You lost the New York laundry. You lost the house with the upstairs. You lost the house with the back porch." She summarized, "No loyal friends or brothers. Savings draining away like time. Can't speak English. Now you've lost the gambling job and the land in China."

Somebody—a Chinese, it had to be a Chinese—dug up our loquat tree, which BaBa had planted in front of the house. He or she had come in the middle of the night and left a big hole. MaMa blamed BaBa for that too, that he didn't go track down the tree and bring it back. In fact, a new loquat tree had appeared in the yard of a house around the corner. He ignored her, stopped shaving, and sat in his T-shirt from morning to night.

He seemed to have lost his feelings. His own mother wrote him asking for money, and he asked for proof that she was still alive before he would send it. He did not say, "I miss her." Maybe she was dead, and the Communists maintained a bureau of grandmother letter writers in order to get our money. That we kids no longer received the sweet taste of invisible candy was no proof that she had stopped sending it; we had outgrown it. For proof, the aunts sent a new photograph of Ah Po. She looked like the same woman, all right, like the pictures we already had but aged. She was ninety-nine years old. She was lying on her side on a lounge chair, alone, her head pillowed on her arm, the other arm along her side, no green tints at her earlobes, fingers, and wrists. She still had little feet and a curved-down mouth. "Maybe she's dead and propped up," we kids conjectured.

BaBa sat drinking whiskey. He no longer bought new clothes. Nor did he go to the dentist and come back telling us the compliments on his perfect teeth, how the dentist said that only one person in a thousand had teeth with no fillings. He no longer advised us that to have perfect teeth, it's good to clamp them together, especially when having a bowel movement.

MaMa assured us that what he was looking forward to was when each child came home with gold. Then he or she (the pronoun is neutral in the spoken language) was to ask the father, "BaBa, what kind of a suit do you want? A silk gown? Or a suit from the West? An Eastern suit or a Western suit? What kind of a Western suit do you want?" She suggested that we ask him right now. Go-out-on-the-road. Make our fortunes. Buy a Western suit for Father.

I went to his closet and studied his suits. He owned gray suits, dark blue ones, and a light pinstripe, expensive, successful suits to wear on the best occasions. Power suits. Money suits. Two-hundred-dollars-apiece New York suits. Businessmen-in-the-movies suits. Boss suits. Suits from before we were born. At the foot of the closet arranged in order, order his habit, were his leather shoes blocked on shoe trees. How could I make money like that? I looked in stores at suits and at the prices. I could never learn to sew this evenly, each suit perfect and similar to the next.

MaMa worked in the fields and the canneries. She showed us how to use her new tools, the pitters and curved knives. We tried on her cap pinned with union buttons and her rubber gloves that smelled like rubber tomatoes. She emptied her buckets, thermoses, shopping bags, lunch pail, apron, and scarf; she brought home every kind of vegetable and fruit grown in San Joaquin County. She said she was tired after work but kept moving, busy, banged doors, drawers, pots and cleaver, turned faucets off and on with *kachunk*'s in the pipes. Her cleaver banged on the chopping block for an hour straight as she minced pork and steak into patties. Her energy slammed BaBa back into his chair. She took care of everything; he did not have a reason to get up. He stared at his toes and fingers. "You've lost your sense of emergency," she said; she kept up her sense of emergency every moment.

He dozed and woke with a jerk or a scream. MaMa medicated him with a pill that came in a purple cube lined with red silk quilting, which cushioned a tiny black jar; inside the jar was a black dot made out of ground pearls, ox horn, and ox blood. She dropped this pill in a bantam broth that had steamed all day in a little porcelain crock on metal legs. He drank this soup, also a thick beef broth with gold coins in the bottom, beef teas, squab soup, and still he sat. He sat on. It seemed to me that he was getting skinnier.

"You're getting skinny again," MaMa kept saying. "Eat. Eat. You're less than a hundred pounds."

I cut a Charles Atlas coupon out of a comic book. I read all the small print. Charles Atlas promised to send some free information. "Ninety-seven-pound weakling," the cartoon man called himself. "I'll gamble a stamp," he said. Charles Atlas did not say anything about building fat, which was what my father needed. He already had muscles. But he was ninety-seven pounds like the weakling, maybe ninety pounds. Also he kicked over chairs like in the middle panel. I filled in the coupon and forged his signature. I did not dare ask him how old he was, so I guessed maybe he was half as old as his weight: age forty-five, weight ninety. If Charles Atlas saw that he was even skinnier than the weakling, maybe he would hurry up answering. I took the envelope and stamp from BaBa's desk.

Charles Atlas sent pamphlets with more coupons. From the hints of information, I gathered that my father needed lessons, which cost money. The lessons had to be done vigorously, not just read. There seemed to be no preliminary lesson on how to get up.

The one event of the day that made him get up out of his easy chair was the newspaper. He looked forward to it. He opened the front door and looked for it hours before the mailman was due. *The Gold Mountain News* (or *The Chinese Times*, according to the English logo) came from San Francisco in a paper sleeve on which his name and address were neatly typed. He put on his gold-rimmed glasses and readied his smoking equipment: the 1939 World's Fair ashtray, Lucky Strikes, matches, coffee. He killed several hours reading the paper, scrupulously reading everything, the date on each page, the page numbers, the want ads. Events went on; the world kept moving. The hands on the clocks kept moving. This sitting ought to have felt as good as sitting in his chair on a day off. He was not sick. He checked his limbs, the crooks of his arms. Everything was normal, quite comfortable, his easy chair fitting under him, the room temperature right.

MaMa said a man can be like a rat and bite through wood, bite through glass and rock. "What's wrong?" she asked.

"I'm tired," he said, and she gave him the cure for tiredness, which is to hit the inside joints of elbows and knees until red and black dots —the tiredness—appear on the skin.

He screamed in his sleep. "Night sweats," MaMa diagnosed. "Fear sweats." What he dreamed must have been ax murders. The family man kills his entire family. He throws slain bodies in heaps out the front door. He leaves no family member alive; he or she would suffer too much being the last one. About to swing the ax, screaming in horror of killing, he is also the last little child who runs into the night and hides behind a fence. Someone chops at the bushes beside him. He covers his ears and shuts his mouth tight, but the scream comes out.

I invented a plan to test my theory that males feel no pain; males don't feel. At school, I stood under the trees where the girls played house and watched a strip of cement near the gate. There were two places where boys and girls mixed; one was the kindergarten playground, where we didn't go any more, and the other was this bit of sidewalk. I had a list of boys to kick: the boy who burned spiders, the boy who had grabbed me by my coat lapels like in a gangster movie, the boy who told dirty pregnancy jokes. I would get them one at a time with my heavy shoes, on which I had nailed toe taps and horseshoe taps. I saw my boy, a friendly one for a start. I ran fast, crunching gravel. He was kneeling; I grabbed him by the arm and kicked him sprawling into the circle of marbles. I ran through the girls' playground and playroom to our lavatory, where I looked out the window. Sure enough, he was not crying. "See?" I told the girls. "Boys have no feelings. It's some kind of immunity." It was the same with Chinese boys, black boys, white boys, and Mexican and Filipino boys. Girls and women of all races cried and had feelings. We had to toughen up. We had to be as tough as boys, tougher because we only pretended not to feel pain.

One of my girl friends had a brother who cried, but he had been raised as a girl. Their mother was a German American and their father a Chinese American. This family didn't belong to our Benevolent Association nor did they go to our parties. The youngest boy wore girls' dresses with ruffles and bows, and brown-blondish ringlets grew long to his waist. When this thin, pale boy was about seven, he had to go to school; it was already two years past the time when most people started

school. "Come and see something strange," his sister said on Labor Day.
I stood in their yard and watched their mother cut off his hair. The hair
lay like tails around his feet. Mother cried, and son cried. He was so
delicate, he had feelings in his hair; it hurt him to have his hair cut. I
did not pick on him.

There was a war between the boys and the girls; we sisters and
brothers were evenly matched three against three. The sister next to me,
who was like my twin, pushed our oldest brother off the porch railing.
He landed on his face and broke two front teeth on the sidewalk. They
fought with knives, the cleaver and a boning knife; they circled the
dining room table and sliced one another's arms. I did try to stop that
fight—they were cutting bloody slits, an earnest fight to the death. The
telephone rang. Thinking it was MaMa, I shouted, "Help. Help. We're
having a knife fight. They'll kill each other." "Well, do try to stop
them." It was the owner's wife; she'd gossip to everybody that our
parents had lost control of us, such bad parents who couldn't get respectable jobs, mother gone all day, and kids turned into killers. "That
was Big Aunt on the phone," I said, "and she's going to tell the whole
town about us," and they quit after a while. Our youngest sister snuck
up on our middle brother, who was digging in the ground. She was
about to drop a boulder on his head when somebody shouted, "Look
out." She only hit his shoulder. I told my girl friends at school that I
had a stepfather and three wicked stepbrothers. Among my stepfather's
many aliases was the name of my real father, who was gone.

The white girls at school said, "I got a spanking." I said we never
got spanked. "My parents don't believe in it," I said, which was true.
They didn't know about spanking, which is orderly. My mother swung
wooden hangers, the thick kind, and brooms. We got trapped behind a
door or under a bed and got hit anywhere (except the head). When the
other kids said, "They kissed me good night," I also felt left out; not
that I cared about kissing but to be normal.

We children became so wild that we broke BaBa loose from his
chair. We goaded him, irked him—*gikked* him—and the gravity suddenly let him go. He chased my sister, who locked herself in a bedroom.
"Come out," he shouted. But, of course, she wouldn't, he having a coat
hanger in hand and angry. I watched him kick the door; the round
mirror fell off the wall and crashed. The door broke open, and he beat
her. Only, my sister remembers that it was she who watched my father's
shoe against the door and the mirror outside fall, and I who was beaten.

But I know I saw the mirror in crazy pieces; I was standing by the table with the blue linoleum top, which was outside the door. I saw his brown shoe against the door and his knee flex and the other brothers and sisters watching from the outside of the door, and heard MaMa saying, "Seven years bad luck." My sister claims that same memory. Neither of us has the recollection of curling up inside that room, whether behind the pounding door or under the bed or in the closet.

A white girl friend, whose jobless and drunk father picked up a sofa and dropped it on her, said, "My mother saw him pushing *me* down the stairs, and *she* was watching from the landing. And I remember him pushing *her,* and *I* was at the landing. Both of us remember looking up and seeing the other rolling down the stairs."

He did not return to sitting. He shaved, put on some good clothes, and went out. He found a friend who had opened a new laundry on El Dorado Street. He went inside and chatted, asked if he could help out. The friend said he had changed his mind about owning the laundry, which he had named New Port Laundry. My father bought it and had a Grand Opening. We were proud and quiet as he wrote in gold and black on big red ribbons. The Chinese community brought flowers, mirrors, and pictures of flowers and one of Guan Goong. BaBa's liveliness returned. It came from nowhere, like my new idea that males have feelings. I had no proof for this idea but took my brothers' word for it.

BaBa made a new special place. There was a trap door on the floor inside the laundry, and BaBa looked like a trap-door spider when he pulled it over his head or lifted it, emerging. The basement light shone through the door's cracks. Stored on the steps, which were also shelves, were some rolled-up flags that belonged to a previous owner; gold eagles gleamed on the pole tips.

We children waited until we were left in charge of the laundry. Then some of us kept a lookout while the rest, hanging on to the edge of the hole, stepped down between the supplies. The stairs were steep against the backs of our legs.

The floor under the building was gray soil, a fine powder. Nothing had ever grown in it; it was sunless, rainless city soil. Beyond the light from one bulb the blackness began, the inside of the earth, the insides of the city. We had our flashlights ready. We chose a tunnel and walked side by side into the dark. There are breezes inside the earth. They blow cool and dry. Blackness absorbed our lights. The people who lived and worked in the four stories above us didn't know how incomplete civilization is, the street only a crust. Down here under the sidewalks and the streets and the cars, the builders had left mounds of loose dirt, piles of dumped cement, rough patches of concrete tamping down and holding back some of the dirt. The posts were unpainted and not square on their pilings. We followed the tunnels to places that had no man-made materials, wild areas, then turned around and headed for the lighted section under the laundry. We never found the ends of some tunnels. We did not find elevators or ramps or the undersides of the buckling metal doors one sees on sidewalks. "Now we know the secret of cities," we told one another. On the shelves built against the dirt walls, BaBa had stacked boxes of notebooks and laundry tickets, rubber stamps, pencils, new brushes, blue bands for the shirts, rolls of wrapping paper, cones of new string, bottles of ink, bottles of distilled water in case of air raids. Here was where we would hide when war came and we went underground for guerrilla warfare. We stepped carefully; he had set copper and wood rat traps. I opened boxes until it was time to come up and give someone else a chance to explore.

So my father at last owned his house and his business in America. He bought chicks and squabs, built a chicken run, a pigeon coop, and a turkey pen; he dug a duck pond, set the baby bathtub inside for the lining, and won ducklings and goldfish and turtles at carnivals and county fairs. He bought rabbits and bantams and did not refuse dogs, puppies, cats, and kittens. He told a funny story about a friend of his who kept his sweater on while visiting another friend on a hot day; when the visitor was walking out the gate, the host said, "Well, Uncle, and what are those chicken feet wiggling out of your sweater?" One morning we found a stack of new coloring books and follow-the-dot books on the floor next to our beds. "BaBa left them," we said. He buried wine bottles upside down in the garden; their bottoms made a path of sea-color circles. He gave me a picture from the newspaper of redwoods in Yosemite, and said, "This is beautiful." He talked about a Los Angeles Massacre, but I wished that he had not, and pretended he had not. He told an ancient story about two feuding poets: one killed the other's plant by watering it with hot water. He sang "The Song of the Man of the Green Hill," the end of which goes like this: "The disheveled poet beheads the great whale. He shoots an arrow and hits a suspended flea. He sees well through rhinoceros-horn lenses." This was a song by Kao Chi, who had been executed for his politics; he is famous for poems to his wife and daughter written upon leaving for the capital; he owned a small piece of land where he grew enough to eat without working too hard so he could write poems. BaBa's luffa and grapevines climbed up ropes to the roof of the house. He planted many kinds of gourds, peas, beans, melons, and cabbages—and perennials—tangerines, oranges, grapefruit, almonds, pomegranates, apples, black figs, and white figs— and from seed pits, another loquat, peaches, apricots, plums of many varieties—trees that take years to fruit.

RAYMOND CARVER

Raymond Carver was born in Clatskanie, Oregon, in 1938, and was raised in Yakima, Washington. His first book of short stories, Will You Please Be Quiet, Please? *(1976), was distinguished by its economic prose and unrelenting honesty of vision. The collection was nominated for the National Book Award. His next two books of stories,* What We Talk About When We Talk About Love *(1981) and* Cathedral *(1983), established Carver as one of America's foremost short fiction writers. Carver published three other short story collections, six volumes of poetry, and* Fires *(1982), a collection of essays, poems, and stories, and an interview. He received a Wallace Stegner Fellowship (1972), two National Endowment for the Arts fellowships (1971, 1980), a Guggenheim (1979), and three O. Henrys. In 1983, he received one of the first Strauss Living Awards, a tax-free three-year stipend from the American Academy and Institute of Arts and Letters. From the close of the 1970s until the end of his life—he died of cancer in 1988—Carver lived with the poet Tess Gallagher, most recently in Port Angeles, Washington. In 1993,* Short Cuts, *a Robert Altman film based on a number of Carver's stories, was nominated for several Academy Awards.*

This selection, a short memoir taken from Fires, *comes to us with Carver's particular virtues—his laconic and evocative way of speaking to us about ultimate matters and how they work out in the complex comings and goings of our days, the ways we guard and share our lives*

*and frailties, reasons why we ought to be good to one another. Carver
is a major American writer.*

MY FATHER'S LIFE

My dad's name was Clevie Raymond Carver. His family called him
Raymond and friends called him C. R. I was named Raymond Clevie
Carver Jr. I hated the "Junior" part. When I was little my dad called
me Frog, which was okay. But later, like everybody else in the family,
he began calling me Junior. He went on calling me this until I was
thirteen or fourteen and announced that I wouldn't answer to that name
any longer. So he began calling me Doc. From then until his death, on
June 17, 1967, he called me Doc, or else Son.

When he died, my mother telephoned my wife with the news. I
was away from my family at the time, between lives, trying to enroll in
the School of Library Science at the University of Iowa. When my wife
answered the phone, my mother blurted out, "Raymond's dead!" For
a moment, my wife thought my mother was telling her that I was dead.
Then my mother made it clear *which* Raymond she was talking about
and my wife said, "Thank God. I thought you meant *my* Raymond."

My dad walked, hitched rides, and rode in empty boxcars when he
went from Arkansas to Washington State in 1934, looking for work. I
don't know whether he was pursuing a dream when he went out to
Washington. I doubt it. I don't think he dreamed much. I believe he
was simply looking for steady work at decent pay. Steady work was
meaningful work. He picked apples for a time and then landed a construction laborer's job on the Grand Coulee Dam. After he'd put aside
a little money, he bought a car and drove back to Arkansas to help his
folks, my grandparents, pack up for the move west. He said later that
they were about to starve down there, and this wasn't meant as a figure
of speech. It was during that short while in Arkansas, in a town called
Leola, that my mother met my dad on the sidewalk as he came out of
a tavern.

"He was drunk," she said. "I don't know why I let him talk to
me. His eyes were glittery. I wish I'd had a crystal ball." They'd met
once, a year or so before, at a dance. He'd had girlfriends before her,
my mother told me. "Your dad always had a girlfriend, even after we

married. He was my first and last. I never had another man. But I didn't miss anything."

They were married by a justice of the peace on the day they left for Washington, this big, tall country girl and a farmhand-turned-construction worker. My mother spent her wedding night with my dad and his folks, all of them camped beside the road in Arkansas.

In Omak, Washington, my dad and mother lived in a little place not much bigger than a cabin. My grandparents lived next door. My dad was still working on the dam, and later, with the huge turbines producing electricity and the water backed up for a hundred miles into Canada, he stood in the crowd and heard Franklin D. Roosevelt when he spoke at the construction site. "He never mentioned those guys who died building that dam," my dad said. Some of his friends had died there, men from Arkansas, Oklahoma, and Missouri.

He then took a job in a sawmill in Clatskanie, Oregon, a little town alongside the Columbia River. I was born there, and my mother has a picture of my dad standing in front of the gate to the mill, proudly holding me up to face the camera. My bonnet is on crooked and about to come untied. His hat is pushed back on his forehead, and he's wearing a big grin. Was he going in to work or just finishing his shift? It doesn't matter. In either case, he had a job and a family. These were his salad days.

In 1941 we moved to Yakima, Washington, where my dad went to work as a saw filer, a skilled trade he'd learned in Clatskanie. When war broke out, he was given a deferment because his work was considered necessary to the war effort. Finished lumber was in demand by the armed services, and he kept his saws so sharp they could shave the hair off your arm.

After my dad had moved us to Yakima, he moved his folks into the same neighborhood. By the mid-1940s the rest of my dad's family —his brother, his sister, and her husband, as well as uncles, cousins, nephews, and most of their extended family and friends—had come out from Arkansas. All because my dad came out first. The men went to work at Boise Cascade, where my dad worked, and the women packed apples in the canneries. And in just a little while, it seemed—according to my mother—everybody was better off than my dad. "Your dad couldn't keep money," my mother said. "Money burned a hole in his pocket. He was always doing for others."

The first house I clearly remember living in, at 1515 South Fifteenth

Street, in Yakima, had an outdoor toilet. On Halloween night, or just any night, for the hell of it, neighbor kids, kids in their early teens, would carry our toilet away and leave it next to the road. My dad would have to get somebody to help him bring it home. Or these kids would take the toilet and stand it in somebody else's backyard. Once they actually set it on fire. But ours wasn't the only house that had an outdoor toilet. When I was old enough to know what I was doing, I threw rocks at the other toilets when I'd see someone go inside. This was called bombing the toilets. After a while, though, everyone went to indoor plumbing until, suddenly, our toilet was the last outdoor one in the neighborhood. I remember the shame I felt when my third-grade teacher, Mr. Wise, drove me home from school one day. I asked him to stop at the house just before ours, claiming I lived there.

I can recall what happened one night when my dad came home late to find that my mother had locked all the doors on him from the inside. He was drunk, and we could feel the house shudder as he rattled the door. When he'd managed to force open a window, she hit him between the eyes with a colander and knocked him out. We could see him down there on the grass. For years afterward, I used to pick up this colander—it was as heavy as a rolling pin—and imagine what it would feel like to be hit in the head with something like that.

It was during this period that I remember my dad taking me into the bedroom, sitting me down on the bed, and telling me that I might have to go live my with Aunt LaVon for a while. I couldn't understand what I'd done that meant I'd have to go away from home to live. But this, too—whatever prompted it—must have blown over, more or less, anyway, because we stayed together, and I didn't have to go live with her or anyone else.

I remember my mother pouring his whiskey down the sink. Sometimes she'd pour it all out and sometimes, if she was afraid of getting caught, she'd only pour half of it out and then add water to the rest. I tasted some of his whiskey once myself. It was terrible stuff, and I don't see how anybody could drink it.

After a long time without one, we finally got a car, in 1949 or 1950, a 1938 Ford. But it threw a rod the first week we had it, and my dad had to have the motor rebuilt.

"We drove the oldest car in town," my mother said. "We could have had a Cadillac for all he spent on car repairs." One time she found someone else's tube of lipstick on the floorboard, along with a lacy handkerchief. "See this?" she said to me. "Some floozy left this in the car."

Once I saw her take a pan of warm water into the bedroom where my dad was sleeping. She took his hand from under the covers and held it in the water. I stood in the doorway and watched. I wanted to know what was going on. This would make him talk in his sleep, she told me. There were things she needed to know, things she was sure he was keeping from her.

Every year or so, when I was little, we would take the North Coast Limited across the Cascade Range from Yakima to Seattle and stay in the Vance Hotel and eat, I remember, at a place called the Dinner Bell Cafe. Once we went to Ivar's Acres of Clams and drank glasses of warm clam broth.

In 1956, the year I was to graduate from high school, my dad quit his job at the mill in Yakima and took a job in Chester, a little sawmill town in northern California. The reasons given at the time for his taking the job had to do with a higher hourly wage and the vague promise that he might, in a few years' time, succeed to the job of head filer in this new mill. But I think, in the main, that my dad had grown restless and simply wanted to try his luck elsewhere. Things had gotten a little too predictable for him in Yakima. Also, the year before, there had been the deaths, within six months of each other, of both his parents.

But just a few days after graduation, when my mother and I were packed to move to Chester, my dad pencilled a letter to say he'd been sick for a while. He didn't want us to worry, he said, but he'd cut himself on a saw. Maybe he'd got a tiny sliver of steel in his blood. Anyway, something had happened and he'd had to miss work, he said. In the same mail was an unsigned postcard from somebody down there telling my mother that my dad was about to die and that he was drinking "raw whiskey."

When we arrived in Chester, my dad was living in a trailer that belonged to the company. I didn't recognize him immediately. I guess for a moment I didn't want to recognize him. He was skinny and pale and looked bewildered. His pants wouldn't stay up. He didn't look like my dad. My mother began to cry. My dad put his arm around her and patted her shoulder vaguely, like he didn't know what this was all about, either. The three of us took up life together in the trailer, and we looked after him as best we could. But my dad was sick, and he couldn't get any better. I worked with him in the mill that summer and part of the fall. We'd get up in the mornings and eat eggs and toast while we listened to the radio, and then go out the door with our lunch pails. We'd pass through the gate together at eight in the morning, and I wouldn't see him again until quitting time. In November I went back to Yakima to be closer to my girlfriend, the girl I'd made up my mind I was going to marry.

He worked at the mill in Chester until the following February, when he collapsed on the job and was taken to the hospital. My mother asked if I would come down there and help. I caught a bus from Yakima to Chester, intending to drive them back to Yakima. But now, in addition to being physically sick, my dad was in the midst of a nervous breakdown, though none of us knew to call it that at the time. During the entire trip back to Yakima, he didn't speak, not even when asked a direct question. ("How do you feel, Raymond?" "You okay, Dad?") He'd communicate, if he communicated at all, by moving his head or by turning his palms up as if to say he didn't know or care. The only time he said anything on the trip, and for nearly a month afterward, was when I was speeding down a gravel road in Oregon and the car muffler came loose. "You were going too fast," he said.

Back in Yakima a doctor saw to it that my dad went to a psychiatrist. My mother and dad had to go on relief, as it was called, and the county paid for the psychiatrist. The psychiatrist asked my dad, "Who is the President?" He'd had a question put to him that he could answer. "Ike," my dad said. Nevertheless, they put him on the fifth floor of Valley Memorial Hospital and began giving him electroshock treatments. I was married by then and about to start my own family. My dad was still locked up when my wife went into this same hospital, just one floor down, to have our first baby. After she had delivered, I went upstairs to give my dad the news. They let me in through a steel door and showed me where I could find him. He was sitting on a couch with a blanket over his lap. *Hey,* I thought. *What in hell is happening to my dad?* I sat down next to him and told him he was a grandfather. He waited a minute and then he said, "I feel like a grandfather." That's all he said. He didn't smile or move. He was in a big room with a lot of other people. Then I hugged him, and he began to cry.

Somehow he got out of there. But now came the years when he couldn't work and just sat around the house trying to figure what next and what he'd done wrong in his life that he'd wound up like this. My mother went from job to crummy job. Much later she referred to that time he was in the hospital, and those years just afterward, as "when Raymond was sick." The word *sick* was never the same for me again.

In 1964, through the help of a friend, he was lucky enough to be hired on at a mill in Klamath, California. He moved down there by himself to see if he could hack it. He lived not far from the mill, in a one-room cabin not much different from the place he and my mother had started out living in when they went west. He scrawled letters to my mother, and if I called she'd read them aloud to me over the phone. In the letters, he said it was touch and go. Every day that he went to work, he felt like it was the most important day of his life. But every day, he told her, made the next day that much easier. He said for her to tell me he said hello. If he couldn't sleep at night, he said, he thought about me and the good times we used to have. Finally, after a couple of months, he regained some of his confidence. He could do the work and didn't think he had to worry that he'd let anybody down ever again. When he was sure, he sent for my mother.

He'd been off from work for six years and had lost everything in that time—home, car, furniture, and appliances, including the big freezer that had been my mother's pride and joy. He'd lost his good name too—Raymond Carver was someone who couldn't pay his bills—and his self-respect was gone. He'd even lost his virility. My mother told my wife, "All during that time Raymond was sick we slept together in the same bed, but we didn't have relations. He wanted to a few times, but nothing happened. I didn't miss it, but I think he wanted to, you know."

During those years I was trying to raise my own family and earn a living. But, one thing and another, we found ourselves having to move a lot. I couldn't keep track of what was going down in my dad's life. But I did have a chance one Christmas to tell him I wanted to be a writer. I might as well have told him I wanted to become a plastic surgeon. "What are you going to write about?" he wanted to know. Then, as if to help me out, he said, "Write about stuff you know about. Write about some of those fishing trips we took." I said I would, but I knew I wouldn't. "Send me what you write," he said. I said I'd do that, but then I didn't. I wasn't writing anything about fishing, and I didn't think he'd particularly care about, or even necessarily understand, what I was writing in those days. Besides, he wasn't a reader. Not the sort, anyway, I imagined I was writing for.

Then he died. I was a long way off, in Iowa City, with things still to say to him. I didn't have the chance to tell him goodbye, or that I thought he was doing great at his new job. That I was proud of him for making a comeback.

My mother said he came in from work that night and ate a big supper. Then he sat at the table by himself and finished what was left of a bottle of whiskey, a bottle she found hidden in the bottom of the garbage under some coffee grounds a day or so later. Then he got up and went to bed, where my mother joined him a little later. But in the night she had to get up and make a bed for herself on the couch. "He was snoring so loud I couldn't sleep," she said. The next morning when she looked in on him, he was on his back with his mouth open, his cheeks caved in. *Gray-looking,* she said. She knew he was dead—she didn't need a doctor to tell her that. But she called one anyway, and then she called my wife.

Among the pictures my mother kept of my dad and herself during those early days in Washington was a photograph of him standing in front of a car, holding a beer and a stringer of fish. In the photograph he is wearing his hat back on his forehead and has this awkward grin on his face. I asked her for it and she gave it to me, along with some others. I put it up on my wall, and each time we moved, I took the picture along and put it up on another wall. I looked at it carefully from time to time, trying to figure out some things about my dad, and maybe myself in the process. But I couldn't. My dad just kept moving further and further away from me and back into time. Finally, in the course of another move, I lost the photograph. It was then that I tried to recall it, and at the same time make an attempt to say something about my dad, and how I thought that in some important ways we might be alike. I wrote the poem when I was living in an apartment house in an urban area south of San Francisco, at a time when I found myself, like my dad, having trouble with alcohol. The poem was a way of trying to connect up with him.

PHOTOGRAPH OF MY FATHER IN HIS TWENTY-SECOND YEAR

October. Here in this dank, unfamiliar kitchen
I study my father's embarrassed young man's face.
Sheepish grin, he holds in one hand a string
of spiny yellow perch, in the other
a bottle of Carlsberg beer.

In jeans and flannel shirt, he leans
against the front fender of a 1934 Ford.
He would like to pose brave and hearty for his posterity,
wear his old hat cocked over his ear.
All his life my father wanted to be bold.

But the eyes give him away, and the hands
that limply offer the string of dead perch
and the bottle of beer. Father, I love you,
yet how can I say thank you, I who can't hold my liquor either
and don't even know the places to fish.

The poem is true in its particulars, except that my dad died in June
and not October, as the first word of the poem says. I wanted a word
with more than one syllable to it to make it linger a little. But more
than that, I wanted a month appropriate to what I felt at the time I
wrote the poem—a month of short days and failing light, smoke in the
air, things perishing. June was summer nights and days, graduations, my
wedding anniversary, the birthday of one of my children. June wasn't a
month your father died in.

After the service at the funeral home, after we had moved outside,
a woman I didn't know came over to me and said, "He's happier where
he is now." I stared at this woman until she moved away. I still remember the little knob of a hat she was wearing. Then one of my dad's
cousins—I didn't know the man's name—reached out and took my
hand. "We all miss him," he said, and I knew he wasn't saying it just
to be polite.

I began to weep for the first time since receiving the news. I hadn't
been able to before. I hadn't had the time, for one thing. Now, suddenly,
I couldn't stop. I held my wife and wept while she said and did what
she could do to comfort me there in the middle of that summer
afternoon.

I listened to people say consoling things to my mother, and I was
glad that my dad's family had turned up, had come to where he was. I
thought I'd remember everything that was said and done that day and
maybe find a way to tell it sometime. But I didn't. I forgot it all, or
nearly. What I do remember is that I heard our name used a lot that
afternoon, my dad's name and mine. But I knew they were talking about

my dad. *Raymond,* these people kept saying in their beautiful voices out
of my childhood. *Raymond.*

RICHARD FORD

*Richard Ford was born in Jackson, Mississippi, in 1944. He left
Jackson and the South to attend Michigan State University and the
University of California at Irvine, where he received an M.F.A. in
creative writing. Ford, who has taught at Williams College, Princeton,
and Harvard, has published his essays and stories in* Esquire, The
New Yorker, *and other magazines. His novels include* A Piece of
My Heart *(1976),* The Ultimate Good Luck *(1981),* The
Sportswriter *(1986), and* Wildlife *(1990). He is also the author
of a collection of short stories set in Montana,* Rock Springs *(1987),
and he wrote the screenplay for the motion picture* Bright Angel. *He
has received a Guggenheim fellowship (1978) and the American Academy and Institute of Arts and Letters Award for Literature (1989).
Ford's latest novel,* Independence Day, *won the 1995 PEN/
Faulkner Award and the Pulitzer prize in fiction. He and his wife,
Kristina, divide their whereabouts among New Orleans, Mississippi,
and central Montana.*

*"They leave with the moon," the mother in "Communist" says,
describing the flight of snow geese. "It's still half wild out here." In
this story from* Rock Springs, *the mother tries to reach out to her
son, the narrator, a Montana teen on the edge of turning tough. "We
have to keep civilization alive somehow," she says, shivering. The
stories in* Rock Springs, *while clearly universal, are also Western to
the bone, struggles in a partways civilized society where the central
characters end up mostly alone.*

COMMUNIST

My mother once had a boyfriend named Glen Baxter. This was in 1961. We—my mother and I—were living in the little house my father had left her up the Sun River, near Victory, Montana, west of Great Falls. My mother was thirty-two at the time. I was sixteen. Glen Baxter was somewhere in the middle between us, though I cannot be exact about it.

We were living then off the proceeds of my father's life insurance policies, with my mother doing some part-time waitressing work up in Great Falls and going to the bars in the evenings, which I know is where she met Glen Baxter. Sometimes he would come back with her and stay in her room at night, or she would call up from town and explain that she was staying with him in his little place on Lewis Street by the GN yards. She gave me his number every time, but I never called it. I think she probably thought that what she was doing was terrible, but simply couldn't help herself. I thought it was all right, though. Regular life it seemed, and still does. She was young, and I knew that even then.

Glen Baxter was a Communist and liked hunting, which he talked about a lot. Pheasants. Ducks. Deer. He killed all of them, he said. He had been to Vietnam as far back as then, and when he was in our house he often talked about shooting the animals over there—monkeys and beautiful parrots—using military guns just for sport. We did not know what Vietnam was then, and Glen, when he talked about that, referred to it only as "the Far East." I think now he must've been in the CIA and been disillusioned by something he saw or found out about and been thrown out, but that kind of thing did not matter to us. He was a tall, dark-eyed man with short black hair, and was usually in a good humor. He had gone halfway through college in Peoria, Illinois, he said, where he grew up. But when he was around our life he worked wheat farms as a ditcher, and stayed out of work winters and in the bars drinking with women like my mother, who had work and some money. It is not an uncommon life to lead in Montana.

What I want to explain happened in November. We had not been seeing Glen Baxter for some time. Two months had gone by. My mother knew other men, but she came home most days from work and stayed inside watching television in her bedroom and drinking beers. I asked about Glen once, and she said only that she didn't know where he was, and I assumed they had had a fight and that he was gone off on a flyer back to Illinois or Massachusetts, where he said he had relatives. I'll admit that I liked him. He had something on his mind always. He was a labor man as well as a Communist, and liked to say that the country was poisoned by the rich, and strong men would need to bring it to life again, and I liked that because my father had been a labor man, which was why we had a house to live in and money coming through. It was also true that I'd had a few boxing bouts by then—just with town boys and one with an Indian from Choteau—and there were some girl-friends I knew from that. I did not like my mother being around the house so much at night, and I wished Glen Baxter would come back, or that another man would come along and entertain her somewhere else.

At two o'clock on a Saturday, Glen drove up into our yard in a car. He had had a big brown Harley-Davidson that he rode most of the year, in his black-and-red irrigators and a baseball cap turned backwards. But this time he had a car, a blue Nash Ambassador. My mother and I went out on the porch when he stopped inside the olive trees my father had planted as a shelter belt, and my mother had a look on her face of not much pleasure. It was starting to be cold in earnest by then. Snow was down already onto the Fairfield Bench, though on this day a chinook was blowing, and it could as easily have been spring, though the sky above the Divide was turning over in silver and blue clouds of winter.

"We haven't seen you in a long time, I guess," my mother said coldly.

"My little retarded sister died," Glen said, standing at the door of his old car. He was wearing his orange VFW jacket and canvas shoes we called wino shoes, something I had never seen him wear before. He seemed to be in a good humor. "We buried her in Florida near the home."

"That's a good place," my mother said in a voice that meant she was a wronged party in something.

"I want to take this boy hunting today, Aileen," Glen said. "There's snow geese down now. But we have to go right away, or they'll be gone to Idaho by tomorrow."

"He doesn't care to go," my mother said.

"Yes I do," I said, and looked at her.

My mother frowned at me. "Why do you?"

"Why does he need a reason?" Glen Baxter said and grinned.

"I want him to have one, that's why." She looked at me oddly. "I think Glen's drunk, Les."

"No, I'm not drinking," Glen said, which was hardly ever true. He looked at both of us, and my mother bit down on the side of her lower lip and stared at me in a way to make you think she thought something was being put over on her and she didn't like you for it. She was very pretty, though when she was mad her features were sharpened and less pretty by a long way. "All right, then I don't care," she said to no one in particular. "Hunt, kill, maim. Your father did that too." She turned to go back inside.

"Why don't you come with us, Aileen?" Glen was smiling still, pleased.

"To do what?" my mother said. She stopped and pulled a package of cigarettes out of her dress pocket and put one in her mouth.

"It's worth seeing."

"See dead animals?" my mother said.

"These geese are from Siberia, Aileen," Glen said. "They're not like a lot of geese. Maybe I'll buy us dinner later. What do you say?"

"Buy what with?" my mother said. To tell the truth, I didn't know why she was so mad at him. I would've thought she'd be glad to see him. But she just suddenly seemed to hate everything about him.

"I've got some money," Glen said. "Let me spend it on a pretty girl tonight."

"Find one of those and you're lucky," my mother said, turning away toward the front door.

"I already found one," Glen Baxter said. But the door slammed behind her, and he looked at me then with a look I think now was helplessness, though I could not see a way to change anything.

My mother sat in the backseat of Glen's Nash and looked out the window while we drove. My double gun was in the seat between us beside Glen's Belgian pump, which he kept loaded with five shells in case, he said, he saw something beside the road he wanted to shoot. I had hunted rabbits before, and had ground-sluiced pheasants and other birds, but I had never been on an actual hunt before, one where you drove out to some special place and did it formally. And I was excited. I had a feeling that something important was about to happen to me, and that this would be a day I would always remember.

My mother did not say anything for a long time, and neither did

I. We drove up through Great Falls and out the other side toward Fort Benton, which was on the benchland where wheat was grown.

"Geese mate for life," my mother said, just out of the blue, as we were driving. "I hope you know that. They're special birds."

"I know that," Glen said in the front seat. "I have every respect for them."

"So where were you for three months?" she said. "I'm only curious."

"I was in the Big Hole for a while," Glen said, "and after that I went over to Douglas, Wyoming."

"What were you planning to do there?" my mother asked.

"I wanted to find a job, but it didn't work out."

"I'm going to college," she said suddenly, and this was something I had never heard about before. I turned to look at her, but she was staring out her window and wouldn't see me.

"I knew French once," Glen said. "*Rosé*'s pink. *Rouge*'s red." He glanced at me and smiled. "I think that's a wise idea, Aileen. When are you going to start?"

"I don't want Les to think he was raised by crazy people all his life," my mother said.

"Les ought to go himself," Glen said.

"After I go, he will."

"What do you say about that, Les?" Glen said, grinning.

"He says it's just fine," my mother said.

"It's just fine," I said.

Where Glen Baxter took us was out onto the high flat prairie that was disked for wheat and had high, high mountains out to the east, with lower heartbreak hills in between. It was, I remember, a day for blues in the sky, and down in the distance we could see the small town of Floweree, and the state highway running past it toward Fort Benton and the Hi-line. We drove out on top of the prairie on a muddy dirt road fenced on both sides, until we had gone about three miles, which is where Glen stopped.

"All right," he said, looking up in the rearview mirror at my mother. "You wouldn't think there was anything here, would you?"

"*We're* here," my mother said. "You brought us here."

"You'll be glad though," Glen said, and seemed confident to me. I had looked around myself but could not see anything. No water or trees, nothing that seemed like a good place to hunt anything. Just wasted land. "There's a big lake out there, Les," Glen said. "You can't see it now from here because it's low. But the geese are there. You'll see."

"It's like the moon out here. I recognize that," my mother said, "only it's worse." She was staring out at the flat wheatland as if she could actually see something in particular, and wanted to know more about it. "How'd you find this place?"

"I came once on the wheat push," Glen said.

"And I'm sure the owner told you just to come back and hunt anytime you like and bring anybody you wanted. Come one, come all. Is that it?"

"People shouldn't own land anyway," Glen said. "Anybody should be able to use it."

"Les, Glen's going to poach here," my mother said. "I just want you to know that, because that's a crime and the law will get you for it. If you're a man now, you're going to have to face the consequences."

"That's not true," Glen Baxter said, and looked gloomily out over the steering wheel down the muddy road toward the mountains. Though for myself I believed it was true, and didn't care. I didn't care about anything at that moment except seeing geese fly over me and shooting them down.

"Well, I'm certainly not going out there," my mother said. "I like towns better, and I already have enough trouble."

"That's okay," Glen said. "When the geese lift up you'll get to see them. That's all I wanted. Les and me'll go shoot them, won't we, Les?"

"Yes," I said, and I put my hand on my shotgun, which had been my father's and was heavy as rocks.

"Then we should go on," Glen said, "or we'll waste our light."

We got out of the car with our guns. Glen took off his canvas shoes and put on his pair of black irrigators out of the trunk. Then we crossed the barbed wire fence, and walked out into the high, tilled field toward nothing. I looked back at my mother when we were still not so far away, but I could only see the small, dark top of her head, low in the backseat of the Nash, staring out and thinking what I could not then begin to say.

On the walk toward the lake, Glen began talking to me. I had never been alone with him, and knew little about him except what my mother said—that he drank too much, or other times that he was the nicest

man she had ever known in the world and that someday a woman would
marry him, though she didn't think it would be her. Glen told me as
we walked that he wished he had finished college, but that it was too
late now, that his mind was too old. He said he had liked the Far East
very much, and that people there knew how to treat each other, and
that he would go back some day but couldn't go now. He said also that
he would like to live in Russia for a while and mentioned the names of
people who had gone there, names I didn't know. He said it would be
hard at first, because it was so different, but that pretty soon anyone
would learn to like it and wouldn't want to live anywhere else, and that
Russians treated Americans who came to live there like kings. There
were Communists everywhere now, he said. You didn't know them,
but they were there. Montana had a large number, and he was in touch
with all of them. He said that Communists were always in danger and
that he had to protect himself all the time. And when he said that he
pulled back his VFW jacket and showed me the butt of a pistol he had
stuck under his shirt against his bare skin. "There are people who want
to kill me right now," he said, "and I would kill a man myself if I
thought I had to." And we kept walking. Though in a while he said,
"I don't think I know much about you, Les. But I'd like to. What do
you like to do?"

"I like to box," I said. "My father did it. It's a good thing to know."

"I suppose you have to protect yourself too," Glen said.

"I know how to," I said.

"Do you like to watch TV," Glen asked, and smiled.

"Not much."

"I love to," Glen said. "I could watch it instead of eating if I
had one."

I looked out straight ahead over the green tops of sage that grew
to the edge of the disked field, hoping to see the lake Glen said was
there. There was an airishness and a sweet smell that I thought might
be the place we were going, but I couldn't see it. "How will we hunt
these geese?" I said.

"It won't be hard," Glen said. "Most hunting isn't even hunting.
It's only shooting. And that's what this will be. In Illinois you would
dig holes in the ground and hide and set out your decoys. Then the
geese come to you, over and over again. But we don't have time for
that here." He glanced at me. "You have to be sure the first time here."

"How do you know they're here now," I asked. And I looked

toward the Highwood Mountains twenty miles away, half in snow and half dark blue at the bottom. I could see the little town of Floweree then, looking shabby and dimly lighted in the distance. A red bar sign shone. A car moved slowly away from the scattered buildings.

"They always come November first," Glen said.

"Are we going to poach them?"

"Does it make any difference to you," Glen asked.

"No, it doesn't."

"Well then, we aren't," he said.

We walked then for a while without talking. I looked back once to see the Nash far and small in the flat distance. I couldn't see my mother, and I thought that she must've turned on the radio and gone to sleep, which she always did, letting it play all night in her bedroom. Behind the car the sun was nearing the rounded mountains southwest of us, and I knew that when the sun was gone it would be cold. I wished my mother had decided to come along with us, and I thought for a moment of how little I really knew her at all.

Glen walked with me another quarter-mile, crossed another barbed wire fence where sage was growing, then went a hundred yards through wheatgrass and spurge until the ground went up and formed a kind of long hillock bunker built by a farmer against the wind. And I realized the lake was just beyond us. I could hear the sound of a car horn blowing and a dog barking all the way down in the town, then the wind seemed to move and all I could hear then and after then were geese. So many geese, from the sound of them, though I still could not see even one. I stood and listened to the high-pitched shouting sound, a sound I had never heard so close, a sound with size to it—though it was not loud. A sound that meant great numbers and that made your chest rise and your shoulders tighten with expectancy. It was a sound to make you feel separate from it and everything else, as if you were of no importance in the grand scheme of things.

"Do you hear them singing," Glen asked. He held his hand up to make me stand still. And we both listened. "How many do you think, Les, just hearing?"

"A hundred," I said. "More than a hundred."

"Five thousand," Glen said. "More than you can believe when you see them. Go see."

I put down my gun and on my hands and knees crawled up the earthwork through the wheatgrass and thistle, until I could see down to the lake and see the geese. And they were there, like a white bandage laid on the water, wide and long and continuous, a white expanse of snow geese, seventy yards from me, on the bank, but stretching far onto the lake, which was large itself—a half-mile across, with thick tules on the far side and wild plums farther and the blue mountain behind them.

"Do you see the big raft?" Glen said from below me, in a whisper.

"I see it," I said, still looking. It was such a thing to see, a view I had never seen and have not since.

"Are any on the land?" he said.

"Some are in the wheatgrass," I said, "but most are swimming."

"Good," Glen said. "They'll have to fly. But we can't wait for that now."

And I crawled backwards down the heel of land to where Glen was, and my gun. We were losing our light, and the air was purplish and cooling. I looked toward the car but couldn't see it, and I was no longer sure where it was below the lighted sky.

"Where do they fly to?" I said in a whisper, since I did not want anything to be ruined because of what I did or said. It was important to Glen to shoot the geese, and it was important to me.

"To the wheat," he said. "Or else they leave for good. I wish your mother had come, Les. Now she'll be sorry."

I could hear the geese quarreling and shouting on the lake surface. And I wondered if they knew we were here now. "She might be," I said with my heart pounding, but I didn't think she would be much.

It was a simple plan he had. I would stay behind the bunker, and he would crawl on his belly with his gun through the wheatgrass as near to the geese as he could. Then he would simply stand up and shoot all the ones he could close up, both in the air and on the ground. And when all the others flew up, with luck some would turn toward me as they came into the wind, and then I could shoot them and turn them back to him, and he would shoot them again. He could kill ten, he said, if he was lucky, and I might kill four. It didn't seem hard.

"Don't show them your face," Glen said. "Wait till you think you can touch them, then stand up and shoot. To hesitate is lost in this."

"All right," I said. "I'll try it."

"Shoot one in the head, and then shoot another one," Glen said. "It won't be hard." He patted me on the arm and smiled. Then he took off his VFW jacket and put it on the ground, climbed up the side of the bunker, cradling his shotgun in his arms, and slid on his belly into the dry stalks of yellow grass out of my sight.

Then, for the first time in that entire day, I was alone. And I didn't mind it. I sat squat down in the grass, loaded my double gun and took my other two shells out of my pocket to hold. I pushed the safety off and on to see that it was right. The wind rose a little, scuffed the grass and made me shiver. It was not the warm chinook now, but a wind out of the north, the one geese flew away from if they could.

Then I thought about my mother, in the car alone, and how much longer I would stay with her, and what it might mean to her for me to leave. And I wondered when Glen Baxter would die and if someone would kill him, or whether my mother would marry him and how I would feel about it. And though I didn't know why, it occurred to me that Glen Baxter and I would not be friends when all was said and done, since I didn't care if he ever married my mother or didn't.

Then I thought about boxing and what my father had taught me about it. To tighten your fists hard. To strike out straight from the shoulder and never punch backing up. How to cut a punch by snapping your fist inwards, how to carry your chin low, and to step toward a man when he is falling so you can hit him again. And most important, to keep your eyes open when you are hitting in the face and causing damage, because you need to see what you're doing to encourage yourself, and because it is when you close your eyes that you stop hitting and get hurt badly. "Fly all over your man, Les," my father said. "When you see your chance, fly on him and hit him till he falls." That, I thought, would always be my attitude in things.

And then I heard the geese again, their voices in unison, louder and shouting, as if the wind had changed again and put all new sounds in the cold air. And then a *boom*. And I knew Glen was in among them and had stood up to shoot. The noise of geese rose and grew worse, and my fingers burned where I held my gun too tight to the metal, and I put it down and opened my fist to make the burning stop so I could feel the trigger when the moment came. *Boom,* Glen shot again, and I heard him shuck a shell, and all the sounds out beyond the bunker seemed to be rising—the geese, the shots, the air itself going up. *Boom,* Glen shot another time, and I knew he was taking his careful time to make his shots good. And I held my gun and started to crawl up the bunker so as not to be surprised when the geese came over me and I could shoot.

From the top I saw Glen Baxter alone in the wheatgrass field, shooting at a white goose with black tips of wings that was on the ground not far from him, but trying to run and pull into the air. He shot it once more, and it fell over dead with its wings flapping.

Glen looked back at me and his face was distorted and strange. The air around him was full of white rising geese and he seemed to want them all. "Behind you, Les," he yelled at me and pointed. "They're all behind you now." I looked behind me, and there were geese in the air as far as I could see, more than I knew how many, moving so slowly, their wings wide out and working calmly and filling the air with noise, though their voices were not as loud or as shrill as I had thought they would be. And they were so close! Forty feet, some of them. The air around me vibrated and I could feel the wind from their wings and it seemed to me I could kill as many as the times I could shoot—a hundred or a thousand—and I raised my gun, put the muzzle on the head of a white goose, and fired. It shuddered in the air, its wide feet sank below its belly, its wings cradled out to hold back air, and it fell straight down and landed with an awful sound, a noise a human would make, a thick, soft, *hump* noise. I looked up again and shot another goose, could hear the pellets hit its chest, but it didn't fall or even break its pattern for flying. *Boom,* Glen shot again. And then again. "Hey," I heard him shout, "Hey, hey." And there were geese flying over me, flying in line after line. I broke my gun and reloaded, and thought to myself as I did: I need confidence here, I need to be sure with this. I pointed at another goose and shot it in the head, and it fell the way the first one had, wings out, its belly down, and with the same thick noise of hitting. Then I sat down in the grass on the bunker and let geese fly over me.

By now the whole raft was in the air, all of it moving in a slow swirl above me and the lake and everywhere, finding the wind and heading out south in long wavering lines that caught the last sun and turned to silver as they gained a distance. It was a thing to see, I will tell you now. Five thousand white geese all in the air around you, making a noise like you have never heard before. And I thought to myself then: this is something I will never see again. I will never forget this. And I was right.

Glen Baxter shot twice more. One he missed, but with the other he hit a goose flying away from him, and knocked it half falling and flying into the empty lake not far from shore, where it began to swim as though it was fine and make its noise.

Glen stood in the stubby grass, looking out at the goose, his gun lowered. "I didn't need to shoot that one, did I, Les?"

"I don't know," I said, sitting on the little knoll of land, looking at the goose swimming in the water.

"I don't know why I shoot 'em. They're so beautiful." He looked at me.

"I don't know either," I said.

"Maybe there's nothing else to do with them." Glen stared at the goose again and shook his head. "Maybe this is exactly what they're put on earth for."

I did not know what to say because I did not know what he could mean by that, though what I felt was embarrassment at the great numbers of geese there were, and a dulled feeling like a hunger because the shooting had stopped and it was over for me now.

Glen began to pick up his geese, and I walked down to my two that had fallen close together and were dead. One had hit with such an impact that its stomach had split and some of its inward parts were knocked out. Though the other looked unhurt, its soft white belly turned up like a pillow, its head and jagged bill-teeth, its tiny black eyes looking as they would if they were alive.

"What's happened to the hunters out here?" I heard a voice speak. It was my mother, standing in her pink dress on the knoll above us, hugging her arms. She was smiling though she was cold. And I realized that I had lost all thought of her in the shooting. "Who did all this shooting? Is this your work, Les?"

"No," I said.

"Les is a hunter, though, Aileen," Glen said. "He takes his time." He was holding two white geese by their necks, one in each hand, and he was smiling. He and my mother seemed pleased.

"I see you didn't miss too many," my mother said and smiled. I could tell she admired Glen for his geese, and that she had done some thinking in the car alone. "It *was* wonderful, Glen," she said. "I've never seen anything like that. They were like snow."

"It's worth seeing once, isn't it?" Glen said. "I should've killed more, but I got excited."

My mother looked at me then. "Where's yours, Les?"

"Here," I said and pointed to my two geese on the ground beside me.

My mother nodded in a nice way, and I think she liked everything then and wanted the day to turn out right and for all of us to be happy. "Six, then. You've got six in all."

"One's still out there," I said, and motioned where the one goose was swimming in circles on the water.

"Okay," my mother said and put her hand over her eyes to look. "Where is it?"

Glen Baxter looked at me then with a strange smile, a smile that said he wished I had never mentioned anything about the other goose. And I wished I hadn't either. I looked up in the sky and could see the lines of geese by the thousands shining silver in the light, and I wished we could just leave and go home.

"That one's my mistake there," Glen Baxter said and grinned. "I shouldn't have shot that one, Aileen. I got too excited."

My mother looked out on the lake for a minute, then looked at Glen and back again. "Poor goose." She shook her head. "How will you get it, Glen?"

"I can't get that one now," Glen said.

My mother looked at him. "What do you mean?"

"I'm going to leave that one," Glen said.

"Well, no. You can't leave one," my mother said. "You shot it. You have to get it. Isn't that a rule?"

"No," Glen said.

And my mother looked from Glen to me. "Wade out and get it, Glen," she said in a sweet way, and my mother looked young then, like a young girl, in her flimsy short-sleeved waitress dress and her skinny, bare legs in the wheatgrass.

"No." Glen Baxter looked down at his gun and shook his head. And I didn't know why he wouldn't go, because it would've been easy. The lake was shallow. And you could tell that anyone could've walked out a long way before it got deep, and Glen had on his boots.

My mother looked at the white goose, which was not more than thirty yards from the shore, its head up, moving in slow circles, its wings settled and relaxed so you could see the black tips. "Wade out and get it, Glenny, won't you, please?" she said. "They're special things."

"You don't understand the world, Aileen," Glen said. "This can happen. It doesn't matter."

"But that's so cruel, Glen," she said, and a sweet smile came on her lips.

"Raise up your own arms, 'Leeny," Glen said. "I can't see any angel's wings, can you, Les?" He looked at me, but I looked away.

"Then you go on and get it, Les," my mother said. "You weren't raised by crazy people." I started to go, but Glen Baxter suddenly grabbed me by my shoulder and pulled me back hard, so hard his fingers made bruises in my skin that I saw later.

"Nobody's going," he said. "This is over with now."

And my mother gave Glen a cold look then. "You don't have a heart, Glen," she said. "There's nothing to love in you. You're just a son of a bitch, that's all."

And Glen Baxter nodded at my mother, then, as if he understood something he had not understood before, but something that he was willing to know. "Fine," he said, "that's fine." And he took his big pistol out from against his belly, the big blue revolver I had only seen part of before and that he said protected him, and he pointed it out at the goose on the water, his arm straight away from him, and shot and missed. And then he shot and missed again. The goose made its noise once. And then he hit it dead, because there was no splash. And then he shot it three times more until the gun was empty and the goose's head was down and it was floating toward the middle of the lake where it was empty and dark blue. "Now who has a heart?" Glen said. But my mother was not there when he turned around. She had already started back to the car and was almost lost from sight in the darkness. And Glen smiled at me then and his face had a wild look on it. "Okay, Les?" he said.

"Okay," I said.

"There're limits to everything, right?"

"I guess so," I said.

"Your mother's a beautiful woman, but she's not the only beautiful woman in Montana." And I did not say anything. And Glen Baxter suddenly said, "Here," and he held the pistol out at me. "Don't you want this? Don't you want to shoot me? Nobody thinks they'll die. But I'm ready for it right now." And I did not know what to do then. Though it is true that what I wanted to do was to hit him, hit him as hard in the face as I could, and see him on the ground bleeding and crying and pleading for me to stop. Only at that moment he looked scared to me, and I had never seen a grown man scared before—though

I have seen one since—and I felt sorry for him, as though he was already a dead man. And I did not end up hitting him at all.

A light can go out in the heart. All of this happened years ago, but I still can feel now how sad and remote the world was to me. Glen Baxter, I think now, was not a bad man, only a man scared of something he'd never seen before—something soft in himself—his life going a way he didn't like. A woman with a son. Who could blame him there? I don't know what makes people do what they do, or call themselves what they call themselves, only that you have to live someone's life to be the expert.

My mother had tried to see the good side of things, tried to be hopeful in the situation she was handed, tried to look out for us both, and it hadn't worked. It was a strange time in her life then and after that, a time when she had to adjust to being an adult just when she was on the thin edge of things. Too much awareness too early in life was her problem, I think.

And what I felt was only that I had somehow been pushed out into the world, into the real life then, the one I hadn't lived yet. In a year I was gone to hard-rock mining and no-paycheck jobs and not to college. And I have thought more than once about my mother saying that I had not been raised by crazy people, and I don't know what that could mean or what difference it could make, unless it means that love is a reliable commodity, and even that is not always true, as I have found out.

Late on the night that all this took place I was in bed when I heard my mother say, "Come outside, Les. Come and hear this." And I went out onto the front porch barefoot and in my underwear, where it was warm like spring, and there was a spring mist in the air. I could see the lights of the Fairfield Coach in the distance, on its way up to Great Falls.

And I could hear geese, white birds in the sky, flying. They made their high-pitched sound like angry yells, and though I couldn't see them high up, it seemed to me they were everywhere. And my mother looked up and said, "Hear them?" I could smell her hair wet from the shower. "They leave with the moon," she said. "It's still half wild out here."

And I said, "I hear them," and I felt a chill come over my bare chest, and the hair stood up on my arms the way it does before a storm. And for a while we listened.

"When I first married your father, you know, we lived on a street called Bluebird Canyon, in California. And I thought that was the prettiest street and the prettiest name. I suppose no one brings you up like your first love. You don't mind if I say that, do you?" She looked at me hopefully.

"No," I said.

"We have to keep civilization alive somehow." And she pulled her little housecoat together because there was a cold vein in the air, a part of the cold that would be on us the next day. "I don't feel part of things tonight, I guess."

"It's all right," I said.

"Do you know where I'd like to go?"

"No," I said. And I suppose I knew she was angry then, angry with life, but did not want to show me that.

"To the Straits of Juan de Fuca. Wouldn't that be something? Would you like that?"

"I'd like it," I said. And my mother looked off for a minute, as if she could see the Straits of Juan de Fuca out against the line of mountains, see the lights of things alive and a whole new world.

"I know you liked him," she said after a moment. "You and I both suffer fools too well."

"I didn't like him too much," I said. "I didn't really care."

"He'll fall on his face. I'm sure of that," she said. And I didn't say anything because I didn't care about Glen Baxter anymore, and was happy not to talk about him. "Would you tell me something if I asked you? Would you tell me the truth?"

"Yes," I said.

And my mother did not look at me. "Just tell the truth," she said.

"All right," I said.

"Do you think I'm still very feminine? I'm thirty-two years old now. You don't know what that means. But do you think I am?"

And I stood at the edge of the porch, with the olive trees before me, looking straight up into the mist where I could not see geese but could still hear them flying, could almost feel the air move below their white wings. And I felt the way you feel when you are on a trestle all alone and the train is coming, and you know you have to decide. And I said, "Yes, I do." Because that was the truth. And I tried to think of something else then and did not hear what my mother said after that.

And how old was I then? Sixteen. Sixteen is young, but it can also be a grown man. I am forty-one years old now, and I think about that time without regret, though my mother and I never talked in that way again, and I have not heard her voice now in a long, long time.

DAVID QUAMMEN

David Quammen, born in 1948, is the author of three novels, a collection of short fiction, and two collections of essays on science and nature. For years he wrote a monthly column for Outside *magazine. In 1987, he received the National Magazine Award in Essays and Criticism for that work. He has lived in Montana since 1973. His recent, much-lauded* The Song of the Dodo *is concerned with the problem of species extinctions on mainlands throughout the world, and the links between that problem and the biological dynamics of islands. In the course of researching the book, he has traveled to Madagascar, New Guinea, Guam, Mauritius, the Galápagos, Krakatau, Sulawesi, Tasmania, the central Amazon, Komodo, and Wyoming.*

Quammen's writings have always been concerned with survival —survival of character, a species, life on our planet. This selection, "Orphan Calves," is taken from "Walking Out," which in its complete version is included in Blood Line: Stories of Fathers and Sons *(1988). Oftentimes, in order for one creature to survive, something else must perish. In understanding this trade-off and in respecting the resultant loss comes true survival: survival of spirit. Quammen says he owes this story "to Barry Gordon, from whose personal experience it derives."*

"ORPHAN CALVES"
FROM "WALKING OUT"

They built a fire. His father had brought sirloin steaks and an onion for dinner, and the boy was happy with him about that. As they ate, it grew dark, but the boy and his father had stocked a large comforting pile of naked deadfall. In the darkness, by firelight, his father made chocolate pudding. The pudding had been his father's surprise. The boy sat on a piece of canvas and added logs to the fire while his father drank coffee. Sparks rose on the heat and the boy watched them climb toward the cedar limbs and the black pools of sky. The pudding did not set.

"Do you remember your grandfather, David?"

"Yes," the boy said, and wished it were true. He remembered a funeral when he was three.

"Your grandfather brought me up on this mountain when I was seventeen. That was the last year he hunted." The boy knew what sort of thoughts his father was having. But he knew also that his own home was in Evergreen Park, and that he was another man's boy now, with another man's name, though this indeed was his father. "Your grandfather was fifty years older than me."

The boy said nothing.

"And I'm thirty-four years older than you."

"And I'm only eleven," the boy cautioned him.

"Yes," said his father. "And someday you'll have a son and you'll be forty years older than him, and you'll want so badly for him to know who you are that you could cry."

The boy was embarrassed.

"And that's called the cycle of life's infinite wisdom," his father said, and laughed at himself unpleasantly.

"Why didn't he?" the boy asked, to escape the focus of his father's rumination.

"Why didn't who what?"

"Why was it the last year he hunted?"

"He was sixty-seven years old," his father said. "But that wasn't the reason. Because he was still walking to work at the railroad office in Big Timber when he was seventy-five. I don't know. We took a bull elk and a goat that year, I remember. The goat was during spring season and every inch of its hide was covered with ticks. I carried it down whole and after a mile I was covered with ticks too. I never shot another goat. I don't know why he quit. He still went out after birds in the wheat stubble, by himself. So it's not true that he stopped hunting completely. He stopped hunting with me. And he stopped killing. Once in every five or six times he would bring back a pheasant, if it seemed like a particularly good autumn night to have pheasant for supper. Usually he just went out and missed every shot on purpose. There were plenty of birds in the fields where he was walking, and your grandmother or I would hear his gun fire, at least once. But I guess when a man feels himself getting old, almost as old as he thinks he will ever be, he doesn't much want to be killing things anymore. I guess you might have to kill one bird in every ten or twenty, or the pheasants might lose their respect for you. They might tame out. Your grandfather had no desire to live among tame pheasants, I'm sure. But I suppose you would get a little reluctant, when you came to be seventy, about doing your duty toward keeping them wild. And he would not hunt with me anymore then, not even pheasants, not even to miss them. He said it was because he didn't trust himself with a partner, now that his hands were unsteady. But his hands were still steady. He said it was because I was too good. That he had taught me as well as he knew how, and that all I could learn from him now would be the bad habits of age, and those I would find for myself, in my turn. He never did tell me the real reason."

"What did he die of?"

"He was eighty-seven then," said his father. "Christ. He was tired."

The boy's question had been a disruption. His father was silent. Then he shook his head, and poured himself the remaining coffee. He did not like to think of the boy's grandfather as an eighty-seven-year-old man, the boy understood. As long as his grandfather was dead anyway, his father preferred thinking of him younger.

"I remember when I got my first moose," he said. "I was thirteen. I had never shot anything bigger than an owl. And I caught holy hell for killing that owl. I had my Winchester .30-30, like the one you're using. He gave it to me that year, at the start of the season. It was an old-looking gun even then. I don't know where he got it. We had a moose that he had stalked the year before, in a long swampy cottonwood flat along the Yellowstone River. It was a big cow, and this year she had a calf.

"We went there on the first day of the season and every hunting day for a week, and hunted down the length of that river flat, spaced apart about twenty yards, and came out at the bottom end. We saw fresh tracks every day, but we never got a look at that moose and the calf. It was only a matter of time, my father told me, before we would jump her. Then that Sunday we drove out and before he had the truck parked my hands were shaking. I knew it was that day. There was no reason why, yet I had such a sure feeling it was that day, my hands had begun shaking. He noticed, and he said: 'Don't worry.'

"I said: 'I'm fine.' And my voice was steady. It was just my hands.

" 'I can see that,' he said. 'But you'll do what you need to do.'

" 'Yessir,' " I said. 'Let's go hunting.'

"That day he put me up at the head end of our cottonwood flat and said he would walk down along the river bank to the bottom, and then turn in. We would come at the moose from both ends and meet in the middle and I should please not shoot my father when he came in sight. I should try to remember, he said, that he was the uglier one, in the orange hat. The shaking had left me as soon as we started walking, holding our guns. I remember it all. Before he went off I said: 'What does a moose look like?'

" 'What the hell do you mean, what does a moose look like?'

" 'Yes, I know,' I said. 'I mean, what is he gonna do when I see him? When he sees me. What color is he? What kind of thing is he gonna do?'

"And he said: 'All right. She will be black. She will be almost pitch black. She will not look to you very much bigger than our pickup. She is going to be stupid. She will let you get close. Slide right up to within thirty or forty yards if you can and set yourself up for a good shot. She will probably not see you, and if she does, she will probably not care. If you miss the first time, which you have every right to do, I don't care how close you get, if you miss the first time, she may even give you another. If you catch her attention, she may bolt off to me or she may charge you. Watch out for the calf when you come up on her. Worry her over the calf, and she will be mad. If she charges you, stand where you are and squeeze off another and then jump the hell out of the way. We probably won't even see her. All right?'

"I had walked about three hundred yards before I saw what I thought was a Holstein. It was off to my left, away from the river, and I looked over there and saw black and white and kept walking till I was just about past it. There were cattle pastured along in that flat but they would have been beef cattle, Herefords, brown and white like a deer. I didn't think about that. I went on looking everywhere else until I glanced over again when I was abreast and saw I was walking along sixty yards from a grazing moose. I stopped. My heart started pumping so hard that it seemed like I might black out, and I didn't know what was going to happen. I thought the moose would take care of that. Nothing happened.

"Next thing I was running. Running flat out as fast as I could, bent over double like a soldier would do in the field, running as fast but as quietly as I could. Running right at that moose. I remember clearly that I was not thinking anything at all, not for those first seconds. My body just started to run. I never thought, Now I'll scoot up to within thirty yards of her. I was just charging blind, like a moose or a sow grizzly is liable to charge you if you get her mad or confused. Who knows what I would have done. I wanted a moose pretty badly, I thought. I might have galloped right up to within five yards before I leveled, if it hadn't been for that spring creek.

"I didn't see it till I was in the air. I came up a little hillock and jumped, and then it was too late. The hillock turned out to be one bank of a spring-fed pasture seepage, about fifteen feet wide. I landed up to my thighs in mud. It was a prime cattle wallow, right where I had jumped. I must have spent five minutes sweating my legs out of that muck, I was furious with myself, and I was sure the moose would be gone. But the moose was still grazing the same three feet of grass. And by that time I had some of my sense back.

"I climbed the far bank of the mudhole and lay up along the rise where I could steady my aim on the ground. From there I had an open shot of less than forty yards, but the moose was now facing me head on, so I would probably either kill her clean or miss her altogether. My hands started shaking again. I tried to line up the bead and it was ridiculous. My rifle was waving all over that end of the woods. For ten minutes I lay there struggling to control my aim, squeezing the rifle tighter and tighter and taking deeper breaths and holding them longer. Finally I did a smart thing. I set the rifle down. I rolled over on my back and rubbed my eyes and discovered that I was exhausted. I got my breath settled back down in rhythm again. If I could just take that moose, I thought, I was not going to want anything else for a year. But I knew I was not going to do it unless I could get my hands to obey me, no matter how close I was. I tried it again. I remembered to keep breathing easy and low and it was a little better but the rifle was still moving everywhere. When it seemed like the trembling was about to start getting worse all over again I waited till the sights next crossed the moose and jerked off a shot. I missed. The moose didn't even look up.

"Now I was calmer. I had heard the gun fire once, and I knew my father had heard it, and I knew the moose would only give me one more. I realized that there was a good chance I would not get this moose at all, so I was more serious, and humble. This time I squeezed. I knocked a piece off her right antler and before I thought to wonder why a female should have any antlers to get shot at she raised her head up and gave a honk like eleven elephants in a circus-train fire. She started to run.

"I got off my belly and dropped the gun and turned around and jumped right back down into that mud. I was still stuck there when I heard her crash by on her way to the river, and then my father's shot.

"But I had wallowed myself out again, and got my rifle up off the ground, by the time he found me, thank God. He took a look at my clothes and said:

" 'Tried to burrow up under him, did you?'

" 'No sir. I heard you fire once. Did you get her?'

" 'Him. That was no cow and calf. That was a bull. No. No more than you.'

"He had been at the river edge about a hundred yards downstream from where the bull broke out. He took his shot while the bull was crossing the gravel bed and the shallows. The moose clambered right out into midstream of the Yellowstone and started swimming for his life. But the current along there was heavy. So the moose was swept down abreast with my father before he got halfway across toward the opposite shore. My father sighted on him as he rafted by, dog-paddling frantically and staying afloat and inching slowly away. The moose turned and looked at him, my father said. He had a chunk broken out of one antler and it was dangling down by a few fibers and he looked terrified. He was not more than twenty yards off shore by then and he could see my father and the raised rifle. My father said he had never seen more personality come into the face of a wild animal. All right, my father said the moose told him, Do what you will do. They both knew the moose was helpless. They both also knew this: my father could kill the moose, but he couldn't have him. The Yellowstone River would have him. My father lowered the gun. When he did, my father claimed, the moose turned his head forward again and went on swimming harder than ever. So that wasn't the day I shot mine.

"I shot mine the next Saturday. We went back to the cottonwood flat and split again and I walked up to within thirty yards of the cow and her calf. I made a standing shot, and killed the cow with one bullet breaking her spine. She was drinking, broadside to me. She dropped dead on the spot. The calf didn't move. He stood over the dead cow, stupid, wondering what in the world to do.

"The calf was as big as a four-point buck. When my father came up, he found me with tears flooding all over my face, screaming at the calf and trying to shoo him away. I was pushing against his flanks and swatting him and shouting at him to run off. At the sight of my father, he finally bolted.

"I had shot down the cow while she stood in the same spring seep where I had been stuck. Her quarters weighed out to eight hundred pounds and we couldn't budge her. We had to clean her and quarter her right there in the water and mud."

His father checked the tin pot again, to be sure there was no more coffee.

"Why did you tell me that story?" the boy said. "Now I don't want to shoot a moose either."

"I know," said his father. "And when you do, I hope you'll be sad too. But the other thing about a moose is, she makes eight hundred pounds of delicious meat. In fact, David, that's what we had for supper."

Through the night the boy was never quite warm. He slept on his side with his knees drawn up, and this was uncomfortable but his body seemed to demand it for warmth. The hard cold mountain earth pressed upward through the mat of fir boughs his father had laid, and drew heat from the boy's body like a pallet of leeches. He clutched the bedroll around his neck and folded the empty part at the bottom back under his legs. Once he woke to a noise. Though his father was sleeping between him and the door of the hut, for a while the boy lay awake, listening worriedly, and then woke again on his back to realize time had passed. He heard droplets begin to hit the canvas his father had spread over the sod roof of the hut. But he remained dry.

THOMAS MCGUANE

Thomas McGuane is a novelist, screenwriter, essayist, and breaker of world-class cutting horses, and as such, has always been several steps ahead of the game. Born in Wyandotte, Michigan, he received a B.A. from Michigan State University in 1962, an M.F.A. from the Yale University School of Drama, and a Stegner Fellowship at Stanford University (1966–1967). With the publication of his first novel, The Sporting Club *(1969), McGuane's acerbic wit and kinetic, stylized language served as a wake-up call to Western writers. In the next ten years, he wrote three critically acclaimed novels and four screenplays (all of which were produced), served as a special contributor to* Sports Illustrated, *and in 1975 even directed the motion picture version of his Key West novel,* Ninety-Two in the Shade. *His later novels are set in the vicinity of the Crazy Mountain in Montana, where McGuane has lived and ranched since the early 1970s. Other novels include* The Bushwhacked Piano *(1971),* Something to Be De-sired *(1984),* Keep the Change *(1989), and* Nothing But Blue Skies *(1992). In addition, he has published a collection of essays on sport,* An Outside Chance *(1980), from which this selection is taken, and a book of short stories,* To Skin a Cat *(1986).*

THE HEART OF THE GAME

Hunting in your own back yard becomes with time, if you love hunting, less and less expeditionary. This year, when Montana's eager frost knocked my garden on its butt, the hoe seemed more like the rifle than it ever had before, the vegetables more like game.

My son and I went scouting before the season and saw some an-telope in the high plains foothills of the Absaroka Range, wary, hanging on the skyline; a few bands and no great heads. We crept around, look-ing into basins, and at dusk met a tired cowboy on a tired horse followed by a tired blue-heeler dog. The plains seemed bigger than anything, bigger than the mountains that seemed to sit in the middle of them, bigger than the ocean. The clouds made huge shadows that traveled on the grass slowly through the day.

Hunting season trickles on forever; if you don't go in on a cow with anybody, there is the dark argument of the empty deep-freeze against headhunting ("You can't eat horns!"). But nevertheless, in my mind, I've laid out the months like playing cards, knowing some decent whitetails could be down in the river bottom and, fairly reliably, the long windy shots at antelope. The big buck mule deer—the ridge-runners—stay up in the scree and rock walls until the snow drives them out; but they stay high long after the elk have quit and broken down the hay corrals on the ranches and farmsteads, which, when you're hunting the rocks from a' saddle horse, look pathetic and housebroken with their yellow lights against the coming of winter.

Where I live, the Yellowstone River runs straight north, then takes an eastward turn at Livingston, Montana. This flowing north is supposed to be remarkable; and the river doesn't do it long. It runs mostly over sand and stones once it comes out of the rock slots near the Wyoming line. But all along, there are deviations of one sort or another: canals, backwaters, sloughs; the red willows grow in the sometime-flooded bottom, and at the first elevation, the cottonwoods. I hunt here for the white-tail deer which, in recent years, have moved up these rivers in numbers never seen before.

The first morning, the sun came up hitting around me in arbitrary panels as the light moved through the jagged openings in the Absaroka Range. I was walking very slowly in the edge of the trees, the river invisible a few hundred yards to my right but sending a huge sigh through the willows. It was cold and the sloughs had crowns of ice thick enough to support me. As I crossed one great clear pane, trout raced around under my feet and a ten-foot bubble advanced slowly before my cautious steps. Then passing back into the trees, I found an active game trail, cut cross-lots to pick a better stand, sat in a good vantage place under a cotton-wood with the ought-six across my knees. I thought, running my hands up into my sleeves, this is lovely but I'd rather be up in the hills; and I fell asleep.

I woke up a couple of hours later, the coffee and early-morning drill having done not one thing for my alertness. I had drooled on my rifle and it was time for my chores back at the ranch. My chores of late had consisted primarily of working on screenplays so that the bank didn't take the ranch. These days the primary ranch skill is making the payment; it comes before irrigation, feeding out, and calving. Some rancher friends find this so discouraging they get up and roll a number or have a slash of tanglefoot before they even think of the glories of the West. This is the New Rugged.

The next day, I reflected upon my lackadaisical hunting and left really too early in the morning. I drove around to Mission Creek in the dark and ended up sitting in the truck up some wash listening to a New Mexico radio station until my patience gave out and I started out cross-country in the dark, just able to make out the nose of the Absaroka Range as it faced across the river to the Crazy Mountains. It seemed maddeningly up and down slick banks, and a couple of times I had game clatter out in front of me in the dark. Then I turned up a long coulee that climbed endlessly south, and started in that direction, knowing the plateau on top should hold some antelope. After half an hour or so, I heard the mad laughing of coyotes, throwing their voices all around the inside of the coulee, trying to panic rabbits and making my hair stand on end despite my affection for them. The stars tracked overhead into the first pale light and it was nearly dawn before I came up on the bench. I could hear cattle below me and I moved along an edge of thorn trees to break my outline, then sat down at the point to wait for shooting light.

I could see antelope on the skyline before I had that light; and by the time I did, there was a good big buck angling across from me, looking at everything. I thought I could see well enough, and I got up into a sitting position and into the sling. I had made my moves quietly, but when I looked through the scope the antelope was 200 yards out, using up the country in bounds. I tracked with him, let him bounce up into the reticle, and touched off a shot. He was down and still, but I sat watching until I was sure.

Nobody who loves to hunt feels absolutely hunky-dory when the quarry goes down. The remorse spins out almost before anything and the balancing act ends on one declination or another. I decided that unless I become a vegetarian, I'll get my meat by hunting for it. I feel absolutely unabashed by the arguments of other carnivores who get their meat in plastic with blue numbers on it. I've seen slaughterhouses, and anyway, as Sitting Bull said, when the buffalo are gone, we will hunt mice, for we are hunters and we want our freedom.

The antelope had piled up in the sage, dead before he hit the ground. He was an old enough buck that the tips of his pronged horns were angled in toward each other. I turned him downhill to bleed him out. The bullet had mushroomed in the front of the lungs, so the job was already halfway done. With antelope, proper field dressing is critical because they can end up sour if they've been run or haphazardly hog-dressed. And they sour from their own body heat more than from external heat.

The sun was up and the big buteo hawks were lifting on the thermals. There was enough breeze that the grass began to have directional grain like the prairie and the rim of the coulee wound up away from me toward the Absaroka. I felt peculiarly solitary, sitting on my heels next to the carcass in the sagebrush and greasewood, my rifle racked open on the ground. I made an incision around the metatarsal glands inside the back legs and carefully removed them and set them well aside; then I cleaned the blade of my hunting knife with handfuls of grass to keep from tainting the meat with those powerful glands. Next I detached the anus and testes from the outer walls and made a shallow puncture below the sternum, spread it with the thumb and forefinger of my left hand, and ran the knife upside down to the bone bridge between the hind legs. Inside, the diaphragm was like the taut lid of a drum and cut away cleanly, so that I could reach clear up to the back of the mouth and detach the windpipe. Once that was done I could draw the whole visceral package out onto the grass and separate out the heart, liver, and tongue before propping the carcass open with two whittled-up sage scantlings.

You could tell how cold the morning was, despite the exertion, just by watching the steam roar from the abdominal cavity. I stuck the knife in the ground and sat back against the slope, looking clear across to Convict Grade and the Crazy Mountains. I was blood from the elbows down and the antelope's eyes had skinned over. I thought, This is goddamned serious and you had better always remember that.

There was a big red enamel pot on the stove; and I ladled antelope chili into two bowls for my son and me. He said, "It better not be too hot."

"It isn't."

"What's your news?" he asked.

"Grandpa's dead."

"Which grandpa?" he asked. I told him it was Big Grandpa, my father. He kept on eating. "He died last night."

He said, "I know what I want for Christmas."

"What's that?"

"I want Big Grandpa back."

It was 1950-something and I was small, under twelve say, and there were four of us: my father, two of his friends, and me. There was a good belton setter belonging to the one friend, a hearty bird hunter who taught dancing and fist-fought at any provocation. The other man was old and sick and had a green fatal look in his face. My father took me aside and said, "Jack and I are going to the head of this field"—and he pointed up a mile and a half of stalks to where it ended in the flat woods—"and we're going to take the dog and get what he can point. These are running birds. So you and Bill just block the field and you'll have some shooting."

"I'd like to hunt with the dog." I had a 20-gauge Winchester my grandfather had given me, which got hocked and lost years later when another of my family got into the bottle; and I could hit with it and wanted to hunt over the setter. With respect to blocking the field, I could smell a rat.

"You stay with Bill," said my father, "and try to cheer him up."

"What's the matter with Bill?"

"He's had one heart attack after another and he's going to die."

"When?"

"Pretty damn soon."

I blocked the field with Bill. My first thought was, I hope he doesn't die before they drive those birds onto us; but if he does, I'll have all the shooting.

There was a crazy cold autumn light on everything, magnified by the yellow silage all over the field. The dog found birds right away and they were shooting. Bill said he was sorry but he didn't feel so good. He had his hunting license safety-pinned to the back of his coat and fiddled with a handful of 12-gauge shells. "I've shot a shitpile of game," said Bill, "but I don't feel so good anymore." He took a knife out of his coat pocket. "I got this in the Marines," he said, "and I carried it for four years in the Pacific. The handle's drilled out and weighted so you can throw it. I want you to have it." I took it and thanked him, looking into his green face, and wondered why he had given it to me. "That's for blocking this field with me," he said. "Your dad and that dance teacher are going to shoot them all. When you're not feeling so good, they put you at the end of the field to block when there isn't shit-all going to fly by you. They'll get them all. They and the dog will."

We had an indestructible tree in the yard we had chopped on, nailed steps to, and initialed; and when I pitched that throwing knife at it, the knife broke in two. I picked it up and thought, *This thing is jinxed.* So I took it out into the crab-apple woods and put it in the can I had buried, along with a Roosevelt dime and an atomic-bomb ring I had sent away for. This was a small collection of things I buried over a period of years. I was sending them to God. All He had to do was open the can, but they were never collected. In any case, I have long known that if I could understand why I wanted to send a broken knife I believed to be jinxed to God, then I would be a long way toward what they call a personal philosophy as opposed to these hand-to-mouth metaphysics of who said what to who in some cornfield twenty-five years ago.

We were in the bar at Chico Hot Springs near my home in Montana: me, a lout poet who had spent the day floating under the diving board while adolescent girls leapt overhead; and my brother John, who had glued himself to the pipe which poured warm water into the pool and announced over and over in a loud voice that every drop of water had been filtered through his bathing suit.

Now, covered with wrinkles, we were in the bar, talking to Alvin Close, an old government hunter. After half a century of predator control he called it "useless and half-assed."

Alvin Close killed the last major stock-killing wolf in Montana. He hunted the wolf so long he raised a litter of dogs to do it with. He hunted the wolf futilely with a pack that had fought the wolf a dozen times, until one day he gave up and let the dogs run the wolf out the back of a shallow canyon. He heard them yip their way into silence while he leaned up against a tree; and presently the wolf came tiptoeing down the front of the canyon into Alvin's lap. The wolf simply stopped because the game was up. Alvin raised the Winchester and shot it.

"How did you feel about that?" I asked.

"How do you think I felt?"

"I don't know."

"I felt like hell."

Alvin's evening was ruined and he went home. He was seventy-six years old and carried himself like an old-time army officer, setting his glass on the bar behind him without looking.

You stare through the plastic at the red smear of meat in the supermarket. What's this it says here? *Mighty Good? Tastee? Quality, Premium, and*

Government Inspected? Soon enough, the blood is on your hands. It's inescapable.

Aldo Leopold was a hunter who I am sure abjured freeze-dried vegetables and extrusion burgers. His conscience was clean because his hunting was part of a larger husbandry in which the life of the country was enhanced by his own work. He knew that game populations are not bothered by hunting until they are already too precarious and that precarious game populations should not be hunted. Grizzlies should not be hunted, for instance. The enemy of game is clean farming and sinful chemicals; as well as the useless alteration of watersheds by promoter cretins and the insidious dizzards of land development, whose lobbyists teach us the venality of all governments.

A world in which a sacramental portion of food can be taken in an old way—hunting, fishing, farming, and gathering—has as much to do with societal sanity as a day's work for a day's pay.

For a long time, there was no tracking snow. I hunted on horseback for a couple of days in a complicated earthquake fault in the Gallatins. The fault made a maze of narrow canyons with flat floors. The sagebrush grew on woody trunks higher than my head and left sandy paths and game trails where the horse and I could travel.

There were Hungarian partridge that roared out in front of my horse, putting his head suddenly in my lap. And hawks tobogganed on the low air currents, astonished to find me there. One finger canyon ended in a vertical rock wall from which issued a spring of the kind elsewhere associated with the Virgin Mary, hung with ex-votos and the orthopedic supplications of satisfied miracle customers. Here, instead, were nine identical piles of bear shit, neatly adorned with undigested berries.

One canyon planed up and topped out on an endless grassy rise. There were deer there, does and a young buck. A thousand yards away and staring at me with semaphore ears.

They assembled at a stiff trot from the haphazard array of feeding and strung out in a precise line against the far hill in a dog trot. When I removed my hat, they went into their pogo-stick gait and that was that.

"What did a deer ever do to you?"
"Nothing."

"I'm serious. What do you have to go and kill them for?"

"I can't explain it talking like this."

"Why should they die for you? Would you die for deer?"

"If it came to that."

My boy and I went up the North Fork to look for grouse. We had my old pointer Molly, and Thomas's .22 pump. We flushed a number of birds climbing through the wild roses; but they roared away at knee level, leaving me little opportunity for my over-and-under, much less an opening for Thomas to ground-sluice one with his .22. We started out at the meteor hole above the last ranch and went all the way to the national forest. Thomas had his cap on the bridge of his nose and wobbled through the trees until we hit cross fences. We went out into the last open pasture before he got winded. So we sat down and looked across the valley at the Gallatin Range, furiously white and serrated, a bleak edge of the world. We sat in the sun and watched the chickadees make their way through the russet brush.

"Are you having a good time?"

"Sure," he said and curled a small hand around the octagonal barrel of the Winchester. I was not sure what I had meant by my question.

The rear quarters of the antelope came from the smoker so dense and finely grained it should have been sliced as prosciutto. We had edgy, crumbling cheddar from British Columbia and everybody kept an eye on the food and tried to pace themselves. The snow whirled in the window light and puffed the smoke down the chimney around the cedar flames. I had a stretch of enumerating things: my family, hayfields, saddle horses, friends, thirty-ought-six, French and Russian novels. I had a baby girl, colts coming, and a new roof on the barn. I finished a big corral made of railroad ties and 2 × 6s. I was within eighteen months of my father's death, my sister's death, and the collapse of my marriage. Still, the washouts were repairing; and when a few things had been set aside, not excluding paranoia, some features were left standing, not excluding lovers, children, friends, and saddle horses. In time, it would be clear as a bell. I did want venison again that winter and couldn't help but feel some old ridge-runner had my number on him.

I didn't want to read and I didn't want to write or acknowledge the phone with its tendrils into the zombie enclaves. I didn't want the New Rugged; I wanted the Old Rugged and a pot to piss in. Otherwise, it's deteriorata, with mice undermining the wiring in my frame house, sparks jumping in the insulation, the dog turning queer, and a horned owl staring at the baby through the nursery window.

It was pitch black in the bedroom and the windows radiated cold across the blankets. The top of my head felt this side of frost and the stars hung like ice crystals over the chimney. I scrambled out of bed and slipped into my long johns, put on a heavy shirt and my wool logger pants with the police suspenders. I carried the boots down to the kitchen so as not to wake the house and turned the percolator on. I put some cheese and chocolate in my coat, and when the coffee was done I filled a chili bowl and quaffed it against the winter.

When I hit the front steps I heard the hard squeaking of new snow under my boots and the wind moved against my face like a machine for refinishing hardwood floors. I backed the truck up to the horse trailer, the lights wheeling against the ghostly trunks of the bare cottonwoods. I connected the trailer and pulled it forward to a flat spot for loading the horse.

I had figured that when I got to the corral I could tell one horse from another by starlight; but the horses were in the shadow of the barn and I went in feeling my way among their shapes trying to find my hunting horse Rocky, and trying to get the front end of the big sorrel who kicks when surprised. Suddenly Rocky was looking in my face and I reached around his neck with the halter. A 1,200-pound bay quarter horse, his withers angled up like a fighting bull, he wondered where we were going but ambled after me on a slack lead rope as we headed out of the darkened corral.

I have an old trailer made by a Texas horse vet years ago. It has none of the amenities of newer trailers. I wish it had a dome light for loading in the dark; but it doesn't. You ought to check and see if the cat's sleeping in it before you load; and I didn't do that either. Instead, I climbed inside the trailer and the horse followed me. I tied the horse down to a D-ring and started back out, when he blew up. The two of us were confined in the small space and he was ripping and bucking between the walls with such noise and violence that I had a brief dis-associated moment of suspension from fear. I jumped up on the manger with my arms around my head while the horse shattered the inside of the trailer and rocked it furiously on its axles. Then he blew the steel rings out of the halter and fell over backward in the snow. The cat darted out and was gone. I slipped down off the manger and looked for the horse; he had gotten up and was sidling down past the granary in the star shadows.

I put two blankets on him, saddled him, played with his feet, and calmed him. I loaded him without incident and headed out.

I went through the aspen line at daybreak, still climbing. The horse ascended steadily toward a high basin, creaking the saddle metronomically. It was getting colder as the sun came up, and the rifle scabbard held my left leg far enough from the horse that I was chilling on that side.

We touched the bottom of the basin and I could see the rock wall defined by a black stripe of evergreens on one side and the remains of an avalanche on the other. I thought how utterly desolate this country can look in winter and how one could hardly think of human travel in it at all, not white horsemen nor Indians dragging travois, just aerial raptors with their rending talons and heads like cameras slicing across the geometry of winter.

Then we stepped into a deep hole and the horse went to his chest in the powder, splashing the snow out before him as he floundered toward the other side. I got my feet out of the stirrups in case we went over. Then we were on wind-scoured rock and I hunted some lee for the two of us. I thought of my son's words after our last cold ride: "Dad, you know in 4-H? Well, I want to switch from Horsemanship to Aviation."

The spot was like this: a crest of snow crowned in a sculpted edge high enough to protect us. There was a tough little juniper to picket the horse to, and a good place to sit out of the cold and noise. Over my head, a long, curling plume of snow poured out, unchanging in shape against the pale blue sky. I ate some of the cheese and rewrapped it. I got the rifle down from the scabbard, loosened the cinch, and undid the flank cinch. I put the stirrup over the horn to remind me my saddle was loose, loaded two cartridges into the blind magazine, and slipped one in the chamber. Then I started toward the rock wall, staring at the patterned discolorations: old seeps, lichen, cracks, and the madhouse calligraphy of immemorial weather.

There were a lot of tracks where the snow had crusted out of the wind; all deer except for one well-used bobcat trail winding along the edges of a long rocky slot. I moved as carefully as I could, stretching my eyes as far out in front of my detectable movement as I could. I tried

to work into the wind, but it turned erratically in the basin as the temperature of the new day changed.

The buck was studying me as soon as I came out on the open slope:
he was a long way away and I stopped motionless to wait for him to
feed again. He stared straight at me from 500 yards. I waited until I
could no longer feel my feet nor finally my legs. It was nearly an hour
before he suddenly ducked his head and began to feed. Every time he
fed I moved a few feet, but he was working away from me and I wasn't
getting anywhere. Over the next half hour he made his way to a little
rim and, in the half hour after that, moved the 20 feet that dropped him
over the rim.

I went as fast as I could move quietly. I now had the rim to cover
me and the buck should be less than 100 yards from me when I looked
over. It was all browse for a half mile, wild roses, buck brush, and young
quakies where there was any runoff.

When I reached the rim, I took off my hat and set it in the snow
with my gloves inside. I wanted to be looking in the right direction
when I cleared the rim, rise a half step and be looking straight at the
buck, not scanning for the buck with him running 60, a degree or two
out of my periphery. And I didn't want to gum it up with thinking or
trajectory guessing. People are always trajectory guessing their way into
gut shots and clean misses. So, before I took the last step, all there was
to do was lower the rim with my feet, lower the buck into my vision,
and isolate the path of the bullet.

As I took that step, I knew he was running. He wasn't in the browse
at all, but angling into invisibility at the rock wall, racing straight into
the elevation, bounding toward zero gravity, taking his longest arc
into the bullet and the finality and terror of all you have made of the
world, the finality you know that you share even with your babies with
their inherited and ambiguous dentition, the finality that any minute
now you will meet as well.

He slid 100 yards in a rush of snow. I dressed him and skidded him
by one antler to the horse. I made a slit behind the last ribs, pulled him
over the saddle and put the horn through the slit, lashed the feet to the
cinch dees, and led the horse downhill. The horse had bells of clear ice
around his hoofs, and when he slipped, I chipped them out from under
his feet with the point of a bullet.

I hung the buck in the open woodshed with a lariat over a rafter.
He turned slowly against the cooling air. I could see the intermittent

blue light of the television against the bedroom ceiling from where I stood. I stopped the twirling of the buck, my hands deep in the sage-scented fur, and thought: This is either the beginning or the end of everything.

RICK DeMARINIS

Rick DeMarinis was born in New York in 1934, grew up in California, and moved to Montana in 1955 as a radar operator for the air force. He worked for Boeing and Lockheed before studying at the University of Montana, where he earned an M.A. in English in 1967 while studying poetry writing with Richard Hugo. The author of six novels and three collections of short fiction, DeMarinis has written The Burning Women of Far Cry *(1986),* The Year of the Zinc Penny *(1989),* Under the Wheat *(1986), which won the 1986 Drue Heinz Prize for short fiction,* The Coming Triumph of the Free World *(1988), and* Voice of America *(1992). He is a recipient of a literature award from the American Academy and Institute of Arts and Letters. Currently, DeMarinis teaches in the creative writing program at the University of Texas at El Paso. Of living in the West, he writes, "The climate is hard, but it satisfies something in me; the sparsity of population is wonderful for the nervous system." His most recent novel,* The Mortician's Apprentice, *was published in 1994.*

"We are western by chance, and remain so by choice. . . . We wear this preference on our pearl-buttoned sleeves. We've been antsy from birth." "Paraiso: An Elegy," from Voice of America, *is a story about survival in the hard-scrabble landscape, a tough, gorgeous place where "we are required to be brave." This story, an elegy for those who are gone yet remain, informs us about how to live Western: "The land owns us, not vice versa."*

PARAISO: AN ELEGY

Hart is dead. Cancer got him. He died well. What I mean is, he died pretty much as he lived, without fear or dread, and he died without the sort of high-torque pain or mind-gumming drugs that would have blunted his ability to find interest in the process of dying. We still talk about him in the present tense. "Hart has presence of mind," we say, and "Hart can't tolerate French movies," and "Hart likes his beer freezer-cold." His gray stare, somewhat quizzical due to the tumors thriving near the occipital region of his brain, asks you to be honest: Never say what you don't mean. If in doubt, remember, silence is incorruptible. You can spend half a day with Hart and maybe trade three opinions. But he likes his jokes. He likes the sharp observation that punctures the gassy balloons of hypocrisy, pomp, and self-importance. As a photographer and poet, that's what he's about. And so he can get you in trouble. He's a little guy with a proud chest. His camera bag, always slung on his shoulder, makes him list ten degrees to port. It makes him walk with a limp.

It began with an omen. We were in Juárez, Christmas 1988, fending off a gang of seasonal pickpockets who had moved into the border town from somewhere in the interior. They circled us like a half-dozen bantamweight boxers, nodding and shrugging, feinting in and dancing back, bumping us, confusing us with large, friendly smiles. Hart pulled out his little Zeiss and started to spend film while our wives, Rocky and Joyce, dealt with the footloose thieves. These wives are tough, friendly women from the bedrock towns of Butte and Anaconda, Montana, respectively. When a quick brown hand slipped into the throat of Rocky's purse, she slapped it away, brisk as a frontier schoolmarm, and my tall, strong-jawed Joyce yanked her purse clear with enough force to start a chain saw. The thieves tap-danced away from the white-knuckled determination of these good-looking *güeras,* with no hard feelings, no need to get righteous. The phrase *No me chinguen, pendejos* was ready on my lips, and I whispered it in rehearsal since I am fluent with set phrases only. And Joyce, who *is* fluent, hissed, "Don't you *ever* say that in this town unless you want to take your gringo whizzer back across the bridge in segments."

Joyce works in a Juárez industrial park, teaching idiomatic, rust-belt American to executives of the *maquiladora* industry who need to travel north. Her company assembles computer components for GM, and pays its workers an average of five dollars a day, which is a full dollar above the Mexican minimum wage. Joyce gets eighteen dollars an hour because she insists on being paid what the job's worth, having come from Anaconda, a town so unionized you can't pour tar on your leaky shed without getting hard stares from the organized roofers. It troubles her that the Tarahumara Indian beggar women on Avenida Diez y Seis de Septiembre can make twice as much on a good day as a worker in a *maquiladora*. That's why she didn't get hysterical over the pickpockets. Their mostly seasonal earnings are on a puny scale compared to what the foreign-owned *maquiladoras* siphon into their profit margins. If anyone was close to hysteria it was me (the gringo instinct to protect and prevail knocking at my heart), not the iron-willed women from Montana. My fists were balled up, and my mind was knotted, too, with such off-the-subject irrelevancies as my honor, my male pride. *¡Lárguense a la chingada!* I felt like saying, but I also knew that if I did things would get serious in a hurry because these thieves from Chihuahua or wherever have a more commanding sense of honor than I do. We gringos might have a more commanding sense of *fair play,* but honor is too abstract to touch off instantaneous grass fires in our blood. It applies to flag and parents and, at one time, to a young man's conduct in the vicinity of decent girls, but it has never functioned as a duty, uncompromising as the survival instinct, to oneself.

And if I did get lucky and scatter them with a few wild punches, then what? The streets were dense with locals who do not think the world of these pale, camera-toting, wise-cracking, uninhibited laughers from a thousand miles north of the Río Bravo. And when a nearby *tránsito*—a black-and-tan-uniformed traffic cop, the local version of the *guardia civil*—strolled by to see what was what, speaking the same street Spanish as the purse-snatchers, whose story did I think would be heard? Who did I think would go to jail? This was before Hart's diagnosis, when we were all planning a succession of trips starting with the thrill-a-minute train ride from Ciudad Chihuahua to Creel and on to the Barranca de Cobre, and later in the year, to Puebla and Vera Cruz. *"Que le vaya bien,"* Joyce called to the retreating pickpockets. And a smiling thief replied, his Spanish courtly and dignified, "And may it also go equally well for you, lady." Rocky, a former parachute journalist who now teaches Bullshit Detection 101, rolled her black Irish eyes and muttered, "Jesus. Joyce must be campaigning for sainthood. The Bleeding

Virgin of the Cutpurse. They wanted to take your MasterCard, honey, not test your Spanish."

We stopped in the Kentucky Club on Avenida Juárez for a round of self-congratulatory margaritas, then crossed back into Texas, purses and wallets intact. We felt generally upbeat. But in the river, on the north bank, we saw a decapitated mule. We hung over the rail, staring at the mud-colored carcass bloating in the silty river, as if this had been the planned high point and ultimate purpose of our tour. Hart said, "Omen, troops." We looked at him. This was one of those moments in life when things get too slippery to catch in a net of words. We looked at each other. An innocence rising up from childhood struck us dumb as Hart attached a long lens to his Zeiss and photographed the headless mule.

2

Joyce and I are on this trip with Hart and Rocky, looking for something in the desert. A kind of comradely spitefulness has made us rowdy and solemnly amused by turns. I guess it is Death we are spiting, though no one comes out and says so. We like each other because we know we are misfits who have found our niche in the friendly halls of universities.

We are western by chance, and remain so by choice. We love cars and rock and roll more than we love fine art and baroque music. We wear this preference on our pearl-buttoned sleeves. We've been antsy from birth: The verb "to go" was the first one we learned to conjugate. We've got Cowboy Junkies in the tape deck and a six-pack of Lone Star balanced on the console between the seats. Drinking and driving is a western birthright. This is Texas, where it's legal to have opened containers in a moving car. This law (known affectionately as the Bubba Law) may be repealed soon, but we're not in a mood to worry about it: the lab report on the biopsies is in and now we all know the worst. Hart has six months, if he's lucky—six months, that is, if the tumors crowding his vertebrae don't break in and vandalize the spinal cord tomorrow or the next day.

Hart has the perfect vehicle for this type of travel. A 1972 Chevy Blazer with the big 350 long-block V-8 throbbing under the hood. The Blazer is a two-ton intimidator. Hart is not into intimidation, but the slender Celicas, Maximas, and Integras that pull into our slipstream don't know that. They tend to keep their distance from the big, rust-brown, generously dented Chevy. Hart and I sit up front, Rocky and Joyce sit in back—a western arrangement not meant to signify the relative status of the sexes. A traveler from New Haven, say, might look into the Blazer and see Hart and me up front in straw hats with beer cans on the dash, and the women eating coffee chews in back, perhaps catch a strain of the Cowboy Junkie's visionary wailing, and think *highway buckaroos and the little women, tsk, tsk.* This is unfair to the Yankees, of course. You might find the same arrangement in a dented Blazer in New Haven. Only in New Haven, I suspect, the highway buckaroo remark might be justified. Two couples riding this way back there *would* be making a statement, whether they wanted to or not. Turning ourselves into an illustrated idea is the last thing in the world the four of us would do.

We're heading in our roundabout way for Tucson, normally a five-hour trek from El Paso, where we live. The sandstorms have raised cubic miles of desert, turning it into coastal fog. Our running lights are on and we've slowed to forty and the wind is making the big Blazer rock and roll. Hart is feeling the strain, having just undergone his first series of radiation treatments, which he found entertaining. ("Star Wars, troops. They levitate you into the center of a big dome where smart machines that know your body better than you do sniff out and then zap the intruders.") I have offered to drive, but no one drives the Blazer except Hart. He loves this truck as a settler might have loved his big-bore buffalo gun, his horse, or his quarter section of homestead bottomland. And so it's decided: We'll turn off at exit 331, get on U.S. 666, and head for my widowed mother's adobe hacienda in Paraiso, Arizona, where Death has left his stain and dull gloom not long ago.

It is late afternoon when we pull into her driveway, and Mom—Sada—is already in her cups. She's been working all morning on *Storm over the Dragoons*, a six-by-three-foot oil painting, and now is drinking ruby port to unwind. Painting has helped fill in the gaps left by the removal of Lenny Burbek, her husband for the last twenty-six years. Cancer got him, too.

Sada pours wine for us at her kitchen table. The house smells of oil paint, even though her studio is out in the attached garage. "Hart, you look fer shit," she says. Sada, at eighty-two, has dispensed with all the social delicacies.

"Fer shit is an improvement over yesterday," Hart says, holding the cup of ruby port but not drinking. The road beers have already given him grief. Alcohol, mixed with the tumor-poisoning chemicals circulating in his system, makes him sick. He's got a tumor in his liver, too, and his liver won't forgive and forget. Hart puts the wine down and takes a picture of Sada. She is a mask of fierce wrinkles and looks more like an old Navajo or Apache squaw than the immigrant Scandinavian that she is. Hart has this theory: The land eventually has its way with us. Live in this desert long enough and sun, wind, sand, and thirsty air will eventually give a native shape to your clay, just as thirty years in Oslo will fade, elasticize, and plump up the austere skin of an Apache. The land works us like a craftsman works maple or oak. Ultimately, the tools and strategies of the craftsman overcome the proud immutability of any hardwood. The land owns us, not vice versa, the current triumph of the capitalist zeitgeist notwithstanding. This is Hart's pet idea. The land owns us and we had better treat it with the proper deference. You can see it in his prints. It is often the text and always the subtext of his poems. "We all need a pet idea," Hart says, "even if it's a stupid one. Even a stupid idea, pursued long enough with enough dedication, so that all its dead ends are discovered, will lead you to the same place as a nifty one." We don't ask Hart what or where that place is. We act like we know, and maybe we almost do. "Besides," Hart says, "*ideas* are ultimately wrong anyway."

Sada fixes her favorite dish that night, linguini with clam sauce, along with big prawns from Puerto Peñasco, down on the Sea of Cortez. Tyrell Lofton, Sada's boyfriend, eats with us. Tyrell is a West Virginia mountain man bent on turning his piece of Paraiso into mountaineer country. He's planted black walnut trees, tulip trees, and a variety of conifers, and has a fecund greenhouse that produces several tons of winter tomatoes. He dreams of building a small still—a genetic mandate. And his house, made of scrap wood, has been half built for twenty years. He's a lean, hard-knuckled seventy-five-year-old widower who also has the weathered Apache look. As we eat, I can tell Hart is planning photography sessions with Tyrell and Sada, for no one we know proves his pet idea better than these two.

After dinner, Sada begins to fidget around. She wants to go dancing. "Have you kids been to the Duck Inn?" she asks coyly. The Duck Inn is a little geezer saloon that caters to the population of Paraiso. "They've got a terrific little band there. The ex-sheriff of Tombstone owns the place. He's also the bandleader."

Sada was a dancer in the Ziegfeld Follies and there is no quit in her. Her bottle-blond hair is startling above her brown, massively grooved, big-cheeked, purse-leather face. "I think we'll pass, Mom," I say.

She scoffs. "Don't be an old fart, sonny, you're not even fifty yet. Come on, we'll have a few laughs."

Tyrell, who always has a twinkle in his faded blue eyes, says, "Goodness me, I don't think they ever had *four* professors in the Duck Inn all at once." Tyrell is quick to spot the potential fun in a given situation, but his remarks are never mean or sour. According to Tyrell, it's okay to take the light view of humanity, since only trees have honest-to-God dignity. It's his pet idea.

"Hart doesn't feel up to it," I say.

"The hell I don't," Hart says, his face drawn, his jaw tight enough to reflect light.

And so we all walk to the bar, surrounded by black night and the thousand unblinking stars of this high desert. Hart amazes me, plodding along, one painful step after another, Rocky hanging on his arm. What amazes me is his placid indifference to the Big Change coming his way, his refusal to let it become the major dramatic event of the season. And then I think of his pet idea, and how the desert might shape a body for pain, too. The Apaches took pain in stride, even sought it out as a measuring stick of their individual worth. The deserts of the Near East have produced prophetic pain-seekers for thousands of years. Jesus, destined for pain, did not pile up annuities or build Alpine retreats to hide himself from it. Blood and sand are the primary colors of the desert. The agonies of crucifixion are storming in Hart's bones and guts, but he won't let us in on this internal secret. I am reminded of Sada's third and last husband, Lenny (another de facto Apache), settling into his easy chair gingerly, as if some wickedness had turned his burly, ex-ironworker's frame into crystal stemware. Lenny and his pal from down the street, also dying of cancer, would sit in their bathrobes and watch the Playboy channel for hours at a time, sampling each other's painkillers. There they were—two old men, all the vigor of their lives sucked into the unappeasable black hole of cancer—denying the sex-hating Intruder by watching the rosy, pile-driving rumps of fornicating youths hour after hour, snacking on chips and *queso,* washing down opiates and tranks with beer, giving a thin cheer now and then to the gymnastic skills of the actors. Lenny died in bed pushing himself up to a sitting position while insisting that he felt much, *much* better.

Paraiso is not exactly a retirement village, though most of the residents are retired. There are a few younger people who commute the ninety miles to Tucson to work. They live here because real estate costs half as much and because the air is about as clean as late-twentieth-century American air can get. A few of these people are in the Duck Inn, dancing and carrying on. Sada knows them all and shouts their names. She backs her straight shots of vodka with draft beer and she has a what-the-hell look in her eyes. Soon she is up on her feet, dancing alone among the younger folk, holding her peasant skirts up over her old hardscrabble knees and yelling, "Yippee, son of a bitch, yippee!" while her carpet slippers flap. Then Tyrell leaps up, his wide pale eyes almost glassy, and does a solo mountaineer buckdance which no one challenges. Rocky is laughing her choppy, nicotine-stained laugh, and Hart, though he's got a white-knuckled grip on his untouched mug of beer, is smiling. Joyce nudges me under the table, whispering, "Hope you feel strong. You and Tyrell are going to have to carry Sada home." And the fiddlers chop down feverishly into their fiddles as if everything now depended on this crazed music.

Later that night, as the coyotes howl and the screech owls make their eerie electronic screams, Joyce and I hear Rocky crying softly through the wall that separates our bedrooms, and under the crying, Hart's laboring snores. Unable to sleep, I get up and prowl the house. It is 3:00 A.M., the hour of the wolf, dead center of night when all of us are naked in our small separate selves. At this hour all the technological wonders and powers of America seem like a feeble dream: the optimistic cities of glass and steel, the superhighways, the elaborate networks of instant communication, and the medical colossus that, for all its precise weapons and collective strategic genius, cannot discourage the barbarous imperialism of a wretched horde of mindless tumors.

The garage light is on. Sada is up, too, working on her big landscape. She doesn't hear me come in, and I watch her drag a broad, paint-fat brush across the base of the Dragoons, the range of mountains where Cochise and his band of righteous Chiricahua warriors held off the U.S. Army for ten years. The mountains are blue-black under the angry flex of muscular storm clouds. All the rage of Sada's eighty-two years is in this canvas, which, the longer I look at it, seems more like a thunderous shout than a painting. "Some painting, Ma," I say.

She whirls around, her leaky Apache eyes burning with a warrior's need to run a spear into the dark gut of the beast.

"It's all I can do now," she says.

3

As we head south toward Douglas and Agua Prieta, I am thinking of the strange girl who lives across the street from Sada. She is sixteen and suffering the pain of boredom and the deeper pain of her own oddness, which will isolate her more than geography ever could. Joyce and Rocky found her lying in the middle of the street, her hair chopped close to her scalp, as if by a hunting knife. Thunderclouds sat on the Dragoons. Joyce thought at first that the girl had been run over, but she was only waiting. I am waiting for something to happen to me, is what she said. Joyce and Rocky left her there, spread-eagled in the road, as the tall clouds moved closer and God's original voice began to rumble with its old no-nonsense authority. Red-tailed hawks lofty as archangels swept down out of the dark sky, choosing among opportunities. Joyce and Rocky decided: Maybe the odd girl was right and was playing her aces now, while she still had them. Maybe we are all waiting for something to happen to us—death or life—but for the girl lying in the street the issue was unclouded by career, marriage, property, and all the other trump cards that must be deferred to before we can clear the slate and move on.

Hart's Blazer pitches and yaws over a rough highway that will take us into the mountains. We have turned onto a narrow, shoulderless road that cuts west into the southern foothills of the Dragoons, as we head now for Bisbee instead of Douglas and Agua Prieta. "I've always wanted to see the Lavender Pit," Hart says.

Traveling by whim is touring at its best.

The old houses of Bisbee cling to the sides of the mountains, prayer-fully as exhausted climbers. And the streets, angled like derailed trains, work their way up to the highest ledge of dwellings. We walk these steep streets, finding level ground in a doorway now and then to catch our breath. Hart's been taking painkillers and tends to stagger against the unexpectedly oblique tugs of gravity that have made the older buildings lean into each other like amiable drunks. He stops now and then to photograph the odd geometry of a ruined hotel, the grit-pocked face of an old miner, the bands of Japanese tourists who photograph everything in their path as if making a visual record of what will one day be all theirs. The four of us often agree that World War Two is still being fought, that the atomic bombings of Japan merely forced a change in weaponry. After Hiroshima and Nagasaki, the tide turned, and now Japanese samurai in three-piece suits, portfolios in hand, are succeeding where Tojo's fanatic armies failed. Choice Hawaiian beachfront and Rockefeller Center are theirs, the great evergreen forests of Oregon are theirs, and lately, giant cattle ranches in Montana. "I could settle down here," Rocky says. "In one of those shacks on the side of the mountain. This place is like Butte, without Butte's winters."

Rocky prides herself for being realistic. She knows we all understand that she is imagining her life without Hart. The terms are hard, but they always have been. We are alone, we have nothing to sustain us but a few pet ideas fueled by a dram of courage. The rest is a pipe dream. Not that pipe dreams are not necessary, we've just got to know the differences. This is Rocky's pet idea, and it's one that she's earned. Ten years ago she survived the removal, from her brain, of a benign plum-sized tumor that made her trade her career in parachute journalism for an academic one.

We are required to be brave. Another pet idea. Also Rocky's.

The Lavender Pit is really two pits, big enough to drop a pair of medium size cities into. On the way out of Bisbee, after getting half-drunk in the Copper Queen Hotel (Hart managing this with a carefully sipped double shot of mescal), we stop with the tourists to gape at this man-made Grand Canyon. Rocky, who has seen her town, Butte, more or less consumed by such a pit, says, "Sucks, don't it?" to a tourist lady from Arkansas. The tourist lady smiles stiffly and turns her camera on her husband and daughter, who backstep dutifully toward the Cyclone fence that guards the lip of the pit and the thousand-foot drop beyond. The red gouge in the earth looks like a fresh wound, the god-size tumor removed, the lake of blood vacuumed out. A lifeless pond at the bottom of the pit glows like iridescent pus. Oh yes, the planet here is dead. It is deader than the moon, because it was once alive.

"I'm losing my buzz, campers," Rocky says. "Let's clear the fuck out." The lady with the camera gives Rocky a murderous look, protecting the innocence of her child. Rocky grins good-naturedly. "Too late for Miss Manners, hon," she says cryptically, swinging her arm out to indicate the pit, the precarious town, the silent witness of the elderly mountains.

4

We skip Tucson and head back, but the Blazer heats up outside of Deming, New Mexico. We were headed for Palomas, the little Mexican town where General Pershing launched his failed attempt to bring a taste of gringo justice to Pancho Villa, but are now stalled in a gas station where two head-scratching mechanics decide the problem is in the fan clutch and that it will take about an hour and a hundred dollars to fix it. It's hot, over a hundred degrees, and we sit inside the crankcase smell of the garage drinking lukewarm Cokes and watching a TV that seems to have only one color: puce. One of the advertising industry's truly horrifying commercials comes on: "Your marriage will never end. Your children will never grow old. Your pets will never die." It's an ad for a video camcorder, showing a family watching their dead past captured and preserved forever. Whatever unhappiness lies ahead, it cannot touch these moments of joy. Mom kissing Dad in the kitchen; Junior chasing a ball; Rover begging for table scraps—immortal, immutable. Old age, sickness, alienation, divorce: all our little hells defeated by videotape. Paradise secure in a cassette, the grim episodes edited out.

We step back into the heat and stroll up the desert road. To the east, the gray humps of the Florida Mountains wobble in the corrugated air. A man, ragged and barefoot, approaches us. He's so far beyond the liberal dream of salvage and social recycling that he almost seems happy. His weak hair and crosshatched sunburned skin make him look sixty but his clear blue eyes put him closer to thirty. He is hashed with small cuts, as if he's been climbing through barbed-wire fences all morning. Hart greets him with the head-on nod of equals. Hart and the ragged man are down to common denominators, and they recognize this in each other. The man asks for a cigarette and Hart gives him one, then lights it for him. As the rest of us stroll on, Hart reaches into his camera bag. When Hart has his camera ready, the man begins to shift his weight from left foot to right and back again. The asphalt road is burning hot and I assume the man is moving oddly because his bare feet are giving him trouble, but then he raises his stick-figure arms as if they were big sunny wings and begins to turn in half-circles, first one way, then the other, his cigarette held delicately in his fingertips. He lifts his face up to the sky to let God see him better, and chants a broken-throated nonsense. It's an Indian dance, or his idea of one. "He didn't want any money," Hart says when he rejoins us. "He said all he needs now is smokes. He gave me permission to take his picture, but only while he was doing his atonement dance."

We continue our stroll; the man, who doesn't need an audience, continues his dance. The sun has baked curiosity out of our thoughts. Curiosity is a luxury of the temperate zone. When a shoeless man in a parched land tells you he's doing an atonement dance, you more or less have to accept him at his word. Besides, there's enough to atone for to keep half of humanity dancing shoeless in the desert for a century while the other half lights cigarettes for them.

A few months later I will think of this moment while looking at Hart's photographs matted and framed on our apartment walls, and it will seem as if all of us are moving to the drumbeat of some privately realized dance—the ducking pickpockets with large incongruous smiles under their stony eyes; Sada and Tyrell holding hands shyly but glaring like unyielding Apaches from their mountain stronghold, determined to make their stand; Rocky tugging defiantly on her cigarette as she fixes something at infinity with wide-open eyes that won't blink; even the headless mule floating near the concrete bank of the Rio Grande like an offering to the indifferent northern gods. And Joyce and me, caught looking at each other with slightly shocked expressions, as if on that very day, before the small white church in Palomas, we grasped for the first time that love is possible only because it must end.

—for Zena Beth McGlashan

GREG PAPE

Greg Pape was born in 1947 in Eureka, California, studied with Philip Levine at Fresno, and did graduate work at the University of Arizona. Both inland California and the desert Southwest figure prominently in his first three books of poetry: Border Crossings *(1978),* Black Branches *(1984), and* Storm Pattern *(1992), all*

published in the Pitt Poetry Series. His latest volume, Sunflower
Facing the Sun *(1992), won the Edwin Ford Piper Award for Poetry
from the University of Iowa Press. Pape has also received Pushcart,
National Endowment for the Arts, and Discovery/The Nation awards
for his work. After teaching in Missouri, Kentucky, Arizona, and
Florida, Pape has moved back to the West, "for good." He teaches
poetry in the writing program at the University of Montana, forty
miles from where he lives with his wife, the poet Marnie Prange, and
their two sons, Coleman and Clay, in the Bitterroot Valley of western
Montana.*

These selections from Sunflower Facing the Sun *are personal
communions about friendships, physical or spiritual, and the monumental importance of naming the details, the actualities.*

SOME NAMES

Nooncaster, Colombini, Abrahms, Perez,
Patigian, Doohan, Eliot, Masterpolo,
Roderick, some names come back tonight.
Nooncaster was a butcher
who drove a red Corvette with a fiberglass
body that shattered like a toy. He always
carried cash, supplied every barbecue
with fresh red meat, and charmed the air
with his quick delivery, bright eyes,
and the odd music—part nasal, part gravel—
of his voice. Colombini had biceps
like baseballs. Abrahms was an unlit
neon sign who could turn it on
when he wanted to and sing like Sam Cooke
or Otis Redding long before they were ghosts,
but spent most of his time in a dark dream
of some childhood road listening. Perez
was cool, no better word for the way
he moved through the hot valley nights
in spit-shined french toes or a lowered
Chevy black as his eyes, his hair slicked back
as if to say the wind, sun, moon, and stars

all stop when I stop. Patigian
was part lion, part wren, but looked
like a bear. Doohan lit the barbecue
with gas splashed from a baby moon hubcap,
and just as we imagined it would happen,
his arm went up in flames. Eliot
drove his loaded Ford on country roads
and raced the trains to crossings
and almost always won. Masterpolo
made a mess of things in the Y Knot Roadhouse
because he wouldn't let it ride, he tore
the antlered heads from the dumb walls.
Old friends, acquaintances, role models
in the badass arts of adolescence.
And Roderick, we called him Red, had
a fine, nervous laugh and hands
quick enough to confuse even his own freckles.
Roderick, one of those names on the wall
in Washington you can find in your own face.

BLESSING AT THE CITADEL

By the time I had walked out of the canyon
toward the end of a day of deep quiet
and daydreams among lizards and wrens,
a day of clarity in the sun and puzzles
in the shadows where I found the petroglyph
of a running animal pecked into the rock
at the base of the canyon a thousand years ago,
the animal I thought at first was a horse,
but after looking awhile and thinking about it
realized was a mountain lion, I was ready
I thought for anything.

I was feeling strong, light, open.
I was ready to sing for a stranger,
or walk into the cinder hills with one
of the spirits of Lomaki, or put on a black

satin cape, step out of my dusty shoes,
croak, and flap off to ride thermals
with the ravens. I was that happy,
as if a new depth had entered my life.

When I came upon the tattooed family
posing for pictures among the walls and rubble
of Box Canyon Pueblo, and noticed
their station wagon with Indiana plates
and the trailer with the words Skin Tattoos
painted carefully in big black letters,
I considered asking the smiling father,
his tattooed belly bulging proudly beneath
his shirt, to make a portrait of the lion
on my chest. I was that happy.
But asked instead, How you doing?
Pretty good so far, he smiled.
And I went on walking across the road,
past a battered pickup, to Nalakihu
and the Citadel, home to the Hisatsinom,
ancestors of the Hopi, guardian spirits
of the land nicknamed America.

I suppose I should keep this to myself,
but there are things in a life that happen
only once and make us who we are,
like being born from one woman
or the first true kiss that makes
all the others possible. I suppose
I should hold my heart hostage
to a regular beat, and if it must go faster,
they say, it should do so gradually
so it isn't strained or damaged
so the whole system starts to break down
and the invisible bird that flies
back and forth between the extremities
bursts into a sudden scattering
of individual feathers.

But there they were, three of them,
standing at the top of the Citadel
in late afternoon light, silhouettes
among the rocks rising like gods
in human figures from the ancient walls.

I stood quietly on the trail below
until one of them came down to me
and put a hand on my shoulder, lowered
his head, opened my shirt, and spoke
in the old way directly to my heart.
Don't go any further heart, he said,
until you are blessed. He rubbed hooma
over my chest and touched my forehead
with the white dust of cornmeal on his fingers.
He poured hooma in my left hand
and placed a sprig of cedar in my right.
Go pray, he said. What for? I asked.
Pray for now, this place, all your relations.
Pray for the hostages.
Then he walked off down the trail
to join the others, not gods
but poor, living men from Moenkopi
here at the home of their ancestors
to pray for the world and bless a stranger.

TESS GALLAGHER

Tess Gallagher writes poetry, screenplays, fiction, and criticism. She has won grants from the Guggenheim Foundation and the National Endowment for the Arts. Her books of poetry include Instructions to the Double *(1976),* Under Stars *(1978),* Willingly *(1984), and*

Amplitude: New and Selected Poems *(1987). A collection of short stories,* The Lover of Horses, *was published in 1986. She has also published a collection of literary essays entitled* A Concert of Tenses *(1986). Gallagher co-wrote and published an as-of-yet unproduced screenplay with her late husband, the writer Raymond Carver, and acted as a consultant to Robert Altman on* Short Cuts, *a 1993 film based on Carver's short stories. Her latest collection of poems,* Portable Kisses: Love Poems, *was published in 1994. She lives in her hometown of Port Angeles, Washington.*

"Cougar Meat" provides a fresh take on the Western hunting ethic. Unlike Kinnell's "The Bear," Ford's "Communist," or Quammen's "Orphan Calves," or the excerpt from Richard Nelson's The Island Within, *this poem isn't about respect for the killed or the equilibrium of the hunt. Instead, it is a deep meditation on the "avalanche of unmeaning" which is trophy hunting. These thematic concerns are echoed in "The Borrowed Ones." Both poems, from* Amplitude, *are ultimately about family and obligation, and acting out the need for nurture in the bloody snow that surrounds us. "The meat was not wasted."*

COUGAR MEAT

Carried this morning in the dodge and swoop
of error, rethinking a breach
with a friend—how I'd failed to staunch harm
with kindness when she needed me
as sacrifice—then you, brother, came in
to say goodbye, hovered in my kitchen
for coffee. You'd been hunting cougar three days
and nights, with your dogs, somewhere
in the mountains back of Gardiner. You hadn't
slept, keeping the fever up until the magic
gave in to you. But on the third day
snow, the invisible current of pursuit
exchanged for tracks. The kill then, baffling
and simple—awesome death made perfunctory
with a shot. I hear you out, know why

you've come, certain of welcome, yet your act
hated for the usual "female" reasons, or so
you think, and are freed of wonder and of
shame. Should I ask, Pharaoh, did you eat
of the heart? Did you find it sweet? Or,
in a bounty of silence, know the pelt
torn away, the carcass unquenchable where it fell
in its blue efficiency, its avalanche of
unmeaning which allows those man-sized footsteps
to point away unknown, yet deeply familiar. Mine
to ask whose wildness we are, whose trust
soon to be plundered? The adrenaline has let you
down. You're bone-weary and back with
the rest of us, diamond bright with hunger,

unfulfilled by the dominant courage here toward
livelihood with all its unedifying hazards.
Should I put aside kinship with the hunted and
the dumb, pray that cougars last for men like you?
Only in the mind's rarefied traffic with the sacred
have I met cougar. Could have gone all day, all
life not thinking *cougar,* had you kept
from here. Wild Horse Annie, in that same untutored
leap, defended mustangs in the Pryor Mountains,
never having laid eyes on one. Enough to guess
spirits of the West surviving in those rugged bands
pursued by helicopters. Her fear—the unseen loss,
more heritage in a Medicine Hat Pinto than
in the frontier mandate to take what

you can. "Good eating too," you say, still
talking cougar. "The word is, it tastes like pork
or veal, not that I'd know." You launch into story:
"That time Dad forgot his lunch and one of the guys
on the dock offered him a sandwich, which he
ate. At poker break, he said to the guy, 'What
kind of sandwich was that, anyway?'
'Me-ow!' the guy said, and he didn't mean pussycat.
Dad looked at him, said 'It's better than snake,

by God, better than flying squirrel, and I've
eat both with appetite to spare.' Cougar meat!" my
brother says, like somebody has handed him a bat
on a skewer. *Not nature, but the visions she*

gave me, Rilke said. I kiss your cheek, brother,
where we stand on the porch. You're off
on your first vacation to an exotic place—Hawaii,
paradise regained, where you will lie down with
the lamb. You tell me you want your son brought up
to hunt cougar. If you die tomorrow in a plane crash,
I'm supposed to see to that. Don't
count on it, I say. Not one iota have I moved you,
but all day I wear dread in your name, and in the name
of Cougar, renewing in heart the biblical sacrifice of
Uzzah, whose unthinking touch on the Ark of the Covenant
was death to him, instruction for us. Recovering
that clear shot in the snow, these intricacies
of undoing, for which language was also given
to say: the meat was not wasted.

THE BORROWED ONES

for Caroline Bock

We, the old children, are now old again
with a new authority. We take
their young hands in ours
and tell them we will stay old, swear
to grow even older, be rust
to their iron. Whose are these
rain barrels in the pasture that fill and over-
fill with softest rain? I knock them aside
and the ground drinks, in its gradual way,
all they give.

We were the motherless, or those who say "Mother"
as "help me," and whatever comes—that sky

with one orange bird, even a wave
that endures moonlight—even these
will do. Finally we did
for ourselves. In our loving we mothered
the men we wanted to be more than. And
though our breasts were still the breasts of
children, we gave ourselves as children
give, with the door wide open, with
the house on fire. Still, our hands were
mothers' hands, were lament and pledge,
a whirl of bells through the sweet gloom of
their foraging, and, yes, something, something was
satisfied.

If at our table those who would have loved us
ate the meal, forgetting to light
the candles, we smiled on them
with the kindness of conquered stars—not
the brightest ones, but those
expendable ones
that fall to gain a share
in the splendor.

Now, if I call you "Daughter," it is not
out of obedience
you will step toward me
but as the ghost of one who bore you,
gazing out—I, who have given you
a daughter's arms.

PART FOUR

BRILLIANT POSSIBILITIES

AT THIS TIME, writing in and about the American West seems to stand at a threshold. While some of the work included here—for instance, that of Leslie Marmon Silko—seems to me enduring, it's almost impossible to predict whether a particular work by a particular writer will necessarily hold up over time (like, say, the *Iliad* or *Bleak House* or some of Rilke or Faulkner or—it's my guess—some poems by Elizabeth Bishop). That's not, of course, the point of things. Usefulness is the point. Helping one another live.

"There is only one question," Mary Oliver writes, "how to love this world." A new and brilliantly capable generation of writers seems to be focusing at least a major portion of its attention on life in the American West. These writers are showing us, continually, by their example, how to attempt cherishing ourselves, one another, and where we are.

CZESLAW MILOSZ

Czeslaw Milosz says, "The act of writing a poem is an act of faith."
He also warns, "Yet if the screams of the tortured are audible in the
poet's room, is not his activity an offense to human suffering?" A poet

who has emphasized art's moral rather than aesthetic imperative, Milosz won the Nobel prize for literature in 1980 for his profoundly influential work. Born in Lithuania in 1911, and raised in Poland, Milosz has lived in the United States since 1960. He published his first collection of poems, Poemat o czasie zastyglym *(Poem of the Frozen Time) at the age of twenty-one, in 1933. Sixty years later, he continues to write, from his home in Berkeley, where he is a professor emeritus at the University of California. The author of more than twenty volumes of poetry—the latest of which is* Facing the River: New Poems *(1995), fifteen collections of essays, and countless translations, he writes in Polish, which is then translated by himself and others (his long-time collaborators include Robert Hass and Robert Pinsky).*

"Polish independence resides in this poet's voice," Joseph Brodsky wrote. When Polish workers in Gdansk unveiled a monument to their comrades shot by the police, two quotations were inscribed on the monument—one taken from the Bible; the other, from a poem by Milosz.

"To Robinson Jeffers," from The Collected Poems *(1988), is about the power of nature and our certain need to both heed and fear power, everywhere. We see, again, that our West is irrevocably connected to a world community. Injustice anywhere, we remember, is our injustice.*

TO ROBINSON JEFFERS

If you have not read the Slavic poets
so much the better. There's nothing there
for a Scotch-Irish wanderer to seek. They lived in a
    childhood
prolonged from age to age. For them, the sun
was a farmer's ruddy face, the moon peeped through a cloud
and the Milky Way gladdened them like a birch-lined road.
They longed for the Kingdom which is always near,
always right at hand. Then, under apple trees
angels in homespun linen will come parting the boughs
and at the white kolkhoz tablecloth

cordiality and affection will feast (falling to the ground at
   times).

And you are from surf-rattled skerries. From the heaths
where burying a warrior they broke his bones
so he could not haunt the living. From the sea night
which your forefathers pulled over themselves, without a
   word.
Above your head no face, neither the sun's nor the moon's,
only the throbbing of galaxies, the immutable
violence of new beginnings, of new destruction.

All your life listening to the ocean. Black dinosaurs
wade where a purple zone of phosphorescent weeds
rises and falls on the waves as in a dream. And Agamemnon
sails the boiling deep to the steps of the palace
to have his blood gush onto marble. Till mankind passes
and the pure and stony earth is pounded by the ocean.

Thin-lipped, blue-eyed, without grace or hope,
before God the Terrible, body of the world.
Prayers are not heard. Basalt and granite.
Above them, a bird of prey. The only beauty.

What have I to do with you? From footpaths in the
   orchards,
from an untaught choir and shimmers of a monstrance,
from flower beds of rue, hills by the rivers, books
in which a zealous Lithuanian announced brotherhood, I
   come.
Oh, consolations of mortals, futile creeds.

And yet you did not know what I know. The earth teaches
More than does the nakedness of elements. No one with
   impunity
gives to himself the eyes of a god. So brave, in a void,
you offered sacrifices to demons: there were Wotan and
   Thor,

the screech of Erinyes in the air, the terror of dogs
when Hekate with her retinue of the dead draws near.

Better to carve suns and moons on the joints of crosses
as was done in my district. To birches and firs
give feminine names. To implore protection
against the mute and treacherous might
than to proclaim, as you did, an inhuman thing.

Berkeley, 1963

N. SCOTT MOMADAY

N. Scott Momaday, a member of the Kiowa tribe, was born in Law-
ton, Oklahoma, in 1934, and spent his childhood on various reser-
vations in the Southwest. His 1969 Pulitzer prize for the novel
House Made of Dawn *(1968) was a defining moment that gave*
heart to Western and Native American writers, indicating that maybe
it was possible their work could be taken seriously by the so-called great
world. He is the author of several other books, including The Ancient
Child *(1989),* The Way to Rainy Mountain *(1969),* The
Names *(1976), and* The Gourd Dancer *(1976). A recipient of*
the Premio Lettario Internazionale Mondello Award, Momaday is
Regent's Professor of English at the University of Arizona.

In this excerpt from his memoir, The Names, *Momaday tells*
us of stories within stories, and reflects on a day in the life of his great-
grandfather, Pohd-lohk, who gifts the author with an Indian name.
In this story, landscape, nature, and tradition all merge into one act
—the act of naming.

FROM *THE NAMES: A MEMOIR*

At four o'clock on the morning of February 27, 1934, in the Kiowa and Comanche Indian Hospital at Lawton, Oklahoma, near the old stone corral at Fort Sill, where my ancestors were imprisoned in 1873 for having fled to the last buffalo range in the Staked Plains, I was delivered into the world by an elderly Indian Service doctor who entered my name on the Standard Certificate of Birth as Novarro Scotte Mammedaty ("Momaday" having first been entered, then crossed out). I have also in my possession a notarized document issued by the United States Department of the Interior, Office of Indian Affairs, Anadarko Area Office, which reads:

> To whom it may concern:
> This is to certify that the records of this office show that Novarro Scott Mammedaty was born February 27, 1934 at Lawton, Oklahoma and is of ⅞ degree Indian blood, as shown on the Kiowa Indian Census roll opposite Number 2035. The official Government agency records further show that his father is Alfred Mammedaty and his mother is Natachee Scott.
> By Act of June 2, 1924 (43 Stat. 253), all Indians born within the territorial limits of the United States were declared to be citizens of the United States.

The first notable event in my life was a journey to the Black Hills. When I was six months old my parents took me to Devil's Tower, Wyoming, which is called in Kiowa Tsoai, "rock tree." Here are stories within stories; I want to imagine a day in the life of a man, Pohd-lohk, who gave me a name.

• • •

The arbor is a square frame building, cool and dark within. Two timbers, like telegraph poles, support the high, pitched roof, which is made of rafters and shingles, warped and weather-stained. Inside, on such a day as this, there are innumerable points of light at the roof, like stars, too small to admit of beams or reflections. The arbor is a place from which the sun is excluded at midday, a room that is like dawn or dusk at noon, and always there is a particular weather inside, an air that is cooler and more fluent than that of the plain, like wind in a culvert, and a deeper, more congenial shade. At times you can hear the wind, for it runs upon the walls and moans, but you cannot know it truly until you are old and have lived with it many years; so they say, who are old. It is the same wind that brings about the chinooks in the old homeland of the Kiowas to the north, the bleak winters and black springs of the whole Great Plains. It is at once the most violent and placid motion in the universe.

There is a clapboard siding to the framework. At the base it is low, rising some three feet or so from the red, earthen floor and giving way to a wide latticework and screens, an open window that encircles the great room. Here and there are certain amenities; an icebox, a cupboard, a low shelf upon which there are metal boxes and basins, shaving mugs and a mirror, a kerosene lamp and a lantern. Adjacent to the northwest corner of the room there is another, smaller block of space, the kitchen, in which there are a stone fireplace and a chimney, a grill, a cutting board, and various implements for cooking. Just now, after the noon meal, there are fragrances of spice, of boiled meat and fried bread, melons, and warm, sweet milk. Here, at this hour, in this season, you do not expect that something extraordinary will happen, only that a bird will call out in a moment, and a low wind arise, carry, and descend.

On this August day, 1934, the old man Pohd-lohk awoke before dawn. For a time he lay still in the darkness beside his wife, Tsomah, not listening to the slow, persistent sound of her breathing in sleep, but leading his mind out and away towards the center of the day. He arose quietly and drew the light, cotton blanket about his naked body, taking up his clothes, which he carried outside and placed on the edge of the porch. At the corner of the house a dog appeared, a rangy, overgrown pup, short-haired and liver-colored, wagging its tail. It seemed a vague epitome of the darkness; he regarded it for a moment, then let it go.

The first light appeared among the trees like smoke and crept upon the hard, bare ground at his feet, blushed upon the skyline to the north and east, where the river made a great bend and the trees grew up in a thicket in a deep crease of the bank. He peered into the dark wall of the grove in the middle distance and saw that it drew slowly upon him in the light and wavered, so it seemed, then settled back into the depths. He thought at such times that the world was centered upon him, that everything near and far must refer to him, drawing close from every quarter upon the very place where he stood. Always he loved to be out and alone in the early morning.

He shivered and huddled over upon himself, bunching the long muscles of his arms and shoulders in the blanket. He had good use of his body still, though now he moved about slowly in his age. He was a good-looking man, having been lively in his youth and closely disciplined in his prime. His body was hard and thick and grew supple in the sun; his eyes were clear and his vision keen. In his face there was reflected all the force of will and intelligence that truly defined him. His sunburned hands were fine and fluent, and with them he could still perform the intricate work of fixing beads and feathers to buckskin, and he made arrows that were precisely delicate and true.

In a moment the sun appeared, and he held his head back and closed his eyes, praying, the long, loose white hair gathering up in the peak and fold of the blanket at his neck.

A rooster crowed among the trees. It was a shrill and vibrant sound, like a cry, that carried for long moments and held like heat on the air. He opened his eyes suddenly and looked after it, but he could not determine where the creature was, and he thought of hunting, of waiting long ago in the same light (or was it a harder, bleaker light, a midwinter dawn?) and listening for such a sound, a thin cry in the distance. Once as a young man he had heard in a high wind the whimper of young wolves, hectic and hollow, and he had known at once, instinctively, where and what they were, and he went to them quietly, directly, so that there should be almost no fear on either side, singing lowly to them. They lay huddled among the rocks, three of them, shuddering with cold, their eyes closed and their fine blue fur gaping in the wind. And he shielded them for a time with his hands and wanted so much to touch them, to hold the soft warm shapes close against him, but he dared not touch them, for fear that he should leave a scent like doom upon them, and after a while he left them alone, as he had found them.

Pohd-lohk, old wolf.

He was awake now and restless. He stepped down from the porch and crossed the yard to the place where he must purify himself, a small, hide-covered framework of eighteen willows, that which is called *seidl-ku-toh*. It stood no higher than his waist, and he entered it on his hands and knees, leaving the blanket outside, and made a fire in the pit. Then, while the stones were heating, he went out again—he felt the sun flaring upon him—to get water and to breathe the last cold air of the night into his lungs.

Later in the bath, while the stones sizzled and steam rose up around him, Pohd-lohk combed out his long hair and braided it. He thought of the dead, of Kau-au-ointy, the mother of his wives, and of Mammedaty, his stepson, of others. Already indistinct in his mind, they happened upon him often now and without substance, like sudden soft winds and shadows in his dreaming, and he imagined who they were and what had happened to them, that they should have been there and then gone forever, and he thought it a strange thing, their going, sad and imponderable at the center. But at the same time the thought of it filled him with wonder, and he saw what it was to be alive. Then, always, his spirit wheeled and ran away with him, out upon an endless, sunlit plain.

Afterwards: the sun was high and the air already heavy and hot. The light was not yet flat, but nearly golden in the yard, where it was broken upon the limbs and leaves of an elm and scattered on the grass and ground. Through a window he saw a magpie drop down among the shadows, gleaming as it settled in the mottled light.

Pohd-lohk began to deal with time, his old age, a restlessness. He went into his room, the room where he and Tsomah slept, and closed the door. He opened a bureau drawer and stood for a moment before it. In it were his best possessions, including a human bone, the forearm of a Crow whose name was Two Whistles. He placed the fingers of his right hand upon it—it was hard and smooth as the stones he heated for his bath—and he caught his breath, as if the bone had quickened to his touch. He removed a book and spectacles; these he kept always together, wrapped round with a red kerchief. The book, a ledgerbook which he had obtained from the Supply Office at Fort Sill, had been in his possession for many years, from the time he was a private in L Troop, Seventh Cavalry, under the command of Hugh Scott, and it meant a great deal to him. He laid his hands to it in a certain way, with precise, familiar care. It was a calendar history of the Kiowa people from 1833.

He could not remember how it was that he came to his special regard for history, or to his resolve that he, Pohd-lohk, should set it down in pictures on a page, but the book had become a serious affair in his life. In it he indicated at first events that had been recorded on an older calendar, a painted hide, then things that had been told to him by his elders or that fell within the range of his own memory. Now that he was old, Pohd-lohk liked to look backwards in time, and although he could neither read nor write, this book was his means. It was an instrument with which he could reckon his place in the world; it was as if he could see in its yellow, brittle leaves the long swath of his coming to old age and sense in the very nature of it—the continuity of rude images in which the meaning of his racial life inhered—a force that had been set in motion at the Beginning. The calendar was a story, or the seed of a story, and it began a hundred years in the past. Beyond that, beyond the notion of a moment in 1833, there was only the unknown, a kind of prehistoric and impenetrable genesis, a realm of no particular shape, duration, or meaning. It was an older, larger story, a story of another people, another reality at last. He believed in it, but he could not take hold of it and set it down. The Kiowas had entered the world through a hollow log; they had known good things and bad, triumph and defeat; and they had journeyed a long way from the mouth of the log. But it was all one moment to Pohd-lohk, as if everything, the whole world, had been created on an afternoon in 1830 or 1832.

He opened the book to the first page, and it was *Da-pegya-de Sai*, November, 1833, and the stars were falling. He closed his eyes, the better to see them. They were everywhere in the darkness, so numerous and bright indeed that the night was shattered. They flew like sparks, he thought, and he thought also of slender, pointed leaves turning in the sun, and of pure light glittering upon water. But as he watched, dreaming, the stars were at last like nothing he had ever seen or should ever see beyond this, the havoc he imagined and remembered in his blood. Truly they were not like sparks or leaves or facets of light upon water. In some older and more nearly perfect synthesis of motion and light the stars wheeled across the vision of his mind's eye. They swung and veered; they drew near and loomed; and they fell slowly and silently away in the void. Silently. Men, women, and children were running here and there in the flashing light, their eyes wide and their mouths twisted with fear, but he could not hear their running, nor even the sound of their cries. And yet it did not seem strange to him that there should be no sound upon the scene. It was as if the earth—or even so much of it as he knew—had fallen off into the still, black depths. Even as this bright catastrophe was somehow the element of his perception just now, in his dreaming, so was silence the element in which the stars moved inexorably. They fell in long arcs and traces, bright delineations of time and space, describing eternity. He looked after them with strange exhilaration, straining to see.

Or it was *Ta'dalkop Sai*, 1839–40, and the designation before him was the crude figure of a man covered with red spots. This was in commemoration of the great smallpox epidemic which began on the upper Missouri in the summer of 1837 and which, in the course of three years, is estimated to have destroyed fully one third of the native inhabitants of the Great Plains.

Always when he thought of it Pohd-lohk could see the bodies of the dead, not their faces, but only their faceless forms, the abstractions of some hideous reality that was a shade beyond his comprehension. More real to him by far were the survivors, those whose grief, he thought, must have been a plague in itself, whose wailing must have been like the drone of locusts in the fields. In his own lifetime, 1892, he had seen a woman kneeling over the body of her child, who had succumbed to measles. She had inflicted bloody wounds upon her arms and shoulders with a knife; she had cut her hair so that it lay close to the scalp and ragged. And all the while that he watched, his rage and shame having come together in a kind of helpless fascination, she emitted cries, hollow, thin, full of wild, incomprehensible grief.

Again, it was 1851–52. That winter there was a hard thing for the coming-out people to bear. A Pawnee boy who had been captured the year before by Set-angya, the great warrior chief of the Kaitsenko society, escaped and took with him the best horse in the tribe, a bay hunter known as Guadal-tseyu, "Little Red." Pohd-lohk had turned this matter over in his mind a thousand times. It might have been a different story among the Pawnees, the story of the boy. But in his own terms, which comprised Pohd-lohk's particular idea of history, it was the story of the horse—and incidentally of the Kiowas at a given moment in time. Moreover, it was a tragic story—nearly as much so from his point of view as was that of the plague, which he imagined no more vividly— inasmuch as it centered upon a whole and crucial deprivation, the loss of a horse, a hunting horse, a loss that involved the very life's blood of the culture. Once upon a time, as he thought of it, there was a horse, and never before had there been such a horse, and it was lost, and with it was lost something of the coming-out people, too, a splinter from the bone. It was a simple story in the telling, but there were many implications, many shadows on the grass. He imagined Guadal-tseyu. Now and then it seemed to him that he had got hold of it, that he could feel the horse under him, the whole strength and whole motion of it. It was hard to hold and half wild in its spirit, but it was all the more congenial to his mind for that, all the more appropriate to the landscape from which it had sprung like a gust of wind. He thought he could see it, the red hunting horse, but it was fleeting. He saw the ghost, the sheer energy of it. Perhaps when it stood still, he thought, it was the ordinary image of a horse, neither more nor less, standing away in the whole hollow of the plain, or away on a ridge, the sky all around it, small and alone, lonely. But when it wheeled and broke into a run, as it did always in his dreaming, it seemed to concentrate the wind and the stars, to gather the splinters of the sun to itself. And someone in his lineage, a man long ago in the Yellowstone, had seen such a thing, a fish flashing at a waterfall in the late afternoon, hurtling high above a dark rainbow on the spray.

Or it was the summer of 1883, in which Sampt'e was killed. Pohd-lohk had known this man and had seen fit to commemorate him, to fix him forever in the scheme of remembered time. But now, as he thought back to that green summer, it was the sun dance that stood out in his mind. It was called *A'dalk'atoi K'ado*, "Nez Percé sun dance." Pohd-lohk was in his twenties at the time. He was then, as he thought of it now, at the end of his youth, as vital and strong as he should ever be, and scarcely concerned to admit of age or illness. *A'dalk'atoi K'ado.* He thought of it as the one time in his life to which he would willingly return from any and all other times; it was simply the best of his memories. The place of the sun dance was pasture land by that time, owned and enclosed by a white cattleman whom the Kiowas called Map'odal, "Split-nose." The lodge was erected on a low rise of dark, rich land on the Washita River where two dense groves of pecan trees grew in a large semicircle. It was a bright, hot summer, a summer of the plains, and it followed upon a hard winter. The camps were gleaming against the dark, shimmering backdrop of the groves, and the arbors, faceted with bright leaves, shone like fire, and there were pennants of red and blue and yellow cloth everywhere, moving in the breeze.

That summer the Nez Percés came. It was then five years since they had been released from imprisonment at Fort Leavenworth and two before they should be allowed to return to their northern homeland. They seemed a regal people, as tall as the Kiowas, as slow to reveal themselves. There was an excitement about them, something of legendary calm and courage. It was common knowledge that, under their great chief Joseph, they had fought brilliantly against the United States and had come very close to victory. It was the first time that Pohd-lohk had seen them, but he had known of them all his life. The Kiowas remembered that, long ago, they had come upon these imposing people, "people with hair cut off across the forehead," in the highlands on the edge of the Northern Plains. This was a part of that larger story in which Pohd-lohk believed. It was a good thing to have the Nez Percés; they were worthy guests, worthy of him, he thought, of his youthful vigor and good looks. For their benefit he strutted about and set his mouth just so, in the attitude of a warrior.

And there were Tsomah and Keahdinekeah, whom he would take for his wives. Keahdinekeah was then twenty-five years old and the mother of the child Mammedaty. She was slender and straight, and she had inherited her mother Kau-au-ointy's strength of will and character. She carried herself with remarkable dignity and grace, so much so indeed that these traits should be apparent even to a child, her great-grandson, sixty years later.

Pohd-lohk sang, for a man sings of such a woman. His dreaming came to an end in the song, and he put the book and spectacles away. His mind turned and drew upon something else now, something that had run through his thoughts for several days, a serious matter. It was time to go, and he set out, walking easily in the heat, towards the trees that grew on Rainy Mountain Creek.

There, in a wide clearing above the bank, Keahdinekeah sat on the edge of the bed in her room. It was late morning, almost noon, and she had been sitting there alone for a long time. It was very hot; even though the window was wide open, the air was heavy and stale in the room. The room smelled of old, settled things, curios and keepsakes that were Keahdinekeah's, having no essence but that of belonging to her. She nodded from time to time, dozing, her eyes closed and her small, crooked hands folded in her lap. She was very small, as if in her waning and weariness all of her little, aged bones had collapsed within her. She was seventy-six years old now, and nearly blind. Unlike Pohd-lohk, she showed her age, seemed even older than she was. Since the death of Mammedaty, her firstborn and favorite son, she had withdrawn into herself—in grief at first, but then as a matter of preference. She had finished with the things that enabled her to live well in the ordinary world; they had passed away from her one by one; and now she was herself waiting to pass away into the darkness that had come upon her and lay like evening at her eyes. It was a long wait—and it would go on for more than a decade—but she kept it with trust and good will. And she was glad to have visitors when they came.

Without knocking, Pohd-lohk opened the door to her room. She looked up, but he knew that she could not see who was there.

Old woman.

Old man!

He paused for a moment in the doorway, wiping the sweat from his forehead.

It is hot.

Yes?

Hot.

There was a dull luster upon the objects in the room, the knobs of metal and hollows of wood, the blocks and wedges of a patchwork quilt, bits of carnival glass. There was a very low amber brilliance, a soft, nearly vibrant glowing, upon the whole setting. The air was close, stifling.

Come, old woman, let's sit outside, in the arbor.

She held out her hand to him, and he helped her to stand and walk. They went out of the house and across the yard, where a speckled hen scratched in the dirt beside a shallow cistern at the well. It raised its head and regarded them sideways. Keahdinekeah walked very softly, in moccasins, on Pohd-lohk's arm.

The arbor was a makeshift affair, nothing but a lean-to, made out of poles and branches. The poles were many years old, smooth and gray, with long, gaping cracks here and there. The branches had been placed on the framework in May or June; the leaves had long since wilted, and most of them were shriveled now and brittle, in spite of the very humid heat. Even so, the arbor afforded them a little shade, and it was soothing. They sat down on a bench at the long table, over the top of which a heavy red oilcloth had been stretched and tacked down. It was ragged and badly faded, but it was cool to the touch. Flies buzzed about them, slowly, as if they were moving against a wind.

How is my sister Tsomah?

Oh, she is all right, very well, in fact. She said to tell you that she is drying some meat, that you ought to come and pay her a visit.

Yes? Well, it may be so, but I don't get out much, you know. I can't see very well at all now.

She looked straight ahead, her eyes open, and he could see in them the milky film of her blindness. A silence fell between them, and she reached for his hand, held it tight, smiling.

Well, Pohd-lohk, it is good to have you here; I am glad that you came.

So, I must go on about my business.

Yes?

It is very important.

Yes?

Oh, yes.

Well, then.

I am on my way to see your great-grandson.

Eh neh neh neh neh!

She clasped her hands together, laughing. And after a moment she was lost in thought, and again there was a silence between them.

And afterwards, when Pohd-lohk had gone, Keahdinekeah sat again on the edge of her bed and thought of Tsoai and of her great-grandson. Neither had she ever seen, but of Tsoai she knew an old story.

Eight children were there at play, seven sisters and their brother. Suddenly the boy was struck dumb; he trembled and began to run upon his hands and feet. His fingers became claws, and his body was covered with fur. There was a bear where the boy had been. The sisters were terrified; they ran, and the bear after them. They came to the stump of a great tree, and the tree spoke to them. It bade them climb upon it, and as they did so it began to rise into the air. The bear came to kill them, but they were just beyond its reach. It reared against the tree and scored the bark all around with its claws. The seven sisters were borne into the sky and they became the stars of the Big Dipper.

Tsoai loomed in her mind; nor could she have imagined it more awesome than it is, the great black igneous monolith that rises out of the Black Hills of Wyoming to a height of twelve hundred feet above the Belle Fourche River. Many generations before, the Kiowas had come upon Tsoai, had been obliged in their soul to explain it to themselves. And they imagined that it stood in some strange and meaningful relation to them and to the stars. It was therefore a sacred thing, Keahdinekeah knew. And her grandson Huan-toa had taken his child to be in Tsoai's presence even before the child could understand what it was, so that by means of the child the memory of Tsoai should be renewed in the blood of the coming-out people. Of this she thought, and she said to herself: Yes, old man, I see; I see now what your errand is.

Pohd-lohk crossed Rainy Mountain Creek on a log, a walnut that he himself had felled the year before. The trees were thick along the creek, the foliage dense. There were shafts of sunlight all about, smoking, so many planes of bright light on the dark shadows of the creek. Birds fluttered up here and there, flashing across the planes and angles of light in the tunnel of trees. Insects made minute, hectic motions on the brown water, which bore up a long, crooked drift, the most fragile mesh of silt and webs. Small white butterflies glittered and bobbed in the humid air, moving in their own way, rising and falling in time to a rhythm too intricate for the old man to follow with his eyes. It was like a dance. He picked his way along a dim, narrow path that led upwards through brier and berry thickets to the top of the land.

Ahead on the highest knoll was the house where Mammedaty had lived in his last years, the arbor and the barn. These, from where he walked now on the first wave of the plain above the creek, stood up against the sky, as if they were the only landmarks in a hundred miles. In the conjugation of distance and light at this hour of the day they might have been little or large, near or far away. It seemed to him that he was forever coming upon them.

In the arbor Pohd-lohk entered among the members of his dead stepson's family and was full of good humor and at ease. He took up the child in his hands and held it high, and he cradled it in his arms, singing to it and rocking it to and fro. With the others he passed the time of day, exchanged customary talk, scattered small exclamations on the air: Yes, yes. Quite so. So it is with us. But with the child he was deliberate, intent. And after a time all the other voices fell away, and his own grew up in their wake. It became monotonous and incessant, like a long running of the wind. The whole of the afternoon was caught up in it and carried along. Pohd-lohk spoke, as if telling a story, of the coming-out people, of their long journey. He spoke of how it was that everything began, of Tsoai, and of the stars falling or holding fast in strange patterns on the sky. And in this, at last, Pohd-lohk affirmed the whole life of the child in a name, saying: Now you are, Tsoai-talee.

I am. It is when I am most conscious of being that wonder comes upon my blood, and I want to live forever, and it is no matter that I must die.

ROBERT HASS

Robert Hass, a recipient of both Guggenheim and MacArthur fellow-ships, has written five books of poetry, including Field Guide, *which won the Yale Younger Poets Award in 1972, and* Praise *(1979) and* Human Wishes *(1989). He has collaborated with Czeslaw Milosz on translations of three books of Milosz's poetry, and has edited the works of Robinson Jeffers and Tomas Tranströmer. His collection of essays,* Twentieth Century Pleasures: Prose on Poetry *(1984), won the National Book Critics Circle Award for criticism. His latest work is* The Essential Haiku *(1994), new translations of classical Japanese haiku.*

Born and educated in northern California, at Saint Mary's Col-lege and at Stanford, Hass has become a world-renowned teacher of poetry. In April of 1995, Hass was appointed poet laureate, and was poet-in-residence at the Library of Congress during his tenure as lau-reate, splitting his time between Washington, D.C., and his home in Berkeley, where he lives with his wife, the poet Brenda Hillman. He uses this role to work as a national advocate for both poetry and en-vironmental sensitivity. He writes a weekly column on poetry for the Washington Post Book World, *and in the spring of 1996 organ-ized the Washington, D.C., Watershed Conference, an influencial gathering of environmental poets and writers.*

Whether the metaphor is prehistoric fish in "On the Coast near Sausalito," from Field Guide, *or wildflowers in "On Squaw Peak," from* Human Wishes, *Hass incites our desire to attempt connecting, and to revere one another.*

ON THE COAST
NEAR SAUSALITO

1

I won't say much for the sea
except that it was, almost,
the color of sour milk.
The sun in that clear
unmenacing sky was low,

angled off the grey fissure of the cliffs,
hills dark green with manzanita.

Low tide: slimed rocks
mottled brown and thick with kelp
like the huge backs of ancient tortoises
merged with the grey stone
of the breakwater, sliding off
to antediluvian depths.
The old story: here filthy life begins.

2

Fish-
ing, as Melville said,
"to purge the spleen,"
to put to task my clumsy hands
my hands that bruise by
not touching
pluck the legs from a prawn,
peel the shell off,
and curl the body twice about a hook.

3

The cabezone is not highly regarded
by fishermen, except Italians
who have the grace
to fry the pale, almost bluish flesh
in olive oil with a sprig
of fresh rosemary.

The cabezone, an ugly atavistic fish,
as old as the coastal shelf
it feeds upon
has fins of duck's-web thickness,
resembles a prehistoric toad,
and is delicately sweet.

    Catching one, the fierce quiver of surprise
and the line's tension
are a recognition.

4

But it's strange to kill
for the sudden feel of life.
The danger is
to moralize
that strangeness.
Holding the spiny monster in my hands
his bulging purple eyes
were eyes and the sun was
almost tangent to the planet
on our uneasy coast.
Creature and creature,
we stared down centuries.

ON SQUAW PEAK

I don't even know which sadness
it was came up
in me when we were walking down the road to Shirley
    Lake,
the sun gleaming in snowpatches,
the sky so blue it seemed the light's dove
of some pentecost of blue,
the mimulus, yellow, delicate of petal,
and the pale yellow cinquefoil trembling in the damp
air above the creek,—
and fields of lupine,
that blue blaze of lupine, a swath of paintbrush
sheening it, and so much of it, long meadows
of it gathered out of the mountain air and spilling
down ridge toward the lake it almost looked like
in the wind. I think I must have thought
the usual things: that the flowering season
in these high mountain meadows is so brief, that

the feeling, something like hilarity, of sudden
pleasure when you first come across some tough little plant
you knew you'd see comes because it seems—I mean
by *it* the larkspur or penstemon curling
and arching the reach of its sexual being
up out of a little crack in granite—to say
that human hunger has a niche up here in the light-cathedral
of the dazzled air. I wanted to tell you
that when the ghost-child died, the three-month dreamer
she and I would never know, I kept feeling that
the heaven it went to was like the inside of a store window
on a rainy day from which you watch the blurred forms
passing in the street. Or to tell you, more terrible,
that when she and I walked off the restlessness
of our misery afterward in the Coast Range hills,
we saw come out of the thicket shyly
a pure white doe. I wanted to tell you I knew
it was a freak of beauty like the law of averages
that killed our child and made us know, as you had said,
that things between lovers, even of longest standing,
can be botched in their bodies, though their wills don't fail.
Still later, on the beach, we watched the waves.
No two the same size. No two in the same arch
of rising up and pouring. But it is the same law.
You shell a pea, there are three plump seeds and one
that's shriveled. You shell a bushelful and you begin
to feel the rhythms of the waves at Limantour,
glittering, jagged, that last bright October afternoon.
It killed something in me, I thought, or froze it,
to have to see where beauty comes from. I imagined
for a long time that the baby, since
it would have liked to smell our clothes to know
what a mother and a father would have been,
hovered sometimes in our closet and I half expected
to see it there, half-fish spirit, form of tenderness,
a little dead dreamer with open eyes. That was
private sorrow. I tried not to hate my life,
to fear the frame of things. I knew what two people
couldn't say

on a cold November morning in the fog—
you remember the feel of Berkeley winter mornings—
what they couldn't say to each other
was the white deer not seen. It meant to me
that beauty and terror were intertwined so powerfully
and went so deep that any kind of love
can fail. I didn't say it. I think the mountain startled
my small grief. Maybe there wasn't time.
We may have been sprinting to catch the tram
because we had to teach poetry
in that valley two thousand feet below us.
You were running—Steven's mother, Michael's lover,
mother and lover, grieving, of a girl
about to leave for school and die to you a little
(or die into you, or simply turn away)—
and you ran like a gazelle,
in purple underpants, royal purple,
and I laughed out loud. It was the abundance
the world gives, the more-than-you-bargained-for
surprise of it, waves breaking,
the sudden fragrance of the mimulus at creekside
sharpened by the summer dust.
Things bloom up there. They are
for their season alive in those bright vanishings
of air we ran through.

GRETEL EHRLICH

*Born in 1946, Gretel Ehrlich was raised in California, went to Wy-
oming as a documentary filmmaker, and ended up staying. She was
educated at Bennington College, the UCLA Film School, and the
New School for Social Research. She has produced four documentaries
and has worked on ranches—lambing, branding, herding sheep, and*

calving. She began writing fulltime in 1979 and has since written two
books of essays, The Solace of Open Spaces *(1985), from which*
"On Water" was taken, and Islands, the Universe, Home
(1991); two books of poetry, Geode/Rock Body *(1970) and* To
Touch the Water *(1981); three short story collections; and the novel*
Heart Mountain *(1988). In 1994, she published* A Match to the
Heart, *a book-length essay ignited by Ehrlich's two near-lethal en-*
counters with lightning.

A rancher tells Ehrlich, "The only way I like my water is if
there's whiskey in it." This essay, about the most basic element and
the Westerner's most primal uses, needs, and reactions to water, shows
the strength and delicacy of Ehrlich's voice and her fluid ability to
create confluences of words which can move us to rethink our priorities
and allegiances, and thus ourselves and our regional society.

"ON WATER,"
FROM *THE SOLACE OF*
OPEN SPACES

Frank Hinckley, a neighboring rancher in his seventies, would rather
irrigate than ride a horse. He started spreading water on his father's
hay- and grainfields when he was nine, and his long-term enthusiasm
for what's thought of disdainfully by cowboys as "farmers' work" is an
example of how a discipline—a daily chore—can grow into a fidelity.
When I saw Frank in May he was standing in a dry irrigation ditch
looking toward the mountains. The orange tarp dams, hung like curtains
from ten-foot-long poles, fluttered in the wind like prayer flags. In Wyoming we are supplicants, waiting all spring for the water to come down,
for the snow pack to melt and fill the creeks from which we irrigate.
Fall and spring rains amount to less than eight inches a year, while above
our ranches, the mountains hold their snows like a secret: no one knows
when they will melt or how fast. When the water does come, it floods
through the state as if the peaks were silver pitchers tipped forward by
mistake. When I looked in, the ditch water had begun dripping over
Frank's feet. Then we heard a sound that might have been wind in a
steep patch of pines. "Jumpin' Jesus, here it comes," he said, as a head
of water, brown and foamy as beer, snaked toward us. He set five dams,
digging the bright edges of plastic into silt. Water filled them the way

wind fattens a sail, and from three notches cut in the ditch above each dam, water coursed out over a hundred acres of hayfield. When he finished, and the beadwork wetness had spread through the grass, he lowered himself to the ditch and rubbed his face with water.

A season of irrigating here lasts four months. Twenty, thirty, or as many as two hundred dams are changed every twelve hours, ditches are repaired and head gates adjusted to match the inconsistencies of water flow. By September it's over: all but the major Wyoming rivers dry up. Running water is so seasonal it's thought of as a mark on the calendar —a vague wet spot—rather than a geographical site. In May, June, July, and August, water is the sacristy at which we kneel; it equates time going by too fast.

Waiting for water is just one of the ways Wyoming ranchers find themselves at the mercy of weather. The hay they irrigate, for example, has to be cut when it's dry but baled with a little dew on it to preserve the leaf. Three days after Frank's water came down, a storm dumped three feet of snow on his alfalfa and the creeks froze up again. His wife, "Mike," who grew up in the arid Powder River country, and I rode to the headwaters of our creeks. The elk we startled had been licking ice in a draw. A snow squall rose up from behind a bare ridge and engulfed us. We built a twig fire behind a rock to warm ourselves, then rode home. The creeks didn't thaw completely until June.

Despite the freak snow, April was the second driest in a century; in the lower elevations there had been no precipitation at all. Brisk winds forwarded thunderclouds into local skies—commuters from other states—but the streamers of rain they let down evaporated before touching us. All month farmers and ranchers burned their irrigation ditches to clear them of obstacles and weeds—optimistic that water would soon come. Shell Valley resembled a battlefield: lines of blue smoke banded every horizon and the cottonwoods that had caught fire by mistake, their outstretched branches blazing, looked human. April, the cruelest month, the month of dry storms.

Six years ago, when I lived on a large sheep ranch, a drought threatened. Every water hole on 100,000 acres of grazing land went dry. We hauled water in clumsy beet-harvest trucks forty miles to spring range, and when we emptied them into a circle of stock tanks, the sheep ran toward us. They pushed to get at the water, trampling lambs in the process, then drank it all in one collective gulp. Other Aprils have brought too much moisture in the form of deadly storms. When a ground blizzard hit one friend's herd in the flatter, eastern part of the state, he knew he had to keep his cattle drifting. If they hit a fence line and had to face the storm, snow would blow into their noses and they'd drown. "We cut wire all the way to Nebraska," he told me. During the same storm another cowboy found his cattle too late: they were buried in a draw under a fifteen-foot drift.

High water comes in June when the runoff peaks, and it's another bugaboo for the ranchers. The otherwise amiable thirty-foot-wide creeks swell and change courses so that when we cross them with livestock, the water is belly-deep or more. Cowboys in the 1800s who rode with the trail herds from Texas often worked in the big rivers on horseback for a week just to cross a thousand head of longhorn steers, losing half of them in the process. On a less-grand scale we have drownings and near drownings here each spring. When we crossed a creek this year the swift current toppled a horse and carried the rider under a log. A cowboy who happened to look back saw her head go under, dove in from horseback, and saved her. At Trapper Creek, where Owen Wister spent several summers in the 1920s and entertained Mr. Hemingway, a cloudburst slapped down on us like a black eye. Scraps of rainbow moved in vertical sweeps of rain that broke apart and disappeared behind a ridge. The creek flooded, taking out a house and a field of corn. We saw one resident walking in a flattened alfalfa field where the river had flowed briefly. "Want to go fishing?" he yelled to us as we rode by. The fish he was throwing into a white bucket were trout that had been "beached" by the flood.

Westerners are ambivalent about water because they've never seen what it can create except havoc and mud. They've never walked through a forest of wild orchids or witnessed the unfurling of five-foot-high ferns. "The only way I like my water is if there's whiskey in it," one rancher told me as we weaned calves in a driving rainstorm. That day we spent twelve hours on horseback in the rain. Despite protective layers of clothing: wool union suits, chaps, ankle-length yellow slickers, neck scarves and hats, we were drenched. Water drips off hat brims into your crotch; boots and gloves soak through. But to stay home out of the storm is deemed by some as a worse fate: "Hell, my wife had me cannin' beans for a week," one cowboy complained. "I'd rather drown like a muskrat out there."

Dryness is the common denominator in Wyoming. We're drenched more often in dust than in water; it is the scalpel and the suit of armor that make westerners what they are. Dry air presses a stockman's insides outward. The secret, inner self is worn not on the sleeve but in the skin. It's an unlubricated condition: there's not enough moisture in the air to keep the whole emotional machinery oiled and working. "What you see is what you get, but you have to learn to look to see all that's there," one young rancher told me. He was physically reckless when coming to see me or leaving. That was his way of saying he had and would miss me, and in the clean, broad sweeps of passion between us, there was no heaviness, no muddy residue. Cowboys have learned not to waste words from not having wasted water, as if verbosity would create a thirst too extreme to bear. If voices are raspy, it's because vocal cords are coated with dust. When I helped ship seven thousand head of steers one fall, the dust in the big, roomy sorting corrals churned as deeply and sensually as water. We wore scarves over our noses and mouths; the rest of our faces blackened with dirt so we looked like raccoons or coal miners. The westerner's face is stiff and dark red as jerky. It gives no clues beyond the discerning look that says, "You've been observed." Perhaps the too-early lines of aging that pull across these ranchers' necks are really cracks in a wall through which we might see the contradictory signs of their character: a complacency, a restlessness, a shy, boyish pride.

I knew a sheepherder who had the words "hard luck" tattooed across his knuckles. "That's for all the times I've been dry," he explained. "And when you've been as thirsty as I've been, you don't forget how something tastes." That's how he mapped out the big ranch he worked for: from thirst to thirst, whiskey to whiskey. To follow the water courses in Wyoming—seven rivers and a network of good-sized creeks—is to trace the history of settlement here. After a few bad winters the early ranchers quickly discovered the necessity of raising feed for livestock. Long strips of land on both sides of the creeks and rivers were grabbed up in the 1870s and '80s before Wyoming was a state. Land was cheap and relatively easy to accumulate, but control of water was crucial. The early ranches such as the Swan Land & Cattle Company, the Budd Ranch, the M-L, the Bug Ranch, and the Pitchfork took up land along the Chugwater, Green, Greybull, Big Horn, and Shoshone rivers. It was not long before feuds over water began. The old law of "full and undiminished flow" to those who owned land along a creek was changed to one that adjudicated and allocated water by the acre foot to specified pieces of land. By 1890 residents had to file claims for the right to use the water that flowed through their ranches. These rights were, and still are, awarded according to the date a ranch was established regardless of ownership changes. This solved the increasing problem of upstream-downstream disputes, enabling the first ranch established on a creek to maintain the first water right, regardless of how many newer settlements occurred upstream.

Land through which no water flowed posed another problem. Frank's father was one of the Mormon colonists sent by Brigham Young to settle and put under cultivation the arid Big Horn Basin. The twenty thousand acres they claimed were barren and waterless. To remedy this problem they dug a canal thirty-seven miles long, twenty-seven feet across, and sixteen feet deep by hand. The project took four years to complete. Along the way a huge boulder gave the canal diggers trouble: it couldn't be moved. As a last resort the Mormon men held hands around the rock and prayed. The next morning the boulder rolled out of the way.

Piousness was not always the rule. Feuds over water became venomous as the population of the state grew. Ditch riders—so called because they monitored on horseback the flow and use of water—often found themselves on the wrong end of an irrigating shovel. Frank remembers when the ditch rider in his district was hit over the head so hard by the rancher whose water he was turning off that he fell unconscious into the canal, floating on his back until he bumped into the next head gate.

With the completion of the canal, the Mormons built churches, schools, and houses communally, working in unison as if taking their cue from the water that snaked by them. "It was a socialistic sonofabitch from the beginning," Frank recalls, "a beautiful damned thing. These 'western individualists' forget how things got done around here and not so damned many years ago at that."

Frank is the opposite of the strapping, conservative western man. Sturdy, but small-boned, he has an awkward, knock-kneed gait that adds to his chronic amiability. Though he's made his life close to home, he has a natural, panoramic vision as if he had upped-periscope through the Basin's dust clouds and had a good look around. Frank's generosity runs like water: it follows the path of least resistance and, tumbling downhill, takes on a fullness so replete and indiscriminate as to sometimes appear absurd. "You can't cheat an honest man," he'll tell you and laugh at the paradox implied. His wide face and forehead indicate the breadth of his unruly fair-mindedness—one that includes not just local affections but the whole human community.

When Frank started irrigating there were no tarp dams. "We plugged up those ditches with any old thing we had—rags, bones, car parts, sod." Though he could afford to hire an irrigator now he prefers to do the work himself, and when I'm away he turns my water as well, then mows my lawn. "Irrigating is a contemptible damned job. I've been fighting water all my life. Mother Nature is a bitter old bitch, isn't she? But we have to have that challenge. We crave it and I'll be goddamned if I know why. I feel sorry for these damned rich ranchers with their pumps and sprinkler systems and gated pipe because they're missing out on something. When I go to change my water at dawn and just before dark, it's peaceful out there, away from everybody. I love the fragrances—grass growing, wild rose on the ditch bank—and hearing the damned old birds twittering away. How can we live without that?"

Two thousand years before the Sidon Canal was built in Wyoming, the Hohokam, a people who lived in what became Arizona, used digging sticks to channel water from the Salt and Gila rivers to dry land. Theirs was the most extensive irrigation system in aboriginal North America. Water was brought thirty miles to spread over fields of corn, beans, and pumpkins—crops inherited from tribes in South and Central America. "It's a primitive damned thing," Frank said about the business of using water. "The change from a digging stick to a shovel isn't much of an evolution. Playing with water is something all kids have done, whether it's in creeks or in front of fire hydrants. Maybe that's how agriculture got started in the first place."

Romans applied their insoluble cement to waterways as if it could arrest the flux and impermanence they knew water to signify. Of the fourteen aqueducts that brought water from mountains and lakes to Rome, several are still in use today. On a Roman latifundium—their equivalent of a ranch—they grew alfalfa, a hot-weather crop introduced by way of Persia and Greece around the fifth century B.C., and fed it to their horses as we do here. Feuds over water were common: Nero was reprimanded for bathing in the canal that carried the city's drinking water, the brothels tapped aqueducts on the sly until once the whole city went dry. The Empire's staying power began to collapse when the waterways fell into disrepair. Crops dried up and the water that had carried life to the great cities stagnated and became breeding grounds for mosquitoes until malaria, not water, flowed into the heart of Rome.

There is nothing in nature that can't be taken as a sign of both mortality and invigoration. Cascading water equates loss followed by loss, a momentum of things falling in the direction of death, then life. In Conrad's *Heart of Darkness*, the river is a redundancy flowing through rain forest, a channel of solitude, a solid thing, a trap. Hemingway's Big Two-Hearted River is the opposite: it's an accepting, restorative place. Water can stand for what is unconscious, instinctive, and sexual in us, for the creative swill in which we fish for ideas. It carries, weightlessly, the imponderable things in our lives: death and creation. We can drown in it or else stay buoyant, quench our thirst, stay alive.

In Navajo mythology, rain is the sun's sperm coming down. A Crow woman I met on a plane told me that. She wore a flowered dress, a man's wool jacket with a package of Vantages stuck in one pocket, and calf-high moccasins held together with two paper clips. "Traditional Crow think water is medicinal," she said as we flew over the Yellowstone River which runs through the tribal land where she lives. "The old tribal crier used to call out every morning for our people to drink all they could, to make water touch their bodies. 'Water is your body,' they used to say." Looking down on the seared landscape below, it wasn't difficult to understand the real and imagined potency of water. "All that would be a big death yard," she said with a sweep of her arm. That's how the drought would come: one sweep and all moisture would be banished. Bluebunch and June grass would wither. Elk and deer would trample sidehills into sand. Draws would fill up with dead horses and cows. Tucked under ledges of shale, dens of rattlesnakes would grow into city-states of snakes. The roots of trees would rise to the surface and flail through dust in search of water.

Everything in nature invites us constantly to be what we are. We are often like rivers: careless and forceful, timid and dangerous, lucid and muddied, eddying, gleaming, still. Lovers, farmers, and artists have one thing in common, at least—a fear of "dry spells," dormant periods in which we do no blooming, internal droughts only the waters of imagination and psychic release can civilize. All such matters are delicate of course. But a good irrigator knows this: too little water brings on the weeds while too much degrades the soil the way too much easy money can trivialize a person's initiative. In his journal Thoreau wrote, "A man's life should be as fresh as a river. It should be the same channel but a new water every instant."

This morning I walked the length of a narrow, dry wash. Slabs of stone, broken off in great squares, lay propped against the banks like blank mirrors. A sagebrush had drilled a hole through one of these rocks. The roots fanned out and down like hooked noses. Farther up, a quarry of red rock bore the fossilized marks of rippling water. Just yesterday, a cloudburst sent a skinny stream beneath these frozen undulations. Its passage carved the same kind of watery ridges into the sand at my feet. Even in this dry country, where internal and external droughts always threaten, water is self-registering no matter how ancient, recent, or brief.

LESLIE MARMON SILKO

Leslie Marmon Silko, a Laguna Pueblo Indian, was born in 1948. She attended law school but decided to become a writer. Her books include Laguna Woman *(1974),* Ceremony *(1977),* Storyteller *(1981), and* Almanac of the Dead *(1991). She received one of the first MacArthur Foundation fellowships, and lives in Tucson, Arizona.*

"I grew up at Laguna listening, and I hear the ancient stories, I hear them very clearly in the stories we are telling right now. Most important, I feel the power which the stories still have, to bring us together, especially when there is loss and grief." Silko manages to keep the tradition of storytelling alive, and the ways we all use it to define ourselves and our cultures, and, finally, our intentions, our politics.

STORYTELLER

Every day the sun came up a little lower on the horizon, moving more slowly until one day she got excited and started calling the jailer. She realized she had been sitting there for many hours, yet the sun had not moved from the center of the sky. The color of the sky had not been good lately; it had been pale blue, almost white, even when there were no clouds. She told herself it wasn't a good sign for the sky to be indistinguishable from the river ice, frozen solid and white against the earth. The tundra rose up behind the river but all the boundaries between the river and hills and sky were lost in the density of the pale ice.

She yelled again, this time some English words which came randomly into her mouth, probably swear words she'd heard from the oil drilling crews last winter. The jailer was an Eskimo, but he would not speak Yupik to her. She had watched people in other cells, when they spoke to him in Yupik he ignored them until they spoke English.

He came and stared at her. She didn't know if he understood what she was telling him until he glanced behind her at the small high window. He looked at the sun, and turned and walked away. She could hear the buckles on his heavy snowmobile boots jingle as he walked to the front of the building.

It was like the other buildings that white people, the Gussucks, brought with them: BIA and school buildings, portable buildings that arrived sliced in halves, on barges coming up the river. Squares of metal panelling bulged out with the layers of insulation stuffed inside. She had asked once what it was and someone told her it was to keep out the cold. She had not laughed then, but she did now. She walked over to the small double-pane window and she laughed out loud. They thought they could keep out the cold with stringy yellow wadding. Look at the sun. It wasn't moving; it was frozen, caught in the middle of the sky. Look at the sky, solid as the river with ice which had trapped the sun. It had not moved for a long time; in a few more hours it would be weak, and heavy frost would begin to appear on the edges and spread across the face of the sun like a mask. Its light was pale yellow, worn thin by the winter.

She could see people walking down the snow-packed roads, their breath steaming out from their parka hoods, faces hidden and protected by deep ruffs of fur. There were no cars or snowmobiles that day; the cold had silenced their machines. The metal froze; it split and shattered.

Oil hardened and moving parts jammed solidly. She had seen it happen to their big yellow machines and the giant drill last winter when they came to drill their test holes. The cold stopped them, and they were helpless against it.

Her village was many miles upriver from this town, but in her mind she could see it clearly. Their house was not near the village houses. It stood alone on the bank upriver from the village. Snow had drifted to the eaves of the roof on the north side, but on the west side, by the door, the path was almost clear. She had nailed scraps of red tin over the logs last summer. She had done it for the bright red color, not for added warmth the way the village people had done. This final winter had been coming even then; there had been signs of its approach for many years.

She went because she was curious about the big school where the Government sent all the other girls and boys. She had not played much with the village children while she was growing up because they were afraid of the old man, and they ran when her grandmother came. She went because she was tired of being alone with the old woman whose body had been stiffening for as long as the girl could remember. Her knees and knuckles were swollen grotesquely, and the pain had squeezed the brown skin of her face tight against the bones; it left her eyes hard like river stone. The girl asked once what it was that did this to her body, and the old woman had raised up from sewing a sealskin boot, and stared at her.

"The joints," the old woman said in a low voice, whispering like wind across the roof, "the joints are swollen with anger."

Sometimes she did not answer and only stared at the girl. Each year she spoke less and less, but the old man talked more—all night sometimes, not to anyone but himself; in a soft deliberate voice, he told stories, moving his smooth brown hands above the blankets. He had not fished or hunted with the other men for many years, although he was not crippled or sick. He stayed in his bed, smelling like dry fish and urine, telling stories all winter; and when warm weather came, he went to his place on the river bank. He sat with a long willow stick, poking at the smoldering moss he burned against the insects while he continued with the stories.

The trouble was that she had not recognized the warnings in time. She did not see what the Gussuck school would do to her until she walked into the dormitory and realized that the old man had not been lying about the place. She thought he had been trying to scare her as he used to when she was very small and her grandmother was outside cutting up fish. She hadn't believed what he told her about the school because she knew he wanted to keep her there in the log house with him. She knew what he wanted.

The dormitory matron pulled down her underpants and whipped her with a leather belt because she refused to speak English.

"Those backwards village people," the matron said, because she was an Eskimo who had worked for the BIA a long time, "they kept this one until she was too big to learn." The other girls whispered in English. They knew how to work the showers, and they washed and curled their hair at night. They ate Gussuck food. She lay on her bed and imagined what her grandmother might be sewing, and what the old man was eating in his bed. When summer came, they sent her home.

The way her grandmother had hugged her before she left for school had been a warning too, because the old woman had not hugged or touched her for many years. Not like the old man, whose hands were always hunting, like ravens circling lazily in the sky, ready to touch her. She was not surprised when the priest and the old man met her at the landing strip, to say that the old lady was gone. The priest asked her where she would like to stay. He referred to the old man as her grandfather, but she did not bother to correct him. She had already been thinking about it; if she went with the priest, he would send her away to a school. But the old man was different. She knew he wouldn't send her back to school. She knew he wanted to keep her.

He told her one time, that she would get too old for him faster than he got too old for her; but again she had not believed him because sometimes he lied. He had lied about what he would do with her if she came into his bed. But as the years passed, she realized what he said was true. She was restless and strong. She had no patience with the old man who had never changed his slow smooth motions under the blankets.

The old man was in his bed for the winter; he did not leave it except to use the slop bucket in the corner. He was dozing with his mouth open slightly; his lips quivered and sometimes they moved like he was telling a story even while he dreamed. She pulled on the sealskin boots, the mukluks with the bright red flannel linings her grandmother had sewn for her, and she tied the braided red yarn tassels around her

ankles over the gray wool pants. She zipped the wolfskin parka.
Her grandmother had worn it for many years, but the old man said
that before she died, she instructed him to bury her in an old black
sweater, and to give the parka to the girl. The wolf pelts were creamy
colored and silver, almost white in some places, and when the old lady
had walked across the tundra in the winter, she was invisible in the
snow.

She walked toward the village, breaking her own path through the
deep snow. A team of sled dogs tied outside a house at the edge of the
village leaped against their chains to bark at her. She kept walking,
watching the dusky sky for the first evening stars. It was warm and the
dogs were alert. When it got cold again, the dogs would lie curled and
still, too drowsy from the cold to bark or pull at the chains. She laughed
loudly because it made them howl and snarl. Once the old man had
seen her tease the dogs and he shook his head. "So that's the kind of
woman you are," he said, "in the wintertime the two of us are no
different from those dogs. We wait in the cold for someone to bring us
a few dry fish."

She laughed out loud again, and kept walking. She was thinking
about the Gussuck oil drillers. They were strange; they watched her
when she walked near their machines. She wondered what they looked
like underneath their quilted goose-down trousers; she wanted to know
how they moved. They would be something different from the old man.

The old man screamed at her. He shook her shoulders so violently that
her head bumped against the log wall. "I smelled it!" he yelled, "as soon
as I woke up! I am sure of it now. You can't fool me!" His thin legs
were shaking inside the baggy wool trousers; he stumbled over her boots
in his bare feet. His toenails were long and yellow like bird claws; she
had seen a gray crane last summer fighting another in the shallow water
on the edge of the river. She laughed out loud and pulled her shoulder
out of his grip. He stood in front of her. He was breathing hard and
shaking; he looked weak. He would probably die next winter.

"I'm warning you," he said, "I'm warning you." He crawled back
into his bunk then, and reached under the old soiled feather pillow for
a piece of dry fish. He lay back on the pillow, staring at the ceiling and
chewed dry strips of salmon. "I don't know what the old woman told
you," he said, "but there will be trouble." He looked over to see if she
was listening. His face suddenly relaxed into a smile, his dark slanty eyes

were lost in wrinkles of brown skin. "I could tell you, but you are too good for warnings now. I can smell what you did all night with the Gussucks."

She did not understand why they came there, because the village was small and so far upriver that even some Eskimos who had been away to school did not want to come back. They stayed downriver in the town. They said the village was too quiet. They were used to the town where the boarding school was located, with electric lights and running water. After all those years away at school, they had forgotten how to set nets in the river and where to hunt seals in the fall. When she asked the old man why the Gussucks bothered to come to the village, his narrow eyes got bright with excitement.

"They only come when there is something to steal. The fur animals are too difficult for them to get now, and the seals and fish are hard to find. Now they come for oil deep in the earth. But this is the last time for them." His breathing was wheezy and fast; his hands gestured at the sky. "It is approaching. As it comes, ice will push across the sky." His eyes were open wide and he stared at the low ceiling rafters for hours without blinking. She remembered all this clearly because he began the story that day, the story he told from that time on. It began with a giant bear which he described muscle by muscle, from the curve of the ivory claws to the whorls of hair at the top of the massive skull. And for eight days he did not sleep, but talked continuously of the giant bear whose color was pale blue glacier ice.

The snow was dirty and worn down in a path to the door. On either side of the path, the snow was higher than her head. In front of the door there were jagged yellow stains melted into the snow where men had urinated. She stopped in the entry way and kicked the snow off her boots. The room was dim; a kerosene lantern by the cash register was burning low. The long wooden shelves were jammed with cans of beans and potted meats. On the bottom shelf a jar of mayonnaise was broken open, leaking oily white clots on the floor. There was no one in the room except the yellowish dog sleeping in the front of the long glass display case. A reflection made it appear to be lying on the knives and ammunition inside the case. Gussucks kept dogs inside their houses with them; they did not seem to mind the odors which seeped out of the dogs. "They tell us we are dirty for the food we eat—raw fish and fermented meat. But we do not live with dogs," the old man once said. She heard voices in the back room, and the sound of bottles set down hard on tables.

They were always confident. The first year they waited for the ice to break up on the river, and then they brought their big yellow machines up river on barges. They planned to drill their test holes during the summer to avoid the freezing. But the imprints and graves of their machines were still there, on the edge of the tundra above the river, where the summer mud had swallowed them before they ever left sight of the river. The village people had gathered to watch the white men, and to laugh as they drove the giant machines, one by one, off the steel ramp into the bogs; as if sheer numbers of vehicles would somehow make the tundra solid. But the old man said they behaved like desperate people, and they would come back again. When the tundra was frozen solid, they returned.

Village women did not even look through the door to the back room. The priest had warned them. The storeman was watching her because he didn't let Eskimos or Indians sit down at the tables in the back room. But she knew he couldn't throw her out if one of his Gussuck customers invited her to sit with him. She walked across the room. They stared at her, but she had the feeling she was walking for someone else, not herself, so their eyes did not matter. The red-haired man pulled out a chair and motioned for her to sit down. She looked back at the storeman while the red-haired man poured her a glass of red sweet wine. She wanted to laugh at the storeman the way she laughed at the dogs, straining against the chains, howling at her.

The red-haired man kept talking to the other Gussucks sitting around the table, but he slid one hand off the top of the table to her thigh. She looked over at the storeman to see if he was still watching her. She laughed out loud at him and the red-haired man stopped talking and turned to her. He asked if she wanted to go. She nodded and stood up.

Someone in the village had been telling him things about her, he said as they walked down the road to his trailer. She understood that much of what he was saying, but the rest she did not hear. The whine of the big generators at the construction camp sucked away the sound of his words. But English was of no concern to her anymore, and neither was anything the Christians in the village might say about her or the old man. She smiled at the effect of the subzero air on the electric lights around the trailers; they did not shine. They left only flat yellow holes in the darkness.

It took him a long time to get ready, even after she had undressed for him. She waited in the bed with the blankets pulled close, watching him. He adjusted the thermostat and lit candles in the room, turning out the electric lights. He searched through a stack of record albums until he found the right one. She was not sure about the last thing he did: he taped something on the wall behind the bed where he could see it while he lay on top of her. He was shriveled and white from the cold; he pushed against her body for warmth. He guided her hands to his thighs; he was shivering.

She had returned a last time because she wanted to know what it was he stuck on the wall above the bed. After he finished each time, he reached up and pulled it loose, folding it carefully so that she could not see it. But this time she was ready; she waited for his fast breathing and sudden collapse on top of her. She slid out from under him and stood up beside the bed. She looked at the picture while she got dressed. He did not raise his face from the pillow, and she thought she heard teeth rattling together as she left the room.

She heard the old man move when she came in. After the Gussuck's trailer, the log house felt cool. It smelled like dry fish and cured meat. The room was dark except for the blinking yellow flame in the mica window of the oil stove. She squatted in front of the stove and watched the flames for a long time before she walked to the bed where her grandmother had slept. The bed was covered with a mound of rags and fur scraps the old woman had saved. She reached into the mound until she felt something cold and solid wrapped in a wool blanket. She pushed her fingers around it until she felt smooth stone. Long ago, before the Gussucks came, they had burned whale oil in the big stone lamp which made light and heat as well. The old woman had saved everything they would need when the time came.

In the morning, the old man pulled a piece of dry caribou meat from under the blankets and offered it to her. While she was gone, men from the village had brought a bundle of dry meat. She chewed it slowly, thinking about the way they still came from the village to take care of the old man and his stories. But she had a story now, about the red-haired Gussuck. The old man knew what she was thinking, and his smile made his face seem more round than it was.

"Well," he said, "what was it?"

"A woman with a big dog on top of her."

He laughed softly to himself and walked over to the water barrel. He dipped the tin cup into the water.

"It doesn't surprise me," he said.

"Grandma," she said, "there was something red in the grass that morning. I remember." She had not asked about her parents before. The old woman stopped splitting the fish bellies open for the willow drying racks. Her jaw muscles pulled so tightly against her skull, the girl thought the old woman would not be able to speak.

"They bought a tin can full of it from the storeman. Late at night. He told them it was alcohol safe to drink. They traded a rifle for it." The old woman's voice sounded like each word stole strength from her. "It made no difference about the rifle. That year the Gussuck boats had come, firing big guns at the walrus and seals. There was nothing left to hunt after that anyway. So," the old lady said, in a low soft voice the girl had not heard for a long time, "I didn't say anything to them when they left that night."

"Right over there," she said, pointing at the fallen poles, half buried in the river sand and tall grass, "in the summer shelter. The sun was high half the night then. Early in the morning when it was still low, the policeman came around. I told the interpreter to tell him that the storeman had poisoned them." She made outlines in the air in front of her, showing how their bodies lay twisted on the sand; telling the story was like laboring to walk through deep snow; sweat shone in the white hair around her forehead. "I told the priest too, after he came. I told him the storeman lied." She turned away from the girl. She held her mouth even tighter, set solidly, not in sorrow or anger, but against the pain, which was all that remained. "I never believed," she said, "not much anyway. I wasn't surprised when the priest did nothing."

The wind came off the river and folded the tall grass into itself like river waves. She could feel the silence the story left, and she wanted to have the old woman go on.

"I heard sounds that night, grandma. Sounds like someone was singing. It was light outside. I could see something red on the ground." The old woman did not answer her; she moved to the tub full of fish on the ground beside the workbench. She stabbed her knife into the belly of a whitefish and lifted it onto the bench. "The Gussuck storeman left the village right after that," the old woman said as she pulled the entrails from the fish, "otherwise, I could tell you more." The old woman's voice flowed with the wind blowing off the river; they never spoke of it again.

When the willows got their leaves and the grass grew tall along the river banks and around the sloughs, she walked early in the morning. While the sun was still low on the horizon, she listened to the wind off the river; its sound was like the voice that day long ago. In the distance, she could hear the engines of the machinery the oil drillers had left the winter before, but she did not go near the village or the store. The sun never left the sky and the summer became the same long day, with only the winds to fan the sun into brightness or allow it to slip into twilight.

She sat beside the old man at his place on the river bank. She poked the smoky fire for him, and felt herself growing wide and thin in the sun as if she had been split from belly to throat and strung on the willow pole in preparation for the winter to come. The old man did not speak anymore. When men from the village brought him fresh fish he hid them deep in the river grass where it was cool. After he went inside, she split the fish open and spread them to dry on the willow frame the way the old woman had done. Inside, he dozed and talked to himself. He had talked all winter, softly and incessantly, about the giant polar bear stalking a lone hunter across Bering Sea ice. After all the months the old man had been telling the story, the bear was within a hundred feet of the man; but the ice fog had closed in on them now and the man could only smell the sharp ammonia odor of the bear, and hear the edge of the snow crust crack under the giant paws.

One night she listened to the old man tell the story all night in his sleep, describing each crystal of ice and the slightly different sounds they made under each paw; first the left and then the right paw, then the hind feet. Her grandmother was there suddenly, a shadow around the stove. She spoke in her low wind voice and the girl was afraid to sit up to hear more clearly. Maybe what she said had been to the old man because he stopped telling the story and began to snore softly the way he had long ago when the old woman had scolded him for telling his stories while others in the house were trying to sleep. But the last words she heard clearly: "It will take a long time, but the story must be told. There must not be any lies." She pulled the blankets up around her chin, slowly, so that her movements would not be seen. She thought her grandmother was talking about the old man's bear story; she did not know about the other story then.

She left the old man wheezing and snoring in his bed. She walked through river grass glistening with frost; the bright green summer color was already fading. She watched the sun move across the sky, already lower on the horizon, already moving away from the village. She stopped by the fallen poles of the summer shelter where her parents had died. Frost glittered on the river sand too; in a few more weeks there would be snow. The predawn light would be the color of an old woman. An old woman sky full of snow. There had been something red lying on the ground the morning they died. She looked for it again, pushing aside the grass with her foot. She knelt in the sand and looked under the fallen structure for some trace of it. When she found it, she would know what the old woman had never told her. She squatted down close to the gray poles and leaned her back against them. The wind made her shiver.

The summer rain had washed the mud from between the logs; the sod blocks stacked as high as her belly next to the log walls had lost their square-cut shape and had grown into soft mounds of tundra moss and stiff-bladed grass bending with clusters of seed bristles. She looked at the northwest, in the direction of the Bering Sea. The cold would come down from there to find narrow slits in the mud, rainwater holes in the outer layer of sod which protected the log house. The dark green tundra stretched away flat and continuous. Somewhere the sea and the land met; she knew by their dark green colors there were no boundaries between them. That was how the cold would come: when the boundaries were gone the polar ice would range across the land into the sky. She watched the horizon for a long time. She would stand in that place on the north side of the house and she would keep watch on the northwest horizon, and eventually she would see it come. She would watch for its approach in the stars, and hear it come with the wind. These preparations were unfamiliar, but gradually she recognized them as she did her own footprints in the snow.

She emptied the slop jar beside his bed twice a day and kept the barrel full of water melted from river ice. He did not recognize her anymore, and when he spoke to her, he called her by her grandmother's name and talked about people and events from long ago, before he went back to telling the story. The giant bear was creeping across the new snow on its belly, close enough now that the man could hear the rasp of its breathing. On and on in a soft singing voice, the old man caressed the story, repeating the words again and again like gentle strokes.

The sky was gray like a river crane's egg; its density curved into the thin crust of frost already covering the land. She looked at the bright red color of the tin against the ground and the sky and she told the village men to bring the pieces for the old man and her. To drill the test holes in the tundra, the Gussucks had used hundreds of barrels of fuel. The village people split open the empty barrels that were abandoned on the river bank, and pounded the red tin into flat sheets. The village people were using the strips of tin to mend walls and roofs for winter. But she nailed it on the log walls for its color. When she finished, she walked away with the hammer in her hand, not turning around until she was far away, on the ridge above the river banks, and then she looked back. She felt a chill when she saw how the sky and the land were already losing their boundaries, already becoming lost in each other. But the red tin penetrated the thick white color of earth and sky; it defined the boundaries like a wound revealing the ribs and heart of a great caribou about to bolt and be lost to the hunter forever. That night the wind howled and when she scratched a hole through the heavy frost on the inside of the window, she could see nothing but the impenetrable white; whether it was blowing snow or snow that had drifted as high as the house, she did not know.

It had come down suddenly, and she stood with her back to the wind looking at the river, its smoky water clotted with ice. The wind had blown the snow over the frozen river, hiding thin blue streaks where fast water ran under ice translucent and fragile as memory. But she could see shadows of boundaries, outlines of paths which were slender branches of solidity reaching out from the earth. She spent days walking on the river, watching the colors of ice that would safely hold her, kicking the heel of her boot into the snow crust, listening for a solid sound. When she could feel the paths through the soles of her feet, she went to the middle of the river where the fast gray water churned under a thin pane of ice. She looked back. On the river bank in the distance she could see the red tin nailed to the log house, something not swallowed up by the

heavy white belly of the sky or caught in the folds of the frozen earth.
It was time.

The wolverine fur around the hood of her parka was white with the
frost from her breathing. The warmth inside the store melted it, and she
felt tiny drops of water on her face. The storeman came in from the
back room. She unzipped the parka and stood by the oil stove. She
didn't look at him, but stared instead at the yellowish dog, covered with
scabs of matted hair, sleeping in front of the stove. She thought of the
Gussuck's picture, taped on the wall above the bed and she laughed out
loud. The sound of her laughter was piercing; the yellow dog jumped
to its feet and the hair bristled down its back. The storeman was watching her. She wanted to laugh again because he didn't know about the
ice. He did not know that it was prowling the earth, or that it had
already pushed its way into the sky to seize the sun. She sat down in
the chair by the stove and shook her long hair loose. He was like a dog
tied up all winter, watching while the others got fed. He remembered
how she had gone with the oil drillers, and his blue eyes moved like
flies crawling over her body. He held his thin pale lips like he wanted
to spit on her. He hated the people because they had something of value,
the old man said, something which the Gussucks could never have. They
thought they could take it, suck it out of the earth or cut it from the
mountains; but they were fools.

There was a matted hunk of dog hair on the floor by her foot. She
thought of the yellow insulation coming unstuffed: their defense against
the freezing going to pieces as it advanced on them. The ice was crouching on the northwest horizon like the old man's bear. She laughed out
loud again. The sun would be down now; it was time.

The first time he spoke to her, she did not hear what he said, so
she did not answer or even look up at him. He spoke to her again but
his words were only noises coming from his pale mouth, trembling now
as his anger began to unravel. He jerked her up and the chair fell over
behind her. His arms were shaking and she could feel his hands tense
up, pulling the edges of the parka tighter. He raised his fist to hit her,
his thin body quivering with rage; but the fist collapsed with the desire
he had for the valuable things, which, the old man had rightly said, was
the only reason they came. She could hear his heart pounding as he held
her close and arched his hips against her, groaning and breathing in
spasms. She twisted away from him and ducked under his arms.

She ran with a mitten over her mouth, breathing through the fur to protect her lungs from the freezing air. She could hear him running behind her, his heavy breathing, the occasional sound of metal jingling against metal. But he ran without his parka or mittens, breathing the frozen air; its fire squeezed the lungs against the ribs and it was enough that he could not catch her near his store. On the river bank he realized how far he was from his stove, and the wads of yellow stuffing that held off the cold. But the girl was not able to run very fast through the deep drifts at the edge of the river. The twilight was luminous and he could still see clearly for a long distance; he knew he could catch her so he kept running.

When she neared the middle of the river she looked over her shoulder. He was not following her tracks; he went straight across the ice, running the shortest distance to reach her. He was close then; his face was twisted and scarlet from the exertion and the cold. There was satisfaction in his eyes; he was sure he could outrun her.

She was familiar with the river, down to the instant ice flexed into hairline fractures, and the cracking bone-sliver sounds gathered momentum with the opening ice until the churning gray water was set free. She stopped and turned to the sound of the river and the rattle of swirling ice fragments where he fell through. She pulled off a mitten and zipped the parka to her throat. She was conscious then of her own rapid breathing.

She moved slowly, kicking the ice ahead with the heel of her boot, feeling for sinews of ice to hold her. She looked ahead and all around herself; in the twilight, the dense white sky had merged into the flat snow-covered tundra. In the frantic running she had lost her place on the river. She stood still. The east bank of the river was lost in the sky; the boundaries had been swallowed by the freezing white. But then, in the distance, she saw something red, and suddenly it was as she had remembered it all those years.

She sat on her bed and while she waited, she listened to the old man. The hunter had found a small jagged knoll on the ice. He pulled his beaver fur cap off his head; the fur inside it steamed with his body heat and sweat. He left it upside down on the ice for the great bear to stalk, and he waited downwind on top of the ice knoll; he was holding the jade knife.

She thought she could see the end of his story in the way he wheezed out the words; but still he reached into his cache of dry fish and dribbled water into his mouth from the tin cup. All night she listened to him describe each breath the man took, each motion of the bear's head as it tried to catch the sound of the man's breathing, and tested the wind for his scent.

The state trooper asked her questions, and the woman who cleaned house for the priest translated them into Yupik. They wanted to know what happened to the storeman, the Gussuck who had been seen running after her down the road onto the river late last evening. He had not come back, and the Gussuck boss in Anchorage was concerned about him. She did not answer for a long time because the old man suddenly sat up in his bed and began to talk excitedly, looking at all of them— the trooper in his dark glasses and the housekeeper in her corduroy parka. He kept saying, "The story! The story! Eh-ya! The great bear! The hunter!"

They asked her again, what happened to the man from the Northern Commercial store. "He lied to them. He told them it was safe to drink. But I will not lie." She stood up and put on the gray wolfskin parka. "I killed him," she said, "but I don't lie."

The attorney came back again, and the jailer slid open the steel doors and opened the cell to let him in. He motioned for the jailer to stay to translate for him. She laughed when she saw how the jailer would be forced by this Gussuck to speak Yupik to her. She liked the Gussuck attorney for that, and for the thinning hair on his head. He was very tall, and she liked to think about the exposure of his head to the freezing; she wondered if he would feel the ice descending from the sky before the others did. He wanted to know why she told the state trooper she had killed the storeman. Some village children had seen it happen, he said, and it was an accident. "That's all you have to say to the judge: it was an accident." He kept repeating it over and over again to her, slowly in a loud but gentle voice: "It was an accident. He was running after you and he fell through the ice. That's all you have to say in court. That's all. And they will let you go home. Back to your village." The jailer translated the words sullenly, staring down at the floor. She shook her head. "I will not change the story, not even to escape this place and go home. I intended that he die. The story must be told as it is." The attorney exhaled loudly; his eyes looked tired. "Tell her that she could not have killed him that way. He was a white man. He ran after her without a parka or mittens. She could not have planned that." He paused and turned toward the cell door. "Tell her I will do all I can for her. I will explain to the judge that her mind is confused." She laughed out loud when the jailer translated what the attorney said. The Gussucks did not understand the story; they could not see the way it must be told, year after year as the old man had done, without lapse or silence.

She looked out the window at the frozen white sky. The sun had finally broken loose from the ice but it moved like a wounded caribou running on strength which only dying animals find, leaping and running on bullet-shattered lungs. Its light was weak and pale; it pushed dimly through the clouds. She turned and faced the Gussuck attorney.

"It began a long time ago," she intoned steadily, "in the summertime. Early in the morning, I remember, something red in the tall river grass. . . ."

The day after the old man died, men from the village came. She was sitting on the edge of her bed, across from the woman the trooper hired to watch her. They came into the room slowly and listened to her. At the foot of her bed they left a king salmon that had been slit open wide and dried last summer. But she did not pause or hesitate; she went on with the story, and she never stopped, not even when the woman got up to close the door behind the village men.

The old man would not change the story even when he knew the end was approaching. Lies could not stop what was coming. He thrashed around on the bed, pulling the blankets loose, knocking bundles of dried fish and meat on the floor. The hunter had been on the ice for many hours. The freezing winds on the ice knoll had numbed his hands in the mittens, and the cold had exhausted him. He felt a single muscle tremor in his hand that he could not stop, and the jade knife fell; it shattered on the ice, and the blue glacier bear turned slowly to face him.

MARILYNNE ROBINSON

Marilynne Robinson was born in Sandpoint, Idaho, in 1944, and burst into the literary world with her first novel, Housekeeping *(1981), which won many accolades and awards, including the Rosenthal Foundation award and the Hemingway Foundation award. The novel was made into a fine film. Robinson is also the author of* Mother Country: Britain, the Nuclear State, and Nuclear Pollution *(1989), a nonfiction account of nuclear tragedy and cover-up. The mother of four sons, Robinson currently lives in Iowa City, Iowa, where she writes and teaches fiction at the Iowa Writer's Workshop.*

Things in Housekeeping *keep returning to water, to cold, immobilizing liquid. Wholly elemental, devoted to the senses, her novel, the opening of which follows, talks about a thing truly Western, the notion that loneliness is bearable, even sacred.* Housekeeping *tells us the story of a female Huck Finn living a woman's equivalent of "the cowboy way," and demonstrates the fear and scorn with which Western society has historically greeted wanderlust and itinerancy in self-sufficient women.*

FROM *HOUSEKEEPING*

I

My name is Ruth. I grew up with my younger sister, Lucille, under the care of my grandmother, Mrs. Sylvia Foster, and when she died, of her sisters-in-law, Misses Lily and Nona Foster, and when they fled, of her daughter, Mrs. Sylvia Fisher. Through all these generations of elders we lived in one house, my grandmother's house, built for her by her husband, Edmund Foster, an employee of the railroad, who escaped this world years before I entered it. It was he who put us down in this unlikely place. He had grown up in the Middle West, in a house dug out of the ground, with windows just at earth level and just at eye level, so that from without, the house was a mere mound, no more a human stronghold than a grave, and from within, the perfect horizontality of the world in that place foreshortened the view so severely that the horizon seemed to circumscribe the sod house and nothing more. So my grandfather began to read what he could find of travel literature, journals of expeditions to the mountains of Africa, to the Alps, the Andes, the Himalayas, the Rockies. He bought a box of colors and copied a magazine lithograph of a Japanese painting of Fujiyama. He painted many more mountains, none of them identifiable, if any of them were real. They were all suave cones or mounds, single or in heaps or clusters, green, brown, or white, depending on the season, but always snow-capped, these caps being pink, white, or gold, depending on the time of day. In one large painting he had put a bell-shaped mountain in the very foreground and covered it with meticulously painted trees, each of which stood out at right angles to the ground, where it grew exactly as the nap stands out on folded plush. Every tree bore bright fruit, and showy birds nested in the boughs, and every fruit and bird was plumb with the warp in the earth. Oversized beasts, spotted and striped, could be seen running unimpeded up the right side and unhastened down the left. Whether the genius of this painting was ignorance or fancy I never could decide.

One spring my grandfather quit his subterraneous house, walked to the railroad, and took a train west. He told the ticket agent that he wanted to go to the mountains, and the man arranged to have him put off here, which may not have been a malign joke, or a joke at all, since there are mountains, uncountable mountains, and where there are not mountains there are hills. The terrain on which the town itself is built is relatively level, having once belonged to the lake. It seems there was a time when the dimensions of things modified themselves, leaving a number of puzzling margins, as between the mountains as they must have been and the mountains as they are now, or between the lake as it once was and the lake as it is now. Sometimes in the spring the old lake will return. One will open a cellar door to wading boots floating tallowy soles up and planks and buckets bumping at the threshold, the stairway gone from sight after the second step. The earth will brim, the soil will become mud and then silty water, and the grass will stand in chill water to its tips. Our house was at the edge of town on a little hill, so we rarely had more than a black pool in our cellar, with a few skeletal insects skidding around on it. A narrow pond would form in the orchard, water clear as air covering grass and black leaves and fallen branches, all around it black leaves and drenched grass and fallen branches, and on it, slight as an image in an eye, sky, clouds, trees, our hovering faces and our cold hands.

My grandfather had a job with the railroad by the time he reached his stop. It seems he was befriended by a conductor of more than ordinary influence. The job was not an especially good one. He was a watchman, or perhaps a signalman. At any rate, he went to work at nightfall and walked around until dawn, carrying a lamp. But he was a dutiful and industrious worker, and bound to rise. In no more than a decade he was supervising the loading and unloading of livestock and freight, and in another six years he was assistant to the stationmaster. He held this post for two years, when, as he was returning from some business in Spokane, his mortal and professional careers ended in a spectacular derailment.

Though it was reported in newspapers as far away as Denver and St. Paul, it was not, strictly speaking, spectacular, because no one saw it happen. The disaster took place midway through a moonless night. The train, which was black and sleek and elegant, and was called the Fireball, had pulled more than halfway across the bridge when the engine nosed over toward the lake and then the rest of the train slid after it into the water like a weasel sliding off a rock. A porter and a waiter who were standing at the railing at the rear of the caboose discussing personal matters (they were distantly related) survived, but they were not really witnesses in any sense, for the equally sound reasons that the darkness was impenetrable to any eye and that they had been standing at the end of the train looking back.

People came down to the water's edge, carrying lamps. Most of them stood on the shore, where in time they built a fire. But some of the taller boys and younger men walked out on the railroad bridge with ropes and lanterns. Two or three covered themselves with black grease and tied themselves up in rope harnesses, and the others lowered them down into the water at the place where the porter and the waiter thought the train must have disappeared. After two minutes timed on a stopwatch, the ropes were pulled in again and the divers walked stiff-legged up the pilings, were freed from their ropes and wrapped in blankets. The water was perilously cold.

Till it was dawn the divers swung down from the bridge and walked, or were dragged, up again. A suitcase, a seat cushion, and a lettuce were all they retrieved. Some of the divers remembered pushing

past debris as they swam down into the water, but the debris must have
sunk again, or drifted away in the dark. By the time they stopped hoping
to find passengers, there was nothing else to be saved, no relics but three,
and one of them perishable. They began to speculate that this was not
after all the place where the train left the bridge. There were questions
about how the train would move through the water. Would it sink like
a stone despite its speed, or slide like an eel despite its weight? If it did
leave the tracks here, perhaps it came to rest a hundred feet ahead. Or
again it might have rolled or slid when it struck bottom, since the bridge
pilings were set in the crest of a chain of flooded hills, which on one
side formed the wall of a broad valley (there was another chain of hills
twenty miles north, some of them islands) and on the other side fell
away in cliffs. Apparently these hills were the bank of still another lake,
and were made of some brittle stone which had been mined by the
water and fallen sheerly away. If the train had gone over on the south
side (the testimony of the porter and the waiter was that it had, but by
this time they were credited very little) and had slid or rolled once or
twice, it might have fallen again, farther and much longer.

After a while some of the younger boys came out on the bridge
and began to jump off, at first cautiously and then almost exuberantly,
with whoops of fear. When the sun rose, clouds soaked up the light like
a stain. It became colder. The sun rose higher, and the sky grew bright
as tin. The surface of the lake was very still. As the boys' feet struck the
water, there was a slight sound of rupture. Fragments of transparent ice
wobbled on the waves they made and, when the water was calm again,
knitted themselves up like bits of a reflection. One of the boys swam
out forty feet from the bridge and then down to the old lake, feeling
his way down the wall, down the blind, breathless stone, headfirst, and
then pushing out from the foot. But the thought of where he was suddenly terrified him, and he leaped toward the air, brushing something
with his leg as he did. He reached down and put his hand on a perfectly
smooth surface, parallel to the bottom, but, he thought, seven or eight
feet above it. A window. The train had landed on its side. He could
not reach it a second time. The water bore him up. He said only that
smooth surface, of all the things he touched, was not overgrown or
hovered about by a cloud of something loose, like silt. This boy was an
ingenious liar, a lonely boy with a boundless desire to ingratiate himself.
His story was neither believed nor disbelieved.

By the time he had swum back to the bridge and was pulled up and had told the men there where he had been, the water was becoming dull and opaque, like cooling wax. Shivers flew when a swimmer surfaced, and the membrane of ice that formed where the ice was torn looked new, glassy, and black. All the swimmers came in. By evening the lake there had sealed itself over.

This catastrophe left three new widows in Fingerbone: my grandmother, and the wives of two elderly brothers who owned a dry-goods store. These two old women had lived in Fingerbone thirty years or more, but they left, one to live with a married daughter in North Dakota and the other to find any friends or kin in Sewickley, Pennsylvania, which she had left as a bride. They said they could no longer live by the lake. They said the wind smelled of it, and they could taste it in the drinking water, and they could not abide the smell, the taste, or the sight of it. They did not wait for the memorial service and rearing of the commemorative stone, when scores of mourners and sightseers, led by three officers of the railroad, walked out on the bridge between handrails mounted for the occasion, and dropped wreaths on the ice.

It is true that one is always aware of the lake in Fingerbone, or the deeps of the lake, the lightless, airless waters below. When the ground is plowed in the spring, cut and laid open, what exhales from the furrows but that same, sharp, watery smell. The wind is watery, and all the pumps and creeks and ditches smell of water unalloyed by any other element. At the foundation is the old lake, which is smothered and nameless and altogether black. Then there is Fingerbone, the lake of charts and photographs, which is permeated by sunlight and sustains green life and innumerable fish, and in which one can look down in the shadow of a dock and see stony, earthy bottom, more or less as one sees dry ground. And above that, the lake that rises in the spring and turns the grass dark and coarse as reeds. And above that the water suspended in sunlight, sharp as the breath of an animal, which brims inside this circle of mountains.

It seems that my grandmother did not consider leaving. She had lived her whole life in Fingerbone. And though she never spoke of it, and no doubt seldom thought of it, she was a religious woman. That is to say that she conceived of life as a road down which one traveled, an easy enough road through a broad country, and that one's destination was there from the very beginning, a measured distance away, standing in the ordinary light like some plain house where one went in and was greeted by respectable people and was shown to a room where everything one had ever lost or put aside was gathered together, waiting. She accepted the idea that at some time she and my grandfather would meet and take up their lives again, without the worry of money, in a milder climate. She hoped that he would somehow have acquired a little more stability and common sense. With him this had so far not been an effect of age, and she distrusted the idea of transfiguration. The bitter thing about his death, since she had a house and a pension and the children were almost grown, was that it seemed to her a kind of defection, not altogether unanticipated. How many times had she waked in the morning to find him gone? And sometimes for whole days he would walk around singing to himself in a thin voice, and speak to her and his children as a very civil man would speak to strangers. And now he had vanished finally. When they were reunited, she hoped he would be changed, substantially changed, but she did not set her heart on it. Musing thus, she set out upon her widowhood, and became altogether as good a widow as she had been a wife.

After their father's death, the girls hovered around her, watched everything she did, followed her through the house, got in her way. Molly was sixteen that winter; Helen, my mother, was fifteen; and Sylvie was thirteen. When their mother sat down with her mending, they would settle themselves around her on the floor, trying to be comfortable, with their heads propped against her knees or her chair, restless as young children. They would pull fringe off the rug, pleat her hem, pummel one another sometimes, while they talked indolently about school or worked out the endless minor complaints and accusations that arose among them. After a while they would turn on the radio and start brushing Sylvie's hair, which was light brown and heavy and hung down to her waist. The older girls were expert at building it into pompadours with ringlets at ear and nape. Sylvie crossed her legs at the ankles and read magazines. When she got sleepy she would go off to her room and take a nap, and come down to supper with her gorgeous hair rumpled and awry. Nothing could induce vanity in her.

When suppertime came, they would follow their mother into the kitchen, set the table, lift the lids off the pans. And then they would sit around the table and eat together, Molly and Helen fastidious, Sylvie

with milk on her lip. Even then, in the bright kitchen with white curtains screening out the dark, their mother felt them leaning toward her,
looking at her face and her hands.

Never since they were small children had they clustered about her
so, and never since then had she been so aware of the smell of their
hair, their softness, breathiness, abruptness. It filled her with a strange
elation, the same pleasure she had felt when any one of them, as a
sucking child, had fastened her eyes on her face and reached for her
other breast, her hair, her lips, hungry to touch, eager to be filled for a
while and sleep.

She had always known a thousand ways to circle them all around
with what must have seemed like grace. She knew a thousand songs.
Her bread was tender and her jelly was tart, and on rainy days she made
cookies and applesauce. In the summer she kept roses in a vase on the
piano, huge, pungent roses, and when the blooms ripened and the petals
fell, she put them in a tall Chinese jar, with cloves and thyme and sticks
of cinnamon. Her children slept on starched sheets under layers of quilts,
and in the morning her curtains filled with light the way sails fill with
wind. Of course they pressed her and touched her as if she had just
returned after an absence. Not because they were afraid she would vanish
as their father had done, but because his sudden vanishing had made
them aware of her.

When she had been married a little while, she concluded that love
was half a longing of a kind that possession did nothing to mitigate.
Once, while they were still childless, Edmund had found a pocket watch
on the shore. The case and the crystal were undamaged, but the works
were nearly consumed by rust. He opened the watch and emptied it,
and where the face had been he fitted a circle of paper on which he
had painted two seahorses. He gave it to her as a pendant, with a chain
through it, but she hardly ever wore it because the chain was too short
to allow her to look at the seahorses comfortably. She worried that it
would be damaged on her belt or in her pocket. For perhaps a week
she carried the watch wherever she went, even across the room, and it
was not because Edmund had made it for her, or because the painting
was less vivid and awkward than his paintings usually were, but because
the seahorses themselves were so arch, so antic and heraldic, and armored
in the husks of insects. It was the seahorses themselves that she wanted
to see as soon as she took her eyes away, and that she wanted to see
even when she was looking at them. The wanting never subsided until

something—a quarrel, a visit—took her attention away. In the same way her daughters would touch her and watch her and follow her, for a while.

Sometimes they cried out at night, small thin cries that never woke them. The sound would stop as she started up the stairs, however softly, and when she reached their rooms she would find them all quietly asleep, the source of the cry hiding in silence, like a cricket. Just her coming was enough to still the creature.

The years between her husband's death and her eldest daughter's leaving home were, in fact, years of almost perfect serenity. My grandfather had sometimes spoken of disappointment. With him gone they were cut free from the troublesome possibility of success, recognition, advancement. They had no reason to look forward, nothing to regret. Their lives spun off the tilting world like thread off a spindle, breakfast time, suppertime, lilac time, apple time. If heaven was to be this world purged of disaster and nuisance, if immortality was to be this life held in poise and arrest, and if this world purged and this life unconsuming could be thought of as world and life restored to their proper natures, it is no wonder that five serene, eventless years lulled my grandmother into forgetting what she should never have forgotten. Six months before Molly left she was already completely changed. She had become overtly religious. She practiced hymns on the piano, and mailed fat letters to missionary societies, in which she included accounts of her recent conversion and copies of two lengthy poems, one on the Resurrection and another on the march of Christ's legions through the world. I have seen these poems. The second speaks very warmly of pagans, and especially of missionaries, ". . . the angels come to roll away / The stone that seals their tomb."

Within six months Molly had arranged to go to China, to work for a missionary society. And even while Molly belabored the air with "Beulah Land" and "Lord, We Are Able," my mother, Helen, sat in the orchard talking softly and seriously to a certain Reginald Stone, our putative father. (I have no memory of this man at all. I have seen photographs of him, both taken on the day of his second wedding. He was apparently a pale fellow with sleek black hair. He appears at ease in his dark suit. Clearly he does not consider himself the subject of either photograph. In one he is looking at my mother, who is speaking to Sylvie, whose back is to the camera. In the other he appears to be grooming the dents in the crown of his hat, while my grandmother,

Helen, and Sylvie stand beside him in a row, looking at the camera.)
Six months after Molly left for San Francisco and thence for the Orient,
Helen had set up housekeeping in Seattle with this Stone, whom she
had apparently married in Nevada. My grandmother, Sylvie said, was
much offended by the elopement and the out-of-state marriage, and
wrote to tell Helen that she would never consider her genuinely married
until she came home and was married again before her mother's eyes.
Helen and her husband arrived by train with a trunk full of wedding
clothes, and with a box of cut flowers and champagne packed in dry
ice. I have no reason to imagine that my mother and father were ever
prosperous, and so I must assume that they went to some trouble
to salve my grandmother's feelings. And yet, according to Sylvie, they
did not spend twenty-four hours in Fingerbone. Relations must have
mended somewhat, however, because a few weeks later Sylvie, in a new
coat and hat and shoes, with her mother's best gloves and handbag and
valise, left for Seattle by train to visit her married sister. Sylvie had a
snapshot of herself waving from the door of the coach, sleek and young
and proper. As far as I know, Sylvie only came home once, to stand
where Helen had stood in my grandmother's garden and marry someone
named Fisher. Apparently no snapshots were made of this event.

One year my grandmother had three quiet daughters and the next
year the house was empty. Her girls were quiet, she must have thought,
because the customs and habits of their lives had almost relieved them
of the need for speech. Sylvie took her coffee with two lumps of sugar,
Helen liked her toast dark, and Molly took hers without butter. These
things were known. Molly changed the beds, Sylvie peeled the vegetables, Helen washed the dishes. These things were settled. Now and then
Molly searched Sylvie's room for unreturned library books. Occasionally
Helen made a batch of cookies. It was Sylvie who brought in bouquets
of flowers. This perfect quiet had settled into their house after the death
of their father. That event had troubled the very medium of their lives.
Time and air and sunlight bore wave and wave of shock, until all the
shock was spent, and time and space and light grew still again and nothing seemed to tremble, and nothing seemed to lean. The disaster had
fallen out of sight, like the train itself, and if the calm that followed it
was not greater than the calm that came before it, it had seemed so. And
the dear ordinary had healed as seamlessly as an image on water.

One day my grandmother must have carried out a basket of sheets
to hang in the spring sunlight, wearing her widow's black, performing

the rituals of the ordinary as an act of faith. Say there were two or three inches of hard old snow on the ground, with earth here and there oozing through the broken places, and that there was warmth in the sunlight, when the wind did not blow it all away, and say she stooped breathlessly in her corset to lift up a sodden sheet by its hems, and say that when she had pinned three corners to the lines it began to billow and leap in her hands, to flutter and tremble, and to glare with the light, and that the throes of the thing were as gleeful and strong as if a spirit were dancing in its cerements. That wind! she would say, because it pushed the skirts of her coat against her legs and made strands of her hair fly. It came down the lake, and it smelled sweetly of snow, and rankly of melting snow, and it called to mind the small, scarce, stemmy flowers that she and Edmund would walk half a day to pick, though in another day they would all be wilted. Sometimes Edmund would carry buckets and a trowel, and lift them earth and all, and bring them home to plant, and they would die. They were rare things, and grew out of ants' nests and bear dung and the flesh of perished animals. She and Edmund would climb until they were wet with sweat. Horseflies followed them, and the wind chilled them. Where the snow receded, they might see the ruins of a porcupine, teeth here, tail there. The wind would be sour with stale snow and death and pine pitch and wildflowers.

In a month those flowers would bloom. In a month all dormant life and arrested decay would begin again. In a month she would not mourn, because in that season it had never seemed to her that they were married, she and the silent Methodist Edmund who wore a necktie and suspenders even to hunt wildflowers, and who remembered just where they grew from year to year, and who dipped his handkerchief in a puddle to wrap the stems, and who put out his elbow to help her over the steep and stony places, with a wordless and impersonal courtesy she did not resent because she had never really wished to feel married to anyone. She sometimes imagined a rather dark man with crude stripes painted on his face and sunken belly, and a hide fastened around his loins, and bones dangling from his ears, and clay and claws and fangs and bones and feathers and sinews and hide ornamenting his arms and waist and throat and ankles, his whole body a boast that he was more alarming than all the death whose trophies he wore. Edmund was like that, a little. The rising of the spring stirred a serious, mystical excitement in him, and made him forgetful of her. He would pick up eggshells, a bird's wing, a jawbone, the ashy fragment of a wasp's nest. He would

peer at each of them with the most absolute attention, and then put
them in his pockets, where he kept his jack-knife and his loose change.
He would peer at them as if he could read them, and pocket them as if
he could own them. This is death in my hand, this is ruin in my breast
pocket, where I keep my reading glasses. At such times he was as forgetful of her as he was of his suspenders and his Methodism, but all the
same it was then that she loved him best, as a soul all unaccompanied,
like her own.

So the wind that billowed her sheets announced to her the resurrection of the ordinary. Soon the skunk cabbage would come up, and
the cidery smell would rise in the orchard, and the girls would wash and
starch and iron their cotton dresses. And every evening would bring its
familiar strangeness, and crickets would sing the whole night long, under
her windows and in every part of the black wilderness that stretched
away from Fingerbone on every side. And she would feel that sharp
loneliness she had felt every long evening since she was a child. It was
the kind of loneliness that made clocks seem slow and loud and made
voices sound like voices across water. Old women she had known, first
her grandmother and then her mother, rocked on their porches in the
evenings and sang sad songs, and did not wish to be spoken to.

And now, to comfort herself, my grandmother would not reflect
on the unkindness of her children, or of children in general. She had
noticed many times, always, that her girls' faces were soft and serious
and inward and still when she looked at them, just as they had been
when they were small children, just as they were now when they were
sleeping. If a friend was in the room her daughters would watch his face
or her face intently and tease or soothe or banter, and any one of them
could gauge and respond to the finest changes of expression or tone,
even Sylvie, if she chose to. But it did not occur to them to suit their
words and manners to her looks, and she did not want them to. In fact,
she was often prompted or restrained by the thought of saving this unconsciousness of theirs. She was then a magisterial woman, not only
because of her height and her large, sharp face, not only because of her
upbringing, but also because it suited her purpose, to be what she seemed
to be so that her children would never be startled or surprised, and to
take on all the postures and vestments of matron, to differentiate her life
from theirs, so that her children would never feel intruded upon. Her
love for them was utter and equal, her government of them generous
and absolute. She was constant as daylight, and she would be unremarked

as daylight, just to watch the calm inwardness of their faces. What was
it like. One evening one summer she went out to the garden. The earth
in the rows was light and soft as cinders, pale clay yellow, and the trees
and plants were ripe, ordinary green and full of comfortable rustlings.
And above the pale earth and bright trees the sky was the dark blue of
ashes. As she knelt in the rows she heard the hollyhocks thump against
the shed wall. She felt the hair lifted from her neck by a swift, watery
wind, and she saw the trees fill with wind and heard their trunks creak
like masts. She burrowed her hand under a potato plant and felt gingerly
for the new potatoes in their dry net of roots, smooth as eggs. She put
them in her apron and walked back to the house thinking, What have
I seen, what have I seen. The earth and the sky and the garden, not as
they always are. And she saw her daughters' faces not as they always
were, or as other people's were, and she was quiet and aloof and watch-
ful, not to startle the strangeness away. She had never taught them to
be kind to her.

A total of seven and a half years passed between Helen's leaving Fingerbone and her returning, and when she did finally return it was on a
Sunday morning, when she knew her mother would not be at home,
and she stayed only long enough to settle Lucille and me on the bench
in the screened porch, with a box of graham crackers to prevent conflict
and restlessness.

Perhaps from a sense of delicacy my grandmother never asked us
anything about our life with our mother. Perhaps she was not curious.
Perhaps she was so affronted by Helen's secretive behavior that even
now she refused to take notice of it. Perhaps she did not wish to learn
by indirection what Helen did not wish to tell her.

If she had asked me, I could have told her that we lived in two
rooms at the top of a tall gray building, so that all the windows—there
were five altogether, and a door with five rows of small panes—overlooked a narrow white porch, the highest flight of a great scaffolding of
white steps and porches, fixed and intricate as the frozen eke of water
from the side of a cliff, grainy gray-white like dried salt. From this porch
we looked down on broad tarpaper roofs, eave to eave, spread like somber tents over hoards of goods crated up, and over tomatoes and turnips
and chickens, and over crabs and salmons, and over a dance floor with
a jukebox where someone began playing "Sparrow in the Treetop" and
"Good Night, Irene" before breakfast. But of all this, from our vantage,

we saw only the tented top. Gulls sat in rows on our porch railing and peered for scavenge.

Since all the windows were in a line, our rooms were as light as the day was, near the door, and became darker as one went farther in. In the back wall of the main room was a door which opened into a carpeted hallway, and which was never opened. It was blocked, in fact, by a big green couch so weighty and shapeless that it looked as if it had been hoisted out of forty feet of water. Two putty-colored armchairs were drawn up in a conversational circle. Halves of two ceramic mallards were in full flight up the wall. As for the rest of the room, it contained a round card table covered with a plaid oilcloth, a refrigerator, a pale-blue china cupboard, a small table with a hotplate on it, and a sink with an oilcloth skirt. Helen put lengths of clothesline through our belts and fastened them to the doorknob, an arrangement that nerved us to look over the side of the porch, even when the wind was strong.

Bernice, who lived below us, was our only visitor. She had lavender lips and orange hair, and arched eyebrows each drawn in a single brown line, a contest between practice and palsy which sometimes ended at her ear. She was an old woman, but she managed to look like a young woman with a ravaging disease. She stood any number of hours in our doorway, her long back arched and her arms folded on her spherical belly, telling scandalous stories in a voice hushed in deference to the fact that Lucille and I should not be hearing them. Through all these tales her eyes were wide with amazement recalled, and now and then she would laugh and prod my mother's arm with her lavender claws. Helen leaned in the doorway, smiled at the floor, and twined her hair.

Bernice loved us. She had no other family, except her husband, Charley, who sat on her porch with his hands on his knees and his belly in his lap, his flesh mottled like sausage, thick veins pulsing in his temples and in the backs of his hands. He conserved syllables as if to conserve breath. Whenever we went down the stairs he would lean slowly after us and say "Hey!" Bernice liked to bring us custard, which had a thick yellow skin and sat in a copious liquid the consistency of eyewater. Helen was selling cosmetics in a drugstore, and Bernice looked after us while she was at work, though Bernice herself worked all night as a cashier in a truck stop. She looked after us by trying to sleep lightly enough to be awakened by the first sounds of fist fights, of the destruction of furniture, of the throes of household poisoning. This scheme worked, though sometimes Bernice would wake in the grip of some nameless alarm, run up the stairs in her nightgown and eyebrowless, and drub our windows with her hands, when we were sitting quietly at supper with our mother. These disruptions of her sleep were not less resented because they were self-generated. But she loved us for our mother's sake.

Bernice took a week off from work so that she could lend us her car for a visit to Fingerbone. When she learned from Helen that her mother was living, she began to urge her to go home for a while, and Helen, to her great satisfaction, was finally persuaded. It proved to be a fateful journey. Helen took us through the mountains and across the desert and into the mountains again, and at last to the lake and over the bridge into town, left at the light onto Sycamore Street and straight for six blocks. She put our suitcases in the screened porch, which was populated by a cat and a matronly washing machine, and told us to wait quietly. Then she went back to the car and drove north almost to Tyler, where she sailed in Bernice's Ford from the top of a cliff named Whiskey Rock into the blackest depth of the lake.

They searched for her. Word was sent out a hundred miles in every direction to watch for a young woman in a car which I said was blue and Lucille said was green. Some boys who had been fishing and knew nothing about the search had come across her sitting cross-legged on the roof of the car, which had bogged down in the meadow between the road and the cliff. They said she was gazing at the lake and eating wild strawberries, which were prodigiously large and abundant that year. She asked them very pleasantly to help her push her car out of the mud, and they went so far as to put their blankets and coats under the wheels to facilitate her rescue. When they got the Ford back to the road they thanked them, gave them her purse, rolled down the rear windows, started the car, turned the wheel as far to the right as it would go, and roared swerving and sliding across the meadow until she sailed off the edge of the cliff.

DAVID LONG

David Long was born in Massachusetts in 1948, but has lived in the
West for more than twenty-five years. A jazz aficionado and an oc-
casional musician, he studied poetry with Richard Hugo and received
an M.F.A. from the University of Montana in 1974. From his home
in Kalispell, Montana, Long has taught in the Montana Poets in the
Schools Program, at Flathead Valley Community College, and at the
University of Montana. Starting out as a poet, Long achieved success
with his collection of stories, Home Fires *(1982), which won the*
Saint Lawrence University prize for short fiction. A second collection,
The Flood of '64, *was published in 1987; a third,* Blue Spruce,
was published in 1994, and recently won the Rosenthal Foundation
award from the American Academy of Arts and Letters.

"Lightning," from Blue Spruce, *is prime evidence of the current*
movement in Western writing toward focusing on the complexities of
interpersonal relationships.

LIGHTNING

"Ivan, he won't do it," Gretchen said from the daybed. "Believe me,
he won't. He's going to let the damn place freeze. You go on up there.
While he's gone."

Now that she was like this—plainly crippled, no longer solely identifiable as his mother—Ivan didn't feel the fight so much, the natural
urge to dig his feet in. Ivan's wife, Phoebe, sat in the rocker by the east
window, one of her fingers stuck in the massive library book she'd been
reading to Gretchen. She straightened her neck and gave him a look:
Do what she's asking. How much can that hurt?

It was mid-November. Ivan and Phoebe had been at the ranch a
week. No one had begged them to come, but they'd come anyway—
Phoebe had talked to Gretchen on the phone, and gotten the sense, she
told Ivan, that things were *this close* to flying apart. So they'd driven up,
and were quartered in the log-walled room off the porch—it smelled of
chinking and forgotten chenille and a desiccated Airwick hanging from
the curtain rod. Ivan had been rising in the sharp cold each morning
and going out to work alongside his father. The tools felt remote in his

hands. *What am I doing here?* he kept thinking—open to evidence that
his father was gratified by his company. But Perry didn't oblige. A film,
a gray mood, had settled on everything. This had been the year of the
fires, dry smoky winds, two thin cuttings of hay. A few dozen Angus
dotted the middle pasture, as animated as glacial till. His father had sold
the herd down, Ivan saw—there'd be scarcely fifty calves in the spring.

Perry had been cooking the meals himself, and then he'd hired a
woman from up the road to come in, a Mrs. Ankli whom Ivan distantly
remembered, but this arrangement had barely lasted a month. Now
Phoebe had taken over the kitchen. "I'm sorry all this is getting dumped
on you," Ivan said. Phoebe shrugged it off. She threw on sweats, grabbed
her hair back in a ponytail, swamped out the worst of it, chewing sunflower seeds, giving off bursts of tuneless humming. After lunch she
tended Gretchen in the bathroom, guided her into the dayroom, fixed
the flotilla of pillows. Gretchen had lost interest in the stacks of novels
spilling from the shelves. "All I want is true stuff," she demanded.
Phoebe drove to town the second afternoon, returned with boxes of
groceries and a book called *Shackleton*. Gretchen inspected it and lay
back. Heroism in the Antarctic, feats of lunatic endurance—it would
do. She listened fiercely, not hectoring in the old way. She stared out
past the blowing yard, past the fences. Across the river the lodgepole
rose up, green-black and prickly, disappearing into the river.

Which thought had led her back to John Andrew? Ivan wondered
from the doorway—he'd been stopped, on his way outside, by the ca-
dences of Phoebe's reading voice.

Gretchen's eyes bore into him. She pressed him again, "Take care
of it, Ivan."

So Ivan took Perry's Jeep up to the hill cabin, banging over the
ruts and shale. The Jeep, too, had deteriorated. The gas pedal had been
replaced by a timber nail that caught in his boot sole. The roof crinkled,
lacquered over with duct tape. Ivan had watched the day go from pearly
to raw; a sleeting wind whipped at the grass. The one wiper made a
wan, jiggling pass across the windshield. No one, Ivan guessed—least of
all, Perry—had gone near the hill cabin since Ivan's brother, John Andrew, had forsaken it. Gretchen (she'd explained to Phoebe, but never
directly to Ivan) had been the only witness to his leaving. She'd been
awake one night in July, late, watching the northern lights while Perry
snored and twisted the bedclothes. Sleep came flukily, grudgingly—she
was stir-crazy, only her thoughts fatigued. So she'd seen John Andrew's

truck barrel down from the hill cabin, headlights out, a denser patch of dark careening across the curve of damp lawn, clipping a corner post without stopping—and only a tap of the brake lights at the cattle guard. "That was it," she'd told Phoebe. "That was his grand farewell. Not so much as a horn toot."

John Andrew's own family—Gala and their two girls—had departed early in May, as the greasy buds of the cottonwoods were finally snapping open, the low spots in the hayfields drying and spiking green. After that, the hill cabin became a hermitage, a welter of bad spirits. Ivan knew that in Perry's world you let a grown man alone with his hurt. He would have stayed away, electing to wait for John Andrew down at the main house each morning, then taking in the puffy face, the jerky drifting eyes, and saying no more than, "You ought to not be hitting it so hard, John." *Weren't they a pair,* Ivan thought. But Perry would shun the place itself, as well, Ivan knew. They'd left a taint on it, Gala and John Andrew.

Ivan nudged through the back door and regarded his brother's leavings. A congealed rancid smell rose off the shredded paper trash fouling the linoleum. A windowpane was smashed out above the sink; porkies had climbed the woodpile and scraped through the hole, ransacked the counters, chewed the rubber stripping off the icebox door—it hung open, the bulb blackened.

On the Hide-A-Bed in the front room lay a sleeping bag, shucked inside out—a child's bag, grimy flannel depicting pheasants and hunters. The bedroom door was pocked with boot-heel-shaped gouges. Ivan toed it open, thinking, *Here will be the mother lode,* but the room was empty and unremarkable, except for dents in the carpet where bureau and bedposts had rested, and a scattering of thin cloth strips. Kneeling, Ivan found these to be the scissored remnants of a summer dress. He should run a stream of gasoline through these rooms, he thought. He should stand out in the crushed shale and feel the front of his clothes bake.

Wouldn't a little joyful noise cut loose in his soul then?

But why be that way? You don't hate John Andrew, he reminded himself—actually it was Phoebe he heard. He drew a breath. He pulled the gloves from his vest pocket, thrust his hands in, wiggled down into the crawl space and crawled. He got Vise-Grips on the valve and shut the water off. Upstairs again, he bled the pipes, filled the toilet tank and traps with Zerex. He taped a square of masonite over the sink window, swept the miscellany into a box and carried it outside, dragged the dead fir limbs from the yard, and, bending, blowing, made a fire of that much.

Standing over it, the black smoke batted by the wind, he thought, *If a story can ruin you, can a story save you?*

His brother's unwound from this exact spot, this one chunk of sanctified earth: a grassy bench along the northwestern fence line, where Perry had gone as a ten-year-old to rain stones down on a bend in the West Fork, where he escaped to as a young married buck, so he could smoke and ruminate and still be within eyeshot of the clamorous, red-roofed house down among the cottonwood. Perry would never have explained this in straight language. But had he not led John Andrew and his bride Gala up here one day in April, pointed out the white-flagged stakes driven into the soft grass, had he not announced that he'd decided to build them a place of their own and this was where? Ivan could see Gala drinking in this news, sparkling—she would touch Perry on his bare forearm, lightly, offering surprise, though she wouldn't be surprised, because all things flowed to Gala. And John Andrew would have his usual nothing to say, his big square face projecting a bashful, manly satisfaction—Perry's number-one son caught in a shower of blessings.

In decent weather, you could see it all from here. Zigzagging, shaped like a child's drawing of lightning, Gretchen had once observed. (Like *which* child's? Ivan wondered.) It was river and foothills and bare-faced mountain on one side, road and government land on the other. Four old skinny homesteads wired together by Ivan's grandfather, worked since the 1950s by Perry and a succession of hands, men like Arch McPheeter—stocky, grousing old Albertan, dead of a stroke long ago now—then by the team of Perry and John Andrew, with various McKee and Santa boys at branding and haying. But the lower piece, sometimes called The Point—where the hypothetical lightning would come scorching down, a sweet cache of twenty-odd acres, out of the wind, thick with red willow and a few old cedars—had become, lately, the property of an orthodontist from Buena Vista, California. He'd strung electric fence around it, erected an unseemly stone and timber gate at the road, hung a sign reading El Rancho Suzette in corny wood-burnt script. Yet no one had consulted Ivan about this transaction. No one had explained why his father would suddenly divest himself of this parcel. Ivan had simply gone to the mail and discovered a check with a note from Perry stapled to it: *This is your part of what I got for the lower piece. I don't care what you do with it. P. W. C.*

In a proper world, Perry and Gretchen would have retired to the hill cabin, settling into what Perry called "his dotage," which only meant he would sleep an hour later and pretend to take orders from John Andrew. Gretchen would spoil her granddaughters at the Sperry Mall, now and then, and otherwise retreat to the cabin's sliver of loft and read herself into a state of grace. She'd be Perry's college girl again, his unexpected treasure. John Andrew and family, meantime, would assume the main house. Gala would insinuate her ownership, gradually, like a medicine time-released into the bloodstream—first the filigreed curtains would go; one by one, new avocado appliances would appear; Gretchen's words of wisdom *(If you want to cry, go in the bathroom and run the water.—E. Roosevelt)* would vanish from inside the cupboard doors, the yellowed Scotch tape effaced with a razor blade.

None of that would happen now.

In a slot in the hutch, Ivan had found the letters, addressed merely *Cook Ranch* in Gala's childish hand. *You realize there's still items John and I have to deal with, like it or not. Really, I just don't see how you can expect me to believe you don't know where he is . . .* pages of it. Ivan had folded them away, wishing he hadn't looked, wishing to remember Gala in her better days, sleek and smart-mouthed, trailing a fragrance that left him in a condition of heated wonderment. Hadn't they all taken to her, even Gretchen—especially, somehow, Gretchen?

Ivan had never known precisely whose idea that union had been —John Andrew's (because Gala was the shining daughter of a surgeon in Sperry, emblem of everything he felt lesser than, having been raised out, away), or Gala's (because John Andrew was as handsome as she was, and had no nonsense in him, no waffling, and because marrying him was a rebellion, yes, but one of the right dimension and heft). Maybe they'd loved each other. Early on, at least, before it had begun to cost.

But then, what did any of this matter? Gretchen, by reason of her illness, was beyond living in the hill cabin, anyway. The tingling along her arms had become, over many months, a heavy dead wasting. Her shoulders curled in. Her calves were like slivers of almond.

Who could you point at, who could you blame for that?

Perry had gone to town after lunch—salve and staples to pick up at Equity, a little banking.

"Look," Ivan had offered, "let me go and do that—what do you say?"

Perry cast him a soured look. "Can't wait to kite out of here again, that it?"

"No, look, Dad—" Ivan started in, felt a hot surge of embarrassment, and let it drop.

Some time after the stock sale, before Ivan and Phoebe arrived, Perry'd taken a fall. Barklike scab graced his cheekbone, and something was wrong with his hip. It surprised no one that Perry declined to have it looked at. All week, Ivan had watched him try not to gimp, seen him squeeze away the stab of pain with his left eye.

"How about stopping at the doctor's?" Ivan said.

Perry stood drinking his coffee, a sheen on his temples, his free hand balled under his arm. "No thanks," he said.

Now lights veered up the West Fork road. Ivan thought that the last thing he wanted was for his father to find him there in John Andrew's mess. But it was a Forest Service truck, not Perry's old brown LeSabre. It rumbled by, vanishing into the road cut.

The wind had ebbed and the sleet had become a fine listless snow. Ivan mushed his boot around in the ashes, scattered them. The yard light clicked on, glowed a deep salmon. Ivan went back to the kitchen, reached in and switched it off. He climbed into the Jeep, fired the engine, and pulled eagerly on the heater knob, which gave a quarter inch, but no more.

If his brother's story spooled out from this one point, so, too, did his. Picture the older boy groomed to be Perry, his fingertips dull with grease, his knuckles nicked and infected, the meat of his shoulders hard-packed from bucking bales, his lips as chapped and straight-lined as his father's. Then picture the other boy, Gretchen's by unspoken default, grilled on spelling words and quadratic equations, asked to scratch thirty lines a day in a private ledger, given Peterson's bird book in his stocking, where John Andrew found shells for his Remington . . . All of that, so that Ivan would wow them in the world-at-large. When he chafed under this regimen, Gretchen stood him back against the coat hooks in the mudroom. "I'm going to tell you something I shouldn't be telling you," she said. "I love both of you to pieces, but you're my smart one. You've got something he won't ever have. Choices, Ivan."

Yes, a feast of choices.

The fall John Andrew married Gala, Ivan inaugurated his five-year carom shot through the university. He took Business and Society, he took Introduction to Major Religious Texts, he took Civil War Battles,

Contemporary Social Problems, Soils. He ignored Perry's threats, assured Gretchen again and again that he was only a handful of credits from graduating. He thinned down, grew his hair. He tended bar, worked on a road crew out of Drummond one summer, sold fireworks, went door to door for the city directory. He missed a Thanksgiving, a Christmas. Then came four or five years when he wasn't home at all. He trailed a barmaid to Fort Collins, drifted east in the aftermath, Omaha, Milwaukee, then up through the hardwood country along Lake Superior, taking work when he found it, quitting without rancor a few weeks or months later. He would just not go in one morning—there would be nothing special about that day, no gripe or grinding hangover or anything to glorify as wanderlust. He'd just feel vaguely, sickeningly lost—as though he'd worn out his welcome.

The first time he saw Phoebe, she was at a round Formica table in the rear of the Ashland, Wisconsin, public library, teaching an older man in blue coveralls to read. Ivan couldn't say why he waited, why he followed her out onto Vaughn Avenue and down to a bakery, and stood watching her clutch a white sack of limpa bread to her chest—except that he'd already fallen in love. Compared to Gala, she was big and plain. Her hair hung. She had thick wrists and skin that blotched at the slightest irritation. It was idiotic. Yet, as near as he could pinpoint such a thing, his attraction had begun the moment he'd seen the man in coveralls shut his book, push his chair back, and say, with a shy bow, "Thank you again, miss."

And what words had rushed from Ivan's mouth so that Phoebe seated herself with him, in one of the booths across from the glass counters, accepting the first cup of coffee? How was it he'd managed to be right about her? "You were dazzled by my inner beauty," Phoebe kidded him whenever the subject arose.

"Uh-huh," Ivan answered. "That's what it was." But the memory terrified him. How can you trust yourself? How do you know to leap?

Lights came on outside the main house. Ivan ground the tires in the pea gravel and let the engine die. No, he did not hate his brother. They were too different for hatred, too ignorant of each other. John Andrew had been almost heedless of Ivan, hellbent on becoming the man he was supposed to become. Ivan, for his part, had fixed his eyes on John Andrew, year after year—he knew how his brother looked with a milk glass tipped to his mouth, or what he'd say when he jammed his feet into cold boots. Ivan could see as little as one wrist, flycasting, and know it was John Andrew's. But that was all he knew—he'd simply memorized John Andrew, the way he'd memorized the lay of the mountains, the river's quirks.

How weird it was, Ivan thought, climbing out, that John Andrew should take his place as the absent son.

Perry still wasn't back. Nonetheless it was dinnertime, and Gretchen was seated at the big table. Sara Dog, the asthmatic setter John Andrew had left behind, was working a path between the kitchen and the buffet, her nails clitter-clattering on the linoleum. Phoebe had tried a curry recipe —the pot had bubbled on low heat all afternoon. She'd put out glass dishes of coconut and peanuts and chopped eggs. She sat, finally, her ears flushed, a fine mist on her cheeks.

Having waited, Gretchen lifted a forkful to her lips, winced, but found it blander than she'd expected.

"What were you burning?" she asked Ivan.

How did she miss nothing, even now? He looked across at her— her hair was cut like a helmet, the color of galvanized nails. Though she'd been out of the sun for months her skin stayed olivy, buffed-looking. Rills of green vein branched across the backs of her hands.

"I just took care of it," Ivan said. "Isn't that what you wanted?"

His mother frowned, paused. "He was gone before he left," she said finally. "One night the two of them were outside at the table after supper, taking coffee, your father and John Andrew. Your brother had the white mug with the broken handle."

Despite himself, Ivan pictured it: the plank boards gone mealy with weather, the green-gold light splashing through the cottonwood leaves.

"They wouldn't look at each other. John Andrew had his hat off. He kept dragging his fingers over his scalp. Your father sat there rubbing his calluses."

She wasn't so much talking as reciting; Ivan knew enough not to interfere. "Your father got up and started for the Quonset, but he stopped and came over behind John Andrew and talked straight into his back. Then he left, and John Andrew didn't so much as take a breath until your father was out of sight, then—"

She turned her head in that way she had now, squeezing a cough from her throat. "Then looked after him—it was an awful, raw look,

Ivan. Like the earth had been cut into. Then he dragged himself back up to the hill cabin and there was only the mug sitting there on the table."

Another cough, two fingers pressed to her mouth. "It's still there. Right outside the window, Ivan. For a while, I couldn't look at it without thinking, John Andrew took that cup down from his lips."

"Oh, now, Gretchen——" Phoebe said.

"But you detach yourself," Gretchen went on. "You see things as they are. A cup sits out in the rain, it catches water. That's what you see."

She looked sharply out toward the kitchen where Sara Dog was wheezing and circling. "Lord, will you put her out," she told Ivan.

Ivan stood.

At the door, the dog swept through his legs, skidded on the glazed incline of Gretchen's ramp, and was gone. Ivan took a few steps into the empty drive. He found himself breathing a downdraft of wood smoke, staring up toward the bench where the hill cabin no longer floated in its pool of chemical light.

Back at the table, he saw Phoebe inspect Gretchen's mostly untouched plate.

"How'd you like some egg custard, Gretchen?" she asked. "I thawed out some raspberries. You don't mind, I hope."

Gretchen gave her daughter-in-law a puzzled, shaken look. Which, in turn, shook Ivan. When the two women were off in the dayroom, he thought, they seemed intimate—traffickers in state secrets. Now Gretchen looked as though she couldn't quite place this woman who'd been rummaging in her freezer.

"But we didn't pick this year," she said, and was quiet.

Ivan didn't know what to say.

Phoebe, finally, asked in a gentle voice, "Do you think we ought to see about Perry?"

Gretchen raised herself, imperial again. "He'll take care of himself," she said. "He's perfectly capable."

Ivan felt a slipping, a little crackle of fear. "Has he been going out like this? Has——"

Gretchen stared.

Okay, then, Ivan thought. *What do I know about any of this?*

He shoved his chair back, feeling Gretchen's eyes still trained on him, as if he were an object to study with an empty mind. A cup with a broken handle, collecting rain.

But an hour elapsed, and another. Sometime in the recent past, a satellite dish had been installed—it stood out in the grass by the pumphouse, aimed up toward the mouth of the valley. (Ivan and John Andrew had been raised on the one weak signal that straggled in from Sperry. Ivan had felt perennially out of it at school—"We don't get that," he was always saying.) Now Gretchen was tucked under her afghan, watching a show about the Amazon. A toothy native man was showing off an eighty-pound nugget of gold that God had allowed him to dig from the ground. Gretchen sat steely-eyed, her lips like rinds, but every minute or so her gaze veered up to the mantel clock.

Ivan couldn't bear it finally. He grabbed a coat from the mudroom and bolted out to the car—once outdoors, he realized, rooting madly in his pockets, that he only had keys for the Jeep, and thought, *Shit anyway*—but rather than go back, he slid in and pumped the nail sticking up through the floorboard. He backed around by the nine-bark, rattled out through the main gate, and followed the river in the direction of town. The headlights were caked with gumbo and issued barely a glow. He kept it floored anyway, hammering over the washboard, through puddles of wet, flattened leaves. Wasn't this asinine, to be out like this, his heart quailing? What did he expect to find, ominous tracks shooting off the embankment? His fingers were freezing, the rims of his ears. He knew this place, knew it the way he knew every old thought in his head. But it felt immensely foreign and chastening tonight, and Perry seemed the most inscrutable thing in it.

He slowed to a crawl, bumped onto a stretch of crumbled blacktop that announced the little settlement of Mullan's Crossing. The mercantile sat tall-fronted at the end of the road, flanked by cabins—dark as slabs of granite. Next door, at Reuben's, chimney smoke bent off toward the clouds.

Perry's car was nowhere in sight, but Ivan stepped onto the flat porch, and squinted through the fogged glass anyway. He saw, as he'd let himself hope, that Terri McKee was behind the bar. She was lost in a tattered paperback—one customer was asleep on his forearms, two others were throwing darts in back. No one he knew—and why should he anymore?

He let himself in.

Terri's head lifted, she recognized him instantly, came and flung her arms around his neck. "Ivan!"

Her hair was red, voluminously frizzed, but going to gray, seized up in two beaded barrettes. But she was still a skinny Minnie, Ivan saw—if he looked much longer, he might decide she couldn't keep any weight on. She and Ivan were old allies, fellow sufferers of the endless bus ride down the West Fork road. One spring they'd stolen a day to run the river, and their raft had dumped them into the roiling water at a narrowing called Sculley's Bend. Freezing, his chest heaving, Ivan found himself on the silted rocks, hugging Terri, kissing her face and eyes, her cold, freckled neck, holding her fiercely; it was their joke later, this sudden passion of Ivan's. Their one kiss. "It's okay," Terri had told him. "You were just amazed you were alive."

She had married straight out of high school; eighteen months later, her husband tripped a wire, walking patrol near An Loc.

Ivan pulled away. "You haven't seen my father?" he asked her.

"He was in here," Terri said. "You didn't pass him?"

Ivan felt a punch of relief, which immediately churned over into resentment.

"What'd he do to himself?" she asked.

"That?" Ivan said. "Fell."

"I mean he looked kind of—"

"I know."

Ivan unsnapped the jacket, which, he realized, was an old one of John Andrew's. It even smelled like him, like solvent or smoke.

"My dad didn't say I was home?" Ivan said.

Terri shook her head. "Not a word. You're the sweetest surprise. Sit, huh?" She gave his hand a pat. "I can't believe I almost missed you. We don't stay open winters anymore."

She'd married Leo Leveque a few years ago, Ivan remembered, the last son of the original Reuben—jowly, sad-looking, barely younger than Perry.

One of the men called from the back, but Terri ignored him. "We go down to see his daughters," she told Ivan. "I don't miss it up here. But then I do. Can't wait to get out, then I go kind of crazy."

She reached around to pour him a shot, hesitated. "Oh, hon, what was it you liked?" she asked.

"Anything's fine," Ivan said.

She leaned in. "How's your girl. You still in love—?"

Ivan flushed, sat finally, letting the relief he felt come ahead.

"Lucky boy."

He raced past the orthodontist's padlocked gate, drew alongside Perry's fence. Off in the dark, higher up, a pulse of yellow caught his eye, then was gone.

Ivan braked and swung onto the property, drove through the turn-around by the main house, and took the hill, his lights bouncing, dinging off the rocks and blowing weeds. He found his father's car, angled into the firs with its door open. Ivan shut it gently, and called out, "Dad?"

Off in back, by John Andrew's shed, he heard a plastic tarp crackling. He walked clear around the cabin, looking, and finally entered through the same door he'd locked that afternoon. He found Perry sitting on the Hide-A-Bed, smoking, his back to the doorway.

"It's me," Ivan said.

Perry made the springs creak, getting the weight off his bad hip. "Leave the lights out," he said.

"What's going on?" Ivan asked.

"She send you out prowling?"

Ivan didn't answer, but approached, waiting for the logic of this business to dawn on him. He could hear Perry's gravelly breathing, but not quite see how his eyes were.

"Why'd you sell that piece?" Ivan heard himself ask. It had not been on his mind to get into that, but there it was.

"What do you care?" Perry said, rolling his shoulders, stifling a grunt.

"You taking anything for that?" Ivan said.

His father mashed the cigarette into the jar lid in his other hand. He appeared to nod.

"That a yes or no?"

"Ivan," Perry said. "You want something to drink?"

"There's nothing."

But Perry said, "The deep freeze."

So Ivan returned to the kitchen, smelling the Pine-Sol he'd used on the countertops, and found a half-full bottle of vodka among the bags of shredded zucchini and freezer-burnt chicken parts Gala had left behind. He popped a wax paper cup from the dispenser by the sink, then another.

Perry drank off the inch or so Ivan gave him, and thrust out his cup for a refill. Ivan balked, but went ahead. He squatted to set the icy bottle on the floor. Perry lunged and grabbed a handful of sleeve, jerking Ivan's face down next to his own. "Where's he gone to?" Perry demanded. "Try and tell me you don't know."

"You're crazy," Ivan said, shaking free. "You think I've been sitting on that all week?" He felt himself careening. "You think he'd ever tell me anything? He didn't tell me a shitting thing."

"Don't talk that way," Perry said.

Ivan went on, a notch softer. "I'm just stating a fact. I'm the last one he'd come to."

Perry made a move to stand—without thinking, Ivan reached out to help, but Perry was past him and into the kitchen, rocking on the sides of his heels.

"I ought to burn all this," his father said.

Ivan had to laugh. "That was my thought," he said.

"It was you been in here?"

"I just picked it up some."

"I guess to Christ you must have."

"Let's just close it up again and go down," Ivan offered.

But Perry cleared his throat violently and spat into the sink. "You don't know what a black day it was he laid eyes on that girl," he said.

Ivan fished around in the shadow, found the back of a chair and sat. Perry's voice came at him through the dark; he pictured that scene his mother had described—Perry talking at the flat of John Andrew's back. "She got all she wanted," Perry said, "then she didn't want it. What kind of way is that? I don't blame her for getting itchy. You feel what you feel. You think your mother never got an itch. For God's sake, think how she feels now—can't hardly stand up. No, Ivan, I blame that girl for spoiling all this for him. She made him hate it. After that, everything was dead for him."

Overhead, fir boughs scraped on the ribs of the steel roof. Ivan thought of John Andrew drinking in the kitchen here and wondering who in hell he was anymore, every noise acute as a needleshaft—and then the shame and panic that must have come as he understood that despite its buildup of history, his life hadn't ever begun, not really. And Gala, too, before that, killing time in her own fashion, watching the girls, resigned, waiting for something, which turned out to be nothing more momentous than the onset of fair weather. None of it was a mystery, just what happens.

Ivan let the dog in. The TV was off, the fire reduced to dull coals. He opened the icebox and stared into it, wondering if he was hungry, then let the door drift closed. What he wanted was to be with Phoebe, lying down with his clothes off, rescued from thought.

Upstairs, he tapped at his mother's door, leaned in. She was in a flannel gown, a dense plaid, buoyed by pillows.

"Don't run off," she said.

Ivan edged in. He'd not been in their room in years. At the foot of the bed, he stood palming the bedpost, old walnut scored like a pineapple.

"He's sitting up there at the hill cabin in the pitch-dark," Ivan said.

Gretchen nodded without surprise.

Ivan wanted to say, I know how you miss John Andrew, but feared her face would snap to life: *No, you don't, how could you possibly know?*

Softly she asked, "Ivan, could you rub my feet?"

He didn't want to touch her. Yet he pulled up the quilt—her feet were encased in pale pink socks specked with shamrocks. Gingerly, he sank onto the comforter and began to knead, his thumbs on the soles, which seemed to radiate cold, even through the fabric.

In a moment his mother said, "At first I thought, *Maybe he'll call Ivan.*"

"John Andrew? You honestly—"

"No, no. I know he didn't."

"He never let loose of anything," Ivan said.

Gretchen seemed to smile. "That's so," she said. "Your father saw how it was all going wrong up there. He thought if John Andrew's money wasn't all tied up with ours, if he didn't have to wait for it. He thought if Gala had a place in town she'd be all right again—she could have that life and John Andrew could still do what he had to do, you see. Then that dentist had been pestering everyone up the road to sell him something on the river. So your father surveyed off that lower piece and cashed it out. I thought it would kill him. I thought it was the last thing on this earth he'd do."

Ivan stared at her.

"But then it didn't change a thing. It didn't make the slightest difference." She moistened her lips. "He thought he could stop the bleeding—that's how he talked about it. But you can't. I told him."

Ivan let his hands relax for a second. But she was right there, "No, Ivan, keep doing that. *Please.*"

Wind rattled the glass as Gretchen's eyes closed. His father had salvaged this bank of windows from a schoolhouse up the draw. Ivan remembered lifting them off the back of the truck, Perry on one side, himself and John Andrew on the other—hoisting them up to the new gabled room with ropes. Perry was smiling, clenching his cigarette in his teeth. Gretchen was up here, where the bed was now, watching, looking down at them, one summer's day.

"They come back on their own sometimes," Ivan said, but she was asleep.

He woke before dawn. Phoebe slept on her back, one hand cupped at her throat. Ivan touched the place on the flannel where her breast was and felt the nipple work its miracle. He found her ear in the muss of hair and whispered into it: "I love you, love you." Her hand slid down his cheek. Ivan swung his feet onto the rag rug and dressed.

The house was quiet. Lacing his boots, out in the kitchen, he saw that the brown Buick had been parked behind the Jeep—so Perry would be upstairs, consigned to sleep, Gretchen beside him.

He set up the coffeemaker, located an old sweater and jacket on a peg in the mudroom, and went outside.

A glaze lay on the fence rails, a wrinkle of ice on the stock pond, broken by a pair of gliding mallards. Ivan walked down to the hay barn and switched on the floodlight. He found gloves that Perry had wedged in the crotch of the timbers, and shook them out.

If there was an off-season, this was it. In a month they'd be kicking bales off the trailer, augering holes in the ponds. And, in another eight weeks, calves.

Ivan noticed that Perry had cut down the rope he and John Andrew had swung on, but a shiny groove still showed on the rafter. He smiled, and let the memory fall away.

An orange cat appeared between the bales. It jumped down and circled Ivan, rubbing hard against his legs.

PATTIANN ROGERS

Pattiann Rogers, born in Joplin, Missouri, in 1940, has taught and lived all over the country, from Austin to Montana to Vermont. She received a B.A. in literature (and a minor in zoology) from the University of Missouri, and an M.F.A. from the University of Houston. Her first book of poetry, The Expectations of Light *(1981), won the Roethke Prize. Since then she has published four more volumes, including* Splitting and Binding *(1989) and* Geocentric *(1993, Peregrine Smith Poetry Series).* Firestarter: New and Selected Poems *was published in 1994. A recipient of Guggenheim and Lannan Poetry fellowships, she is the mother of two grown sons. Except for the fall semester, when she teaches poetry at the University of Arkansas, she lives with her husband in Colorado.*

Rogers, one of the finest environmental poets in America, concerns herself with metaphysics and geophysics, with the dance of atoms and the music of the celestial spheres and flowers and butterflies. As in "A Passing" and "Why Lost Divinity Remains Lost," both from Geocentric, *Rogers's poetry is a hymn to the intricacies of the cosmos.*

A PASSING

Coyotes passed through the field at the back
of the house last night—coyotes, from midnight
till dawn, hunting, foraging, a mad scavenging,
scaring up pocket gophers, white-breasted mice,
jacktails, voles, the least shrew, catching
a bite at a time.

They were a band, screeching, yodeling,
a multi-toned pack. Such yipping and yapping
and jaw clapping, yelping and painful howling,
they *had* to be skinny, worn, used-up,
a tribe of bedraggled uncles and cousins
on the skids, torn, patched, frenzied
mothers, daughters, furtive pups

and, slinking on the edges, an outcast
coydog or two.

From the way they sounded they must have smelled
like rotted toadstool mash and cow blood
curdled together.

All through the night they ranged and howled,
haranguing, scattering through the bindweed and wild
madder, drawing together again, following
old trails over hillocks, leaving their scat
at the junctions, lifting their legs on split
rocks and witch grass. Through rough-stemmed
and panicled flowers, they nipped
and nosed, their ragged tails dragging
in the camphorweed and nettle dust.

They passed through, all of them, like threads
across a frame, piercing and pulling, twining
and woofing, the warp and the weft. Off-key,
suffering, a racket of abominables
with few prospects, they made it—entering
on one side, departing on the other.
They passed clear through and they vanished
with the morning, alive.

WHY LOST DIVINITY
REMAINS LOST

I look for it, but there are always
distractions—eleven magpies cawing, rocking,
crowded in one small-boned locust tree.

I search, but my concentration
is broken by the pattern of leaf shadows

moving on the wall, the fragrances of pine sugar,
sage, dry red grasses in the air.

I say prayers, but the evening thunder,
the gully wind . . . I have to stop
and check the sky.

Once I shouted the word, called out
across the field, "Divinity?"
But if there was an answer, five prairie dogs
rising on their haunches beside their mounds
at that moment to stare straight at me
took my attention completely.

Some holy men and some holy women
can sit on spires and nails and try
to remember for days at a time
without being distracted. Even that mountain goat
we saw yesterday appearing suddenly
out of the rocks on the edge of the cliff,
even her kid appearing just as suddenly
at her udder, couldn't cause those holy
ones to blink. But I don't know how
to know what they know.

I try to meditate. I try to set my mind
firmly on the task. Again, just devils
I suppose—the night that is nothing
soothing around my face, my hair,
and the stars, seeded by an uneven hand,
so profuse, so demanding, so clearly
insistent in their silence.

GARRETT HONGO

Garrett Hongo, born in Volcano, Hawaii, in 1951, grew up in Los Angeles, and was educated at Pomona College (B.A.) and the University of California at Irvine (M.F.A.). Since 1989, Hongo has been a professor and director of creative writing at the University of Oregon. His books of poetry include Yellow Light *(1982) and* The River of Heaven *(1988). He has had several plays produced, among them* Nisei Bar and Grill *(1976).* Volcano, *a memoir centered on going back to investigate the story of his family in Hawaii, was published in 1995, to critical acclaim.*

Hongo, an energetic man with obsessive passions and considerable political common sense, has labored for decades on behalf of Oriental and other minority writers, as can be seen in his work as an editor and anthologist in books that include Songs My Mother Taught Me *and* The Open Boat: Poems from Asian America *(1993). Those same concerns, reflecting both his Los Angeles upbringing and his Hawaiian-Japanese heritage, resonate in the poems here, from* Yellow Light. *Hongo says, "I wanted to become a doctor of pure magic." Or, we think, a poet who could help cure the world.*

YELLOW LIGHT

One arm hooked around the frayed strap
of a tar-black patent-leather purse,
the other cradling something for dinner:
fresh bunches of spinach from a J-Town *yaoya*,
sides of split Spanish mackerel from Alviso's,
maybe a loaf of Langendorf; she steps
off the hissing bus at Olympic and Fig,
begins the three-block climb up the hill,
passing gangs of schoolboys playing war,
Japs against Japs, Chicanas chalking sidewalks
with the holy double-yoked crosses of hopscotch,
and the Korean grocer's wife out for a stroll
around this neighborhood of Hawaiian apartments
just starting to steam with cooking

and the anger of young couples coming home
from work, yelling at kids, flicking on
TV sets for the Wednesday Night Fights.

If it were May, hydrangeas and jacaranda
flowers in the streetside trees would be
blooming through the smog of late spring.
Wisteria in Masuda's front yard would be
shaking out the long tresses of its purple hair.
Maybe mosquitoes, moths, a few orange butterflies
settling on the lattice of monkey flowers
tangled in chain-link fences by the trash.

But this is October, and Los Angeles
seethes like a billboard under twilight.
From used-car lots and the movie houses uptown,
long silver sticks of light probe the sky.
From the Miracle Mile, whole freeways away,
a brilliant fluorescence breaks out
and makes war with the dim squares
of yellow kitchen light winking on
in all the side streets of the Barrio.

She climbs up the two flights of flagstone
stairs to 201-B, the spikes of her high heels
clicking like kitchen knives on a cutting board,
props the groceries against the door,
fishes through memo pads, a compact,
empty packs of chewing gum, and finds her keys.

The moon then, cruising from behind
a screen of eucalyptus across the street,
covers everything, everything in sight,
in a heavy light like yellow onions.

WHAT FOR

At six I lived for spells:
how a few Hawaiian words could call
up the rain, could hymn like the sea
in the long swirl of chambers
curling in the nautilus of a shell,
how Amida's ballads of the Buddhaland
in the drone of the priest's liturgy
could conjure money from the poor
and give them nothing but mantras,
the strange syllables that healed desire.

I lived for stories about the war
my grandfather told over *hana* cards,
slapping them down on the mats
with a sharp Japanese *kiai*.

I lived for songs my grandmother sang
stirring curry into a thick stew,
weaving a calligraphy of Kannon's love
into grass mats and straw sandals.

I lived for the red volcano dirt
staining my toes, the salt residue
of surf and sea wind in my hair,
the arc of a flat stone skipping
in the hollow trough of a wave.

I lived a child's world, waited
for my father to drag himself home,
dusted with blasts of sand, powdered rock,
and the strange ash of raw cement,
his deafness made worse by the clang
of pneumatic drills, sore in his bones
from the buckings of a jackhammer.

He'd hand me a scarred lunchpail,
let me unlace the hightop G.I. boots,

call him the new name I'd invented
that day in school, write it for him
on his newspaper. He'd rub my face
with hands that felt like gravel roads,
tell me to move, go play, and then he'd
walk to the laundry sink to scrub,
rinse the dirt of his long day
from a face brown and grained as koa wood.

I wanted to take away the pain
in his legs, the swelling in his joints,
give him back his hearing,
clear and rare as crystal chimes,
the fins of glass that wrinkled
and sparked the air with their sound.

I wanted to heal the sores that work
and war had sent to him,
let him play catch in the backyard
with me, tossing a tennis ball
past papaya trees without the shoulders
of pain shrugging back his arms.

I wanted to become a doctor of pure magic,
to string a necklace of sweet words
fragrant as pine needles and plumeria,
fragrant as the bread my mother baked,
place it like a lei of cowrie shells
and *pikake* flowers around my father's neck,
and chant him a blessing, a sutra.

ROBERT WRIGLEY

*A native of southern Illinois, Robert Wrigley has spent the last twenty
years in the Northwest, mainly in Idaho and Montana. He studied
under Richard Hugo at the University of Montana, where he received
his M.F.A. and was the editor of* Cutbank *magazine. A two-time
winner of writing fellowships from the National Endowment for the
Arts, as well as a winner of two Pushcart prizes and a Guggenheim
fellowship in 1995, Wrigley has published four collections of poetry,
including* The Sinking of Clay City *(1979),* Moon in a Mason
Jar *(1986), and, most recently,* In the Bank of Beautiful Sins
*(1995). He is a professor of English and poet-in-residence at Lewis
and Clark State College in Lewiston, Idaho, not far from where he
lives with his wife, the writer Kim Barnes, and their children, at
Omega Bend in the canyon of the Clearwater River.*

In "Ravens at Deer Creek," from What My Father Believed
(1991), and in "Majestic," from In the Bank of Beautiful Sins
*(1995), Wrigley writes about men and animals and their fates; we're
incited to reimagine the ancient connections, and driven to pity and
fearfulness and, perhaps, reassurance.*

RAVENS AT DEER CREEK

Something's dead in that stand of fir
one ridge over. Ravens circle and swoop
above the trees, while others
swirl up from below, like paper scraps
blackened in a fire. In the mountains
in winter, it's true: death is a joyful flame,
those caws and cartwheels pure celebration.
It is a long, snowy mile I've come
to see this, thanks to dumb luck or grace.
I meant only a hard ski through powder,
my pulse in my ears, and sweat, the pace
like a mainspring, my breath louder and louder
until I stopped, body an engine
ticking to be cool. And now the birds.

I watch them and think, maybe I have seen
these very ones, speaking without words,
clear-eyed and clerical, ironic, peering in at me
from the berm of snow outside my window,
where I sprinkled a few crumbs of bread. We
are neighbors in the neighborhood of silence.
They've accepted my crumbs, and when the fire was hot
and smokeless huddled in ranks against
the cold at the top of the chimney. And they're not
without gratitude. Though I'm clearly visible
to them now, they swirl on and sing,
and if, in the early dusk, I should fall
on my way back home and—injured, weeping—
rail against the stars and the frigid night
and crawl a while on my hopeless way
then stop, numb, easing into the darkening white
like a candle, I know they'll stay
with me, keeping watch, moving limb to limb,
angels down Jacob's ladder, wise
to the moon, and waiting for me, simple as sin,
that they may know the delicacy of my eyes.

MAJESTIC

The only word for it, his white Lincoln's arc
from the crown of the downriver road
and the splash it bellied in the water.
Two other passersby and I waded out and pulled him
from the half-sunk wreck, the high collar
of his vestments torn away for breathing,
a rosary knotted in his left hand.
It's an endless wait for an ambulance
there, that serpentine road between distant towns,
night coming on, August, the rocks we laid him on
still fired by the sun. And so we came
to know one another, three living men
touching tenderly the dead one's body,
tending mouth and chest, making

a pillow for the head. He did not look,
we understood, like any man of God.
It was Roy, the mill-hand from Orofino,
who saw the tattoo first—no cross at all
but Christ Himself hung out, crucified
to the pale, hairless flesh by needles of India ink.
Jim, the prison guard, had seen it all in his time,
and looked up sweaty from the breath-kissed face
only long enough to say "Keep pumping."
I cupped my hands behind the doughy neck
to hold the airway straight and knew
as the others knew there was no point at all
for him in what we did. After a while
we just stopped, and Jim began to talk about time
and distance, the site of the nearest phone,
the speed of the first car he'd sent there.
Roy lit a cigarette, traced the flights of nighthawks,
and I waded back out to the Lincoln,
in the open driver's door
a little eddied lake of papers and butts,
where the river lapped the deep blue dash,
a sodden Bible and a vial of pills.
There was something we should say
for him, we must all have been sure,
for later on, when the lights came in sight
around the last downriver corner,
we gathered again at the body
and took one another's hands,
bowed, our eyes closed,
and said each in his turn
what we thought might be a prayer.
Something huge sliced through the air then,
but no one looked up,
believing owl, saying owl,
and at last opening our eyes
just as the day's final light ripened purple
and the black basalt we knelt on disappeared.
In that one moment, that second

of uncertainty, nothing shone
but the cold flesh of the priest,
and on the breast, almost throbbing
with the out-rushing dark—
the looming, hand-sized tattoo of Jesus
we could just as suddenly not see.
Bless the owl then, for passing
over once more and returning to us
the breathable air, the new, unspectacular night,
and the world itself, trailing beneath its talons,
still hanging on and making its bleats
and whimpers, before the noise
and the night above the river
swallowed it all.

ALBERTO RIOS

*Alberto Rios, born in 1952, is a native of Arizona and a recipient
of the Arizona Governor's Arts Award. He has received National
Endowment for the Arts and Guggenheim fellowships, and has won
four Pushcart prizes. His most recent book is* Teodoro Luna's Two
Kisses *(1990). Other books include* Whispering to Fool the Wind
(1982), Five Indiscretions *(1985),* The Lime Orchard Woman
(1988), The Iguana Killer *(1984), and* The Warrington Poems
(1989).

*Rios, one of the foremost authors in the recent emergence of Chi-
cano writing, is also recognized for his connections with Latin American
magic realism. In "The Secret Lion," from* The Iguana Killer, *Rios
remembers growing up, the innocence of unknowing, where young boys
find nature and call it heaven, call it good, only to find it's not a place
they can own, or even inhabit for long. It's a story about growing up
in the West, about a lesson learned, a paradise lost, a lion found.*

"THE SECRET LION,"
FROM *THE IGUANA KILLER*

I was twelve and in junior high school and something happened that we didn't have a name for, but it was there nonetheless like a lion, and roaring, roaring that way the biggest things do. Everything changed. Just that. Like the rug, the one that gets pulled—or better, like the tablecloth those magicians pull where the stuff on the table stays the same but the gasp! from the audience makes the staying-the-same part not matter. Like that.

What happened was there were teachers now, not just one teacher, teach-erz, and we felt personally abandoned somehow. When a person had all these teachers now, he didn't get taken care of the same way, even though six was more than one. Arithmetic went out the door when we walked in. And we saw girls now, but they weren't the same girls we used to know because we couldn't talk to them anymore, not the same way we used to, certainly not to Sandy, even though she was my neighbor, too. Not even to her. She just played the piano all the time. And there were words, oh there were words in junior high school, and we wanted to know what they were, and how a person did them— that's what school was supposed to be for. Only, in junior high school, school wasn't school, everything was backward-like. If you went up to a teacher and said the word to try and find out what it meant you got in trouble for saying it. So we didn't. And we figured it must have been that way about other stuff, too, so we never said anything about any- thing—we weren't stupid.

But my friend Sergio and I, we solved junior high school. We would come home from school on the bus, put our books away, change shoes, and go across the highway to the arroyo. It was the one place we were not supposed to go. So we did. This was, after all, what junior high had at least shown us. It was our river, though, our personal Mis- sissippi, our friend from long back, and it was full of stories and all the branch forts we had built in it when we were still the Vikings of Amer- ica, with our own symbol, which we had carved everywhere, even in the sand, which let the water take it. That was good, we had decided; whoever was at the end of this river would know about us.

At the very very top of our growing lungs, what we would do down there was shout every dirty word we could think of, in every combination we could come up with, and we would yell about girls, and all the things we wanted to do with them, as loud as we could—we didn't know what we wanted to do with them, just things—and we would yell about teachers, and how we loved some of them, like Miss Crevelone, and how we wanted to dissect some of them, making signs of the cross, like priests, and we would yell this stuff over and over because it felt good, we couldn't explain why, it just felt good and for the first time in our lives there was nobody to tell us we couldn't. So we did.

One Thursday we were walking along shouting this way, and the railroad, the Southern Pacific, which ran above and along the far side of the arroyo, had dropped a grinding ball down there, which was, we found out later, a cannonball thing used in mining. A bunch of them were put in a big vat which turned around and crushed the ore. One had been dropped, or thrown—what do caboose men do when they get bored—but it got down there regardless and as we were walking along yelling about one girl or another, a particular Claudia, we found it, one of these things, looked at it, picked it up, and got very very excited, and held it and passed it back and forth, and we were saying "Guythisis, this is, geeGuythis . . .": we had this perception about nature then, that nature is imperfect and that round things are perfect: we said "GuyGodthis is perfect, thisisthis is perfect, it's round, round and heavy, it'sit's the best thing we'veeverseen. Whatisit?" We didn't know. We just knew it was great. We just, whatever, we played with it, held it some more.

And then we had to decide what to do with it. We knew, because of a lot of things, that if we were going to take this and show it to anybody, this discovery, this best thing, was going to be taken away from us. That's the way it works with little kids, like all the polished quartz, the tons of it we had collected piece by piece over the years. Junior high kids too. If we took it home, my mother, we knew, was going to look at it and say "throw that dirty thing in the, get rid of it." Simple like, like that. "But ma it's the best thing I" "Getridofit." Simple.

So we didn't. Take it home. Instead, we came up with the answer. We dug a hole and we buried it. And we marked it secretly. Lots of secret signs. And came back the next week to dig it up and, we didn't know, pass it around some more or something, but we didn't find it. We dug up that whole bank, and we never found it again. We tried.

Sergio and I talked about that ball or whatever it was when we couldn't find it. All we used were small words, neat, good. Kid words.

What we were really saying, but didn't know the words, was how much that ball was like that place, that whole arroyo: couldn't tell anybody about it, didn't understand what it was, didn't have a name for it. It just felt good. It was just perfect in the way it was that place, that whole going to that place, that whole junior high school lion. It was just iron-heavy, it had no name, it felt good or not, we couldn't take it home to show our mothers, and once we buried it, it was gone forever.

The ball was gone, like the first reasons we had come to that arroyo years earlier, like the first time we had seen the arroyo, it was gone like everything else that had been taken away. This was not our first lesson. We stopped going to the arroyo after not finding the thing, the same way we had stopped going there years earlier and headed for the mountains. Nature seemed to keep pushing us around one way or another, teaching us the same thing every place we ended up. Nature's gang was tough that way, teaching us stuff.

When we were young we moved away from town, me and my family. Sergio's was already out there. Out in the wilds. Or at least the new place seemed like the wilds since everything looks bigger the smaller a man is. I was five, I guess, and we had moved three miles north of Nogales where we had lived, three miles north of the Mexican border. We looked across the highway in one direction and there was the arroyo; hills stood up in the other direction. Mountains, for a small man.

When the first summer came the very first place we went to was of course the one place we weren't supposed to go, the arroyo. We went down in there and found water running, summer rain water mostly, and we went swimming. But every third or fourth or fifth day, the sewage treatment plant that was, we found out, upstream, would release whatever it was that it released, and we would never know exactly what day that was, and a person really couldn't tell right off by looking at the water, not every time, not so a person could get out in time. So, we went swimming that summer and some days we had a lot of fun. Some days we didn't. We found a thousand ways to explain what happened on those other days, constructing elaborate stories about the neighborhood dogs, and hadn't she, my mother, miscalculated her step before, too? But she knew something was up because we'd come running into the house those days, wanting to take a shower, even—if this can be imagined—in the middle of the day.

That was the first time we stopped going to the arroyo. It taught us to look the other way. We decided, as the second side of sum-

mer came, we wanted to go into the mountains. They were still mountains then. We went running in one summer Thursday morning, my
friend Sergio and I, into my mother's kitchen, and said, well, what'zin,
what'zin those hills over there—we used her word so she'd understand
us—and she said nothingdon'tworryaboutit. So we went out, and we
weren't dumb, we thought with our eyes to each other, ohhoshe'strying-
tokeepsomethingfromus. We knew adult.

We had read the books, after all; we knew about bridges and castles
and wildtreacherousraging alligatormouth rivers. We wanted them. So
we were going to go out and get them. We went back that morning
into that kitchen and we said "We're going out there, we're going into
the hills, we're going away for three days, don't worry." She said, "All
right."

"You know," I said to Sergio, "if we're going to go away for three
days, well, we ought to at least pack a lunch."

But we were two young boys with no patience for what we thought
at the time was mom-stuff: making sa-and-wiches. My mother didn't
offer. So we got our little kid knapsacks that my mother had sewn for
us, and into them we put the jar of mustard. A loaf of bread. Knives-
forksplates, bottles of Coke, a can opener. This was lunch for the two
of us. And we were weighed down, humped over to be strong enough
to carry this stuff. But we started walking, anyway, into the hills. We
were going to eat berries and stuff otherwise. "Goodbye." My mom
said that.

After the first hill we were dead. But we walked. My mother could
still see us. And we kept walking. We walked until we got to where the
sun is straight overhead, noon. That place. Where that is doesn't matter;
it's time to eat. The truth is we weren't anywhere close to that place.
We just agreed that the sun was overhead and that it was time to eat,
and by tilting our heads a little we could make that the truth.

"We really ought to start looking for a place to eat."

"Yeah. Let's look for a good place to eat." We went back and forth
saying that for fifteen minutes, making it lunchtime because that's what
we always said back and forth before lunchtimes at home. "Yeah, I'm
hungry all right." I nodded my head. "Yeah, I'm hungry all right too.
I'm hungry." He nodded his head. I nodded my head back. After a good
deal more nodding, we were ready, just as we came over a little hill.
We hadn't found the mountains yet. This was a little hill.

And on the other side of this hill we found heaven.

It was just what we thought it would be.

Perfect. Heaven was green, like nothing else in Arizona. And it wasn't a cemetery or like that because we had seen cemeteries and they had gravestones and stuff and this didn't. This was perfect, had trees, lots of trees, had birds, like we had never seen before. It was like "The Wizard of Oz," like when they got to Oz and everything was so green, so emerald, they had to wear those glasses, and we ran just like them, laughing, laughing that way we did that moment, and we went running down to this clearing in it all, hitting each other that good way we did.

We got down there, we kept laughing, we kept hitting each other, we unpacked our stuff, and we started acting "rich." We knew all about how to do that, like blowing on our nails, then rubbing them on our chests for the shine. We made our sandwiches, opened our Cokes, got out the rest of the stuff, the salt and pepper shakers. I found this particular hole and I put my coke right into it, a perfect fit, and I called it my Coke-holder. I got down next to it on my back, because everyone knows that rich people eat lying down, and I got my sandwich in one hand and put my other arm around the Coke in its holder. When I wanted a drink, I lifted my neck a little, put out my lips, and tipped my Coke a little with the crook of my elbow. Ah.

We were there, lying down, eating our sandwiches, laughing, throwing bread at each other and out for the birds. This was heaven. We were laughing and we couldn't believe it. My mother *was* keeping something from us, ah ha, but we had found her out. We even found water over at the side of the clearing to wash our plates with—we had brought plates. Sergio started washing his plates when he was done, and I was being rich with my Coke, and this day in summer was right.

When suddenly these two men came, from around a corner of trees and the tallest grass we had ever seen. They had bags on their backs, leather bags, bags and sticks.

We didn't know what clubs were, but I learned later, like I learned about the grinding balls. The two men yelled at us. Most specifically, one wanted me to take my Coke out of my Coke-holder so he could sink his golf ball into it.

Something got taken away from us that moment. Heaven. We grew up a little bit, and couldn't go backward. We learned. No one had ever told us about golf. They had told us about heaven. And it went away. We got golf in exchange.

We went back to the arroyo for the rest of that summer, and tried to have fun the best we could. We learned to be ready for finding the grinding ball. We loved it, and when we buried it we knew what would happen. The truth is, we didn't look so hard for it. We were two boys and twelve summers then, and not stupid. Things get taken away.

We buried it because it was perfect. We didn't tell my mother, but together it was all we talked about, till we forgot. It was the lion.

JIMMY SANTIAGO BACA

Jimmy Santiago Baca, born in 1952, is a Chicano poet, essayist, playwright, and screenwriter from New Mexico. He has written several volumes of poetry, including Swords of Darkness *(1981),* Black Mesa Poems *(1989), and* Immigrants in Our Own Land *(1990). A collection of long poems,* Martín and Meditations on the South Valley *(1987), won an American Book Award. Baca also wrote and co-produced* Bound by Honor *(1992), a feature film depicting Hispanic gang culture in the barrios of East Los Angeles and the violent race relations among prisoners in California's federal prisons. He splits his time between Los Angeles and his home in Black Mesa, New Mexico.*

"Martín," from Martín and Meditations on the South Valley, *provides a slice of the Chicano experience as this manchild of urban blight yearns for a different West, a version more spiritual, more elemental, dedicated to social justice and freedoms.*

FROM "MARTÍN," IN *MARTÍN AND MEDITATIONS ON THE SOUTH VALLEY* [SECTION V]

Years pass.
Cattle cars in the downtown freightyard
squeal and groan, and sizzling grills

steam the Barelas Coffee House cafe windows,
as the railroad workers with tin hard hats
stop for coffee, hours of dawn
softly click on grandfathers' gold pocket watches
in Louey's Broadway Pawnshop, hocked
to get a cousin or brother out of jail.
City workers' tin carts and long-handled dust pans
clatter in curb gutters
as buses spew smoldering exhaust as they stop beneath
Walgreen's neon liquor sign.
I lean against an office building brick wall,
nothing to do, no where to go,
comb my hair in the blue tinted office windows,
see my reflection in the glinting chromed cars,
on a corner, beneath a smoking red traffic light,
I live—

> blue beanie cap snug over my ears
> down to my brow,

in wide bottomed jean pants trimmed with red braid,
I start my daily walk,

> to the Old Town Post Office,
> condemned Armijo school building,
> Río Grande playa,
> ditches and underpasses—

de-tribalized Apache
entangled in the rusty barbwire of a society I do not
understand,
Mejicano blood in me spattering like runoff water
from a roof canale, glistening over the lives
who lived before me, like rain over mounds of broken
pottery,
each day backfills with brown dirt of my dreams.

I lived in the streets,
slept at friends' houses, spooned
posole and wiped up the last frijoles with tortilla
from my plate. Each day
my hands hurt for something to have,
and a voice in me yearned to sing,

and my body wanted to shed the gray skin of streets,
like a snake that grew wings—
I wished I had had a chance to be a little boy,
and wished a girl had loved me,
and wished I had had a family—but these
were silver inlaid pieces of another man's life,
whose destiny fountained over stones and ivy
of the courtyard in a fairytale.

Each night I could hear the silver whittling blade
of La Llorona,
carving a small child on the muddy river bottom,
like a little angel carved into ancient church doors.
On Fridays, Jesus Christ appeared
on La Vega road, mounted on a white charger,
his black robe flapping in the moonlight
as he thrashed through bosque brush.
Sometimes Walleí, the voice of water, sang to me,
and Mectálla, who lives in the fire, flew in the air,
and Cuzál, the Reader of Rocks, spoke with a voice
jagged as my street-fighting knuckles.

A voice in me soft as linen
unfolded on midnight air,
to wipe my loneliness away—the voice blew open
like a white handkerchief in the night
embroidered with red roses,
waving and waving from a dark window
at some lover who never returned.

I became a friend of the old women
who hung out by the bars
on Central,
    Broadway,
    Isleta,
    and Barcelona,
blue tear drops tattooed on their cheeks,
initials of ex-lovers on their hands,
women drawn out from the dark piss-stinking rooms

they lived in,
by the powerful force of the moon,
whose yellow teeth tore the alfalfa out of their hearts,
and left them stubbled,
parched grounds old goats of Tecatos and winos
nibbled.

All my life the constant sound of someone's bootheels
trail behind me—thin, hard,
sharp sounds scraping frozen ground,
like a shovel digging a grave.
It's my guardian, following me through the broken branches
of the bosque, to the door
of the Good Sheperd Home on south 2nd. street,
for a hot meal.

RAY GONZALEZ

*Ray Gonzalez is the author of three books of poetry, including, most
recently,* The Heat of Arrivals *(1994), and a collection of essays,*
Memory Fever: A Journey Beyond El Paso Del Norte *(1993).
He is the editor of twelve anthologies, including* Currents from the
Dancing River: Contemporary Latino Writing *(1994),* Under
the Pomegranate Tree: Latino Erotica *(1995), and* This Is Not
Where We Began: Essays by Chicano Writers *(1994). He received a 1993 Before Columbus Foundation American Book Award
for excellence in editing.*

*Gonzalez has worked hard on behalf of other Chicano writers
(as can be seen in his work as an anthologist), and his poetry reflects'
their concerns. In both "Snakeskin (A Dream)," from* The Heat of
Arrivals, *and "Talk with the Priest," from* Twilights and Chants
*(1987), his Chicano heritage—the fusion of North American insights
and customs and imported European beliefs—creates a confusion of*

belonging, a confusion to be remedied through an embrace of nature,
through finding "new life in the green flesh of the world."

SNAKESKIN (A DREAM)

I thought the rattler was dead
and I stuck my finger in its mouth,
felt the fangs bite down,
penetrate me without letting go,
the fire removing my eyes,
replacing them with green light
of the reptile illuminating my hand.

It entered my bone and blood,
until my whole body was green and damp,
my whole left side turning
slick and cool as I tried
to pull it out of my body.

I peeled my skin back to find
my veins were green and held
tightly what I believed,
what forced itself into me,
what I allowed to be given
without knowing I carried that secret,

crawled over the ground,
became sinew the sun steps on.
I leaned against a huge boulder,
sweated, waited, slept,
and, by morning, found a new way
of embracing that rock,
new life in the green flesh of the world.

TALK WITH THE PRIEST

He says the mountains have changed.
The shadow of prayer now falls
off the wings of the canyons
to enter the mind like a bad dream,
like a lost man wandering
across *El Jornado del Muerto*,
the stretch of desert where
the secret well has never been found,
the water that trickles down the rocks
and seeps into the skeleton
of the mountain to retrieve
oaths from the dead.

He covers his face with a black hood
and points to the lightning
striking north of the mission,
miles from where we stand,
trying to find reasons for confession,
waiting for the desert to respond
to the electric sky by opening
new canyons in the mountains,
flash floods sweeping toward us.

His right hand cuts the air, as he blesses
me with the sign of the cross,
then closes the heavy doors of the mission.
I see my talk with the old one
will never confirm me,
and the confession will find me
on the other side of the flood,
beyond the land the priest
and his congregation claim
when the sun comes out to dry
the fresh wounds of running, muddy arroyos.

JAMES GALVIN

James Galvin, born in 1951, is the recipient of Guggenheim and National Endowment for the Arts fellowships, and has published four books of poetry: Imaginary Timber *(1980),* God's Mistress *(1984),* Elements *(1988), and* Lethal Frequencies *(1994). Galvin teaches poetry at the University of Iowa Writer's Workshop in Iowa City, where he received his M.F.A. and where he now lives with his wife, the Pulitzer prize–winning poet Jorie Graham, and their daughter, Emily.*

The Meadow (1992) is a book Galvin says he wrote for Emily, so she could have some idea of the world he grew up in and why he values what he values. It is a mixture of memoir and novelistic storytelling in which Galvin details for us his impressions of an isolated territory and a tiny but enduring community at Tie Siding, in the highlands on the Colorado/Wyoming border, a place to which, when he can, Galvin returns, a place where people are responsible for saving their own lives—to the degree that they can—over and over again. It seems to me to be one of the most emotionally accurate books ever written about the American West, and a dream of possibility.

WATER TABLE

How shy the attraction
of simple rain to east wind
on the dry east side
of the Neversummer Mountains.
Each afternoon clouds sidle in
just so, but rain is seldom.
Here what they call the water table
is more like a shooting star.
Streams that surface in the spring
are veins of fool's gold.
The water we count on
is run-off from high snows
gone underground.

The rest, the rain,
is a tinker's damn.

                              ★

My mother is favored
in being buried here, where she was born.
My father is from the east.
He tried to understand these hills
by building miles of roads and fences,
looking for water in unlikely places.
When we had enough fence
he kept building roads—
up canyons, through timber,
with axe and bar.
Sometimes he found old mining roads
unused in years.
Such innocence terrifies stones.

                              ★

Midyear,
if you drive on the pasture,
the grass won't spring back anymore,
so come September we saw the tracks
of everywhere he'd been since then.
To the rain it would have looked like a child's first attempt
to write his name.

Once he found an infant's grave
near a failed claim.
The writing on the stone
was also like a child's hand,
written by someone
who didn't know anything
about writing in stone.
It didn't say a name, it said,
She never knew a stranger.

Before the snow one September,
a man who lived here years ago

came to pay a visit.
He wore a white shirt,
sleeves rolled to the elbows,
and trousers the color of autumn grass.
He wouldn't come inside
or lean across the fence
the way a neighbor will.
He didn't care to stay,
although he'd lived here thirty years
and made this place from nothing
with his hands.

He showed my father a hidden spring
with fool's gold in the water.
He showed me how to use a witching-wand.
He said he mined for thirty years
and never found a thing worth keeping,
said the time to sink a well
is a dry year, in the fall.
The next we heard he'd died
somewhere west of here.
Then I had this dream:

*

In the driest month of a dry year
my father took it in his mind
to dig out fallow springs
all across the mountains.
He had roads to all of them.
He thought someone might be thirsty.
I asked how people stayed alive
before he came here
from the east.
He guessed they must have died.

*

I could say I understand
what goes on underground:
why all old men are miners

and children turn to gold-flecked water;
I could explain the weather,
like when the wind comes out of the east
and meets the simple rain.
The wind is strong.

The rain has slender shoulders.
The rain can't say
what it really means
in the presence of children
or strangers.

COMING INTO HIS SHOP FROM
A BRIGHT AFTERNOON

Like a local flurry or stars too small to use that spilled, iron
filings stain the dirt floor silver.
                          In the center of the floor,
the forge, in the center of the forge, the rose the bellows
angers.

He lights a cigarette on rose colored steel then hammers the
steel over the anvil's snout.
                          Red sprays of sparks splash from
each strike.
            One gummy, fly-specked window begins to allow a
sprawl of wrenches, brushes, punches, chisels, taps, gauges . . .

Coalsmell.
            Sweat.
                  The distant blue his eyes are.
                                          There is a lathe
and milling machine, both homemade from scraps.
                                          He chooses a
lighter hammer.

Now I can read the names on varnish cans and see
how the walls are layered under sawblades, snowshoes, an
airplane propeller, a loom.

On the other side of the door at my back, the
light I came in from grows white like a blizzard or hot steel.

Hammer blows ring across the meadow too much like bells.

He is

shaping a piece of earth.

He is hammering it into what he wants.
He thrusts it back into the fire when it loses its blush.

FROM *THE MEADOW*

App sits in the open doorway of the claim shack with his bum leg in
the sun, slowly rubbing it up and down and thinking. It is only the first
of March, but when the sun shines with no wind it is always hot. App
thinks his swollen, stiffened leg is like a tree trunk that the early spring
warmth will draw the sap up into.

As he sits in the doorway hour after hour he tries to make himself
remember only the good things, tries for a little warmth in his soul. He'd
started out pretty strong, as strong and capable as any man. He'd had a
beautiful young wife, a green mountain ranch, children, cattle, horses,
hay, and he'd lost it, or most of it, just by trying to hang on. He'd
married a second time, but the hard luck dogged him and the doctor
bills and lean years ended up taking everything he'd dreamed and found
and built, except for his three boys.

He tries to concentrate on the early days, before the run of hard
winters and disease. In those days he used to wake each morning feeling
completely indestructible. The good green memories, those warm winter
sunshine memories make him smile in the sunlight with his eyes closed,
and he can see the moving pictures of the times they made love down
by the flume he'd built to irrigate the patch of meadow on the far side
of the creek. Right out in the open sunshine in the greenness of all the
different kinds of grasses that still grew in that meadow. They could hold
hands and run buck naked through all that green with no way in hell
anyone was going to see them cutting up like damn fool kids. But it

was living that far away that killed her, App thinks, that sent her farther away yet, like she is now, only reachable in memories and dreams.

The smile has left his face and he opens his eyes and looks down at the lumber his leg has become, sticking out the front door into the barren sunshine, and he looks down at the legs of his wooden chair sunk slightly into the dirt floor of the claim shack that isn't his, that is built on a strip of land between two borders that two states refused to claim, and he thinks of the cold cellar dark out back, hung with jerked venison, and with a small hill of blind potatoes. He bakes six each morning in the coals of the heater and gives two to each of his boys as they leave in the Model-T for school, to warm their hands until they get there and to eat for lunch.

Suddenly a little breeze picks up and makes App shiver, then a small cloud covers the sun and chills him through. He starts to think of the time on Sheep Creek when he told Marie to wait supper for him, when three feet of snow had fallen during the night and it was just the end of October. He still had cows up near Bull Mountain. Most of them were smart enough to come down when it snowed, but not all. He decided to ride out and bring the stragglers down.

The horse's belly dragged in the snow, but it was a light, dry powder. The horse was strong and plowed through the drifts with his head down like a doubtless pilgrim. App's boots were making their own runnels alongside the horse's big furrow. The weather seemed like it would hold clear and cold, and he didn't notice that his feet were frozen by the time he made it up to the big meadow on Sand Creek where he expected to find his strays. They were nowhere to be seen so he pushed on when he should have turned home. His legs were numb all the way to his knees before he realized they were cold. So intent had he been, scanning the hypnotic white ridges and draws for his stock, that it was near dark before he knew that he'd gone too far, that he was in trouble.

His horse was still strong, but they were too far from any timber to build a fire, the snow was deep, and he could not feel anything from the waist down.

He rode into an arroyo and up the other side. He saw a young antelope, not yet a yearling, separated from the herd somehow, standing above him on a high spot of ground. She was unable to go anywhere, unable to reach the grass beneath the snow anymore, so played out and exposed that she just stood there shivering like a wet dog on the back porch, looking right at App, too tuckered out to run or show any fear.

App rode slowly up to the antelope child. Since he could not dismount any more than the antelope could run, he dropped the loop of his lariat over the antelope's neck and hoisted her up onto the saddle and laid her across his legs like a lamb. Then he turned his horse for home. His legs thawed out some because of the critter on his saddle, and the antelope decided she liked it better where she was now than where she was before. She never struggled when App carried her into the house after midnight and laid her in his wife's lap.

The antelope that App figured had saved his life got named Misty. She hardly went out of the cabin that winter, but lapped up pans of sugared milk and ate hay from Marie's hand. Misty slept on a blanket next to the stove. By spring she was going outside to graze on the new shoots of grass making their way up through the sagebrush, and she knew to come when called by name.

That summer they left her outside nights. She'd bed down and disappear in the sage until Marie said her name. Then she'd spring up, long-legged and skittish, and bounce up to lick the salt from Marie's palm.

When the antelope herded up that fall, App wondered what Misty would do. She went with them. One morning the following summer, though, Marie said an antelope ewe with twins at her side came strangely near the cabin, sniffed, and kind of perked up when Marie called "Misty" and held out her hand. Then she bolted and ran with the two miniatures of herself zigzagging and playing tag like two kites she was trying to get to fly.

TERRY TEMPEST WILLIAMS

Terry Tempest Williams is a native of Utah and the author of several books, most recently An Unspoken Hunger *(1994), a collection of nonfiction essays, portraits, and stories. Her previous works include*

Refuge: An Unnatural History of Family and Place *(1991) and*
Coyote's Canyon *(1989). She is a naturalist-in-residence at the*
Utah Museum of Natural History. In 1993, she received a fellowship
from the Lannan Foundation. A politically and environmentally com-
mitted writer, Williams reminds us that "Perhaps the most radical act
we can commit is to stay home." Her home is in Salt Lake City.

"The Clan of One-Breasted Women," the epilogue from Refuge, *presents us with a new version of the West—a landscape made*
toxic through our willingness, even eagerness, to experiment with dis-
aster. Resonating with outrage, courage, and lessons for survival, this
essay energized political sensibilities throughout the West.

"THE CLAN OF ONE-BREASTED WOMEN," FROM *REFUGE: AN UNNATURAL HISTORY OF FAMILY AND PLACE*

I belong to a Clan of One-Breasted Women. My mother, my grandmothers, and six aunts have all had mastectomies. Seven are dead. The
two who survive have just completed rounds of chemotherapy and
radiation.

I've had my own problems: two biopsies for breast cancer and
a small tumor between my ribs diagnosed as a "borderline malig-
nancy."

This is my family history.

Most statistics tell us breast cancer is genetic, hereditary, with rising
percentages attached to fatty diets, childlessness, or becoming pregnant
after thirty. What they don't say is living in Utah may be the greatest
hazard of all.

We are a Mormon family with roots in Utah since 1847. The
"word of wisdom" in my family aligned us with good foods—no coffee,
no tea, tobacco, or alcohol. For the most part, our women were finished
having their babies by the time they were thirty. And only one faced
breast cancer prior to 1960. Traditionally, as a group of people, Mormons have a low rate of cancer.

Is our family a cultural anomaly? The truth is, we didn't think about it. Those who did, usually the men, simply said, "bad genes." The women's attitude was stoic. Cancer was part of life. On February 16, 1971, the eve of my mother's surgery, I accidentally picked up the telephone and overheard her ask my grandmother what she could expect.

"Diane, it is one of the most spiritual experiences you will ever encounter."

I quietly put down the receiver.

Two days later, my father took my brothers and me to the hospital to visit her. She met us in the lobby in a wheelchair. No bandages were visible. I'll never forget her radiance, the way she held herself in a purple velvet robe, and how she gathered us around her.

"Children, I am fine. I want you to know I felt the arms of God around me."

We believed her. My father cried. Our mother, his wife, was thirty-eight years old.

A little over a year after Mother's death, Dad and I were having dinner together. He had just returned from St. George, where the Tempest Company was completing the gas lines that would service southern Utah. He spoke of his love for the country, the sandstoned landscape, bare-boned and beautiful. He had just finished hiking the Kolob trail in Zion National Park. We got caught up in reminiscing, recalling with fondness our walk up Angel's Landing on his fiftieth birthday and the years our family had vacationed there.

Over dessert, I shared a recurring dream of mine. I told my father that for years, as long as I could remember, I saw this flash of light in the night in the desert—that this image had so permeated my being that I could not venture south without seeing it again, on the horizon, illuminating buttes and mesas.

"You did see it," he said.

"Saw what?"

"The bomb. The cloud. We were driving home from Riverside, California. You were sitting on Diane's lap. She was pregnant. In fact, I remember the day, September 7, 1957. We had just gotten out of the Service. We were driving north, past Las Vegas. It was an hour or so before dawn, when this explosion went off. We not only heard it, but felt it. I thought the oil tanker in front of us had blown up. We pulled over and suddenly, rising from the desert floor, we saw it, clearly, this golden-stemmed cloud, the mushroom. The sky seemed to vibrate with an eerie pink glow. Within a few minutes, a light ash was raining on the car."

I stared at my father.

"I thought you knew that," he said. "It was a common occurrence in the fifties."

It was at this moment that I realized the deceit I had been living under. Children growing up in the American Southwest, drinking contaminated milk from contaminated cows, even from the contaminated breasts of their mothers, my mother—members, years later, of the Clan of One-Breasted Women.

It is a well-known story in the Desert West, "The Day We Bombed Utah," or more accurately, the years we bombed Utah: above ground atomic testing in Nevada took place from January 27, 1951, through July 11, 1962. Not only were the winds blowing north covering "low-use segments of the population" with fallout and leaving sheep dead in their tracks, but the climate was right. The United States of the 1950s was red, white, and blue. The Korean War was raging. McCarthyism was rampant. Ike was it, and the cold war was hot. If you were against nuclear testing, you were for a communist regime.

Much has been written about this "American nuclear tragedy." Public health was secondary to national security. The Atomic Energy Commissioner, Thomas Murray, said, "Gentlemen, we must not let anything interfere with this series of tests, nothing."

Again and again, the American public was told by its government, in spite of burns, blisters, and nausea, "It has been found that the tests may be conducted with adequate assurance of safety under conditions prevailing at the bombing reservations." Assuaging public fears was simply a matter of public relations. "Your best action," an Atomic Energy Commission booklet read, "is not to be worried about fallout." A news release typical of the times stated, "We find no basis for concluding that harm to any individual has resulted from radioactive fallout."

On August 30, 1979, during Jimmy Carter's presidency, a suit was filed, *Irene Allen v. The United States of America.* Mrs. Allen's case was the first on an alphabetical list of twenty-four test cases, representative of nearly twelve hundred plaintiffs seeking compensation from the United States government for cancers caused by nuclear testing in Nevada.

Irene Allen lived in Hurricane, Utah. She was the mother of five children and had been widowed twice. Her first husband, with their two oldest boys, had watched the tests from the roof of the local high school.

He died of leukemia in 1956. Her second husband died of pancreatic cancer in 1978.

In a town meeting conducted by Utah Senator Orrin Hatch, shortly before the suit was filed, Mrs. Allen said, "I am not blaming the government, I want you to know that, Senator Hatch. But I thought if my testimony could help in any way so this wouldn't happen again to any of the generations coming up after us . . . I am happy to be here this day to bear testimony of this."

God-fearing people. This is just one story in an anthology of thousands.

On May 10, 1984, Judge Bruce S. Jenkins handed down his opinion. Ten of the plaintiffs were awarded damages. It was the first time a federal court had determined that nuclear tests had been the cause of cancers. For the remaining fourteen test cases, the proof of causation was not sufficient. In spite of the split decision, it was considered a landmark ruling. It was not to remain so for long.

In April, 1987, the Tenth Circuit Court of Appeals overturned Judge Jenkins's ruling on the ground that the United States was protected from suit by the legal doctrine of sovereign immunity, a centuries-old idea from England in the days of absolute monarchs.

In January, 1988, the Supreme Court refused to review the Appeals Court decision. To our court system it does not matter whether the United States government was irresponsible, whether it lied to its citizens, or even that citizens died from the fallout of nuclear testing. What matters is that our government is immune: "The King can do no wrong."

In Mormon culture, authority is respected, obedience is revered, and independent thinking is not. I was taught as a young girl not to "make waves" or "rock the boat."

"Just let it go," Mother would say. "You know how you feel, that's what counts."

For many years, I have done just that—listened, observed, and quietly formed my own opinions, in a culture that rarely asks questions because it has all the answers. But one by one, I have watched the women in my family die common, heroic deaths. We sat in waiting rooms hoping for good news, but always receiving the bad. I cared for them, bathed their scarred bodies, and kept their secrets. I watched beautiful women become bald as Cytoxan, cisplatin, and Adriamycin were injected into their veins. I held their foreheads as they vomited green-

black bile, and I shot them with morphine when the pain became inhuman. In the end, I witnessed their last peaceful breaths, becoming a
midwife to the rebirth of their souls.

The price of obedience has become too high.

The fear and inability to question authority that ultimately killed
rural communities in Utah during atmospheric testing of atomic weapons
is the same fear I saw in my mother's body. Sheep. Dead sheep. The
evidence is buried.

I cannot prove that my mother, Diane Dixon Tempest, or my
grandmothers, Lettie Romney Dixon and Kathryn Blackett Tempest,
along with my aunts developed cancer from nuclear fallout in Utah. But
I can't prove they didn't.

My father's memory was correct. The September blast we drove
through in 1957 was part of Operation Plumbbob, one of the most
intensive series of bomb tests to be initiated. The flash of light in the
night in the desert, which I had always thought was a dream, developed
into a family nightmare. It took fourteen years, from 1957 to 1971, for
cancer to manifest in my mother—the same time, Howard L. Andrews,
an authority in radioactive fallout at the National Institutes of Health,
says radiation cancer requires to become evident. The more I learn
about what it means to be a "downwinder," the more questions I
drown in.

What I do know, however, is that as a Mormon woman of the fifth
generation of Latter-day Saints, I must question everything, even if it
means losing my faith, even if it means becoming a member of a border
tribe among my own people. Tolerating blind obedience in the name
of patriotism or religion ultimately takes our lives.

When the Atomic Energy Commission described the country north
of the Nevada Test Site as "virtually uninhabited desert terrain," my
family and the birds at Great Salt Lake were some of the "virtual
uninhabitants."

One night, I dreamed women from all over the world circled a blazing
fire in the desert. They spoke of change, how they hold the moon in
their bellies and wax and wane with its phases. They mocked the pre-
sumption of even-tempered beings and made promises that they would
never fear the witch inside themselves. The women danced wildly as
sparks broke away from the flames and entered the night sky as stars.

And they sang a song given to them by Shoshone grandmothers:

Ah ne nah, nah	Consider the rabbits
nin nah nah—	How gently they walk on the earth— /
ah ne nah, nah	Consider the rabbits
nin nah nah—	How gently they walk on the earth—
Nyaga mutzi	We remember them
oh ne nay—	We can walk gently also—
Nyaga mutzi	We remember them
oh ne nay—	We can walk gently also—

The women danced and drummed and sang for weeks, preparing them-selves for what was to come. They would reclaim the desert for the sake of their children, for the sake of the land.

A few miles downwind from the fire circle, bombs were being tested. Rabbits felt the tremors. Their soft leather pads on paws and feet recognized the shaking sands, while the roots of mesquite and sage were smoldering. Rocks were hot from the inside out and dust devils hummed unnaturally. And each time there was another nuclear test, ravens watched the desert heave. Stretch marks appeared. The land was losing its muscle.

The women couldn't bear it any longer. They were mothers. They had suffered labor pains but always under the promise of birth. The red hot pains beneath the desert promised death only, as each bomb became a stillborn. A contract had been made and broken between human beings and the land. A new contract was being drawn by the women, who understood the fate of the earth as their own.

Under the cover of darkness, ten women slipped under a barbed-wire fence and entered the contaminated country. They were trespassing. They walked toward the town of Mercury, in moonlight, taking their cues from coyote, kit fox, antelope squirrel, and quail. They moved quietly and deliberately through the maze of Joshua trees. When a hint of daylight appeared they rested, drinking tea and sharing their rations of food. The women closed their eyes. The time had come to protest with the heart, that to deny one's genealogy with the earth was to com-mit treason against one's soul.

At dawn, the women draped themselves in Mylar, wrapping long streamers of silver plastic around their arms to blow in the breeze. They wore clear masks, that became the faces of humanity. And when they arrived at the edge of Mercury, they carried all the butterflies of a sum-mer day in their wombs. They paused to allow their courage to settle.

The town that forbids pregnant women and children to enter because of radiation risks was asleep. The women moved through the streets as winged messengers, twirling around each other in slow motion, peeking inside homes and watching the easy sleep of men and women. They were astonished by such stillness and periodically would utter a shrill note or low cry just to verify life.

The residents finally awoke to these strange apparitions. Some simply stared. Others called authorities, and in time, the women were apprehended by wary soldiers dressed in desert fatigues. They were taken to a white, square building on the other edge of Mercury. When asked who they were and why they were there, the women replied, "We are mothers and we have come to reclaim the desert for our children."

The soldiers arrested them. As the ten women were blindfolded and handcuffed, they began singing:

> *You can't forbid us everything*
> *You can't forbid us to think—*
> *You can't forbid our tears to flow*
> *And you can't stop the songs that we sing.*

The women continued to sing louder and louder, until they heard the voices of their sisters moving across the mesa:

> *Ah ne nah, nah*
> *nin nah nah—*
> *Ah ne nah, nah*
> *nin nah nah—*
> *Nyaga mutzi*
> *oh ne nay—*
> *Nyaga mutzi*
> *oh ne nay—*

"Call for reinforcements," one soldier said.

"We have," interrupted one woman, "we have—and you have no idea of our numbers."

I crossed the line at the Nevada Test Site and was arrested with nine other Utahns for trespassing on military lands. They are still conducting nuclear tests in the desert. Ours was an act of civil disobedience. But as

I walked toward the town of Mercury, it was more than a gesture of peace. It was a gesture on behalf of the Clan of One-Breasted Women.

As one officer cinched the handcuffs around my wrists, another frisked my body. She did not find my scars.

We were booked under an afternoon sun and bused to Tonopah, Nevada. It was a two-hour ride. This was familiar country. The Joshua trees standing their ground had been named by my ancestors, who believed they looked like prophets pointing west to the Promised Land. These were the same trees that bloomed each spring, flowers appearing like white flames in the Mojave. And I recalled a full moon in May, when Mother and I had walked among them, flushing out mourning doves and owls.

The bus stopped short of town. We were released.

The officials thought it was a cruel joke to leave us stranded in the desert with no way to get home. What they didn't realize was that we were home, soul-centered and strong, women who recognized the sweet smell of sage as fuel for our spirits.

RICHARD K. NELSON

Richard K. Nelson, born in 1941, is an anthropologist who spent many years studying relationships to the natural world among the Inupiaq Eskimo and Athabaskan Indian people in Alaska. His books on Native Alaskan lifeways include Hunters of the Northern Ice *(1969),* Hunters of the Northern Forest *(1973),* Shadow of the Hunter *(1980), and* Make Prayers to the Raven *(1983). The latter is the clearest explanation of beliefs of an animist culture I've come across.*

The Island Within *(1989), from which this selection is drawn, received the 1991 John Burroughs Medal for nature writing. It is a personal, intimate look at the nature of life in Nelson's adopted home country on the coastline of southeastern Alaska. In 1991, Nelson was*

*awarded a National Endowment for the Arts creative nonfiction writing
fellowship. A book about deer and hunting is forthcoming in 1997.*

"THE GIFTS OF DEER,"
FROM *THE ISLAND WITHIN*

Cold, clear, and calm in the pale blue morning. Snow on the high peaks
brightening to amber. The bay a sheet of gray glass beneath a faint haze
of steam. A November sun rises with the same fierce, chill stare of an
owl's eye.

I stand at the window watching the slow dawn, and my mind fixes
on the island. Nita comes softly down the stairs as I pack gear and
complain that I've slept too late for these short winter days. A few
minutes later, Ethan trudges out onto the cold kitchen floor, barefoot
and half asleep. We make no direct mention of hunting, to avoid acting
proud or giving offense to the animals. I say only that I'll go to the island
and look around; Ethan says only that he would rather stay at home
with Nita. I wish he would come along so I could teach him things,
but know it will be quieter in the woods with just Shungnak.

They both wave from the window as I ease the skiff away from
shore, crunching through cakes of fresh-water ice the tide has carried in
from Salmon River. It's a quick run through Windy Channel and out
onto the freedom of Haida Strait, where the slopes of Kluksa Mountain
bite into a frozen sky. The air stings against my face, but the rest of me
is warm inside thick layers of clothes. Shungnak whines, paces, and looks
over the gunwale toward the still-distant island.

Broad swells lying in from the Pacific alternately lift the boat and
drop it between smooth-walled canyons of water. Midway across the
strait a dark line of chop descends swiftly from the north, and within
minutes we're surrounded by whitecaps. There are two choices: either
beat straight up into them or cut an easier angle across the waves and
take the spray. I vacillate for a while, then choose the icy spray over the
intense pounding. Koyukon elders often told me it's wrong to curse the
wind or complain about the cold, but this morning I do it anyway.

A kittiwake sweeps over the water in great, vaulting arcs, its wings
flexed against the surge and billow of the air. As it tilts its head passing
over the boat, I think how clumsy we must look. The island's shore lifts

slowly in dark walls of rock and timber that loom above the apron of snow-covered beach. Approaching the shelter of Sea Lion Point, the chop fades and the swell diminishes. I turn up along the lee, running between the kelp beds and the surf, straining to see if any deer are grazing on seaweed at the tide's edge.

Near the end of the point is a gut that opens into a tight, shallow anchorage. I ease the boat between the rocks, with lines of surf breaking close on either side. The waves rise and darken, their edges sparkle in the sun, then long manes of spray whirl back as they turn inside out and pitch onto the reef. The anchor slips through ten feet of crystal water to settle among the kelp fronds and urchin-covered rocks. On a strong ebb the boat would go dry here, but today's tide range is only six feet. Before launching the punt, I pull the binoculars from my pack and warm them inside my coat so the lenses won't fog. Then I spend a few minutes scrutinizing the broad, rocky shore and the sprawls of brown grass along the timber's edge. A bunch of rock sandpipers flashes up from the shingle and an otter loops along the windrows of drift logs, but there are no signs of deer.

I can't help feeling a little anxious, because the season is drawing short and our year's supply of meat is not yet in. During the past few weeks, deer have been unusually wary, haunting the underbrush and slipping away at the least disturbance. I've come near a few, but these were young ones I stalked only for the luxury of seeing them from close range. Now that the rutting season has begun, there's a good chance of finding larger deer, and they'll be distracted by the search for mates.

A bald eagle watches from a tall hemlock as we bob ashore in the punt. Finally the bird lurches out, scoops its wings full of dense, cold air, and soars away beyond the line of trees. While I trudge up with the punt, Shungnak prances back and forth hunting for smells. The upper reaches are layered and slabbed with ice; slick cobbles shine like steel; frozen grass crackles underfoot. I lean the punt on a snow-covered log, pick up my rifle and small pack, and slip through the leafless alders into the forest.

My eyes adjust to the darkness, the deep green of boughs, and the somber, shadowy trunks. I feel safe and hidden here. The forest floor is covered with deep moss that should sponge gently underfoot. But today the softness is gone: frozen moss crunches with each step and brittle twigs snap, ringing out in the crisp air like strangers' voices. It takes a while to get used to this harshness in a forest that's usually wet and velvety and silent. I listen to the clicking of gusts in the high branches and think that winter has come upon us like a fist.

At the base of a spruce tree is a familiar white patch—a scatter of deer bones: ribs, legs, vertebrae, two pelvis bones, and two skulls with half-bleached antlers. I put them here last winter, saying they were for the other animals, to make clear they were not being thoughtlessly wasted. The scavengers soon picked them clean, the deer mice have gnawed them, and eventually they'll be absorbed into the forest again. Koyukon elders say it shows respect, returning animal bones to a clean, wild place instead of throwing them away with trash or discarding them in a garbage dump.

The long, quiet, methodical process of the hunt begins. I move deeper into the forest, ever mindful of treading the edge between protracted, eventless watching and the startling intensity of coming upon an animal, the always unexpected meeting of eyes. A deer could show itself at this moment, in an hour, in several hours, or not at all. Most of hunting is like this—an exercise in patient, isometric endurance and keen, hypnotic concentration. I lift my foot, step ahead, ease it down, wait, step again. Shungnak follows closely, as we work our way through a maze of windfallen trees, across the clear disks of frozen ponds, and around patches of snow beneath openings in the forest canopy. I remind myself there is probably a doe or a buck somewhere in this stretch of woods, perhaps close enough to hear a branch snap or a bough scratch against my clothes. Deep snow has forced the deer off Kluksa Mountain and Crescent Peak, so they're sure to be haunting these lowlands.

We climb a high, steep scarp that levels to a wooded terrace. After pausing to catch my breath, I stand atop a log and peer into the semi-open understory of twiggy bushes, probing each space with my eyes. A downy woodpecker's call sparks from a nearby tree. Several minutes pass. Then a huckleberry branch moves, barely shivers, without the slightest noise, not far ahead.

Amid the scramble of brush where I saw nothing a few minutes ago, a dim shape materializes, as if its own motion had created it. A doe steps into an open space, deep brown in her winter coat, soft and striking and lovely, dwarfed among the great trees, lifting her nose, looking right toward me. For perhaps a minute we're motionless in each other's gaze; then her head jerks to the left, her ears shift back and forth, her tail flicks up, and she turns away in the stylized gait deer always use when alarmed.

Quick as a breath, quiet as a whisper, the doe glides off into the forest. Sometimes when I see a deer this way I know it's real at the moment, but afterward it seems like a daydream.

As we move farther into the woods, I hope for another look at her and think a buck might have been following nearby. Any deer is legal game and I could almost certainly have taken her, but I'd rather wait for a larger buck and let the doe bring on next year's young. Shungnak savors the ghost of her scent that hangs in the still air, but she has vanished.

Farther on, the snow deepens to a continuous cover beneath smaller trees, and we cross several sets of deer tracks, including some big prints with long toe drags. I poke my fingers into one track and feel its edges: still soft and fluffy, with no hint of the crustiness that develops in a few hours when snow is disturbed in cold weather. The powder helps to muffle our steps, but it's hard to see very far because the bushes are heavily loaded. The thicket becomes a lattice of white on black, every branch spangled in a thick fur of jeweled flakes. We move through it like eagles cleaving between tumbled columns of cloud. New siftings occasionally drift down when the treetops are touched by the breeze.

I stop for a while, not to watch for deer so much as to catch my balance in this feathery mosaic of snow, with its distracting beauty and dizzying absence of relief. A Koyukon word keeps running through my mind: *duhnooyh*, "clumps of powdery snow clinging on branches." In the old days, pregnant women drank water melted from this snow, so their children would grow up to be nimble and light-footed. For the same reason, I heard people advise the young boys to drink water melted from surface powder, not from the dense, granular snow, called *tliyh*, which forms underneath during the course of winter. Koyukon elders sometimes told riddles to help teach their children these words, to test their cleverness, and to sharpen their attention to details of the natural world:

> *Wait, I see something: We are sitting all puffed up across from each*
> *other, in coats of mountain sheep skin.*
> *Answer:* duhnooyh.

Slots between the trunks ahead shiver with blue where a muskeg opens. I angle toward it, feeling no need to hurry, picking every footstep carefully, stopping often to stare into the jumbled crannies, listening for any splinter of sound, keeping my senses tight and concentrated. A raven calls from high above the forest, and as I catch a glimpse of it the same old questions run through my mind. It lofts and plays on the wind, then folds up and rolls halfway over, a strong sign of hunting luck. Never mind the issue of knowing; I'll assume the power is here and let myself be moved by it.

I turn to look at Shungnak, taking advantage of her sharper hearing and magical sense of smell. She lifts her nose to the fresh but nebulous scent of deer who must have come through here this morning. I watch her little radar ears, waiting for her to focus in one direction and hold it, hoping to see her body tense as it does when something moves nearby. But she only hears the twitching of red squirrels on dry bark. Shungnak and I have a very different opinion of the squirrels. They excite her more than any other animal because she believes she'll catch one someday. But for a hunter, they make distracting spurts of movement and sound, and their sputtering alarm calls alert the deer.

We approach a low, abrupt rise, covered with obscuring brush and curtained with snow. A lift of wind hisses in the high trees, then drops away and leaves us in near-complete silence. I pause to choose a path through a scramble of blueberry bushes and little windfalls ahead, then glance back at Shungnak. She has her eyes and ears fixed toward our left, directly across the current of breeze. She stands very stiff, quivering slightly, leaning forward as if she has already started to run but cannot release her muscles. I shake my finger and look sternly into her eyes as a warning to stay.

I listen as closely as possible, but hear nothing. I work my eyes into every dark crevice and slot among the snowy branches, but see nothing. I stand perfectly still and wait, then look again at Shungnak. Her head turns so slowly I can barely detect the movement, until finally she's looking straight ahead. Perhaps it's just another squirrel. I consider taking a few steps for a better view.

Then I see it.

A long, dark body appears among the bushes, moving up into the wind, so close I can scarcely believe I didn't see it earlier. Without looking away, I gently slide the breech closed and raise the rifle to my shoulder, almost certain that a deer this size will be a buck. Shungnak, now forgotten behind me, must be contorted with the suppressed urge to give chase.

The deer walks silently, determinedly along the little rise, never looking our way. Then he turns straight toward us. Thick tines of his antlers curve over the place where I have the rifle aimed. I remember the Koyukon elders saying that animals come to those who have shown them respect, allowing themselves to be taken, in what is both a physical and spiritual passage. At a moment like this, it's easy to sense that despite my abiding doubt there is an invisible world beyond this one, a world filled with power and awareness, a world that demands recognition and exacts a price from those who ignore it.

It is a very large buck. He comes so quickly that I have no chance to shoot, and then he is so close I haven't the heart to do it. Fifty feet away, the deer lowers his head almost to the ground and lifts a slender branch that blocks his path. Snow shakes onto his neck and clings to the fur of his shoulders as he slips underneath. Then he half lifts his head and keeps coming. I ease the rifle down to watch, wondering how much closer he'll get. Just now he makes a long, soft rutting call, like the bleating of a sheep, except lower pitched and more hollow. His hooves tick against dry twigs hidden by the snow. I can almost feel the breeze blowing against his fur, the chill winnowing down through close-set hairs and touching his skin.

In the middle of a step he raises his head all the way up, and he sees me standing there—a stain against the pure white of the forest, a deadly interloper, the one utterly incongruous thing he has met here in all his life. He reaches his muzzle forward and draws in the affliction of our smell. A sudden spasm stuns him, so sharp and intense it's as if his fright spills out into the forest and tingles inside me like electricity. His front legs jerk apart and he freezes all askew, head high, nostrils flared, coiled and hard. I stare at him and wait, my mind snarled with irreconcilable emotions. Here is a perfect buck deer. In the Koyukon way, he has come to me; but in my own he has come too close. I am as congealed and transfixed as he is, as devoid of conscious thought. It's as if my mind has ceased to function and only my senses remain.

But the buck has no choice. He instantly unwinds in a burst of ignited energy, springs straight up from the snow, turns in midflight, stabs the frozen earth again, and makes four great bounds off to the left. His thick body seems to float, relieved of its own weight, as if a deer has the power to unbind itself from gravity.

The same deeper impulse that governs the flight of a deer governs the predator's impulse to pursue it. I watch the first leaps without moving a muscle. Then, not pausing for an instant of deliberation, I raise the rifle back to my shoulder, follow the movement of the deer's fleeing form, and wait until he stops to stare back. Almost at that moment, still moving without conscious thought, freed of the ambiguities that held me before, now no less animal than the animal I watch, my hands warm and steady and certain, acting from a more elemental sense than the ones that brought me to this meeting, I carefully align the sights and let go the sudden power.

The gift of the deer falls like a feather in the snow. And the rifle's sound has rolled off through the timber before I hear it.

I walk to the deer, now shaking a bit as accumulated emotions pour through me. Shungnak is already next to it, whining and smelling, racing from one side to the other, stuffing her nose down in snow full of scent. She looks off into the brush, searching back and forth, as if the deer that ran is somewhere else, still running. She tries to lick at the blood that trickles down, but I stop her out of respect for the animal. Then, I suppose to consummate her own frustrated predatory energy, she takes a hard nip at its shoulder, shuns quickly away, and looks back as if she expects it to leap to its feet again.

I whisper thanks to the animal, hoping I might be worthy of it, worthy of carrying on the life it has given, worthy of sharing in the larger life of which the deer and I are a part. Incompatible emotions clash inside me—elation and remorse, excitement and sorrow, gratitude and shame. It's always this way: the sudden encounter with death, the shock that overrides the cushioning of the intellect. I force away the sadness and remember that death is the spark that keeps life itself aflame: these deer we eat from, and the fish, and the plants that die to feed us.

It takes a few minutes before I settle down enough to begin the other work. Then, I tie a length of rope onto the forelegs, run it over a low branch, back down through a loop in the rope, and up over the branch again like a double pulley, so I can raise the animal above the ground. This done, I cut the dark, pungent scent glands from its hind legs, to prevent their secretions from tainting the meat. Next, I make a small incision through the belly skin, insert my hand to shield the knife blade from the distended stomach, and slice upward to make an opening about a foot long. Reaching inside, I loosen the stomach and intestines, then work them out through the incision, pulling carefully to avoid tearing the thin membranes and spilling stomach contents into the body cavity. The deer's inward parts feel very hot, slippery, and wet, as I suppose my own would if I could ever touch them. Finally the viscera slide out onto the ground: soft, bladderlike stomach and flaccid ribbons of intestine; a gray, shining mound, webbed with networks of veins and lacy fat, steaming into the cold, saturating the air with a rich odor of plant mulch and body fluids.

Next, I roll up my jacket sleeve and thrust my arm deep inside the deer, until I feel the diaphragm, a sheet of muscle that separates the abdomen from the chest. When I slice through it, a thick, hot rush of blood flows down my arm and sloshes into the vacant belly. There is a hollow, tearing sound as I pull the lungs free; and reaching up inside the chest, I can feel the firm, softball-sized muscle of the heart. The lungs are marbled creamy-pink and feel like soft, airy sponge. As I lay them beside the other organs, I whisper that these parts are left here as food for the animals. Shungnak wants to take some for herself but I make her stay away. Koyukon elders say the sensitivity and awareness leave an animal's remains slowly, and there are rules about what should be eaten by a dog. Shungnak will have her share of the scraps later on, when more of the life is gone.

The inside of the deer is now empty, except for the heart and the dark-purple liver, which I've left attached. I tie a short piece of cord around the end of the lower intestine to keep the remaining blood from flowing out when I carry the animal on my back. Then I poke a series of holes in the hide along either side of the belly incision and lace it shut with another cord. After lowering the deer onto the ground, I cut through the "knee" joints of the forelegs, leaving them attached by a stout tendon, then slice a hole in the hock—a space between the bone and tendon of the hind leg—and I toggle the forelegs through these openings. This way I can put my arms through the joined legs and carry the deer like a pack—not a trick to be used if there is the slightest chance another hunter might be around and mistake my burden for a live animal.

I barely have enough strength to lift the buck and trudge along, but there is plenty of time to work back toward the beach, stopping occasionally to rest and cool down. During one of these breaks, I hear two ravens in an agitated exchange of croaks and gurgles, and I wonder if those black eyes have already spotted the remnants. No pure philanthropist, if Raven gave this luck to me, it was only to create luck for himself. I remember how difficult it was, at first, to accept the idea of a sanctified creature having such a contradictory personality. The Raven described by elders like Grandpa William was both good and evil, sage and fool, benefactor and thief—embodiment of the human paradox. When Joe Stevens described an American president of dubious character, he said, "Just like Raven."

Half an hour later, sweating and exhausted, I push through the low boughs of the beachside trees, lay the animal down, and find a comfortable seat on the driftwood. Afternoon sun throbs off the water, but the north wind takes every hint of warmth out of it. Little gusts splay dark patterns across the anchorage; the boat paces on its mooring line; the strait races with whitecaps. I take a good rest, watching a fox sparrow flit among the alders and a bunch of crows hassle over some bit of food near the water's edge. At this low tide, Sea Lion Point has expanded to a flat sill of rock reaching out several hundred yards from the island's shore. The point has such scant relief that higher tides reduce it to a fraction of this size. The anchorage is nothing more than a gouge in the rocks, closely rimmed with breakers and jagged boulders, so it's only accessible to small skiffs whose pilots are either reckless or foolish. Despite its barren appearance, Sea Lion Point has extensive tide flats, ponds, and beds of estuarine grass that attract congregations of birds, especially during the spring and fall migrations.

Today, hundreds of gulls have gathered on the outer reaches of the point, all sitting with their beaks into the wind. They appear sluggish and languid, as if their sole purpose is to huddle together against the chill. But they're also keeping watch. When the breeze slacks to a momentary calm, a black foil sweeps out from the forest's edge. The eagle leans sharply down, half folds its wings, banks toward the gulls, and builds speed, falling and blurred and sinister. Gulls and crows swirl up like a handful of salt and pepper thrown into the wind. Clusters of ducks spray off the water in opposite directions. Shorebirds dazzle over the tangled skeins of kelp. A close formation of oystercatchers babbles across the anchorage in front of us.

The eagle shears through the scattering swarm, looking ponderous and clumsy, oddly outclassed by its darting prey. Carried into a steep climb by its momentum, the eagle swings around and drops again, legs dangling, unsheathed talons gaping in the frosted air. But the birds have whirled away, leaving an empty void like the eye of a storm. Its voice mingles with the cries and wails of the gulls, a shrill complaint amid easy laughter. Finally the eagle flaps off to a high perch. Swaying back and forth, jerking and flexing its wings for balance, it watches the crows dwindle away over the rocks, the gulls float down onto the flats again. All of the birds seem calm and unhurried, as if nothing of significance has happened, as if the whole thing has been only a game. The hoary quiet of winter returns, and the wait begins once more.

Though I feel satisfied, grateful, and contented sitting here, much remains to be done, and at this time of year the daylight ebbs quickly. Hunters are allowed more than one deer, so I'll stay on the island and take another look around tomorrow. As we idle from the anchorage, we pass within a few yards of lovely surf peeling across a smooth, triangular reef. If I had a surfboard and wetsuit it would be impossible to resist, no matter how frigid the air and water might be. I stop to watch a few waves pour over the shoals like liquid silver; then I follow the shore toward Bear Creek. By the time I've anchored and unloaded the boat, the wind has diminished and a growing winter chill sinks down in the pitched, hard shadow of Kluksa Mountain.

Bear Creek cabin is situated in a thicket well back from shore, hidden in summer but easily seen once the leaves have fallen. I split some half-dry wood, which hisses and sputters in the rusty stove, then reluctantly gives way to flames. After the fire starts crackling, I walk down to the creek. Dipping a bucket into a clear pool, I notice a few salmon bones scattered among the rocks and pebbles. I'm surprised to see them, but also surprised that so little would remain from the hordes of fish I watched here this fall. I had a similar feeling recently, when I went looking for the sperm whale carcass that beached last summer near Tsandaku Point. At first it seemed the storm swells had washed it away, but then I found a bare vertebra and a rib among the rocks. Eventually, I came across the skull—about ten feet long and weighing hundreds of pounds—half buried in the driftwood. Six months after the whale came ashore, scavengers and decay had taken every bit of flesh, gnawed or carried off the smaller bones, and left only a few fragments to wash in the surge.

After fetching water, I carry the deer inside the cabin and hang it from a low beam. Better to work on it now than wait, in case tomorrow brings more luck. The animal is dimly lit by a kerosene lantern and a blush of daylight through the windows. I feel strange in its presence, as if it still watches, still glows with something of its life, still demands that nothing be done carelessly and no offensive words be spoken in its presence. Grandpa William told me that a hunter should never let himself be deluded by pride or a false sense of dominance. It's not through his own power that a person takes life in nature, but through the power of nature that life is given to him.

After sharpening the knife, I slit the deer's skin along the whole length of its underside and down each leg to the hoof. Then I peel the soft hide away, using the blade to separate it from the muscles underneath, gradually revealing the inner perfection of the deer's body. When the skinning is finished, I follow an orderly sequence, cutting through crisp cartilage, severing the leg joints, brisket, ribs, vertebrae, and pelvis, following the body's own design to disarticulate bone from bone. Everything comes apart smoothly and easily, as deer becomes meat, animal becomes food, the most vital and fundamental transformation in all of living existence. There is no ugliness in it, only hands moving in concert with the beauty of an animal's shape. While I work with the deer, it's as if something has already begun to flow into me. I couldn't have understood this when I was younger and had yet to experience the process of one life being passed on to another.

Before I lived with the Eskimo people, I had never hunted and had never seen how game is prepared. But I was immediately fascinated by their skill at taking an animal into its component parts. The Eskimos always watched me closely and found my mistakes entertaining. If I did something uncharacteristically well, someone was likely to look bemused and declare: "Accident." They were passionate hunters and incredibly hard workers. When they hunted walrus, it took only a short while to stalk the animals but many hours to butcher them. As we pulled the skin-covered boat onto the ice, someone was sure to say, "Well, the excitement's over. Now it's time for the real work." But somehow, it never seemed like work to me, this deeply engaged process of learning about animals from the inside and out, of binding my own existence more closely to the lives that sustained me.

By the time I went to live with Koyukon people, I could skin and butcher animals; but I knew little about the delicate matter of keeping a right mind while working with them. Sarah and Joe Stevens were especially scrupulous about treating each animal as a sentient being and butchering it according to the traditional pattern, which was not only a technique but also a ritual of respect. They made certain that no usable part was wasted or tossed carelessly aside, that the meat was covered to keep dogs and scavengers away, and that it was well cached so nothing would spoil. Once, I met Sarah carrying a platter of meat to her neighbor's house, with a piece of cloth over it. She explained, "It wouldn't be right to leave this open to the air, like it doesn't mean anything." In this and other ways, she treated meat as a sacred substance, a medium of interchange between herself and the empowered world in which she lived. It seemed that everything she did in relationship to nature was both an activity and a prayer.

When I've finished with the deer, I put two slices from the hind-quarter in a pan atop the stove. Scraps of meat and fat boil in a separate pot for Shungnak. She whines impatiently, perhaps remembering her sled dog days, when she lived mostly on meat and fish and bones. As soon as she's been fed, I sit on a sawed log and eat venison straight from the pan. No meal could be simpler, more satisfying, or more directly a part of the living process. I also savor a deep feeling of security in having this meat, bringing it home to freeze or can for the year ahead—pure food, taken from a clean, wild place, and prepared by our own efforts. There is a special intimacy in living directly from nature, nourishing my body from the same wildness that so elevates my spirit.

I wish Ethan were here to share this meal, so I could explain to him again that when we eat the deer, its flesh becomes our flesh. Each time we eat we should remember the deer and feel gratitude for what it has given us. And each time, we should carry a thought like a prayer inside: "Thanks to the animal and to all that made it—the island and the forest, the air, and the rain . . ." I would tell Ethan that in the course of things, he and Nita and I are all generations of deer and of the life that feeds us. Like the deer, we also come from the island, and from the earth that sustains us and gives us breath.

Later, perched atop rocks near the mouth of Bear Creek, Shungnak and I look out over Haida Strait to the sea beyond. A distant winter sun sprawls against the horizon, thins to a mound of shivering flame, and drowns itself in the cold Pacific. The sky fades to violet, darkens, and relaxes, like a face losing expression at the edge of sleep. Silence hovers in the brittle woods.

A great blue heron glides down into the anchorage cove and stands motionless in the shallows, like the shadow of a pterodactyl against the Mesozoic sky. Every few minutes I notice the bird's stance and position have changed, but invisibly, like a clock's hands, so that I never actually see its legs move. Then I notice its head slowly lowering, its body tilting, its neck stretching forward. Suddenly it flashes out and draws back, and a fish wriggles on the dripping spear of its beak. The recoiling heron stands erect, flips the fish lengthwise, gulps it, and resumes hunting. Over the next few minutes, the bulge of the fish gradually moves down its serpentine neck.

I've watched herons many times before, admiring them as elegantly plumed, primeval works of art. But I never thought about their impeccable skill and patience as hunters. This event gives me a better sense of the way they live—the measured and timeless stalks, the penetrating eyes fixed at the water's edge, the shadows of prey moving below, the saber beak striking down, the sudden consummation of predatory impulse. Given a choice of birds, I would be a heron, or an owl, a falcon, an eagle. I love these quick, canny animals, perhaps because they seem closest to my own kind. To feel otherwise about predators would be like shrinking from the face in the mirror.

Dusk settles on the waters of Haida Strait, swallows the far peaks and inlets, drifts down through the surrounding forest, takes the island inside itself, and joins it with the sky. Sitting in the darkness, I feel overcome with gratitude and wish for a way to express it. Words seem frail and empty; offerings seem foreign and artificial. Perhaps just being here is enough, becoming wholly engaged with this place, touching it, eating from it, winding my life as tightly as possible into it. The island and I, turning ourselves ever more inside out.

Warm in my sleeping bag, I let the fire ebb to coals. The lamp is out. The cabin roof creaks in the growing chill. I drift toward sleep, pleased that there is no moon, so the deer will wait until dawn to feed. On the floor beside me, Shungnak jerks and whimpers in her dog's dreams.

Dawn. The cold fire of winter sun climbs a pallid wall of sky. Mountains stand out as sharp and clear as the sound of shattering glass. Clouds of steam rise above the open riffles of Bear Creek. The silver calm of Haida Strait is splotched with dark blue where an uncertain breeze touches down against it. Three goldeneye ducks drift in the anchorage, like smudges on a sheet of polished iron.

The temperature is twenty degrees, perhaps much colder back away from shore. Although it rarely drops to zero along this coast, sea humidity and gusty winds often intensify the chill. But even so, our winter is a far cry from that of Koyukon country, where temperatures average below zero for five months of the year and may hover at forty to sixty below for weeks. Not surprisingly, Koyukon elders treat cold weather as a conscious thing, with a potent and irritable spirit. They warn the younger ones to speak carefully about cold, lest they incite its frigid wrath. In the old days, children were even told not to throw snowballs, because the frivolity or annoyance could bring on bitter weather.

When Shungnak was born it was so cold that one of her littermates froze stiff. Thawed out behind the wood stove, he survived, although his tail eventually fell off. Perhaps because she grew up in that climate, and because the frozen landscape meant freedom and adventure for a sled dog, Shungnak still loves winter weather. As we walk back to the cabin, she prances around me, full of excited energy, anxious to get started with the day.

An hour later, I anchor the boat at Sea Lion Point. After paddling the punt ashore, I follow Shungnak to where our tracks from yesterday enter the woods. Just beyond the place of the buck, a pair of does drifts at the edge of sight and disappears. For an hour we angle north, then come slowly back deeper into the woods, moving crosswise to a growing easterly breeze. In two places, deer snort and pound away, invisible beyond a shroud of brush. Otherwise there is nothing.

We keep on in the same direction, probing first through snowy thickets, then through heavy forest with bare, frozen moss underneath. In a dense maze of young spruce, I come face to face with a red squirrel, clinging to the trunk of a dead tree. Luckily, Shungnak has lagged a few yards behind. And instead of scurrying to a high branch, the squirrel stays put, bold, curious and confident, apparently unconcerned about my intentions. I inch ahead, wait, then move again, until he's so close I could ruffle his fur if I blew hard enough.

The squirrel twitches this way and that on his skinny white tree, first head up, then head down, leaning out as if to get a closer look at me. He sticks effortlessly to the smooth wood, or actually hangs from it by the tips of his curved claws. Never satisfied to simply observe, I wonder how his claws can possibly be so sharp, and what keeps them from getting dull? The squirrel spends a long minute checking me out, constantly in motion, scratching up the tree and back down again, jerking from one angle to another, stitching his little feet, shaking his frizzy tail, shivering his long black whiskers. Then he jumps to a spruce just as close but with a slightly different angle. I can see the crenulations of his nose, the fine hairs on his snout, the quick pumping of his ribs, and my face reflecting on his bright indigo eye. When he's seen enough, he turns and jitters to a place above my head. I can tell he's ready to burst into a chatter, as squirrels often do after some deliberation, so I edge past and leave him alone.

A short while later we follow a familiar stretch of trail through a copse of shore pines and cedars. I kneel down to examine a bunch of deer bones in the snowless patch under a tree. Darkened by age and half covered with moss, they're hardly visible anymore. I first came across them several years ago, when they still had a blanched white color, with bits of clinging skin, cartilage, and tufts of fur. It looked as if the deer had died only a few months before, and because the nearby tree trunk was heavily clawed, I guessed a bear had either killed the animal or scavenged its carcass. I always looked at the bones when I passed by, but never touched them because I wanted to see how long it took an animal's remains to vanish from the forest floor. Each year, a few more bones were missing or were cloaked over by the moss.

Last summer, I walked through here with a friend and showed him the bones. He touched several of them and pulled one out from the moss. Both of us were stunned by what he found: a hind-leg bone that had been fractured in several places while the deer was alive. It was so badly shattered that a piece the thickness of my index finger had stuck out almost two inches from the wound, as indicated by a line where healing flesh had closed around it. The deer must have lived a long time after its terrible injury. Long enough so the fragments knitted themselves together, as if liquid bone had seeped into the wound and solidified as a porous, bulging, convoluted mass. Though gnarled and misshapen, the fused bone seemed almost as strong as a healthy one. But the deer's leg was considerably shortened and had a hollow ivory splinter piercing out from it. As we turned the bone in our hands, I marveled at the determination of living things, and of life itself, to carry on, to mend, and to become whole again after being torn apart.

What could have caused such a wound? It might have been a bad fall, an unskilled hunter's bullet, or a bear. Hardest of all to imagine was the agony this deer went through, the days and weeks of unrelievable pain, endured in solitude, through nights of rain and storm, burdened by the omnipresent danger of being discovered by a bear. Of course, it might have been another bear that eventually killed the animal. After my friend and I left the bones, the forest seemed less beautiful for a while, less a place of shelter than of violence and tragedy. At that same moment, some other animal was probably suffering toward death not far away—perhaps severed by an eagle's beak or broken by a bear, perhaps old and weakened, perhaps riven with disease—biting the moss in torment and fear. I thought, there is little mercy in nature, little to relieve the pain or loneliness of death. Many of the tragedies found in the human world are also found here. Then I realized that loving nature meant loving it all, accepting nature exactly as it is, not idealizing it or ignoring the hard truths, not reducing it to an imaginary world of peace and perfection. How could I crave the beauty of the flame without accepting the heat that made it?

Shortly after noon we come into a narrow muskeg with scattered shore pines and a ragged edge of brushy, low-growing cedar. I squint against the sharp glare of snow. It has that peculiar look of old powder, a bit settled and touched by wind, very lovely but without the airy magic of a fresh fall. I gaze up the muskeg's easy slope. Above the encroaching wall of timber, seamed against the deep blue sky, is the peak of Kluksa Mountain, with a great plume of snow streaming off in what must be a shuddering gale. It has a contradictory look of absoluteness and unreality about it, like a Himalayan summit suspended in midair over the saddle of a low ridge.

I move slowly up the muskeg's east side, away from the breeze and in the sun's full warmth. Deer tracks crisscross the opening, but none of the animals stopped here to feed. Next to the bordering trees, the tracks join as a single, hard-packed trail, showing the deer's preference for cover. Shungnak keeps her nose to the thickly scented snow. We come across a pine sapling that a buck has assaulted with his antlers, scattering twigs and flakes of bark all around. But his tracks are hardened, frosted, and lack sharpness, indicating they're at least a day old.

We slip through a point of trees, then follow the edge again, pausing long moments between footsteps. A mixed tinkle of crossbills and siskins moves through the high timber, and a squirrel rattles from deep in the woods, too far off to be scolding us. Shungnak picks up a strong ribbon of scent, but she hears nothing. I stop for a few minutes to study the muskeg's raveled fringe, the tangle of shade and thicket, the glaze of mantled boughs.

Then my eye barely catches a fleck of movement up ahead, near the ground and almost hidden behind the trunk of a leaning pine— perhaps a squirrel's tail or a bird. I slowly lift my hand to shade the sun, stand dead still, and wait to see if something is there. Finally it moves again.

At the very edge of the trees, almost out of sight in a little swale, small and furry and bright-tinged, turning one direction and then another, is the funnel of a single ear. Having seen this, I soon make out the other ear and the slope of a doe's forehead. Her neck is behind the leaning pine, but on the other side I can barely see the soft, dark curve of her back above the snow. She is comfortably bedded, gazing placidly into the distance, chewing her cud.

Shungnak has stopped twenty yards behind me in the point of trees and has no idea about the deer. I shake my finger at her until she lays her ears back and sits. Then I watch the doe again. She is fifty yards ahead, ten yards beyond the leaning tree, and still looking off at an angle. Her left eye is visible and she refuses to turn her head away, so it might be impossible to get closer. Perhaps I should just wait here, in case a buck is attending her nearby. But however improbable it might be under these circumstances, a thought is lodged in my mind: I can get near her.

My first step sinks down softly, but the second makes a loud budging sound, like stepping on a piece of toast. She snaps my way, stops chewing, and stares for several minutes. It seems hopeless, especially out here in an open field of crispy snow with only the narrow tree trunk for a screen. But she turns away and starts to chew again. I move just enough so the tree blocks her eye and the rest of her head, but I can still see her ears. Every time she chews they shake just a bit, so I watch them and step when her hearing is obscured by the sound of her own jaws.

Either this works or the deer has decided to ignore me, because after a while I've come close enough so the noise of my feet has to reach her easily. She should have jumped up and run long ago, but instead she lies there in serene repose. I deliberate on every step, try for the softest snow, wait long minutes before the next move, stalking like a cat toward ambush. I watch beyond her, into the surrounding shadows and across to the muskeg's farther edge, for the shape of a buck deer; but there is nothing. I feel ponderous, clumsy-footed, out of place, inimical. I should turn and run away, take fear on the deer's behalf, flee the mirrored image in my mind. But I clutch the cold rifle at my side and creep closer.

The wind refuses to blow and my footsteps seem like thunder in the still sunshine. But the doe only turns once to look my way, without even pointing her ears toward me, then stares off and begins to chew again.

I am ten feet from the leaning tree. My heart pounds so hard I think those enchanted ears should hear the blood rushing in my temples. Yet a strange assurance has come into me, a quite unmystical confidence. Perhaps she has decided I am another deer, a buck attracted by her musk or a doe feeding gradually toward her. My slow pace and lapses of stillness would not seem human. For myself, I have lost awareness of time; I have no feeling of patience or impatience. It's as if the deer has moved slowly toward me on a cloud of snow, and I am adrift in the pure motion of experience.

I take the last step to the trunk of the leaning pine. It's bare of branches, scarcely wider than my outstretched hand, but perfectly placed to break my odd profile. There is no hope of getting any closer, so I slowly poke my head out to watch. She has an ideal spot: screened from the wind, warmed by the sun, and with a clear view of the muskeg. I can see muscles working beneath the close fur of her jaw, the rise and fall of her side each time she breathes, the shining edge of her ebony eye.

I hold absolutely still, but her body begins to stiffen, she lifts her head higher, and her ears twitch anxiously. Then instead of looking at me she turns her face to the woods, shifting her ears toward a sound I cannot hear. A few seconds later, the unmistakable voice of a buck drifts up, strangely disembodied, as if it comes from somewhere underneath the snow. I huddle as close to the tree as I can, press against the hard dry bark, and peek around its edge.

There is a gentle rise behind the doe, scattered with sapling pines and bushy juniper. A rhythmic crunching of snow comes invisibly from the slope, then a bough shakes . . . and a buck walks easily into the open sunshine.

Focusing completely on the doe, he comes straight to her and never sees my intrusive shape just beyond. He slips through a patch of small trees, stops a few feet from where she lies, lowers his head and stretches it toward her, then holds this odd pose for a long moment. She reaches her muzzle to one side, trying to find his scent. When he moves up behind her she stands quickly, bends her body into a strange sideways arc, and stares back at him. A moment later she walks off a bit, lifts her tail, and puts droppings in her tracks. The buck moves to the warm ground of her bed and lowers his nose to the place where her female scent is strongest.

Inching like a reptile on a cold rock, I have stepped out from the tree and let my whole menacing profile become visible. The deer are thirty feet away and stand well apart, so they can both see me easily. I am a hunter hovering near his prey and a watcher craving inhuman love, torn between the deepest impulses, hot and shallow-breathed and seething with unreconciled intent, hidden from opened eyes that look into the nimbus of sun and see nothing but the shadow they have chosen for themselves. In this shadow now, the hunter has vanished and only the watcher remains.

Drawn by the honey of the doe's scent, the buck steps quickly toward her. And now the most extraordinary thing happens. The doe turns away from him and walks straight for me. There is no hesitation, only a wild deer coming along the trail of hardened snow where the other deer have passed, the trail in which I stand at this moment. She raises her head, looks at me, and steps without pausing.

My existence is reduced to a pair of eyes; a rush of unbearable heat flushes through my cheeks; and a sense of absolute certainty fuses in my mind.

The snow blazes so brightly that my head aches. The deer is a dark form growing larger. I look up at the buck, half embarrassed, as if to apologize that she's chosen me over him. He stares at her for a moment, turns to follow, then stops and watches anxiously. I am struck by how gently her hooves touch the trail, how little sound they make as she steps, how thick the fur is on her flank and shoulder, how unfathomable her eyes look. I am consumed with a sense of her perfect elegance in the brilliant light. And then I am lost again in the whirling intensity of experience.

The doe is now ten feet from me. She never pauses or looks away. Her feet punch down mechanically into the snow, coming closer and closer, until they are less than a yard from my own. Then she stops, stretches her neck calmly toward me, and lifts her nose.

There is not the slightest question in my mind, as if this was sure to happen and I have known all along exactly what to do. I slowly raise my hand and reach out.

And my fingers touch the soft, dry, gently needling fur on top of the deer's head, and press down to the living warmth of flesh underneath.

She makes no move and shows no fear, but I can feel the flaming strength and tension that flow in her wild body as in no other animal I have touched. Time expands and I am suspended in the clear reality of the moment.

Then, by the flawed conditioning of a lifetime among fearless domesticated things, I instinctively drop my hand and let the deer smell it. Her black nose, wet and shining, touches gently against my skin at the exact instant I realize the absoluteness of my error. And a tremor runs through her entire body as she realizes hers. Her muscles seize and harden; she seems to wrench her eyes away from me but her body remains, rigid and paralyzed. Having been deceived by her other senses, she keeps her nose tight against my hand for one more moment.

Then all the energy inside her triggers in a series of exquisite bounds. She flings out over the hummocks of snow-covered moss, suspended in effortless flight like fog blown over the muskeg in a gale. Her body leaps with such power that the muscles should twang aloud like a bowstring; the earth should shudder and drum; but I hear no sound. In the center of the muskeg she stops to look back, as if to confirm what must seem impossible. The buck follows in more earthbound undulations; they dance away together; and I am left in the meeting place alone.

There is a blur of rushing feet behind me. No longer able to restrain herself, Shungnak dashes past, buries her nose in the soft tracks, and then looks back to ask if we can run after them. I had completely forgotten her, sitting near enough to watch the whole encounter, somehow resisting what must have been a prodigious urge to explode in chase. When I reach out to hug her, she smells the hand that touched the deer. And it seems as if it happened long ago.

I walk slowly from the spot, letting the whole event roll through my mind again and again, remembering the dream that began many months ago, that I might someday touch a deer. After trying and failing with the naive little fawn earlier this fall, I'd begun to think the idea was farfetched, perhaps even foolish. But now, totally unexpected and in a strange way, it has happened. Was the deer caught by some reckless twinge of curiosity? Had she never encountered a human on this wild island? Did she yield to some odd amorous confusion? Then I realize I truly do not care. I would rather accept this as pure experience and not give in to a notion that everything should be explained.

Koyukon elders simply accept what comes to them. They teach that everything in the natural world has its own spirit and awareness, and they give themselves to that other world, without expecting voices, without waiting for visions, without seeking admission to the hidden realms.

I am reminded of something that happened the last time I hunted with Grandpa William. While we sat talking at the edge of a meadow, an unusual bird started singing and chattering in a nearby treetop. At first it looked like a small hawk, but there was something different about its color and shape. When I asked what it was, he listened closely to its calls, then took my binoculars and watched it for a long while, intrigued and perplexed. "I don't know," he muttered, mostly to himself; then he suggested a difficult Koyukon name I'd never heard before. Shortly, his interest darkened to concern: was the arrival of this strange bird a sign, an omen?

Suddenly he began addressing the bird at length in the Koyukon language, speaking in a soft, gentle voice. "Who are you," he wondered, "and what are you saying to us?" He walked out into the meadow, still talking, still trying to establish that the loquacious bird was something ordinary, not an ominous stranger. "Wish us good luck, whoever you are," he said. "Wish us well, and surround us—your grandchildren—within a circle of protection." By this time I'd lost interest in identifying the bird, and my whole attention was focused on Grandpa William: a man imploring mercy and protection from a bird, addressing a feathered emissary in a treetop.

Those moments epitomized everything I had learned from Koyukon people, everything they had tried to tell me about living in a natural world filled with spirit and power. I've had few experiences that so moved me. For how many thousand generations, I wondered, have people spoken and prayed to the natural beings around them, as a customary part of daily life? At any other time in human history, this event would be as ordinary as talking to another person. To me, Grandpa William represented the universal man beseeching the powers that pervade his living world, powers so recently forgotten among my own people. More than anything else, I wished it had seemed quite unremarkable for me, wished my ancestors hadn't forsaken what Grandpa William still understood.

Neither Grandpa William nor I ever knew what that bird was, though I later concluded it must be a young northern shrike. And if the bird did carry an omen, who was it for?

I stop in the shadows along the muskeg's upper edge, and think back over the years with Koyukon people. What stands out for me at this moment is a special wisdom of their tradition—to expect nothing of nature, but to humbly receive its mystery, beauty, food, and life. In return, Koyukon people show the same respect toward nature that is shown toward humans, acknowledging that spirit and sacredness pervade all things. If I understand correctly, their behavior toward nature is ordered around a few simple principles: Move slowly, stay quiet, watch carefully, be ever humble, show no hint of arrogance or disrespect. And if they follow one overarching commandment, it is to approach all life, of which humans are a part, with humility and restraint. All things are among the chosen.

As I reflect on the experiences of yesterday and today, I find an important lesson in them, viewed in the light of wisdom taken from the earth and shaped by generations of elders. Two deer came and gave the choices to me. One deer I took and we will now share a single body. The other deer I touched and we will now share that moment. These events could be seen as opposites, but perhaps they are identical. Both are founded on the same principles, the same relationship, the same reciprocity. Both are the same kind of gift.

Koyukon elders would explain, in words quite different from my own, that I moved into two moments of grace, or what they would call luck. This is the source of success for a hunter or a watcher; not skill, not cleverness, not guile. Something is only given in nature, never taken.

Well soaked and shivering from a rough trip across the Sound, we pull into the dark waters of Anchor Bay. Sunset burns on the spindled peak of Antler Mountain. The little house is warm with lights that shimmer on the calm near shore. I see Nita looking from the window and Ethan dashes out to wait by the tide, pitching rocks at the mooring buoy. He strains to see inside the boat, knowing that a hunter who tells his news aloud might offend the animals by sounding boastful. But when he sees the deer his excited voice seems to roll up and down the mountainside.

He runs for the house with Shungnak, carrying a load of gear, and I know he'll burst inside with the news. Ethan, joyous and alive, boy made of deer.

ADRIAN C. LOUIS

Adrian C. Louis was born and raised in Nevada, the eldest of twelve
children, and is an enrolled member of the Lovelock Paiute Indian
Tribe. Louis received his B.A. and M.A. degrees in creative writing
from Brown University. A former journalist and a co-founder of the
Native American Press Association, he has been the editor of four tribal
newspapers and, since 1984, has been teaching English at Oglala
Lakota College on the Pine Ridge Reservation of South Dakota. A
recipient of honors, including fellowships from the Wurlitzer Founda-
tion, the Bush Foundation, and the National Endowment for the Arts,
he has written several books of poetry, including Fire Water World
(1989) and Among the Dog Eaters *(1992). A novel,* Skins, *was*
published in 1995.

Louis is a powerful stylist who is deservedly angry about the plight
of the modern Native American. The poems here, from Among the
Dog Eaters, *are strong as acid, ironic and hard-edged, and yet full of*
yearning, pathos.

IN THE GHETTO ON THE PRAIRIE
THERE IS UNREQUITED LOVE

In the imperfect prefecture
of stone and sky
the sauna breath of August
simmers commonplace dogs.
They circle paths through the sun
softened asphalt of Sioux
Nation Shopping Center
where stretched out in the shade
of the loading dock
winos bask and bake
in the luxuriant miasma
of slow death
and the only thing
separating me from them

is my growing need for you
and the fear that I might die unloved.

SOMETIMES A WARRIOR
COMES TIRED

> WHEN THE LAST RED MAN shall have perished from the
> earth and his memory among the white men shall
> have become a myth, these shores shall swarm with
> the invisible dead of my tribe.   —Chief Seattle

Sometimes a warrior comes tired
in the guise of prepositions
of propositions and says
of thee I sing when he means
what's the use . . . our race is doomed.

And let's face it.
In any waking dream about the most beautiful
Indian girl on Mother Earth I'm going to use
a rubber and blubber about it later
in the memories of nightmares
of the plain wonderful women
I lost at the cost of never being responsible
for something I don't
quite remember now.

Who listens and who cares less
than those gods who dance
with one hand on your ass
and the other pinching their noses
offended by your body stink?

These white men strut into our lives
with invisible robes.
Their imaginary halos encircle our throats
until we look like those African women

in *National Geographic*
with stretched necks.

We like their credo of dominion.
We gratefully accept the results: knives
into our wives, children
dumped along the highway and refrigerators
lined with government cheese.
Yes, we know what is best and stage the old ways
unaware of our blasphemy,
unaware of our Grandfather snickering.

AMERICA LOOMED BEFORE US

Lester Hawk dumped a couple hundred pound sacks of corn meal into the trough. I gravied buckets of curdled milk from a fifty gallon drum over it and forty hogs went ape-shit, drooling, farting, scarfing up in minutes the food that the Gods had brought. "What a bunch of pigs," Lester said and then began shouting, "Soooooeeeee, Sooooooooeeeeeee, you capitalist pigs!" The hogs started running in circles, led by one big scroungy monster with gnarled fangs. They wouldn't stop, even after Lester quieted. They were going mad, so we picked up rocks and threw high, hard ones at the leader. Lester beaned him squarely on the right eye. He staggered and toppled to the ground, screaming, thrashing, flipping bits of crushed eye ooze into the sky. Lester got a big boulder and bashed his brains in. Took a buck knife from his Levis and slit open the huge hog stomach. Stinking guts naked onto the thirsty soil. The other hogs, shocked momentarily, soon attacked like piranha. In ten minutes there was nothing left but a pile of gristly bones and hide. We gathered those up and hid them in a gully. The white rancher would never know of our murder, but our childhood had been consumed with the hog flesh. America loomed before us.

SHERMAN ALEXIE

*Sherman Alexie, a Spokane/Coeur d'Alene Indian, received a Lila Wallace Foundation Award in 1994. The author of three books of poetry—*I Would Steal Horses *(1992),* Old Shirts & New Skins *(1993), and* First Indian on the Moon *(1993)—Alexie has also published a collection of poetry and prose called* The Business of Fancydancing *(1992) and a collection of short stories,* The Lone Ranger and Tonto Fistfight in Heaven *(1993). His first novel,* Reservation Blues, *was published in 1995.*

Sherman Alexie at present lives in Seattle, where he devotes great energy and time to promoting Native American writers and interests. As these selections demonstrate, Alexie is one of the most imaginatively innovative while politically tough-minded of the next generation of Native American writers, and clearly one of the most vital and interesting of the many first-rate emerging writers in the American West.

THE BUSINESS OF
FANCYDANCING

After driving all night, trying to reach
Arlee in time for the fancydance
finals, a case of empty
beer bottles shaking our foundations, we
stop at a liquor store, count out money,
and would believe in the promise

of any man with a twenty, a promise
thin and wrinkled in his hand, reaching into the window of our car. Money
is an Indian Boy who can fancydance
from powwow to powwow. We
got our boy, Vernon WildShoe, to fill our empty

wallets and stomachs, to fill our empty
cooler. Vernon is like some promise
to pay the light bill, a credit card we

Indians get to use. When he reach-
es his hands up, feathers held high, in a dance
that makes old women speak English, the money

for first place belongs to us, all in cash, money
we tuck in our shoes, leaving our wallets empty
in case we pass out. At the modern dance,
where Indians dance white, a twenty is a promise
that can last all night long, a promise reaching into back pockets of unfamiliar Levis. We

get Vernon there in time for the finals and we
watch him like he was dancing on money,
which he is, watch the young girls reaching for him like he was Elvis in braids and an empty
tipi, like Vernon could make a promise
with every step he took, like a fancydance

could change their lives. We watch him dance
and he never talks. It's all a business we
understand. Every drum beat is a promise
note written in the dust, measured exactly. Money
is a tool, putty to fill all the empty
spaces, a ladder so we can reach

for more. A promise is just like money.
Something we can hold, in twenties, a dream we reach.
It's business, a fancydance to fill where it's empty.

MY HEROES HAVE NEVER BEEN
COWBOYS

1.

In the reservation textbooks, we learned Indians were
invented in 1492 by a crazy mixed-blood named Columbus.
Immediately after class dismissal, the Indian children traded
in those American stories and songs for a pair of tribal shoes.

These boots are made for walking, babe, and that's just what they'll do. One of these days these boots are gonna walk all over you.

2.

Did you know that in 1492 every Indian instantly became an extra in the Great American Western? But wait, I never wondered what happened to Randolph Scott or Tom Mix. The Lone Ranger was never in my vocabulary. On the reservation, when we played Indians and cowboys, all of us little Skins fought on the same side against the cowboys in our minds. We never lost.

3.

Indians never lost their West, so how come I walk into the supermarket and find a dozen cowboy books telling me *How The West Was Won?* Curious, I travel to the world's largest shopping mall, find the Lost and Found Department. "Excuse me," I say. "I seem to have lost the West. Has anybody turned it in?" The clerk tells me I can find it in the Sears Home Entertainment Department, blasting away on fifty televisions.

4.

On Saturday morning television, the cowboy has fifty bullets in his six-shooter; he never needs to reload. It's just one more miracle for this country's heroes.

5.

My heroes have never been cowboys; my heroes carry guns in their minds.

6.

Win their hearts and minds and we win the war. Can you hear that song echo across history? If you give the Indian a cup of coffee with six cubes of sugar, he'll be your servant. If you give the Indian a cigarette and a book of matches, he'll be your friend. If you give the Indian a can of commodities, he'll be your lover. He'll hold you tight in his arms, cowboy, and two-step you outside.

7.

Outside it's cold and a confused snow falls in May. I'm watching some western on TBS, colorized, but the story remains the same. Three cowboys string telegraph wire across the plains until they are confronted by the entire Sioux nation. The cowboys, 19th century geniuses, talk the Indians into touching the wire, holding it in their hands and mouths. After a dozen or so have hold of the wire, the cowboys crank the portable generator and electrocute some of the Indians with a European flame and chase the rest of them away, bareback and burned. All these years later, the message tapped across my skin remains the same.

8.

It's the same old story whispered on the television in every HUD house on the reservation. It's 500 years of that same screaming song, translated from the American.

9.

Lester FallsApart found the American dream in a game of Russian Roulette: one bullet and five empty chambers. "It's Manifest Destiny," Lester said just before he pulled the trigger five times quick. "I missed," Lester said just before he reloaded the pistol: one empty chamber and five bullets. "Maybe we should call this Reservation Roulette," Lester said just before he pulled the trigger once at his temple and five more times as he pointed the pistol toward the sky.

10.

Looking up into the night sky, I asked my brother what he thought God looked like and he said "God probably looks like John Wayne."

11.

We've all killed John Wayne more than once. When we burned the ant pile in our backyard, my brother and I imagined those ants were some cavalry or another. When Brian, that insane Indian boy from across the street, suffocated neighborhood dogs and stuffed their bodies into the reservation high school basement, he must have imagined those dogs were cowboys, come back to break another treaty.

12.

Every frame of the black and white western is a treaty; every scene in this elaborate serial is a promise. But what about the reservation home movies? What about the reservation heroes? I remember this: Down near Bull's Pasture, Eugene stood on the pavement with a gallon of tequila under his arm. I watched in the rearview mirror as he raised his arm to wave goodbye and dropped the bottle, glass and dreams of the weekend shattered. After all these years, that moment is still the saddest of my whole life.

13.

Your whole life can be changed by the smallest pain.

14.

Pain is never added to pain. It multiplies. Arthur, here we are again, you and I, fancydancing through the geometric progression of our dreams. Twenty years ago, we never believed we'd lose. Twenty years ago, television was our way of finding heroes and spirit animals. Twenty years ago, we never knew we'd spend the rest of our lives in the reservation of our minds, never knew we'd stand outside the gates of the Spokane Indian Reservation without a key to let ourselves back inside. From a distance, that familiar song. Is it country and western? Is it the sound of hearts breaking? Every song remains the same here in America, this country of the Big Sky and Manifest Destiny, this country of John Wayne and broken treaties. Arthur, I have no words which can save our lives, no words approaching forgiveness, no words flashed across the screen at the reservation drive-in, no words promising either of us top billing. Extras, Arthur, we're all extras.

BARRY LOPEZ

Barry Lopez was born in Port Chester, New York, in 1945, grew up in southern California, and received both his B.A. and M.A. degrees at the University of Notre Dame, in South Bend, Indiana. Postgraduate work at the University of Oregon brought him out west, and he's never left. Lopez is the author of two books of essays, Crossing Open Ground *(1988) and* The Rediscovery of North America *(1991); two books of nonfiction,* Of Wolves and Men *(1978) and* Arctic Dreams *(1986), which won the National Book Award; and five works of fiction, including* Winter Count *(1981), and the children's book (also useful for grown-ups)* Crow and Weasel *(1990), which was winner of the 1990 Parents' Choice Award. He lives in the Cascade Mountains of Oregon.*

"The Passing Wisdom of Birds," from Crossing Open Ground, *takes us from "the grotesqueness and unmitigated violence" of the Spanish conquistadors in Iztapalapa, Mexico, in 1519 to an imagined world of true communion with nature in the next millennium.*

"Contemporary American culture," Lopez warns, "has become a culture that devours the earth." This essay, like much of his writing, is an impassioned plea for sanity, conservation, and, primarily, respect for the world above and around us.

THE PASSING WISDOM
OF BIRDS

On the eighth of November, 1519, Hernando Cortés and four hundred Spanish soldiers marched self-consciously out of the city of Iztapalapa, Mexico, and started across the great Iztapalapan Causeway separating the lakes of Xochimilco and Chalco. They had been received the afternoon before in Iztapalapa as demi-gods; but they stared now in disbelief at what lay before them. Reflecting brilliantly on the vast plain of dark water like a landscape of sunlit chalk, its lines sharp as cut stone in the dustless air at 7200 feet, was the Aztec Byzantium—Tenochtitlán. Mexico City.

It is impossible to know what was in the facile, highly charged mind of Cortés that morning, anticipating his first meeting with the reluctant

Montezuma; but Bernal Díaz, who was present, tells us what was on the minds of the soldiers. They asked each other was it *real*—gleaming Iztapalapa behind them, the smooth causeway beneath their feet, imposing Tenochtitlán ahead? The Spanish had been in the New World for twenty-seven years, but what they discovered in the Valley of Mexico that fall "had never been heard of or seen before, nor even dreamed about" in their world. What astounded them was not, solely, the extent and sophistication of the engineering that divided and encompassed the lakes surrounding Tenochtitlán; nor the evidence that a separate culture, utterly different from their own, pursued a complex life in this huge city. It was the depth and pervasiveness of the natural beauty before their senses.

The day before, they had strolled the spotless streets of Iztapalapa through plots of full-blossomed flowers, arranged in patterns and in colors pleasing to the eye; through irrigated fruit orchards; and into still groves of aromatic trees, like cedar. They sat in the shade of bright cotton awnings in quiet stone patios and marveled at the robustness and the well-tended orderliness of the vegetable gardens around them. Roses glowed against the lime-washed walls of the houses like garnets and alexandrites. In the hour before sunset, the cool, fragrant air was filled with the whirr and flutter of birds, and lit with birdsong.

That had been Iztapalapa. Mexico City, they thought, even as their leader dismounted that morning with solemn deliberation from that magical creature, the horse, to meet an advancing Montezuma ornately caparisoned in gold and silver and bird feathers—Mexico City, they thought as they approached, could only outdo Iztapalapa. And it did. With Montezuma's tentative welcome they were free to wander in its various precincts. Mexico City confirmed the image of a people gardening with meticulous care and with exquisite attention to line and detail at the edge of nature.

It is clear from Díaz's historical account that the soldiers were stunned by the physical beauty of Tenochtitlán. Venice came to their minds in comparison, because of its canals; but Venice was not as intensely fresh, as well lit as Mexico City. And there was not to be found in Venice, or in Salamanca or Paris for that matter, anything like the great aviaries where thousands of birds—white egrets, energetic wrens and thrushes, fierce accipiters, brilliantly colored parrots—were housed and tended. They were as captivating, as fabulous, as the displays of flowers: vermilion flycatchers, copper-tailed trogons, green jays, blue-throated hummingbirds, and summer tanagers. Great blue herons, brooding condors.

And throughout the city wild birds nested.

Even Cortés, intensely preoccupied with politics, with guiding a diplomacy of conquest in the region, noticed the birds. He was struck, too, by the affinity of the Mexican people for their gardens and for the measured and intricate flow of water through their city. He took time to write Charles V in Spain, describing it all.

Cortés's men, says Díaz, never seemed to tire of the arboretums, gardens, and aviaries in the months following their entry into the city. By June 1520, however, Cortés's psychological manipulation of Montezuma and a concomitant arrogance, greed, and disrespect on the part of the Spanish military force had become too much for the Mexicans, and they drove them out. Cortés, relentless and vengeful, returned to the Valley of Mexico eleven months later with a larger army and laid siege to the city. Canal by canal, garden by garden, home by home, he destroyed what he had described to Charles V as "the most beautiful city in the world." On June 16, in a move calculated to humiliate and frighten the Mexican people, Cortés set fire to the aviaries.

The grotesqueness and unmitigated violence of Cortés's act has come back to me repeatedly in reading of early European encounters with the landscapes of the New World, like a kind of darkness. The siege of Mexico City was fought barbarously on both sides; and the breathtaking parks and beautiful gardens of Mexico City, of course, stood hard by temples in which human life was regularly offered up to Aztec gods, by priests whose hair was matted with human gore and blood. No human culture has ever existed apart from its dark side. But what Cortés did, even under conditions of war, flies wildly in the face of a desire to find a dignified and honorable relationship with nature. It is an ambitious and vague longing, but one that has been with us for centuries, I think, and which today is a voice heard clearly from many different quarters —political science, anthropology, biology, philosophy. The desire is that, our colonial conquests of the human and natural world finally at an end, we will find our way back to a more equitable set of relationships with all we have subjugated. I say back because the early cultures from which Western civilization evolved, such as the Magdalenian phase of Cro-Magnon culture in Europe, apparently had a less contentious arrangement with nature before the development of agriculture in northern Mesopotamia, and the rise of cities.

The image of Cortés burning the aviaries is not simply for me an image of a kind of destructive madness that lies at the heart of imperialistic conquest; it is also a symbol of a long-term failure of Western civilization to recognize the intrinsic worth of the American landscape, and its potential value to human societies that have since come to be at odds with the natural world. While English, French, and Spanish explorers were cruising the eastern shores of America, dreaming of feudal fiefdoms, gold, and political advantage, the continent itself was, already, occupied in a complex way by more than five hundred different cultures, each of which regarded itself as living in some kind of enlightened intimacy with the land. A chance to rediscover the original wisdom inherent in the myriad sorts of human relationships possible with the nonhuman world, of course, was not of concern to us in the sixteenth century, as it is now, particularly to geographers, philosophers, historians, and ecologists. It would not in fact become clear for centuries that the metaphysics we had thrown out thousands of years before was still intact in tribal America. America offered us the opportunity to deliberate with historical perspective, to see if we wished to reclaim that metaphysics.

The need to reexamine our experience in the New World is, increasingly, a practical need. Contemporary American culture, founded on the original material wealth of the continent, on its timber, ores, and furs, has become a culture that devours the earth. Minerals, fresh water, darkness, tribal peoples, everything the land produces we now consume in prodigious amounts. There are at least two schools of thought on how to rectify this high rate of consumption, which most Western thinkers agree is unsustainable and likely wrongheaded if not disastrous. First, there are technical approaches. No matter how sophisticated or innovative these may be, however, they finally seem only clever or artful adjustments, not solutions. Secondly, we can consider a change in attitude toward nature, adopting a fundamentally different way of thinking about it than we have previously had, perhaps ever had as human beings. The insights of aboriginal peoples are of inestimable value here in rethinking our relationships with the natural world (i.e., in figuring out how to get ourselves back *into* it); but the solution to our plight, I think, is likely to be something no other culture has ever thought of, something over which !Kung, Inuit, Navajo, Walbiri, and the other traditions we have turned to for wisdom in the twentieth century will marvel at as well.

The question before us is how do we find a viable natural philosophy, one that places us again within the elements of our natural history. The answer, I believe, lies with wild animals.

II

Over the past ten years it has been my privilege to spend time in the field in North America with biologists studying several different kinds of animals, including wolves, polar bears, mountain lions, seals, and whales. Of all that could be said about this exercise, about people watching animals, I would like to restrict myself to but one or two things. First, although such studies are scientific they are conducted by human beings whose individual speculations may take them out beyond the bounds of scientific inquiry. The animals they scrutinize may draw them back into an older, more intimate and less rational association with the local landscape. In this frame of mind, they may privately begin to question the methodology of Western science, especially its purported objectivity and its troublesome lack of heart. It may seem to them incapable of addressing questions they intuit are crucial. Even as they perceive its flaws, however, scientists continue to offer such studies as a dependable source of reliable information—and they are. Science's flaws as a tool of inquiry are relatively minor, and it is further saved by its strengths.

Science's strength lies with its rigor and objectivity, and it is undoubtedly as rigorous as any system available to us. Even with its flaws (its failure, for example, to address disorderly or idiosyncratic behavior) field biology is as strong and reliable in its way as the collective wisdom of a hunting people actively involved with the land. The highest order of field work being done in biology today, then, from an elucidation of the way polar bears hunt ringed seals to working out the ecology of night-flying moths pollinating agaves in the Mojave Desert, forms part of the foundation for a modern realignment with the natural world. (The other parts of the foundation would include work done by anthropologists among hunter-gatherer people and studies by natural geographers; philosophical work in the tradition of Aldo Leopold and Rachel Carson; and the nearly indispensable element of personal experience.)

I often search out scientific reports to read; many are based on years of research and have been patiently thought through. Despite my regard, however, I read with caution, for I cannot rid myself of the thought that, even though it is the best theoretical approach we have, the process is not perfect. I have participated in some of this type of work and know that innocent mistakes are occasionally made in the data. I understand how influential a misleading coincidence can become in the overall collection of data; how unconsciously the human mind can follow a teasing parallel. I am cautious, too, for even more fundamental reasons. It is hard to say exactly what any animal is *doing*. It is impossible to know when or where an event in an animal's life begins or ends. And our human senses confine us to realms that may contain only a small part of the information produced in an event. Something critical could be missing and we would not know. And as far as the experiments themselves are concerned, although we can design and carry out thousands of them, no animal can ever be described as the sum of these experiments. And, finally, though it is possible to write precisely about something, this does not automatically mean one is accurate.

The scientific approach is flawed, therefore, by its imposition of a subjective framework around animal behavior; but it only fails, really, because it is incomplete. We would be rash, using this approach exclusively, to claim to understand any one animal, let alone the environment in which that animal is evolving. Two remedies to this dilemma of the partially perceived animal suggest themselves. One, obviously, is to turn to the long-term field observations of non-Western cultural traditions. These non-Aristotelian, non-Cartesian, non-Baconian views of wild animals are stimulating, challenging, and, like a good bibliography, heuristic, pointing one toward discovery. (They are also problematic in that, for example, they do not take sufficiently into account the full range of behavior of migratory animals and they have a highly nonlinear [though ultimately, possibly, more correct] understanding of population biology.)

A second, much less practiced remedy is to cultivate within ourselves a sense of mystery—to see that the possibilities for an expression of life in any environment, or in any single animal, are larger than we can predict or understand, and that this is all right. Biology should borrow here from quantum physics, which accepts the premise that, under certain circumstances, the observer can be deceived. Quantum physics, with its ambiguous particles and ten-dimensional universes, is a branch of science that has in fact returned us to a state of awe with nature, without threatening our intellectual capacity to analyze complex events.

If it is true that modern people desire a new relationship with the natural world, one that is not condescending, manipulative, and purely utilitarian; and if the foundation upon which the relationship is to be built is as I suggest—a natural history growing largely out of science and the insights of native peoples—then a staggering task lies before us.

The initial steps to be taken seem obvious. First, we must identify and protect those regions where landscapes largely undisturbed by human technology remain intact. Within these ecosystems lie blueprints for the different patterns of life that have matured outside the pervasive influence of myriad Western technologies (though no place on earth has escaped their influence entirely). We can contemplate and study endlessly the natural associations here, and draw from these smaller universes a sophisticated wisdom about process and event, and about evolution. Second, we need to subscribe a great public support to the discipline of field biology. Third, we need to seek an introduction to the reservoirs of intelligence that native cultures have preserved in both oral tradition and in their personal experience with the land, the highly complex detail of a way of life not yet torn entirely from the fabric of nature.

We must, too, look out after the repositories of our own long-term cultural wisdom more keenly. Our libraries, which preserve the best of what we have to say about ourselves and nature, are under siege in an age of cost-benefit analysis. We need to immerse ourselves thoughtfully, too, in what is being written and produced on tape and film, so that we become able to distinguish again between truthful expression and mere entertainment. We need to do this not only for our own sake but so that our children, who too often have only the half-eclipsed lives of zoo animals or the contrived dramas of television wildlife adventure before them, will know that this heritage is disappearing and what we are apt to lose with it.

What disappears with a debasement of wild landscapes is more than genetic diversity, more than a homeland for Henry Beston's "other nations," more, to be perfectly selfish, than a source of future medical cures for human illness or a chance for personal revitalization on a wilderness trip. We stand to lose the focus of our ideals. We stand to lose our sense of dignity, of compassion, even our sense of what we call God. The philosophy of nature we set aside eight thousand years ago in the Fertile Crescent we can, I think, locate again and greatly refine in North America. The New World is a landscape still overwhelming in the vigor of its animals and plants, resonant with mystery. It encourages, still, an enlightened response toward indigenous cultures that differ from our own, whether Aztecan, Lakotan, lupine, avian, or invertebrate. By broadening our sense of the intrinsic worth of life and by cultivating respect for other ways of moving toward perfection, we may find a sense of resolution we have been looking for, I think, for centuries.

Two practical steps occur to me. Each by itself is so small I hesitate to set it forth; but to say nothing would be cowardly, and both appear to me to be reasonable, a beginning. They also acknowledge an obvious impediment: to bridge the chasm between a colonial attitude toward the land and a more filial relationship with it takes time. The task has always been, and must be, carried into the next generation.

The first thought I would offer is that each university and college in the country establish the position of university naturalist, a position to be held by a student in his or her senior year and passed on at the end of the year to another student. The university naturalist would be responsible for establishing and maintaining a natural history of the campus, would confer with architects and grounds keepers, escort guests, and otherwise look out after the nonhuman elements of the campus, their relationships to human beings, and the preservation of this knowledge. Though the position itself might be honorary and unsalaried, the student would receive substantial academic credit for his or her work and would be provided with a budget to conduct research, maintain a library, and produce an occasional paper. Depending on his or her gifts and personality, the university naturalist might elect to teach a course or to speak at some point during the academic year. In concert with the university archivist and university historian, the university naturalist would seek to protect the relationships-in-time that define a culture's growth and ideals.

A second suggestion is more difficult to implement, but no less important than a system of university naturalists. In recent years several American and British publishers have developed plans to reprint in an extended series classic works of natural history. These plans should be pursued; the list of books should include not only works of contemporary natural history but early works by such people as Thomas Nuttal and William Bartram, so that the project has historical depth. It should also include books by nonscientists who have immersed themselves "beyond reason" in the world occupied by animals and who have emerged with stunning reports, such as J. A. Baker's *The Peregrine*. And books that offer us a resounding and affecting vision of the landscape, such as John Van Dyke's *The Desert*. It should also include the writing of anthropologists who have worked, or are working, with the native peoples of North America to define an indigenous natural history, such as Richard Nelson's *Make Prayers to the Raven*. And a special effort should be made to unearth those voices that once spoke eloquently for parts of the country the natural history of which is now too often overlooked, or overshadowed, by a focus on western or northern North American ecosystems: the pine barrens of New Jersey, the Connecticut River Valley, the White Mountains of New Hampshire, the remnant hardwood forests of Indiana and Ohio, the Outer Banks, the relictual prairies of Texas, and the mangrove swamps and piney woods of Georgia.

Such a collection, it seems to me, should be assembled with several thoughts in mind. It should be inexpensive so that the books can fall easily into the hands of young people. It should document the extraordinary variety of natural ecosystems in North America, and reflect the great range of dignified and legitimate human response to them. And it should make clear that human beings belong in these landscapes, that they, too, are a part of the earth's natural history.

III

The image I carry of Cortés setting fire to the aviaries in Mexico City that June day in 1521 is an image I cannot rid myself of. It stands, in my mind, for a fundamental lapse of wisdom in the European conquest of America, an underlying trouble in which political conquest, personal greed, revenge, and national pride outweigh what is innocent, beautiful, serene, and defenseless—the birds. The incineration of these creatures 450 years ago is not something that can be rectified today. Indeed, one could argue, the same oblivious irreverence is still with us, among those who would ravage and poison the earth to sustain the economic growth of Western societies. But Cortés's act can be transcended. It is possible to fix in the mind that heedless violence, the hysterical cries of the birds, the stench of death, to look it square in the face and say that there is more to us than this, this will not forever distinguish us among the other cultures. It is possible to imagine that on the far side of the Renaissance and the Enlightenment we can recover the threads of an earlier wisdom.

Again I think of the animals, because of the myriad ways in which they have helped us since we first regarded each other differently. They offered us early models of rectitude and determination in adversity, which we put into stories. The grace of a moving animal, in some ineluctable way, kindles still in us a sense of imitation. They continue to produce for us a sense of the Other: to encounter a truly wild animal on its own ground is to know the defeat of thought, to feel reason overpowered. The animals have fed us; and the cultures of the great hunters particularly—the bears, the dogs, and the cats—have provided the central metaphors by which we have taken satisfaction in our ways and explained ourselves to strangers.

Cortés's soldiers, on their walks through the gleaming gardens of Tenochtitlán, would have been as struck by the flight paths of songbirds as we are today. In neither a horizontal nor a vertical dimension do these pathways match the line and scale of human creation, within which the birds dwell. The corridors they travel are curved around some other universe. When the birds passed over them, moving across the grain of sunlight, the soldiers must have stopped occasionally to watch, as we do. It is the birds' independence from predictable patterns of human design that draws us to them. In the birds' separate but related universe we are able to sense hope for ourselves. Against a background of the familiar, we recognize with astonishment a new pattern.

In such a moment, pausing to take in the flight of a flock of birds passing through sunshine and banking gracefully into a grove of trees, it is possible to move beyond a moment in the Valley of Mexico when we behaved as though we were insane.

ALLEN GINSBERG

Allen Ginsberg, a self-avowed Buddhist Jew with attachments to Krishna, Siva, Allah, Coyote, and the Sacred Heart, has been expanding minds (his own included) with his hybrid brand of poetry—involving heavy doses of spirituality, invective, and prophecy—for some forty years. Born in Newark, New Jersey, in 1926, his father a poet and his mother a Communist, Ginsberg was educated in the public schools of Paterson. One of his earliest friends there (and first

*in a long series of mentors) was the poet William Carlos Williams.
In New York City, where Ginsberg earned a B.A. from Columbia
University in 1948, he received an equally valuable education from
the work and exuberant example of his friends William Burroughs,
Jack Kerouac, and Gregory Corso. In 1953, bearing a letter of introduction to Kenneth Rexroth from Williams, Ginsberg headed to San
Francisco. In 1956, the first edition of* Howl *was published, by
Lawrence Ferlinghetti's City Lights Press; it has been in print ever
since. Later poems, such as the long eulogy for his mother,* Kaddish
*(1961), have cemented his reputation as a poet with both a wide
popular reputation and critical acceptance. A comprehensive volume of
his collected poems was published in 1984. Ginsberg has also published
voluminous excerpts from journals kept during his world travels, as
well as books of letters, essays, and more recently,* Snapshot Poetics,
*a collection of his Beat-era photographs. "A Supermarket in Califor-
nia" connects back to Whitman, with visions of a new American
beginning, and forward to a commodified future where we dream "of
the lost America of love."*

A SUPERMARKET IN CALIFORNIA

What thoughts I have of you tonight, Walt Whitman, for I walked down
the sidestreets under the trees with a headache self-conscious looking at
the full moon.
In my hungry fatigue, and shopping for images, I went into the neon
fruit supermarket, dreaming of your enumerations!
What peaches and what penumbras! Whole families shopping at night!
Aisles full of husbands! Wives in the avocados, babies in the
tomatoes!—and you, Garcia Lorca, what were you doing down by the
watermelons?

I saw you, Walt Whitman, childless, lonely old grubber, poking among
the meats in the refrigerator and eyeing the grocery boys.
I heard you asking questions of each: Who killed the pork chops? What
price bananas? Are you my Angel?
I wandered in and out of the brilliant stacks of cans following you, and
followed in my imagination by the store detective.
We strode down the open corridors together in our solitary fancy

tasting artichokes, possessing every frozen delicacy, and never passing the cashier.

Where are we going, Walt Whitman? The doors close in an hour. Which way does your beard point tonight?
(I touch your book and dream of our odyssey in the supermarket and feel absurd.)
Will we walk all night through solitary streets? The trees add shade to shade, lights out in the houses, we'll both be lonely.
Will we stroll dreaming of the lost America of love past blue automobiles in driveways, home to our silent cottage?
Ah, dear father, graybeard, lonely old courage-teacher, what America did you have when Charon quit poling his ferry and you got out on a smoking bank and stood watching the boat disappear on the black waters of Lethe?